Born in Hobart, ~~~~~~~~~~~~~~~~~~~~~~~~~~~~~ he Royal Hong Kong ~~~~~~~~~~~~~~~~~~~~~~~~~~~~~ ed as a Launch Commander in the Marine Division and was a Platoon Commander in the Police Tactical Unit.

In 1984, Bruce moved to Sydney and began his career as a writer of film and television scripts. He is also well known to Australian and international audiences as an actor. His television credits include *Blue Heelers*, *Wildside*, *Water Rats*, *Minder*, *Always Greener* and *Murder Call*, and he's appeared in films such as *Paperback Hero* with Hugh Jackman and Claudia Karvan, *Evil Angels* with Meryl Streep, and *On Our Selection* with Geoffrey Rush and Leo McKern.

Bruce's first novel was *A Necessary Evil*, a story of vice and corruption, set in Sydney during the rock and roll years of the '50s and '60s. His second novel was *The Time of the Dragons*, part one of his Hong Kong trilogy, part two of which is *Two Tigers, One Mountain*.

Also well known as a poet, a collection of his works entitled *The Spirit of the Bush* was published in 2003 and on Anzac Day 2007 Bruce was invited to attend the Anzac Memorial Ceremony at Lone Pine in Gallipoli, where he read his remembrance poetry, *The Gallipoli Sonnets*, soon to be published by the Department of Veterans' Affairs publishing unit.

Bruce lives on the Central Coast with his wife, actress and international best-selling author Judy Nunn.

Also by Bruce Venables

A Necessary Evil
The Time of the Dragons
The Spirit of the Bush (poetry)

TWO
TIGERS,
ONE
MOUNTAIN

BRUCE VENABLES

An Arrow book
Published by Random House Australia Pty Ltd
Level 3, 100 Pacific Highway, North Sydney NSW 2060
www.randomhouse.com.au

First published by Random House Australia in 2007
This edition first published by Arrow in 2008

Addresses for companies within the Random House Group can be found at
www.randomhouse.com.au/offices

National Library of Australia
Cataloguing-in-Publication Entry

Venables, Bruce.
Two tigers one mountain.

ISBN: 978 1 74166 616 8 (pbk.)

A823.3

Cover illustration: 'The Ming Tigers' by Tanya Creer, Pen and Think
Cover design by Darian Causby/Highway 51 Design Works
Typeset in 11.5/14 pt Sabon by Midland Typesetters, Australia
Printed and bound by Griffin Press, South Australia

Random House Australia uses papers that are natural, renewable and
recyclable products and made from wood grown in sustainable forests.
The logging and manufacturing processes are expected to conform to
the environmental regulations of the country of origin.

10 9 8 7 6 5 4 3 2 1

In Memoriam

This book is dedicated
to the memory of
Paul Lincoln Everard
7 March 1971–10 October 2006

Requiescat in Pace

PREFACE

I am a storyteller. I write to entertain. Once again, I hope to transport readers to a time and place unfamiliar to them, the city of Hong Kong during the 1950s and '60s.

This novel presents the middle years in the saga of the Merchant family of Hong Kong. It centres on the lives of James Merchant, his adopted brother Lee Kwan Man Hop, and their offspring, who are all governed by forces from the past. It is the second of a three-book saga called the Hong Kong Trilogy. *Two Tigers, One Mountain* is the sequel to the first book, *The Time of the Dragons*, and it picks up the story during the Korean War.

I have mentioned real characters and events to give an historical perspective to the narrative and in doing so I hope readers get a sense of those turbulent times in China's history – the rise of Communist China, the rise of Nationalist Taiwan, and the survival, against all odds, of the little British capitalist enclave of Hong Kong.

I was an Inspector in the Royal Hong Kong Police Force during the 1970s and although that was many years ago, the memories I have of that wonderful time are still vivid in my mind. For me, as a young man, Hong Kong was the most exciting city on earth.

From 1845 until 1997, the British Crown Colony of Hong Kong was an anachronism. It was unique. It was a place out of time, originally used, nefariously, by the British East India Company as a gateway for trade with China. 'The Company' traded opium from the sub-continent for China tea, which it sold to the dining salons of Europe at enormous profit, and in doing so turned half the population of China into drug addicts. But it was not only the British who traded in opium; the Dutch, Portuguese, Germans, French and Americans all followed suit. The guilt was well spread. But Hong Kong survived its immoral birth and flourished. It became the most famous city of Asia, the brightest beacon in the South China Sea, and in the minds of men, a place of adventure, romance and high drama. Sought by the bold and dreamed of by the meek, Hong Kong was, for two hundred years, a magnet to mayhem, money, misfits and fortune-hunters. She was Britain's shining jewel in the Far East.

One result of my time in Asia is a limited knowledge of the Cantonese language. Throughout this book I have, as I did in *The Time of the Dragons*, italicised all Cantonese dialogue in an attempt to capture the wonderful sense of humour and the refreshing candour of the people of Hong Kong. To those who might find fault, I would explain that I have used it as a device to give the reader a sense of belonging to the time and place of which I write.

It is very easy to make a fool of yourself when embarking on a conversation in a foreign language and the Cantonese showed great patience when I did so. They helped me when I stuttered and stammered my way through a linguistic nightmare, and laughed, with great affection I'm sure, at the way I so often abused their language, and for that I remain deeply grateful.

Bruce Venables
Sydney, Australia

THE STORY SO FAR

In 1925 a young Englishman, Richard Brewster, arrived in the Far East to join the Hong Kong Police Force. During a terrible fire in the island's warehouse district, he saved the life of a small Chinese boy, Lee Kwan Man Hop. The boy was the grandson of the leader of a triad society and, as a result of his humanitarian action, Richard found himself at the centre of a triad war.

In an act of self-preservation, and upon the advice of his Chinese friends, Richard founded the Society of Golden Dragons, the *Gaam Lung Tong*, an illegal secret society comprised solely of police officers. He was aided in his endeavours by the woman with whom he was to have a passionate affair, Elanora Merchant, the beautiful Eurasian widow and owner of the Merchant Company, a Hong Kong trading house.

Elanora gave Richard and his fellow triad members four statues, each of solid gold, and each with eyes of fabulous gemstones – one of rubies, one of diamonds, one of emeralds and one of sapphires. The property of the Nationalist Party of China many years before, the statues were thought to be lost at sea, but it was not the case. They were stolen by fortune-hunters and remained hidden in Hong Kong until Elanora discovered their existence.

After the defeat of his enemies, Richard's fortunes flourished, as did those of Elanora. Combining brilliant business acumen with illicit money, courtesy of the triad society, Elanora became known throughout Asia and Europe as the Merchant Mistress. And Richard Brewster, a mere Police Inspector to most, discovered power beyond his wildest dreams. In 1930s Hong Kong, a world of intrigue, corruption, violence, triads and piracy, Richard's Golden Dragons ruled supreme.

By now, as Elanora's lover, Richard controlled the upbringing and education of her son, James, and her adopted son, the boy he had rescued, Lee Kwan Man Hop. From the age of six the boys were trained in *Shaolin*, the oldest and purest form of the Chinese martial arts. At thirteen they were adopted into the Society of Golden Dragons, and at sixteen performed their first assassination for the society on Richard Brewster's orders.

Prior to the outbreak of World War II the brothers were separated. Lee Kwan Man Hop returned to China to fight with the Nationalist Forces of Ch'iang Kai-shek against the invading Japanese, and James joined the Royal Air Force as a fighter pilot. Their extraordinary fighting skills became legendary. James, as a fighter ace, won the Distinguished Flying Cross in the Battle of Britain, and Lee, revered by his compatriots for his ferocity in battle, became known throughout China as the Dragon of Shanghai.

When Hong Kong was invaded in December 1941, Elanora, at her lover's insistence, fled to Australia. Richard remained to fight in the Battle of Hong Kong and on Christmas Day 1941, when the British Crown Colony surrendered to the Japanese, he and his compatriots were interned in Stanley Prison.

And so ended *The Time of the Dragons*.

What became of the boys, James and Lee, caught up in the winds of war? What became of Elanora and the Merchant Company? What became of the fabulous, golden statues? And what became of Richard Brewster, left languishing in a Japanese prisoner-of-war camp? Read on in *Two Tigers, One Mountain*, Book Two of the enthralling Hong Kong Trilogy.

Hong Kong Song

There's a city up in Asia
And it has a hold on me,
Where the women wear the *cheung saam*
That is split from hip to knee.
I found all the tea in China
In an oriental play,
And a China girl to love me
But there was a price to pay.

Yes, I paid the Chinese piper,
You can be assured of that.
For the Orient it seized me
Like the wind can snatch a hat.
But the price I paid was worth it,
For the passion in the song
That old China's voice sang to me
In the city called Hong Kong.

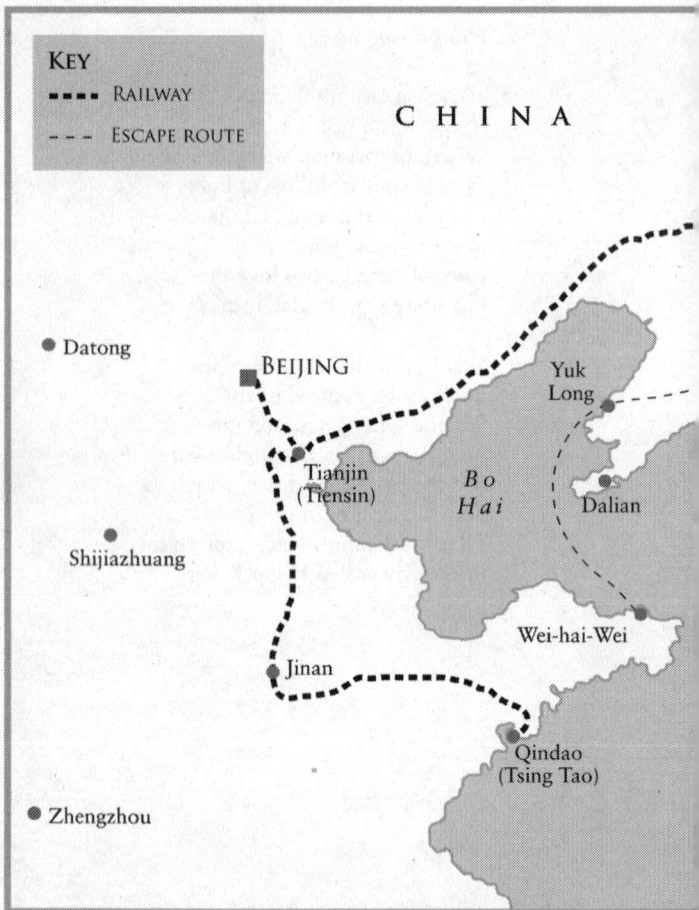

CHINA

Datong

BEIJING

Yuk Long

Tianjin
(Tiensin)

Bo Hai

Dalian

Shijiazhuang

Wei-hai-Wei

Jinan

Qindao
(Tsing Tao)

Zhengzhou

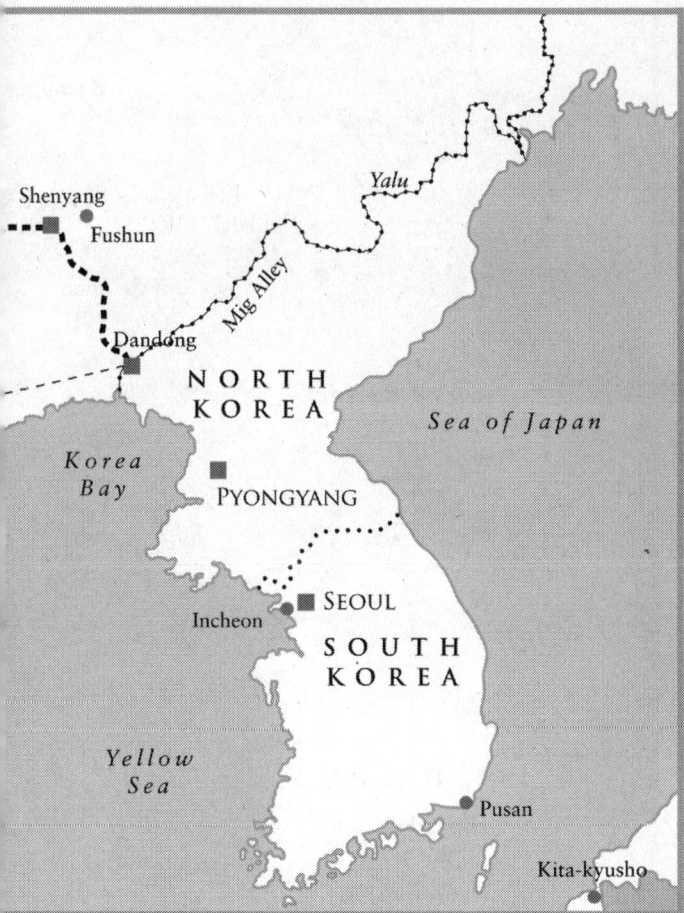

Shenyang
Fushun
Yalu
Mig Alley
Dandong
NORTH KOREA
Sea of Japan
Korea Bay
PYONGYANG
Incheon
SEOUL
SOUTH KOREA
Yellow Sea
Pusan
Kita-kyusho

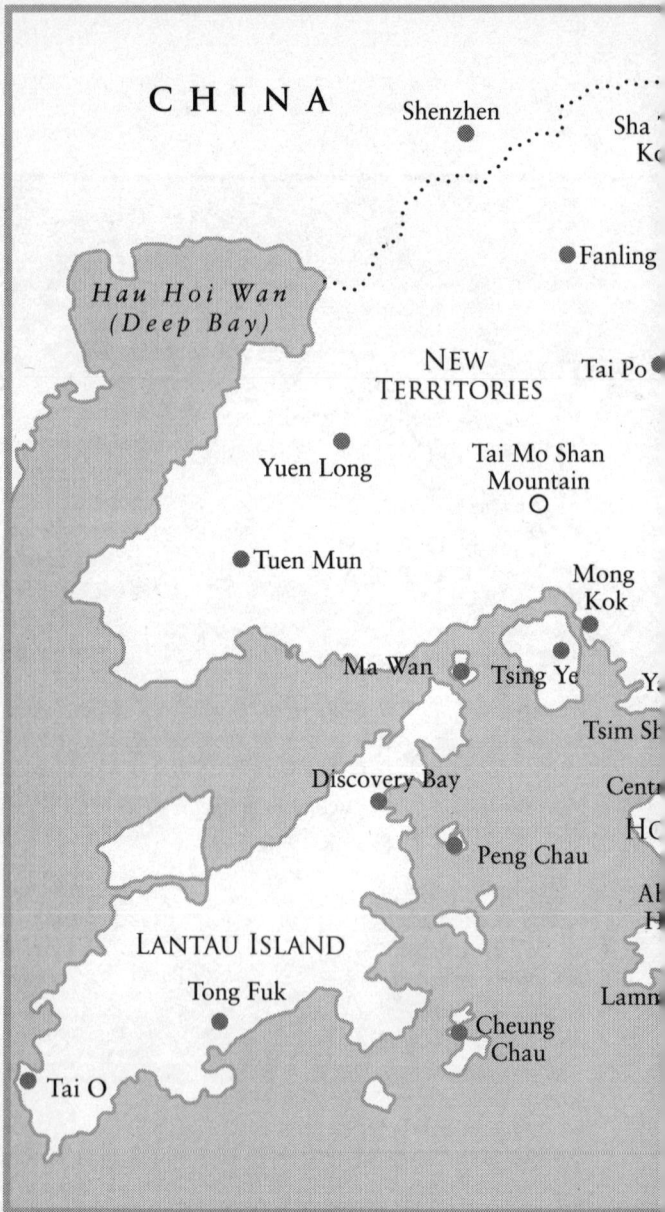

CHINA

Shenzhen

Sha ⸳
K⸱

Fanling

Hau Hoi Wan
(Deep Bay)

NEW
TERRITORIES

Tai Po

Yuen Long

Tai Mo Shan
Mountain
O

Tuen Mun

Mong
Kok

Ma Wan   Tsing Ye   Y⸱

Tsim Sh⸱

Discovery Bay   Centr⸱

HO

Peng Chau   A⸱
H

LANTAU ISLAND

Tong Fuk

Lamm⸱

Tai O   Cheung
Chau

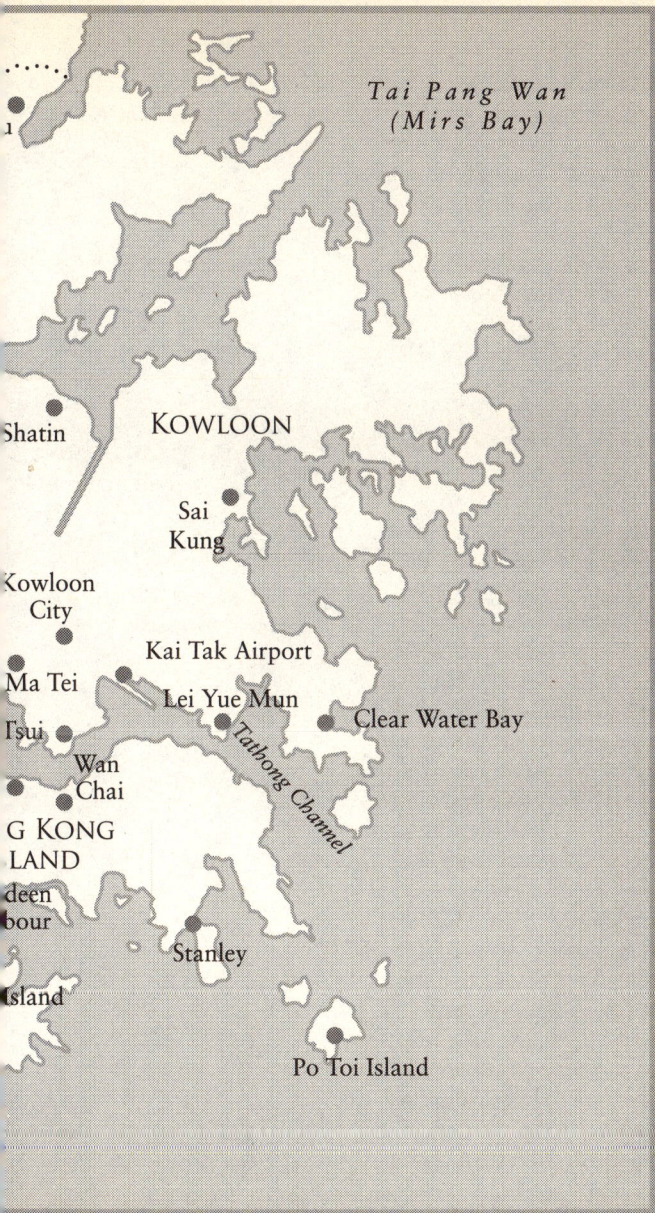

Tai Pang Wan
(Mirs Bay)

KOWLOON

Shatin

Sai
Kung

Kowloon
City

Kai Tak Airport

Ma Tei

Lei Yue Mun

Tsui

Clear Water Bay

Wan
Chai

Tathong Channel

G KONG
LAND

deen
bour

Stanley

Island

Po Toi Island

PROLOGUE

Portuguese Macau, 1967

'*Homo humus, fama fumus, finis cinis,*' Father Raphael murmured, looking across the open grave at the woman standing opposite him.

'Man is dust, fame is smoke, the end is ashes,' she said and he nodded.

High on a windswept hillside on the island of Coloane, the Jesuit intoned a final prayer for the repose of the soul of Richard Brewster. As his words were swept away on the warm morning breeze, his gaze lingered upon the widow.

Even at sixty-six, he thought, Elanora Maria Escaravelho de Ruiz Merchant Brewster was a remarkable looking creature, with the ageless beauty peculiar to Eurasian women. His mind wandered back to 1914, the year they'd first met.

Of Portuguese-Chinese stock, Elanora had been fourteen years old and the most exquisitely beautiful creature he'd ever seen when, as a young priest, Raphael had been charged by her father, the wealthy businessman Don Rodrigo Escaravelho de Ruiz, to arrange her passage to Portugal to complete her education.

After her return to Macau near the end of the Great War, he had presided over her arranged marriage to John Merchant, the wealthiest of Hong Kong's company bosses, known as *taipans*. Then, the following year, Raphael had baptised their only son.

John Merchant had been killed by pirates when the boy, James, was only six. The young widow had taken the reins of the Merchant Company and, displaying brilliant business acumen, had ruled it with an iron fist until she'd become known from Hong Kong to London as the Merchant Mistress.

Their paths had crossed many times since, but he remembered that first meeting vividly and now, over fifty years later, as he watched her in profile gazing out over the South China Sea, he was still of the same opinion. Even in grief, Elanora's beauty radiated like the brightest sun.

Elanora Brewster's thoughts were exactly forty miles away from Coloane. Her gaze was drawn irresistibly eastward, away from the beautiful blue vista of the South China Sea, across the sunlit Pearl River Estuary, through the distant haze, to the British Crown Colony of Hong Kong. For it was there, in Merchant House, her first husband's opulent mansion high on Victoria Peak, that she'd first laid eyes on Richard Brewster, the young Police Inspector destined to be the love of her life.

'Richard, my love,' her lips fashioned the words. She saw his face in the sparkling waters of the estuary and heard again his sweet whispered endearments. It was not the wind, but his breath, that now fanned her cheek. And neither was it the breeze that moved the black silk of her mourning dress, it was Richard's hands moving proprietorially over her body.

'Richard, my love,' she whispered again. He was there with her. She could feel his presence. It cannot be, she told herself. It's impossible. Panic rose in her. She thought she might be losing her mind. But Richard, her lover, her husband, was near. The feeling grew so intense it threatened to overwhelm her.

Then she saw the figure of a man further down the narrow track that led up to the grave. He was dressed in black with a hat pulled low over his face, and he was walking slowly but surely towards her. She knew this man. Good God, her mind screamed, I *am* going mad. It's Richard. But it can't be.

Elanora's eyes remained fixed on the black clad figure now standing some twenty yards distant beneath the only tree on the otherwise barren hillside. Slowly the man removed his hat. It was not Richard, she knew, but her Chinese heart had almost convinced her otherwise.

People did not return from the dead, not even Jesus, she chastised herself, glancing at the dear old Jesuit, Father Raphael. Since she'd been a little girl she'd tried many times to take the leap of faith her father's religion required. Throughout her life she'd been subjected to the doctrines of Christianity, Buddhism, Taoism and Confucianism, but the mystical Chinese world of gods and legends taught to her by her Chinese mother and house servants was strongest in her heart. It was the reason she'd panicked, believing for one fleeting moment, that Richard was alive and near her.

The face of the man looking at her from beneath the tree caused her to smile. It was Lee, her darling Lee.

Lee Kwan Man Hop, given the harsh realities of life in Hong Kong, would not have survived his childhood had it not been for the man now lying in the grave. At Richard Brewster's suggestion, Elanora Merchant had taken six-year-old Lee into her household, at first as a servant and companion for James, but as the little Chinese boy had endeared himself more and more to both Elanora and her son, she had arranged to become his official guardian. With James, Lee had been educated in one of England's finest schools and afforded all the privileges life in a wealthy family could bring. With the single stroke of a bureaucratic pen, Elanora had changed Lee Kwan's life completely.

Father Raphael concluded his service and moved discreetly some distance away. Elanora remained motionless. She gazed again at her husband's grave then looked down the hillside towards Lee Kwan and beckoned to him.

Lee walked up the narrow track and into Elanora's waiting arms. She hugged him for some time before taking him by the hands. *'The funeral was to be private, Ah Lee,'* she said in Cantonese. *'I wanted no one here except me and the priest.'*

'I did not know. I am sorry.'

'Did your daughter say or not say to you that I wanted no one here?'

'Perhaps,' he shrugged apologetically, *'but I did not hear her. I thought only of you. I was compelled to come.'*

'I'm glad you're here.'

'*I set out from Tai Mo Shan the moment I heard of his death.*'

'*All the way from your mountain top. Thank you.*'

'*The wheel of life turns for us all, Elanora.*' He looked into the open grave.

'*Yes.*' Elanora nodded. She drew in a breath, held it, and stretched herself to full height as her hands tightened their grip on his. She stared out over the estuary below and as Lee watched, she seemed to reach a decision. The elderly beauty slowly exhaled and looked at him. '*You are my adopted son, but we have not spoken for ten years, Lee.*'

'*I told you I would not return from the mountain, Elanora. Society is not for me. I made that decision and will remain true to it. I could find no peace in the world, so I chose a secluded place and sought peace from within, and I found it. I live high on the side of Tai Mo Shan and I am content.*'

'*You have been selfish.*'

'*My son Jet has visited you many times and my daughter Su-lin has lived with you. It is not as if I did not have contact, true or not true?*'

'*Not true, Ah Lee. Your children are my grandchildren, but they are not you.*'

'*I thank you for giving them that great honour.*' Lee bowed his head.

'Don't play the humble Chinese peasant with me!' The brutality of the English language cut through the air like a knife. 'I am the Merchant Mistress, or have you forgotten?'

'I'm sorry, Elanora.' Her vehemence shocked him.

'Mother! You will address me as Mother, for that is what I am to you.'

'Yes, Mother.' Ten years of serenity on Tai Mo Shan, highest of the Kowloon Mountains, had caused Lee to forget the power Elanora could exude. Now, at forty-eight years of age, he was being rudely reminded.

'*Your arrival is timely.*' Elanora's demeanour softened as she reverted to Cantonese. '*I was going to send for you today.*'

'*What is the matter?*' Lee sensed her anxiety.

'*I have need of you, son. I need to talk to you and tell you of the troubles that burden me.*' Elanora looked at Father Raphael, who'd moved off down the hill out of earshot, but she lowered her voice nonetheless. '*I need to talk of dragons, understand or not understand?*'

'*Understand,*' Lee replied as a feeling of uneasiness crept over him. The world of men was dragging him back and he was powerless to stop it. He saw the worry on Elanora's face and for one moment he wanted to turn and run, but he could not ignore the plea in her eyes. If his mother, the Merchant Mistress, needed him, then something must be terribly wrong. '*But why should we talk about dragons, Mother?*' Lee indicated the open grave beside him. '*The last dragon is dead. His remains will lie undisturbed in the ground at our feet, true or not true?*'

'*True, Lee.*' Elanora looked him in the eye. '*But the remains of other dragons are being disturbed.*'

'*Other dragons?*'

'*Yes. Golden Dragons. That is why we must talk.*'

BOOK ONE

THE ASCENT

CHAPTER ONE

Kenjong, South Korea, 31 December 1951

Wing Commander Richard Beckham, DFC, British Royal
Air Force, stood in the freezing wind and watched the
two US Air Force F-86 Sabre jet fighters drop their wheels and
hit the runway, side by side. He continued to watch as they
taxied off the runway and moved towards him. He'd never
seen the American jets up close and he was more than
impressed. In fact, he was mesmerised. He stood stock still as
the sinister looking war-birds rolled closer.

He would never get used to aircraft without propellers, he
decided, they appeared so cold and impersonal. Unlike Spitfires and the American Mustangs he'd flown until recently,
jets were cold and evil looking. One could form a bond with
a propeller driven aircraft, he mused, just as one did with a
horse. You could pat a Spitfire and whisper good morning to
it, and sense that it registered your presence. You can't do
that with a jet, he thought, jets are machines – machines
made to kill. The science of aeronautics had moved on, he
realised sadly. Man had discarded the propeller driven plane
just as he'd discarded the horse with the invention of the
motor car.

The Sabres came to a standstill in front of him, their
engines screaming like banshees. The gaping holes at their
noses that acted as air-intakes looked like the maws of great
white sharks. For one foolish moment, Beckham imagined
they were huge carnivorous beasts come to devour him. He
shivered. But it was not the thought, nor the biting wind, that
made him hop from toe to toe and clap his arms around his

shoulders. Richard Beckham was as excited as a schoolboy. He knew who was flying one of the aircraft.

He laughed self-consciously and glanced about, embarrassed, but no one was looking at him. The ground crews receiving the incoming aircraft were busy surrounding them with various machines for refuelling, mechanical inspection and re-armament. The screams of the jet engines began to subside, whining lower and lower, and Richard saw the aircrafts' canopies slide back and the pilots remove their helmets. And printed along the canopy line of one jet, in black letters, was the name: Wing Commander J. Merchant R.A.F.

'Dickie boy!' James Merchant yelled as he strode towards Richard Beckham. 'You're a sight for sore eyes, lad!'

Beckham was crushed in a bear hug. 'I didn't believe it,' said Beckham when James Merchant let him go. 'When I read your name on the Incoming Flight List I just didn't believe it. My God, Sir, it's good to see you!'

'Sir?' James replied. 'What's this Sir business? We're the same rank now, Dickie.'

'Are we?'

'You are a Wing Commander now, are you not?'

'Oh, er, yes. Of course,' Beckham stammered. 'By God, but I'm amazed you got those planes onto the ground in this wind, Sir. I've just ordered the runway closed until it eases.'

'They're remarkable aircraft, Dickie,' James shouted. 'We live in a different age. Oh,' he indicated the young man who joined them, 'this is my wingman Captain Johnnie Wilson, United States Air Force. He's from Texas.'

'I'm very pleased to make your acquaintance, Captain Wilson.' Richard Beckham extended his hand and received an almighty slap on the back.

'The name's Johnnie,' the young American yelled over the howling wind. He pronounced it *Jarnie*. 'And you're Dick right? Dick Beckham? Jimbo here's told me all about you. You flew Spits together in the Battle of Britain.'

'We certainly did,' Beckham managed to reply. 'I was merely a humble Flight Sergeant back then.' He would never get used to the informality displayed by American servicemen. Rank seemed to hold no meaning for them. They all called each other Mac, or Buddy, or Pal, without any acknowledgement of seniority.

'Jesus H. Christ!' the American declared. 'It's colder here than in Suwon.'

'He's right,' James concurred. 'Got any scotch, Dickie?'

'Oh, yes. Right you are, Sir . . . um, I mean James. Joint Operations with the Americans is wonderful. Their Officers' Club here has everything, and I mean *everything*.' He smiled at his former Commanding Officer and the three men pressed into the wind and set off for the distant buildings that constituted Kenjong United States Air Force Base under the command of the United Nations Armed Forces, Korea.

'Happy New Year, Dickie,' James said when he and Beckham were seated indoors. Johnnie had gone to secure their accommodation, saying he would rejoin them soon. He raised his drink in a salute and downed half of it. 'By Christ, Beckers old man,' he continued after looking around the expansive USAF Officers' Club. 'The bloody Yanks could teach the R.A.F. a thing or two about housing their officers, eh? I thought their Suwon Base was decent enough, but it's not a patch on this place.'

'Don't be fooled, James. The rest of the place is a sea of frozen mud and the accommodation, my God!' He laughed humourlessly. 'No matter what your rank, it's primitive to say the least – flimsy wooden huts, freezing in winter and stiflingly hot in summer.'

'Some things never change, eh Dickie?'

'I got the shock of my life when I heard you'd re-activated your commission,' Dickie said. 'I thought you'd have had enough air combat to last you a lifetime. And here you are in Korea, and not only that but seconded to the mighty United States Air Force, flying Sabres, you lucky sod.'

'And you're flying Gloster Meteors with the Aussie 43rd Squadron.' James laughed and drained his scotch. 'Can't help bad luck, old boy.'

'Being posted to Kenjong was more than bad luck.' Dickie sipped his whisky and placed his glass on the table that separated them. 'Air combat missions in Meteors around this neck of the woods are downright bloody dangerous.'

He's rattled, James thought, as he sat back and savoured the comfort of his armchair. After two hours in a Sabre cockpit, it felt like heaven against his back. He watched Dickie light a cigarette and drag furiously on it, before drinking the rest of his scotch.

'It's that bad is it?'

'The Meteor is no match for the Mig-15.' Dickie shook his head and puffed again on his cigarette. 'Quite simply, the Russian jet is a modern-day fighter and the Meteor is a bastard born of World War II. Can I get you another?' He indicated the empty scotch glasses. James nodded and watched Dickie head for the bar.

He's rattled all right, James thought. He lit a cigarette and surveyed his sumptuous surroundings, now being decorated for New Year's Eve. The USAF Officers' Club at Kenjong had to be seen to be believed. It was part of a massive two storey complex built by the Americans to house the USAF Fighter-Interceptor Communications Centre and the Australian 43rd Fighter Squadron HQ. It had the best of everything, except good aircraft, James mused. It was nothing like the R.A.F. bases he'd been used to sharing. Glass topped tables and comfortable chairs were set around a dance floor and they even had two potted palm trees inside the front doors. The bandstand had potted plants along its front too, and, James assumed, judging by the amount of music stands and instruments on it, a big band would be playing that night. The whole set up was more like a London nightclub than a recreation room at an air base.

And the Americans had this wonderful thing called a PX, which apparently stood for Post Exchange, where one could purchase anything one could think of from cigarettes and alcohol, to silk stockings and satin neckties. James decided Americans didn't simply fight wars, they lived them. And, he thought, they never really had to leave their homeland to do it; wherever they went, they took the United States with them.

In World War II, unlike many others in the R.A.F., James had had little contact with Americans, but since re-enlisting and arriving in Korea as part of the United Nations Forces, he'd been seconded to the USAF 8th Tactical Fighter Group at Suwon, south of Seoul. The Americans' logistic skills and their organisational capability had him awestruck. They had the best aircraft and equipment, mainly because they'd invented most of it, and they had the best communications and support he'd ever seen. And they were generous to a fault, which was the reason he was sitting where he was, in Kenjong Officers' Club about to drink his second whisky. The wing of six Sabre jets he commanded had been seconded to Kenjong to assist the Australians.

'Here you go.' Dickie Beckham handed him a large scotch, sat down and lit yet another cigarette. He inhaled deeply, then exhaled, and attacked his scotch like a thirsty camel.

'Go easy on that stuff, Dickie,' James cautioned. 'I didn't fly in from Suwon to spend New Year's Eve with an unconscious man.'

'Don't worry about me, old boy, I'm not rostered to fly for another seventy-two hours.'

'You never drank at all in the old days, Dickie . . .'

'Christ alive, James!' Beckham snapped. 'I'm flying fighter missions along the Yalu River in a fucking Meteor!' He sat back in his armchair and heaved a sigh. 'I'm sorry, old man, I didn't mean to swear like that, but . . . damn it all, James, you've no idea what it's like flying through Mig Alley – that's what they call the Yalu River Valley by the way – with the threat of Russian Mig-15s constantly hanging over you.'

'Well your troubles are over, Dickie boy.' James pulled an official looking envelope from his pocket and threw it on the table. 'UN Strategic Air Command has seen fit to transfer Johnnie Wilson and me, and those two F-86 Sabres parked out on the tarmac, to 43rd Squadron Kenjong. We're to be your nursemaids.'

'I say!' Dickie Beckham exclaimed. He sat upright and snatched the envelope. 'You're not pulling my leg are you, old boy?'

'Call it a belated Christmas present from Uncle Sam. Our American commanders know the limitations of the Meteor jet, Dickie. That's why they've sent Sabres as high cover.'

Beckham ran his eyes over the orders, replaced them in the envelope and handed them back to James. 'It's good news, James, it really is – I mean the fact that you're here – but it's also laughable you know? Sending fighters to escort fighters? The Aussies I fly with are brilliant pilots flying obsolete aircraft. It's not their fault the Meteor is no match for the Mig. And I'll tell you what: if they had Sabres, there wouldn't be a Mig left in the sky in a month.'

'They're that good, are they, Dickie?'

'Don't doubt it for a minute. Mind you, they have no respect for command. In fact, they have no respect for authority whatsoever. And believe you me, when they find out that High Command has sent them nursemaids, they will not be amused. They're very proud young men.'

'Well, Dickie,' James leaned back in his chair, 'I hope they're as good as you say they are, because they're going to need to be.'

'Why's that, old boy?' Dickie asked, as he lit yet another cigarette.

'Because as from tomorrow, the Australian 43rd Squadron and their 77th Squadron at Kimpo will be re-classified as a low level ground attack squadron.'

'Oh, Christ.' Dickie Beckham's glass stopped halfway to his mouth. 'By low level I take it you mean knocking out anti-aircraft batteries?'

'Precisely.' James nodded. 'I believe the new term for it is anti-aircraft suppression. Johnnie and I will fly above you as fighter-interceptors.'

'Two Sabres for high cover? Is that it?'

'No. I'll have a wing of six. Four more Sabres will join us in about a week.'

'Ground attack, eh? What a spectacular way to die.' Dickie's smile held everything but humour. 'The Migs will be diving all over us like seagulls after breadcrumbs.'

'Don't worry, old boy, they'll have to get through us first. We'll be right over the top of you, all the way.'

'Oh well, for king and country.' Dickie drained the last of his whisky. 'If it has to be done, it has to be done. Stiff upper lip and all that, eh what?'

'Hey, fly-boy!' Johnnie Wilson threw himself into a chair and spun a gleaming Colt .45 self-loading pistol on his finger in the style of a cowboy in a western movie. Then he tossed it in the air, caught it by the barrel and offered the handle to James. 'There you are, Jimbo. I arranged for it to be sent here to Kenjong. I told you I'd get you one, didn't I? It was easier than ropin' a calf.'

James inspected the firearm; it was a silver-plated semi-automatic, intricately engraved with pearl handle grips, and it had his name and rank engraved along the barrel. He removed the magazine and opened the breech, ensuring it was unloaded before handing it to Dickie.

'I say, old man, weapons in the Mess? Not on, James. Simply not done,' blustered Dickie.

'Relax, Dickie,' James replied. 'This is not the R.A.F.'

'Well . . . um, it's a beautiful sidearm, I'll say that.' Dickie inspected it and handed it back to James. 'A work of art, in fact.' He looked at Johnnie Wilson. 'Where on earth did you acquire it?'

'As I keep telling Jimbo, Dick,' the American winked at him, 'the American military, apart from being the greatest fighting machine in the world, is also the greatest black market in the world. There ain't nothin' . . . and I mean *nothin'* . . . you can't get if you know the right people.'

'In that case,' Dickie snorted, 'I'll have a Sabre if you've got a spare one lying about.'

'Well, now, that's a mighty tall order, Wing Commander,' the Texan drawled, looking at James. 'If you're serious I could arrange one, but it might take a few weeks. And you'd have to have some place to hide it.'

'I was joking,' Dickie stated flatly.

'Well, in that case, so was I . . . sorta.' Johnnie Wilson leaned back in his chair, drained his scotch and grimaced.

'Goddammit, boys! But I ain't never gonna get used to scotch whisky. Ain't you fellas ever tried good ol' Tennessee sour mash?'

'I'm not even aware of the term,' Dickie replied.

'Well, it's about time you were, pardner.' Johnnie Wilson got to his feet. 'It's New Year's Eve for cryin' out loud, time to break out the sour mash and have us a celebration. I'll just wander over yonder and get us a bottle of Tennessee's finest, and we'll do some serious sippin' till the clock strikes twelve and the flares go up.' He headed off towards the bar and an awkward silence developed between the two Englishmen.

James Merchant was aware that his young American wingman was deliberately using an appalling Texan accent in order to restore the sense of bonhomie that had existed before he'd produced the Colt handgun. John Wilson, Captain USAF, had spent two years at Oxford University and spoke perfectly modulated and almost accentless English when he wished. He probably should have warned Johnnie that Dickie was a bit of a stick in the mud, James thought irritably, especially when it came to military protocol.

He's a typical product of the British military, James thought, still using terms like 'stiff upper lip', 'king and country', and all the other garbage he'd been indoctrinated with to justify the simple fact that he was professionally involved in the kill-or-be-killed business of war.

'You're not seriously thinking of keeping that thing are you?' Dickie finally broke the silence.

'The handgun?' James picked it up from the table and read the inscription, *'To James, in case you hit the deck – from Johnnie, Korea 1951.* I most certainly am.'

'It's in direct contravention of UN Standing Orders, you know?'

'Dickie, I couldn't give a "flying fuck", to quote my American friend.' James put the weapon in his inside coat pocket. 'If I am destined to crash land in a rice paddy and die in a gunfight with the North Korean Army, I intend to do it with a bit of style.'

Dickie Beckham had to smile. He'd never known anyone like James Merchant. The man had simply walked through the horror of World War II like anyone else would stroll through a park. He was the greatest fighter pilot he'd ever known. When James was at the controls of an aircraft he became an invincible killing machine, cold blooded, calculating and ruthless. And on the ground too, he could, when the occasion warranted, be precisely the same. Dickie's smiled widened at the memory.

龍

Flight Sergeant Dick Beckham walked into the packed Tangmere Fighter Base Pilots' Mess at about eight o'clock on an evening in August 1940. The Battle of Britain was raging and everybody's nerves were at breaking point. Only that afternoon the squadron had lost two pilots over the Channel.

Dickie noticed Flight Lieutenant James Merchant standing alone at the end of the bar, observing several other pilots playing darts, and decided to join him.

Young O'Halloran's first two darts missed narrowly, but the third struck dead centre and a chorus of cheers erupted.

'Christ, O'Halloran,' Dickie heard James say, a little too loudly, 'it's a shame you can't hit Messerschmitts like that.'

Dickie watched uneasily as several of the pilots involved in the game turned their eyes upon James.

'I suppose you could do better, Merchant,' one of the men remarked.

'I could do that with my eyes shut,' James said, flatly.

'You're insufferable, Merchant,' another pilot said. 'You really are a pompous bastard.'

'I'm not here to play stupid bar games,' James replied. 'I'm here to eradicate German aircraft from the sky. However, to prove it was no idle boast.' He took the darts from young O'Halloran's hand, stood in front of the dart board, took a deep breath, exhaled slowly, closed his eyes and delivered all three darts into the bullseye.

'Good God,' someone muttered among the gasps of shock and amazement.

'It's a simple accomplishment,' James said. 'Any idiot can achieve it with a bit of practice.' He looked at O'Halloran. 'There's no element of risk involved. After all, the dart board's not going to outmanoeuvre you and fire back, is it?'

'Now steady on, Merchant,' another pilot remarked.

'All I'm saying is, if O'Halloran, and the rest of you for that matter, could target Messerschmitts the way you target dart boards, the air war at least would be over in a month. Your problem is that you miss nine out of ten times because you let fear get the better of you.'

Even Dickie gulped at the outrageous statement and the Mess, which contained thirty or more men, fell silent.

'Are you calling us cowards?' a tall New Zealander asked.

'Of course not,' Richard replied. 'I'm simply saying . . .'

The New Zealander threw the first punch and Dickie stood dumbstruck at what ensued.

During the melee that followed, five other men had hurled themselves at James Merchant intent on doing him some serious damage, but Dickie had watched, dumbstruck, as James had retaliated with a blur of fists and feet. He'd rendered the New Zealander and the other five unconscious, or incapable of continuing, without them landing a single blow on him.

When Dickie later enquired, James explained that since childhood he'd studied a discipline called *kung fu*, which was part of an ancient Chinese philosophy called the *Way of Shaolin*. Apparently, he practised the mental and physical exercises every morning of his life.

龍

The memory of that night had stayed with Dick Beckham for two reasons. Firstly, because he'd never witnessed its like before or since and secondly, because that event had made James Merchant a pariah. He'd been sent to Coventry by his fellow pilots, but it hadn't seemed to worry him in the slightest. James had kept on killing, coldly and efficiently, until he'd been awarded the Distinguished Flying Cross and was transferred to the Prime Minister's Office and paraded around the country as a hero. And that had been the last Dickie had seen of him.

'You're a cool customer, James,' he chuckled. 'Tell me, do you still do those Chinese things,' he waved his hands about theatrically, 'you used to practise at Tangmere?'

'If by "Chinese things" you mean the teachings of *Shaolin*, the answer is yes, Dickie. I am still very much a disciple. I was born and raised in Hong Kong, after all.'

'Well, God help the North Koreans is all I can say!' Dickie laughed. 'By Jove, I remember that stoush you were in at Tangmere, do you remem – '

'Gentlemen,' Johnnie Wilson interrupted, 'it is my profound pleasure to introduce you to the Flower of the South. I refer, my friends, to the beautiful little lady that sits housed in that there bottle.' He winked at the young waiter he'd led back to their table, who was bearing a tray of drinks. 'Why don't you just do the honours, son?'

'Yessir!' the young man replied, placing three shot glasses on the table followed by three bottles of Budweiser beer. Then he opened the bottle of Kincaid's Tennessee Sour Mash Whiskey and filled each glass to the brim.

'That'll be all, son. And you can leave the bottle.' As the waiter turned and left, the American pilot raised his shot glass and offered a toast. 'Gentlemen, here's to the United Nations Forces Korea, the British, the Australians,' he saluted the room aware he was being watched by predominantly Australian pilots, 'and us good old boys from the US of A.'

The two British pilots watched as he downed the whisky.

'Aaah!' Johnnie Wilson exclaimed. 'Chug-a-lug, chug-a-lug! Now that, boys, is the real thing! Genuine Tennessee sour mash sippin' whisky. Only you don't sip it. Where I come from in Texas, what I just did is called chug-a-lug.' He put his glass on the table and drank a hefty mouthful of beer.

'Well,' James replied. 'When in Rome, Dickie.'

'Right you are, James.'

'Chug-a-lug!' They chorused in unison.

龍

It was three o'clock in the morning on New Year's Day, 1952, when the pilots staggered out of the Officers' Club. They'd drunk and sung their way to midnight and beyond, dancing with a number of young Korean women imported for the night's party. And now, wrapped in USAF issue fur-lined winter parkas, and armed with a case of Tennessee whisky Johnnie had stolen from behind the bar, they stumbled across the tarmac towards the two Sabre jets sitting ominously in the bright moonlight. The wind had finally dropped to a whisper, but the Korean winter night was still freezing.

A night crew of enlisted personnel was gathered around a forty-four gallon drum trying to draw warmth from the fire they'd lit in it. Upon the approach of the officers, the men pretended to be busy.

'There's no need for that, gentlemen,' James said as he sat on an empty ammunition box. 'It's 1952, come and have a drink.' He held up a bottle of Tennessee whisky. 'To no one in particular,' he stated. It was soon grabbed and, before long, ten men had gathered around the fire and were quietly drinking.

'I thought we were going to call it a night?' Dickie Beckham shrugged. 'Oh well, here's to no one in particular,' he said. He swigged some sour mash from a bottle but the liquid had lost its magic. He believed he'd actually drunk himself sober.

'A last look at the war-birds, Dickie, and that full Korean moon.' James took a bottle from the case and opened it up. 'Drink that. It's an order.' He handed it to one of the ground crew and began opening another.

'Goodonya, mate,' came the high speed reply.

'Ah,' James looked at the ground crew member who'd taken the bottle, 'an Antipodean, unless my ears deceive me?'

'That's right, Sir. I'm an Australian, from Sydney.'

'Sydney, eh?' James clunked his bottle against the one he'd

given the Australian. 'Here's to no one in particular . . . and Sydney, I'm sure it's a wonderful city.' They both drank from the bottles. 'My mother had property in Sydney . . . er,' he squinted at the man's uniform insignia, '. . . Sergeant, but after the war we had to sell every asset we owned.'

'Yeah.' The Sergeant took a hefty swig and nodded. 'The bloody war didn't do anyone any good. And now we're in another one.' The comment invoked silence and the men shuffled on their seats, or moved about trying to keep warm.

'Would no one in particular like something to eat?' The Sergeant continued the joke. 'I've got some septic rations here.' He held up an American ration pack.

'Septic rations?' Dickie muttered. 'What on earth are septic rations? They sound disgusting.'

'Septic, Sir, septic tank. It's rhymes with . . .'

'Oh, I see,' Dickie interrupted. 'Rhyming slang, got you now. Like the Cockneys use. I'd forgotten the Aussies' fondness for it. Septic tank, eh? What's it rhyme with?'

'Yank.'

Johnnie Wilson, who had not uttered a word since arriving at the aircraft, stood up. 'Septic tank? Rhymes with Yank?' he asked in his broadest Texan drawl. 'Am I hearin' you right, Sergeant?'

'Oh, shit,' the Australian muttered. 'Not all Americans, Sir,' he said quickly. 'Only those from the Northern States.'

'Well, that's okay,' Johnnie Wilson smiled, 'I myself am from the Lone Star State of Texas and my ancestors, on my Momma's side, hail from the good old State of Georgia and we are therefore, *not* Yankees. If anything we are Good Ol' Boys and that's a fact.'

They fell into silence, sipping vigorously at their whisky until, eventually, a young Aussie spoke up. 'I'll bet those North Korean soldiers out there,' he nodded vaguely into the darkness beyond the fire, 'would give their right arms for one of them US ration packs.' He took a grateful sip from the bottle offered to him by his Sergeant. 'I've heard it said they eat rats because they don't get any proper food.'

'Hey, you know what?' Johnnie Wilson decided to lighten the mood again. 'We could steal ration packs from the Quartermaster and take 'em on combat missions and drop 'em in Mig Alley. All we'd need to do is set up a bank account in Switzerland and the North Korean Government could forward payment by post.' The remark caused a laugh. 'Whaddaya say, Jimbo? After the war we could retire on the profits.'

'I'd say the profits would be enormous,' James replied. What an intriguing idea, he thought. 'But if I operated a business like that, I'd be disinclined to make the deliveries myself, Johnnie. It would be too dangerous. I'd do a deal with the Chinese. Let's face it, they're running the war for the Koreans. I'd send the goods overland from Hong Kong through China and sell them across the Yalu River border.'

'Whadda you say, Dickie?' Johnnie turned to Richard Beckham. 'You wanna make some money?'

'Hmm? I'm sorry, I'm falling asleep. If you gentlemen will excuse me, I might trot off to bed. I'm freezing, and neither the fire nor the whisky is doing anything to alter that fact.' This statement caused the silence to fall yet again and it lasted a full minute until the young Aussie spoke.

'Fuckin' oath I'm cold.' He said it more to himself than anyone else.

First there was a snigger and then laughter broke out in full. They laughed at the inanity of the remark; they laughed because it was true; and they laughed to ward off the thought that they were cold and alone and far from home.

'Johnnie, why don't you warm the lads up?' James winked, nodding at the aircraft not thirty yards from them. 'You're their Senior Officer after all, and it's New Year's Eve for God's sake.'

'It's as good as done, pardner.' Johnnie Wilson saluted, got up and headed for his Sabre, then while the group watched he threw several switches on a machine linked up to the aircraft, climbed into the cockpit and fired up the engine.

'Oh, shit, he's not gonna . . . Jesus fucking wept!' the Aussie Sergeant exclaimed over the boom of the engine ignition. 'He'll get us all court-martialled.'

The jet engine screamed, like an angry dragon woken from its slumber, and flames roared from its tail. One of the young ground crew just managed to escape the blast and several empty boxes were blown twenty yards from where they'd been standing.

'Good God!' Dickie yelled, suddenly quite sober. 'What on earth does he think he's doing? He'll have the Military Police out here in no time flat!'

No sooner had Dickie issued the warning than several military Jeeps came around the corner of a hangar several hundred yards distant and rushed towards the aircraft with spotlights blazing.

James waved a hand at Johnnie, who was grinning at him from the cockpit. He made a sign like cutting his throat and the engine began to shut down, whining and growling.

Six USAF MPs arrived fully armed and leapt from the Jeeps, but when they saw the drunken group of airmen and the whisky bottles, they visibly relaxed.

'Okay! Who's the wise-guy?' a young American Lieutenant asked.

'It was no one in particular, Lieutenant.' Johnnie Wilson continued the lame joke as he emerged from the shadows beneath the fuselage of the plane, causing another round of laughter.

'With all due respect, Captain, Sir,' the MP began, aware now that he was not the Senior Officer present, 'I'll have to report this. Standing Order Number one-oh-six-eight forbids – '

'Okay, okay. I accept full responsibility for what occurred, Lieutenant. My name is Captain John Wilson and I expect to be flying a combat mission in this airplane tomorrow morning. I was concerned the freezing temperature tonight might be detrimental to my aircraft. I came out to the plane, saw that some ice had formed on her and thought I might warm her up.'

The young Lieutenant looked about at the other members of the group and noticed the two British Wing Commanders present. Jesus, he thought to himself, what are they having here, a Joint Chiefs of Staff meeting? Then he noticed the four bottles of whisky remaining in the case.

'I see you got plenty of fuel there too, Captain. You gentlemen look like you've had a good night.'

'Lieutenant.' It was James. He stood and smiled at the young MP. 'I was wondering if you could take that fuel there,' he indicated the whisky, 'and get rid of it for us?'

'Yes, Sir! I'm sure I could do that for you, Wing Commander.' The MP nodded to one of his subordinates who picked up the case in an instant and put it in the back of a Jeep.

'I take it there'll be no report, Lieutenant?'

'A report, Sir?' All of the MPs were smiling. 'About what?' He issued a smart salute. 'Happy New Year, gentlemen. I hope it's a good one for you all.'

When the MPs had gone the party broke up and beds and sleep were swiftly sought. But James Merchant could not sleep. Despite the long night, the alcohol and the dancing, he was unable to find that peaceful oblivion. His mind kept returning to the drunken conversation he'd had with Johnnie Wilson, before the MPs broke up their little party. He lay thinking until the first rays of winter sunlight crept through his window. Only then did sleep catch him unawares.

龍

James sat in the cockpit of his Sabre jet and lit a cigarette, fully aware of the apprehension he was creating amongst his ground crew. During the three months since his arrival at Kenjong Base, he'd pretty much given cigarettes up, but being genuinely excited at the day's prospects, he'd acquired one from an MP and was smoking it furiously.

'I don't want to tell you your job, Sir,' the Aussie ground crew Sergeant remarked as he climbed onto the wing, 'but cigarettes and jet aviation fuel ain't a good mix.'

'Ordinarily I'd agree with you, Sergeant, but today is a very special day . . .'

'It is for me too, Sir, and I intend to stay alive to enjoy it. Begging your pardon, Sir,' the Aussie took the cigarette from

James' fingers and spat on it to extinguish it, 'you know the old saying, "one flash and you're ash"?'

'Fair enough, Sergeant.' James laughed as the man reached around him and made sure the straps of his ejector seat were firmly buckled.

'So, you're off on Special Ops today, Sir?' The Sergeant continued with his last minute checks of cockpit controls and safety procedures.

'Yes, if ever my wingman decides to show up.'

'Captain Wilson said to tell you he's over at the Maintenance Depot and will be about five minutes.' The Sergeant patted his pilot on the shoulder and leapt from the wing to the ground. 'Ground crew on standby for ignition, Sir,' he called back and threw a brief salute.

James made himself as comfortable as the cockpit would allow and looked again, across the flight field to the row of cherry trees alive with pink blossoms along the distant perimeter fence line.

Spring had come to Korea. And not before time, James thought, wishing desperately that he would not have to suffer another Korean winter. The weather he'd experienced had been the worst he'd encountered in his life. Even sitting in the warm, spring sunshine he shuddered involuntarily at the memory, as he reflected on the last three months.

龍

Conflicting political ideologies had been briefly forgotten during the freezing winter of 1952. The great armies of East and West, massed on the Korean Peninsula, sought shelter from the harsh conditions that had held all of Korea in a snow white grip.

The state of the war seemed to be less intense since the 8th Army had landed at Inchon and broken out of the Pusan Perimeter. There were several major battles, but for the most part confrontations between the Communist and UN Forces had been smaller, more fragmented affairs.

The first time James flew through Mig Alley he'd been bitterly disappointed. Not only did he cop no ground fire, he didn't engage a single Mig-15. There were none in the air. He'd been anticipating at least a scrap of some sort, but nothing had eventuated. The Yalu River Valley was a blanket of snow and ice, as empty and uninviting as the North Pole.

At altitude he'd seen any number of Migs sitting smugly on the deck at Antung, the Chinese air base on the Manchurian side of the border, but under UN Standing Orders that was strictly a 'no fly zone'.

Rules in warfare were an absurdity in James' opinion. The Mig-15s were sitting ducks, ripe for the plucking, but if he crossed into Chinese air space and opened fire, the Chinese would righteously claim it was an 'act of war' and the United Nations itself would declare his actions an 'unauthorised act of aggression against a neutral power'.

The thought of China and Russia being neutral powers in the Korean War had caused James to laugh out loud into his oxygen mask as he'd turned his Sabre and headed for home.

Several days later he and Johnnie had escorted two Meteors of 43rd R.A.A.F. Squadron, one flown by Dickie Beckham, on a photo-reconnaissance mission gathering information on North Korean and Chinese Army troop movements and supply lines. The photos had revealed practically nothing, apart from some North Korean Army units dug in for the winter, and the UN Intelligence Unit analysts, in their wisdom, had declared the Chinese must have closed their supply lines because of the winter weather. They based this profoundly stupid declaration on the fact that no vehicles were evident in the photos.

James, part Chinese himself, knew them too well to believe such rubbish. He knew beyond any doubt the Chinese would continue to operate their supply lines, no matter what adversity they faced, and his faith in their ingenuity was rewarded.

He'd noticed tracks in the snow where the Chinese had assembled during the preceding night, but there were no vehicles to be seen. He'd crossed the area at low level several times before the penny dropped. The Chinese had driven their vehicles straight through the walls of farmhouses, barns, stables, and in many instances, straight into haystacks, and covered the evidence of entry with canvas or snow. It was brilliantly simple and typical of the cunning Chinese mentality James knew so well. All they needed was for snow to fall and cover their tracks, and their concealment from reconnaissance cameras was complete. But the previous night there had been no snowfall, and their ploy had been revealed.

James had returned to Kenjong and expressed his views to Fighter Command. As a result, that same afternoon, the six Sabres that made up James' Fighter-Interceptor Wing, along with other squadrons from Suwon and Kimpo, began attacking indiscriminate targets. The results had been spectacular. Napalm attacks and heavy machine-gun fire had revealed military vehicles and personnel in eight out of every ten instances. Massive explosions had revealed hidden ammunition stores. He'd watched the tiny figures of soldiers in the snow scatter in all directions, frantic to extinguish their flaming uniforms. Eventually, the entire frozen landscape had been littered with trucks, buildings and haystacks alike, all burning furiously and emitting long columns of black smoke high into the winter air.

Later that night in the Officers' Club at Kenjong, the pilots had rejoiced, swapping stories, and, like excited children with their arms extended, flying imaginary jets, they had relived the events of the day.

It was late February before James saw any actual fighter-to-fighter aerial combat. His squadron of Sabres had been flying high cover for Dickie Beckham's Wing of Gloster Meteors as they performed ground attacks, mainly on supply vehicles. It had been dangerous work, all the more so because a Meteor had to be held smooth and level on its firing run for its gyro-stabilised gun sight to operate accurately, making the aircraft vulnerable to ground fire.

It was eagle eyed Johnnie Wilson who'd made the first call of enemy contact. 'Bogies at twelve o'clock high!'

James' reaction was instantaneous and the direct opposite of any other pilot in the sky. There was no sense of fear, no rising heart rate, no muscle tension; instead, his mind began to prepare for battle. A sense of calm engulfed him. Already he'd broken formation and his aircraft was climbing under full power seeking higher altitude. *Relax,* the voice of Lo Shi-mon, his *Shaolin* master, whispered inside his head. *Let your mind take control of your body. Use your senses, detect the threat, choose the correct response, strike, withdraw, defend. Detect the next threat. Strike, withdraw, defend. Detect, strike, withdraw, defend. Relax, Little Brother.* He felt a soft, sensual thrill as he relaxed more and more, until the aircraft became an extension of his being. His body became a conductor of impulses from his brain to his hands and feet, and his aircraft became a dragon, screaming through the sky, prepared to vent its wrath upon any who would dare challenge it.

At thirty-five thousand feet, James rolled his Sabre and sought combat, but even he was not prepared for the sight that met his gaze. The silver wings of Mig-15s flashed in the sunlight all through the sky. There must be forty or more, he thought, far too many for six Sabres to engage in a dog fight.

'Red Leader, Red Leader,' he called to Dickie Beckham in his reconnaissance aircraft far below, his voice cold and clear. 'This is Blue Leader. Abort mission and return to base.'

'Roger Wilco, Blue Leader.' Dickie's voice came back through James' headset. 'Mission completed, withdrawing. Will stay under twenty thousand.' Under twenty thousand feet in the thicker atmospheric conditions nothing could catch the Meteors.

'Blue Wing, Blue Wing,' James called to his pilots. 'This is Blue Leader. Shoot your way clear. Disengage and withdraw.'

As his pilots acknowledged his orders, James dived on a Mig, closing rapidly to less than a hundred yards before opening fire. His Sabre shuddered as bullets from the six Browning M3 fifty-calibre machine guns mounted in its nose tore into the Russian jet's wing and fuselage. The effect was instantaneous. The Mig-15 erupted in a ball of flame as the armour-piercing incendiary shells exploded on impact with its fuel tank.

'You got him, Blue Leader.' Johnnie Wilson's excited voice crashed in James' ears.

'Let's get out of here, Johnnie, there're too many of them.'

'You've got a Roger to that from me, Skip. Okay, Blue Wing,' Johnnie called to the other Sabre pilots. 'You heard the man, let's skedaddle outta here! Last one home buys the booze.'

It was several hours later in the Officers' Club at Kenjong after the mission debriefing when Johnnie Wilson slapped his C.O. on the back and called for drinks.

'But none of that sour mash stuff for me,' James said. 'A beer will be more than sufficient.' He fell into an armchair and put his booted feet up on the table. Johnnie Wilson flopped down next to him as did Andrew Macdonald, another of his Sabre pilots.

'That was good shooting, Skipper,' the young Scot said. 'That Mig just blew apart. They're built like brick shithouses, you know. You must have hit his fuel tank. I've tried twice to down one. I put more holes in one of them than a Swiss cheese, but it wouldn't blow.'

'It's strange,' James said. 'The pilot never attempted to evade me. In fact, I don't believe he was even aware I was on him.'

'Well, if he wasn't aware of it then,' Johnnie Wilson drawled in his worst accent, 'he sure as hell ain't aware of it now!' The remark caused a lot of laughter and they were joined at the table by the rest of Blue Wing and several of the Australian Meteor pilots. Congratulations were offered by many and soon a celebration was under way.

James was not in a party mood and hoped he made it obvious by moving to the next table. As he sat down he noticed Johnnie disappear only to return several minutes later with a box containing six brand new Austrian cameras. The result, it went without saying, of his latest foray into the military black market, James thought. Johnnie sold the lot in ten minutes.

There was no doubt in James' mind, as he watched the young Texan pack his wallet with cash, that Johnnie Wilson was a born horse-trader, utterly without morals, driven by the excitement of the illegal exchanges, and ruled by the love of money.

But apart from a mildly amused interest in Johnnie Wilson's business acumen, James' mind remained detached from the party swelling around him. He couldn't get his mind out of the sky. Several other pilots in the debriefing had estimated the number of Mig-15s between a hundred and a hundred and fifty and James was intrigued. During the debriefing he'd adjusted his own estimate to seventy or eighty at least, but he couldn't understand why so many had been in the sky. And with so many, why had they failed to shoot down any UN aircraft? They'd been outnumbered by at least ten to one and yet his squadron and the six Meteors had escaped unscathed.

'Penny for your thoughts, old man?' Richard Beckham placed two beers on the table and sat down next to James, who couldn't help but notice that Dickie also had a large glass of whisky.

'Oh, hello, Dickie.'

'One of those beers is for you. You looked like you were miles away. Thought I'd wake you up. Why the furrowed brow?'

James picked up a beer. 'Cheers,' he offered, and sipped it. 'You know, Dickie, not one of us should have got out of that scrap today alive and yet here we all are,' he indicated by waving the beer around in the air. 'Something like a hundred Migs in the sky, Dickie, and they never fired a shot. Why? Answer me that?'

'I have a theory, if you'd care to indulge an old soldier.'

'Fire away.'

'Well,' Dickie lit a cigarette and puffed rapidly on it. 'You said in the mission debriefing that the fellow you shot down seemed to be unaware he was under attack, am I right?'

'Yes.' James nodded. 'He didn't appear to have a clue. No reaction whatsoever. No evasion tactics at all, nothing. A lamb to the slaughter.'

'In other words,' Dickie murmured, 'a total novice?'

'Exactly.'

'And that's part of my theory right there,' Dickie nodded and gulped his beer. 'I believe that Mig base at Antung, just across the Yalu from Sinuiju, contains a pilot training facility. Jet conversion training, I'd bet my socks on it.'

'Pilot training?' James scoffed. 'Directly beneath Mig Alley? You can't be serious?'

'Can you think of a better place to learn aerial combat tactics? That's providing you're a good enough pilot in the first place.'

'It's certainly unconventional, but – '

'Unconventional!' Beckham scoffed. 'It's immoral, that's what it is!' He took a drink of whisky before continuing. 'It's the Communists. They're utterly ruthless. They fight wars with a total disregard for casualties or conventions. It's because they have more manpower than they know what to do with. They'll throw men and machines at us until there's not one of them left, and by that time there'll be hardly any of us left.' Dickie leaned towards James and lowered his voice, warming to his topic of discussion. 'I've been trying to tell the Brass for six months, but like you they scoffed at me. The Chinese Military Commander in Manchuria is a typical Communist soldier. He's unconventional. He doesn't play by the rules. Look at the way he kept his supply lines active all through winter. Farm-house and haystack concealments for God's sake! It's unheard of. It's Hamlet and the bloody burning wood!'

'I think that was Macbeth and Birnam Wood, Dickie.'

'Yes, yes, whatever,' Dickie said abruptly, irritated by the interruption. 'But the fact remains, James, that if it weren't for your eagle eye last month, he'd still be getting away with it. He's a damned clever fellow, bold and resourceful with the ability to think outside the square. In short, old boy, he's a formidable adversary. But do you think anyone at HQ will listen? Oh no, not them.'

'You've voiced these opinions at GHQ have you, Dickie?' James sipped his beer and watched Dickie light another cigarette.

'Haven't you been listening to me, James?' Beckham snapped. 'I've been at them for the past six months. General

Hargreaves had the temerity to suggest I was being too emotional when I voiced my concerns.' Dickie looked about the Club before continuing. 'Too emotional? What sort of a bloody reply is that? Honestly, James, I wanted to hit the man.'

And he would have deserved it, James thought, for not recognising combat fatigue when it was thrust in his face. Dickie Beckham wasn't fit to fly. He was an emotional wreck. James had been well aware of the excessive drinking and smoking, but he'd not seen Dickie this upset before. He'd have to have a word with someone before the man cracked completely.

James decided to humour him for the moment and have a word with the Medical Officer after dinner. 'So what do you think he's up to at Antung?' he asked.

'Who?'

'This Chinese Commander.'

'Oh. Yes. Think? I don't think, James, I bloody well know!' Dickie Beckham had worked himself into a rage. 'Any idiot who can read a calendar couldn't help but know. Every four weeks to the day, there's a hundred or more Migs in the sky without fail. I've been marking the days on my calendar for six months and it's a twenty-eight day cycle. Week one, no Migs. Week two, several Migs, but they never cross the Yalu. Week three, a few more, but still, they rarely cross the border. Then week four, bingo – it's graduation day and over they come. This Commander, whoever he is, has arranged for his young Chinese pilots to do a four-week jet conversion training course right on our doorstep, because he knows we'll maintain the border protocols and observe the no fly zone. Then, when their training is completed, he has them take off en masse, climb to thirty thousand feet, wander over the border into Mig Alley and practise their crash course in air combat tactics.'

'And where,' said James, 'if they get into trouble, they can turn tail, open the throttle and be back in their own air space in sixty seconds.'

'Precisely! If they're good enough.' Dickie downed his beer

and signalled the bar that two more beers were required. 'But every squadron will have its lame ducks,' he continued, a little too loudly, 'and I believe this Commander chappie knows it. He is deliberately sending his planes over towards us to sort the wheat from the chaff.'

'You mean only the good pilots get home. Survival of the fittest, Dickie?'

'Exactly. And he's got us doing the sorting for him. There will always be some who are simply not good enough, like the one you got today.'

'Yes. He certainly wasn't good enough.'

'But eventually, James, my theory will prove correct!' Dickie's voice was now very loud. 'You mark my words. The Communist Commander is a clever fellow. You saw those Migs today, all those wings flashing in the sunlight. It's like flying through a crystal chandelier. And pretty soon it'll be like putting your head in a hornet's nest. Oh yes! Eventually they'll randomly open fire, all at once, and everyone in the bloody sky, them and us, will be damned to hell!'

'Take it easy, old fellow,' James murmured, aware other pilots were now paying attention. Several of the Australians looked at each other knowingly.

'Yes,' Dickie replied softly, now conscious of the silence around them. 'Right you are, James. I'd actually decided to give up discussing my theory until you happened to mention it and I'm afraid I got a bit wound up.'

A waiter arrived with two beers and placed them on the table.

'I'll get these, Dickie,' James said, taking the bar chit from the waiter and signing it. 'Let's drop the subject and tie one on. What do you say?'

'If you don't mind, James,' Dickie said, rising from his chair, 'I might call it a day, actually. I've got a splitting headache.'

James watched the man leave the Club as the noise of the party resumed. Dickie had been gabbling, there was no other word for it – but he had to admit his idea that Antung was a training base was probably right. The rest of his tirade, however, had manifested itself as symptoms of emotional distress, James thought. Dickie Beckham was a disturbed man, there was no doubt about it.

James had little time for weak men, especially those who allowed fear of combat to get to them. Not that he didn't understand the mental process himself – that moment of self-doubt, that first twinge of fear that could lead to a complete loss of courage – but a man simply had to learn to control himself. He remembered the one and only time he'd experienced it, just for a few brief seconds. It had been during the Battle of Britain.

My God, what a day that had been, he thought, smiling at the memory of it. He'd won the Distinguished Flying Cross, saved a friend's life, then crashed and met the woman he'd marry, all in one day.

He'd taken off in his Spitfire without a parachute and had been shot down trying to rescue Dickie Beckham, of all people. Unable to jump from the burning aircraft as it dived towards the ground, for several seconds he'd been frozen with fear until his *Shaolin* training had forced him to relax and concentrate on safely grounding the Spitfire.

He'd crash landed in the grounds of Stawell Manor, the ancestral home of Katherine Billings, niece and sole heiress to Sir Herbert, and the moment the grand house had come into view, he'd realised that he'd been there before. It had been in that very house, as seventeen-year-olds, that he and Lee Kwan, his adopted brother, had carried out their first assassination for the Society of Golden Dragons upon the orders of their *Shan Chu*, Richard Brewster. And there he was again, standing on the front door steps being introduced to the wealthy young aristocrat who would become his wife.

James drank long and hard, enjoying the freezing cold American beer. It amused him to think that Katherine had never known, and didn't to this day, that he'd murdered her uncle for an illegal triad society.

He'd chosen Katherine Billings for his wife because of her bloodlines. She was pure English aristocracy and James had decided she would bear his children. She'd been a pushover –

beautiful, wealthy and intelligent, but a pushover nonetheless. He'd seduced her and wed her during the latter stages of the war.

Their marriage had been good at first, he thought, but after the war, when he took her home to Hong Kong, and the twins, Paul and Georgina, were born, his passion for her had waned. She'd served her purpose by supplying him with a son and heir, although what sort of heir Paul would make was anybody's guess, he frowned. The boy was weak.

Katherine had made no attempt to understand the Chinese side of Hong Kong and he'd quickly given up trying to explain it. And he'd never mentioned the society – that would always remain a secret from her.

The Society of Golden Dragons, he thought, and the familiar surge of frustration ran through him. It had been part of his life since he was a child.

His step-father, Richard Brewster, as a young policeman, had created the *Gam Loong Tong*, the Society of Golden Dragons. It had become the most powerful triad in Hong Kong and Richard had been its *Shan Chu*, its Master. From the age of six, James and Lee Kwan had been instructed in the martial arts of *Shaolin* by Richard's closest friend and ally, Sergeant Lo Shi-mon. They had been trained to be the society's enforcers and assassins.

The scar on James' left upper arm itched as it often did. He scratched at it, his mind wandering back to his thirteenth year when he and Lee had been adopted by the Dragons in an initiation ceremony in the old Walled City on Kowloon side. The brand of a dragon had been burned onto a shoulder of each boy and they'd sworn undying loyalty to the society they believed would last forever.

But the Society of Golden Dragons had died, James thought bitterly. It had died on Christmas Day 1941, when the British Colonial Government of Hong Kong had surrendered to the invading Japanese Army. Of the founding First Five Dragons, only two had survived as far as James knew. Sergeant Lo Shi-mon had escaped to Mainland China, and had never been heard of again. And Richard Brewster was still alive, certainly, but to what purpose? He might as well have been slaughtered like the others. Three years in Stanley POW camp had destroyed him. Richard had been James' idol when he was young, but the war had changed all that. James had returned home full of hope for the future, only to find Richard a broken cripple, a weak man bereft of any hope or ambition. James despised weak men and his contempt for Richard Brewster knew no bounds.

After the war, James had returned to Hong Kong and suggested to Richard that they restore the society, but Richard had ignored him.

'Damn him!' James got to his feet and patted his pockets searching for a cigarette. He rarely smoked, but thinking about the Dragons – and Richard – had made him angry.

'Would you like one of mine, Sir?'

'Oh, thank you, Andrew.' James took a cigarette from the packet extended to him by his Flight Lieutenant Andrew Macdonald.

'Can I have a word in your ear, Skipper?' The young Scot's tone was conspiratorial.

'By all means,' James replied and indicated they both sit down. He began patting his flight jacket pockets, and Macdonald produced an American Zippo lighter and snapped it open. After accepting the light, James sat back in his chair, regarding the young man. 'Well, what is it, lad? Do you have a problem?'

'Oh, no, Sir, the problem's not mine.'

Macdonald's accent had a lilting quality to it. Probably Edinburgh or Dundee, James guessed, and immediately felt irritated for not knowing Macdonald's home town. It was a bad officer who didn't know the men under his command. The boy had been posted to Kenjong more than a month previously and James had yet to even read his Record of Service.

'Then whose problem is it? Get to the point, Macdonald.'

'Well, Sir,' the Scot's tone was hesitant, 'I could not help overhearing your conversation with Wing Commander Beckham – '

'Eavesdropping is a nasty habit,' James interrupted.

'With all due respect, Sir,' the Scot was affronted, 'it was hardly eavesdropping. I'd not be surprised if they heard him in Seoul.'

'All right,' James replied tersely. 'I'll withdraw the remark, but if you intend to offer an opinion on a Senior Officer, Macdonald, I'll warn you right now, I won't stand for it.'

'I had no such intention, Sir.' The Scot rose to his feet. 'It's obvious this is not a convenient time for me to – '

'Sit down immediately!' James cut the young officer off mid-sentence. They stared at each other for several seconds before the young man broke eye contact and sat, reluctantly. James continued to stare until eye contact was re-established. 'I misunderstood your intentions, Andrew,' he said evenly. 'I'm sorry. I've got a lot on my mind.'

'That's okay, Skipper.'

James smiled at his subordinate. 'Now, what's this problem?'

'Well, it's not exactly a problem, Sir,' the Scot replied, 'but I think it's something you should be aware of.'

'Go on.' James sipped his beer and placed the glass on the table.

'Well, Sir, when I was in transit from the UK to Seoul, I was delayed for a couple of days at Kai Tak R.A.F. Base in Hong Kong.'

'That's my home town.'

'Exactly. The officers at Kai Tak Mess were only too quick to point that out.'

'Really?' James was intrigued.

'Yes, Sir. When I told them I was on my way to Korea they told me you were stationed here and I should look out for you. Apparently the Merchant family is very famous in Hong Kong?'

'That's true. My family had many business concerns before the war and when my father died my mother took control of the Merchant Company and built it into an international trading house.' James paused and picked up his drink. 'But I'm afraid the war took care of the family fortune. My mother is hardly poor, but the family egg, so to speak, is miniscule compared to what it was before the war. Might I ask where this is all leading, Macdonald?'

'I'll get to the point, Sir, I promise, but allow me to continue?'

'Yes, yes, by all means.' James sipped his beer. 'Go on.'

'They also told me you had a brother?'

'Adopted brother,' James corrected. 'He's Chinese.'

'And he was a Captain in the Kuomintang?'

'Yes. He believed in Ch'iang Kai-shek and the Nationalist cause, as many Chinese patriots did, but he changed his allegiance after the fall of Hong Kong. The last I heard he was a Major in the People's Liberation Army living in Peking, but that was a long time ago. I haven't seen him for something like fifteen years and would doubt that he's still in the Army.'

'Have you ever had any sort of contact with him, Sir?'

James stiffened in his seat. He put his beer back on the table and stared at Andrew Macdonald. 'This conversation is becoming quite personal, Mr Macdonald. I think it might be wise for you to get to the point.'

'It's regarding the conversation you were having with Wing Commander Beckham. I thought your brother might be the General he was goin' on about.'

'Don't be ridiculous.' James lowered his voice, looking around as he replied.

'Sir, I would never have mentioned it if I didn't think it was a possibility.'

'And what makes you think it is a possibility?'

'Well, Sir – '

'Give me another cigarette.'

'Yes, Sir.' Macdonald handed his cigarettes and lighter to his Commanding Officer and waited until he'd lit one.

'Go on, Andrew.' James exhaled smoke and leaned towards the young Scot.

'Well, one particular officer in Hong Kong . . . I don't remember his name . . . he was a wee bit drunk, you know. Well, he was goin' on about a fellow called Lee Kwan who was an officer in the Chinese Army. According to him, this Lee Kwan was your mother's adopted son and he didn't think it was right for him to be fighting against the British in Korea.'

'And what makes you think he's the Commander in Manchuria to whom Beckham was referring?'

'Well, when I was in Seoul, I overheard a Yankee Air Force Colonel talking about a General Lee Kwan. Apparently he's the Commanding Officer Military Operations Manchuria and I thought it was a hell of a coincidence, Sir, that he had the same name as your brother.'

'That's all it is, Andrew, a coincidence,' James said. 'Both Lee and Kwan are very common Chinese names. In fact, the whole population shares about one hundred surnames in all. If I know my adopted brother, and I think I do, he would have left the Army when the People's Republic was created in 1949. Despite his war experiences, Lee is a dedicated pacifist, who finds the very idea of military conflict abhorrent.'

'Right you are, Sir.' Andrew Macdonald could not help but notice the tone of finality in his CO's voice. 'I'm sure it's just a coincidence. I mean to say, this Chinese General over the border is hardly a pacifist, is he?' The Scot laughed. 'More like the Antichrist according to Mr Beckham.'

'That's far enough, Andrew!' James rose from his seat.

'Yes, Sir.' Macdonald rose with his superior. 'I'm sorry, Sir.'

'Keep your opinions to yourself, lad. And as for your theory regarding my brother,' James picked his hat up from the table and placed it under his arm, 'I suggest you forget it. The very notion that he's a General in Manchuria is absurd.'

'Yes, Sir.'

'Now if you'll excuse me, I've got a mountain of paper-work to catch up on.' He patted the young Scot on the shoulder. 'Perhaps I'll see you at dinner.' James walked out of the Officers' Club into the cold, bright, spring sunshine.

So, Lee's a General now, he thought. And not only a General, but the General Commanding Military Ops in Manchuria. James wasn't remotely surprised. Anyone who knew Lee Kwan knew, also, that his rise through the military ranks of Mao Tse-tung's Army had been inevitable.

He walked on, deep in thought, finally stopping near the Air Maintenance building where he leaned against the wall and stared vacantly out towards the horizon. A plan was forming in his mind. It had been there since the early hours of New Year's Day when he'd sat on the apron beside Johnnie's Sabre, drinking whisky. But, in order to make it work, he had to telephone people in Hong Kong. And more importantly, he had to get to Hong Kong.

龍

'Hong Kong, here we come,' Johnnie Wilson yelled as he ran past James' Sabre and climbed up the access ladder into his own. His ground crew gathered on either wing ensuring he was correctly strapped to his seat, then leapt to the ground as the engine screamed into life and flames roared from its exhaust outlet.

James smiled and shook his head in amusement. Then, after giving Johnnie the thumbs-up signal, both Sabres taxied slowly to the runway.

James had been careful in his approach to Johnnie Wilson. When he'd told Johnnie that they were to fly to Hong Kong, he'd casually suggested that there may be the chance for some black market profiteering and Johnnie had been all for it. The following day he'd upped the ante in Johnnie's mind from trading in silk stockings and cameras to something slightly more substantial.

'Like what, Jimbo?' Johnnie had asked.

James' reply had caused the young American to hyperventilate. When he'd recovered, they shook hands and the partnership was sealed.

'Let's fly, Blue Leader.' Johnnie's voice came sharply through James' headset, as the jets thundered down the runway.

'Oh, you're going to fly all right, Captain Wilson,' James replied. 'You're going to fly higher than you've ever flown before.'

'Yeehaa!' The Texan's rebel yell shattered the airwaves as the Sabres roared into the bright blue morning sky and headed south.

CHAPTER TWO

The old man made himself comfortable. He nestled his knees into the sand and took his prize from the bag beside him. It is beautiful, he thought, or maybe magnificent. There is no word to describe it. But then again, there is one word to describe everything that exists, he reasoned, except that which cannot be described. So how does a man decide that which can be described and that which cannot? The five senses are the tools by which a man can assess what he is experiencing and that assessment creates emotions. Joy and anticipation were human emotions that came immediately to mind because he was experiencing both of them, but how did one describe joy and anticipation? Were they describable? Could one simple word truly describe an emotion? He decided that some things were beyond his intellectual capacity, so he would use the only word he could think of to describe his prize.

'Fish!' He called out in Cantonese over the dark water of the South China Sea. 'I describe this as a fish! A beautiful fish. A magnificent fish! An indescribable fish! And I am going to eat it for my dinner.'

Satisfied, he set about cleaning it and was immediately confronted with the question of how to cook it. Cooking was a great art in his native China. Cooking techniques had been developed, nurtured and handed down over the centuries. Cooking was indeed a noble art. How will I cook the fish, he asked himself.

The old man suddenly stopped cleaning the fish and stared out over the water. I think too much, he thought, and I don't have a smart brain. If I had a smart brain I would still be rich.

And if I was still rich I would not be living in a stone hut on Po Toi Island on the south side of Hong Kong Island. I will let my old friend Ho jai decide how to cook it. I will simply eat it and give thanks to the gods for allowing me to catch such an indescribable fish.

Tin Hau, the Goddess of the Sea, was indeed deserving of his thanks. He looked up into the night sky and wondered if he called to her, would she answer him? He didn't think she would, because she never had before, but you never knew with gods.

The gods were a rather stupid lot in his experience. They seemed to have made more mistakes than he ever had. They wore expensive silk slippers, but spent most of their time treading in shit. The thought made him laugh. Yes, he decided, they were stupid. Dangerous, but stupid. Mind you, he'd never say that out loud.

'Tin Hau?' he called. 'Are you listening or not listening to an unworthy soul like me? If you are listening, thank you for this indescribable fish.'

Tin Hau's immediate answer caused him to forget the fish entirely.

Two USAF Sabre jets thundered past Po Toi Island at a height of five hundred feet and The Admiral, The One Eyed Woo, once the most feared pirate in the South China Sea, ran for his stone hut as fast as his seventy-year-old legs would carry him.

龍

'UN Blue One, this is Kai Tak tower. We have you on screen, you are clear to land, over.'

'Roger, Kai Tak,' James Merchant transmitted. 'You should have us visual in twenty seconds, we're over Tathong Channel, altitude five hundred feet.'

The two jets screamed along the channel in the deepening twilight. Below, terrified bright light fishermen, setting their candlelit glass bowls on the water, looked up from their bobbing sampans.

Approaching Junk Island, James tilted his wings to port

and dropped below two hundred feet. The two jets then flew through Lei Yue Mun Pass, the narrow passage of water at the end of Tathong Channel that constituted the eastern entrance to Victoria Harbour, and the lights of Kai Tak runway appeared before them.

James looked to his left where the island of Hong Kong lay glittering like a million diamonds on folds of black satin. He felt a surge of sheer joy rush through him.

Three days, he thought, as he felt the landing gear of his aircraft lock into place. Three days and so much to do, but he would complete his mission. Getting to Hong Kong had been much simpler than he'd anticipated. All it had taken was a call to his mother.

Elanora Merchant Brewster, the Merchant Mistress, had no trouble convincing the Governor of Hong Kong that more awareness should be made of the part Britain was playing in the UN military operations in Korea. 'With the death of King George VI and young Queen Elizabeth's Coronation scheduled for next year,' she'd told him, 'it is imperative that the public be reassured of the power of the monarchy.'

To start the ball rolling she suggested a gala dinner, at her expense, to raise money for the troops, and then suggested that perhaps the people of Hong Kong would be interested in seeing the newest type of jet fighter being flown by the British boys in Korea.

The thought of Sabre jets on display at Kai Tak was a stroke of genius in the Governor's eyes. 'The latest in military aircraft technology on show for all the people to see,' he'd said, 'especially the Communists, will serve as a reminder that the British flag still flies proudly over the Colony.' He set the wheels in motion and within a month James had been summoned to Seoul and ordered to fly himself and one other under his command to Hong Kong.

The two jets had refuelled on the southernmost Japanese island of Honshu and again in Taipei, on the island of Formosa, the stronghold of Ch'iang Kai shek and the remains of his Chinese Nationalist Army. The whole journey, including fuel stops, had taken less than a day.

'Welcome to Hong Kong, Johnnie my lad,' James said as his wheels touched down.

'Thanks, pardner,' came the American's reply as he landed behind James. 'She sure is a pretty lady. I can't wait to meet her.'

龍

Richard Brewster sat on the balcony of the Merchant House, high on the top of Victoria Peak. After dispatching his chauffeur to the airport to collect James, he'd watched the US jets land with his new twenty-by-eighty binoculars. They were a birthday gift from Elanora and since he'd received them, the balconies of the Merchant mansion, with their panoramic views of Hong Kong, had become his favourite place. He watched the comings and goings of ocean liners, warships and commercial aircraft and had even started keeping a log book of unusual or important occurrences.

He'd known the arrival time of the UN jets – it had been in all the papers, and the excitement they'd aroused in the Colony was palpable. At the Hong Kong Club there'd been talk of nothing else. The wealthy members of that famous whites-only institution included retired military officers, prominent businessmen and a fair share of Britain's lords, earls, barons and other aristocratic types, pretenders or otherwise, who had decided to spend their remaining years in the Far East. The jets, they declared, were a show of military might and would serve as a reminder to Mao Tse-tung, and his jumped up set of sycophantic supporters, that Britain still ruled the waves. The fact that the jets were the property of the United States of America was not mentioned.

Richard looked out over the vista that lay before him. It was a beautiful spring night in April, his favourite month, and below him the city of Hong Kong glittered, like a myriad of tiny gold coins spread on jewellers' cloth. Victoria Harbour, the stretch of water that separated Hong Kong Island from Kowloon Peninsula, was a hive of lights and activity. Ocean liners and cargo boats were being serviced by barges and tiny sampans, bustling around them like bees. United States and

British warships sat silently at anchor, dark and dangerous shadows, as Hong Kong's brightly lit Star Ferries hustled past them carrying passengers between the Island and Kowloon.

Richard's gaze moved north to the mountain range that gave the peninsula its name. *Gau Loong*, the Cantonese words, mispronounced 'Kowloon' by the first British residents, meant nine dragons. He smiled at the memory of his old mentor Quincy Heffernan telling him the ancient legend of the nine dragons.

Hong Kong, Quincy had told him, was once only a small village that manufactured incense, hence its name *Heung Gong*, meaning 'fragrant harbour' in Cantonese. The nine dragons were sent from heaven to guard the village from marauding pirates. The dragons were apparently so successful in their mission they soon had nothing to do, so they sat on the beach and waited to be called home to heaven. However, the gods forgot them and they wandered about, filled with sadness, until they finally fell asleep. And, his teacher had insisted, the nine dragons were still there sleeping.

Richard continued to stare at the mountains in the moonlight. There are many more than nine dragons sleeping there now, he thought sadly.

The Battle of Hong Kong had commenced on those peaks in December 1941. Richard and his friends, all part of the Hong Kong Volunteer Defence Force, had confronted the Japanese Army at Shing Mun Redoubt on Smugglers' Ridge and they'd been slaughtered. Over the ensuing two weeks the Colony had been battered into submission and on Christmas Day the formal surrender had taken place in Central Square on Hong Kong Island.

Richard remembered that day with awful clarity. He'd stood with the other prisoners and watched, humiliated, as Sir Mark Young, the Governor and Commander-in-Chief, had surrendered to Lieutenant General Takashi Sakai of the Imperial Japanese Army. The Union Jack had been lowered and the Rising Sun raised, and all present had been forced to bow in recognition. It was the first time a British Colony had ever been surrendered to an enemy.

Richard gazed again at the harbour below and recalled the day, several weeks before the Japanese invasion, when Elanora had left the Colony. His last sight of her, in the open launch that had ferried her to the Pan-Am flying boat bound for Australia, had almost broken his heart.

Elanora had taken with her not only Lee Kwan's wife Lin Li and their little boy, but also Old Soong, Ah Po the *amah*, and Li Ping, the devoted mistress of Robert McCraw, Richard's great friend who'd died on Smugglers' Ridge. Elanora had begged Richard and Lee Kwan to accompany her, but both men had steadfastly refused. James, at that time, had been fighting the Germans in Britain.

Richard had watched the vessel carry her all the way out to the floating aircraft and he'd continued watching until the huge amphibious plane had disappeared from his view.

Nearly four years under the boot of the Kempetai, the Japanese Military Police, had destroyed him. He'd watched his friends beaten, starved, and in some cases beheaded by the brutal Japanese guards. On two separate occasions he'd had a leg broken, and one other time, after some perceived insolence on his part, his skull was fractured and he was bayoneted and left for dead. He'd survived the physical assaults, but tropical ulcers, berri-berri and psychological distress had destroyed his will to live. When Stanley Prison was liberated in 1945 he'd emerged a crippled wreck.

Richard was drawn from his reverie by the sound of Elanora's shoes on the wooden balcony. He turned and watched her approach. At fifty she was as beautiful as ever – raven haired, almond eyed, the perfect blend of east and west. Her beauty was timeless.

'James will be here any minute, darling.' She kissed his cheek and her hand lingered lovingly on his sleeve. 'Katherine is going to put all the lights out and the twins are going to surprise him in the entrance hall with their new battery torches.'

'Well, we mustn't miss that,' Richard replied. He stood, retrieved his walking stick from the balcony railing and took her arm. 'Come along, or we'll be floundering down the stairs in the dark.'

They went inside and walked along the landing towards the top of the grand staircase. Richard looked down at the black and white tiled floor of the magnificent foyer and squeezed Elanora's arm. There, crouched behind an enormous fountain made up of four elephants, their tails together and water spouting from their trunks, were Paul and Georgina, James and Katherine's twin children. In pyjamas and robes, clutching their new battery torches, they huddled conspiratorially waiting for their daddy to arrive. Katherine stood at the front doors with her hand on the light switch listening for the sound of the car.

They were halfway down the curved staircase when Katherine waved and put her index finger to her mouth.

'He's here,' she hissed and flicked off the lights.

Richard and Elanora sat on the stairs and the children began to giggle, unable to contain their excitement.

'Shhh!' Katherine hissed again, and Richard saw two figures loom into view at the frosted glass front doors.

'This is your house?' Richard heard an American voice exclaim. 'Jesus H. Christ, it's bigger than the White House.'

'Well, this is a fine how do you do.' It was James. He'd opened the door. 'A chap comes home from fighting the war and there's no one to welcome him.'

'Surprise!' the twins screeched, and raced from behind the fountain, torch beams searching frantically for their father.

'Over here,' James called. The torch beams found him, then Katherine flicked on the lights and he was flattened by a sea of little arms and legs. 'Oh my God!' he exclaimed. 'I'm being attacked by monsters!'

'No, you're not, Daddy,' Georgina squealed, 'it's only us. Georgina and Paul. Don't be frightened, Daddy.' James rolled on the floor with them, wrestling and tickling. The little eight-year-old Georgina loved the rough play with her father, but her twin brother, Paul, cried out as if in pain and his father pushed him away.

'For God's sake, Paul,' James snapped. 'Don't be such a sissy.'

'All right. That's enough,' Katherine said quickly, as Georgina threatened to go into hysterics.

'Darling!' James got up and took his wife into his arms. He kissed her and pressed his index finger into a pressure point on her buttock.

Long dormant desire shot through Katherine like a lightning bolt, but it was accompanied by a hot flash of irritation. Damn it, she thought, can't he even finish saying hello? She broke the kiss and, breathless, pointed to the staircase.

'Mother!' James exclaimed, striding across the foyer to take her in his arms. 'And Richard,' his voice suddenly lost some of its enthusiasm. 'How good to see you.'

'Hi, all. I'm Johnnie.' The American put his bag down and extended his hand to Katherine.

'Of course you are,' Katherine replied, shaking his hand. 'James mentions you in his letters. It's as if I've known you forever.'

'What a beautiful thought,' Johnnie replied. What a beautiful thought indeed, he thought. Katherine Brewster was a very attractive woman, but she was nothing compared to the vision floating across the foyer towards him, hand extended.

'Captain Wilson.' Elanora stopped before him and smiled. 'Welcome to my house.'

Johnnie Wilson was lost for words. She can't be his mother, was all he could think. She didn't look a day over thirty. He'd heard that Elanora Merchant was beautiful and he'd expected handsome good looks, but Elanora was an exotic mixture of east and west and the combination was something he'd never experienced.

'Mrs Merchant Brewster,' he managed to stammer.

'Oh, please, call me Elanora,' she said softly.

Johnnie suddenly realised her hand was still extended and he groped for it clumsily. 'I'm very pleased to meet you, Elanora.' It felt warm and smooth. 'And thanks for letting me stay in your house, it will be a welcome change. Military accommodation in Korea ain't all that flash, Ma'am.'

Richard Brewster watched, amused. His wife's beauty had

a great effect on every young man who met her, and Captain Wilson was proving to be no exception.

'Have you eaten?' he asked James.

'Oh, Richard,' James replied with Georgina struggling in his arms, 'food is the last thing on my mind. We've been in the air all day.' He looked at Katherine. 'I think a good sleep would be much more beneficial.'

'How about you, Captain?' Richard asked.

'Me?' Johnnie replied. 'I could eat a horse, Sir!'

Elanora laughed. 'Well, come along then, Captain, I think we've got a horse in the pantry. I'll have the kitchen staff kill it and put it in the wok.' She turned to Katherine. 'Why don't you take your family upstairs, Kate? I'm sure you've got lots to catch up on.' The look of understanding that passed between the two women went unnoticed by the men. 'Give the children to their *amah*. I'll look in on them later.'

'Right you are, Mother.' It was James who replied. 'What say we all catch up for breakfast on the balcony?'

'A wonderful suggestion, darling.' Elanora kissed her son on the cheek. 'And tomorrow night I'm throwing a ball. And don't give me that look!'

'What look?' James raised his eyebrows.

'You know very well what look. The ball is to raise money for the British Forces in Korea and you will attend. You two will be representing your respective Air Forces as the guests of honour and you *will* attend. Do I make myself clear, James?'

'Yes, Mother,' James replied evenly, 'but I have some business to . . .'

'*When you ask for favours, James,*' Elanora interrupted in Cantonese, '*you must expect to repay them, true or not true, ah?*'

'Yes, Mother,' his jaw went rigid.

To lighten the mood, Elanora turned to the American. 'Well, Captain Wilson?' She offered her most brilliant smile. 'How about you? I hope the thought of dancing with every notable beauty in Hong Kong is not abhorrent to you?'

'Ma'am,' the American produced his best Texan drawl, 'if them thar ladies is as purdy as the two that's here right now, I'll dance the darn spurs clean off my boots!'

'Spoken like a true Texan!' Elanora declared. She took the American pilot's arm. 'Come along, now, and we'll find you that horse.'

'If you'll excuse me, Elanora, I might turn in,' Richard said. 'This leg of mine is giving me hell.'

'Of course, darling. You go off to bed. I'll join you as soon as I find the cook and get this young man fed.'

Richard watched them all disappear, Elanora and the American through to the kitchen, and James and his family up the staircase. Favours? Elanora's outburst in Cantonese was ringing in his ears. What had Elanora been referring to when she'd spoken to James of favours that needed to be repaid? She'd said nothing to him.

James was up to something and obviously had his mother's support. Well, he thought, if Elanora hasn't smelled a rat it must be above board. If she'd thought anything was wrong she would have discussed it with him well before James' arrival. Still, an uneasy feeling ran through him. James was in Hong Kong for a reason and knowing James as he did, Richard knew that could only mean trouble.

War changed people, Richard knew, but he'd never realised how much it had changed James until he had returned to Hong Kong. He'd wanted Richard to reform the Golden Dragons and when Richard had refused, saying he had no interest in it, James' attitude towards him had shifted dramatically. He could sense the man's loathing for him every time their eyes met. James' greed and selfishness were palpable.

龍

It was a ball all right, but a ball the like of which Johnnie Wilson had never experienced before. He was no stranger to wealth – his father was a successful surgeon in Dallas and owner of a cattle ranch near Amarillo – but the sheer opulence of the ballroom in the Merchant mansion left him breathless.

Three massive chandeliers dominated the room, each ten feet in diameter and set forty feet apart. A quick calculation suggested the ballroom was fifty yards long. Men in formal attire and women in the latest fashions danced around the room as the orchestra, with at least twenty members, played the big band music of Glenn Miller. Chinese waiters with trays of chilled champagne and *hors d'oeuvres* moved skilfully amongst the guests as the procession of dancing couples was reflected in huge mirrors set equidistant along the rear wall.

Johnnie secured a glass of champagne and found himself a secluded spot near one of the many sets of French windows leading into the gardens.

'Enjoying yourself, partner?' It was James.

'I sure am, pardner.' Johnnie laughed. 'I'll say one thing for your momma, she sure as hell knows how to throw a party.'

'Yes.' James' smile faded. 'This lot,' he indicated the room full of people with a casual wave of his champagne glass, 'represents the *crème de la crème* of Hong Kong society. Lords, ladies, barons, earls, wealthy bankers, retired generals, prominent businessmen, you name it.'

'And their wives.'

'And more importantly, Johnnie, their daughters.'

'Right. Let's not forget their daughters.' Johnnie raised his glass in mock salute and sipped. 'I haven't seen this many beautiful girls in one room since the Dallas Debutantes' Ball. I feel like a kid in a candy store, Jimbo.'

'And all you have to do is ask them.' James offered the advice through the corner of his mouth as he bowed towards an elderly woman passing. 'Lady Daphne,' he murmured.

'You're pullin' my leg, right, pardner?' Wilson whispered back.

'Oh, no.' James smiled and shook his head. 'Believe me, John, the children of Hong Kong's social elite are an independent, bored and highly promiscuous lot and you have all the credentials required to take your pick.'

'How's that?'

'You're young, handsome and in uniform.'

'Oh, come on,' Johnnie chided, 'these girls must have seen plenty of uniforms in Hong Kong. What makes me so special?'

'Two things. Firstly, you're the pilot of one of the Sabre jets parked at Kai Tak, which happen to be the talk of the town at the moment.' James sipped his drink and feigned an end to the conversation, pretending to take interest in the crowds of dancing couples.

'Well?' Johnnie elbowed his friend. 'Out with it, Jimbo. What's the second thing?'

'You're also guest of honour at a party thrown by the Merchant Mistress.' James smiled and raised one eyebrow. 'And that makes you the number one ticket in town, old boy.'

'Really?'

'If I know Hong Kong women, you'll very quickly find yourself in a secluded part of the garden with one of these bored beauties.' James stopped a waiter, took an *hors d'oeuvre* from a tray, popped it in his mouth and sipped his champagne. He watched the young American's eyes scour the room. The look on his face suggested a religious experience. 'All you need do is ask one of them to dance,' he winked.

'How about your mom?' Johnnie Wilson realised his mistake immediately. As the words left his mouth the *hors d'oeuvre* and champagne sprayed from James' mouth. 'Oh, Christ! I'm sorry, James. I don't know what made me say that. I'm so sorry.'

James fought for control of both his amusement and the food that remained in his mouth. 'It's all right, John,' he said when he'd recovered. 'You're not the first of my friends to fall in love with my mother.'

'No, really.' Johnnie Wilson was mortified. 'That's the worst thing I've ever said in my life. Your mother is the most beautiful, most gracious – '

'It's all right, John.'

' – and I don't mean that in a sexual way . . . I mean . . .'

'I said it's okay, John.' James took a handkerchief from his pocket and wiped food from his mouth and a speck of his spittle from Johnnie Wilson's lapel. 'Listen to me. I'm not offended.' He laughed again. 'I've got some business to attend to here tonight, so you enjoy yourself. Test my theory and ask someone to dance.' He patted the American on the shoulder. 'Just don't ask my mother.'

James watched Elanora walk across the dance floor and engage several of her friends in conversation. There's no doubt about it, he thought. Even in her fifties, his mother was still the best looking woman in the room by a country mile. He wondered idly if she took lovers. He hoped she did, often, for Richard's sake, the weak bastard.

'You're the Yankee jet pilot, aren't you?' Johnnie felt a tap on his shoulder and, turning, gazed into the face of a very pretty young woman.

'Would you like to dance, Ma'am?' Johnnie Wilson took the girl's arm as his grin spread from ear to ear.

James took another champagne from a waiter and made his way through the crowded party towards the very end of the room. He stopped at the final set of French windows that led onto the large patio outside and caught his mother's eye. Elanora was chatting gaily to several women but her gaze remained firmly fixed on James. He smiled at her, raised his glass and mouthed the words, 'Lovely party', at which she haughtily raised her chin and turned abruptly back to her companions.

Ho Man-lai stood on the patio of Merchant House and gazed at the city lights far below. Hong Kong, he thought, the city of streets paved with gold where rich men eat fat pork. It was the phrase with which most Communists referred to the capitalist enclave of Hong Kong, although some preferred the expression 'a running sore on the underbelly of China'. Hong Kong represented everything abhorrent in Communist ideology and Ho Man-lai was the quintessential Communist.

He was a banker, employed at the offices of the Bank of China in De Veux Road Central. He had a very respectable wife, and two children who attended the Communist School in Cause Way Bay. He lived in a standard housing estate flat in North Point and espoused the views of Mao Tse-tung to his family, and anyone else who'd listen, at every given opportunity. To most who knew him, Ho Man-lai was ostensibly the perfect Communist, but to those few who knew him well, Ho Man-lai was a spy, and a very good one.

Espionage, to the citizens of Hong Kong, was just as much a part of daily life as Cantonese operas, fireworks and *yum cha*. Geographically speaking, it was the perfect place for foreign powers to spy on China and conversely, it was the perfect place for China to spy on them. The art of spying held no fascination for the Hong Kongese. Everybody claimed to know, or at least to have met a spy, and everybody knew the buildings from which they worked. This was particularly the case for Communist China's Secret Service. Even the poorest peasant could tell you that they worked from the Bank of China building.

Ho Man-lai was head of China's Secret Service in Hong Kong. He had a spacious office on the tenth floor of the China Bank building with a beautiful view of the harbour. He had not one, but two secretaries, both of whom were his mistresses, when they were not sleeping with the enemy on Ho's instructions. And he had access to three bank accounts, two official ones that funded the clandestine activities of his trade and one – unofficial – that accumulated the personal bribes he so often negotiated as part of his services. And tonight another profitable negotiation will take place, he thought. He took a cigarette from a gold case and lit it.

'*Ah Ho*,' James said in Cantonese. '*Do you have or not have a cigarette for an enemy of your country?*'

'*Have*,' Ho replied as required in Cantonese with the positive part of the verb. He chuckled as he offered James Merchant a cigarette. The phrase 'an enemy of your country' had been a standing joke between them since childhood when they'd played war games along with Lee Kwan on the very patio they now stood upon. Ho Man-lai and Lee Kwan would play various Chinese generals or emperors and James would always be the leader of the British Army.

'*Thank you.*' James accepted a light and puffed on the cigarette.

'But, Ah James, I can hardly call you an enemy of my country if the deal you've proposed comes to fruition, true or not true?'

'True. Have you spoken to my brother?'

'Yes.'

'He knows that the equipment is not new, true or not true?'

'True. He is aware some of it may be broken, but he has the men available to repair it.'

'So he is happy with the deal, true or not true?'

'True, Ah James. Lee Kwan is delighted with the deal. He has had the matter approved by the highest power in Peking. All you have to do is deliver.'

'The circle is almost complete, Ah Ho. I have only to organise the transportation of the equipment from Hong Kong to Canton and that will be arranged later tonight. From Canton onwards the transportation is your problem, true or not true?'

'True.' Ho nodded.

'And the money?'

'The money will be paid in cash to the Woo twins as you requested.'

'United States dollars?'

'Of course.'

'And the amount, just so there is no misunderstanding later?'

'Twenty-five thousand per shipment.' Ho Man-lai gave a slight cough. 'Less my five per cent of course.'

'Two.'

'Three?'

'Done.'

'And my Government can expect one shipment every month?'

'Yes, Ah Ho. That is correct. The United States Military machine is a giant. It consumes men and equipment like a monster. The radios and other equipment you are purchasing is all second hand, but there is nothing wrong with most of it. It is capitalism at its very best: supply and demand, keep *up the turnover so the industrialists in America who make the equipment keep making more money.'*

'In my Government's eyes it is disgusting,' Ho Man-lai smiled, *'but personally speaking, capitalism is the whore I would fuck, if only she would allow me into her bed.'*

'She is expensive, my friend,' James replied, *'but she's wild, wet and willing, true or not true?'* Both men laughed at their respective jokes.

'But seriously, Ah James, you do the People's Republic a great service. I have been told to inform you officially that this service will not be forgotten.'

'With the money, Ah Ho, I will be making investments in Hong Kong. It is then that I will need the People's Republic to remember.'

'It will be remembered,' Ho replied loudly in English, as several people moved onto the patio behind them. 'Every party your mother throws is remembered. Is she not, after all, the Merchant Mistress?'

'She is indeed, Mr Ho.' James laughed at the swift change of subject. 'She is indeed.'

龍

Johnnie Wilson was in the gardens behind a row of conifers with his pants around his ankles when he heard his name being called. The girl on her knees in front of him recognised the voice.

'Oh my God!' She hissed as she stood up. 'It's Mrs Merchant.' The pretty girl, whose name Johnnie had not yet discovered, took off into the night like a startled gazelle as he fumbled with his clothing.

'Captain Wilson?' The voice rang out again.

'Ah, right here, Ma'am.' He strolled into view trying to effect a casual air.

'Have I disturbed you?' Elanora asked as he appeared from behind the fir trees.

'No, Ma'am. I was just having a quiet smoke like us cowboys do now and again.'

'Really?' Elanora said, then burst out laughing as his

trousers slipped down around his thighs, exposing his boxer shorts.

Johnnie looked down, mortified. 'Would you excuse me for one moment, Ma'am?' With what dignity he could muster, he pulled his trousers up again and moved back behind the conifers. He corrected the problem and strode back into view.

'Tell me, Captain, is it the custom of cowboys to remove their trousers when they smoke?'

'No, Ma'am.' He decided to brazen it out. 'We usually wait till they're actually on fire.'

Elanora laughed at the witticism, so casually delivered. The young American was delightful. He was brash and bold like so many of his countrymen. And he has the looks of a movie star to go with it, she thought. No wonder young Margaret Huxtable had dragged him into the garden. Mind you, the girl had the morals of an alley cat, not unlike her mother's.

Elanora suddenly realised she'd felt a twinge of jealousy, an emotion she'd not experienced for many years. How silly, she thought angrily, I'm old enough to be his mother. She immediately tried to dismiss the notion from her mind, but it lingered.

'Is there something you wanted, Ma'am?'

'What?' Elanora realised with some horror that she'd been staring at the young man.

'I asked if there was something you wanted, Ma'am.'

'Yes, there is.' Elanora recovered her composure very quickly. 'Of course there is. I'm not a Peeping Tom, Captain Wilson.'

'I'm sure you're not.' Johnnie stared at her. He sensed she was suddenly uncomfortable.

'I sent servants to find you but they failed.' Her voice was stern. 'And I'm not surprised, given where you were and what you were doing. The Chinese consider displays of public affection distasteful and when carried to the lengths you seem to have been achieving, disgusting.'

'And they're right, Ma'am. I can only offer my most humble apology. I was way outta line.'

'Your presence is required in the ballroom, Captain.' Elanora found herself adopting the tone she reserved for her servants. The young American had unsettled her and now she had him on the back foot, she felt an overwhelming urge to put him in his place. 'A speech is to be given in honour of your country, and I thought you should at least be there to hear it.'

'Yes, Ma'am.' Johnnie Wilson stared at her for a moment then his face broke into a long, slow smile. She felt her face flush as his eyes roved over her body like a big cat surveying its next meal.

Elanora felt as if she was being undressed. 'Come along then,' she said tersely. She turned on her heel and began walking back through the garden. She could sense him walking behind her, watching her, so she hurried along the path, up onto the terrace and across the patio. She stopped at the open French doors and turned to him.

'I suggest you stand near the bandstand, Captain. After the Governor's speech, a brief acknowledgement from you will be required.'

'Yes, Ma'am,' the young American whispered as he passed and his voice felt like a caress against her throat.

Elanora didn't follow him. She stepped back out onto the patio and breathed in the warm night air. She stared down at the harbour lights trying to analyse the emotional experience she'd just had. She'd not felt such overwhelming desire for some years and it had confused her.

She breathed deeply again and tried to relax. For a moment back there in the garden she'd actually wished the young American would drag her into the bushes and ravish her. What was it about the American that had brought about these feelings? Other young men had had no such effect on her. Why Johnnie Wilson? She could not answer the question and she felt foolish.

Richard, her beloved husband, had not made love to her for many years. Not since the war. It had destroyed him. He'd returned to her a physical and emotional cripple and try as she may, she had not been able to help him. A deep-rooted sense of morbidity pervaded his being and neither love nor understanding had been able to break down the wall. She adored him with every fibre of her being and would stay with him until she drew her last breath, but although the passing years had been emotionally satisfying, she still sometimes yearned for physical love. Elanora realised that the young American fighter pilot was only serving as a window to the past, when she and Richard had been young and beautiful. Richard had had his youth stolen from him. He was an old man, old before his time. But time had been good to Elanora. She still felt young and she still felt beautiful.

'Hello, Mother,' James said as he walked onto the patio. 'Not interested in what our good Governor has to say? He's started his speech.'

'I'm sure he's saying all the right things, dear.' Elanora turned and kissed her son on the cheek. 'Like I'm sure you said all the right things to Ho Man-lai.'

'We talked about old times. That's all. We did go to school together, you know?'

'For God's sake, James, he's the head of the Chinese Secret Service and you're a Wing Commander with the United Nations Forces in Korea! I know you better than that.' Her eyes challenged him. 'What are you up to?'

'Nothing.' He held her eyes until she shrugged and looked away. 'All right, the business I have to conduct will be later tonight and it's nothing to do with the Chinese Secret Service. I'm taking Johnnie out on the town and while he's carousing, I'll be seeing a couple of people.'

'Who?'

'That's not your concern . . . yet.' And it never will be, Mother, dear, James thought. My plans for after the war will not include you, or your pathetic husband. 'I've got an idea for a new business venture and I want to set a few things in motion so they'll be ready when my tour in Korea is over. How's that?'

'All right. I believe you.' She didn't. She didn't believe him at all. Elanora knew her son only too well; he was scheming some sort of deal. But rather than pursue the subject any further she let it go. 'I found our young American friend in the garden with Margaret Huxtable, a girl with rather dubious moral standards, to say the least.'

'Do forgive him, Mother,' James said. 'He's only a boy really and he's barely spoken to a western woman for nearly a year, let alone touched one.'

'You're right, of course.' Elanora brushed a lock of hair from her eyes. 'He's only a boy.' She was suddenly sick of the ball. She was sick of the formality. And she was sick and tired of the hypocrisy she experienced in every conversation. She wanted to take a hot bath, then sip jasmine tea on the balcony and catch the night breeze. She wanted the world to walk without her for a while.

'Come along, James.' Elanora took his arm. '*I am the Merchant Mistress,*' she continued in Cantonese, '*and you are my son. We have guests and family honour demands we serve them.*'

龍

Tsang Leng-Leng was bored. She sat in a cubicle and toyed with the mahjong tiles spread on the table before her. She'd been winning handsomely, but the late night customers had started arriving and she and the other girls were told to stop playing and cater to them. The *Mama-san* was not to be disobeyed. She ruled the bar with an iron fist and any girl who dared challenge her would find herself, very quickly, on the street and unemployed.

The place was a typical Hong Kong girlie-bar with dim, but garish, coloured lighting and several ceiling fans rotating slowly. A bar sat in one corner and around the walls of the room, cubicles for six people abutted one another separated by thin bamboo curtains. A brand new Wurlitzer jukebox sat next to the entrance to the single toilet and twenty young Chinese girls in *cheung sams*, high collared and split from knee to hip, pretended to be fascinated by the lies the customers were telling them.

Several groups of military servicemen entered the bar, mostly sailors from the warships at anchor in the harbour, but two other *gwai loh* entered with them and Leng-Leng immediately smelled money. Real money, not the few Hong Kong dollars the Army and Navy boys would spend on drink and sex. These two foreign devils were the genuine article and Leng-Leng, who had Jenny, her five-year-old daughter to support, made a bee-line for them.

'The *Heroes* of Waterloo?' Johnnie Wilson asked James Merchant. 'How could anyone name a bar the *Heroes* of Waterloo? There was only *one* hero of Waterloo.'

The two men had left Elanora's ball at midnight, changed out of uniform and taken a taxi down to Wanchai, Hong Kong Island's waterfront red light district. They'd located a nightclub called the Heroes of Waterloo in Jaffe Road and now, as they approached the bar, Johnnie looked about him as James spoke in rapid-fire Cantonese to an old woman sitting on a barstool counting out money. The woman stuffed the cash into her pocket then almost leapt off the stool and scurried through a beaded curtain behind the bar.

'Sorry, John,' James yelled in competition with the music blaring from the jukebox. 'What was that you said?'

'I said, who would name a bar the *Heroes* of Waterloo?'

'I did. To stop an argument.'

'There was only *one* hero at Waterloo, Jimbo, and that was Wellington. If there were any others they didn't give their names.'

'*Leung ji Tsing Tao bei jau, mgoy.*' James indicated to the barman with two fingers.

'Hum guy?' Johnnie asked. 'Is that Chinese for bartender?'

'No,' James shook his head. 'I ordered two Tsing Tao beers and said *mgoy*. Make an 'm' sound as in hum and add 'goy' and it means thank you in Cantonese. Actually it means a little thank you. You use it for small services like ordering a drink. If you want to say a big thank you, it's *doh jei*.'

'*Mgoy*, small, *doh jei*, big. Gotcha.'

James indicated a cubicle. 'Let's get a seat and I'll tell you the real story of the Heroes of Waterloo.'

Leng-Leng beat them to the cubicle by a split second. She slid onto the bench seat, grabbed Johnnie by the arm and dragged him down next to her. James, who was carrying both bottles of Tsing Tao beer, sat opposite them.

'Dis is special table only reserve for me,' Leng-Leng exclaimed. 'You wanna use it you pay me ten dollar, okay?'

'That's okay by me, sweetie,' Johnnie said.

'You buy me drink?' the girl continued. 'I am your Fukien fantasy, okay?'

'You're my what?' Johnnie laughed.

'She said "Fukien", John.' James was laughing too. 'It's a province in China. I'd say she comes from there. As for "fantasy" I don't think she'd even know the meaning of the word. Probably picked up the phrase from a customer and personalised it.'

'Well, honey,' Johnnie turned to the girl. 'If you wanna be my Fukien fantasy, that's all right by me.'

'Okay you buy me drink, okay? Only fi' dollar.' She held up the five fingers of her open hand.

'*You stupid dog-fucking slut!*' The *Mama-san* came from nowhere, screaming in high pitched Cantonese. '*Do you want your cunt cut out and fed to the pigs?*' She turned to James and bowed slightly. '*I am sorry, big boss. This stupid girl does not know who you are. She still has the dirt from the rice paddies between her toes.*'

'*There is no problem, Mama-san.*' James reassured her with a pat on the arm. '*She is amusing me and she will give great enjoyment to my American friend, true or not true?*'

'*True, big boss,*' the old hag cackled as relief flooded through her. The foolish girl could have caused her to lose great face. '*I told my bosses you are here, Mister Merchant.*' She grabbed Leng-Leng by the wrist and pulled her across the table. '*This man is the big boss of the Merchant Company and the son of the Merchant Mistress,*' she hissed. '*You will do whatever he asks of you or you will be dead by morning, and so will your daughter. Understand or not understand?*'

'*Understand, Mama-san.*' Leng-Leng's face was drained of colour. The man opposite her was the Merchant *taipan*. She sat terrified, watching the old woman return to her stool at the bar.

'Who, or what, was that?' Johnnie asked.

'That was the *Mama-san*. It's an American–Japanese slang word meaning Madam. It's used in girlie-bars throughout Asia, thanks to American sailors.

'She runs the bar girls, right?'

'Yes, including this one. *What is your name, Little Sister?*' James asked the girl clutching Johnnie's arm.

'*Leng-Leng. I am sorry, Elder Brother,*' she whispered. She spoke the words Elder Brother very deliberately. It was a term of respect for anyone of a higher position in the social order. '*I did not know who you were. I meant no disrespect.*'

'*There was no disrespect, Leng-Leng,*' James reassured her. '*Do me a favour tonight, and give me great face, can or can not?*'

'*Can, Elder Brother.*' Leng-Leng nodded furiously and offered a silent prayer to the gods. This foreign devil spoke immaculate Cantonese, better than her, and he was a genuine *taipan*. He was son of the Merchant Mistress what's more, the most powerful woman in Hong Kong, and the woman who'd helped her when she'd arrived penniless from Canton and with a baby girl to feed. This was good joss. The smell of money was returning.

'*My young friend is from America and if you treat him like an emperor tonight, you will be well rewarded. Understand or not understand?*'

'*Understand big boss. It is not often great men walk in my world. I will do whatever you wish. The American will travel to Heaven and return.*'

'Would somebody mind telling me just what's goin' on?' Johnnie complained. 'I don't speak the lingo, remember, *compadre*. If we was speakin' Texas Mexican things might be a little different, but I don't know any Chinese except *mgoy* and *doh jei*, remember?'

'This little lady,' James patted the girl on the shoulder and winked at her, 'has just informed me that she fell in love with you the minute you walked through the door.'

'You don't say?' The American looked at the girl who was nodding eagerly. 'What's your name, honey?'

'My name is Leng-Leng.'

'That's a pretty name, what's it mean?'

'My name is Very Beautiful.'

'It sure is, honey, just like you, but what's it mean?'

'Leng means beautiful,' James explained. 'It can get complicated, but basically, when you repeat certain words in Cantonese it means even more so. Her name is Beautiful Beautiful. Mind you, used with a different tone it also means good for nothing, but given that she's in love with you, I'm sure you'll be forgiven if you mispronounce it.'

'Well, Miss Leng-Leng, I need to talk to my pardner here. Why don't you head on over to that bar yonder and get yourself a drink. And while you're at it,' he wiggled his half empty beer bottle in front of her nose, 'get us a couple more of these here Tsing Tao beers? Put 'em on my tab.'

'No tab!' The girl squeezed herself over his lap making sure she hit the spot on the way. She stood up and turned to him. 'You no need pay money, okay? You are wiv da' Merchant *taipan*. Da't make you special customer, okay?'

'*Taipan*?' Johnnie said when the girl had left. 'That's an Aussie snake, isn't it? One of the Aussie pilots at Kenjong has got that name painted on his fuselage.'

'In Cantonese it means big boss.'

'Well now, big boss, I can only suppose the reason we're in this joint has something to do with our little bit of electrical business in Hong Kong?'

James was about to answer when he noticed an odd expression come over the American's face.

'Please tell me I ain't drunk, James?'

'What?'

'Am I seeing double?'

James looked in the direction that Johnnie was staring and smiled. The Woo twins arrived at the table and stood grinning at him.

'No, you're not drunk, and you're not seeing double. Johnnie, I'd like you to meet two old friends of mine, Wellington and Napoleon Woo.'

'Aah, the *Heroes* of Waterloo, right? Gotcha.' Johnnie

smiled at James and stood. He shook hands with both men and offered them his seat, which they declined with identical shakes of their identical heads. They were exactly the same in every way, including their dress. About forty years of age, both were five feet five inches tall, slightly balding and slightly overweight. Both wore smart tuxedos with emerald green waistcoats and bow ties and both were smoking cigars.

'I am Wellington Woo,' the twin closest to him said. 'I am the elder by ten minutes. This is my brother Napoleon. We welcome you to our humble establishment Captain Wilson. Any friend of the Merchant *taipan* is a friend of ours. Our families go back a long way.'

The old *Mama-san* arrived with two cocktails on a tray. Each twin took a martini glass of cherry coloured liquid with a paper umbrella in it and they raised them simultaneously.

'Would you like a strawberry daiquiri, Captain? My brother and I drink nothing else.'

'Ah, no thanks, Wellington.'

'I am Napoleon.'

'I'm sorry,' Johnnie said. 'It's very difficult to tell one of you from the other.'

'Is not so difficult.' Napoleon pointed to his left ear. 'Our father had the same trouble, so he cut off my earlobe to make us different.'

'Jesus,' was all Johnnie could think of to say.

'No, not like Jesus. Our father was a bad man, Captain Wilson,' Wellington explained. 'He was a pirate, a villainous cutthroat and a particularly bad parent.'

'You don't say?'

'*Where is The Admiral these days?*' James asked in Cantonese.

'*Go and fuck your mother's smelly cunt,*' Wellington replied. The phrase was not an insult, but rather a common expression used by the Cantonese that could mean anything from 'Oh my gosh' to 'Damn it' or even 'Would you believe it?' '*We finally got rid of the old vagina licker,*' Wellington continued. '*He's living on Po Toi Island with Ho jai, his mad first mate, and a couple of the older girls from the bar who had no juices left in them. The servicemen who come here only like the young girls.'*

'To our new enterprise, Mister James.' Napoleon offered the toast in English.

'Why not? It looks like we're in the electrical business, John.' James and Johnnie downed their beers and the twins sipped their daiquiris. 'I take it all the arrangements I requested have been made?'

'Oh yes, Mister James.' It was Wellington who replied. 'The information supplied by Captain Wilson proved to be first class. We contacted the American officer he recommended and he was only too willing to discuss the used radio equipment in his possession. Apparently he is required to arrange for its destruction. When we suggested we dump it at sea for him, he was delighted. He understood our suggestion completely. In exchange for five hundred US dollars he assured us the warehouse containing the used equipment would be unattended tomorrow night.'

'I have procured a fast junk, Mister James,' Napoleon continued, 'and a reliable crew who will ask no questions. They will have the equipment in Canton by the following morning. After that it will become the problem of the People's Liberation Army.'

'Good,' James nodded. 'The same business will take place every month from now on, unless I call from Korea and tell you otherwise.'

'Excuse me, Elder Brothers.' Leng-Leng brushed past the twins and placed beers on the table before sitting next to Johnnie.

'Well, gentlemen,' James picked up a bottle of beer and raised it towards Johnnie Wilson. 'It would seem we're in business. Here's to it.' They all sipped in acknowledgement of the toast and Johnnie almost choked as, beneath the table, Leng-Leng's hand found his groin.

'Everything all right, John?' James gave his friend a wry smile.

'Oh, yeah!' The American nodded rapidly. 'You wouldn't believe how all right.'

'Good, because I'm going to leave you with Leng-Leng.'

'Where are you going?'

'Unfortunately, duty calls. I have a wife and family, remember?' James stood up. 'Leng-Leng has instructions she must follow that will culminate with your safe return to my mother's house. I suggest you place yourself in her loving hands.'

'I'm already in one of them, pardner.' Johnnie's face was beginning to flush.

'Well, I'll see you at breakfast. Enjoy yourself, *partner*.' James winked and turned to the twins. 'Good night, gentlemen.'

CHAPTER THREE

The young soldier felt very proud of himself. He had only been in the new People's Liberation Army for six months and here he was driving none other than General Kwan Man Hop, the most famous soldier in all of China, on an inspection. He concentrated, making sure the GAZ he was driving moved at exactly five miles per hour maintaining a straight line. The GAZ was a canvas-top Russian-made military vehicle similar to the American Jeep. It had very direct steering and he knew that even the slightest pressure on the steering wheel would cause it to swerve violently.

'*Relax, Private Chou.*' Lee Kwan spoke to his young driver in Mandarin. '*You are doing very well.*'

'*Thank you, General,*' the young soldier replied and the GAZ immediately changed direction. '*Sorry, Elder Brother,*' he cried, correcting the wheel. '*I'm so sorry, General.*'

'*It's all right, Little Brother.*' Lee patted the boy on the leg. '*We are in Manchuria, not Tien An Men Square in Peking, and Our Great Leader Mao is not watching.*'

The boy concentrated even harder, as he slowly drove the GAZ between rows of Mig-15s lined up on either side of the jet runway at Antung Air Base. As they passed each aircraft the pilot standing beneath its nose came to attention and saluted the General.

Even concentrating as hard as he was, the young man could not help but take occasional glances at his General. *He is so young,* was all the boy could think, barely more than thirty. *How could he have achieved so much? He is as famous in the Army as Mao Tse-tung himself.* In 1937 as a young

Captain in the Kuomintang, it was rumoured he'd killed a thousand Japanese at the Battle of Shanghai and even more during the Siege of Nanking. He was also believed to be a master in the arts of *Shaolin*. The boy glanced at the General's hands, noticing the calluses on each knuckle that could only come from years of training in a martial art. Yes, he thought, it must be true, the General is a master of *kung fu*.

'*That completes the inspection,*' Lee Kwan's voice caused Private Chou to swerve violently again. '*Take me to the main office block and drop me at the front door. Then, Private Chou, might I suggest you go somewhere and relax?*'

'*Yes, Elder Brother!*'

The boy did as he was ordered and when he stopped in front of the three storey concrete building he leapt from the vehicle and saluted. '*May I say, Sir, it was an honour for you to have driven me on this inspection.*'

'*I didn't drive you, Private Chou, you drove me,*' Lee laughed. He returned the salute and patted the embarrassed boy on the shoulder before trotting up the front steps of the Antung Military Operations and Administration building.

Three salutes later, Lee reached his office on the first floor looking forward to a pot of hot tea. He took his hat off as he entered and was about to throw it at the hat stand when he stopped dead in his tracks.

'Good morning, Comrade General.' The Russian Military Advisor spoke in guttural English.

'Good morning, Comrade Major.'

Lee couldn't stand Major Petrov. He was the worst type of sycophant and a back-stabbing, traitorous, middle-ranked officer who would sell his own mother for a promotion, or even a mere pat on the back from his Soviet Commanders. Petrov had been posted to Lee's command as an advisor on jet-fighter tactics and Lee was stuck with him.

What he knows about jet-fighter combat tactics could be written on the back of a train ticket, Lee thought as he hung his hat on the stand. *The man can't even fly, for Christ's sake.* Lee had never seen him at the controls of an aircraft and when he'd challenged Petrov on the matter, the Russian had told him an ear infection, suffered several years before, had permanently grounded him. Petrov was a counter-espionage officer in the *Komitet Gosudarstvennoi Bezopasnosti*, better known by its acronym, KGB, and Lee Kwan detested him.

Lee was convinced Russia had started the conflict in Korea, and that China, wrongfully blamed, had copped the brunt of the international condemnation which had followed. He had no doubt that Josef Stalin, a criminal lunatic in Lee's opinion, had convinced his puppet protégé President Kim Il Sung to send the North Korean Army into democratic South Korea as a test of American political resolve in the Far East. Stalin obviously believed the Americans would do nothing, but he could not have been more wrong. The move had backfired with horrendous consequences for all concerned. United Nations Forces, led by the American Military megalomaniac General Douglas MacArthur, had come to the assistance of South Korea, and China, as a new Communist nation, had had no option but to back North Korea. All out war had ensued and was now in its third year.

'These are yours,' Petrov said throwing a packet of letters on the desk. 'I found them in the mail room. Obviously one of your clerks allowed them to accumulate, probably because he didn't know the name of his own Commanding Officer. He is typical of the ignorant peasants you fill your ranks with, yes?' The Russian laughed, which brought on a fit of coughing. When he'd recovered he continued. 'I noticed the letters are from Peking and probably from your wife, so I brought them to you directly.'

'Thank you, Major.' Lee ground his teeth, seething with anger. The envelopes had been opened and clumsily resealed and he had no doubt Petrov would have memorised every word in them. Images of his family flickered through his mind as he stared at the pile of letters. He had not seen his wife and children for over a year and the sight of Lin Li's neat handwriting brought with it a feeling of intense shame. As a professional soldier, he'd dragged his family from one war-torn province to another, and he'd left them alone and unprotected for long periods of time.

Lee hated war and yet he'd been engaged in it ever since he'd returned to China from England in 1937. He'd first fought for China in Ch'iang Kai-shek's Nationalist Army against the Japanese, but the harsh brutality of Ch'iang's regime had driven him into the arms of the more people-friendly Communist forces of Mao Tse-tung. With Japan's defeat at the end of World War II, he'd fought in Mao's Red Army against the Nationalists until China had been liberated. Now as a General in the newly named People's Liberation Army he was being forced to fight yet again, and this time against the United Nations, in a war started on the political whim of a Russian psychopath.

'I've been meaning to ask you,' Petrov began. He crossed the room to gaze out the window as Lee sat down at his desk. 'I have noticed that the radio transmission sets your troops are using are United States Military issue. How can this be? Where does your Logistics Officer get them?'

'I have no idea, Comrade Major, nor do I care and neither would my Logistics Officer. All I know is that they are superior in quality and design to their Russian equivalent and are proving their worth in the field.'

'That may be so, Comrade General.' Petrov turned from the window. He hadn't missed the hostile jibe. 'But that is not what I asked. I asked where the PLA got them from.'

'Why don't we get straight to the point, Major?'

'And what would that point be, General?' Petrov offered Lee a supercilious smile.

'I'd bet my last round of ammunition that you already know not only where the radios come from, but who is supplying them.'

'My superiors in Moscow – '

'You mean the KGB,' Lee interrupted. The two men stared at each other for several seconds, their mutual dislike evident.

'As I was saying, Comrade, my superiors in Moscow are not stupid. They are fully aware of what has transpired between you and the infamous Woo twins of Hong Kong.'

Petrov turned back to the window and took his time lighting a cigarette before continuing. 'You are to be commended, General Kwan, you are a true patriot, as are your Hong Kong friends with the ridiculous names, even though they masquerade as lackeys of the British Imperialists.'

Lee got up and crossed to his filing cabinet, switched on an electric fan, took off his tunic and loosened his tie. The summer heat of August was sticky and the office air stifling. He should have known the deal would not remain a secret forever. No doubt some stupid party bigwig in Peking had shot his mouth off at a Russian Embassy dinner and the conversation had been recorded. But did Petrov know about James' dealing in the matter? He hung his tunic up and sat back down. The answer was not long in coming.

'According to Moscow, Wing Commander James Merchant, the British war hero, is your brother. Is this correct, General?'

'I was adopted into his family, Major, but I'm sure you already knew that too.'

'Hmm.' Petrov was enjoying himself. He gazed out across the airfield over the six rows of Mig-15 jets and the ant-like figures attending them like drones to queen bees. 'Did you know he is currently stationed at Kenjong near Seoul, flying Sabre jets for the United Nations Forces?'

'No, I didn't.' The lie came easily to Lee. 'I haven't seen my brother for many years, Comrade Major.' And that's the absolute truth, he thought. All my dealings with James have been through third parties. 'Not since before World War II.'

'But surely you have written to him?'

'I don't write letters from China, Major,' Lee murmured, picking up the packet of his wife's letters. 'Too many people read them before they reach the addressee.'

'Addressee?' Petrov turned from the window puffing on his Russian cigarette. The smoke was starting to make Lee feel sick. 'I do not know this word, addressee.'

'It means the person to whom a letter is addressed.'

'But of course.' Petrov nodded and immediately turned his back again. 'So you are saying that your brother was never the addressee of your letters?'

'Major.' Lee was becoming exasperated. 'I have not seen James Merchant since we were schoolboys together in England.'

'Ah yes, your English education paid for by your capitalist guardian, the renowned beauty and socialite, Elanora Merchant. Is this not so?'

'I would strongly suggest we leave my mother out of this conversation, Major!' The warning in Lee's voice was distinct.

'As you wish.' The Russian shrugged his shoulders, and did not bother turning back from the window. He enjoyed interrogation. He enjoyed making people uncomfortable and then angry, before crushing them.

'I would also suggest that you get to the point, Major, as I believe I suggested you do some ten minutes ago. I have a military campaign to run that includes both Army and Air Force operations. In short, I'm a very busy man!'

'Your brother,' Petrov turned to face Lee, 'has supplied the Chinese Government with six deliveries of stolen radio parts and equipment for which he has received the sum of one hundred and fifty thousand United States dollars.'

'All right, Petrov. So there's a deal in place, so what? Get to the point!'

'My Government has suggested to yours that the arrangement with James Merchant remains in place, but that there should be a change in commodity.'

'To what?'

'Something a little larger in size, and infinitely more interesting.'

Lee was shocked. Some idiot official in Peking must have revealed the whole story of the deal he'd arranged between James and the Chinese Government. He had been assured it would remain top secret but now here he was, discussing the matter quite openly with none other than a Russian KGB agent.

'Really? Like what for instance?'

'Like a United States F-86 Sabre jet fighter.'

'Ha!' Lee's outburst was involuntary. 'A Sabre? You're out of your mind,' he managed to say. 'It's one thing to deal in second hand radios . . . but a Sabre jet?'

'That is what your Government wants.'

Lee gave a wry smile as the penny finally dropped. 'My Government?' he sneered. 'What would my Government want with a Sabre jet? My Government doesn't even manufacture aircraft.'

Petrov crossed to the desk, placed his palms on it and leaned provocatively towards Lee. 'But my Government does, Comrade General, and the Sabre fighter is proving a match for the Mig-15. Your air combat casualty statistics over the last six months must have told you that?'

'I'm only too aware of my combat casualties, Major. The list of young Chinese pilots dying over the Yalu River grows longer every day. And, I might point out, it is because of the insistence of their Soviet instructors that they cross the Yalu to gain combat experience.'

'The UN pilots are shooting Migs down faster than we can supply them to you, General. So we must have possession of a Sabre in order to examine it. It is the only way we can refine the Migs' performance and correct the tactical imbalance.'

'And you expect my brother to steal one for you?'

Petrov sat in a chair opposite Lee. 'Is he not already stealing radios and other electrical equipment? Why not a jet?'

This time it was Lee who sought the view from his window. He crossed to gaze out at the aircraft on the field. Petrov was right. Lee's inexperienced pilots had proven no match for the UN pilots since the Sabre had entered the war. Lee had tried demanding more advanced training for them from their Soviet instructors but to no avail. More and more young men were dying every day. Petrov had a point, he had to admit. A Sabre in the hands of the Russian aviation experts could reduce the number of Chinese pilots being killed.

Lee had fought long and hard with his conscience when the proposal from James had first been delivered to him. Their mutual old school friend Ho Man-lai, now head of China's Secret Service in Hong Kong, had made secure contact earlier in the year. The radios James was offering to sell were of inestimable value to the ill-equipped Chinese Army. And when he'd learned the equipment was second hand and destined for destruction anyway, he'd decided the welfare of his men in battle was more important than his concern about James' risky dealings or lack of patriotism.

Would James steal a Sabre and sell it? Yes, he would, Lee thought as he looked at the Russian Migs stretched out across the airfield. Of course he would, and Lee knew why. Lee knew his brother better than anyone alive.

Lee had tried to maintain contact with Elanora throughout the years, although rarely by correspondence – Communist China was not a good place to commit your thoughts to paper. Rather, he'd made use of telephones. It had been difficult. The contacts had been brief and intermittent, but at least they'd kept in touch. The last time they had spoken at any length was four years previously in 1948 and he'd learned of James' crushing disappointment and frustration with Richard's failure to show any desire to resurrect the Merchant Company. The fact that the man was ill and crippled and traumatised had apparently not entered into James' calculations.

Yes, Lee concluded, James would do almost anything for the money to restore the Merchant Company to its former glory, and that included betraying his country.

'Well, Comrade?' Petrov was losing patience with the Chinese soldier who had not spoken for several minutes, but simply stood staring at his airfield.

'So what part would our masters have me play in all this, Major?' Lee suddenly felt tired. He returned from the window and sat behind his desk.

'You are ordered, by Peking, to have your brother acquire for us an F-86 Sabre jet.'

'And just how do they suggest I go about that?'

'You will contact your brother and tell him to defect.'

'Defect?' Lee laughed out loud. 'My dear Major, defectors are idealists, people whose actions are governed by a conscious change of belief or allegiance, people driven by a sense of morality. The only thing that drives my brother is greed.'

'If he refuses, his other treasonous behaviour will be revealed to the relative authorities in London.'

'Forget it, Major!' Lee scoffed. 'James is far too clever for those games. He was raised in Hong Kong, the corruption capital of the world. No one would ever connect him to an illegal act, be it treason or anything else. You can be sure the chain of evidence would not even contain his shadow. Besides which, he's a war hero. They'll never believe he's a traitor. Why don't we stop the charade and get to the heart of the matter?' He leaned forward, placed his elbows on his desk, locked his fingers beneath his chin and smiled at the Russian. 'How much money have you been authorised to offer him?'

'I have not been authorised to offer him money,' Petrov lied.

'Please, Major, don't insult my intelligence. I know how your organisation works. How much are you authorised to offer?'

Petrov gave a resigned shrug as he lit another cigarette. 'My Government would be prepared to pay half a million dollars.'

'Make it a million US dollars, in cash.'

'A million? Are you insane?'

'Major Petrov, my brother would never give the Russian Air Force a Sabre jet, but – knowing him as I do – for a million dollars in cash, I believe he'd do anything.'

龍

Hutong, an old Mongol word meaning 'passageway', had been used to describe the narrow lanes that separated water wells and dwellings in the forever shifting tent cities of the ancient, nomadic Mongol hordes. To the citizens of Communist Peking, however, the word described a suburban slum area. The several thousand *hutongs* of Beijing were mazes of lanes and alleyways, some as narrow as five feet, where people lived in squalid, unsanitary conditions, jammed together in the former suburbs built by the Manchus.

In the seventeenth century when the Manchus had swept down from the north and seized control of China, they had built their tent cities outside the walls of Peking. But as the decades passed and the Manchus had continued to rule, the wealthy middle classes had replaced their tents with permanent dwellings, large stone houses with even larger courtyards, and, fanatical about their privacy, they'd built walls around them.

The Ch'ing Dynasty, the last to rule, had fallen in 1911 and Sun Yat-sen had declared China a republic. Some Manchus had fled the retribution they knew would come, others had assimilated into the local population and their *hutongs* were flooded with the poor and homeless Chinese, who, in turn, built even more walls, within the walls of the larger dwellings, for their own privacy, thus creating an unfathomable maze. Where one wealthy family had lived in style and comfort, ten poor families now shared the same space, and the *hutongs* surrounding the walls of Peking had slowly but surely evolved into slums.

Lin Li was hurrying to a *hutong* just outside 'The Gate Facing the Sun' or Great Southern Gate of the Outer Peking Wall. She was being followed.

Earlier that morning she had decided to act upon the instructions her husband, Lee Kwan, had made her commit to memory in case of an emergency. She had released a homing pigeon that would warn of her arrival, pinned a badge on her cap that showed the ancient symbol of old Shanghai and set off for the *hutong*. Now, as she walked quickly towards the packed bazaars and trading tents at the bottom of Tiananmen Square, she struggled with her fear, fighting the overwhelming urge to run.

The particular *hutong* she was going to was known colloquially as Little Shanghai, because its inhabitants were, in the main, Shanghai refugees who had fled their city after the Japanese invasion in 1937. When the Sino-Japanese war had ended in 1945 and civil war had erupted, many had chosen not to return to their native city and had gathered together in one suburb, thus creating Little Shanghai.

Like a good citizen of the new Republic of China, Lin Li
wore her boiler suit and cap to indicate to all other good
citizens of the Republic that she was a devoted follower of
their beloved Chairman Mao and the Chinese Communist
Party. Her long black hair was combed tightly across her
skull and fell down her back in a plait, and she wore strong
black leather shoes acquired from the Military by her
husband, a hero of the People's Republic, General Lee Kwan
Man Hop.

She pushed her way into the packed bazaars, stepping over
caged chickens and past tethered goats, all the while keeping
her eyes fixed on the enormous structure of the Great
Southern Gate in the Outer Peking Wall, until finally she
found herself standing before it. The Peking Wall was fifty
feet thick and thirty feet high and on top of the archway that
constituted the gate sat a five storey building. Adorning the
building's façade was a massive portrait of Chairman Mao.

Lin Li stopped for a moment to look up at the smiling face
of China's new leader, her heart pounding, desperate to know
if the two men were still following her, but she dared not turn
around. She'd first become aware of them when she'd entered
Tiananmen Square. They had been watching her apartment
block for over a week and now they were following her all
the way from the suburb she lived in, west of the Forbidden
City.

The men were Intelligence agents of the People's Liberation
Army, she was sure of it. But why were they watching and
following her? When she first became aware of them she'd
assumed they were interested in someone else in the apartment block. It had not occurred to her that she was the object
of their interest. Then she realised that her mail had been
opened and clumsily resealed, and when the local fruit
vendor had told her the two men had been asking questions
about her and Lee Kwan, her fears had begun to multiply.
The final straw had been her children returning home from
school complaining about being interrogated with questions
about their mother and father.

Lin Li had not heard from Lee Kwan in nearly six months

and her fears had grown daily until, that very morning, she'd decided on her course of action. She had to find out what was going on and only Lee Kwan would know the answer. It was then she'd released the pigeon and headed for Little Shanghai.

Without looking back, she continued on her way, terrified, and when she reached the end of the markets she ran across the expanse of open ground towards the gate. She dodged the rickshaws and pedal-cabs and pushed her way into the throng of people flowing through the massive archway.

People from all over China surrounded her. Tibetans, Ugurs and Kazakhs were all arriving and departing the great city; people in colourful tribal dress, soldiers in uniform, and even a Mongolian camel train was making its way through the arch, the camels spitting and groaning as they swayed through the mass of humanity surrounding them.

When she emerged on the other side of the gate, Lin Li began running again, as fast as she could across another wide open space towards the low grey walls of Little Shanghai.

Like all *hutongs*, and indeed Peking itself, Little Shanghai was topographically flat, a low-rise suburb, and overwhelmingly confusing to those unfamiliar with it. Crooked, narrow alleys intersected meandering laneways with no semblance of order or direction, so much so that even some of the long-time inhabitants failed to navigate them successfully. *Hutongs* are traditionally painted grey and Little Shanghai was no exception, but the dull, uninteresting colour of its walls and structures was in vast contrast to the sea of colourful life that thrived within.

Lin Li dived through the nearest doorway in the wall and was suddenly immersed in the host of people packed into the narrow lane. On either side hawkers plied their trade, children shrieked, piglets squealed, chickens squawked and shopkeepers clacked wooden blocks together to attract the attention of passers by. Myriad cooking smells assailed her nostrils, mingling with the smoke of incense sticks lit to appease the temperament of all manner of gods who kept watch over households, shops and people alike.

Lin Li continued on thirty yards to the first laneway, turned the corner and hid behind a pile of bamboo baskets, gasping for breath. She waited ten full minutes but neither of the men appeared. Confident she'd eluded them she pulled a crudely drawn map from her pocket and examined it.

Lin Li knew exactly where she was. She was in Rosewood Lane and the next alley she encountered would be Red Lacquer Street. Then she would turn right into Wooden Flute Alley. Indeed, as she moved forward, she began to hear music. It was the sounds of a singsong cabaret, old Peking's favourite form of entertainment.

The music got louder as she entered Wooden Flute Alley and she saw a number of old men in Mao jackets sitting on benches around a particular window in the alley wall that served as a teashop, and which was also Lin Li's destination. Several men played flutes and one was playing an *ehru*, a single stringed instrument that functioned like an upright violin. Two other old men stood singing, in high-pitched voices, a song from a Shanghai opera.

Lin Li crossed to the hole in the wall. '*Please you? A cup of tea and a bowl of sunflower seeds,*' she ordered from the old woman whose face appeared at the window. '*I have walked a long road and my shoes are worn thin.*'

'*Your face is very red,*' the old woman said. '*Have you been running?*'

Lin Li sagged with relief, the question was very appropriate, but it was also the question she was hoping to hear. It was the beginning of a recognition code. '*I have been running for most of my life, Old Mother,*' she replied, continuing the exact conversation her husband had taught her.

'*Did you run from the ancient capital?*'

'*Yes, I ran from Nanking in the Year of the Ox.*'

The old woman nodded as she handed Lin Li her tea. '*If you know Nanking, then you must know of the Living Goddess, true or not true?*'

'*True, Old Mother, the Living Goddess was an American woman named Minnie Vautrin. She was a Christian missionary at Ginling College.*'

'*Good.*' The old woman gave Lin Li the bowl of sunflower seeds then asked the penultimate question. '*What was the gift of the Living Goddess?*'

'*A gold ring.*' Lin Li could see it before her eyes, a gold signet ring Wilhelmina Vautrin had given her husband when they'd escaped from the Japanese occupation of Nanking in 1937.

'*And who received the gift?*'

'*The Dragon of Shanghai.*'

'Okey dokey.' The old woman was very proud of her only English phrase, picked up from American GIs stationed in Peking before the Communists took power. Her face creased into a generous smile. '*You come through the door,*' she said, taking back the tea and seeds and indicating the wooden entrance to Lin Li's left.

'*I dare not.*' Lin Li shook her head. '*I was followed.*'

'*The pigeon arrived this morning and we sent people to watch for the sign of Shanghai.*' The old woman indicated the badge on Lin Li's cap. '*You were only followed as far as the markets in Tiananmen,*' she cackled. '*The Government spies who followed you were dragged into an argument about an injured goat and beaten severely for their ignorance of goat-herding before they fled back to their masters. Forget about them and come inside.*'

Lin Li pushed against the time-worn wooden door. It creaked open and she stepped back two centuries into a large courtyard edged by covered verandahs with tiled roofs that had seen better days. At the centre of the yard was an obviously disused well, now home to a miscellany of potted plants and flowers. The old woman ushered her across the stone flagging and bade her sit at a table on a verandah.

'*You are a friend of the Captain?*' the old woman asked.

'*He is a General now,*' Lin Li said proudly, placing her tea and sunflower seeds on the table.

'*Ah yes, but to those of us from Shanghai he will always be known as Captain Lee Kwan, the Dragon of Shanghai. He killed ten million Turnip Heads!*' The old woman cackled at the derogatory term used to describe Japanese soldiers.

Lin Li's relief at finding her husband's friends over-whelmed her and the woman's grin was infectious. She felt herself relaxing. *'I don't think it was quite that many.'*

'Perhaps it was only five million, I tend to exaggerate.' The old woman sat down and stared at her young guest. *'Do you serve under the Captain?'*

Lin Li could not contain her snort of laughter. *'You could say that, Old Mother,'* she replied boldly, *'I am his wife.'* Normally she would not have dared indulge in smutty talk – she was a General's wife and usually surrounded by people in the higher echelons of the Communist Party – but she was born the daughter of a Suchow innkeeper and could not resist the vulgar retort. And the joke seemed more than appropriate to the old Shanghai peasant, because she cackled raucously.

'I have not heard a better joke, since before I was married. Husband!' She yelled at the top of her voice. *'Come and meet a rare flower, a Communist with a sense of humour.'*

'All Communists have a sense of humour!' The deep and sonorous voice came from behind Lin Li and seemed to spread over her shoulders like the warmth from an open fire. *'They must all have a sense of humour! Have you seen or not seen pictures of their Chairman?'*

'Husband, this is – ' The old woman cackled again and raised her hands in the air. *'I'm sorry. I do not know your honourable name.'*

'My name is Lin Li.'

'Husband, this is Lin Li, the wife of Captain Lee Kwan.'

Behind Lin Li there was an audible intake of breath. She turned and saw a big man with both hands placed over his heart. He had a full beard and moustache and wore a strange set of clothing: a bright red leather coat, a yellow woollen hat and scarf, knitted trousers and high soft leather boots.

'Elder Sister – ' the big man began, and Lin Li flinched involuntarily at his approach.

'Do not be afraid,' the old woman said. *'My husband is a Kazakh, he comes from the mountains in the far-west.'*

'Elder Sister, it is a great honour to meet you.' He spoke

Chinese with a heavy accent as he pressed his palms together and bowed.

'*I am also honoured.*' Lin Li stared at him for far too long. From what she'd heard he was too tall to be a Kazakh. '*Forgive my impudent eyes, Sir,*' she apologised, '*but I have never spoken with a Kazakh before.*'

'*They are outer barbarians who eat their newborn children,*' the old woman shouted. '*Kazakh women fuck with wolves. That is why he is so hairy.*' She thought her remarks were hilarious and cackled again.

'*Please ignore my wife,*' he said, but there was a gleam of laughter in his eyes. '*Soo-Soo is from Shanghai and therefore knows nothing of any consequence. I am only part Kazakh on my mother's side. And my father was not a wolf. He was a Pathan from beyond the roof of the world. My name is Jun Khan and my life belongs to your husband, Captain Lee Kwan.*'

'*Were you in the Army with him?*'

'*No, he saved my life in Sikiang Province in 1939.*'

'*Really?*' Lin Li remembered the winter of that year. She had been pregnant with her son, Jet, when Lee had been banished by the Nationalists to Sikiang in the far-west for what the Army termed 're-education' after he'd been absent without leave.

'*Yes,*' the big man answered. '*The town policeman shot my camel.*'

'*Oh?*'

'*So I shot the policeman. But to my eternal shame the bullet did not kill him. My camel's spirit, hovering above, would have been disgusted with such a poor shot. He once witnessed me kill a Tibetan at a distance of half a mile. The Tibetan was very small and I took the shot in a high wind.*'

'*Oh dear.*' Lin Li was beginning to wonder if she'd contacted the right people. They seemed an eccentric pair to say the least, but Lee had assured her that if she was ever in trouble she was to find a big bearded Kazakh named Jun Khan. '*He is a good friend,*' Lee had told her, '*and you can trust him with your life.*'

She believed she had not panicked and undertaken Lee Kwan's emergency instructions lightly. She had written him many letters and had received nothing in reply and she was worried sick, not only for his safety, but for the welfare of their two children who were being interrogated at school.

Their son, Jet, and daughter, Su-lin, were both boarders at the Ba-yi School, which was established in 1947 during the Civil War, specifically for the children of senior Communist Army officers. In the northwest Beijing suburb of Haidian, it was China's largest and most prestigious educational institution.

The students of the Ba-yi School were considered China's leaders of tomorrow and as such Lin Li's children were subject to close scrutiny and questioning from teachers and party officials. They were expected to have full knowledge of the rank, positions held, and contributions made by their parents in the Communist Party of China, but the questions her children had been subjected to seemed far deeper and more personal than the norm.

Her son, Jet, was not so much of a problem. He was a very wise and savvy thirteen-year-old, and if he had any fears for his father's well-being, he was careful not to show them. But her six-year-old daughter, Su-lin, was a different matter. Her distress at being interrogated and anger at her mother's inability to answer questions about her father's well-being had finally overwhelmed Lin Li.

'*I was incarcerated,*' Jun Khan continued his tale, unaware he'd lost his audience, '*in a very small gaol, and told I was going to be shot the following morning, but your Captain set me free in the middle of the night. He obviously understood the value of a camel over that of a wounded policeman. I owe your Captain my life.*'

'He saved my life too. In the Siege of Nanking,' Lin Li said, faltering. She began to cry as the pressure she'd been under finally caught up with her.

'*Aaaiiyaaah!*' The old woman leapt from her seat and berated her husband. '*See what you've done to our Elder Sister now with your bragging! You oaf!*'

'*I am so sorry, Elder Sister.*' Jun Khan placed his hand on Lin Li's shoulder.

'*To my shame,*' Lin Li continued, tears unabated, letting her fears and emotions run unchecked, '*I was abused by the Japanese in Nanking and Lee Kwan saved me. He took me to Minnie Vautrin at Ginling College in the International Safety Zone and defeated the demons that possessed my mind.*' She cried, silently and earnestly, as the fear and anxiety of the last week spilled forth. '*I could not speak for a year,*' she continued, sobbing. '*Lee took me with him, first to Hangkow, and later to Chungking. He nursed me back to health, then I was blessed by the gods to receive his love and he made me his wife.*' Lin Li looked up at the big bearded Kazakh standing over her. '*I have heard nothing from him for six months,*' she wailed. '*He is fighting in Manchuria and I am alone, separated from my children for days at a time and living in a building surrounded by people I cannot trust. And now I am being watched! I have been to the Ministry of the Army to enquire about my husband . . .*' she paused momentarily. '*I cannot get past the bureaucrats to anyone in authority. Lee could be dead! May the gods not make it so!*'

'*Cease your tears, Elder Sister,*' old Soo-Soo murmured as she sat next to Lin Li and put her arms around the young woman. '*The Dragon of Shanghai is engaged in the war in Korea. He is fighting yet again for his country and as a General this time. Generals are always very busy, true or not true? I'm sure he would contact you if he could. And as for the People's Army,*' she spat on the ground, '*they are no better than the Nationalists or the dogs that came before them.*'

Lin Li sobbed, as the old woman rocked her like a distressed child. '*I have a letter for him,*' she said finally, pulling a crumpled envelope from her pocket and offering it blindly.

Soo-Soo's immediate sympathy for the young woman was obvious in the groan that escaped her lips. '*Oh, my child,*' she crooned. '*We women of China are destined to be the real victims of war. We make homes for men, we serve their needs, we have their children and how are we repaid for these deeds? By watching them die in wars.'* She scowled at her husband as her sympathy was supplanted by anger. *'First it was the old emperors, then the Manchus, then the feudal lords. Next came the Nationalists and the Japanese and now the Communists, and they are presently fighting for the glory of the Russian puppet, Kim Il Sung!'* Soo-Soo's anger was beginning to get the better of her. *'I met that similarity to a pig's cunt years ago in Shanghai when we were fighting the Japanese,'* she cursed. *'At that time he was in the Russian Army, which proves his mother was raped by monkeys! He was an idiot then and he's an idiot now! His first wife was the one with the brains, but the Turnip Heads killed her!'*

'Enough!' Jun Khan interrupted. It was an order and Soo-Soo knew better than to ignore her husband when he adopted such a tone. *'The Captain's wife does not need to hear your opinions. She came to us for help and that is what she will get.'* Without waiting for an answer the big man knelt in front of Lin Li and placed his hands upon her shoulders, forcing her to look at him. *'Elder Sister,'* he began softly. *'Dry your tears and return to your home. I will find the Captain. I will deliver your letter and make him aware of your fears.'*

'But, Jun Khan, my husband is many miles from this place – '

'Do not concern yourself, Elder Sister,' Jun Khan interrupted softly, as if to a child. *'Have I not walked across the roof of the world? The Korean border is only a train journey away.'* He looked at his wife. *'I will take the Gobi Express to Tientsin and then north to Shenyang at the top of the Yellow Sea. From there I will travel south to Dandong on the Yalu River. Antung Air Base is not one mile from there. Three days and two nights will see me sitting at your husband's table, Elder Sister.'*

'My husband will reward you, Jun Khan, I am sure of it.' The relief in Lin Li's voice was obvious.

'He has already given me the gift of life,' he replied. *'It is I who must reward him, if only by relieving the anxiety of his wife and children.'*

Lin Li sprang up from the old woman's embrace and began to pace the verandah, her hands clasped before her, as the thoughts she wished to share with Lee Kwan began rushing through her mind. *'Please be so kind as to tell my husband that his children are safe and . . .'* she began.

'He will do so, Elder Sister.' Soo-Soo smiled as she watched the veil of fear lift from the young woman's face.

'. . . and tell him to contact us, his daughter, Su-lin, especially, as she is still very young and pines for him. Find out if he needs new socks and other clothing . . .'

The old Shanghai woman watched and listened as Lin Li gave Jun Khan a list of instructions he could not possibly remember. It is good to let her ramble on about trivialities, she thought. It will get rid of the tension that must have been building within her small frame for a long time.

Soo-Soo did not envy the girl's situation. Lin Li was married to a national hero, a legend before he was twenty, who had been appointed the youngest General ever in the PLA by Mao Tse-tung himself. But Soo-Soo knew Lee Kwan would remain an icon only as long as the war in Korea continued, and that would not be for much longer. A truce had been in place since the previous year – not that either side was observing it – and although peace negotiations were going slowly, an armistice was inevitable. An end was in sight and that end would mean disfavour and persecution for the Dragon of Shanghai.

Lee Kwan had been raised in the capitalist environment of Hong Kong and had been a Nationalist before he defected to the Communists. Soo-Soo knew they would never forget it, no matter how many battles he won for them. Already they had spies monitoring the activity of his wife and Soo-Soo had no doubt that when Lee Kwan returned to Peking, he would be criticised and made to *kow-tow* before the very people he had risked his life for a hundred times. She nodded, agreeing with herself. Revolution and betrayal walk hand in hand, true or not true?

Soo-Soo, uneducated Shanghai peasant though she was, had a remarkably acute political instinct, honed in the trenches during the war against the Japanese. She had worn the Nationalist uniform and fought in Ch'iang Kai-shek's Army alongside Captain Lee Kwan and many other officers during the war. Then, in 1945 with the Japanese defeated, she had watched in horror as her country had dissolved into civil war. Sick and tired of conflict, Soo-Soo, like many other women, both Nationalist and Communist, had discarded her uniform and awaited the coming of peace, any sort of peace. She could not have cared less who won.

The victory, when it finally came in 1949, was a Communist victory. Ch'iang Kai-shek and the tattered remnants of his Nationalist Army retreated south and eventually escaped to the island of Taiwan. On 1 October, Soo-Soo had stood with thousands of others and watched Mao Tse-Tung declare China a Communist People's Republic from atop Tiananmen Gate.

She remembered the time so vividly. The killing had commenced immediately, as she knew it would. Mao and his Chinese Communist Party needed to establish total control, just as Ch'iang would have done had he been victorious, and that meant re-educating the masses and eradicating all dissent.

From the outset the new Government had been very clever. They had given the working classes the right to judge their former landlords and employers. The workers across the country had formed 'people's courts' and so far they had accused, judged, humiliated, flogged or executed more than a million people.

And it will not stop with landlords, Soo-Soo thought. She looked again at the young girl, avidly giving her impossible instructions to Jun Khan. Next they will attack the middle classes, then the intellectuals, and then the ranks of the Military, just like the Marxists had done in Russia. And Lee Kwan would be caught in the web. She nodded sadly. Revolution and betrayal walk hand in hand, true or not true?

CHAPTER FOUR

The chauffeur driven car was a black 1948 Buick with the Union Jack flying above each headlight on little flag poles, and James found it rather ironic that the official car of the British Ambassador to South Korea was of American manufacture. It had picked them up from Kenjong Air Base and was taking them into Seoul to a British Embassy cocktail party, and James had no idea why.

He sat comfortably on the enormous back seat and watched the neon world of night-time Seoul pass by. The streets still bore evidence of the invasion and recapture of Seoul two years before by the US Marine Corps and General Infantry Divisions. Bullet and artillery holes decorated the walls of some buildings and bomb craters were still in evidence, probably because those public service departments that still functioned regarded them as the least of the city's current worries.

The streets of downtown Seoul were packed with soldiers and civilians alike. Prostitutes were evident and obvious, dressed in split silk dresses and high-heeled shoes, plying their time-worn trade. Markets and street stalls lit by bare electric bulbs flourished in every doorway and alley, attended by soldiers of many nations, who, bored with the bars and the booze, searched for native souvenirs to remind them of their time in war. Australians in slouched hats, GIs in their fashionable baseball style caps so sought after by the locals, French paratroopers, Italians, and soldiers of ten or more other countries with UN affiliation all lounged on street corners or stood in groups, smoking endless cigarettes, discussing anything but war.

Johnnie Wilson had his head stuck out of the rear window of the Buick. Although he'd been stationed in Korea for nine months, like many other pilots, he'd had little opportunity to see the capital city that was now fascinating him. He'd already identified Central Seoul Railway Station, the Capital, South Korea's parliamentary building, Duk Soo the royal palace, and several other palaces including Chung Dak and the Royal Gardens.

'Damn, Jimbo!' Johnnie gasped, his face flushed with boyish enthusiasm. 'There's more palaces in this city than on the goddamn Rhine River and the Danube put together.'

James smiled. 'What did you expect? Korea was ruled by various dynasties for two thousand years. In fact Korea once ruled most of China.'

'Really?'

Johnnie's earnest enquiry made James laugh. 'Yes. At one time a people from here ruled half of Asia. They were called the Khitai. That's why Marco Polo called China Cathay – he mispronounced Khitai.'

Johnnie shook his head. 'Is there anything you don't know?'

'Yes. I don't know why we're going to a cocktail party at the British Embassy.'

'Hell, who cares? Anything's better than another night in Kenjong Officers' Club.' Johnnie laughed and stuck his head back out of the window.

James was not quite so sure.

The streets had suddenly become darker and narrower than the tree lined boulevards of central Seoul. The houses were now mansions, set back off the street with high iron fences and gates. They stared out imposingly at any who dared to pass.

The big Buick then turned slowly into a driveway and came to a halt in front of a large set of steps covered by a portico. James' door was opened by a Korean boy dressed in fine pressed white linen.

As they walked up the steps a young British Navy Lieutenant greeted them.

'Good evening, Sir,' the young man saluted. 'I'm Lieutenant Les Bird, Aide-De-Camp to Ambassador Woodruff.'

'Good evening, Lieutenant.' James returned the salute. 'I am Wing Commander James Merchant and this is Captain John Wilson, United States Air Force. The Captain is my date for this evening. I'm afraid eligible young ladies are in rather short supply at Kenjong Air Base.'

'Ha, ha, very good, Sir,' the young officer chuckled politely as he shook Johnnie's outstretched hand. 'You're more than welcome, Captain Wilson.'

'How's it goin', Les?' the American replied in a pure Texan drawl. 'Sorry about the uniform, but my cocktail dress is being cleaned for my coming out party.'

'Ha, ha,' the Lieutenant chuckled again, and then turned his attention back to James. 'His Excellency asked me to watch for your arrival, Commander. I'm to take you straight to him.'

'Tell me,' James enquired as the young man ushered them through the front doors, 'do you have any idea why I was invited tonight?'

'Yes, Sir.' Lieutenant Bird indicated the ornate stairway he wished them to ascend. 'It would seem the French Ambassador, M'sieur Jacques DuFresne, has developed a very sudden interest in air combat theory and asked Ambassador Woodruff if he could meet you, hence the invitation.'

'Really?' James offered a raised eyebrow to Johnnie Wilson as they climbed the stairs.

'I'm not surprised, Sir,' the young officer babbled on. 'You are something of a celebrity, you know. Your exploits have been recorded in the newspapers recently, most notably in the *South China Morning Post* and indeed the *London Times*. Five kills in six months. That makes you an "ace".'

'It's six, as of yesterday,' Johnnie interjected.

'Oh, I say, Sir, well done,' the young man gushed as they reached the top of the stairs. 'Madame DuFresne will be beside herself.'

'*Madame* DuFresne?' This time it was Johnnie Wilson who raised an eyebrow to James.

'Yes, Sir.' Lieutenant Bird halted at the top of the stairs and lowered his voice to a conspiratorial whisper. 'I believe air combat theory has actually become the passion of a number of Embassy wives of late, and particularly the French Ambassador's wife, Francine.' He smiled knowingly at James. 'I'm afraid modern air warfare might be a bit beyond the French Ambassador. He's more of your bi-planes and barrage balloons era, if you know what I mean?'

'Hey, Jimbo.' Johnnie nudged him in the ribs. 'I think you've been set up, pardner.'

'It's one of the chores of being an ace fighter pilot, John.' James winked at the American. 'Women seem to throw themselves at one's feet. As an officer and a gentleman one can't simply leave them lying there, unattended, can one?'

'Oh, it must be frightfully awful for you, old boy,' Johnnie replied in his worst Etonian English accent.

'King and country, old man.' James grinned lasciviously and slapped the American on the back. 'With damsels and particularly French damsels, *je suis bien obligé*, you understand? One is simply obliged to do it.'

'Indubitably, old fellow,' Johnnie crowed. 'Indubitably.'

They entered a spacious salon containing thirty or forty fashionably dressed guests, delicately sipping from flutes of champagne. Beneath crystal chandeliers, and surrounded by heavy brocades and the finest antique furniture, they were ushered through the crowd to a distinguished looking silver-haired gentleman in a dinner suit bedecked with medals.

'Your Excellency,' Lieutenant Bird began obsequiously, 'may I present Wing Commander James Merchant and Captain John Wilson, United States Air Force? Gentlemen, His Excellency the British Ambassador, Sir Beaufort Woodruff.'

'Merchant, you're here at last.' The tall Englishman offered his hand.

'It's an unexpected honour, Sir,' James responded, shaking the man's hand.

'Delighted to meet you, Merchant. So good of you to come.' Woodruff turned to the American. 'And you, Captain

Wilson. America's doing a damned fine job in this war, what?'

'Thank you, Your Excellency,' Johnnie replied in perfectly modulated mid-Atlantic English. 'Great Britain and the United States will always be brothers in arms. United we stand, divided we fall, Sir. I'm sure you'll agree.'

'Indeed I do, Captain,' the Ambassador chortled. 'Well said, Sir.'

James had to smile. Johnnie Wilson was a total chameleon, changing from saloon sidekick to salon chevalier in the twinkling of an eye. It's an ability I'll put to good use, James thought, when this bloody war is concluded.

The Korean War was becoming a nuisance to James, and a dangerous nuisance at that. He and Johnnie were doing very nicely thanks to the deliveries made by the Woo twins, and the last thing he needed was for either him or Johnnie to be killed in a dog fight over the Yalu River.

The North Korean Army had seized the whole of South Korea in 1950, then the UN had intervened and fought them all the way back to the Manchurian border. China had then entered the war and by 1951 had pushed the UN Forces back to the 38th Parallel and a stalemate had ensued. A truce had been announced and peace negotiations had begun in the border town of Panmunjong.

James, like everyone else in the conflict, was sure an armistice was not far off. None of the countries involved could afford the cost of continuing such a meaningless war. But, typical of all truces, in James' opinion, the peace negotiations had developed into a game of cat and mouse being played out at a snail's pace.

'I believe the French Ambassador is most anxious to meet you, Merchant,' Woodruff said as he summoned a drink waiter with an imperious wave of his very long arm. 'Would you do me a favour and corner the fellow at some stage this evening?'

'I'll make it my business, Sir.' James took a flute of champagne from a tray and raised it to the Ambassador. 'Anything I can do to help the war effort, Your Excellency.'

'What?' Woodruff's attention had been elsewhere. 'Oh, yes, quite. Well said, Wing Commander. Mind you, lad, he's as deaf as a post. You'll have to shout.' He began waving at someone across the room. 'Would you two young men excuse me? My wife is demanding my presence. Talk to the ladies and have a good time.'

James watched the tall, gangly diplomat make his way through the crowd then suddenly became aware of the array of attractive women in the room, most of whom were staring at him. One particular woman's stare demanded reciprocation.

She's from Indochina, James thought, French-Indochinese, or Cantonese. Yes, a Viet definitely, with French-Cantonese bloodlines, he was sure of it. And probably the mysterious Madame DuFresne, if his instincts were correct.

'Excuse me, Wing Commander?' It was the young Lieutenant again. 'His Excellency asked me to introduce you to the French Ambassador.'

'Yes, by all means, Mr Bird.' James turned to Johnnie, whose gaze was wandering the room like a drunken gunsight. 'Captain Wilson, will you excuse me for a minute?'

'I certainly will, Wing Commander,' the Texan replied without breaking his surveillance.

'On second thoughts, I think you'd better come with me.'

'What was that, pardner?'

'I said,' James nudged him in the ribs, 'you'd better come with me.'

'What for?'

'If I have to sing for my supper, you jolly well can, too.'

'But . . .'

'No buts about it, Johnnie my lad.' James grabbed the American by the arm. 'The French Ambassador wants to discuss jet-fighter tactics and you're a jet-fighter pilot, are you not?'

'Aw, gimme a break, Jimbo . . .'

'Lead the way, Mr Bird.'

'*Enchanté, Commandeur. Parlez-vous français, M'sieur?*' the Ambassador enquired as they were introduced.

'*Oui, M'sieur l'Ambassadeur,*' James replied in perfectly modulated French, before switching to English. 'But my American companion does not speak French, Sir. And considering our host, the fact that we're in the British Embassy and the fact that I'm wearing the Queen's uniform, perhaps we should converse in English?'

'*Pardon, M'sieur?*' The point of diplomatic etiquette was completely lost on the Frenchman.

'Fortunately for you, the Ambassador is slightly deaf,' a voice behind him murmured.

James knew who it would be and their eyes locked again as he turned.

'Good evening, Madame . . . ?' He offered his hand to the beautiful young woman.

'DuFresne,' she replied taking his hand. 'Francine DuFresne.' Then she totally unsettled him, whispering in faultless Cantonese. '*The man you are trying to insult is my husband. Fortunately for you, he is as deaf as a bell-ringer's dog.*'

'*Fortunately for him, Little Sister,*' James whispered with a sardonic smile, '*the English half of me has no heart for the French and my Chinese half is indifferent.*' He reverted to English. 'I'm . . . er . . . delighted to meet you, Madame DuFresne,' he said loudly, looking around to see if anyone had heard or understood their exchange. Johnnie Wilson had already engaged a young woman in conversation and the deaf Frenchman, his face creased in an irritated Gallic frown, was the only one paying them any attention.

'Jacques,' Francine DuFresne said loudly, leaning to her husband's ear. 'I believe M'sieur Woodruff wishes to speak with you.'

'*Oh, merci, Francine. Excusez-moi, Commandeur Merchant,*' the man grunted and peremptorily thrust an empty champagne flute into his wife's hand before wandering off through the crowd.

'That was a lie, wasn't it?'

'Yes,' she replied, placing her husband's empty glass on the tray of a passing waiter.

James looked at the young Eurasian. She has to be thirty years younger than her husband, he thought. Barely five feet tall, Francine Dufresne was dressed in traditional Indochinese formal attire. She wore silk ankle length trousers, apricot in colour and close fitting, with a full-length gown of the same material split to the hip on either side. Her jet black hair was swept up and a minimum of makeup highlighted the amber colour of her skin. She stared back at him, her eyes inquisitive, like those of a cat confronted by something new and intriguing.

'Madame DuFresne, I do believe Eurasians are the most beautiful people in the world, wouldn't you agree?' He made the observation *sotto voce*, ensuring it was for her ears only.

Her laugh was sexy. 'Considering my antecedents, and indeed yours, M'sieur Merchant, I would be a fool to say otherwise.'

'Ah, but do you agree?' James teased.

'True beauty lives in the heart, M'sieur, it has no shape or form. It cannot be seen in a mirror, it can only be seen through the eyes of love.'

'Then I must be in love, Madame.' James bowed slightly.

'You are a fighter pilot, are you not?' She offered him a sparkling, mischievous smile. 'That makes you a predator, M'sieur, and predators cannot afford to love. It colours their judgement and makes them hesitate at the kill.'

'Not only beautiful,' James smiled easily, 'but a tigress as well. Your husband is a very lucky man.'

'My husband is a racist,' Francine DuFresne replied, the light of humour dying in her eyes, 'and a fool, who symbolises the bigoted righteousness of the French bourgeoisie.'

'I see.' James was taken aback. Hearing Marxist doctrine spoken with such vehemence from an Embassy wife was beyond his experience. Just who am I dealing with here, he wondered.

'I am Indochinese, a Viet, M'sieur Merchant,' she said forcefully, her eyes defiant. 'I love *my* people and *my* country. The French are colonialists of the worst type, even more so than the English, but their time is at hand.'

'If you dislike the French so much, Madame, may I ask why you married one?'

'He bought me, M'sieur, as one would buy a pig or a goat. My mother sold me to him in return for work and shelter.'

'Your mother sold you?'

'Have you ever slept in a pool of mud surrounded by pigs?' Her question was rhetorical. 'My mother and I did. I was twelve years old and we were destitute. Do you understand, M'sieur? Twelve years old, need I say more?'

'No.' James tried to sound sympathetic, but he didn't really care. He'd heard the story, or variations of it from other Asians, a thousand times before. 'It must have been awful for you.'

'Oh, well,' she shrugged, smiled and sipped her champagne. 'I'm sure everyone has awful times, even yourself.'

'Me?' James laughed. 'Good God no, I can't remember anything really awful, far from it.'

'What about the Battle of Britain?'

'I was just a fighter pilot.'

'In a newspaper article I once read, a man called Dowding was quoted as saying you were more than a fighter pilot. He described you as an aerial assassin.'

'Air Marshall Dowding said that? What a dreadful thing to say.'

'Do you think it's possible, Commander?'

'What? That I'm an assassin?'

'Yes,' Francine said. 'The art of assassination intrigues me, in fact it fascinates me. I once read the exploits of a true life assassin. He described the moment he killed as the moment of ultimate fulfilment. Better even than sex.' She stared straight into his eyes. 'Do you find that is true for you, Wing Commander? What does it feel like to kill? Is the moment of execution truly . . . fulfilling?' She let the words hang in the air.

Was this woman playing mind games with him, or merely flirting? Was she simply a bored Embassy wife, or did she know more about him than might prove healthy for her?

He'd decided to answer her truthfully and study her reaction when his thoughts were suddenly interrupted.

'Hey, Jimbo.' Johnnie Wilson arrived with a pretty young girl on his arm. 'This party is gonna fold at twenty-two hundred hours, buddy. Can you believe that?'

'Well, Embassy cocktail parties usually do, old boy.' James offered a look of apology to Francine. 'Excuse me, Madame. May I introduce my wingman, Captain John Wilson? John, this is Madame DuFresne, wife of the French Ambassador.'

'The pleasure is all mine, Ma'am.' Johnnie took her hand and kissed it, which started a giggling fit in the young woman accompanying him. 'Oh, by the way,' he turned to the giggling girl, 'this is Miss Connie Bufalo from Des Moines in the good old State of Iowa. Connie's pappy is a Marine Colonel, James. He's stationed right here in Seoul and Connie's over from Stateside for a little visit, aren't you, sweetie?'

'This is my first time overseas,' the girl managed to say from behind her gloved hand.

At the completion of the introductions, Francine touched Johnnie lightly on the arm. 'Well, Captain Wilson, I'm throwing a small supper party tonight and I was just about to invite Wing Commander Merchant. It's at the Embassy's summer residence in the hills to the north of the city. Perhaps you and Miss Bufalo would care to attend?'

'You can count us in, Ma'am.'

'Oh,' the girl managed to mutter. 'I'd have to ask Daddy's permission.'

'I thought you might,' Francine murmured, catching James' eye.

'Well, why don't we just go right on over and do that?' Johnnie took the girl's hand and disappeared as quickly as he'd arrived, leaving James and Francine staring at each other.

'Why do I have the distinct feeling that your husband will not be attending tonight?'

'My husband never goes to the summer residence. He prefers to remain in the Embassy apartment. He doesn't like the hills.'

'And what if I don't like the hills?' His voice was soft, but with a dangerous undertone.

'I arranged for your attendance here tonight, Commander – ' Francine began.

'I was beginning to suspect as much,' he interrupted.

'Please let me finish.' Francine glanced about, nervously. 'I went to a great deal of trouble and effort to get you to Seoul and I can assure you, if you accept my invitation it may prove to be very . . . gratifying.'

'For who, Francine?' James kept his voice low and switched to Cantonese. *'The Viet Min, or the People's Liberation Army? Which side are you on?'*

'I do not understand,' she lied.

'Little Communists should not play games with dragons, understand or not understand?' James took her hand in his.

'I am not playing games, Elder Brother,' she answered with all the respect she could muster. Then she felt it, a warm tingling sensation. It began in the palm of her hand and slowly crept up her arm. Suddenly she was very frightened. She became lost in his gaze. James Merchant seemed, in her eyes, to be taking over the whole room; her surrounds were disappearing. He emanated power from his whole being. Francine knew it was her imagination playing tricks, but the tingling sensation was not. It had reached her throat and was turning rapidly to severe pain.

'Swear to me, little Communist, on your mother's life, that you are not playing games.'

'I . . . I . . . swear, Elder Brother,' she managed to whisper. He dropped her hand and the pain ceased immediately, then he looked at her and smiled benignly, but it only added to her terror.

'In that case, Madame,' James murmured, returning to English, 'I would be delighted to accept your invitation.' He made a show of kissing her hand and she flinched when he recaptured it and pressed it to his lips. 'That is of course, if it is still on offer?'

'It most certainly is, Wing Commander,' Francine managed to reply with forced gaiety. She could see, over James

Merchant's shoulder, her husband approaching and he was seemingly the worse for alcohol.

'*Ma cherie,*' Jacques DuFresne dribbled. 'Will you forgeeve an old man?' he clumsily attempted in heavily accented English. 'I am returning to zee Embassy immediately. Urgent business, eh?'

'Of course, my darling,' Francine's face wore a fixed smile.

'Enjoy your leetle *soirée ce soir, ma cherie.*' He clumsily kissed her hand. 'I weel expect you back at zee Embassy tomorrow evening, *oui?*'

'*Certainement.*' Francine patted her husband's sleeve with false affection. '*Bonne nuit, Jacques,*' she whispered and watched him stagger off through the last of the guests.

'Madame, you are extraordinary, a genuine mercenary.' James inclined his head, his voice mocking her. 'Shall we collect my wingman and his idiot girlfriend and toddle off?'

Francine took his arm. As they walked towards the exit, she prayed that things would go as she had planned. She was only too aware she had a dragon by the tail, and a very dangerous one at that.

龍

The sports car, a 1949 Delahaye 175 two-door cabriolet, began the winding climb into the hills north of the city with powerful ease and James enjoyed its speed and grace as much as the fresh night air in his face. The girl gunned the engine as she came out of each turn. He had to admit, she was a damned fine driver. He relaxed into the leather seat and lit a cigarette.

Marine Colonel Bufalo had apparently refused his daughter permission to attend the summer house and Johnnie had gone off with her family to a nightclub. It was just as well, James thought. He was beginning to smell a rat, and if anything went wrong he would rather there were no witnesses to muddy the waters.

They had barely spoken since leaving the British Embassy and James could sense the tension in the girl as he watched her deftly spinning the steering wheel. He'd put the fear of

God into her earlier and had done so with good reason. She was a Communist all right, she'd made that obvious. Probably a member of the *Viet Min*, Ho Chi Min's ragtag army of peasants now fighting their French masters in Indochina, and that would make her, in all probability, a spy. The ramifications of his theory fascinated him.

Francine DuFresne, if his assessment of her proved true, was a serious threat to the whole United Nations community in Korea. As the wife of the French Ambassador she was in a position to spy to her heart's content and relay any valuable information she gleaned to the *Viet Min*, who would no doubt pass it on to their Communist brothers in North Korea. She was officially his enemy, and were he to do his duty as an officer in the United Nations Armed Forces, she would probably be arrested, tried and shot.

But, he mused, she had mentioned the word gratifying.

He would bide his time and find out just what was in store for him at the French Embassy's summer residence. If tonight's dealings met with his approval, he would dismiss from his conscience any frivolous idea he may have entertained that she was a spy. However, if things did not meet with his approval, he would kill her and anyone connected with her, then accept his just and well-earned reward for exposing a Communist spy-ring, from a grateful UN High Command.

Not an unenviable position to be in, he thought, as he drew on his cigarette. He looked down at the lights of Seoul spread out across the plain below, then allowed his gaze to drift to the profile of Francine DuFresne. She's a very beautiful woman, he thought, and his eyes roved to her legs. If the worst comes to the worst I'll seduce her before I kill her.

Francine could feel his eyes upon her as she slammed the gear-shift down one ratio and threw the car into a bend. James Merchant was a dangerous man, an entirely different animal to the statesmen and academics she was used to charming information from at Embassy dinners. James Merchant was a cold blooded assassin. Her orders had been so simple. Get him to Seoul, get him to the summer residence and leave him sitting alone on the balcony. What transpired after that was none of her business. But even the simplest of plans could go wrong, couldn't they? And if this one did, Francine knew she would die.

She fought down an overwhelming urge to stop the car and run for her life.

'Is it much further?' James interrupted her thoughts.

'No.' Francine dropped the car back through the gears. 'In fact, we are here.' She slowed the vehicle almost to a stop and turned into a driveway.

The Ambassador's summer residence was a magnificent single storey house built in the French Colonial style with a long, low, vine covered front verandah, set among beautifully manicured lawns and gardens. The property was in darkness and as she negotiated the front steps James waited by the car, admiring the distant lights of Seoul through the trees that screened the house from the road.

Francine opened the front door and suddenly the gardens were swathed in soft golden light emanating from a series of French windows set along the verandah.

'Would you care to sit out here, M'sieur Merchant?' She stood in the doorway. 'It is such a beautiful night. It would be a shame to waste it.'

'While we wait for your friends, no doubt,' James replied mockingly. He moved along the verandah, sat in one of two seats at a small table and gazed out at the gardens.

Francine took a deep breath. 'You are correct, M'sieur,' she answered and the ten seconds of silence that followed seemed to her like a lifetime, until James finally turned and gazed at her.

'Why am I not surprised?' His tone again mocked her.

'I will have the houseboy bring you a glass of wine,' she said. 'I would like to change out of this formal attire, if you will excuse me?'

'*Certainement, Madame.*'

'*A bientôt,*' she replied and disappeared inside.

James breathed deeply and let his body relax. Whatever

happened next, he would be ready for it. He allowed his *Shaolin* training to take over his mind. His senses heightened, he took in the surroundings, analysing obstacles and escape routes. His skin felt the faint breeze against his face. His brain began to filter the night noises around him: a bird some distance off, the rustling of vine leaves, frogs in a pond, a gecko in the eaves, the houseboy's approaching footsteps on the verandah . . . and a slight footfall in the shrubbery to his right.

'Good evening, Sir.' The houseboy placed an ice bucket and two glasses on the table.

James nodded, but he did not reply. The boy was interfering with his concentration. His senses continued to search for sound or movement in the garden as the boy poured a glass of white wine then re-entered the house.

James breathed rhythmically, feeling his heart rate slow as his body prepared for action, and the words of his teacher Lo Shi-mon came into his mind reciting the principles of combat. *Detect, assess, strike, defend,* he heard his Shaolin master say. *Concentrate, James. Detect, assess, strike, defend. Search for the threat.*

'*Detect, assess, strike, defend. Concentrate, James.*'

For a moment James thought his mind was playing tricks with him, then he heard the soft voice nearby as it once again repeated Lo Shi-mon's words in Cantonese.

'*Detect, assess, strike, defend. Concentrate, Ah James, you lazy boy.*'

James smiled. '*It has been a long time, Little Brother, true or not true?*' he replied.

'*True,*' the voice of Lee Kwan agreed. '*And I am not your Little Brother. I am only three days younger than you and deserve more respect.*'

James laughed softly at their life-long joke. '*And you are a General now, also true?*'

'*Also true. Forgive me if I do not join you in the light, Ah James, but South Korea is not a good place for the Commander of Military Operations in North Korea.*'

'*Then I will join you in the darkness.*' James stood.

'*Do not bother, Ah James.*' Lee's voice was much closer, he'd moved to the end of the verandah. '*Sit down and enjoy the wine.*'

James sat again. 'I see,' he switched to English. 'If I don't see your face I won't be forced to lie about it later, right?'

'There is that,' Lee answered, 'but also there is a sniper in the bushes and he'll shoot you if you come within three feet of me.'

'That is totally unnecessary, Lee!' James snapped.

'I know that,' Lee replied evenly. 'I don't like it any more than you do, but the people who smuggled me into South Korea think otherwise.'

'So this is not a social visit?' James responded sarcastically then sipped his wine. 'How disappointing.' He put his glass on the table and searched his pockets for a cigarette.

'I have five minutes, James, then I'm off to catch a boat back to China. Please listen carefully. I would like nothing more than to embrace you and talk for hours the way we did as children, but circumstances will not permit such a luxury. I have taken a great risk in order to speak to you personally.'

'I'm sorry. Hearing your voice came as a shock.' James lit his cigarette. 'It's been nearly fifteen years, Lee. I've missed you,' he said with genuine sincerity.

'As I have missed you, James.' Lee Kwan heard the affection in his brother's voice and thoughts of their happy childhood came flooding back. 'One day when the war is over, we will meet again and rejoice in each other's well-being. But now is not the time . . .'

'I know,' James interrupted. 'I realise the risk you have taken, so say what you have to say then get to that boat, for both our sakes.'

'The deals we put in place are known by the KGB – '

'Oh, shit!' James coughed up a lungful of smoke.

'Loose talk by some fat ignorant politician or other in Peking was all it took.'

'And the bloody Russians got wind of it?'

'Exactly. I should have foreseen it, James. I should never have agreed to buy the radio parts from you – '

'Never mind that,' James interrupted. 'What does the bloody KGB want?'

'That is why I came to you personally. What they want is a far cry from second hand radio parts.'

'I half expected as much.' James flicked his unfinished cigarette into the shrubbery. 'I knew when I set up the deal that it wouldn't remain a secret forever. But you know me,' he shrugged, 'the thought of all that profit was irresistible.' James put his hands on the verandah railing and sighed. 'So what do they want?'

'A Sabre jet.'

'*What?!*' James gasped.

'An F-86.'

'That's preposterous! It's out of the question!'

'They're prepared to pay you one million in cash,' Lee said softly. In the darkness he smiled at the silence that followed. He knew James Merchant better than any man alive.

'US dollars?' James managed to whisper. The sum astounded even him.

'Yes,' Lee answered and more silence followed.

'Christ on the Cross!' James' whispered exclamation, when it finally came, was a favourite expression of the two when they were schoolboys. Lee snorted involuntarily.

'What are you laughing at?' James demanded.

'You, my wonderful brother. You never fail to delight me.'

'It's no laughing matter, Lee,' James retorted in earnest. 'I could get into serious trouble for stealing a jet!'

The understatement was the undoing of Lee Kwan and silent laughter racked his body. 'I know,' he said, struggling for control. 'It's called treason.'

'Not if I steal from the Americans,' James reasoned with utter sincerity. 'I'm English. My Sabre jet is the property of the United States Government. The British Crown doesn't own any Sabre jets – it can't afford them – so technically speaking – '

'Oh, don't!' Lee groaned.

'What *is* the matter with you?'

Lee gasped for breath. 'Wait a minute.' He took several deep breaths through his nose and finally regained his composure. 'James,' he said affectionately, 'if only all soldiers in this world were as morally corrupt as you, there would be no war.'

'Well, you've got to admit, Lee,' James was beginning to see the funny side of the exchange himself, 'war does get in the way of business . . .'

'It certainly does, James.'

'. . . unless of course, you're into arms dealing.'

'Ha!' The witticism set Lee off again. 'You're incorrigible, James, absolutely incorrigible!'

'I mean to say,' James smiled, enjoying his adopted brother's mirth, 'how often does one get the chance to sell a jet?'

'So, I take it your answer is yes?'

'Of course it is!'

'Good.'

'And payment is in cash you say?'

'Yes, in cash.'

'By God, Lee, right at this moment, given the embargo on China, I could buy half of Hong Kong for a million US . . .'

'And restore the Merchant Company to its rightful place as the noble house of Hong Kong?'

'Exactly!' James chose to ignore the slightly sarcastic tone in Lee's voice. 'In one fell swoop, I could have it all.' He took up his wine glass and drank it dry.

'Wasn't it Paul the Apostle who wrote, "For the love of money is the root of all evil"?' Lee asked, all trace of humour gone from his voice.

This time James retaliated. 'Don't you dare lecture me, *Sai Loh*,' he sneered, deliberately emphasising the term Little Brother. 'You may find contentment in this world with only a cloak for warmth and a rice bowl, but I won't. Without money and the power that comes with it, life holds no interest for me.' He turned in Lee's direction and glared into the darkness. 'And I make no excuses for that fact. I am what I am, Lee, and you of all people should know that, so don't you *dare* quote the Bible to me. You're not even a Christian, for Christ's sake!'

James stared down at the twinkling lights of Seoul trying to maintain his rage, but the inanity of his final retort had dawned on him and he reddened in embarrassment. He could hear Lee's breathing and realised the remark had not escaped him either.

'Are you laughing at me again?' There was no conviction in his voice.

'Yes,' was the muffled reply from the darkness.

'It was a stupid thing to say, wasn't it?'

'Yes.'

James continued to stare down at Seoul, his anger dissipated, replaced by a feeling of affection for his brother, in the nearby darkness. 'I'm sorry, Lee,' he said finally, 'we haven't spoken for so very long and after two minutes, I start an argument.'

'I started the argument, James,' Lee replied. 'It was petty of me, sanctimonious and entirely unnecessary.'

James smiled. It was typical of Lee Kwan's forgiving nature. He was the only person James had ever known whom he could describe as a truly good soul. He had been blessed by the gods at birth. Even as a boy, Lee had a maturity and wisdom far beyond his years, qualities James had admired, but had never been able to fully comprehend, let alone emulate. They had shared a wonderful friendship until war had separated them. As teenagers, Lee had gone to China and James had joined the R.A.F., and although they had not seen each other since, James could sense the bond they shared was as strong as ever.

He turned and leaned his back against the verandah railing. 'How is your family?' he asked. 'How is Lin Li?' James was suddenly desperate to know. 'And your children, Jet and Su-lin? Are they well?'

'We have no time, James – '

'Please,' he interrupted. 'Just for a minute, can you tell me – '

'They are living, but things do not go well for them in Peking, or Beijing, as we now must call it. I am a General in the Army and that protects them for the while, but they are being watched and when the war is over and I am no longer of any value, I fear things will change for the worst.'

'Is there anything I can do?'

'Yes, you can make my superiors happy by stealing a Sabre jet.'

'Consider it stolen, Little Brother,' James said. 'I take it you have a plan?'

'Yes, a plan that will see you safely at Antung and one million dollars richer.'

'Antung?' James' voice held concern. 'That's across the Yalu.'

'Trust me, James.'

'Very well. How much does the DuFresne woman know?'

'Nothing. She simply facilitated our meeting.'

'Right. Well, you'd better explain your plan, then go and catch your boat, Little Brother.'

龍

Francine DuFresne stood at the windows in the darkened library and gazed out into the rear garden, lit up in bright moonlight. She had no idea what had transpired on the front balcony, but she knew it was over. Ten minutes before, she'd seen four shadowy figures run into the trees beyond the back fence of the property and disappear.

She was confused and frightened. She stood rooted to the floor clutching a tumbler of whisky to her chest with both hands. Had one of those men been James Merchant, she wondered, or was he perhaps dead on the front balcony? The idea of finding out terrified her. What would she do? Report it to the police? Ring her husband? Try to get rid of the body? She was alone, except for the houseboy, and he was still a child. She had no instructions and could not seek them using the phone at the summer residence; her controller would kill her for breaching the security protocols.

But then, what if nothing had happened at all and he was still sitting on the verandah waiting for her? She couldn't possibly just tell him to get into the car and then drive him back to Seoul. She had played the *agent provocateur* in luring him to the hills, making it fairly obvious that she was attracted to him. Would she have to have sex with him? She had to admit, back at the British Embassy, she had found herself physically drawn to him. That was, until he'd threatened her.

What if they hadn't killed him? The thought hit her like a freight train and a shiver ran through her body. What if they'd botched the job and he was lurking somewhere, wounded and waiting to take his revenge? Her mind raced with so many possibilities she couldn't think straight. She shivered again and the ice in her glass tinkled.

'Hello, Francine,' James whispered. She felt his hand grasp the nape of her neck. She stood frozen to the spot, staring blindly into the garden, waiting for that final sound, the snapping of her neck. Her body was incapable of responding, no fight, no flight, nothing.

'Don't tell me you've been standing in the dark spying on your comrades, Little Communist?' he whispered in Cantonese.

Where had he come from? She hadn't even heard him enter the library let alone approach and now he stood immediately behind her, his powerful fingers massaging her neck.

'Don't worry, Francine. Your secret is safe with me, if my secret is safe with you.'

'I do not know your secret, Elder Brother,' she managed to reply and was surprised by the even tone of her voice.

'Then you have nothing to be afraid of, Little Sister.' He reached around her and placed the palm of his free hand on her abdomen.

They stood still, neither moving a muscle and Francine began to relax. Then she felt it, the same tingling sensation he had induced in her earlier at the Embassy. A warm feeling began to extend from beneath his palm outward, upward and downward through her limbs until it reached the furthest extremities of her body. Her toes, fingers and even her ears tingled. She fixed her gaze on the garden outside, but her mind would not respond; it was being slowly and surely seduced by the growing sensations in her body. She felt her knees weaken and his arm responded, taking some of her body weight, and her breathing became shorter, quicker.

His hand stopped massaging her neck and slowly moved around her waist, taking more of her weight as his fingers captured a breast, while his palm on her abdomen moved slightly lower. The feeling he was creating became even stronger and seemed to centre itself between her legs. She began to gasp for breath, then her gasps turned to sighs, and her sighs turned to moans. Then, suddenly, both her mind and body lost control as wave after wave of orgasmic pleasure surged through her.

Francine was lost in a world she had never before known. For a full minute euphoria and ecstasy collided, making her mind reel out of kilter, then slowly the sensations began to recede. She felt the polished wooden floor beneath her feet and strength began to flow back into her legs. His arms moved to her shoulders, helping her remain upright until her breathing finally slowed.

'*Remember, at the Embassy, you asked me what it feels like to kill?*' he whispered in her ear. '*That is what it feels like, Little Sister.*' She felt him move away, and in the time it took her to turn, he was gone.

Francine found him seated on the verandah, sipping a glass of wine. She clipped the end from the cigar she was carrying, lit it and offered it to him. 'It's Cuban.' She spoke in English. 'Jacques gets them imported through the American Army, at great expense.'

James merely nodded, took the cigar and puffed on it.

'How did you do that?' She sat at the table opposite him.

'Do what?'

'Don't tell me you were not aware of what just happened to me in there, M'sieur.'

'I didn't do anything,' he replied. 'Have you got any brandy?'

She stared at him for a moment then nodded. She went back into the house and a minute or so later returned with a bottle of cognac and two brandy balloons.

James poured the drinks, fully aware that she was staring at him.

'Are you going to explain?' She took a balloon from him and inhaled the brandy fumes.

'You did it to yourself. It was what your body wanted, Francine. My hands were merely the catalyst.' James held the cigar smoke in his mouth and placed the brandy balloon to his lips. He allowed the smoke to dribble from his mouth and it spread across the top of the brandy like a thick morning mist on a river. He held the balloon at arm's length watching the smoke ripple gently on the brandy, then quickly drank it down, inhaling the smoke through his nostrils at the same time.

'I've seen it before, James,' she offered a gentle sneer. 'Sniffing the mist is a disgusting English habit. Tell me,' she leaned forward, 'tell me how you do it? You created the same sensation in my body at the Embassy, but then you inflicted pain. How is it possible for you to do that?'

'I'm not going to tell you my secrets, Madame.' James smiled at her through a plume of cigar smoke.

'Why not?'

'Because you're a spy,' he replied flatly and his face lost all expression.

A tingle of fear returned as she looked into his eyes. There it is again, she thought, the look of the predator.

'I am not a spy, James.'

'Then what are you, Francine?'

'I am a pawn,' she held her thumb and forefinger up with barely any space between them, 'a tiny, tiny pawn in the game of political and military chess that is Asia.' She placed her glass on the table and gazed out at the bright night sky for some time before continuing. 'Tonight was the first time I ever did anything dangerous. Usually I just listen to conversations and report anything I think may be relevant to my controller.'

'What was dangerous about tonight?'

'You, James,' her tone was serious. 'You are dangerous. I have been terrified since the moment you hurt me at the cocktail party. And when you came into the library just now, I thought you were going to kill me.'

'Kill you?' James sipped his brandy and smiled. 'I have no reason to kill you.'

'I know.' She looked at him, accusingly. 'But what if I had not hid in the house as I was ordered? What if I had learned what went on out here on the verandah tonight? What would you have done then?'

'You don't know what transpired on the verandah, do you?'

'Of course I do not.'

'Then your question is not worth answering.'

'Oh!' Francine stood and took several deep breaths before turning to him. 'Your refusal to answer is an answer in itself. You would have killed me if you had deemed it necessary. You don't care about anyone or anything, do you?'

'No.'

'You are incapable of it, aren't you?'

'I believe so,' he nodded.

'Then you should not have done what you did to me in the library.'

'Why not?' James puffed on the cigar. 'I got the feeling you enjoyed it.'

'Of course I enjoyed it,' she said, exasperated. 'I have never experienced anything like it in my life.' She fell silent and stared at him.

'You were tense,' he shrugged. 'I released that tension from your body.'

'I have only ever had one man touch my body, James.' Her voice was softer, appealing.

He paused, cigar in midair. 'What, you mean Jacques?'

'Of course, Jacques.' She looked at him quizzically. 'Who else? He's my husband.'

'Never any boyfriends, when you were younger?'

'He bought me when I was twelve, remember?' She sat and sipped her brandy.

'Oh, yes, that's right.' He nodded and tried to look sympathetic.

'What I did not tell you was that he raped me.' She looked out at the night sky. 'Then he married me in order to ensure my silence, and has barely touched me since.' And I need to be touched, she thought.

'I'll make love to you, Francine.' James used what he thought was the appropriate tone. He didn't mean it. Lee's plan and the million dollars was all he could think about. He briefly considered taking her on the verandah, but quickly dismissed the idea. He wanted solitude to plan his financial assault on Hong Kong. Damn the woman. He'd given her an orgasm in the library. Wasn't that enough?

'I'd like to very much,' he continued, 'but I must be back at Kenjong Air Base by oh nine hundred hours tomorrow and, as I don't have any means of transportation, you realise you'll have to get up early and drive me.'

Her reaction was most extraordinary, he thought. She placed the glass on the table, and lowered her head into her hands. He watched her for several minutes unable to comprehend then she suddenly sat upright, brushed the hair from her face and wiped away what appeared to be tears.

'I thank you for your offer, James, but I've had enough emotional experiences for one night.' She stood and drank down the last of her brandy. 'I'll get my car keys and take you home now.' She smiled at him, then turned and headed for the front door. 'I'm not good in the mornings,' she called back, 'and it would not do for you to be late.'

CHAPTER FIVE

'*General Kwan!*' The frightened crewman's voice woke Lee instantly. He leapt from his bunk and flung open his cabin door.

'*What is it?*' he asked, struggling into his shirt, but before the crewman could answer an artillery shell screamed overhead and an explosion, in the water close by, rocked the boat.

'*It's an American battleship, General.*'

Lee pushed past the terrified man and made his way out onto the deck of the fishing boat. He followed the gaze of the others on deck and saw, about a half mile astern, a Class II gunboat of the Chinese Navy.

'*It's all right, Ah Sing,*' he called up to the skipper on the poop deck of the junk. '*It's the Chinese Navy. Get the new national flag up the mast, cut the engine and let her drift.*'

'*Yes, General.*'

Lee went up on the poop deck as the skipper gave the necessary orders to his crew. '*And tell your men not to worry, they won't fire again,*' he assured the frightened Captain.

As soon as the words left his mouth the gunboat fired again. Lee heard the scream of the shell and then an enormous explosion erupted in the water not fifty feet from them.

'*You said they wouldn't fire again!*' the skipper screamed as he ducked behind the stern railing.

'*Get the Chinese flag up!*' Lee yelled back. '*And drop your sail. Show them we are complying with their wishes.*'

'*Drop the sail,*' the skipper screeched at his crew, cowering, safely hidden behind the railing.

'*Come here,*' Lee commanded.

'*Yes, Sir.*' The skipper rose and backed towards Lee, never taking his eyes from the gunboat, now less than two hundred yards astern.

'*How long is it since you first became aware of them?*' Lee patted Mr Sing on the shoulder to calm him down.

'*About ten minutes,*' the man replied.

'*How long have they been signalling you?*'

'*About ten minutes,*' the skipper said, turning towards Lee. '*They've been flashing a light and sounding their siren.*'

'*Well why didn't you stop?*'

'*I hoped they'd go away.*'

'Christ on the Cross!' Lee cursed in English. '*Wait until they heave to then put your ship alongside,*' he snapped in Cantonese. '*All they want to do is check your papers. And whatever you do, when they come aboard, don't call me General. I don't want them to know who I am.*'

'*Yes, General.*'

Lee looked at the simple fisherman and felt immediately sorry for showing his irritation. The man was not very bright, but his loyalty could not be questioned. Mr Sing had taken him from Wei-hai-Wei in Shantung Province to the Korean Coast and then almost back again, without once ever questioning why.

'*I'm sorry, Ah Sing.*' He patted the poor fellow on the arm. '*You have done a fine job and you will be well rewarded for your effort when you return to Wei-hai-Wei. I could not have asked for a better skipper. Thank you.*'

'*It is not necessary to say thank you, Elder Brother,*' Sing replied. '*You are the Dragon of Shanghai, true or not true? You killed ten thousand Japanese soldiers during the war. We people of Shanghai can never repay the debt we owe you.*'

Lee shook his head and turned away. He had long ago given up trying to correct the absurd exaggerations of his exploits against the Japanese. He went to the stern rail and stood staring at the gunboat, then he waved at the officers on its bridge. He could see them quite clearly now, and one of them waved back. Thank God for that, he thought, and cursed his own stupidity. He looked at his watch. It was nearly eight o'clock in the morning. He should have been up and on deck earlier, keeping his own lookout; they couldn't be more than fifteen miles from the Shantung Coast and the safety of Wei-hai-Wei.

Lee had left his command in Antung a week earlier after working out a precise plan with Major Petrov.

'You will have no trouble getting to the front line. Once you cross it, we have South Korean operatives who will take you to Seoul,' Petrov had said.

'But how do I get into Kenjong Air Base, Major?'

'There will be no need. Your brother will be persuaded to go to a suitable meeting place and my operatives will take you there and get you back to the border.'

'And just who is going to persuade him?'

'A beautiful woman – '

'Ha!' Lee's interjection was humourless. 'That ought to do it.'

'We Russians are masters of the covert situation,' Petrov boasted. 'And have no fear, General, you will be carefully guarded.'

'Oh, I'm sure I will be,' Lee had replied with just a hint of sarcasm. And probably shot in the back of the head, he thought, leaving you free to disappear with your Government's money. He had no illusions about Petrov. The man was a complete scoundrel and a million United States dollars would be irresistible to him, no matter what the risk.

'All that remains to be decided, Comrade General, is the date of your departure, so I can arrange the meeting with your brother.'

'I'll set off as soon as the money is in my possession.'

'What?' Petrov was caught completely off guard.

'My brother will require assurances, Major.' Lee smiled innocently. 'And I will not lie to him. I want to be able to tell him that the money will be his the minute he delivers the jet.'

'I do not think that will be possible, General Kwan. My superiors – '

'Major!' Lee cut him off. 'If your superiors want an F-86

Sabre jet, they'd better produce a million dollars in cash, or the deal is off. James Merchant is a very clever man, one not easily fooled. He trusts me completely and I will not jeopardise that trust. He will want my assurance that he will not be double-crossed and to give that assurance honestly, I must have the cash in my possession for safekeeping.'

Petrov had not liked the ultimatum, but he'd had no option. The money had been delivered to Lee's office, a Military receipt was given to Petrov, and the wheels had been set in motion.

One week ago he'd told Petrov that he was setting off to cross the Yalu River as they'd planned and would travel south through Korea to Seoul, but he'd never had the slightest intention of following the Russian's plan. He had a plan of his own. Immediately after leaving Antung, he'd made his way overland through China to Shantung Province.

Disguised as a Private in the PLA on leave from the front, he'd travelled around the Bo Hai, the finger of water that was the northwestern extremity of the Yellow Sea. Taking the train, he'd gone first north to Shenyang, then south via Tianjin into Shantung Province. Once there he had made his way to the fishing port of Wei-hai-Wei on the extreme tip of Shantung Peninsula. In Wei-hai-Wei, with the help an old and trusted friend, Lee had acquired the services of Mr Sing and his fishing boat and sailed due east to the Korean Coast near Seoul.

Once in South Korea, he'd headed for the prearranged border crossing point and made contact with Petrov's Korean KGB agents. The agents, unaware that he'd arrived by sea, had taken him to the meeting with James in the hills north of Seoul. Immediately following the meeting, the KGB agents had escorted him back to the border assuming he would travel north again, overland, back into Manchuria. Lee, however, had doubled back and boarded the fishing vessel. He would retrace his steps and return to Antung by land and Petrov would be none the wiser.

Lee watched the boarding crew assemble on the deck of the Chinese gunboat as Sing manoeuvred his junk alongside it.

He was not particularly worried. Their interception was an unexpected circumstance, but the chances of him being identified were remote. The boarding party would carry out a simple search and identification procedure and allow them to be on their way.

'*I want the full crew on deck,*' the young Lieutenant in charge of the boarding party ordered as he jumped onto the junk. '*Who is in command of this vessel?*'

'*I am,*' old Sing answered.

'*Bring me your vessel's registration papers.*' The officer stood with his legs astride, hands on hips, as his men began to search the junk.

'*What sort of papers?*' Sing asked and Lee's heart sank.

'*This vessel has to be registered in accordance with the new Regulations of the People's Republic of China for Vessels at Sea,*' the sailor replied. '*If it is not registered, you and your crew are in serious trouble.*'

'*Do you eat raw meat, sailor?*'

'*Oh no,*' Lee moaned, losing all hope. The idiot was asking metaphorically, if the Lieutenant took bribes.

'*What are you talking about?*' the officer asked.

'*How much money would it cost me to get out of this serious trouble?*' Sing asked.

'*Are you offering me a bribe?*' The young Lieutenant was clearly affronted.

'*No, I'm offering you money to get out of serious trouble.*' Sing's remark caused everyone on the junk with the exception of Lee and the young officer to laugh out loud.

'*You're under arrest,*' the Lieutenant roared, '*and your vessel is confiscated.*'

'*You can't do that!*' Sing roared back.

'*Why not?*'

'*Because he's a General.*' Sing smiled victoriously and pointed at Lee.

龍

Kimjang, which occurs in the autumn harvest season, is the most important annual social event in Korea. During this time, as tradition demands, women all over the country gather in groups to spend hours cutting, washing and salting cabbage and white radishes. These two main ingredients are dosed liberally with red pepper and garlic, then pickled. The concoction is buried in huge earthenware crocks to keep it fresh yet fermenting through the winter months. Then, in the spring, when the time comes to feast upon the final product, it is fiery hot.

'Jesus H. Christ!' Johnnie Wilson managed to gasp as his mouth turned to fire and tears flooded his eyes. He dropped his spoon and took a handkerchief from his pocket.

Dickie Beckham roared with laughter. 'Don't blow your nose, whatever you do,' he called as he pushed the stricken young American from the cushion he was sitting on. 'Koreans consider it the height of bad manners. Get out in the street.'

Johnnie rolled on the floor and staggered the ten feet to the open front of the restaurant they were in and stepped out onto the dusty dirt road. He blew his nose repeatedly and walked in circles, head up, trying to recover his breath.

'I thought you said you liked hot food,' James Merchant called out from the restaurant.

'That's not food, it's goddamn aviation gas.' Johnnie returned to sit on his cushion and a young Korean girl poured him a cup of water which he gulped greedily. 'What in the name of damnation is it?'

'It's *kimchi*, old boy,' Dickie explained as he and James spooned more of the hot liquid into their mouths, 'Korea's most famous dish. Fermented cabbage and red peppers. The Koreans make it, then bury it in the ground during the winter, then when spring comes – '

'They should leave it buried.' Johnnie stared at the wooden bowl on the squat table in front of him. 'I can't eat it, Jimbo. It's got me beat.'

James smiled distractedly. It was Saturday morning, one week after his meeting with Lee. He sat with John and Dickie in a ramshackle, open fronted food stall in a dusty street immediately outside the Kenjong Air Base perimeter fence. The street was the main thoroughfare of a small town that had, by virtue of supply and demand, sprung up at the edge of the base. It contained four little restaurants, three local arts and crafts shops, two very cheap bars, one laundry and nine brothels.

James loved the little town with no name and was a regular visitor to the Kimchi Stall. Although the town was officially off limits to air base personnel, the Military Police never enforced the law and the meticulously clean and well-serviced brothels in particular did a roaring trade.

'They serve a milder *kimchi* for nancy boys,' Dickie sneered at the young American. 'Would you care for a bowl of that?'

'I'm just fine thanks,' Johnnie replied and drank another cup of water.

'Well, I must say,' Dickie continued to tease, 'that was a rather fine song and dance you put on. I mean, you, of all people, after going on about hot Mexican food, have one sip of *kimchi* and you carry on like a sissy.'

'I already told ya,' Johnnie drawled, 'that ain't food.'

James smiled at the friendly banter between the two, but his mind was busy contemplating another matter. Lee's plan to steal the Sabre was set to commence that very afternoon. He looked again at his friends. There was every chance he would not be seeing them after today and, he'd decided, he was genuinely going to miss them.

He'd known Dickie Beckham since the tempestuous days of the Battle of Britain when they'd flown Spitfires together and, James realised, although they'd never been particularly close, poor old Dickie was one of the few males he could actually describe as a friend of sorts. The thought disturbed him momentarily. He racked his brain trying to remember other friends he'd acquired, but he finally had to admit to himself that there were none. Apart from Lee Kwan, James had never had a real male friend. That was, until recently.

He looked at Johnnie Wilson and felt a genuine tug of affection. The brash young Texan had replaced Lee in his life. The thought struck home with some force. He had not realised it until now, but Johnnie had become like a younger brother to him. Why now? he asked himself. Is it perhaps because there's a chance I might not see him again? Or is it because I spoke to Lee the other night for the first time in years and realised how much I'd missed him? Either way, he thought, I'll miss this young American. But, he thought again, I'll get over it.

James had briefly considered telling Johnnie of his meeting with Lee and the outrageous million dollar plan he'd embarked upon. They were, after all, business partners together in the black market, but just as briefly he'd dismissed the idea as dangerous. Johnnie was a villain, but he wasn't a traitor, and James had no doubt he'd scream the walls down if he knew what was going to happen, possibly that very afternoon.

'A penny for your thoughts, Jimbo.' Johnnie's voice startled him.

'What?' James asked, distractedly.

'Wake up, old man,' Dickie chimed. 'You were miles away there, James.'

'Sorry,' James smiled. 'I was just thinking how lucky we three are.'

'How so my dear fellow?' Dickie asked.

'We can fly,' James said. Both men stared at him for several seconds, perplexed by his reply. 'Like birds, high in the clouds, separated completely from the world and the foolish beings that inhabit it, by five miles of clean, fresh air. If you can fly, you need answer to no man or deity. And we can fly, gentlemen.'

'Yes, right, we certainly can,' Dickie replied utterly perplexed. 'And speaking of flying,' he looked at his watch, 'we'd better get back to base, eh? We're in the air at fifteen hundred hours.'

龍

'*Both engines ahead three quarters,*' Captain Lao Sha ordered his helmsman and instantly felt the gunboat he commanded surge through the water in response. He set a course due north into Korea Bay and sat back in his Captain's chair, fully satisfied with the day's work.

What a stroke of luck, he thought, happily. Of all the people in China the last he expected to meet on a fishing junk in the middle of the Yellow Sea was General Lee Kwan Man Hop. It would look good on his Record of Service, the rescue at sea of China's most famous General. He might even be awarded an Order of the Hero of the People's Republic for his actions. He felt, quite rightly, impressed with himself.

He'd been surprised by the youth of the General. He could be no more than thirty-five years old at the most, he thought, and obviously as deadly as the stories of him suggested. What he'd done to young Lieutenant Ji had been nothing short of astounding and it had confirmed the tales he'd heard of General Lee Kwan's ability in the ancient art of *Shaolin kung fu*.

Captain Lao had heard the commotion on the deck of the junk when Lieutenant Ji had boarded it. He'd stepped out onto the flying bridge to watch the proceedings that followed and although he'd not been able to hear what was said, he'd seen the Lieutenant draw his firearm and aim it at the old skipper of the junk. What had happened next he would never forget. A deck hand on the junk had flown through the air like an enraged dragon and in a split second, Lieutenant Ji had been disarmed and flattened and two of the boarding crew who'd attempted to help him had been knocked unconscious. The whole affair had been thrilling to watch.

Later, when he'd come on board, General Kwan had apologised most graciously for his behaviour, but had explained that he did not want the crew of the junk harmed and had therefore been forced into action. He had also apologised to the young Lieutenant and the two crew members, which Captain Lao thought was going a bit far. As far as he was concerned they got what they had deserved for being incompetent at their task. He'd warned them many times not to underestimate the crews of junks and trawlers, they were one step up from pirates, and today's little episode would serve as a warning to them to be more vigilant in future. The Captain chuckled to himself. Lieutenant Ji and his boarding party would not forget today in a hurry.

What a story he had to tell when he got back into port. By all the gods, the General had been fast. He'd never seen such speed of movement or such fluidity in action. So that is *Shaolin*, he thought. He'd never seen it before, but now having witnessed a master in action he prayed he would never be confronted with it. May my first born son's penis fall off before I witness it again, he wished fervently.

'*Set a course for Dairen – sorry – I mean Dalian,*' he ordered his coxswain. Damn the new Government, he thought, although he would never utter such a curse out loud. The names of half the ports on the China Coast had been changed to the Mandarin language and the navigator in him was being driven mad by it. Tsing Tao is now Qingdao, Foochow is Fuzhou, Amoy is Xiamen, Swatow is Shantou. The list is endless, he thought angrily. He understood the need for unifying the national language, but why did it have to be in Mandarin? Because that fat Communist bastard Mao Tse-tung speaks Mandarin, he thought. He quickly looked about the bridge to see if his thoughts were being read. He had to be careful these days; anyone with any position of power or authority had to think very carefully before they opened their mouth, because the lowest scum in their vicinity could howl them down and accuse them of being an enemy of the people. You couldn't be too careful.

General Kwan had ordered him to set a course for Dalian and if that was what the General wanted, that was what the General would get. Dalian was a port on the tip of Liaodong Peninsula, a piece of the Chinese Mainland that extended southwest, forming an arm that separated Korea Bay to the east from Bo Hai, the body of water that was the westernmost reach of the Yellow Sea. It was the obvious port for the General to disembark at, because it was only about two hundred miles by land from Dandong, the General's Headquarters, but, more importantly for Captain Lao, it was the only port his gunboat could navigate with any degree of safety. The northern shores of Korea Bay were a maze of shallows and mudflats.

The ship's cook entered the bridge and all thoughts of navigation were instantly dismissed as the smell of food assailed

Captain Lao's nostrils. Pots of rice, pork dumplings, fish and steamed vegetables were placed on the chart table alongside a plate of crispy fried duck from the Captain's private stores. Two chilled bottles of Tsing Tao beer sat side by side and Lao's palate began to water in anticipation as he admired them, glistening in the sunlight that was streaming through the starboard bridge portholes.

He leapt to his feet as General Kwan entered.

'Something smells good, Captain,' Lee remarked. He offered his hand and the Captain shook it vigorously.

'It is a poor example of a duck, General, from the markets in Tenggu. I had it taken from my private larder and prepared especially for you.' He indicated the food on the chart table and offered Lee a pair of chopsticks.

'I'm sure the duck will be magnificent, Mr Lao,' Lee replied. He had not eaten since the previous evening and was ravenous. He took up the Captain's offer and began by serving himself some boiled rice.

'It is not often I have the chance to entertain such esteemed company as yourself, Sir.' The Captain poured two glasses of beer and placed one in front of Lee.

The two men ate in silence for some minutes, staring out over the shining water of the Yellow Sea until Lee finally spoke.

'We are on course for Dalian, Captain Lao, true or not true?'

'True, General. Just as you ordered.' Lao moved several of the dishes on the chart table. *'We are here, Sir.'* He indicated a point on the chart. *'If we maintain course and speed we should arrive in Dalian about midnight.'*

'Excellent,' Lee nodded as he plucked a choice piece of crispy duck from the bowl. *'This lunch is also excellent. My congratulations to your cook.'*

'I will tell him so, Sir,' Lao replied and they resumed eating in silence.

Finally Lee set aside his chopsticks and bowl, sipped from his beer glass and sighed contentedly, as he gazed out at the flat glassy sea.

'I envy you, Captain Lao.'

'You, General? You envy me?'

'You must get great enjoyment from your job, sailing the oceans and keeping the shores of our great country safe from the Imperialists?'

'I merely do my duty, General, but I must admit, most of the time it is an enjoyable life. Mind you, I hardly sail the oceans, my patrols are limited to the northern reaches of the Yellow Sea.'

'Have you ever made contact with the foreign forces that oppose us in Korea?'

'No, Sir, they would not sail their battleships this far north and my orders do not allow me to sail south and confront them.'

'Lucky for them I say, Captain. I'm sure if you did, you'd do our great nation proud.'

'I believe I would, General.'

'I suppose you've been wondering what the General in Command of Chinese Forces in Manchuria was doing on a fishing junk on the middle of the Yellow Sea?'

'No, Sir!' Lao was most vociferous in his reply. 'I would not dream of questioning your actions. I do not doubt that you are on some sort of secret mission of great importance that far exceeds my small understanding of this war.'

'You are obviously a man well schooled in the art of war, Captain Lao,' Lee said loudly, giving the man great face in front of his helmsman. He clinked his glass against Lao's. 'I am indeed on a secret mission and when you drop me off in Dalian it will be completed.'

'I am honoured to be a part of it, General.'

'And I trust you have made no entries concerning the matter in the ship's log?'

'Not yet, Sir.'

'And you have reported nothing by radio?'

'No, Sir.'

'Good.' Lee looked at the helmsman steering the ship, then turned to Lao and lowered his voice to a conspiratorial whisper. 'And you will not do so.'

'But, Sir – ' Lao began to protest.

'Listen carefully, Captain,' Lee hissed. 'No one, and I mean no one,' he glared at Lao, 'is to know I've even been in the Yellow Sea, let alone on this vessel. It is a state secret and it will remain a state secret. Understand or not understand?'

'Understand, Sir. I certainly understand.' The look from the General had chilled him to the bone. Gone was the tale of rescue he had had to tell. Better to keep my silence than to lose my head, he thought.

'You will advise your crew accordingly and warn them that the punishment for releasing state secrets is death.'

'Yes, Sir!'

'Good!' Lee exclaimed loudly for the benefit of the helmsman. 'The meal was excellent, Captain.' He crossed to the helm and patted the helmsman on the back. 'Move aside, Little Brother,' he smiled at the young man, 'and let me hold course for you.' He took the wheel from the startled young man and whistled cheerily as he steered for Dalian.

龍

It was two o'clock by the time James entered the hangar that housed his Sabre and the one flown by Johnnie Wilson. He'd wanted to get there even earlier but had had trouble putting on his 'G' suit, the tight fitting coverall worn by pilots that helped resist the gravitational forces exerted on the body when flying jets. He hated the damned thing, but without it he would be helpless against the unconsciousness brought on by dives and tight turns, so he always ensured it was properly fitted.

As he'd hoped, there were no members of his ground crew present and the hangar was empty. He climbed up to the cockpit and dropped several extra packs of emergency rations and a map of Manchuria onto the seat, then went to the small office at the rear of the hangar to get extra ammunition from the weapons locker.

He loaded five extra magazine clips for the silver-plated Colt .45 Johnnie had given him and placed them in every pocket and gap he could find about his body. He worked the breech mechanism several times, loaded it, applied the safety catch and put it in his shoulder holster. It was at that moment he heard the sound of someone coughing out in the hangar.

James quickly strapped the mission flight plan to his thigh front and went to investigate.

'I say, old man,' Dickie Beckham said as he climbed back down from James' Sabre's cockpit, map in hand. 'Maps of Manchuria? Extra ration packs?' He laughed at James. 'What's the go, Jamie lad? Going to defect are we? Ha ha ha.'

'Not exactly,' James said evenly. He glanced at the hangar doors ensuring no one was watching. 'I'm going to sell the aircraft to the Russians for a million dollars.'

'Ha, very funny James,' Dickie scoffed. 'Come on, old boy, tell me what's going – '

They were the last words Richard Beckham uttered. The knife-like edge of a hand struck him behind the ear, snapping his neck. As he fell forward into James' arms, his face wore an expression of utter bewilderment.

James dragged the body to the oil pit at the side of the hangar and threw it in. He jumped into the six feet deep concrete slot in the floor used for vehicle maintenance and grabbed Dickie's head by the hair. He slammed it into the concrete wall and leaned back puffing from his exertions.

'Sorry, old chap,' he whispered, taking the map of Manchuria from Dickie Beckham's lifeless hand and stuffing it into a pocket of his flight suit, 'but your timing, as usual, was appalling.' He offered the corpse a wry smile. 'And a million dollars is a lot of money.'

'Hey, Captain Wilson.' James heard the voice of his ground crew Sergeant. 'You flying at fifteen hundred, Sir?'

'Yes, I am, Sergeant,' he heard Johnnie reply. 'Have you seen Mr Merchant?'

'Johnnie!' James yelled at the top of his voice.

'What are you doin' in there, Jimbo?' Johnnie peered into the pit.

'For God's sake, get a bloody ambulance! Dickie fell into the oil pit,' James said, as Johnnie jumped down beside him.

'Call the Medics, Sergeant,' Johnnie yelled as he crouched over Dickie's body. 'How is he?'

'I think he's dead.' James replied solemnly. 'His neck looks broken.'

'One hell of a way to start a mission,' Johnnie said, visibly shocked. 'I sure hope it ain't gonna be one of those bad luck days.' The American looked down at the lifeless form of his friend. In the short time they'd known each other, he'd come to like the stuffy Englishman. He reached down and closed the eyes of Dickie Beckham, removing the shocked expression the man had offered in death.

'There's no such thing as bad luck,' James muttered.

'Oh, yeah? Try tellin' that to Dickie. He just fell in a fucking oil pit and broke his neck!'

'Dickie just did what destiny required of him. No more no less.' James climbed out of the pit.

'Are you sure you're up for it, James?' Johnnie asked, as Dickie's body was placed in the ambulance. 'The mission I mean. Don't you think you should stand yourself down?'

'On what grounds?'

'Your friend just died, James!'

'You can't stop a war, John, just because someone dies. Even if that someone happens to be a friend.' James watched the ambulance, red lights flashing, move towards the Admin building. It travelled slowly. It had no cause to hurry. No amount of emergency medical treatment would help Richard Beckham.

Ashes to ashes, James thought, as he imagined the vehicle as a hearse conveying the body of his friend to its final resting place. And dust to dust. *Vale* Richard Beckham.

'You're a cold bastard, James. I gotta hand it to ya.'

James turned to find Johnnie Wilson staring at him. 'Oh? And what would you have me do, Captain Wilson, burst into tears?'

'Well, Jesus no,' Johnnie laughed humourlessly, 'but the

least you could do is show some emotion. He was your friend, for Chrissakes. Don't you feel anything?'

'Yes, I do.' James turned towards his cockpit ladder. 'I feel like taking to the air and killing people.'

'Ha!' Johnnie snorted. 'Well, it's not quite the sort of emotion I had in mind, Jimbo,' he shook his head, 'but it'll do. I'm with you, Blue Leader! We'll shoot one down for Dickie.' He ran towards his waiting Sabre yelling, 'I'll see ya top side. Gun sight on and safety off!'

龍

It took Lee twenty-four hours to cover the two hundred miles from Dalian to Dandong. After leaving Captain Lao, he'd first taken a bus, which broke down, then he'd ridden thirty miles in a farmer's cart before hitching a ride in a Military Stores truck on its way to Dandong Military HQ.

It was midnight when he arrived in the town. He got out of the truck about half a mile from the camp gates and gave the driver some coins for his trouble. He wanted to approach the main gates on foot. It would not only test his camp's perimeter security, but it was a subtle way of alerting all under his command that he was back. The news of his arrival would spread like wildfire through the ranks despite the late hour.

He walked along the dirt road in the still night air and was only a hundred yards from the guardhouse when a figure emerged from the trees beside the road. Lee Kwan stood stock still, his *Shaolin* training coming to the fore as his breathing slowed. He prepared himself for battle.

'I've been in this wretched dog infested town for a week waiting for you,' a deep voice growled.

'Jun Khan?' Lee answered.

'I can't stand Manchurians. The men are effeminate and the women are ugly!'

'Jun Khan!' Lee gasped as the big Kazakh grabbed him in a bear-like embrace and lifted him off his feet.

'I thought you were the General in charge of this brothel?' the big man grumbled. He placed Lee back on his

feet and held him at arm's length. '*What are you doing wandering the dark roads like a peasant? Have you been dismissed?*'

'*What are you doing here?*' Lee replied as fear shot through him. '*Is it Lin Li, or the children? Has something happened to them?*'

'*Calm yourself, Elder Brother, your family is safe for the moment, but they have not heard from you for months and your woman came to me for help.*'

'*What's wrong?*' Lee grabbed the man's arm. '*I told Lin Li never to go near Little Shanghai unless something was wrong.*'

'*Calm yourself, Lee Kwan!*' the Kazakh ordered. '*Your wife is lonely, and frightened, that is all. She suddenly became aware, for the first time, I suppose, that all-important Communist Party Members and their families are regularly spied upon. So I promised her I would seek you out and deliver her letter to you. Your family is safe, do not worry.*' He smiled in the moonlight. '*It is I who am in trouble.*'

'*You're always in trouble.*' Lee's fear abated with the big man's smile. '*What's the problem this time?*'

'*I've got the pox.*'

'*You've always got the pox.*'

'*The girls at your local inn gave it to me.*'

'*Well, that's what you get when you lie down with prostitutes,*' Lee smiled. Jun Khan had always been able to make him smile.

'*What else would you have me do, Lee Kwan? Your guards informed me that you were absent and did not know when you would be back. When I told them I was your greatest friend and insisted they give me shelter until your return, they told me to go and lick my sister's rectum.*' Jun Khan eyed Lee with great solemnity. '*Unfortunately I do not have a sister or I would have done so.*'

'*Don't be disgusting,*' Lee laughed. '*Come, let's get a drink and you can tell me of my family.*' He pushed the Kazakh towards the main gate. '*So what have you been doing for the past week?*'

Jun Khan raised his arms to the heavens dramatically. *'I've been wasting my life, sleeping on the earth and sharing my loneliness with the stars. Three times I have returned to this gate but as yet I've had no satisfaction.'*

'Well, why don't you try again?' Lee asked mischievously and pushed Jun Khan towards the pool of light they were approaching.

The big man needed no further urging. He approached the gate and yelled, *'It is I, Jun Khan, great friend of your Commander, General Lee Kwan.'*

'You're a pig fucker, that's what you are!' came the reply from within. *'Take your testicles back to where you came from.'*

'What do you want now?' another voice asked.

'I have this letter,' Jun Khan held up a crumpled envelope. *'It is for General Lee Kwan, the Dragon of Shanghai, and I intend to deliver it personally.'*

'Well, you can't, because he's not here.'

'Oh, yes he is.' Jun Khan flashed a brilliant grin and held the letter aloft.

'Is that for me?' Lee stepped into the pool of light, took the letter and glared up at the gate. *'Do you speak to everyone who approaches the gate like that?'*

'Oh, shit!' came the horrified reply and the main gate flew open.

龍

Mig Alley was a maelstrom. James could count at least a hundred Mig-15s flashing through the sky like angry hornets. Dickie Beckham's theory had proven right again. It was the start of week four and a new batch of Chinese pilots had been flung over the border for a taste of combat.

Lee had given James a four-day period starting today in which to steal the Sabre and his reasoning was obvious; nobody in the sky would have a clue who had shot whom. The air was full of flashing wings and tracer bullets.

'Blue Wing, Blue Wing, this is Blue Leader,' James spoke through his oxygen mask. 'Engage, engage.'

Blue Squadron needed no further invitation. They dived headlong into the fray, wheeling, diving and turning as they sought out the enemy.

'Blue Two, stay on me,' James called to his wingman.

'I'm right with you, Blue Leader,' Johnnie replied. 'Go get 'em, pardner.'

It was a turkey shoot. The Chinese pilots threw their Migs around sloppily like the novices they were. James engaged them one after another at close range and scored hits on two, but failed to down them. Unlike the Sabres, the Migs were heavily armoured, and could take far more punishment.

James climbed and deliberately headed back into the thick of the action. He placed himself in a position of vulnerability and two Migs opened fire on him. He barely managed to avoid the shells that raced past his fuselage, but the action had given him his opportunity. He put his Sabre into a shallow dive and continued to lose altitude and headed northwest to where the Yalu River opened into Korea Bay.

'Jimbo, are you okay?' Johnnie ignored radio protocol as he began to suspect all was not right with his leader.

'My instrument panel is lit up like a Christmas tree, Blue Two,' James replied. 'I must have taken hits.'

'Try to climb, James.' Johnnie spoke urgently. 'You'll need altitude to bail out. Try to climb. You're getting way too low.'

'I'm losing power, Blue Two, fuel flow irregular, hydraulics gone. I can't climb.'

'Bail out, James!' Johnnie yelled. 'For Christ's sake, bail out, James!'

James saw the shallows of Korea Bay directly in front of him and smiled. He was right where he wanted to be. 'My ejection seat's failed.'

'It can't have, it's got a separate power source, James! Try it again.'

'It's no use, John, I've lost power altogether and I'm well under a thousand feet, too low to bail out now. My only chance, if I can clear the hills ahead of me, is a wheels-up landing on those mudflats in Korea Bay.'

'That's Commie territory, Jimbo!'

'Wait until I'm down, Captain Wilson,' James ordered in an even, measured tone, 'then use your cannons to destroy the aircraft.'

'Not until you're clear of it, Sir. Not for a million dollars.'

Even in the madness of the moment James nearly laughed out loud. 'Whether I get clear or not,' he replied. 'This aircraft cannot be allowed to fall into enemy hands. Report its position and destroy it, Captain. That's an order.'

'Sorry, Blue Leader, I didn't copy. Your transmission is weak. If you are receiving me, when you're clear of the aircraft I will remain overhead for as long as I can. Put her down as close to the shoreline as possible and I'll try to cover you, until you reach the trees at least.'

That's my boy, Johnnie, James thought, a man of honour, and therefore predictable. 'You will destroy this aircraft, Captain Wilson. That is an order. Do you read me? Over.'

'You're breaking up, Blue Leader. I did not copy your last. Please repeat. Over.'

James smiled grimly as he lined up the crash landing. That's the difference between you and me, Johnnie, he thought, you still believe there is something more important than self. Then the underbelly of his Sabre smacked into three feet of water and flew like a bullet across the surface.

龍

Lee sat at his office desk and read Lin Li's letter yet again. He missed her and the children terribly and Jun Khan's lecture to him the night before had done nothing to assuage his feelings of guilt. His wife had had no mail from him in six months although he'd written to her at least once a week. The damned Intelligence Service had obviously intercepted his letters and kept them – not that there was anything incriminating in them, he was too careful for that. But Lin Li had become aware of spies watching the flat, it was something he should have warned her about and it added to his feelings of guilt. Then when the children had come home from boarding school complaining of being interrogated, she'd been pushed over the edge and gone to Little Shanghai.

'*Government agents followed her as far as the hutong, Elder Brother,*' Jun Khan had told him the previous night. '*We must assume they'll be watching our hutong from now on. If she comes anywhere near Little Shanghai again, especially with your children, they'll place her under house arrest.*'

'*I understand,*' Lee had replied. '*You must return and tell her not to worry. Tell her harassment is a common tactic of the Intelligence Service. They do it in the hope that someone in a senior official's family will panic and say something they shouldn't say. Tell her to carry on as normal, because as long as I am of use to the Government, no harm will come to any of us. Make sure she understands. No one will trouble her while this war continues, and I remain in favour with Chairman Mao.*'

'*You must write her a letter explaining all this, General –*' Jun Khan began.

'*Don't be ridiculous,*' Lee had snapped. '*What if you were caught with the letter? It would become nothing short of a death warrant for both your family and mine.*'

'*I am sorry, General Kwan,*' the big Kazakh replied, '*I am not a clever man. I will return home immediately and tell your wife what you have told me.*'

'*No.*' Lee's mind was working overtime. '*I have another job for you first, Jun Khan. I am involved in another matter and have need of your services.*'

'*Anything you ask of me I will do, General.*' Jun Khan bowed as he replied.

'*I want you to remain in Dandong, take lodgings at the inn you're so fond of and await a visitor.*' Lee patted the big man on the shoulder. '*Go to the canteen and get yourself some breakfast, then come back and see me. I'll have more instructions for you. And Jun Khan, thank you for bringing me the letter, I am in your debt.*'

The Kazakh turned at the door. '*You will never be in my debt, Captain,*' he said before disappearing.

Lee looked at the letter again. He could not blame Lin Li for panicking. He could see her, sitting alone in their flat composing the letter to him, haunted by her fears, terrified.

He stood up, tore the letter into small pieces and dropped them in the waste basket, then moved across to the window.

How long will this bloody war last? he asked himself, yet again. Will there ever be a time when I can live peacefully with my family? The questions were rhetorical. The war would not last another year he knew, and there would be no peace for Lee Kwan upon his return to Peking. In the eyes of the Communist Party faithful Lee would always be a 'grasshopper', a man who changed his political allegiance from Nationalism to Communism and, therefore, a man who could never be trusted.

'Good afternoon, Comrade General.'

'Don't you ever knock?' Lee hated the way Petrov always entered his office unannounced.

'The door was open.' Petrov shrugged.

'What do you want?' The Russian was the last person Lee felt like talking to.

'Your brother didn't waste any time, did he?'

'What do you mean?'

'His Sabre is sitting on the mudflats in Korea Bay.'

'Where is my brother?'

'He is in the camp infirmary, but don't worry.' Petrov lit another of his foul smelling Russian cigarettes and flicked the match into Lee's bin. 'He has only a mild concussion and I have ordered him to be transferred to the interrogation block.'

'You what?!' Lee was furious that Petrov had been informed of the Sabre crash and the capture of James before he had been informed himself. Someone's head will roll for this, he thought. He'd left strict instructions with the Air Controllers that he was to be informed of any such incident, but somehow Petrov had beaten him to the punch.

'I took the liberty of ordering constant air cover over the Sabre until it can be recovered. No doubt the UN Command will have ordered fighters to destroy it.'

'You have overstepped your authority, Major,' Lee said ominously. He moved towards the Russian with his fists clenched until they were face to face. 'Be careful, Russian,' he whispered, 'or you may see a side of me you are unfamiliar with. A side, I can assure you, you will not like.'

'But, Comrade, I only anticipated your – ' Petrov began.

'Get out of my way!' Lee ordered. The Russian obeyed and Lee stood motionless for several seconds, glowering at him, before he walked out the door.

龍

James lay motionless in the bed, his left wrist handcuffed to the side rail. His memory of the crash landing was vague. He concentrated, causing his heart rate and breathing to slow. He was obviously in a ward of a hospital of some sort, probably in the Antung Military Base. A ceiling fan spun slowly above him and as he watched the blades his mind searched his body for injuries. Apart from a headache, he detected nothing.

Images began to flick through his brain. He remembered the tremendous thud as his Sabre had hit the water and careened off the surface like a skipping stone, and he remembered the spray of salt water hitting his face, but after that he must have blacked out. Memories of PLA soldiers running towards his plane were mixed with hands pulling him from the cockpit and he remembered being thrown onto the wing of his jet, but after that, nothing.

He heard a door slam somewhere in the building, then the stamp of booted feet on a wooden floor. The footsteps got louder and the door to his room burst open. A doctor and nurse entered, followed by Lee Kwan.

James remained motionless as the nurse came to his side and took his pulse.

'*Sixty-four beats a minute, Doctor,*' she said in Mandarin.

'*Extraordinary,*' the doctor replied.

'What is your name?' Lee demanded in English. He winked as he approached the bed.

'Merchant, James,' he replied, continuing the charade. 'Wing Commander Royal Air Force.'

'And who is that?' Lee pointed to the bed next to him.

James turned his head and his heart skipped a beat. 'That is Captain John Wilson, United States Air Force.'

CHAPTER SIX

It was eight o'clock the following morning when Johnnie Wilson awoke. James was sitting up in bed eating noodles with his free hand, when he heard Johnnie groan.

'James?' Johnnie struggled to raise his head, then moaned, and let it drop back on the pillow.

'I wouldn't move if I were you, John,' James replied. 'You're a bit of a mess.'

'I'm chained to the bed. Where are we?'

'Well, it's not the Peninsula Hotel in Hong Kong,' James replied with not a little acerbity. 'I can assure you of that!'

'Okay. So take another guess.'

'We – and I stress the word *we* – are in the infirmary of Antung Military Base as prisoners of war. And before you ask,' he snapped, 'I have concussion, and you had a broken arm and nose, both of which were reset under anaesthetic.'

'Jesus,' Johnnie exclaimed. 'What's botherin' you?'

'Would you like me to make you a list?' James threw the bowl of noodles across the room and it smashed against a wall. 'I've got a good mind to break your bloody neck for good measure!'

'Hey!' Johnnie cried. 'I was only trying to cover your ass and I got hit! It was no more than you'd do for me, right?'

'Wrong!' James exploded. 'I gave you explicit orders to destroy the grounded Sabre and get the hell out of there. But that wasn't good enough for you, was it? Oh no! You had to play the hero! And as a result, we're both prisoners of war, and I can only suppose the People's Republic of China is now in possession of two bloody Sabre jets!'

'Not a chance, pal,' Johnnie snapped angrily. 'They didn't get mine. When I got hit I took her way up high and made sure she blew after I ejected. They didn't get mine!'

'All right. So they didn't get your jet, but they got you.'

James' head began to ache. He lay back on the bed, sighed deeply and stared at the ceiling fan. What do I do now? he thought angrily. Johnnie's presence had changed the game. Do I carry on with my plan and leave him here? Do I carry on with my plan and take him with me? Or do I tell him the truth? Telling Johnnie would indeed be a risk. A risk for Johnnie that is, he thought, not me.

If the young American reacted badly to the story, James would have no option but to kill him. He couldn't possibly leave anyone alive to tell the tale. But then again, he thought, perhaps the natural born criminal instinct that dwells in Johnnie's soul is more powerful than his love of country? If that proved to be true and Johnnie decided to join him in his nefarious enterprise, it would bind the young Texan to him forever.

'You would have done precisely what I did, Jimbo,' Johnnie reiterated. 'You know it.'

'Yes, you're probably right,' James said. 'But I wouldn't have been shot down.'

'I had no chance, James. I made one pass over your bird and there were soldiers all over you and Migs all over me. It was like they appeared from nowhere. If I didn't know better I'd say they were waiting for us.'

'It's all water under the bridge now, anyway.' James quickly changed the subject. 'Why don't you get some rest, John, while I figure out a way for us to get out of here?'

'You mean escape?'

'Yes. Why not?'

'Nobody escapes from North Korea, Jimbo,' Johnnie replied. 'At least nobody I knew ever did. You know, I heard tell they bundle you into a bamboo box and leave you to rot.'

'There isn't a prison in this world that can hold me, John.'

'Oh, really,' Johnnie chuckled then groaned. 'Ooh, don't make me laugh, it hurts.'

James was suddenly standing over Johnnie's bed, with a set of handcuffs dangling from his index finger.

'I said, there's not a prison in this world that can hold me, Johnnie.'

'Wow!' Johnnie exclaimed. 'How'd you do that?'

'It's a trick I learned from a dragon.'

'A dragon?'

'That's right.' James smiled then returned to his bed. 'You're in China now, Johnnie, the home of dragons.' He continued speaking as he re-handcuffed himself to the rail. 'You know, I wouldn't be at all surprised if you meet one in the next few days. In fact,' James laughed, 'I'd be surprised if you didn't.'

龍

It was another twenty-four hours before James spoke with Lee again.

Two uniformed PLA soldiers came to the infirmary and handcuffed him. They marched him across a large square from where he could see, out on the airstrips, several hundred aircraft, many of them Mig-15s. He was taken into the Main Administration building, up several sets of stairs and put in what he assumed was an interrogation room, judging by the microphone on the table before him. He was pushed into a seat and left under the eye of a very young and very nervous soldier.

'You are very tense, young man,' James said softly in English. The soldier's eyes widened dramatically. 'Don't worry, I won't bite you.'

'He does not speak English, Wing Commander.'

The guttural Russian-accented voice came from a speaker, set on the wall. James turned and looked at his own hand-cuffed image in what was obviously a two-way mirror.

'Ah,' James replied, 'a friendly voice at last. KGB no doubt, and not before time I might add. I believe we have a deal to conclude?'

'A deal, Wing Commander?' the voice answered. 'Ah yes, our deal. I'm afraid complications have arisen with our deal – '

The Russian's voice was suddenly cut off and James heard a loud pop and squeal through the speaker as if the equipment had been broken or suddenly disconnected.

He remained seated as the implications of what he'd heard began to sink in. Had his own brother lied to him? Had he been tricked into delivering a Sabre jet to the Russians? Surely not, he thought. If there was one person on earth who never lied, it was Lee Kwan. Lee had struck a deal with him and Lee was a man of honour, perhaps the only man of honour James had ever known.

His anxiety deepened as he analysed the situation. He had not seen Lee for fifteen years. People changed. But not Lee, he thought, definitely not Lee. He was the one constant in James' life. The only person James was sure he could always trust. But the KGB, James thought, is another kettle of fish altogether. Perhaps they had some hold over Lee. Lin Li and his kids would be the obvious one. He shook his head trying to make sense of his thoughts. No, not even a threat of that magnitude would induce Lee to betray him. It had to be the Russians.

The door opened and the young soldier jumped to attention as Lee entered the room.

'It's all right, James,' Lee said as he sat at the table. 'Don't worry about the Russian. I have disabled the recording equipment and told him not to interfere. We can speak freely.'

'What's going on?' James searched Lee's eyes, seeking signs of betrayal, but he could detect nothing.

'*Speak Cantonese, understand or not understand?*' Lee spoke in a calm even tone and nodded in the direction of the young guard. '*Just to be safe. No one speaks it in this part of the world, especially Russians.*'

'*The arrival of my wingman has complicated our problem.*'

'*Your problem, James. He is of no concern to me. My only concern is the deal.*'

'*I have completed my part of the deal, Little Brother.*'

'*And I have completed mine, James,*' Lee replied.

'Then what am I doing in handcuffs?'

'The deal I struck with you did not include escape.'

'Please say that again?'

'The Russians have the jet and I have the money – '

'So when do I get it?' James cut him off.

'When you make your escape from this camp,' Lee replied, enjoying the shocked look on James' face.

'You are saying a joke, true or not true, aaah?' James sang the question mark forcefully in true Cantonese fashion, letting the syllable hang in the air to emphasise his astonishment.

'Not true,' Lee replied. 'I told you I had a plan that would see you safely at Antung and one million dollars richer. I do not remember discussing your actual escape.'

'Of course we discussed it!' James cracked his handcuffs on the table, causing the young guard to flinch. 'I am to go via Shantung Peninsula across the Yellow Sea back into South Korea. You said you would arrange it.'

'Oh, yes,' Lee replied. 'I've arranged all that.'

'So you remember discussing my escape?'

'Yes. I remember discussing your escape route from China. I've even arranged a guide to escort you. But we never discussed your escape from this camp.'

'I do not understand,' James said, giving his brother a surly look.

'I think you do, James,' Lee said. 'I am the Commander of Antung Military Base and I will not knowingly put any man under my command at risk unless it is in battle. How you get out of here is entirely your concern, but I must insist that no one is killed.'

'A matter of honour, Little Brother, true or not true?' James sneered.

'True, James. Now listen. At the moment you are housed in the infirmary, not the prison block, but you will be transferred to the prison tomorrow, so I would suggest you escape tonight. At the moment the only thing between you and freedom is a gate, and a convoy of trucks will pass through that gate at twenty-one hundred hours tonight. Therefore, a man with your skill and training should have no trouble escaping without injuring anyone, true or not true?'

'And what happens when I'm through the gate?'

'Not far from here is the town of Dandong. There you will find an inn called the Three Willows. Seek out a man called Jun Khan. He is easily recognisable, a big Kazakh with a thick moustache and beard. He is expecting you and will be your guide.'

'And what about the money?'

'It is waiting for you in Shantung, James. You must find an old Buddhist temple in the village of Wei-hai-Wei – '

'Wei-hai-Wei?' James gave a quizzical look. 'Isn't that the family village of Lo Shi-mon?'

'Correct.' Lee looked him straight in the eye. 'It is Ah Lo who guards your money.'

'Are you telling me our teacher survived the war?' James was genuinely happy at the news. 'It will give me great joy to see him again.' Then his smile slowly faded. 'Does he know what I've done?'

'Yes.' Lee continued to stare at his brother.

Their eyes locked. 'Did you tell him the truth?'

'I always tell the truth, James.'

'Did it have to be Lo Shi-mon?' James' tone was accusatory.

'Yes. I knew our story would break his heart, but I could think of no one else to trust with that amount of money.'

'You could have lied, just once.'

'Believe me, I thought about it, but you cannot lie to Lo Shi-mon. I told him the truth. And when I saw the look of disappointment in his eyes, I felt ashamed.'

'And what effect do you think that look will have on me, Lee?'

'On you?' Lee shook his head. 'None. But if you want to collect the money, you'll have to experience it. And perhaps one day, when you are a wealthy man living in Hong Kong, that city of streets paved with gold where rich men eat fat pork, the memory of it will serve as a reminder to you that your life of ease came at the cost of your honour.'

'*Ha!*' James scoffed, but the knowledge that his *Shaolin* master Lo Shi-mon knew of his treason had disturbed him profoundly. '*Are you saying there is honour in war, Little Brother?*'

'*No,*' Lee replied with a tinge of sadness.

'*Then what are you saying?*' James was becoming angry at himself for becoming angry, but he could not control his feelings. '*Damn you, Lee! And damn your "honour"! You sought me out, remember? You came to me and offered me a million dollars, knowing I would accept it. You gave me the rope to hang myself, true or not true?*'

'*That is true,*' Lee nodded. '*Lo Shi-mon accused me with the same questions.*'

'*So tell me, how did your answers comply with your sense of honour?*'

The door opened before Lee could answer and Major Petrov entered.

'Comrade General, I must insist this interrogation be conducted in English.'

'*This man is your enemy, James. Trust me and play the fool.*'

'I insist, General!' Petrov demanded.

'Of course, you're right,' Lee replied pleasantly. 'Major, this is Wing Commander Merchant R.A.F. Wing Commander, this is Major Petrov, the man who is buying your Sabre.'

'Excellent.' James took Lee's cue seamlessly. He got to his feet and extended his cuffed hands. 'So, when do I get my money, Major?'

'Er . . . there are complications,' he stammered. 'Er . . . certain protocols must be observed before it can be handed over, Wing Commander.'

'Protocols?' James laughed out loud. 'What protocols could you possible associate with theft? I stole you a Sabre from the United States Air Force and you will now pay me a million dollars, in US currency. I hope there will not be any problems, Major?' James looked at Lee. 'You told me there would be no problems, Lee.'

'I have to inform my superiors that I am in possession of the Sabre before we complete the transaction,' Petrov interjected.

'And I'm afraid the aircraft will need to be inspected. Those are the protocols to which I refer, Wing Commander.'

'Is he telling the truth, Lee?' James asked innocently.

'Yes, he is, James. Don't worry. The money is here on the base.'

'It had better be, Little Brother.'

'It is. It should only be a matter of a day or two until it's released. Isn't that right, Major?'

'Yes, yes,' Petrov produced a silly grin, 'only a day or two.'

'Do I have your word on that, brother?' James asked Lee.

'Yes, James.'

'Very good,' James replied. 'I can't say I'm happy with the arrangement, but as it's only a couple of days I'll go along with it. Now, if we've concluded our business,' he said to both men, 'I think I'll return to the infirmary, if that's all right?'

'Yes, of course it is,' Lee replied then broke into rapid Mandarin. '*Soldier,*' he snapped at the young room guard, '*take this prisoner back to the infirmary.*'

When James had gone Lee turned back to discover Petrov lighting yet another of his filthy cigarettes.

'Tell me, Comrade General,' the Russian asked through a cloud of smoke, 'is your brother . . .' He paused and spat tobacco from his lip. ' . . . How can I put it politely? Is your brother a foolish romantic, or something of that nature?'

'My brother,' Lee wanted to laugh, 'a foolish romantic?'

'I do not understand the English mentality. Does he not realise the hopelessness of the situation he is in? We have the aircraft and he is a prisoner of war.'

'My brother is frightened, Comrade.' Lee hated lies, but lying to Petrov came easily. 'Like any man would be. What you just witnessed was an act of false bravado. He has kept his part of the bargain and now must rely on me to keep mine.' Lee walked to the door. 'And whether I do or not remains to be seen, Major,' he added cryptically, and left.

龍

The escape was simplicity itself, at first.

'Johnnie.'

'What?' Johnnie Wilson sat bolt upright in his bed. 'What is it?'

'We're leaving,' James replied.

'What's going on?' The young American was out of bed before he realised his handcuffs had been removed. 'What do you mean, we're leaving?'

'Put these on.' James threw a pair of trousers at him and a padded military jacket. He'd stolen two uniforms from the guards' bathroom down the corridor. 'We're going to hitch a ride out of here.'

'Slow down, Jimbo, and let me catch up.'

'We are to be transferred to the prison tomorrow, which will make any escape we attempt ten times harder, so we're going tonight.'

'I take it you've got some plan in mind, pardner?'

'Yes, but there's no time to discuss it now.' James opened the door and checked the corridor. 'Come on, Johnnie. There's no time to waste.'

The two men stepped into the corridor and Johnnie nearly fell over their room guard slumped over on his chair. 'What's with him?' he whispered.

'I just put him to sleep,' James replied and headed for the rear of the building.

They had not gone twenty yards when two men, naked but for the towels wrapped round their waists, stepped out of the washroom. Johnnie watched in amazement as James stepped between them and seized each by the neck. In a matter of seconds, they lay on the floor utterly still, staring at the ceiling.

'Jesus,' Johnnie gasped. 'Are they dead, or what?'

'No.' James headed for the rear door. 'Paralysed, but they'll be up and about soon.'

Johnnie stared at the soldiers for several seconds. 'How did you do that?' he asked, looking up, but James had disappeared through the door.

Johnnie caught up to him outside the building. He was crouched in the shadow of a water tower.

'If you don't keep up, I'll leave you here,' James hissed as Johnnie knelt beside him. 'You see those trucks over there?' James pointed across a wide square lit up by flood lighting.

'Yeah,' Johnnie nodded.

'They'll be going out of the main gates in convoy at nine o'clock and we're going to be on one, Johnnie my lad.'

'You mean *in* one?'

'No, I mean *on* one.' James pointed his finger skyward to the platform on the water tower directly above them. 'Start climbing, lad,' he grinned and leapt upward into the darkness as if he had springs on his heels.

It took Johnnie several harrowing minutes to climb the thirty feet to the platform that held the water tank. His left arm, in plaster from elbow to wrist, was weak and his fingers were unable to grasp hold of the wooden beams. Finally, he sprawled out on the deck, gasping.

'Shh!' James hissed. 'Do you want the entire PLA to know where we are?'

'You're that guy, right?' Johnnie whispered. 'The guy in the comic books. Where did you learn to climb like that?'

Before James could reprimand him again, their attention was drawn by the sound of truck engines starting up. Voices yelled and several horns honked as the convoy began to rumble towards them.

'They'll pass close to the tower. The jump will be ten feet out and ten feet down,' James said. 'Will you be able to manage that?'

'Are you giving me a choice?'

'Yes,' James said. 'Escape, or spend your foreseeable future in a POW camp somewhere in the glorious People's Republic of North Korea.'

'I'll jump, thanks, *amigo*.'

'Good.' James helped him to his feet. 'I didn't fancy walking a thousand miles through China on my own.'

'Hey.' Johnnie's smile was not convincing, he looked terrified. 'Tourism's what I do best, *hombre*. Maybe we'll see all that tea that's supposed to be in China.'

'Humour. Very good.' James nodded, looking at him. 'Nervous are we?'

'You can bet your tight *cojones* on that one, *compadre*.'

'Right, well listen up. We've got one shot at it, John.' James pointed at the convoy rumbling past. 'They're soft-tops, so we should be all right. The last truck is the only one that's any good to us, because we'll be getting off again outside the gates and we don't want any of the drivers seeing us.'

'*Comprendo.*'

'Are you aware that you speak Spanish when you're nervous?'

'*Si.*'

They stood watching the canvas topped trucks pass and when the last one was beneath them, they jumped. Their aim was good, but the canvas wasn't. It parted like rice paper and both men crashed into the rear of the truck.

'*Fuck your mother!*' they heard a voice exclaim. '*What was that?*'

The truck stopped, both doors slammed and they heard the driver and guard hurry towards the tail flap of the vehicle.

'*I thought for a moment, the water tower had fallen on us,*' the driver complained.

The rear canvas flap was flung back and James struck. His left foot caught the man on the jaw and, as he dropped to the ground, unconscious, James leapt out of the truck to engage the other soldier. Before the startled man could react, James hit him in the head and he too fell unconscious to the ground.

Johnnie watched from the truck as James dragged each of the men into the nearby shadows, picked up one of the soldiers' hats and sprinted for the truck cabin. Then the American fell flat on his back again as the truck lurched forward and increased speed to catch the convoy.

'Damn it!' James snarled as the last truck in the convoy passed through the gate and a guard began to close it. He beeped the horn continuously and increased speed intending to crash through it. Fortunately, the gate guard made a rude

gesture with his fingers in response to the beeping and began
to push the gate back open.

'*Your mother sits on candlesticks!*' James heard the gate
guard yell as he drove the truck through the gates.

'*Your mother licks them clean!*' James yelled back and was
relieved to see, in the rear view mirror, the gate guard double
over with laughter.

He caught up with the convoy about halfway along the
mile of road that led to the town of Dandong. He slowed
down, adjusting to the convoy's speed, and desperately tried
to think of his next move. Lee had told him to find the Three
Willows Inn and a Kazakh called Jun Khan, but he was more
concerned about what to do with the truck he had stolen.
Their escape would be reported before much longer because
he hadn't killed the driver and guard.

Damn Lee and his damned rules of escape, he thought.
At first he'd tried to figure out a way of escaping without
anyone being aware of him, but it had been a fool's errand.
He'd had to take care of the room guard and then he'd been
forced to incapacitate the naked men whose uniforms he'd
stolen. Then he'd had to flatten the soldiers from the truck.
Damn Lee! he cursed again. If he'd been able to kill all five
of the men and hide their bodies, no one would have known
he was gone until the next morning, and that would have
given him at least an eight-hour start.

The convoy began to pass through Dandong and James
kept a lookout hoping to spot the Three Willows Inn. It
would make things easier if he knew where it was. But his
first decision was to keep on going through the town and
abandon the truck a mile or two past it. If he dumped it in
the town there would be soldiers all over it in an hour and
he'd have no chance of returning to find the Kazakh. But
if he hid the truck, they'd think he was still with the convoy
and go after it.

His next disappointment was the Three Willows Inn. It
was a disgusting place if the exterior was anything to go by.
He stared forlornly as he drove past it. Built of mud-brick
and stone, it was a sorry sight to behold. The windows were

smashed, the door hung off its hinges, and even the walls were lopsided and askew, squashed between several other slightly taller buildings. He prayed it would not be indicative of the man he was to find there. The last thing he needed was a drunk for a guide.

At least there's activity within, he thought. The place was packed and several fights were in progress. Two women screamed as several drunken men chased them into the street, but James was unable to tell if their shrieks expressed horror or delight. Probably the latter, he supposed.

On the far side of Dandong, he slowed the vehicle and gradually dropped off the pace until the convoy was no longer in sight. He chose a dirt side road and drove up it several miles to a wooded area that would conceal the truck. He stopped the vehicle between several stands of bamboo and turned off the engine. He sat quietly gathering his thoughts before heading back to Dandong, when he heard a groan and realised he'd forgotten he had a passenger.

'That was one helluva ride, pardner,' Johnnie's face appeared at the driver's window. 'Where the hell are we?'

'We're in Manchuria and we have to get to Shantung,' James replied dryly.

'Right,' Johnnie nodded. 'No problems. That explains everything. For a minute there I thought we were in trouble.' He gently felt the tape holding his broken nose cartilage in place.

'How is it?'

'It hurts.'

'How's your arm?'

'It hurts too, but I don't think there's any more damage.'

'Good.' James got out of the truck. 'Try to keep the plaster cast covered, it's a dead giveaway. And take that tape off your nose.' He began to walk back towards the east.

'Where are we going?' Johnnie asked as he pulled the tape off and began to follow.

'We've got a decent hike, cross-country back to Dandong.'

'Back to Dandong?' Johnnie was puzzled. 'Ain't that the wrong way?'

'Do you know the way to Shantung Province?' James yelled back over his shoulder.

'No.'

'Then I suggest you stop asking questions and follow me.'

It was nearly midnight when they arrived in Dandong. James had deliberately kept to the hills for the most part then they'd made their way down through rice paddies and ploughed fields until they were on the outskirts of the town. They crept silently through several lanes that led them to the side of a building directly opposite the Three Willows Inn.

'Jee-sus,' Johnnie muttered as he looked across the street. The only living thing not drunk, in or around the inn was a dog. Its inebriated master and two other drunken customers were asleep. 'Don't they have homes to go to?'

James ignored Johnnie's attempt at levity and looked left and right. The street was empty, the town silent, and James could not help but be surprised. Surely their escape must have been reported by now?

'How come nobody's looking for us?' Johnnie asked as if he'd read James' mind. 'I'd a' thought this place would be crawling with Commie soldiers.'

The reason was obvious when James gave it some thought. Of course the escape would have been reported, but Lee had not sent anyone to look for them. And the Russian would be the first one to agree with his lack of action. Petrov had the Sabre so he'd be the last one to kick up a fuss. They were home and hosed.

'Wait here, John,' James said and strolled casually across the street to the inn.

The dog sniffed at James' trouser leg as he stepped over several drunks to peer through the broken doorway. The inn was empty except for two old men who sat either side of a barrel playing Chinese chequers, and a young woman cleaning up behind the bar. He entered and approached her. She sensed his presence and turned.

'The inn is closed,' she said, her eyes appraising him. 'Are you Chinese?'

'My father was Chinese, my mother was Korean,' he replied.

'Ah, that explains your looks,' she nodded. 'Your father must have had weak seed, you don't look very Chinese. Where are you from?'

'The Military camp.'

'I've never seen you in here before. You must be new, true or not true?'

'True, Sister,' he answered as he leaned on the decrepit wooden bar. 'I seek a man called Jun Khan. Do you know him?'

'The Kazakh,' she said with some disgust. 'He gave all the girls here the pox! The innkeeper has banned him.'

'Do you know where he is?'

'He's sleeping in the barn, that is if he's not buggering one of the pigs. Even they are not safe from that hairy foreign devil.'

'Thank you, Sister,' James nodded his head respectfully and began walking towards the door.

'Hey, soldier,' the girl called. 'Have you got any money?' She pulled aside her blouse and revealed a pretty young breast. 'He didn't give me the pox.'

'Perhaps not,' James turned and smiled at her, 'but he gave it to me.'

'You speak big words,' she laughed, meaning he was telling a lie, 'and I don't believe them. If you want somewhere to sleep, come back and see me. I've got a comfortable mattress here.' She tilted her head indicating she slept on the floor behind the bar. 'And it won't cost you anything.'

'I know you would be like a gift from the gods, princess,' James said softly and bowed to her, 'but I have important work to do.'

'Please come back,' she pleaded, 'if you can.' She was suddenly very young, sad and lonely. 'My husband was killed by the foreign army in Korea and I don't want to be alone.'

James stared at her for a moment, but he could think of nothing to say. He turned and left.

Outside he signalled to Johnnie, and they both walked down to a side lane fifty yards along the street. James presumed it would lead to the night alley that serviced the inn and he was right. They found the darkened barn and entered, warily.

No sooner had they done so than Johnnie was seized in a vice-like grip and a knife was placed against his throat.

'*Tell me your business,*' a deep voice growled in Mandarin, '*or this man will leave the world of men for a better place.*'

'*We seek a man called Jun Khan,*' James answered.

'*What business would you have with him?*'

'*The Dragon of Shanghai told us this man would . . .*' James paused, '*. . . give us the pox.*'

A deep-throated laugh came from the darkness, and Johnnie was thrown into the pool of moonlight at the entrance to the barn. Then a match was struck and a lantern lit.

'*I am the man you seek, but the Dragon told me there would only be one man.*'

'*Well, there are two of us. Things got a bit complicated, understand or not understand?*'

'*One or two, it is of little concern to me. I am merely the escort.*' He stepped forward and handed James his silver-plated Colt .45. '*The Dragon told me to return this to you.*'

'Do you speak English?' James asked, taking his firearm and tucking it in his belt.

'I was born in British India, Sahib,' the big Kazakh sang in a deep but lilting Indian accent. 'In a place that, because of the accursed Division, is now known as northwest Pakistan. But I was born in the golden age of colonial rule, before that stick insect Gandhi began his seditious preaching that brought about independence.'

'My name is James Merchant, I'm a Wing Commander in the Royal Air Force. And this,' he indicated Johnnie who was still rubbing his neck, 'is Captain John Wilson. He's an American fighter pilot.'

'You're a British officer.' Jun Khan was impressed. 'I knew it. You have the voice of authority, Sahib, that once ruled the world. I am most graciously pleased to meet you both.' He beamed his best smile. 'And now we must go.'

'Go where?' Johnnie asked.

'To the village of Yuk Long,' the big man declared with an expansive wave of his arm. 'I am ordered to take you there. It is on the Bo Hai Coast over one hundred and fifty miles from here as the birds fly, and therefore a long walk. So, we must go now while the darkness protects us. My orders are to travel only at night, and therefore, the journey will take us two weeks at least.'

'Orders?' Johnnie asked. 'You have orders? From who?'

'General Lee Kw – '

'Do you want to escape or not?' James snapped at the American before the Kazakh could finish. 'If you do, then stop asking irrelevant questions.'

'But . . .' Johnnie began.

I'm sorry, James turned to the Kazakh, *'but the less the American knows the better.'*

Jun Khan nodded. 'We must go immediately, Sahib. The journey will take many days.'

'I've got a better idea,' James said. 'There is an army truck several miles from here, we'll use that.' He looked at Johnnie. 'We could be in Yuk Long in, what – ?' He snapped his fingers. 'Come on, work it out.'

'. . . Call it three hours back to the truck,' Johnnie continued. 'Thirty-five miles an hour, make it two hundred miles . . . six hours . . . call it seven . . . I'd say twelve hours.'

'It's all mountains between here and Yuk Long, so let's call it twenty-four hours to be on the safe side. What do you say, Jun Khan?' said James. 'It beats walking.'

'I once walked across the roof of the world,' Jun Khan declared proudly, 'but it took me a year. I therefore bow to your superior logistic experience. The truck is a most brilliant suggestion, Sahib.'

In the end it only took eighteen hours, including two rest intervals, for James to drive across the mountains. Johnnie couldn't operate the crash gearbox and Jun Khan simply didn't know how to drive. They stood on a hill overlooking the tiny fishing village of Yuk Long. It consisted of several small stone huts separated by a cobbled road that led down to aricketty wooden jetty at which several fishing junks were moored.

Apart from a number of treacherous mountain roads, they had encountered no trouble on the drive from Dandong to the Bo Hai Coast. Even when they'd passed the convoy their truck had originally been part of, no one gave them a second glance. James had to admit the whole escape so far had a surreal quality to it. When the truck ran out of petrol on the hill only just above Yuk Long he was not remotely surprised. The whole series of events seemed to him preordained, but he remained vigilant. He knew their luck would run out eventually – luck had a nasty habit of doing just that.

'How can such a small place have so many dogs?' Johnnie asked as they walked through the village. They'd counted fifty or more black furry dogs on their way down the cobbled road to the jetty.

'China is a country of many dogs,' Jun Khan replied.

'You can say that again.' Johnnie laughed. 'Hey, they've got black tongues! What kind of dogs have black tongues?'

'The breed is called *Chau*,' James informed him. He and Jun Khan shared a look. Neither had the heart to tell the young American that, apart from fish, they were probably the villagers' main source of food. *Chau* dogs were bred to be eaten and considered a delicacy.

'*Good evening, Sirs,*' an old fisherman called. He jumped from his junk onto the pier and walked towards them. '*What is your honourable name?*' he asked James.

'*Who is asking?*' James enquired.

'*My name is Sing,*' the fisherman replied. '*The Dragon of Shanghai asked me to wait for the one named Merchant. I've been waiting for three days.*'

'*What did this dragon request of you?*' Jun Khan asked.

'*I am to take the one called Merchant down the Bo Hai to Shantung Peninsula.*'

'*To the village of Wei hai Wei,*' James said.

'*True, Elder Brother. But I was told there would only be one Merchant. Are you all called Merchant?*'

'What's going on, James?' Johnnie asked. 'I don't speak the lingo, remember?'

'I've offered this old man money to take us south,' James lied.

'You can't do that. We haven't got any money.'

'Might I remind you that we are escaped prisoners of war, John?' James was irritated by the interruption. 'We are hundreds of miles inside enemy territory and I really think that the fact we have no money is of little consequence given our circumstances, don't you?'

'Okay, James,' Johnnie snapped. 'Keep your shirt on. I was only asking what's going on because I don't speak Chinese, okay?'

'*I am Merchant,*' James said, turning to old Sing, '*and these two men are my travelling companions. They, too, are going to Wei-hai-Wei.*'

'*Then you'd better get on board,*' the old man said. '*The sun is setting. Soon it will be dark and so will be a good time for us to get under way.*'

'Get on board, Johnnie.' James indicated the large junk. The American did so without comment, but Jun Khan remained on the pier.

'*Is that your truck?*' old Sing asked pointing up to the vehicle so obvious on the hill. '*I do not think it is your truck, Elder Brother.*'

James looked towards Jun Khan, who had made no attempt to board the junk. He had positioned himself on the end of the jetty and was staring at the setting sun.

'I take it you are not coming with us, Jun Khan?' James joined the big Kazakh.

'You are correct as always, Sahib,' the man replied as he took in the glorious sky and the sun's crimson light reflecting off the water. 'The part I play in your journey has ended. The old man Sing will take you to Wei-hai-Wei. I have other business I must do for the General.' He pointed west into the sunset.

'His family?' James asked.

'Yes,' the big man turned, 'do you know them?'

'I have met them.' James was deliberately non-committal. If Lee had not considered it necessary to tell the Kazakh of their relationship, he would not complicate matters. The less the Kazakh knew the better, not only for his sake, but for all concerned.

'I bid you farewell,' Jun Khan offered his hand, 'and may your god protect you, Wing Commander.'

'And yours protect you.'

They shook hands and James began heading back to the junk. 'Oh, I almost forgot.' He returned to the Kazakh. 'Take this.' He took a box from his pocket and offered it.

'What is it?'

'It's a box of penicillin tablets I took from Antung infirmary. They'll cure you of the pox.'

'But I do not wish to be cured, Sahib.'

'Why on earth not?'

'I have actually suffered it for years. The pox and I reached a compromise a long time ago. Each of us is content to suffer the other.'

'Really?' James was horrified at the thought.

'As much as I love my wife, may God protect her, if you saw her, Sahib, you would understand completely.'

James was still smiling ten minutes later as he waved farewell.

龍

The junk motored south-southwest all night at a speed of eight knots and morning found it well down the Bo Hai. Old Sing changed course to southeast and told James that, barring any unforeseen incidents, they'd be in the fishing village of Wei-hai-Wei by sunset.

'Good morning, Johnnie,' James said as the American came on deck. James had been up since dawn, uneasy at the prospect of being so exposed on the sea during daylight. He sat in the bow drinking tea and smoking one of old Sing's supposedly English cigarettes. Where he'd acquired them from James hardly dared to imagine. They were not very good and they were most certainly not English.

'Yeah, mornin',' Wilson grunted making it obvious to James that he was not happy.

'All right, John.' James flicked his cigarette into the water as Johnnie sat next to him. 'Spit it out. What's eating you?'

'A lot of things, Skipper, if you really want to know.'

'Well, I've got nothing better to do today, except to watch for the PLA.' James tried to sound jovial, but the thought that he may have to kill John Wilson in the next few minutes was not helping. 'Why don't you tell me what's on your mind?'

'Well,' Johnnie began, 'don't get me wrong, I mean I'm grateful that we got out of that camp, but . . . well . . . we didn't do it on our own, did we?'

'No one else disabled five men in that escape, and we stole a truck, John.'

'Yeah, I been chewing that one over, but there's more.'

'Like what?'

'Like, how did you know that convoy was leaving the camp at nine o'clock?'

'I not only speak five Chinese languages, John,' James replied after sipping his tea, 'I also read it. The movement order for that convoy was on the main notice board in the Admin building they took me to.'

'Okay,' Johnnie nodded. 'I'll accept that one, but I've got a whole bunch of others. Jun Khan was expecting you.'

'Was he?' James smiled, but it held no warmth.

John stared at him. 'For Chrissakes, James, the gun he gave you is the same goddamn gun I gave you at Kenjong!'

'Hmmm.' James stood up and emptied the dregs of his tea over the bow. 'That one could take a bit more explaining.'

'Let me finish, first,' said John, getting to his feet. 'The old guy who owns this boat was waiting for us, too.'

'It could have appeared that way, yes.' James placed his tea cup in the scuppers.

'When you told me you was offerin' him money to take us south, I knew you were lyin'.'

'Would it do any good if I denied it all?' James began to slow his breathing. *Detect, assess, strike, defend*, his mind repeated.

'Well, here comes the sixty-four thousand dollar question, old buddy. Jun Khan mentioned the name General Lee Kwan. Your mother, Elanora, that night of the ball in Hong Kong, told me all about your brother. She's very proud of you both.'

'You're a clever lad, John.' James began pacing, never taking his eyes off the American. 'And you're right on the money, old son. You've caught me out. Yes, Lee Kwan is my brother, by adoption and – '

'I ain't finished, James,' Johnnie interrupted. 'I got to thinkin' last night while I was layin' down in the cabin. I started thinkin' about you goin' down in your Sabre.'

Here it comes, James thought. 'What about it, Johnnie?' he asked softly, dangerously.

'Well, I'm a pretty good wingman, wouldn't you say?'

'Yes, you are. A natural, one of the best I've ever flown with.'

'Well, I didn't see you get hit.' Johnnie looked at James. 'There, I said it.'

'Said what, exactly, John?'

'What I'm really gettin' at, pardner – and I emphasise the word *pardner* – is if you were gonna steal a fuckin' jet, why in hell's name didn't you tell me?'

The two men stared at each other for several seconds until a smile creased James' lips and he began to laugh.

'And as for stealin' the Sabre, well, I'll tell you, James, I couldn't give a goddamn one way or the other.'

'Really? I must say I'm surprised.' James was more than surprised, he was delighted. Johnnie Wilson was revealing himself to be even more mercenary than James had first thought.

'I've killed three men in aerial combat as far as I know and that's fair enough.' Now it was Johnnie's turn to pace the deck. 'But I've killed a heck of a lot more in strafing runs, including women and children, and I'm ashamed of my actions. Whoever said that war was honourable never strafed farmhouses and bombed people's homes. That's indiscriminate killing. It's murder.' He stopped pacing and stared out over the waters of the Bo Hai. 'The love of country imbued in me by my parents, and the sense of duty instilled by military training, are not enough to condone what I've done. I feel ashamed. I'm sick of war altogether. And this war in particular, because it should never have happened in the first place. It's a stupid, stupid war.'

'I agree with you,' James said, noting that Johnnie Wilson's Texan accent disappeared when he talked from the heart. 'War itself is stupid.'

Johnnie sat again, on the bow rail. 'Surely, you'd think the A-Bombs we dropped on Hiroshima and Nagasaki would have served as an indication to people of what we are now capable of in war. One bomb killed a hundred thousand people, most of them civilians.'

'Those bombs ended the war, John. They made the invasion of Japan unnecessary.'

'I know that. They saved a lot of American lives. But the point I want to make is: it won't stop there. We've already improved on those bombs and in twenty years' time humans will have a bomb capable of killing a million people. Can you imagine what will happen if anybody explodes such a bomb – or worse still – a dozen of them?

'I want to live before I die, James. I want to be comfortable somewhere, enjoying myself. I want money and power and beautiful women, before I become a victim of atomic warfare.' Johnnie looked up at James. 'I guess that's enough "speechifyin'" as my granddaddy would say. I sure went on a bit didn't I?'

'It was the most eloquent "speechifyin'" I've heard in a long time, John.'

'Well, Jimbo?' The two men stared at each other.

'Well, what?'

'Well, are you gonna tell me just what the hell you've been up to, pardner?'

'Are you sure you want to know?'

'In for a dime, in for a dollar, as my daddy used to say. If we're partners, Jimbo, I'd better know it all.'

'Well it started when the KGB found out we were selling radios to the Chinese – '

'The KGB? Damn!'

'Yes.' James told him the whole tale concluding with the unfortunate appearance of Richard Beckham. 'And the rest you've experienced for yourself.'

'It's a damned shame Dickie had to come along right at that moment.'

'Yes. Poor Dickie,' James said. 'That wasn't supposed to happen. It was an accident, John.' He looked Wilson straight in the eye. 'He was furious. He said he was going to report me. I grabbed him by the sleeve.' James paused and shook his head. 'We struggled and he fell into the pit and broke his neck.'

'Yeah, that was a real shame.' Johnnie's voice dripped sarcasm. He didn't believe the lie for a second. Struggled, my ass, he thought. James Merchant was a martial arts expert. Johnnie had seen it for himself during the escape from Antung Base.

'What do you mean by that?' James asked softly.

'Dickie Beckham had been around aeroplanes and hangars far too long to go falling in a maintenance pit all by himself, Jimbo.'

'Meaning?' *Detect, assess, strike, defend.* James stood directly in front of Johnnie.

'Meaning *pardners* don't lie to one another.' Johnnie stood up and faced James nose to nose. 'I don't give a flyin' god-damn what happened in that hangar, James. I just want the truth, so at the end of the day I know what I'm lookin' at.'

James' face broke into a smile. 'Fair enough, John.' He moved back to the opposite bow rail and sat on it. 'He caught me, red-handed, stealing the bloody jet. He saw the maps of Manchuria, the ration packs and the extra ammunition I'd put in the cockpit. Dickie would never have let it lie. It was him or me – or, more accurately, him or me on a treason charge.'

'So you threw him in the maintenance pit.'

'No, I broke his neck,' James looked across at the young American, 'then he *accidentally* fell in the maintenance pit. That's the only bit you have to remember when we get back to a heroes' welcome in Seoul.'

'Right,' Johnnie nodded. He turned his face into the wind, took a deep breath of salt air and gazed out over the blue waters of the Bo Hai. He'd made his bed and now he had to lie in it. He was as guilty as James. And that's probably the reason I'm still alive, he thought. He needs me to verify the jet crash and the escape. Like it or not, John boy, he mused, you and James Merchant are joined at the hip from now on and where your life's headed, only time will tell.

'So what do you think?' James said finally.

Johnnie looked up. 'About what? About ol' Dickie? Or stealing an F-86 from the United States Air Force?'

'Both really,' James shrugged.

'Well, if Dickie hadn't gone and *accidentally* fallen into the maintenance pit, you'd have had to kill him anyway right?'

'That's right.'

'And as far as stealing the F-86 goes, well, it just depends on how much you got paid for that bird, Jimbo?'

'The truth?'

'The truth.'

'One million United States dollars.'

'Jesus *died,* Mary *cried* and Joseph *shit a nail*!'

龍

Petrov was angry. He strode down the corridor and burst into Lee's office like an enraged bull, allowing the door to slam into a filing cabinet.

Lee jumped to his feet. 'How many times must I tell you to knock, Major?'

Petrov stood there fuming. 'Don't play games with me, you little Chinese upstart.'

'I beg your pardon?' Lee's voice was full of venom.

'I just spoke with your Camp Auditor and Accountant, Colonel Kwok. I asked for the money belonging to my Government to be returned to me.'

'Oh, I see.' A devious smile spread across Lee's face.

Petrov extended his chin and worked an index finger into

the high collar of his uniform. 'Colonel Kwok refused to even discuss the matter. He suggested I talk to you.'

'What do you want to know?'

'I simply want the one million dollars returned that was entrusted to me by my Government!'

'But you in turn entrusted it to me.' Lee stared at the Russian.

Petrov eyed Lee suspiciously. 'I want that money back,' he growled. 'You seem to forget that I have a receipt for that money, Comrade General, a carbon copy of which is in your official camp records.' He took a paper from his tunic pocket and waved it at Lee. 'Here it is. It has been in my personal possession since I deposited the money into your care. And it is countersigned by you!'

Lee perused the paper and handed it back to the Russian. 'That is a receipt for nine hundred thousand dollars, Comrade, not one million.'

'What?' Petrov gasped. He examined the receipt closely then looked at Lee, utterly dumbfounded. 'But that is impossible. I signed a deposit slip for one million dollars.'

'No, you didn't, Major,' Lee grinned malevolently. 'You signed a deposit slip for nine hundred thousand dollars.'

'What are you talking about?' The Russian's face was still white, but the rage had gone, replaced by a look of sickening realisation.

'It is the oldest trick in the book of Chinese accounting. You should always check the amount before you sign, and always make sure you're the last to sign. When you gave the book to me for countersignature, I changed the figure one into a dollar sign and changed the first zero to a nine, then gave you your copy. As far as I am concerned, and I'm sure the KGB will agree, the amount deposited was nine hundred thousand United States dollars.'

Petrov stood glaring for what seemed an eternity as he tried to consider all the ramifications of Lee's sleight of hand. 'Very well,' he nodded, 'you have helped yourself to one hundred thousand dollars, General. You have my congratulations, but I must insist you now return the other nine hundred thousand.'

'Why? Your Government has the jet, for which I will tell them I handed over nine hundred thousand dollars, as you instructed me to do.'

'But I gave you no such instructions.'

'But, I'll say you did.'

'I must have that money back!' Petrov's voice cracked. 'All of it!'

'For you to return to the Russian Government?' Lee's tone dripped sarcasm.

'Of course.'

'Don't make me laugh, Petrov. You intended all along to keep it for yourself.'

'That is not true!'

'Ha!' Lee scoffed. 'You're in serious trouble, my friend. You'll be in front of a firing squad before you can draw breath. I'll spell it out for you. Your Government gave you a million dollars in cash. I will tell them that the amount received by the Camp Accounts Department was nine hundred thousand dollars, which I duly paid to my brother. Therefore, any shortfall could only have occurred before the money was received at this base. In other words, you stole one hundred thousand dollars from the KGB.'

'Comrade,' Petrov offered a thin-lipped smile. 'We are both men of the world. Let us lay our cards upon the card playing table, as they say in the western movies of America.'

'Why don't we do just that, Major.'

'You have realised my ambitious plan, but look at the situation. My Government is in possession of the aircraft it so desperately desired. Your brother has fled in fear of his life. I will share the million with you, fifty-fifty.'

'So you can retire to the shores of the Black Sea and live a life of ease?' Lee snorted derisively.

'Please, Comrade, don't make jokes.' Petrov tried to chuckle but he failed miserably, he was beginning to feel sick. 'Let us agree to split the money as I said, fifty-fifty.'

'But I no longer have the money, Major.'

'What?'

'I went ahead and made the transaction myself, on your

Government's behalf. I gave the money to my brother. Two weeks ago to be exact.'

'What are you saying?' the Russian gasped. '*All* of it?'

'Yes, Major Petrov, *all* of it.' Lee sat at his desk and felt a brief twinge of sympathy for the Russian. But he'd brought it all on his own head. He'd played a game for high stakes and lost. And the reason for his loss had been his own greed and arrogance. He'd taken his KGB masters and Lee for fools and it would cost him his life.

Lee had assumed all along that Petrov would attempt to steal the money. That was why he'd insisted the cash be secured at Antung before he left for South Korea. From that moment on, the game had become a *fait accompli*. The Russian had believed the cash was in the camp safe and his intention would have been to retake possession of it and head for parts unknown. But Lee had taken the money with him on the first part of his trip, carefully covering his tracks as he went, and had hidden it for James to collect after his capture and escape.

The Russian stood in the middle of Lee's office his shoulders slumped in defeat.

'You're a dead man, Major. All you can do is run. Now, if you'll excuse me, I have work to do and a great many things to think about,' he smiled thinly at the man, 'as I'm sure you have too.'

BOOK TWO

THE SUMMIT

CHAPTER SEVEN

Macau and Hong Kong, 1956

Elanora came out of the pantry wiping her hands on a cloth. She tossed it playfully at her kitchen maid and picked up a large tray with Richard's breakfast on it.

'I will take this to the Master, Sally.'

'Yes, Mistress,' the young girl smiled brightly. The Mistress seemed happy this morning and that made Sally happy. She adored Elanora, who had rescued her from a life of drudgery in her father's laundry business and taken her on as a maid in the beautiful *Lung Fa Yuen*, the Dragon's Garden, as the house she lived and worked in was known.

Elanora had purchased the house in Macau and had moved from Hong Kong permanently the year before because of the personal differences between Richard and her son James. The newly acquired three storey residence sat in pride of place above the Praia Grande, the beautiful boulevard that represented Macau's waterfront. The building was Sino-Portuguese in style, old and elegant, with balconies on every floor that captured beautiful views of the port and estuary. It was also a sensuous house, its high, arched windows featured heavy wooden shutters to block the lashing wind and rain from summer typhoons, but on balmy, tranquil days, they allowed the warm summer air to caress lace curtains and silk bed sheets as it moved through the house. Another fine feature was a beautiful rear garden enclosed by walls ten feet high from which several small water fountains sprang. Elanora simply adored the place.

'*You will visit your mother this morning,*' Elanora ordered.

'*Yes, Mistress,*' the girl replied.

Elanora made sure Sally visited her mother every two weeks. The old woman lived in Baak Ma Hong Street at the rear of her husband's laundry in the old Sao Lorenqo area. And, because Sally hated going anywhere near her father, as an incentive Elanora made the girl take the household laundry and insisted her mother wash and iron it personally. For the service, Elanora paid Sally's father the going rate and paid her mother a further sum of money, of which Sally's father knew nothing.

'*But I want you back in the house by lunchtime,*' Elanora warned. '*I am taking the one o'clock ferry to Hong Kong and will not return until tomorrow afternoon, understand or not understand?*'

'*Understand, Mistress.*'

'*You and the other staff must take good care of the Master, or I will be very angry.*'

'*Yes, Mistress,*' the girl replied and with a slight bow went off to the laundry.

Elanora placed the tray in the dumb waiter, pulled the rope until it reached the third floor and went into the main hallway. She climbed the three flights of stairs, recovered the tray and took it into Richard's bedroom.

'Good morning, darling,' she called to her husband.

'Good morning, good morning,' he called back cheerfully from the balcony.

Elanora stepped out into bright early spring sunshine, placed the tray on the balcony table and kissed Richard on the cheek.

'Did you sleep well, my dear?' Richard asked. It had been Richard's idea that they occupy separate bedrooms.

'Wonderfully, thank you,' she replied. But Elanora had not slept well at all. She'd tossed and turned most of the night, angry with herself at the anticipation she was experiencing about her trip to Hong Kong.

'You've got your Annual General Meeting today, haven't you?' Richard asked as he buttered a piece of toast.

'Tomorrow morning, actually,' she replied pouring them both tea. 'But I'm taking the ferry this afternoon.'

'Will you be staying at the Peninsula?'

'Yes, but only for tonight. I'll be back tomorrow afternoon to look after you.' Elanora took a seat opposite Richard and smiled at him as she sipped her tea. 'I'll only be a phone call away if you should need me.'

'Really, my love,' he replied nibbling at the crisp toast. 'You shouldn't fuss over me as you do. I'm quite all right, on my own. Besides which, the house is teeming with servants if I should need anything.'

'It's because I love you,' Elanora said, not without a tinge of sadness. She put her cup down and gazed out over the beautiful vista of the Pearl River Estuary. Forty miles east lay the city of Hong Kong and her suite at the Peninsula where tonight, she would luxuriate in a marble bath and indulge herself with a massage and fine food and wine. But, she reminded herself, the company AGM was scheduled for the following morning and she was not looking forward to that one bit.

James would be his usual bombastic self. Nobody really got the chance to say anything in the meetings because he had turned into a complete megalomaniac. He bought and sold, imported and exported as he chose, without ever advising his board of directors, of which Elanora was one. He took off on mysterious business trips all over the place without ever bothering to tell anyone, not even his wife, Katherine, where he was going. And, Elanora knew, his nocturnal behaviour left a great deal to be desired. He was an inveterate woman-iser and a gambler.

But, she had to admit he was a brilliant businessman. He'd returned from Korea a hero all over again after escaping from a prisoner-of-war camp. He bought several Hong Kong companies at rock bottom prices and had never looked back. Where he'd appropriated the money for those first purchases he never did explain and, strangely enough, none of her spies had ever been able to find out. It was rare for Elanora to be in the dark about anything, business or social, that went on in Hong Kong, but try as she might, she'd never been able to find out where he got his original stake.

In the three years since the end of the Korean War, James had restored the Merchant Company to its former glory, but he'd made sure he gained complete control in the process. He held most of the shares; Elanora's percentage was eighteen per cent, but his was somewhere near fifty. And he'd made sure Richard had absolutely no shares in the new company and had absolutely no input. Not that it had bothered Richard. Her husband had not cared remotely.

'To hell with him,' Richard had said to her. 'He's no good, Elanora. Your son is greedy and cruel. He'll rule the Merchant Company and, indeed, probably all of Hong Kong with an iron fist, but I'll warn you now, my love, no good will come of it.'

She had argued with her husband during the first two years, but eventually she had to admit his forecast was proving to be only too accurate. Elanora had watched in horror as James had gobbled up companies left, right and centre. He'd never once offered financial help to anyone, including those who were once his friends. She'd watched him destroy people who had struggled to resurrect their careers and fortunes after World War II only to be hammered again by the United Nations–imposed embargo on trade with China during the Korean conflict. He'd bought them out with what had seemed like an endless supply of money and showed no emotion as, one after another, they'd found-ered on the rocks of financial ruin.

Elanora slowly realised her son was an avaricious beast. A corporate tiger who tore and destroyed anyone or any-thing that stood in his path, and did so without the slightest remorse.

'Will you be seeing Katherine and the twins?' Richard interrupted her disturbing reflections.

'Yes. At least, I hope to.' Elanora hated lying but she knew how much Richard adored her grandchildren.

Before they'd been forced to move from their house on the Peak in Hong Kong, Richard had spent hours playing with the twins on the balconies and throughout the gardens that surrounded the Merchant House. Paul and Georgina had replaced Lee and James in his heart as the children he'd never had. He adored the twins and had spoilt them at every given opportunity. In fact, his behaviour with them had been the straw that broke the camel's back in his relationship with James.

James' jealousy had been obvious to all but Richard, and to hit back, like a vicious child, James had taken every opportunity to start quarrels and arguments, not only with Richard but with Elanora too. The unhealthy and unhappy atmosphere that pervaded the Merchant House had reached a peak the previous year and had brought about Elanora's decision to leave Hong Kong for Macau.

She had sold the Merchant Mansion to her son. She had demanded an exorbitant amount of money for it and James, as she knew he would, had paid it. His pride and arrogance would not allow him to do otherwise. And Elanora had then, unbeknown to James, twisted the knife even further.

At first she'd only wanted to get back at him for his treatment of Richard. She had wanted to teach him a lesson and the only way to do that, she knew, was financially. But when she had received the money, another idea had occurred to her that she'd found irresistible. Elanora had opened a bank account in Switzerland in the name of Katherine Merchant and given her all of the money.

Katherine had been horrified at first, and terrified of what James would say, but Elanora had invited her and the twins to Macau and spoken with her long into the night.

'He'll demand I give it back to him, El,' Katherine had said. Katherine was the only person in the world Elanora allowed to call her El.

'Then don't tell him you've got it, my dear,' had been the reply. 'Just let it sit there in Switzerland gathering interest. There may come a time when you'll need it, or perhaps when your children will need it.'

'Oh,' Katherine had laughed self-consciously, 'whatever would I need it for?'

Elanora hated the way James had bullied his wife during their marriage, but Katherine had never mentioned it. The girl had been brilliant and feisty when they'd first met, but over the years his continuous brow-beating and criticism had turned Katherine from a strong, independent young woman into a timorous mouse, who dared not say a word in front of her husband.

'Katherine,' Elanora had stared into her eyes. 'Your husband is not a nice man.'

'Oh, El,' the younger had woman gasped. 'He's your son!'

'Don't you think I know that?' Elanora's eyes had glowered. 'The discussion we're about to have is long overdue, my girl.'

And what a discussion it had been, Elanora thought as she sipped her tea and watched the activity along the Praia Grande below. Elanora had told Katherine precisely how she felt and after the tears and sobbing, Katherine had revealed how she, too, truly felt. That night had forged a bond between the two women that would stand the test of time.

'Would you tell Ah Po I'd like to see her this afternoon?' Richard asked.

'Certainly, darling,' Elanora replied. She knew what would transpire. Richard had resorted to using opium as a painkiller for the last six months and Ah Po got it for him. The old *amah* had been in service to the Merchants since Elanora had been young and had told her immediately. Ah Po would never do anything without Elanora's knowledge and permission.

Elanora, and Richard too, had always detested the insidious drug and its soul destroying effects. It seemed to Elanora a sad irony that Richard was now addicted to the dreadful poppy juice, but she knew how much pain his crippled leg afforded him. Late at night she would hear him groaning and then he'd leave his bedroom and disappear to the floor below. If it gave him relief, what could she say?

'I have so many things to do,' Elanora professed as she tidied his breakfast tray and picked it up. 'I must give instructions to the household staff and I have several letters to write before I take the ferry, so I'll say goodbye while I have the chance.'

'Very well, my dear,' Richard replied and the love in his eyes hurt her to the quick.

When Elanora had gone, Richard sat for some minutes staring at his hands, suddenly aware they were clasped neatly in his lap. His fingers were old, his hands wrinkled and his nails gnarled, a symbol of just what he'd become: a cripple, broken and beaten before his time.

He stood up, sighing as the pain knifed through him. He shuffled across to the balcony rail in an attempt to exercise his leg and caught his reflection in the glass doors. The man staring back at him was nothing like the young man who'd arrived in Hong Kong all those years ago, the young fire-brand who had risen through the ranks of the Hong Kong Police Force to make a life for himself as the most powerful man in the Far East.

Richard had, with four other police officers, created the secret society known as the *Gaam Lung Tong*, the Society of Golden Dragons, and together they'd vanquished their enemies, both Chinese and British, and virtually ruled Hong Kong.

But that rule had been benign, Richard thought. The society had been formed as a means of mutual protection for its members. The fact that he and the others had become rich as a result was, to Richard, of secondary importance.

James didn't want a benevolent triad. He wanted a business cartel with which to rule Hong Kong for his own selfish reasons. That was why Richard had refused to help re-establish it. The days of the society had been a golden era in Richard's life and he didn't want the memory, or the name of the Dragons, sullied.

'And now look at you,' Richard sneered at his reflection. His fortunate life had ended abruptly with the Japanese invasion in 1941. Nearly four years as a prisoner of war had broken him, just as the war had broken the Society of Golden Dragons. He stared at his twisted leg and a feeling of utter loathing swept through him.

Elanora had returned to Hong Kong from Sydney after the war and found him, half starved and despondent, living like a hermit in the grand entrance hall of the Merchant Mansion up on Victoria Peak. The once magnificent house had been a burnt out shell, ravaged during the Battle of Hong Kong and looted by the Japanese invaders. It was the only place he could think of to go after British rule had been re-established with the arrival in Hong Kong Harbour of Sir Cecil Harcourt and the British Fleet. The Colony had been a mess and after several months of Red Cross food and sleeping in an over-crowded Victoria Barracks, Richard had simply wandered up to the house, not really knowing what else to do.

Elanora had swept into the ruined mansion like a summer storm, swept him into her arms, and her entourage of house-hold staff had scrubbed the scars of war from the walls. She'd loved him and fed him and calmed his fears, but all the while he'd sunk deeper into a state of morbid melancholia. The black dog of depression had appeared and it had stalked him ever since.

Elanora had spent a fortune returning the house to its former glory and she'd spent even more trying to get him interested in new business ventures, thinking it may draw him back to the land of the living. She'd thrown parties and surrounded him with old friends, but it had all been to no avail. Richard hadn't cared. It had been as simple as that. Nothing, including Elanora's love, could make him care. Something had died within him and try as he most certainly had, he could not resurrect it.

James' return to the Colony after the war had not improved matters. James had been full of enthusiasm and grand business ideas for him and Richard to pursue, including the restoration of the Society of Golden Dragons, but when James had realised Richard Brewster had no heart for it he'd finally made his feelings obvious.

Richard looked again at his reflection and cringed at the memory of their confrontation.

He had been sitting on the upper balcony of the Merchant House watching the comings and goings of ships in the harbour below and making notes of their arrival and departure times. It was a pastime he found relaxing and had developed it into a hobby over several years. As he wrote neatly in his journal, James, fresh from showering, had walked out onto the balcony wearing only a bath towel around his waist. With another he was drying his hair. It was then that Richard had noticed he wore no jewellery around his neck and made what he thought to be an innocent enquiry.

'Do you still have the medallion I gave to you?'

'What medallion?' James had asked from beneath the towel.

'The medallion of the golden dragon. Don't you remember? I gave one each to you and Lee when you were little, before you left to attend school in England.'

'I gave it away,' James had said. 'It wasn't important, was it? Besides, the Society of Golden Dragons is long dead, isn't it?'

'Yes, the Dragons are dead,' Richard replied evenly, 'but that medallion was a personal gift from me, to you. I thought you might have valued it . . .'

'The Dragons are dead!' James had ripped the towel from his head, his eyes blazing with clear contempt. 'Just like you!'

'I was simply enquiring about – '

'What in Christ's name's the matter with you, man?' James yelled, but Richard ignored him. 'I asked you a question,' he snapped, angry at the lack of response. 'Mother and I have done everything humanly possible to help you help yourself, Richard. She has offered you directorships. I have offered you a partnership. We have work to do. We have an empire to rebuild. And it could include the resurrection of the society. Don't you understand – '

'And when will you understand?' Richard interrupted sharply, irritation getting the better of him. 'I want no part of your blasted empires or triad societies.'

'You're pathetic!' James sneered. 'What happened to my *Shan Chu*? What happened to the master of the *Gaam Lung Tong*? Where is the dragon that once ruled Hong Kong?'

'Look at me.' Richard struggled onto his crippled leg gripping the balcony rail for support. 'Look at what I've become. I am not the person you knew before the war.'

'You don't need legs, man!' James yelled. 'I'll do any running that needs to be done. All you need is a mind to re-establish a dynasty.' He picked up the book Richard had been writing in and waved it under his nose. 'For God's sake, stop playing childish games. You're not a bloody harbour master, you are *Blue Star*, master of the Society of Golden Dragons.' He threw the book across the balcony and watched in horri-fied fascination as it slid to a stop at Elanora's feet.

'What's going on here?' His mother's voice was as cold as ice.

'What's going on here?' James mimicked her cruelly. 'I'll tell you what's going on here.' He pointed at Richard. 'This pathetic excuse for a man – '

'That will be enough out of you!' Elanora's voice sliced through the air.

'I've just been informed that – '

'That will be enough, I said!' Elanora trembled with rage.

'Very well, Mother,' James replied evenly, 'if you insist.' He drew himself to full height and stared at Richard. 'But I'm done with you, *Sir*,' he sneered. 'I am done with you!'

Richard remembered standing on that balcony gripping the rail, just as he was doing now, only this time the pain in his leg was even worse than it had been then. His gaze drifted down to the Praia Grande below where he caught sight of Elanora and Ah Po buying vegetables from a street vendor and the pain worsened.

龍

Conrad Vaas, concierge of the celebrated Peninsula Hotel, knew only too well the identity of the woman walking across the carpet towards him. She was the Merchant Mistress, a living legend in Hong Kong.

'Good evening, *Merchant tai tai*,' he said as he extended his hand to her. 'Your suite is ready, Madame, as always.'

'Thank you, Conrad,' Elanora smiled as she shook hands with him. Elanora had a permanent booking at the Penin-sula. Situated on the tip of the Kowloon Peninsula at the very centre of Hong Kong, it had seen the famous and infamous pass through its doors during its long and luxurious existence, including the Japanese Army during World War II. The hotel offered the very best of everything, and discretion was its byword.

'I have an important meeting tomorrow morning, so I will dine in my suite and have an early night. I will require a massage at six o'clock. Please make sure that I am not otherwise disturbed.'

'Certainly, Madame, it will be as you wish.'

Elanora took the lift to the fourth floor and entered her suite. She threw her hat on the *chaise longue*, went to the windows and pulled back the curtains to gaze at the island she so loved. As it always did, the sudden panorama of Hong Kong across the harbour, bathed in late afternoon sunlight, took her breath away.

She smiled at the enormous Coca-Cola bottle adorning a ten storey building in Wanchai and the optical illusion it created by appearing to sit on the roof of Fenwick Pier, immediately in front of it. She ran her eyes along the foreshore marvelling at the ever increasing number of massive neon signs atop the ever increasing number of high-rise office buildings. And above the tops of those buildings, even more buildings, high-rise apartments, like silent sentinels watching from the island's Mid-Levels. Then her gaze swept up to Victoria Peak, towering over the city like an ancient pyramid, a temple dedicated to commerce.

Hong Kong had risen from the ashes of World War II as she knew it would. Even Communism in China and the Korean embargo had only slowed its progress temporarily. Construction sites dotted the island, businesses sprouted from every street front and once again the business of money-making reigned supreme. Free trade, the first love of Hong Kong's citizens, was reborn and thriving and it was as if the island knew it. The pearl of the South China Sea glittered and gleamed, preening in anticipation as twilight approached to admire her.

A young woman arrived and commenced setting up a massage table in the main living room. Elanora went into the study that served as her office. She took a number of papers from her briefcase and arranged them tidily on the desk, then went back through the living area to the bedroom.

'*I will not be long,*' she called to the young masseuse.

'*Yes, Mistress,*' the girl replied. She was excited at the prospect of a big tip. The Merchant Mistress was famous for her generosity.

Elanora fell asleep during the massage. The young girl's powerful hands kneaded and rubbed her into a state of euphoria. Her mind wandered drowsily down the corridors of her life, stealing glimpses into rooms and through windows at things long forgotten, until oblivion stole them back.

'*Mistress,*' the girl cooed as she gently shook Elanora's shoulder. '*Mistress, you will please wake up now?*'

'*That was indescribable,*' Elanora murmured and the young girl glowed with pride.

She signed the girl's service book acknowledging payment of the massage and gave her an impressive tip. When she had packed and departed, Elanora poured herself a scotch and soda and did a half hour's work in the study.

Her meal arrived promptly at seven-thirty p.m. She ate slowly, deliberately, enjoying every morsel interspersed with sips of a fine Bordeaux. The food and wine were first class as usual. When she'd finished her repast she bathed, taking her time luxuriating in the marble tub and then spent half an hour brushing her long jet black hair.

Eventually, she went to the wardrobe and chose a beautiful apricot coloured silk dressing gown. She slipped it over her naked body, turned off all the lights and lay on the bed, enjoying the sensuous feel of the silk against her skin.

It was ten o'clock precisely when she heard the key turn in the lock. She took a deep breath and butterflies teased her stomach as she waited. She heard the rattle of ice in a bucket, then a champagne cork popped. Her breathing quickened.

She saw him in silhouette framed by the bedroom doorway in the half light from the lounge room windows, and she watched as he placed the champagne flute on the dresser and began to disrobe. Her heart raced as he crossed to where she lay, and she closed her eyes.

How long their love-making went on Elanora had no idea. She was transported, delirious. She was lost in a tempest of emotions raging across a sexual sea. She heard her voice, crying, pleading, begging, for release. 'Richard,' she cried out, and felt herself tossed upon a sandy shore by waves of pure bliss. Eventually, she felt the warmth of his body against her back and his arms enfolded her. She sighed, content and drifted into a dreamless sleep.

It was after midnight when she awoke. She reached for him but he was not there. She leapt out of bed, threw on her dressing gown and hurried into the living room. He was sitting in the half light on the *chaise longue*, naked, sipping a whisky.

'You called me Richard again.' He patted the space beside him.

'I didn't, did I?' She sat beside him and placed her palm on his thigh. 'I'm sorry, John.'

'It's all right, Missy.' Johnnie Wilson used his pet name for her. 'You can't help who you love.' He sipped his drink and chuckled ruefully. 'Nobody can.'

Their affair had started the previous year. Johnnie had returned to the United States after Korea, but James had invited him to Hong Kong in 1954 and he'd made the Colony his home. He was deeply involved with the Merchant Company, having made himself indispensable to James. He was on the board of directors of the company along with Elanora and several others of the Colony's elite, and he was considered the most eligible bachelor in the Far East. And he was the secret lover of Elanora Merchant Brewster, the Merchant Mistress.

'I love you, too, John,' Elanora replied. 'As much as it is possible for me to love any other man, I love you. Never doubt it.' She took the glass from his hand. 'Let me freshen that up.' She stood and went to the bar.

'But not like you love Richard, eh?'

'We've been through this before,' she answered firmly, as she added whisky to his glass and poured one for herself. 'I cannot give you any more of myself.'

'I know, I know.' Johnnie raised his palms defensively. 'But my problem is I love you, like you love Richard.'

'Well, you shouldn't.' Elanora made a fuss of putting ice cubes in the glasses. 'I will not hurt him, John. He must never know.' She turned, folding her arms across her chest. 'Besides, I'm too old for you. You should find someone your own age and have children.'

'Don't lecture me, Missy,' Johnnie said. 'I'm not your son. I'm your lover, remember?' He stared at her, his expression hardening. 'Say it,' he demanded.

'You are my lover,' she repeated. She knew what was coming. She understood him completely. She knew he truly loved her and that the pain and frustration he suffered because of their illicit affair was tearing him apart. But she could never allow it to become anything else, so she prepared herself to play the game. His game, the game that allowed him to exert sexual control over the woman he loved.

'That's right! I'm the one who screws you and you love it. Don't you?'

'Yes.'

'You worship it, don't you?' He stood up and walked towards her, his arousal already obvious.

'Yes.' Her heart ached for him. He was caught in a one sided love affair and Elanora knew only too well what it was like to suffer unrequited love. She had loved Richard for many years before he had returned it, but they had been of similar age, and time had corrected the imbalance. For Johnnie Wilson there would be no such experience.

Elanora undid the silken cord of her dressing gown and let it part. She knew now she should never have let things go this far.

At first she'd been flattered by his obvious attempts to seduce her; it became a game with them. But Johnnie soon awakened her long dormant physical needs and she had succumbed. Now he had become an addiction to Elanora.

'I came here tonight and played it your way. Now we'll play it mine, Missy.' He moved slowly closer to her. 'Beg me.' He stopped inches in front of her and she felt him hard against her abdomen.

'Please,' she whispered.

'That's not good enough. You know what I want to hear.'

'Fuck me,' she whispered, hating the words he needed to hear as they passed her lips.

'Louder,' he demanded. 'Say it louder.'

'Fuck me!' She despised this game they played, but her addiction was strong. 'Fuck me, Johnnie!' She hissed the words. 'Fuck me! Fuck me! . . . And . . .' Her body ached for him, but her heart couldn't cope with the anguish she saw in his eyes '. . . please don't be angry with me?'

She felt him tense, then his expression softened. He stared at her for a moment then fell to his knees and wrapped his arms about her, burying his face in her abdomen. The game had stopped, she realised. He was crying.

'Angry with you, Elanora?' She felt his wet lips move against her skin. 'I could never be angry with you.' He looked up at her. 'I worship the ground you walk on. If these nights are all you will give me, then I'll take them gladly.'

Tears sprang from her eyes and washed over her cheeks. She looked down at him, then, taking his face in her hands, she sank slowly to the floor, drawing him on top of her.

'*These nights are yours, my lord,*' she whispered in Cantonese. '*These nights are yours.*'

龍

The young man walked out of Kowloon Railway Station and stood motionless, awestruck at the sight that greeted his seventeen-year-old eyes. The junction of Salisbury Road and Nathan Road was a bustling array of motor cars, buses, rickshaws and pedicabs, the brightly painted rickshaws crazily attached to English bicycle frames, pedalled by fearless men. The Peninsula Hotel, directly opposite, was ablaze with lights and next to it, on a small hill, Tsim Sha Tsui Police Station, a beautiful three storey Georgian building, seemed to being standing guard over the peninsula of Kowloon and its citizens.

Across the harbour, glittering in the early evening in all its majesty, sat Hong Kong Island. It was just as his mother had described it. *'One day you will see it, and it will take your breath away, Jet, my son,'* she had said so often. *'It has more lights than the night sky and the Peak soars into the air like a mighty celestial dragon.'*

'Jet,' his father called, interrupting his dreamy state.

'Yes, Sir,' he turned and ran back to his parents and younger sister, Su-lin. *'It is just like you said it would be, Mother.'*

'More lights than the night sky, true or not true?' Lin Li smiled at her son. He was a young adult now and she was so proud of him. The last two months had been hard on them all and Jet had never once complained.

'Jet,' Lee said, pointing at the two hessian sacks that contained the family's entire worldly possessions, *'take one of the bags and cross over to Nathan Road.'* Lee Kwan pointed across the intersection to the main road that bisected Kowloon Peninsula from south to north. *'We must catch a motor bus to Tai Kok Tsui.'*

'Yes, Father,' the boy replied.

'And help your sister across the road. She is tired from the train journey.'

'Yes, Father.' Jet shouldered the hessian sack with ease and took his ten-year-old sister by the hand. *'Come along, Little Sister.'*

They crossed the road and Jet was suddenly lost in a world of magic. He stared into a jeweller's window. Hundreds of gold and silver watches gleamed like a pirate's treasure. He marvelled at the beautiful fabrics and clothing accessories hung in rows along a series of tailors' shops. And he stared in open-mouthed fascination at the beautiful girls gathered at the door of a bar.

He had never seen such beautiful creatures. Their eyes and lips were painted in bright colours and they wore traditional, high collared Chinese dresses, similar to those of the Beijing

Opera stars he had once seen. But these dresses, unlike opera dresses, did not fall to ankle length, these dresses barely reached the knee and they were slit on either side to the hip, leaving little of the female form to his vivid teenage imagination.

'*They are women of ill repute,*' Lee said to his son. '*They consort with men for money.*' He pointed to a bus further up the street. '*Come. That is the transport we must board.*'

Su-lin came to life in the motor bus that carried them up Nathan Road. Both she and Jet stared in wonder at the tall buildings and the brightly dressed shop windows as Lee Kwan pointed out various landmarks.

'*What is that, Baba?*' Su-lin pointed to a strange building on her left.

'*That is a mosque,*' her father answered. '*It is a type of church where Muslims go to pray.*'

'*What is a Muslim?*' Su-lin's curiosity was in overdrive.

'*Do you remember Jun Khan?*' Lin Li asked her daughter.

'*Yes, I do,*' Jet answered automatically, but his mind still lingered on the beautiful girls he had seen. '*Jun Khan, who walked across the roof of the world.*'

'*The giant with the beard,*' Su-lin replied.

'*That's right.*' Lee smiled. '*Well, he is a Muslim. And that is a Catholic church,*' Lee pointed to his right, '*and see, behind it is the Royal Observatory. That is where men study the moon and the stars.*'

As the motor bus travelled north though the intersection of Nathan Road and Gascoigne Road, parkland spread away to their right, dominated by a hill several hundred feet high, and on the left the tall buildings gave way to one and two storey structures, both small business and residential.

'*That is King's Park you're looking across, Su-lin,*' Lin Li said. '*It is a special place reserved for children to run and play in. And that hill is known as Danger Flag Hill because –* '

'*Are these hutongs?*' Jet interrupted, gesturing at the low buildings to their left. '*The lanes are very narrow, like the ones in Little Shanghai.*'

Lee recognised Kwong Wa Hospital as the bus crossed Dundas Street and he urged his family to their feet. *'Be quick,'* he said, pushing them through the passengers towards the front of the vehicle. *'We must get out near the police station at Mong Kok Road.'*

'The police station?' Su-lin asked in a trembling voice. The last three years had left their scars. *'We must not go near a police station, Baba. Mother, you said we should never go near police stations.'*

'Not the police stations in Hong Kong, child,' Lin Li said, trying to calm her. *'Policemen in Hong Kong will not hurt you.'*

They walked in a westerly direction towards the water, down Mong Kok Road to where it became much narrower and its name changed to Anchor Street. Directly in front of them lay the waterfront of Tai Kok Tsui. Its main features were the Cosmopolitan Dock where rich foreigners had their big yachts repaired, and an oil depot. To their left, flat sandy ground ran away for several hundred feet to the Yau Ma Ti typhoon shelter with its huge sea wall, known as the Refuge Boundary.

Unlike a *hutong* in Peking, the laneways of Tai Kok Tsui were all straight, but otherwise it was utterly the same, a squalid mess of single storey buildings built of any material available. It was one of the many tiny suburbs for the poor of Hong Kong and it throbbed with humanity. Just like Little Shanghai in Peking, its tiny lanes were full of stalls selling anything and everything. Hawkers plied their wares, musicians played, chickens cackled, pigs squealed, smells of cooking filled the air and street urchins scampered through the alleys, unchecked by adult control. But there was one striking difference between Tai Kok Tsui and Little Shanghai. Red, white and blue Nationalist flags adorned all of the shop fronts and houses.

Lin Li and Su-lin sat on the low stone wall of Anchor Street that separated the compacted suburb of Tai Kok Tsui from the sandy ground between it and the typhoon shelter. Lee placed the two bags of belongings beside them and stood staring out past the oil storage depot, over the western reaches of the harbour.

'*Do we have or not have somewhere to sleep, Father?*' Jet asked. '*Su-lin is falling asleep, she needs to lie down.*'

'*Soon, Jet,*' Lee replied.

Jet was tired too, but his mind was filled with the sexual creatures in split dresses he had observed in Nathan Road. He sat on the wall gazing into the lanes of the brightly lit little suburb until he realised that several men had gathered at the end of one lane and were staring at his family.

Lee was aware of them too. He watched from the shadows as several more men joined them and a whispered conversation took place. Eventually one of the men began to cross the road in a very cautious manner.

'*Excuse me, traveller,*' the man called from the middle of the street. '*Do you have or not have business in Tai Kok Tsui?*'

'*I have travelled from the northern capital to the far south in search of someone,*' Lee answered, '*a man of strange appearance.*'

'*No two men look exactly alike, stranger, unless they are identical twins, true or not true?*'

'*True,*' Lee replied, '*but if the man I seek is a twin, then his sibling has only one ear.*'

'*I know of a man with three ears, but to my knowledge he has no twin. Could this be the man you seek?*'

'*It sounds like the man I seek,*' Lee said. '*Where can I find him?*'

'*This man is an important man in Tai Kok Tsui,*' the villager replied. '*He does not give audiences readily.*'

'*But you will get him for me, true or not true?*'

'*What makes you think that, stranger?*'

'*Because if you don't, Sergeant Wing,*' Lee stepped out of the shadows, '*I will rip out your heart and feed it to my family.*'

'*Captain Lee Kwan!*' the man exclaimed. '*Is it really you! Aaiiyaaahh!*' he yelled, throwing his arms in the air. He spun on his heels and yelled at the group he'd been whispering with. '*It is Captain Lee Kwan! It is the Dragon of*

Shanghai! Go and find Three Eared Loong. The Dragon commands it!'

Jet, who had been listening to the conversation with growing alarm, could not believe his eyes. The group of men opposite began leaping about and slapping each other on the back. They all ran across the road and surrounded his family and the one who'd been first to talk would not stop shaking his father's hand. Then it was Jet's turn. The men all shook his hand and called him Little Dragon and they patted his mother and half awake sister on the shoulders.

Jet was amazed at the respectful attention his father commanded as even more people arrived to stare and smile at him, but he was even more amazed by the appearance of a fat man who was running up Anchor Street towards them. The fellow had two ears on one side of his head. Jet watched dumbfounded as the crowd parted and the fat man fell to his knees, puffing and panting in front of his father.

'*Captain, Sir, Elder Brother!'* the man gasped. '*We heard rumours. We heard bad stories. Some said you were dead, some told us you were disgraced and your heart was broken. Of course, I did not believe it but –* '

'*Master Sergeant Loong,'* Jet heard his father say. '*Get off your knees at once! That is no way for a soldier of China to behave.'* A voice of authority cracked through the still night air. It sounded nothing like his father's voice.

'*Yes, Sir!'* Loong said and Jet watched him scramble to his feet, stand at attention and stare his father in the eye.

'*I am neither dead, disgraced, nor broken hearted!'*

'*Yes, Sir!'* Loong's head snapped back at the force of his own reply.

'*I need food and lodging for my family.'*

'*Yes, Captain. A room awaits you. Three rooms, in fact, a small house,'* Three Eared Loong replied. The poor man had been born with a full flap and lobe of a third ear on the left side of his head and he tugged at it nervously and gestured vaguely behind him in the direction of the village. '*Since word first filtered through that you were heading for Hong Kong I have not been idle.'*

'Good.' Lee nodded. 'Do you still have or not have something else in your possession, something that belongs to me?'

'I have, Captain.'

'Excellent.' Lee nodded. 'You have done well, Loong. We will take care of business tomorrow, but now, my wife and children need sleep.'

'If you will follow me,' Loong bowed. 'I will show you to your house.'

It was hardly a house by Merchant family standards, but to Lee it was more than adequate. Set in the middle of a narrow street between a laundry and a tiny herbalist's shop, it consisted of a living room, which one entered directly off the street, and a kitchen, which led into a small walled backyard. A rickety set of stairs led up to a tiny bedroom.

Lin Li was delighted with the little house. It was clean and tidy, with a slight smell of jasmine, and she was overcome at the sight of several baskets of food, including fresh vegetables, which the family had not eaten in months. She immediately set about cooking.

By the time they'd eaten and sat around chatting avidly like children in a dormitory it was ten o'clock. Jet and Su-lin were soon comfortably asleep on the living room floor and Lin Li lay on a straw mattress upstairs with Lee asleep beside her. She listened to the lively night sounds of the little suburb, and in a half dream, saw herself in a small boat, drifting idly into a sheltered harbour after an eternity on an ocean of terrible storms.

Her storms had started in the autumn of 1953, almost three years ago to the day, when Lee had returned from Korea.

龍

No sooner had the war ended than the Communist Party began its purge of the military. Lee had predicted as much and he was the first to be accused. Along with several other high ranking soldiers and a number of Peking intellectuals he'd been taken to Tiananmen Square and publicly ridiculed. Stripped to the waist, hands tied behind his back and forced to wear a sign around his neck declaring him an enemy of the people, he'd been stoned with rotten eggs and vegetables while his alleged crimes had been announced over a public address system.

Lin Li had watched his humiliation and had never loved him more. He wore the insults and injury with silent dignity and serenity worthy of Buddha himself, aware that his children were in a Communist boarding school and any retaliation on his part would endanger them. House arrest had followed, which included the children being banished from the Ba-yi School, and then, to make matters worse, Lin Li's father had turned up in Peking.

Lin Li had not seen or even heard from him for fifteen years, not since the night the very young Captain Lee Kwan, then on his way to defend Nanking from the Japanese, had walked into her father's tavern in Suchow. Her father had told her to attach herself to Lee Kwan, who appeared to be a well educated young officer and potential husband, or face death in the freezing winter snow because she was a 'useless mouth' and he would no longer care for her. Lee had arranged work for her at the hospital in Nanking and she'd tasted freedom and independence for the first time in her life. But the Japanese invasion of the city had destroyed all that. She'd been raped by Japanese soldiers in the courtyard of the hospital and that was where Lee had discovered her, lying at the bottom of a pile of dead nurses. He'd nursed her back to health and, a year later, had married her.

When Lin Li's father turned up on their doorstep, Lee, in true Chinese fashion, had insisted the old man be taken into their family home and cared for, but it wasn't long before the old fool was bragging around Peking of his famous son-in-law and boasting of how he'd once owned a tavern in Suchow. It was all the Party spies had needed. Her father had been publicly condemned as a landlord and executed, then Lin Li herself had been forced to admit publicly that she had shared in her father's wealth. Jet and Su-lin had been taken from them and put into foster homes and Lee and Lin Li had been banished to a labour camp. Two and a half years of hell had followed.

They were sent to a tiny village high in the windswept mountains of Shansi Province, about four hundred miles southwest of Peking. Forced to live in a cave, they had toiled twelve hours a day trying to grow crops in a place where constant northwesterly winds had long ago removed any top soil that might support growth. They lived on maize and sorghum which Lin Li made into thin soups, and if it had not been for the generosity of several villagers they would have starved. Their children were allowed visits only during school holidays and it took two years before Lee could finally plot their escape.

Six months earlier they had been allowed to move into a small hut and, when the children had arrived for a brief visit, Lee had faked a catastrophe. He had dug up a recently buried family of four and set fire to them in the hut. They had watched the blaze from a distant hill and prayed for the souls of that family until only ashes remained, then they'd set off to walk a thousand miles to Hong Kong.

龍

Lin Li rolled over and cuddled up to her husband's back. She placed her palm on his stomach and stroked his skin until he awoke. They made love, tenderly, silently, as a cacophony of suburban Hong Kong sounds drifted through the window of their new home.

The following morning, Lee Kwan arose at six o'clock refreshed after the first, decent night of sleep he'd had in a long time. He left Lin Li sleeping, roused his children and together they went into the small courtyard behind their tiny house and practised *Shaolin* exercises and disciplines for two hours.

The family had been on the run for two months and, apart from snatched moments of meditation, they had been unable to practise the arts of *Shaolin*. Even Lee, who had practised them since he was six years old, found the disciplines demanding after the long lay-off. He took it slowly and insisted the children do likewise, but he made sure the full practice session was completed before they went in to breakfast.

They sat together in the small front room and Lin Li delighted in the relish with which Jet and Su-lin ate. Good food had been a rare commodity in their lives over the last two years, but now there was plenty and they wasted no time in clearing their full plates with gusto. Lee watched them eat too. Finally neither could eat any more and they both sat back with contentment written all over their faces.

'Now that we are finally here in Hong Kong,' Lee said, 'we will speak only English when we are together in our new house. Is that understood?' The children nodded. 'For you to succeed in this city your English must be perfect so we will practise it at all times. And I will re-establish your regular *Shaolin* training sessions beginning next week, but for the next few days I will allow you some extra free time.'

'Thank you, Father,' Jet and Su-lin chorused in English.

'I realise you are anxious to explore, but I want you both to remember what I say now. Hong Kong is a big city with much vice, and much of that vice is to be found in Kowloon, so I expect you to be watchful at all times.'

'Yes, Father.'

Lee was not concerned about them being molested. He'd trained them well since they were babies and the very thought of anyone attempting to assault them actually made him smile. Jet was competent in the physical arts of *Shaolin*, but Su-lin's skills were extraordinary for a ten-year-old. In fact Su-lin was so good that Lee had often engaged her in extra practice sessions simply to watch her move; she had such grace and style, and the ferocity she displayed reminded him of a tiger. Su-lin would bare her teeth, and with fire blazing in her eyes strike at him with the speed of a snake. With all due respect for Jet, who struggled to be a good disciple, Su-lin was without doubt the finest student Lee had ever had the privilege of training.

Lee had no concerns for their physical safety, but he had to ensure that they stayed close to home for other reasons. He wanted anonymity not only for himself, but for the children as well. Tai Kok Tsui was a village made up entirely of expatriate Shangtung families from the cities of Shanghai and Nanking and they were Nationalists to the core. Hong Kong was a microcosm of China's Civil War and as far as its Chinese citizens were concerned, the matter had yet to be resolved. The city was evenly divided between Nationalist sympathisers and Communists and Lee was determined not to become involved with either. The politics of China no longer interested him.

'When you are out in the streets, you will never discuss your family name and never identify yourselves with me. Is that understood?'

'But why, Father?' Jet did not like what he was hearing. 'You are famous. I saw people who greeted you last night, they were – '

'That is exactly why, Jet,' Lin Li interrupted.

'The less people know about us outside this small suburb the better,' Lee continued. 'As far as the Government of China is concerned, we no longer exist, and here in Tai Kok Tsui the people will deny our existence to any who may ask. We are safe here.'

'But Father – ' Jet began to protest.

'Jet!' Lee's voice brooked no defiance. 'I have been a soldier of China since I was seventeen, first for the Nationalists and then for the Communists. In all that time I have known nothing but war and misery. We are going to live as a family in Tai Kok Tsui where I will find work and you and your sister will go to school and have a normal life.'

'Yes, Father,' Jet mumbled.

'You and Su-lin clean up the breakfast table,' Lin Li said, 'and then you can both go exploring.'

Three Eared Loong arrived huffing and puffing not long after the children had left. He knocked on the open door of the tiny house in the narrow laneway known as Elm Street and waited patiently to be summoned. He placed the locked satchel he'd been carrying on the ground and put his foot on it. It was the property of Captain Lee Kwan and he had no intention of losing it now, not after having been its guardian for the last three years.

'*Come in, Sergeant Loong.*' He complied instantly. '*Have you eaten or not eaten rice yet?*' Lee asked as he entered. It was a common form of greeting in Cantonese based on the fact that if one has eaten breakfast then presumably one is well.

'*Eaten. Thank you, Elder Brother,*' Loong replied. He bowed politely.

'*Then have a cup of jasmine tea.*' Lee poured two cups from a teapot. '*My wife made it before she left for the market, it is still quite hot. And sit down, Ah Loong,*' he said. '*You look tired. Have you been running?*'

'*Yes, Captain,*' the man replied and sat gratefully on a chair at the table.

'*I wish to say a big thank you for your efforts. This small house is perfect for me and my family and you even supplied food. I am grateful.*'

'*It is not necessary to say thank you, Captain.*' Loong sipped at his tea. He had always been nervous in the presence of Lee Kwan. He had not seen him since the Battle of Shanghai nearly twenty years previously, but still his mere presence unnerved him. '*Half of the people in Tai Kok Tsui would not be alive if it were not for the help and protection you gave to their families in Shanghai and Nanking. You saved many lives, Captain, and they will never forget you.*'

'*How do they feel about me being a grasshopper?*' Lee looked at the stocky man over the rim of his teacup.

'*The opinion of most is that you did what you thought was best for China, Elder Brother,*' Loong replied. '*It has been a topic of discussion on many occasions, Captain. Many in this village believe Ch'iang Kai-shek deserted Nanking in its hour of need and even though they remain loyal to the Nationalist cause, they will never forgive him for it. And they believe that is the reason you offered your allegiance to the Communists.*'

'*That is partly true.*' Lee nodded and sipped his tea.

'*But they are also saying that, now you have been humiliated by Mao Tse-tung and his regime, you will return your support to the Nationalist cause.*'

'*There is no Nationalist cause,*' Lee said firmly. '*General*

Ch'iang and his army will remain on the island of Taiwan until they rot. They will never retake China. It is a fool's dream.'

Three Eared Loong was shocked by the statement and began tugging nervously at the lobe of his third ear. He had been dreading this conversation, but many in the suburb of Tai Kok Tsui wanted to know the intentions of the Dragon of Shanghai and, as village spokesman, he was expected to find out.

'With respect, Sir,' Loong said deferentially, *'many of the population of Hong Kong are Nationalists and like the people of Taiwan they believe General Ch'iang will re-establish his army on the Mainland and will – '*

'Two tigers cannot live on one mountain, Ah Loong,' Lee interrupted, *'true or not true?'*

'True, Elder Brother, but we believe General Chi'ang will defeat Mao.'

'Victory depends upon the support of the people and Mao has their support.'

'But how can that be true, Captain?' Loong was beginning to feel miserable, he was being dragged into the argument he had been dreading. *'The Communists killed millions of innocent people – '*

'So did the Nationalists!' Lee was exasperated. *'Between them and the Communists they killed half the population of China in thirty years!'*

'Ah, Elder Brother,' Loong spoke softly, *'you are educated and I must bow to your knowledge of history.'*

'When will people finally realise the Civil War was fought and won seven years ago? It is over, Ah Loong. China was torn to pieces for forty years, but now at least it has a single form of government. Whether that government is Communist or Nationalist doesn't matter. What the people of China need is peace to survive and prosper, understand or not understand?'

'Forgive my ignorance, Captain Kwan, I do not know enough to discuss the matter and neither do the people of this village. They all fought for what they were told was right and

they have personal histories and harbour old wounds that will not heal. And some who heard you were coming to Hong Kong believed you would feel the same way and support them.'

'What would they say if I told them I had no intention of supporting anyone, neither Communist nor Nationalist?' Lee placed his cup on the table.

'You saved many lives, Sir,' Loong replied lamely.

'That is not an answer to my question,' Lee said. He poured himself more tea and waved the pot at Loong who placed his cup beneath the spout.

'Those of us in the village who fought with you in Shanghai would understand your decision,' Loong replied cautiously as he watched the Captain pour him tea. *'And those who knew you in Nanking and remember your kind acts would support you, but . . .'* Loong paused searching for words.

'But what?' Lee placed the teapot on the table and looked at his old compatriot.

'It's the younger generation, Captain, those who were not involved in the wars. They have adopted the cause of Nationalism and truly believe that a new era is beginning right now – an era in which they will rise up against the Communists here in Hong Kong and then join with General Ch'iang's army and overthrow the rulers in Peking.'

'That's madness.'

'It is to you and me, Captain, and to any other man who experienced the bloodshed of the Civil War, but I am talking about young fanatics. Their goal is not only to rise up against the local Communists, but it includes overthrowing the British and using Hong Kong as a foothold for Ch'iang's army on the Mainland of China.'

'By all the gods!' Lee exclaimed. *'Do they know or not know what the Communist Party of China will do if they try it?'*

'They do not know.' Loong shook his head. *'And they cannot be told.'*

'The PLA will have fifty divisions on the Shum Chun River

before the world can count to ten, and when they invade Hong Kong it won't matter what flag people wave at them, they'll slaughter anyone standing in their path, including the British. These young hotheads you speak of are crazy to even consider such action.'

'I agree, Captain, but words on the wind say that this will happen very soon.'

'How soon?' Lee felt a chill of apprehension. The phrase, 'words on the wind', was a triad phrase and that could mean only trouble.

'Do you know what today is?'

'I have been on the run for weeks, Ah Loong. I don't even know what month it is.'

'You have arrived in Hong Kong on a most auspicious day, Elder Brother. Today is the tenth day of the tenth month in the foreign calendar.'

'Ten Ten Day,' Lee muttered, in English, 'I should have known.' He slapped the palm of his hand against his forehead as he suddenly realised the significance of all the Nationalist flags decorating the village. The tenth of October 1956 would mark the forty-fifth anniversary of the uprising that overthrew the Ch'ing Dynasty and the last Emperor. It was the biggest day of celebration in the Nationalist calendar.

'I do not know what is planned, Elder Brother.' Loong shook his head. *'But I heard that perhaps there is a plan to create civil disorder, and the Green Pang have been hired to cause trouble for the British.'*

'The Green Pang.' Lee nodded. He knew of the Green Pang, a triad society also known as the Shanghai Greens. Most of them had been slaughtered by the Communists after their victory in Shanghai and the remaining rabble had made their way to Hong Kong.

'They have grown powerful again since the old days in Shanghai,' Loong said. *'The Green Pang and the Fourteen-K are the most powerful societies in Hong Kong.'*

'The Fourteen-K?' Lee asked. *'I've never heard of them.'*

'They started after the Japanese left. They named themselves after the weight of gold – you know, fourteen carat.'

'Will they be involved?'

'I do not know, Elder Brother.' Loong shook his head. 'As you wisely said, two tigers cannot live on one mountain and it is true, because the Green Pang and Fourteen-K are always fighting against each other, but who can tell? I know the loyalty of the Green Pang will be paid for. Perhaps the loyalty of the Fourteen-K will be purchased, too.'

'Well, I don't care, Sergeant Loong. I want no part of it. They can do what they like as long as it doesn't concern me.'

'Yes, Sir.' Loong was feeling decidedly ill. 'But Captain, news of your arrival spread like wildfire across Kowloon last night.'

'Your face has gone as white as a funeral dress,' Lee said. 'What are you trying to say?'

'You are known as the Dragon of Shanghai, Captain,' Loong began to sweat, 'and the Angel of Nanking. And because of the stories told by those of us who knew you during the wars, you are a living legend to the young Nationalist fanatics and . . .' Loong faltered, appalled by the expression on Lee Kwan's face.

Lee put his cup on the table and held his head in his hands. 'Go on, Sergeant. What do they want?'

'They believe that you have returned to the Nationalist cause and will want to seek revenge for your humiliation by the Communists . . .'

'No.' Lee groaned.

'. . . and,' Loong rushed to finish, 'your arrival on such an auspicious day is an omen from the gods and they want you to lead them in their glorious endeavour.'

Lee stood up and took the teapot and cups into the kitchen. He leaned on the tiny bench and stared at his reflection in the bowl of water Lin Li had used to clean vegetables. The face he looked at seemed not his own, it was gaunt and weary like an old man's. Will I ever escape the clutches of war? he asked himself. Am I destined to be forever surrounded by conflict and hostility?

When he was only eighteen he'd faked his own death to escape the Nationalists, but, for the sake of his wife and unborn child, had been forced to reveal his lie. Then only recently he'd done the same thing to the Communist Party in order to escape from China, only to now find himself facing another confrontation that would lead to his exposure.

'All you can do is run again,' he whispered softly to his reflected face, 'and you'd better do it quickly.'

'*Are you all right, Captain?*' Loong called from the other room.

'Yes,' Lee replied as he entered. '*I want you to tell the Green Pang, or whoever it is that expects my services, that I'm not interested.*'

'Yes, Sir.' Loong nodded, rising from his seat. '*But they won't like it, Captain.*'

'*Then you will explain to them that it would not be wise to incur the wrath of the Dragon of Shanghai.*' Loong shivered at the ominous tone of Lee's voice. It was the last thing he wanted to incur himself. '*Tell them that if my name is even mentioned in connection with any event they may be considering, I will seek them out one by one and put them to death, understand or not understand, Sergeant?*'

'I understand completely, Sir,' the old soldier answered. He had seen the wrath of Lee Kwan before and wanted no part of it. '*They will hear of your desire within the hour, Captain.*'

'*Just a moment,*' Lee said as Three Eared Loong turned to go. '*Do you have or not have something for me?*'

Three Eared Loong's face drained of all colour. '*Aaaaii-iyaaahh!*' He practically dived out the front door and fell upon the locked satchel still sitting on the ground where he'd placed it.

'*What's the matter with you?*' Lee stood in the doorway looking down on the stocky old man clutching a locked satchel in his arms. '*Have demons entered your mind?*'

'*I'm sorry, Captain Kwan!*' was all the terrified man could say as he stood and handed the satchel to Lee.

'*Do you know what this satchel contains, Sergeant?*' Lee reached beneath his shirt and took a leather necklace from around his neck from which dangled an old black key.

'No, Sir!' Loong barked. 'And please don't tell me. It has remained locked since you sent it to me. I have guarded it with my life.'

'Until ten minutes ago, Sergeant, when you left it in the street outside my door, true or not true?'

'True, Sir. I am sorry.'

'It is good that you are sorry.'

'Thank you, Sir.'

'Now go and deliver my message.'

'Yes, Sir.' the old soldier snapped to attention then took off down the lane.

Lee returned to the table, unlocked the satchel, lifted the flap and took out a steel box, using the same key to unlock it. Inside the box, as good as new, sat twenty-five thousand dollars in United States bank notes. He sat staring at it for several minutes then put his mind to the problem that now confronted him. For the next hour he concentrated, working out the plan for what he hoped would be his final move.

'Husband,' Lin Li gasped from the open doorway. 'Where did you get that?' She dropped her meagre bag of shopping on the floor and moved to sit down, her face already grey with worry. She stared, mesmerised by the notes in the steel box. 'It is a fortune. Where did you get it?'

'I cannot tell you, wife,' Lee answered. 'It is not stolen and I earned it, but how I earned it is a secret that must remain with me.'

'Then that is how it must be, husband,' Lin Li nodded, 'but just assure me of one thing.'

'What is it?'

'This money has nothing to do with what is happening in Sham Shui Po, does it?'

'What is happening in Sham Shui Po?' Lee's voice was tinged with concern. The large suburb of Sham Shui Po was immediately north of Tai Kok Tsui, barely half a mile away.

'Everybody is talking about it,' Lin Lui replied. 'There is trouble in Block G of Li Cheng Uk resettlement estate, trouble between the Nationalists and the Communists.

A Government official, a Resettlement Officer I think, pulled down some Kuomintang propaganda posters that were stuck on the outside of the concrete verandahs, and some Nationalists didn't like it.'

'Is that all?' Lee's anxiety began to evaporate.

'No,' Lin Li shook her head. *'That was only the start of it. I was just told the Resettlement Estate Office is surrounded by rioters and they've set fire to it.'*

'Guard this. It contains our future,' Lee said. He closed the steel box and pushed it across the table to Lin Li. *'I must find the children.'*

'What is wrong?' she cried, grabbing him by the arm. *'Is it anything to do with this money?'*

'It has nothing to do with the money, but we are in danger and must leave Tai Kok Tsui.'

'Father!' They both turned to the distressed call and saw Jet standing in the doorway with blood streaming down his face.

'What has happened?' Lee demanded as Lin Li screamed.

'Some men have taken Su-lin!'

CHAPTER EIGHT

News of the kidnapping of Kwan Su-lin had spread like wildfire in Tai Kok Tsui. Some of the older people in the suburb knew of Lee Kwan's connection to the House of Merchant and to them, the kidnapping of anyone and especially a child, with ties to the Noble House was an act of sheer stupidity. It was folly enough to anger the Dragon of Shanghai, people whispered, but to invite the wrath of his entire house was more than stupid, it was suicidal.

The villagers learned what had happened after hearing Lin Li's screams. It was bad *joss*, they all agreed as they gathered outside the doorway of Lee's house to offer their help and learn more of the crime.

Joss roughly translated meant luck or fortune, good or bad, but it had a much wider connotation to the Hong Kong Chinese. In a philosophical sense, it related vaguely to the idea of cause and effect and could be the prediction, result, or even simply the name given to any set of circumstances, ranging from gambling to birth and death. But whatever its meaning, to the villagers of Tai Kok Tsui, the circumstances of Kwan Su-lin's disappearance was *joss*, and it was very, very bad *joss*.

'*Someone will have their testicles removed over this,*' one villager proclaimed solemnly from within the group of thirty or forty people gathered outside the little house in Elm Street.

'*And they'll be placed in an urn and returned to his place of birth,*' another added and those about him nodded earnestly. It was bad *joss*, they all agreed, *fucking bad joss*.

The Cantonese were a gregarious people and quick to offer opinions, therefore any remarks made aloud in Hong Kong invariably led to public debate and the statements regarding testicles proved no exception to the rule. One woman had said that her husband had one testicle removed and it had changed his whole outlook on life. Another declared that she'd seen a pair of testicles delivered to her grandfather although they'd not been his own. And a third citizen, an old man, had said that people in the far-west of China considered human testicles a delicacy, but that was to be expected because the people of the far-west, not having been born near the Yellow River, were barbarians.

As the debate raged outside, a doctor inside the little house gave Lin Li a sedative, then began putting stitches in Jet's forehead.

Meanwhile, Lee organised several groups into search parties. He sought, for group leaders, the men of his old command, those who had greeted him the previous night. They had seen Su-lin and would be able to recognise her. Then, when the groups of villagers had moved off to search for the child, Lee turned his attention to Three Eared Loong who had not been allocated a group.

'*I want to talk to you.*' Lee pointed directly at the terrified man. '*Go out into the backyard and wait for me.*'

When the man had gone, Jet and Lin Li watched in horror as Lee took a carving knife from the kitchen and moved towards the back door.

'*What are you going to do?*' Lin Li recognised the expression on Lee's face. She had not seen it often in all the years they had been married and it frightened her.

'*I'm going to get my daughter back,*' Lee replied without looking around.

'*Forgive me, Elder Brother,*' Three Eared Loong wailed as he saw Lee emerge from the house, knife in hand. '*I know nothing of this terrible deed.*'

Lee grabbed him by the throat and, with a vicious flick of the knife, corrected Loong's birth deformity. The man barely had time to see the flap and lobe that was his third ear fall into the dust when Lee struck again. The knife embedded itself an inch into Loong's stomach and remained there.

'*You have dared to disturb a dragon.*' Lee's face loomed in front of the man's tear-filled eyes. '*You'd better tell it what it wants to know, or your agony will be indescribable.*'

'*It was the Green Pang, Captain,*' the man wailed, then screamed as Lee turned the knife blade ninety degrees.

'*That is a lie. The men of the Green Pang are merely drones. They work for someone, or a committee perhaps, a committee of young Nationalists, true or not true?*'

'*True, Captain.*'

'*Tell me their names.*'

'*The Green Pang will kill me.*'

'*No one will kill you, Loong. As of this moment you belong to me, the Dragon of Shanghai, remember?*' Lee licked the man's cheek lasciviously dribbling saliva. '*You taste good, Loong.*' Lee made a hissing noise through his teeth. '*Tonight I will dine of your flesh.*' Loong's eyes flared in horror, then he screamed again as the knife turned another ninety degrees.

'*I swear it, Captain Kwan! I do not know their names. The Green Pang approached me last night with orders from the Brotherhood of Warriors –*'

'*Are they the ones who kidnapped my daughter?*'

'*Yes, Captain, Sir. It would have been them, because you refused to join them. They sent me orders to inform you that they expected you to –*'

'*Expected?*' Lee snapped.

'*Yes, Sir, they are arrogant young men, they do not know you as I do.*'

'*Go on.*'

'*They believed you would lead them today. I tried to tell the men of the Green Pang that you would not, but they just laughed and told me to deliver the message to you. I tried to tell you this morning, Sir, but when I saw your face, I had no heart for it and could not explain properly. I was frightened.*'

Lee stared into the man's eyes. '*I believe you,*' he said and withdrew the knife. '*Sit.*' He let go of Loong's throat and watched as he slumped weeping to the ground.

'*Forgive me, Captain –* ' the man began.

'*I said sit!*' Lee roared.

The fat soldier began crying like a child as he struggled onto his haunches holding his bleeding stomach. '*Forgive me,*' he whimpered, his eyes following Lee, who was slowly circling him.

'*You will listen, Two Ears Loong,*' Lee spoke softly as if to a small child, '*and you will obey. You will seek out a member of the Green Pang and tell him to inform the Brotherhood of Warriors that the Dragon of Shanghai wants his child back immediately. There will be no compromise. If they do not return my child unharmed, they will all die.*'

'*Yes, Sir,*' Loong whimpered. The pain, in his gut especially, was excruciating.

'*If you find out the identity of any of this Brotherhood,*' Lee sneered the word, '*you will return and tell me immediately. If you do not, you will not be at fault. I know you will have done your best.*'

'*Thank you, Sir.*'

'*Jet,*' Lee said softly. He knew his son and wife had been watching from the back door, but there was no answer.

Jet was stunned by the violence he'd witnessed. He would never have believed his father was capable of treating anyone like that had he not witnessed it with his own eyes.

'*Lin Li?*'

'*Yes, husband.*'

'*Is the doctor still here?*'

'*Yes.*'

'*Tell him to come out here and sew up the Sergeant's gut.*'

After six years the walls of the dams that contained Hong Kong's two rival political factions had finally burst and their vitriolic waters had flooded through the streets of Sham Shui Po, sparing no one.

龍

Jeremy Bent knew practically nothing about the recent political history of China. He'd heard of the Nationalist, Generalissimo Ch'iang Kai-shek – how could one forget a grandiose name like that – and the Communist Chairman, Mao Tse-tung – his name was mentioned by someone every ten minutes. He also knew the Left had won a civil war and the Right had run off to the island of Taiwan, but that was about the extent of his knowledge and he was currently wishing he knew a little more.

Recently arrived in Hong Kong, Jeremy was on his first official patrol as a newly appointed Inspector in the Hong Kong Police Force. The Land Rover he was travelling in pulled up outside Li Cheng Uk Resettlement Estate in Sham Shui Po and, as he got out and looked up at the sixth floor of Block G, his hand reflexively reached to caress the lucky necklace he wore tucked under his collar.

The Station Sergeant at Sham Shui Po had received a telephoned report from a Government official who said he was being threatened, and from what Jeremy could see the caller had not exaggerated his situation. Angry people packed the sixth floor balconies, all waving Nationalist flags and making a lot of noise, and an even nastier mob was surrounding the Resettlement Estate office, a squat building directly in front of him.

Jeremy followed his Patrol Sergeant and two Police Constables as they walked across the road. The PCs forced their way through the noisy crowd to find the windows of the office had all been smashed and several angry citizens were trying to drag a screaming official out through the window.

'Well, we'd better put a stop to that for a start, Sergeant,' Jeremy ordered ten seconds too late.

The Sergeant had already decided on a course of action, and as Jeremy spoke, he whacked one of the crowd on the head with his baton. His two PCs did likewise to a round of general abuse from the crowd, which became decidedly uglier.

'All right! All right!' Jeremy used English which was entirely useless given the fact that he was surrounded by more than a hundred screaming Chinese, but the Cantonese he'd learned in the Police Training School had deserted him.

The crowd surged forward pressing him against a wall and

he was suddenly very concerned for his welfare. He drew his service revolver and fired a shot in the air. The effect was instantaneous, the crowd fell back several feet and the sudden silence crashed against his eardrums.

'*Dang yat jang,*' he yelled, suddenly remembering the phrase for wait one minute.

'*Ho ho, Dai Loh.* Very good, Elder Brother,' his Sergeant congratulated him, 'but please not to use da' gun again,' he continued in halting English, 'I fink we shou' go away from he'ah, very soon. How you fink abou' dat, Ah Sir?'

'I think we will get to the bottom of this problem . . .'

'I fink you are coll'ect, Ah Sir,' the Sergeant said nervously.

'Good.'

'I fink we will be unda' neaf dis plo'blem,' he pointed at the crowd, 'very soon, *Dai Loh.* So we take dis man,' he indicated the official, 'and go.'

'*That snot-eating licker of Government arseholes,*' a man in the crowd yelled, '*pulled down our Ten Ten Day signs.*'

'*That is true,*' another yelled, and then the whole crowd joined in.

'*It is illegal to paste posters on Government property,*' the official retaliated.

'*Shut your cunt kissing mouth,*' the nervous Sergeant yelled at the official.

'*He's a shit eating Communist,*' another called. '*He should be made to set off a string of fire-crackers to mark his regret at defacing the Kuomintang flag.*'

Jeremy had had enough. Never had the expression 'discretion is the better part of valour' held more meaning for him. 'Let's go,' he yelled to his men, 'and bring him with you.' He pointed at the bleeding official the two PCs were now supporting. Jeremy and his Sergeant literally kicked and fought a way through the crowd, then all four policemen and the terrified official got into the Land Rover and made a hasty retreat.

As the vehicle moved off, chased by sixty or more screaming rioters, for that's what they'd become in Jeremy's opinion, he saw a fire break out in the Resettlement office and, in the second before they turned the corner, he noticed flames flaring from the windows.

Several minutes later, when his Land Rover pulled into the compound of Sham Shui Po Police Station, he leapt out and explained the situation to his Chief Inspector.

'It doesn't sound good,' was his boss's reply, which, Jeremy often remarked in later years, turned out to be the understatement of the decade.

龍

By dusk an air of uneasy calm had fallen over Kowloon. Lee Kwan's search parties had returned to Tai Kok Tsui, unable to find any trace of Su-lin, but with them they brought tales from Sham Shui Po of Nationalist-inspired rioting and looting. They were unanimous in their opinion that the civil unrest had only just started and it would be worse by nightfall.

Lee's feelings of inadequacy gained momentum as he sat despondently in his living room with Jet and Lin Li. He had walked the streets of Mong Kok and Sham Shui Po searching in vain for his daughter, knowing all the while the futility of his efforts. She would be alive, he didn't doubt it, but he knew she would be imprisoned somewhere to be used as a bargaining tool. The thought that she might be injured was fuelling his fury to the point where his mind refused to think clearly.

Two Ears Loong, as the villagers of Tai Kok Tsui were already calling him, stood in Lee's living room with bandages wrapped round his head and abdomen.

'Well?' Lee snapped at the old Sergeant.

'I have not been approached all day, Captain,' the wounded man replied. 'I have remained at my house awaiting a reply from the Brotherhood, but they have obviously deemed your warning to be unimportant.'

'The Brotherhood?' Lin Li asked.

'The group of young Nationalist fanatics who have kidnapped Su-lin,' Lee replied.

'Who are they?' she asked quickly. 'Where do they live?'

Lee's fist smashed the table top as he replied. *'If I knew that, do you think or not think I would be sitting here like an impotent fool?'*

'It is not necessary to speak to Mother that way,' Jet said, shocked at his father's reaction.

'Do not speak!' Lee's eyes blazed with fury. *'This situation is your fault. You were responsible for your sister's welfare,'* he shouted, leaping to his feet. *'It is your fault she was kidnapped!'*

'That is not true!' Lin Li protested angrily. *'Jet was hit from behind and knocked unconscious. He is lucky to be alive.'*

The sound of Lin Li's raised voice stunned Lee. In all their years together she had rarely spoken in anger. He sat down, breathing heavily, and stared at them both as the rage slowly drained from his system.

'I am sorry, my son,' he said. *'What I said was not true. It was the raving of an angry man fearful for his child's welfare. None of this matter is your fault.'*

Jet nodded in understanding, but tears welled in his young eyes as the three sat in unhappy silence for several minutes.

'Anger is not your way, husband,' his wife said when she was satisfied Lee had calmed down. She spoke softly hoping her tone would restore his equilibrium. *'It is not the way of Shaolin.'*

'My concern for our daughter is clouding my brain, wife.' Lee's eyes conveyed an apology for his outburst.

'I understand,' she nodded. *'Completely,'* she added. *'I also understand that the way of Shaolin is the way of Su-lin's salvation, true or not true? And are you or are you not a master of Shaolin?'*

'That is true,' Lee replied and smiled contritely. *'And a master of stupidity, it would seem also.'*

'Not also,' she shook her head and reached for his hand. *'You lost your way momentarily,'* she whispered, *'but now it has returned, true or not true?'*

'True.' Lee stood up suddenly. *'And I know what I must do.'*

龍

Ekatarina Popova found herself alone for the first time in the Chairman's office, with her buttocks squashed against his desk, his hand up her dress and both of hers pushing gently against his chest.

'It's your soft husky Russky accent that excites me,' James whispered into her hair, 'even more than your formidable beauty.'

'Pleese, Meester Merchant,' she murmured, 'Meester Veelson vill be back very soon.'

'Keep talking. Your accent is driving me mad with desire,' James breathed onto her neck. 'And don't worry about "Meester Veelson",' he mimicked, 'I've sent him to fetch a file that is already on my desk. He'll be hours yet.'

'But other people from the cocktail party could walk in, James.' She pronounced his name 'Jemms' and she spoke in a tone she hoped would not offend him.

'No one would dare,' he muttered. 'I'd sack them on the spot.'

Like you will sack me if I resist your advances, Katya thought.

Ekatarina Popova was a prostitute. At least she had been until that very morning. Katya was born in 1926, the only child of wealthy White Russian parents in the city of Shanghai. Her family had lived in a beautiful Georgian mansion on The Bund, the wide boulevard that graced Shanghai's waterfront, similar to the Praia Grande in Macau, only much bigger. She'd had a good private education, but when the Japanese had invaded China in 1937, Shanghai had been the first city to fall and over the next few years, so had Katya.

The beautiful Russian girl had been orphaned and was penniless in 1944 and fallen on hard times that led her into a life of high class prostitution, and eventually to the city of Hong Kong and a fateful meeting with an American, through whom she had, that very morning, secured a job with the famous Merchant Company.

Katya had seduced Johnnie Wilson during a series of

arranged liaisons in expensive hotels. She had been searching for just such a man and considered herself lucky to have found him before the bloom of youth eluded her. She had impressed him, not only with her knowledge of the bedroom, but of the boardroom as well. Katya had inherited her father's business sense and was multilingual, a valuable asset in Asia. She soon found herself spending more time in her customer's study than his boudoir, discussing the intricacies of oriental business practice. And that very morning she'd been appointed as his private secretary and taken onto the payroll of the Merchant Company.

Just as Katya decided to scream for Johnnie to come and rescue her, the phone rang.

'Damn!' James cursed as he pulled away from her. 'Don't go away,' he whispered and picked up the receiver. 'Hello?' A huge smile creased his face. 'Lee? Is that you? Wait one second.' He looked at Katya and said flatly, 'That will be all for now, Miss Popova, you may go.'

James watched the girl walk all the way across the room. She is very beautiful, he thought as she closed the door behind her, and Johnnie is a very lucky man.

'You owe me twenty-five thousand dollars, *Sai Loh*.' He deliberately used the Cantonese for Little Brother as he joked down the line.

'I need help, James,' Lee replied.

James had never in his life heard fear in Lee Kwan's voice. 'Spit it out, *Sai Loh*,' he replied evenly, 'anything you need, you will get.' He listened with growing apprehension as Lee related his story.

'Ring me back in an hour, Lee,' James said when the line went silent. 'I'll have their names. I'll have *all* their names. Oh, and Lee,' he said quickly, before his brother could hang up, 'watch yourself in Kowloon, especially Sham Shui Po. I've got a feeling that's where they'll be, and there's a riot going on.'

James hung up as Johnnie Wilson came through the door. 'The file's supposedly on your desk,' he began, then noticed the ashen look on James' face. 'Jesus, what's the matter with you?'

'Lee's in Hong Kong and he's in trouble,' James said as he picked up the phone. 'Connect me with the Heroes of Waterloo nightclub. It's in Jaffe Road, Wanchai,' he demanded of the switchboard operator.

龍

It was nearly midnight when Lee Kwan scaled the fire escape of the building on the corner of Yen Chow Street and Lai Chi Kok Road. He pushed his way through a crowd of curious onlookers, most of them laughing, cheering and waving Nationalist flags as they peered over the parapet down into the chaos below.

Sham Shui Po Police Station on the adjacent corner was under siege with people throwing bottles and rocks at the windows and doors. Tear gas filled the air and five thousand rioters, most sporting Nationalist flags, packed the inter-section, the streets extending from it, and a large block of open land beyond the police station. Buses and cars were at a standstill and sirens screamed on police cars and fire engines, while private vehicles caught in the traffic were being set alight and bursting into flames.

Tear gas was a misnomer of the worst kind, Lee thought, as clouds of it wafted up from the street below. He paused every so often to face what breeze there was and forced his eyes open wide, causing the tears to well up and flush the fine particles of irritant dust from his eyes.

While he controlled the effects of the tear gas, he carefully and slowly surveyed the scene below. They will be here, somewhere, he thought of the men he was seeking. People hung out of the windows and balconies of every building, watching the mayhem in the streets below as screams and shouting echoed all about.

He identified the address James had given him. It was two doors up Yen Chow Street from the police station and, as he examined it, he noticed there was no one on its roof. Every other roof for as far as he could see was packed with people.

Lee moved to the rear of the roof and scaled back down

the fire escape. He hurried along the narrow lane and turned left into Kweilin Street and began forcing his way through the crowd. When he reached Lai Chi Kok Road, completely jammed with people and cars, he was forced to climb over a fire engine to continue on his way.

He soon found the rear of the building he was after and entered through the public back door. It was a four storey residential block, its narrow hallways filled with the tears and laughter of children placed there for safety, while their parents went to join in the excitement. Lee pushed his way through them to the stairwell.

The scene was the same on the second and third floors, but he found only two young men in the stairwell above. By their stance and scowling faces they were making it obvious they did not wish him to advance any further.

Lee didn't hesitate. He leapt into the air and, while seizing one man by the throat, locked the other's head in his thighs. He controlled the fall of all three of them down the stairway to the landing below, still maintaining his vice-like grip on each. When they came to a collective stop, Lee was sitting upright with his back against the wall and the two men found themselves face to face, their noses inches apart, struggling in vain to break free. He released his grip on the man's throat, grabbed him by the hair, drew a knife from a scabbard behind his neck and shoved it against the man's throbbing jugular vein.

'*Where is the young girl, Kwan Su-lin?*' he hissed.

'*Do you know who you are offending?*' the young member of the Brotherhood squeaked, feeling his hair separating from his scalp.

Lee's blade slashed across his throat and blood spurted all over the face of the other man's head, still caught between Lee's legs. He gasped, sputtered and spat out his friend's blood.

'*You have ten seconds,*' Lee whispered viciously. He placed the point of the bloodied knife blade in the corner of the man's eye, next to the nose. '*Where is the young girl, Kwan Su-lin?*'

The man could not speak because of the pressure of Lee's thighs, but he pointed up the stairs. Lee relaxed his grip slightly.

'*In the room at the end of the corridor,*' the horrified man whispered hoarsely.

'*How many are in the room?*'

'*Six or seven,*' he managed to reply before he looked up into the eyes of a dragon and lost what was left of his reason.

'*Excellent,*' Lee answered, before driving the knife into the man's brain.

He stood up, drenched in blood, and leaned his back against the cold concrete stairwell. *Detect, assess, strike, defend,* his mind whispered, overpowering the other tiny voice that was trying to scream *murder*. His mind continued the mantra, *detect, assess, strike, defend,* until the tiny voice was stilled.

Lee's breathing slowed, his heart rate dropped and he moved stealthily up the stairs. He looked to his right. There were no lights in the hall of the top floor, but it was eerily lit up by the flickering light of flames from the street below. He moved cautiously but quickly, then stopped as a door not ten feet from him opened. A man stepped out.

'*If the boss heard you say that, you'd be fed to his dogs,*' the man laughed and closed the door behind him before becoming aware of the shadowy figure in the hall. '*Who are you –* ' he began, but a knife flew through the air and pierced his throat, cutting off the sound of his last words.

Lee closed the ground between them and pulled the blade from the lifeless body. He listened intently at the doorway. Six or seven, the man had told him. One was already on the floor before him.

Lee was overwhelmed by the urge to open the door, but he had to have more information. He moved ten feet further down the corridor and stepped through an open door onto the empty balcony. He looked down again into Yen Chow Street. From this perspective the scene was even worse, the police station was completely surrounded and the vacant land next to it, now directly opposite him, was a seething mass of Nationalist flags and angry people.

He turned away and peered through the balcony windows into the room the man had been in and counted six men seated at a table, playing cards. Beyond them, he could see his daughter lying on a blanket on the floor. Her wrists were bound together and she appeared to be asleep. Relief flooded through him momentarily. But then he saw it: blood dribbling from her inner thigh to gather in a pool beneath her hip.

'Rage is your worst enemy, Lee Kwan,' the voice of his master Lo Shi-mon whispered in his mind as he struggled to quell his horror. *'It is the first messenger of defeat. Control it and use it as a source of energy,'* the voice commanded. *'Divorce your mind from emotion until the battle is won.'*

Lee moved back to the door, leaned against the wall and forced himself to breathe deeply. *'Slow your body chemistry, Lee Kwan,'* the voice urged. *'Find the calm eye within the storm. That is good. There is no storm, there is no sky, there is no earth. There is only space,'* the voice soothed, *'nothing but space all around you. That is good. Now, turn to the door and open it.'*

The six men playing cards took little notice as the door opened, thinking their friend who had left only minutes before had returned. Then, suddenly, there was silence as they all looked at the intruder.

'What do you want?' one said.

'Who are you?' asked another.

'I am the Dragon of Shanghai,' Lee replied softly and moved closer to the table.

'Ha! The great Lee Kwan,' the first sneered.

'So, you've decided to accept our invitation, have you?' a third man enquired and several of the others sniggered at his joke.

'No,' Lee answered. *'I've decided to take your lives.'*

Two of the men never made it to their feet. Lee cut one's throat then reversed the blade in his hand and plunged it into another man's temple. He leapt onto the table top and struck another with the edge of his foot, snapping his neck, then somersaulted onto the floor, blocking a roundhouse blow and killing his fourth attacker with a fist to the sternum.

The punch was delivered with such force it caused the man's heart to fibrillate. He spun on one heel and adopted the stance of the crouching tiger, facing the last two.

'*Baba,*' Su-lin screamed, and Lee was distracted long enough for the other two men to bolt out the door. But the corridor was a far as they got. Lee watched as the young Jet Kwan struck one a fierce blow to the head, knocking him unconscious, then sent the other reeling out onto the balcony with a roundhouse kick to the head. He followed the man and hit him again, sending him over the balcony to his death.

Lee pulled the knife from the dead man's temple and went to his daughter.

'*Everything is all right, Su-lin. Baba has come to take you home.*' He quickly cut the rope that bound her, wrapped her in his jacket and gathered her into his arms.

'*Are they dead?*' Lee said as Jet entered the room.

'*One is. He fell from the balcony. The other is rendered useless.*'

'*Good. You should not have followed me.*'

'*I am your son,*' the young man replied as he surveyed the carnage wrought by his father, '*and Su-lin is my sister.*'

'*And that is reason enough. Thank you.*' They exchanged a look. Lee was disturbed by the light he saw in Jet's eyes. The lad was on fire, he realised, and it was not merely the drama of combat. Jet had enjoyed himself.

'*We must get Su-lin to a hospital, Father.*'

'*That man hurt me, Baba,*' Su-lin keened, pointing to the man on the floor who had succumbed to a heart attack. '*He hurt me while I was tied up and could not defend myself.*'

'*He will not hurt you anymore, little princess,*' Lee said softly as he carried her through the doorway. '*He is gone to the world of darkness and will never return.*'

'*I hurt two of them, Baba,*' the girl sobbed, '*and Jet would have defeated them all, but someone hit him from behind.*'

'*I know. Your brother is a very brave man.*'

'*They put a cloth over my face and it stung my eyes, and . . .*' she stumbled with the words, '*. . . and then I went to sleep. The cloth made me sleep.*'

It was only three-quarters of a mile back to Tai Kok Tsui, but it took them nearly half an hour because the streets of Sham Shui Po were a nightmare. Cars were burning all along Lai Chi Kok Road and Communist shops and restaurants had been smashed and looted. People lay injured in the streets and gangs of flag-waving Nationalist youths wandered aimlessly looking to cause more trouble.

Would China's heartaches never cease? Lee wondered as he took in the carnage around him. Would its people never realise the futility of conflict? He handed Su-lin carefully to her brother and stood staring at two dead bodies being wept over by a woman in a shop doorway. How many times had he seen such sights? How many more must he look upon before he found the peace he so desperately longed for? Would he ever find it? He turned and watched his son carrying Su-lin. Then, shaking his head sadly, he followed them down the smoke-filled road.

Double Ten Day 1956 opened old wounds that would bleed freely for three days, leaving sixty-two people dead and hundreds injured.

CHAPTER NINE

It was a week after the Sham Shui Po riots when James ran down the gangway and leapt onto the Star Ferry, just as the boat boy began to raise the gangplank. He found himself a seat on the open sided ship and sat watching the frantic activity all around as it pulled away from Queen's Pier. It was a beautiful autumn day, James' favourite time of year, and a tingle of excitement ran through him. He watched the shoreline of Hong Kong recede as the ferry made its way across the harbour to Kowloon side.

As the double-decked passenger vessel cruised along he looked about avidly. Things he'd taken for granted he suddenly saw with new eyes. Great passenger ships, cargo boats and warships were anchored throughout the harbour and flotillas of barges and sampans attended them, loading and unloading goods and people. Sailors shouted, boat boys grinned and seagulls filled the air. And through all this wonderful, frantic activity, a beautiful old sailing junk with red sails nudged its way westward, as if blissfully unaware of the maritime madness that was Hong Kong Harbour.

James could not stop grinning. Business and family can go to hell, he thought happily, I'm off to Kowloon to spend the whole day with my brother. A frown creased his forehead momentarily as he thought of Lee's daughter. The poor young girl had been raped, a vile act that no woman, let alone a child, should ever be subjected to. But, he smiled again, he'd managed to save her from an even worse fate. She'd been hospitalised for several days and would no doubt carry the trauma and humiliation of the assault for many years, but she was alive and that was all that really mattered.

He would personally ensure she had the best treatment and advice over the coming years. It was the least he could do for Lee. And for the family too, he thought. He was, when all was said and done, patriarch of the Merchant clan and that included the Kwan family. The image of father figure appealed to him and he smiled at a small boy who sat staring at him from his mother's lap. Yes, he smiled happily, he was the Merchant patriarch and it was his duty to care for them all.

He leaned back in his seat and enjoyed the ride. He took in the harbour, the island and its Peak and the sprawl of Kowloon, and a rush of pride surged through him as he realised he probably owned nearly half of it. Most men, he mused, would cringe at the sheer arrogance of such a thought, but all he felt was a slight disappointment that he did not, as yet, own all of it. He was proud of his achievements and believed Hong Kong should be proud of him for having done so much for it.

The ferry docked and James was first to disembark. He leapt onto the gangway and hurried up and out of the terminal. He stepped into the sunlight again and made his way past the railway station and post office on his right and headed up Canton Road, looking up at the beautiful Georgian building that was Tsim Sha Tsui Police Station, set on a hill to his immediate right. It was his favourite building in Hong Kong and he would give his right arm to purchase it and make it his residence. But the bloody Hong Kong Government was touchy about anything like that. Oh well, he mused, one day perhaps. Who knows?

'Whenever la la la,' he sang softly, 'I la la la.' He couldn't remember the words so he whistled the happy tune from a new movie he'd recently seen in New York. It had starred Deborah Kerr as a beautiful governess, and a bald Russian fellow with a weird name who played the King of Siam. James had identified with the character of the King instantly; he didn't have quite so many children, but he did have the same wealth and power and, of course, the same over-whelming sexual drive and charisma.

He continued to whistle the happy tune as he made his way through hawkers' carts, street urchins and rickshaws and turned right into Haiphong Road. To his left stretched a beautiful piece of open parkland and on his right were furniture shops and goldsmiths. He stopped for a few moments, as he had done so many times as a boy, and watched the old *doh yau* sitting in the sunshine crafting their tiny gold statues and engraving rings. It never ceased to amaze him that opium addicts made the best goldsmiths. It was probably because they'd lost any future, he thought. They knew they'd destroyed their lives with the filthy habit and were happy to sit in the sunshine and toil away.

James had tried opium once when he was a young man about town and member of the jazz set. He'd seduced a nightclub singer and she'd taken him to her home and given him several pipes, but when he'd arrived home he'd been hallucinating and his mother had taken one look at his eyes and realised instantly. She'd been furious. She'd called in an old family apothecary who had purged him of the drug and he'd promised never to touch it again, and he hadn't. He'd had a lucky escape and he knew it. Just look at those *doh yau*, he thought, there but for the grace of God go I.

James crossed Nathan Road and entered Humphrey's Avenue, then walked fifty yards to a crazy five-way intersection of narrow streets where Humphrey's, Hart and Prat avenues collided with Carnavon Road. James told everybody it was his favourite eating place in all of Hong Kong. It housed the best collection of *dai paai dong*, little street stalls, that served the best *yum cha* in Kowloon. The fact that he hadn't been there for twenty-five years didn't enter his equation.

'*Joh san, Sai Loh.*' James heard a soft voice in his ear. He spun to his right and crushed Lee Kwan in a bear hug.

'Good morning to you, too,' James growled as he lifted Lee off the ground. 'And just for today I'll let you keep calling me Little Brother.' He put Lee down, held him at arm's length and surveyed him with a critical eye. 'You look none the worse for wear, Lee Kwan,' he smiled, 'and you are a sight for sore eyes.'

'And you look like a militant coolie,' Lee quipped.

'Long live the People's Republic of China,' James shouted, tipping the PLA peaked cap with red star he was wearing, along with the peasant shirt and three-quarter length trousers of Hong Kong's poor waterside workers.

'Considering recent events, it's probably not the most auspicious time to be yelling that out,' Lee remarked. 'You're asking for trouble, you know?'

'It's blatant provocation, brother. I'd love some bloody Nationalist or other to make a comment, I really would.'

'Where in God's name did you get a PLA cap?'

'You probably don't know,' James smirked, 'but I was a prisoner of the Chinese in the Korean War. I took this hat from a soldier when I made my escape from a Manchurian army base. I have kept it as a memento of my brief, and highly profitable, I might add, period of incarceration as a POW.'

'I think the less said about that little episode the better, don't you?' Lee remembered the Sabre jet transaction vividly. His part in the affair had been one of the topics of interrogation in Beijing during his arrest as an enemy of the people, but his brother's happy mood was infectious, so he let the subject pass.

'Speaking of Manchurian prisons,' James said, laughter welling up inside him, 'you owe me twenty-five thousand US dollars, General Kwan.'

'Shhh,' Lee hushed and cast a look around them. 'No more Generals, no more Captains,' he waved a hand in the air to emphasise his irritation, 'no more Dragons of Shanghai, or Angels of Nanking. I'm fed up with ranks and titles. They've given me nothing but trouble. And you've given me trouble too, especially with that blasted aircraft,' he added, thinking again about the Sabre.

'Yes, yes, all right,' James replied. 'Let's drop the subject, find somewhere to sit and order *yum cha*.'

They moved among tables scattered about the intersection, which slowly but surely over the years had become an unofficial mall. Traffic simply didn't use the streets except in the several hours before dawn, when the stalls were closed. The narrow five-way junction was known locally as the Place of Five Sighs, because no matter which direction you took when you left, you sighed at the thought of leaving good food and companionship.

They found a small table and ordered a number of dishes from different stalls. Taro filled dumplings, rice noodles, egg rolls, turnip cake, and *char siu baau*, little buns filled with barbecued pork, and to wash it all down, *heung pin*, a jasmine flavoured tea.

'So how is my niece, Su-lin?' James thought he'd better ask as chopsticks clacked, mahjong tiles rattled and people chattered noisily all around them. The Cantonese, he reminded himself yet again, were the noisiest people in the world.

'I will be forever grateful to you for the information you supplied, James,' Lee said as the food arrived.

'Don't thank me.' James glanced at Lee, then looked away. 'It was the Woo twins who supplied it.'

'Without it I would never have found her.'

'*Or had the satisfaction of killing her tormentors, true or not true?*' James whispered in Cantonese.

'I am not like you, James,' Lee said in a sombre tone. 'I did what had to be done to save my child. I did not enjoy it.'

'You killed six men in the space of five minutes, according to my sources,' James replied defensively. 'For someone who does not enjoy it, that's a veritable feast of killing.'

'Don't goad me, James.' Lee, who had begun eating, stopped abruptly, chopsticks in midair. 'The only source capable of telling you that information would be the sole survivor. He was knocked unconscious and escaped. Have you spoken to him?'

'You don't miss a thing, do you?' James smiled. 'You're right. I happened to run into him in the car park beneath the Merchant building.'

'Where?' Lee nearly choked on his food.

'He fell out of a black sedan right at my feet. It was an extraordinary stroke of luck.'

'Extraordinary,' Lee said, raising an eyebrow. 'Where is he now?'

'He's gone on a fishing trip,' James smirked.

'Well, good for him,' Lee said sarcastically. 'I hope he's enjoying himself.'

'He won't be. He's the bait.'

Lee placed his chopsticks on the table. 'James, there is no need for you to involve yourself in the matter. It is over.'

'Oh no, it's not! Old Chinese saying, *Sai Loh: a snake is not dead till you cut off its head*. You only cut off its tail, Lee. Fortunately for you, I cut off its head. Your real enemy was a young firebrand named Wu Kai-wah who lived in Mong Kok and was the leader of the Brotherhood of Warriors.'

'Was?'

'Yes,' James nodded. 'He, too, fell out of the black sedan, and he, too, went fishing.'

'So, you killed him, too?'

'He was responsible for my niece being raped!' James' tone was indignant. And one more witness to be eradicated, he thought.

'Do you know of any others?'

'Drop it, Lee,' James said softly. 'You've had your revenge and I've had mine.' He hoped his tone was sincere. The last thing James wanted was for Lee to pursue the matter any further. 'Of course there would be others,' he continued, desperate to put an end to Lee's curiosity. 'But they would be young and inexperienced and what you did to their leaders would obviously have frightened them. They've no doubt gone to ground and probably won't trouble you any more, but don't go looking for them whatever you do, will you? They are still members of a triad, and triads never forget a wrong.'

'I didn't do *them* wrong!' Lee exclaimed.

'Well,' James offered a false chuckle as he poured the tea, 'you certainly didn't do them any good. Anyway, enough of that. Cheers,' he said, and they clinked their cups and savoured the aroma of jasmine before sipping the hot liquid.

They ate silently, during which time Lee stole quick glances at his brother, who was looking about and smiling at everyone. He's a child again, just for the day, Lee thought. He's escaped from his responsibilities for a few hours and he's reliving our past. Lee was touched by the look of joy on his brother's face. If only Elanora was here, he thought. It would be as if they'd stepped back in time.

When they were kids, Lo Shi-mon, their *Shaolin* master, would take them up into the Kowloon Mountains on Saturdays and they'd camp overnight. He'd run them ragged over the hills, stopping only to teach them the name of a plant, shrub, or tree, or show them an insect, or point out an animal. He'd explain to them that everything had a reason for being and that true harmony with life could be gained from that understanding. And when they'd return to Kowloon on Sunday mornings, Elanora would meet them and bring them here, to the Place of Five Sighs for *yum cha*.

James had changed from the last time he'd seen him in Manchuria, Lee thought. He'd put on weight, not too much, but enough that it showed. And there was something else that Lee could not quite identify. Was it an air of ruthlessness? James had always been arrogant and boldly so, which had delighted the introverted Lee Kwan. And there was the overt masculinity to which so many women had fallen prey, which had always been there, too. Lee searched James' face intently and realised the answer was in his eyes. They were cold and hard like a shark's, windows to a dark and compassionless soul. James' eyes made Lee feel sad.

'Do you realise we've only seen each other twice in nearly twenty years?' Lee asked, placing his chopsticks down and pouring them more tea.

'And both times it was on business,' James laughed, 'and during a bloody war!' He was really enjoying himself now the conversation about Su-lin's kidnap was out of the way.

'What happened to you?' Lee asked.

'What do you mean?' James looked at his brother with a puzzled expression. 'Nothing happened to me. What makes you think something happened?'

'Maybe "happened" is the wrong word, but I can sense a change in you – '

'Seven or eight years of aerial combat didn't help,' James interrupted. He put down his chopsticks and stared at Lee. 'War changes people, *Sai Loh*, or haven't you noticed?'

'Don't get upset, *Dai Loh*,' Lee chided.

'All right, you want the truth?' James wiped his mouth with a paper serviette and leaned back in his seat. 'I got so good at killing people that I started to enjoy it. Then I lost whatever vague faith or sense of spirituality I may have had and decided to surround myself with money and power, and wallow in the physical pursuits of hedonism.'

'That is very sad,' Lee replied solemnly. 'I feel sad for you, James. The world is an unforgiving place and we as individuals must search – '

'Oh, please!' James snapped. 'Don't give me platitudes. Not you, and especially not in that bloody Buddhist monk monotone. You've killed more people than anyone I ever knew. If half of the stories I've heard about you over the years are true, you should hold the fucking world record.'

Lee stared at his brother. 'You swore,' he said accusingly. He was truly shocked. For all James' faults Lee could never remember him being foul mouthed. At least not in English anyway, he thought. In Cantonese, if you couldn't swear, you couldn't converse.

'So what?' James sneered. 'What are you going to do, tell Mummy?' The absurdly childish remark hung in the air as they glared at each other.

James fought frantically with his facial muscles as a smile forced its way to the surface. Lee began with a grin that turned into a full-faced smile and finally both men erupted into gales of laughter. They roared, causing looks and knowing glances from every direction, until finally the laughter subsided. They wiped away the tears, caught sight of each other's weeping faces and began laughing all over again.

James felt foolishly happy. He had allowed himself, if only for a moment, to laugh. Normally, laughing held no place in his life; it was a childish indulgence.

Lee was happy too. He knew the value of unrestrained laughter and accepted it gratefully and often. It had the power to rejuvenate the mind and body, thereby extending the lifetime of a man.

And so they laughed together, blissfully unaware of the philosophical abyss that separated them as they sat in the Place of Five Sighs, surrounded by their childhood memories, drinking jasmine tea.

'Hey, *Sai Loh*,' James said, throwing some extra money on the little table. 'Let's go for a prowl through the Walled City. Come on, it'll be fun. Remember when we used to go in there as kids?'

'The Walled City is a dangerous place, James,' Lee cautioned as they began walking up Carnavon Road. 'What if we are attacked by robbers?'

'Ha!' James laughed. 'That's very funny.'

'What is?'

James stopped and looked at his brother. 'You're serious, aren't you?'

'Yes,' Lee nodded, 'the Walled City is a dangerous place, as you of all people should know, James.'

'I thought you were making a joke.'

'I wouldn't joke about something like that.'

James placed his hands on Lee's shoulders. 'Can't you see the ridiculousness of what you just said?' He looked into Lee's eyes. 'I mean, giving consideration to what we just discussed, don't you find your remark just a bit silly?'

'I don't understand.'

'No,' James shook his head, 'you really don't, do you? You've fought the Communists, the Japanese, the Nationalists and the combined United Nations, you're a martial arts expert and you've done more killing than Genghis Khan, yet you're worried about taking a walk in the Walled City. Can't you see the humour in that?'

'Now you've analysed it,' Lee nodded, 'I suppose I can see how it would seem funny, from a Westerner's perspective.'

James put his arm around his brother's shoulder and they

continued walking. 'East is East and West is West and never the twain shall meet, eh?'

' "Till Earth and Sky stand presently at God's great Judgement Seat",' Lee quoted. 'I remember that poem from Gladstone School.'

James grinned and continued on, ' "But there is neither East nor West, Border, nor Breed, nor Birth".'

' "When two strong men stand face to face" . . .' Lee faltered.

' "Though they" . . .' James encouraged Lee with a wave of his hand.

'. . . "though they come from the ends of the Earth!" ' they chorused together loudly as they rolled up the street.

'When was the last time you got drunk, Lee?'

'I've never been drunk.'

'Never?'

'No,' Lee shook his head, 'never. Wait,' he corrected himself. 'I am wrong. Once, when we were at school in London and the house was empty, I drank a decanter of Charles Higgins' port to experience the effects of alcohol.'

'And . . . ?'

'I experienced dizziness, and vomited.'

As they crossed Cameron Road, hilarity hit again and they collapsed like drunks against a shop window.

龍

'Kuda ve egyor cha?' the Russian voice demanded.

'I beg your pardon?'

'I'm sorry, you startled me, I asked, where are you going? You can't go in there.'

'And who might you be?' Elanora said, pausing at the door to James' office.

'My name is Ekaterina Popova.' She moved to Elanora's side and pulled the office door closed. 'I am personal secretary to Mr Wilson.'

'Really?' A flicker of jealousy ran through Elanora as she stepped back and looked the young woman up and down.

'Yes,' Katya sensed the animosity. 'And who might you be?'

'My name is Elanora – '

'Do you have business here?' Katya broke in. She did not like this woman's haughty manner.

'As I was saying, my name is Elanora,' she paused. 'Elanora Merchant.'

'Oh, my God. Mrs Merchant?'

'Correct.'

'*The* Mrs Merchant, the Merchant Mistress?'

'Correct again.'

Johnnie Wilson saved Katya from further embarrassment when he opened the door to James' office from within and stood beaming at the women. 'Good morning, Elanora.'

'Good morning, John.'

'Have you met Katya?'

'We just introduced ourselves,' Elanora said and strode into James' office.

'Excellent,' he winked at Katya who was standing with one palm at either temple, open mouthed. 'Tell one of the office girls to get downstairs immediately, find the nearest fruit stall and buy some lychees. And you, *nanushka*, rustle up some jasmine tea.'

'She is beautiful, Johnnie,' Elanora remarked as he closed the door. She stood at the window, gazing down over Ice House Street at the Star Ferry Pier. 'White Russian, born in Shanghai, no doubt?'

'Yes, and she's bright.'

'You don't say?'

'She's my new personal secretary.'

'How personal?' Elanora turned and smiled tartly as she met his gaze.

'Isn't it great that Lee's in town?' Johnnie remarked cheerfully, wanting to change the subject.

'What?' All colour drained from Elanora's face.

'You mean, James hasn't told you?'

'Where is he?'

'Who, James?'

'Where is Lee Kwan?' Elanora demanded.

'Uh oh,' Johnnie took her arm and guided her to a sofa. 'You'd better sit down. Boy, have I got a story for you.'

Fifteen minutes later Katya entered, pushing a silver tea trolley. Johnnie's cross examination came to an end. He'd started off telling Elanora about Lee's adventures, but pretty soon she had begun asking questions and it had turned rapidly into an interrogation.

'And that's about it,' Johnnie was saying, sensing Elanora's growing anger. He smiled an apology at Katya and nodded for her to serve.

'Lee's been here a week and his daughter's been raped?'

'Yes,' Johnnie nodded solemnly, 'I'm afraid so.'

'Where's James?' Elanora was furious. How dare he, she fumed. Lin Li and Jet were in Hong Kong, too, and her grand-daughter Su-lin, whom she'd never met. And she's been raped for God's sake, Elanora thought angrily. Lin Li must be out of her mind with worry. I must go to them.

'James didn't show up to work,' Johnnie answered. 'I mean, he's usually here before eight every morning, rain, hail or shine, but today he didn't show.'

'Do you know where the family is living in Kowloon?'

'Not exactly,' Johnnie shrugged.

'They are in Tai Kok Tsui, Mrs Merchant,' Katya said.

'You pronounced that very well,' Elanora said as she was handed a cup of tea. *Do you speak or not speak Cantonese?*'

'I speak a little,' Katya replied, holding her hand up with thumb and forefinger about an inch apart. *'My Mandarin is better.'*

'She is smart, this girl,' Elanora said to Johnnie. And tough, she thought. I liked the way she demanded to know who I was. The other women who work here would never show such initiative, or courage. She looked at the Russian. 'You will be an asset to the company, Miss Popova.'

'Thank you,' Katya said.

Elanora placed her tea cup on the tray and picked up her handbag. 'And now I must go,' she said to the American. She moved to him and whispered as she pecked him on the cheek. 'You have chosen well, John. I will miss you.'

'Where are you going?' he asked as she headed for the door.

'I'm going to Tai Kok Tsui to see my grandchildren.'

'I wouldn't do that if I were you, Elanora. I mean, Kowloon's a pretty dangerous place right now, what with the riots and all.'

Elanora opened the door and turned to face him. *'I am the Merchant Mistress, Little Brother, or have you forgotten? I go wherever I want, understand or not understand?'*

'I'm sorry, Elanora, my Cantonese is a little bit shaky. What was that?'

'Just say *ming bak*, Mr Wilson,' Katya advised.

'Ming bak?' Johnnie looked at her. 'What is *ming bak* again?'

'It means "understand".'

'Oh. Okay, gotcha.' He looked at Elanora who was smiling at the exchange. *'Ming bak,'* he said and waved to her.

'I like you, Katya,' Elanora said. *'You and I will be friends, true or not true?'*

'True, Merchant Mistress. Thank you.'

'Your boss, there,' Elanora indicated Johnnie with a flick of her chin in typical Cantonese fashion, *'he is very close to my heart. Make sure you never hurt him or we will be enemies.'*

'I understand, Mistress. He is very close to my heart, too.'

'I know. It is obvious.' Elanora smiled sadly and looked at Johnnie. 'Goodbye Johnnie Wilson,' she said and blew him a final kiss.

龍

As children, the poorer suburbs of Hong Kong Island had been the boys' escape from the affluence of Victoria Peak and the Merchant Mansion, but to cross the harbour to Kowloon side, an act strictly forbidden to them by Richard and Elanora, was considered the greatest escape of all. The back streets, lanes and alleyways of the peninsula represented a world of dramatic adventure to James and Lee, and one place in particular proved irresistible, luring them like moths to a lantern.

The infamous Walled City was talked about by everyone who'd ever visited Hong Kong.

It is a den of iniquity, they whispered, a home for every villain on the South China Coast, owned by many yet governed by none.

Originally a fort, built by an emperor long ago to display the imperial flag of Peking in the remote wilds of Southern China, it had been rebuilt in 1847 to keep a watch on the British across the harbour on Hong Kong Island. It had six watchtowers, walls fifteen feet thick, held a garrison of several hundred soldiers and was presided over by a third ranked mandarin.

When the British signed a ninety-nine year lease over the New Territories in 1898, the garrison moved out and sovereignty of the tiny city became a political dilemma never solved by either side. Nobody was quite sure who governed it, so it was politely ignored, and as the years rolled by it was simply referred to as the Walled City, for want of a better name.

Not one hundred yards from Kai Tak Airport and less than two hundred yards north of the border separating British Kowloon and the leased New Territories, the Walled City became the haunt of misfits and villains. A maze of narrow lanes and alleys, gas pipes and illegal electric wires, it was a rabbit warren filled to the brim with the worst guttersnipes and criminals the burgeoning port of Hong Kong could offer. In short, it was a disgusting slum.

The two brothers wandered along Carpenter Road through the shops and produce stalls of Kowloon City Markets then scurried down the steps of South Wall Road into the old fort.

They, like many before them returning to the Walled City, had forgotten just how small it was. The lanes were only four or five feet wide and twisted and turned in all directions, making it seem far bigger in size. They made it to the *ya'man*, the original administrative office in the centre of the tiny city, in less than a minute and stood gazing at the old stone building, their memories working overtime.

The *ya'man* had been the place where the original *Gam Loong Tong*, the Society of Golden Dragons, had gathered to induct two thirteen-year-old boys into their ranks.

'*Your heart is what colour?*'James whispered reverently.

'*My heart is blue.*' Lee recited the first answer in the identification code.

'*Your soul is what colour?*'

'*My soul is golden.*'

'*Your master is who?*'

'*The Golden Dragon,*' Lee said forcefully, as the memories flooded back.

'*He has how many brothers?*' James quickened the pace.

'*Four.*'

'*His brothers came from where to here?*'

'*From the four foreign cities.*'

'*They brought what with them?*'

'*They brought the truth.*'

'*And their eyes are which colours?*'

'*Red, blue, green and white,*' Lee finished. His cheeks were flushed and his eyes bright.

'They were great days, weren't they, *Sai Loh?*' James too, could feel the excitement reciting the recognition code of the Dragons.

'They certainly were,' Lee murmured.

Both men sat on the short stone wall that formed the verandah of the *ya'man* remembering the night Lo Shi-mon had branded their upper arms with the mark of the dragon. At thirteen they had been made the enforcers, the assassins of an illegal secret society made up entirely of policemen. And, at sixteen years of age, they'd killed to protect it.

'What are you thinking about?' Lee asked.

'Sir Herbert Billings,' James replied, remembering the night in London when they'd broken in to Stawell Manor. He'd poisoned the old politician as he was sleeping and they'd watched him die, almost instantaneously.

'So was I.' Lee nodded. 'I've often wondered what that poison was, haven't you?'

'No.'

'It was remarkably efficient stuff, wasn't it?'

'Yes.' James remembered the night vividly. 'One drop on the lips, then two snores, and his eyes flew open as the poison hit his system. Remember?' He looked at Lee. 'He clutched at his heart and his whole body stiffened as if he was being electrocuted.' The episode had taken less than thirty seconds, but after thirty years, James could still see that man's eyes.

'He was your wife's uncle, wasn't he?'

'No,' James exclaimed defensively. 'Well, yes, technically. But I killed him years before I married Katherine,' he added earnestly. 'It's not like I knew him.'

'Ha!' Lee began to laugh. 'How could you ever have known him? The first time you laid eyes on him you killed him.'

'What are you laughing at?'

'What you just said. It's very funny.'

'Well, I don't find it remotely amusing,' James said with some indignation.

'East is East, eh, *Dai Loh*?' Lee slapped his knee to make the point. 'If you told that story in China, everyone would laugh.'

An old man with a broom in his hand approached the brothers and stood not ten feet away, staring at them.

'What are you looking at, Old Uncle?' James asked.

'You should not touch that building,' the old man squeaked. *'It is bad luck to touch that building. I would rather fuck my wife's dead sister than touch that building. I am serious.'*

'Why is that, Old Uncle?' Lee asked.

'Because she was ugly,' the old man replied, and spat on the ground.

'Ha!' James hooted. 'Now that's funny,' he said, slapping Lee on the back.

'Why should we not touch the building, Uncle?' Lee tried again.

'*It is haunted by dragons.*'

Both Lee and James had been smiling at the old man's antics and his reply caught them off guard.

'*What makes you think that?*' James asked softly.

'*I do not think it, I know it.*' The old man waved his hand around in the air. '*They were here before the Turnip Heads came.*'

'*The Japanese?*' Lee asked.

'*What other race of people do you know who look like turnips?*' The old man emitted a high pitched cackle. '*Are you blind as well as stupid? Have you seen or not seen a Japanese?*'

'*He's killed a few,*' James said pointing at Lee.

'*That is good,*' he cackled again. '*I ate one once.*'

'Jesus,' James muttered. He'd heard stories of starving Hong Kong locals eating Japanese soldiers during the war, but he'd never met anyone who'd admitted to it. '*What do they taste like?*'

'Stop it, James,' Lee pushed him on the shoulder. '*Tell me, Old Uncle, did you see or not see those dragons you say were here?*'

'*See!*' the old fellow affirmed. '*They all were policemen, you know. The Turnip Heads hunted them like dogs and they never came back. But their ghosts did, and they live in there.*' He pointed to the *ya'man*.

'*This man is a dragon,*' James said, putting his arm around Lee. '*Have you heard or not heard of the Dragon of Shanghai?*'

'*Waaaahh!*' the old man wailed excitedly. '*Heard, heard, certainly heard.*' He nodded his head furiously and danced about. '*You are the boy warrior, true or not true? You are the Shanghai Dragon, true or not true?*'

'*True,*' Lee nodded, giving James a dirty look.

The old man stopped dancing and suddenly gave them a baleful stare. '*How do I know you are truly who you say you are?*' He wagged a gnarled finger at them. '*How do I know you are not bad and disrespectful boys telling lies to an old man?*'

'*I do not tell lies, Old Uncle,*' Lee answered.

'People say the Dragon of Shanghai is a master of Shaolin. If this is so, then you are a master of Shaolin, true or not true? And only a master of Shaolin could perform the Flight of the Crane, also true? I have never seen it and I'm told it is beautiful, so,' he gave a cunning grin and pointed at Lee, 'if you are the Shanghai Dragon, you will show me the Flight of the Crane.'

'I am who I say I am,' Lee said, 'but I do not perform for old men, or monkeys.'

'Ha!' the old man danced rapidly about. 'I got you,' he declared. 'You have lost great face. You are just an impudent boy who tells lies to old men.'

'Is this what you want to see?' James threw himself forward, rolling on one shoulder to rise immediately and spin through the air in a complete twisting somersault. He landed, arms extended high behind and above him with one knee raised, giving the appearance of a crane, on one leg, airing its wings.

'Waaaah!' the old man wailed.

James moved through the routine, and the intricate series of movements he'd practised so many times in his life became faster and faster. He leapt and wheeled through the air, striking and retreating, then stopped in front of the old man in the original starting stance.

The old man stood, mesmerised, staring into James' eyes until something drew his gaze. James followed it and saw Lee in the starting stance. James dropped his arms, stood beside the old man and watched. Lee's performance was faultless. It was poetry. It was perfect.

For James, the routines of the Shaolin style of fighting were just that, routines. He'd learned them as a child and had practised them all his life, but to Lee, they had always been something else entirely. Lee didn't simply do the exercise, he became the crane. There was no other way to describe it, and James envied him.

'Come on, James,' Lee said softly when he had finished straightening his shirt. 'Let's get out of here.'

龍

A dove grey Rolls Royce rolled down Mong Kok Road and stopped in Anchor Street in the suburb of Tai Kok Tsui. Like all unusual occurrences, news of it spread quickly and a curious crowd, mostly women chattering in high speed Cantonese, soon gathered. They all knew the owner of this particular car.

Elanora told her chauffeur to wait and a respectful hush fell over the crowd as she got out of the vehicle. She smiled and surveyed the sea of faces for a moment then pointed to a woman somewhat older than the rest, with presumably her grandson on her hip.

'What is your honourable name, Mother?' Elanora asked.

'My name is Yeung Kip-lee, Mistress.'

'Your grandson is beautiful,' Elanora said as she took the child from the old woman's arms and rested it on her own hip. *'The Yeung family is blessed to have such a handsome male child, true or not true?'*

'True, Mistress,' the old woman chuckled nervously. She looked about her at the faces of the other villagers, proud to have been chosen as a spokesperson by the famous woman. *'And Tai Kok Tsui is blessed to be honoured with your presence, Merchant Mistress. You have done many kind works for the women here, including my sister who has a wooden leg where she once had no leg at all. If there is anything we can do for you or your noble house, please ask.'*

'I seek the house of Lee Kwan Man Hop – '

'I will show you the way,' the old woman interrupted.

' – but first I will drink tea with you and the other ladies, good or not good?' This statement by Elanora caused great excitement and she was bustled by the crowd into Lime Street and soon seated among twenty or so respectfully attentive women.

'What brings the Merchant Mistress to our poor suburb?' a woman asked politely.

'Lee Kwan Man Hop and his family hold a place in my heart.' Her reply caused a flurry of nodding heads. *'I have not seen them for many years and have heard they have trouble.'* She cast her eye over those seated around her. *'I am*

the Merchant Mistress and need to know the reason for this trouble so I can help the family.' This remark caused more head nodding and knowing looks. *'But,'* Elanora held up her hand, *'I need the open, common-sense talk of women, not the evasive talk of men who believe in keeping foolish secrets. Men can be ridiculous, true or not true?'*

Thirty minutes later, for the cost of tea and a tray of fresh *naai wong baau*, buns with egg yolk and cream, Elanora had far more information than her brain could immediately absorb.

The women of Tai Kok Tsui owed a debt of gratitude to the Merchant Mistress and were determined to pay it back ten-fold. They spoke of Ten Ten Day, the Green Pang triad society, the Brotherhood of Warriors and the Sham Shui Po riots, and agreed that women would never behave so foolishly. Their disgust at the treatment of little Su-lin and their heartfelt sorrow for Lin Li manifested itself in sisterhood and they revealed information to Elanora she would rather not have heard, information with sinister overtones that made her sick with foreboding.

龍

'Hello, grandson,' Elanora said softly. She'd recognised him straightaway. She'd been standing in the doorway for a full minute watching the young man seated at the table. He is seventeen now, she thought. How he has grown. He was no longer the little boy who'd lived with her in Sydney during the war.

Jet Kwan could not see the face of the woman standing in his doorway because of the bright daylight from the street behind her, but he recognised the voice that had once murmured bedtime stories and sung him to sleep.

'Grandmother?' Jet's voice was tentative. He had last seen Elanora in 1946 when he and his mother had taken the train from Hong Kong to Peking to join his father. *'Grandmother!'* he yelled, and flew into her arms.

'How is my little Jet?' she cooed, rocking him in her arms, but the boy could not answer. Jet had shared a special bond

with his grandmother and it flooded back into him from the warmth of her bosom.

'*Where is your father?*' Elanora asked.

'*I don't know,*' Jet replied pulling away from her, embarrassed by his childish display of affection. '*He's been gone all day.*'

'*And your mother?*'

'*She has gone to the hospital to fetch medicine for Su-lin.*'

'*And you are taking care of your sister, true or not true?*'

'*True, Grandmother,*' Jet nodded his head. '*She is upstairs sleeping.*'

'*Then you make some tea,*' she said softly, thinking it would give the embarrassed young man time to regain his composure, '*and I will go and watch her.*'

Jet went into the kitchen and Elanora mounted the tiny staircase. At the top, she found her granddaughter sleeping peacefully on a straw mattress. She knelt on the floor and felt tears coursing down her cheeks. You have suffered, child, she thought, as she gazed at the pretty little girl. But your grandmother is here now, and you will suffer no more.

She looked around her, noticing two tidy bundles of clothing. They must belong to Lee and Lin Li, she thought. A small vase of flowers sat on a wooden box next to the bed, and several books, brand new by the look of them, sat piled neatly on the floor. Apart from that, the room was unfurnished and sterile, with no pictures or other personal mementos.

Elanora knew little of what had transpired in the lives of Lee Kwan and his family during the past ten years. She knew he'd been a General in the PLA and because of that, she had automatically assumed the family would have led quite a comfortable lifestyle. But her brief observation suggested a different reality. Was this all they owned, some clothing and some books? What were they doing in Hong Kong? She'd had no contact with Lee since the end of the Korean War and that had only been a brief telephone conversation from an army base in Manchuria.

'*Who are you?*' Su-lin had opened her eyes and was staring at a beautiful woman.

'I am your grandmother,' Elanora answered. 'I've come to look after you.'

'I have been hurt,' the girl said.

'I know.'

'My body was violated. It was a bad experience, but I have decided to forget it. The weight of such a memory would be too much to bear. I will be much stronger without it.'

'Yes, you will,' was all Elanora could reply. Her granddaughter's analysis of what must have been a horrendous experience and her decision to dismiss it from her memory for the sake of her mental well-being was extraordinary. The girl sounded like an adult.

'Do you know good stories?' Su-lin was suddenly a little girl again.

'Do I know good stories, you ask?' Elanora wiped the tears from her eyes. She immediately felt foolish crying in front of the child-woman. 'I am your grandmother, and all grandmothers know good stories. Do you know the Romance of the Three Kingdoms?'

'No,' Su-lin answered shyly, shaking her head.

'Well, I must tell it to you. It is long and involved. It will take me three years to tell it, so I will begin immediately. One thousand years ago in a kingdom far away, there lived a man called Kwan Gung – '

'Was he a good man or a monster?' Su-lin asked with wide eyes.

'Oh, he was a good man. He became Kwan Dai, the god of books and stories, but that happens later. First, he met two other good men in a peach orchard . . .' Elanora continued with the famous old tale for ten minutes before her granddaughter drifted back into sleep, then she rose and went downstairs.

On the living room table sat a pot of tea and cups, and on either side sat Jet and his mother Lin Li. The young woman looked up, then walked into Elanora's arms, bursting into tears.

龍

'How are Elanora and Richard?' Lee asked as they strolled down Nathan Road towards the harbour.

'They are both well,' James lied. He couldn't be bothered discussing Richard, it would mean explaining his pathetic outlook on life and he just didn't want to. 'They live in Macau now, you know? Oh, that reminds me, I've not told Mother you're in Hong Kong.'

'Why not?' Lee was surprised.

'Well, what with the riots in Sham Shui Po last week and the curfew in place, I didn't think it was a good idea her being in Hong Kong, especially Kowloon. I'll phone her and tell her this evening, how's that?'

'Fine,' Lee nodded. He was longing to see Elanora and Richard. 'You know, we've walked and talked for hours, James,' Lee said. 'But in all that time you have never mentioned Lo Shi-mon.'

'No, I haven't.'

'You mentioned that I owe you twenty-five thousand dollars, so I assume you found your money?'

'I found *him* first.' James had stopped walking and was pointing enigmatically into the front window of a shop.

'Who?' Lee asked, mystified.

'Him,' James pointed at a statue beaming at them from the shop window. 'You told me to find an old Buddhist temple in Wei-hai-Wei and he,' he said, indicating the Smiling Buddha, 'was sitting right in the middle of it.'

'He's hardly an uncommon sight in Buddhist temples, James.'

'But he wasn't smiling, Lee,' James was suddenly serious. 'And neither was Lo Shi-mon.'

'Well I warned you, didn't I?' Lee said. 'So, tell me, what happened?'

龍

James had left Johnnie Wilson aboard Old Sing's fishing junk, telling him he wouldn't be long and had gone off in search of the temple. The sun was just beginning to set when he found the old ruin. He'd walked up the steps into the roofless temple and been confronted by the statue of a Smiling Buddha, one of many in various stages of decay lining the walls.

James realised he was not alone. A shiver ran down his spine as his senses warned of a presence immediately behind him. *Detect, assess, strike, defend,* his mind began the mantra.

'Lo Shi-mon, is that you?' he asked.

'*You are too late to defend yourself, James,*' a deep voice replied.

'*Do I need to?*'

'*No.*'

James felt a hand on his shoulder. He turned and was stunned by what he saw.

'*It is good to see you, teacher,*' he said. '*I thought you had died in the war.*'

'*I did,*' Lo said. '*My wife and our child were killed by the Japanese in Canton and my heart went with them. I returned here to my family village to await death, but as you can see, it has not yet come.*'

James could not believe the change in Lo Shi-mon. He'd been a big man who had exuded power and energy from every pore, but seeing him now came as a shock. He is only seven years older than Richard Brewster, James thought, which would make him about sixty, but he looks far older. Lo seemed to have shrunk, his back was bowed and his hair and long beard were as white as snow.

'*Are you well?*' James asked. He had always liked and respected Lo Shi-mon.

'*I exist,*' Lo replied.

'Well . . . Where do you live?'

'*I have a hut by the shore behind this temple. It is only small, but it's all I need.*'

'*Lee told me you are the watchman of this place,*' said James as he walked around the old temple.

'*Yes,*' Lo nodded. '*Sometimes people come here to take the statues and anything else they might find, so I ask them not to.*'

'*But that would not be often, true or not true, ah?*' James let the question hang in the air as he wondered who would possibly want any of the damaged statues. '*Who would want to steal anything from here?*' he asked.

'*To some people, stealing is necessary.*' James could not help but notice Lo's accusatory tone. '*They need to take things of value and convert them to money, so they can make more money to support their addiction –* '

'*Addiction to what?*' James interrupted.

'*For some it is drugs, for some it is the flesh of women, and for others it is the simple, yet unreasonable, fear of poverty.*'

'*You're talking about me, aren't you, teacher?*' James grinned at his former mentor. '*What is my addiction?*'

'*As it always was and always will be,*' Lo replied. '*Money, because it will give you power. And power is what you always desired most.*'

'*And what's wrong with power, Master?*' James sat on a solid wooden box at the foot of a statue and searched Lo's face for the disappointment Lee had told him would be there.

'*Nothing, if it is physical ability and nothing more,*' Lo's face gave away little. '*If you are capable of breaking a large stone to use to build a house, that is good, especially if you also help others who do not have the same capability. If you use power to remove an obstacle that blocks your path, the same rule applies. And if you use it to defend yourself from an assailant, that is good, too, providing you also defend others who cannot defend themselves. But if you use power to control men's lives, that is a crime.*'

'*Ha!*' James scoffed. '*Against who?*'

'*Against all men, but particularly, those whose lives you choose to control.*'

'*That sounds like a quote from K'ung Fu-tzu.*' James remembered Lo Shi-mon had been in the habit of quoting Confucius years ago in Hong Kong. Many of the sayings of the famous old Chinese scholar and teacher were woven into the teachings of *Shaolin*.

'*No, I do not quote K'ung Fu-tzu, but he had a similar philosophy.*' Lo Shi-mon approached James and stood looking down at him. *'He lived around here, you know. Over two thousand years ago Shantung Province was the small feudal state of Lu. He probably walked the same ground we are standing on while considering his philosophy.'*

'Philosophers have caused nothing but trouble, Ah Lo. And to me, eastern philosophies make no more sense than western philosophies. They are primitive responses to un-answerable questions thought up by old men who had nothing better to do.'

'Like me?' Lo asked.

'Only you know the answer to that, old man.' James had had enough of the conversation. *'Do you have or not have something for me?'*

'Have,' Lo nodded. *'You are sitting on it.'*

James knelt and looked at the box he'd been on. It had a steel latch on the front but no locking device of any sort. *'Do you know what it contains?'* he asked.

'Of course, the box is full of money. I would not guard a box without knowing what it contained. That would be stupid.'

James sprung the latch and lifted the lid. Bound packs of neat, new US currency stared up at him and the mixture of relief and excitement he felt was a heady brew indeed. *'That is one million dollars, Ah Lo,'* he sighed happily.

'No, it's not.' Lo Shi-mon shook his head.

'How much is it then?' James asked, a twinge of concern creasing his brow.

'I counted it several times over the last week. I found it a most satisfying exercise. It is good to know I can still count to such high numbers.'

'How high?' James was losing his patience with the old fool.

'Each time the amount was the same, which proved my ability to –'

'How much is here?' James interrupted, through clenched teeth.

'The box contains nine thousand seven hundred and fifty pieces of paper, not counting the wrappings, and each piece

of paper has a value of one hundred dollars in United States currency, which makes the sum total nine hundred and seventy-five thousand dollars.'

'Well, *that's close enough for me,'* James said with some relief.

'*I continued to count until I got to a million,'* Lo continued. '*I felt it was foolish to get so close and stop, because I might never count so high again, so I kept going until I reached seven figures.'*

'Good for you,' James muttered in English as he stared at the cash.

'*Yes, it was, thank you,'* Lo replied. '*Counting clears the mind. It is a healthy exercise that I would recommend to those of advanced age who suffer short periods of memory loss. Would you like or not like to eat some barbecued pork?'*

'*Do you have barbecued pork?'* James suddenly realised he was hungry.

'*No,'* Lo said, '*but you and Lee Kwan used to eat it all the time when you were boys. I have some rice in my hut and a dried fish.'*

James was overwhelmed by a sudden urge to get out of the temple and away from this wizened old man he no longer knew. It was obvious that Lo had entered the stage of mental decline that signalled the onset of senility. He felt a tinge of sadness for the old fellow, but it was momentary. They had not seen each other for over twenty years and James felt no responsibility for his former teacher's welfare, and besides, he could not allow it to interfere with his mission. He'd stolen the jet, been paid, and now all he had to do was sail across the Yellow Sea to South Korea and a hero's welcome. And then Hong Kong, he thought. Hong Kong with a million US dollars to spend.

'*Do you or do you not wish to ask me if I took your missing money?'* Lo asked.

'*I do not.'* Lee closed the lid of the box.

'*Why not? The money is important to you, true or not true? It will ensure your future as a great man, also true?'*

'I know who took the twenty-five thousand,' James

replied. He relatched the box and hefted it onto his shoulder, surprised that it was nowhere near as heavy as he'd imagined a million dollars would be, and walked out into the late evening. He looked at the stars and imagined the city of Hong Kong ablaze with light. Then, without even bothering to say goodbye, he began walking back down the path to the fishing village.

He'd gone half a mile and was passing down a narrow cobbled street when he was startled to see Lo Shi-mon standing there staring at him. He must have taken a short cut, James assumed. But then, how could he? There was no short cut. The temple was on a tiny, narrow, bluff-like peninsula. The only way to get off it was by the path James had taken. What Lo seemed to have done defied logic.

'*I see you have not lost the* way, *Ah Lo,*' James said, hoping his knowing tone suggested he understood the mysteries that surrounded *Shaolin* and knew what had transpired.

'*The* way *cannot be lost, Ah James,*' Lo replied, '*once it has been found.*'

'*How did you do that?*' James' exasperation was obvious.

'*How did I do what?*' Lo seemed genuinely puzzled by James' question.

'*I left that temple before you did, but here you are standing in front of me. How did you do it?*'

'*Have you forgotten all I taught you?*' Lo Shi-mon said. '*When a man looks, what does he see?*'

'*The eyes only see what the brain expects to see.*' James automatically recited the *Shaolin* principle he'd been taught as a child.

'*When a covert movement is necessary, what do you do?*'

'*Become as one with the elements around you.*'

'*And . . . ?*'

'*Be black as night, or white as light. Wear the environment as a cloak.*'

'*And still you do not understand?*'

'*No, I do not understand* ' Now James could feel scorn emanating from the older man. '*There has to be more to it than that!*'

'There is nothing more,' Lo said, 'if you understand the way of Shaolin. But you never understood the way, and you never will.'

'Then please explain. Teach me.'

'There is nothing to teach. That is what you don't understand.' Lo shook his head. He felt genuine pity for his former pupil. 'You turned your back on me and walked out of the temple with your money, true or not true?'

'True.'

'Then you stood on the temple steps dreaming of what your money would do for you, also true?'

'Also true,' James admitted.

'You were so overcome by your greed you did not see me pass. I walked down the path and waited here. That is what happened. That is the truth. That is the way of Shaolin.'

'I see,' James lied. Lo Shi-mon was deliberately talking in riddles, not wanting to share his secrets.

'You do not see,' Lo corrected him. 'You did not see when you were small and you still cannot see. All you ever took from my teaching was what you thought would prove valuable to you, the superior fighting skills of Shaolin, because they gave you power, power to control the lives of others, remember? Lee Kwan understood the way, because he had the mind to embrace it. But you never took the way, because the way was beyond your understanding and it always will be, understand or not understand?'

'No.' James just wanted to get on the boat and leave. Lee had often talked to him in this quasi-philosophical way and he'd hated it.

'Aaah!' Lo Shi-mon vented his frustration. 'Take your box of money and go away. What you did to get it disgusts me. And when it provides the world of wealth and power you wish for and you find yourself drowning in foolish, meaningless excess, perhaps then you will begin to understand.'

龍

'James?' Lee patted his brother on the shoulder.

'What?' James was startled from his reverie.

'I asked you what happened when you saw Lo Shi-mon.'

'Oh,' James quickly recovered. 'It was good to see him. We talked late into the night about all sorts of things. He shared his rice with me . . . and a dried fish.'

'Has he aged?'

'You can say that again, *Sai Loh*,' James agreed wholeheartedly. His memory of the wizened old man in the temple was not a pleasant one.

'It was the loss of his wife and child in Canton that did it,' Lee continued. 'He loved them very much and the Japanese killed them. All the fight went out of him after that and he went home to Shantung. What did you talk about?'

'We talked about the *way* of *Shaolin*,' James said airily with a wave of his hand. He began walking again and Lee skipped to catch up. 'You know,' James went on waving his hand airily, 'the ethos of the old *Shaolin* monks, their beliefs that relate to the *way*.'

'Really?' Lee was pleasantly surprised, he had no idea that James took the *way* so seriously. In fact he'd never been quite sure if James even understood it.

'Yes,' James said. 'It's something that I've always held within me, you know,' he tapped his chest for effect, 'the *way*, that is. It's not something I'm comfortable talking about, because it's . . . it's . . .' he searched for a word, '. . . insubstantial, isn't it? Um . . . ephemeral might be even better.' He hoped.

'I think I know what you mean.' Lee struggled with James' description. The *way* was something he'd never thought to describe before. It was simply the *way*. Thinking about putting it into words as James had just done stirred his intellect.

'Yes, well, never mind,' James said hastily. 'Whenever la la, la la, la la my la la la . . .' He began singing his happy tune and increased his walking pace. The last thing he wanted was a philosophical discussion, especially with Lee, of all people.

'I believe,' Lee started, as he skipped to catch up with his brother, 'the *way* could best be described as acceptance . . .'

'. . . and whistle la la, la la la la la, I'm afraid.'

'. . . Acceptance of life as it surrounds you, perhaps?' Lee warmed to his theory. 'But it's more than that. It's a state of mind. No, it's much more, a state of existence, I think. Yes, that's closer, it's existing – '

'Does my twenty-five thousand dollars still exist?' James interrupted sharply.

'Yes,' said Lee, surprised by James' question.

'I knew it. You're incredible,' James laughed as he strode along. 'You haven't spent a cent of it, have you?'

'No, not yet,' Lee replied sincerely. 'Do you want it back?'

'Of course not, keep it,' James replied. 'I'll consider it your two and a half per cent commission. You earned it, *Sai Loh*, believe me, you earned it.'

'I took it as a safeguard for my family.' Lee felt he had to explain. 'I thought I could use it to bribe my way out of the Communist Party if things went wrong, which they did, but I foolishly sent it to Hong Kong for safekeeping and then I couldn't get access to it when I needed it.'

'That was dumb,' James said. 'For a smart person, you can be stupid, Lee.'

'I know,' Lee agreed with a shrug.

'It's a large sum of money in this town at this time, brother. What do you think you'll do with it?'

'I think I'd like to give it back to you.'

'Don't!' James stopped walking and held his index finger up in front of Lee's nose. 'Don't start, Lee. I know what you're going to say next and I don't want to hear it.' He strode on with his nose in the air. 'You want to rid yourself of your guilt, and then you can begin the assassination of my character with the word "treason". Then you'll get to "dishonour" and "theft". Well, I can tell you now, you'll be wasting your breath. It won't mean a thing to me. It'll be water off a duck's back.'

'I was not going to criticise you, James. I'd just feel better if I gave – '

'*Fuk sui laan sau, Sai Loh!*' He glared at Lee. 'Or as it's said in English, the die is cast, Little Brother. The jet was stolen, the money was paid. *Ngoh hai ngoh, lei hai lei, ming-m-ming bak, aaaah?'* James virtually wailed the question for two or three seconds to signal his irritation. 'I am me, you are you, understand?' he repeated in English. 'And, as Kipling said, "never the twain shall meet". So you can just bloody well drop it!'

'All right.' Lee held his hands up defensively. 'Keep your shirt on.'

They walked on for several minutes before Lee broke the silence.

'I was thinking of using the money to purchase the old Kap Lung retreat.'

'Good idea,' James said as they turned right from Nathan Road into Mong Kok Road. 'Richard's the man you should talk to.' He pointed directly ahead. 'You live down here in Tai Kok Tsui, don't you?'

'Yes, in Elm Street.' Lee was puzzled. 'Talk to Richard?'

'Yes.' James stopped abruptly and held out his hand. 'Well, I'll leave you here and catch the Hong Kong Island ferry from Sham Shui Po Pier, okay?'

'Is there a ferry to the island from there?' Lee asked shaking his brother's hand. 'There never was when we were kids.'

'That was over twenty years ago, Lee.' James' feelings of brotherly love and child-like enjoyment were dissolving by the minute. 'You can also catch one from Mong Kok Tsui Pier in the typhoon shelter which is only two hundred yards from the squatters' suburb you live in. I might do that myself, it'd be quicker for me.' He was suddenly desperate to get back to Hong Kong Island.

He'd spend the night in his private apartment in Wanchai, he decided, with one of his mistresses – the tall one from North Point with the beautiful breasts, if he could remember her name. He'd ring Katherine and tell her he was going to work late into the night, and would stay in the city.

'Don't you want to call in and see my family?' Lee asked as they reached Tong Mi Road that constituted the water-front of the Yau Ma Tei Typhoon Shelter.

'I'd love to, Lee, but there's a ferry now.' James pointed to where a green and yellow ferry was moored alongside Mong

Kok Tsui Pier. 'But we'll catch up soon,' he yelled over his shoulder as he ran for the boat. *'Joi kin, Sai Loh.'*

'Yes, goodbye,' Lee yelled back. He stood watching his brother run flat out along the waterfront and remained there until he was sure James had caught his ferry. Then he turned and walked down Anchor Street into Tai Kok Tsui.

龍

Lin Li had talked non-stop for two hours, by which time Elanora had gleaned the full story of the family's past ten years. She found the tale of the last three, in the windswept and inhospitable mountains of Shensi Province, and their dreadful escape to Hong Kong, particularly harrowing.

'Thank God none of you died,' was all Elanora could say.

'Yes,' Lin Li nodded, 'we were lucky.' She tried to sound solemn and subdue her happiness at seeing Elanora, but she could not, and kept grinning broadly throughout her tale. After three nightmare years she'd almost given up believing peace in her life was possible, but now the wonderful Elanora had appeared her hopes were rekindled.

'Lee will do what in Hong Kong?' Elanora asked in Cantonese.

'Please, Mother, we must speak English,' Lin Li requested.

'All right,' Elanora's exasperation was clear. Why does the girl insist in speaking English, she wondered. She'd tried several times to converse in Cantonese, but Lin Li had insisted. 'What does Lee intend to do in Hong Kong?'

'I do not know, Mother,' Lin Li replied. 'He see many bad thing. He is unhappy in here.' She touched her breast. 'He wants peace. He wants a quiet time.'

'Oh!' Elanora gasped as she looked at the man standing in the doorway.

'Hello, Elanora,' said Lee.

'Oh, Lee!' she wailed. 'Oh Lee, my boy, you're here at last.' She stood and opened her arms in invitation.

Lee could only smile. She was more beautiful than ever. 'Will you never grow old?' he said, as they embraced.

Jet came in, wondering at the commotion, and Su-lin crept

down the stairs. Elanora was in her element. She hugged them all in turn and bade Su-lin sit on her lap. She made a fuss of making Jet sit beside her at the table and beamed her radiant smile at them all in turn.

'What a wonderful family you are,' she gushed. 'I'm so happy you're here. You're all coming to Macau tomorrow to stay with me.'

'I don't think that will be possible – ' Lee began.

'*It is possible!*' Elanora snapped in Cantonese. '*Who are you to say it is not possible? What sort of a son denies his mother the right to see her grandchildren?*'

'*I'm just saying –* '

'*You will say nothing!*' Elanora continued. '*I must return home, now, to prepare my house for your visit. I will send the Merchant Company junk for you tomorrow. It will be at Mong Kok Tsui Pier at ten o'clock and you'd better be on it when it gets to Macau! Understand or not?*'

'Yes, Mother,' Lin Li answered in English for her stunned husband.

'Good,' Elanora nodded. She raised her chin and glared at Lee. 'You can do whatever you like,' she continued, 'but your family is staying with me! Do I make myself clear?'

Lee could only burst out laughing, which set everyone else off. 'All right, I give up,' he said, raising one hand high above his head as he shrugged.

Lee's surrender caused Su-lin to squeal with delight. 'I am going to O Mun to stay with Ju Mo,' she screamed using the Cantonese words for Macau and grandmother.

'That's right,' Elanora said, smiling at Lee. 'You are coming to O Mun to stay with Ju Mo.' She touched her son's cheek. 'And Ju Mo can't wait.'

When Elanora had gone, Su-lin sat on her father's lap.

'Ju Mo is the most beautiful lady I have ever seen, Father. Is she a princess?'

'She is much more than that, my child, she is the Queen of the East and the Star of the West. She is the Merchant Mistress.'

CHAPTER TEN

The faith of the Church of Rome arrived in the Far East in the mid-sixteenth century and developed a foothold in the Portuguese colony of Macau, where it has remained, balancing precariously on one toe, ever since. At first the Chinese embraced Christianity, as they had embraced all things religious in their long history, and generously tossed it into the pot of theological soup that fed the oriental mind. But when told by the pious teachers of Catholicism that they must reject all other gods in favour of the one true God, most Chinese dismissed the idea as unpalatable. They already had Buddhism and Taoism, plus gods for everything that walked, talked, swam, flew, ate or breathed, they said, and the suggestion they give all of them up for one single god, and especially a god who insisted on monogamy, was definitely *chi sin*, crazy, they all decided.

What if Christ turned out to be a fake? they asked. Where would they be then? *'Goo ju yat jak!'* they exclaimed loudly. Putting all your eggs in one basket wasn't a smart thing to do, and putting all your faith in one god wasn't either. Furthermore, the priests that espoused Christianity also practised celibacy which, they decided, was probably the reason they never laughed. And how could a priest of any persuasion, they asked, offer counsel on matters such as life and death if he didn't have a sense of humour?

To the oriental mind Christianity seemed to be based on grief and unhappiness, and the paradox, that man will find joy through suffering, was unfathomable. If the only joy on offer was in the next life, they asked, why didn't Catholics simply commit suicide? And when they were told that suicide was forbidden, they decided the whole philosophy was incomprehensible and reeked of bad *joss*.

As a result of such eastern logic, the Catholic priests who roamed China pedantically preaching that there was no god but the one true God were usually ignored, or dismissed as *mong cha cha*, which, roughly translated, meant somewhere between dizzy and hallucinatory. But in the tiny colony of Macau, where Portuguese merchants and Government officials sat like fat ducks ripe for the plucking on the pond of commerce and trade, many Chinese declared vociferously that there was no god but the one true God. However, they still kept *ba'ak wa* mirrors at their front doors to ward off evil spirits and still placed their ancestors' bones in urns on hillsides to give them a better view of the world they'd already departed.

The great 16th century Catholic Cathedral of Sao Paulo in Macau had been a fine example of the Manueline style of early Portuguese architecture until it was destroyed by fire after a typhoon in 1835, leaving only its façade. The massive three-tiered front wall stood staring out over the Pearl River Estuary like a giant tombstone, perhaps indicating the last resting place of Christianity in China.

Kwan Su-lin stood gazing up at the façade's intricate stone carvings, which included a seven-headed dragon being trampled by a woman, but it was the gaping holes that once held stained glass windows that impressed her most. To the young girl staring up, they looked like the mouths of people screaming in purgatory.

'Did people die here?' she asked her grandmother.

'People die everywhere, Su-lin. Just as people are born, so must they die,' Elanora replied. 'It is how life works.'

'Does it hurt to die?' the little girl asked, looking up again at the church façade.

'No,' her father replied, as he sat down next to Elanora on the massive front steps of Sao Paulo, 'the body is too smart for that. It would not inflict pain on itself, so don't worry about it.'

'I won't,' Su-lin said decisively. 'Did you know there are sixty-six steps on this stairway, *Ju Mo*?' she asked her grandmother. 'I counted them.' She put her heel on a higher step, placed her hands on her upper leg and leaned on them, stretching her hamstring muscle. Five times she pressed down, changed legs and repeated the exercise, then she adopted a *Shaolin* fighting stance and leapt across the stairs, practising her technique.

'Is she good at that?' Elanora asked, as she watched the young girl pirouette and land like a butterfly.

'Oh, yes,' Lee answered. Elanora could hear the pride in his voice. 'She is far more than good at it, Mother. I already have trouble defending myself when we practise the fighting techniques, and she's only ten.'

'Really?' Elanora was impressed. Lee had never offered praise freely.

'She is a rare child, Elanora,' he continued. 'Her ability to understand the principles of *Shaolin*, even its most complicated philosophies, is extraordinary. She has a remarkable intellect. Her mind is so quick and agile.'

'She accepts the *way*, is that what you are trying to tell me?'

'Yes,' Lee nodded intently, delighted by his mother's perception, 'that's exactly it. I am glad you understand. She learns fast, analyses what she is taught, dismisses what she doesn't accept and retains the rest. And her fighting skills are truly breathtaking,' he said. 'When she is grown I would not like to be in the shoes of anyone who threatens her. She will make a terrifying adversary.'

'Yes, well,' Elanora patted her son's leg, 'it's nice to know she'll be able to *kill* anyone who threatens her, dear,' her voice dripped sarcasm. 'But *trained assassin* is hardly the thing a young lady of refinement wants written on her social resumé, is it? What about her education? Have you given any thought to that?'

'I will take your advice on that matter. I want you to oversee her education.'

'Oh?' Elanora was surprised. 'That's not like you, Lee.'

'It was Lin Li's idea actually,' he replied. 'She is, like you,

Mother, a touch ambivalent about Su-lin's fascination with things eastern and believes you can correct matters.'

'By eastern I take it you mean *Shaolin*?' Elanora got to her feet and breathed in the crisp autumn air. October and November were her favourite months of the year in Macau. The stultifying heat and humidity of summer were gone, replaced by clean air, blue skies and fresh southeasterly afternoon breezes.

'Yes,' Lee replied, hoping Elanora would sense his own ambivalence. 'But I do not think she should give it up. The *way* is so strong in her, Mother. I believe it will serve her well in life.'

'I believe it already has.' Elanora looked down at her son who had folded Su-lin's jacket and placed it on his lap. He was stroking it with an absent-minded affection. 'She told me, in the house at Tai Kok Tsui, that she had dismissed the trauma of the sexual assault from her mind because it would serve no purpose to remember it. For a moment I couldn't believe my ears. I thought I was listening to a forty-year-old woman. I had to remind myself she is only ten.'

'As I said before, Mother, she is a rare child.'

'But *is* she a child?' Elanora wondered aloud.

'Of course she is,' Lee stood up. 'And she is conspicuously feminine. She talks to her rag doll, has tea parties with a stuffed donkey, and spends hours each night brushing her hair and rabbiting on to her mother about princesses, dragons, swordsmen and fairies. How much more child-like can you get?'

'And what of Jet?' she asked. 'He is a young man now. We should think of his future, too.'

'I have spoken with him, Mother, and he wishes to remain with me and study. He wants to, one day, teach *Shaolin*.'

'And will he?'

'No.' Lee shook his head. 'Jet has neither the intelligence nor the skill of his sister.'

'Then why not send him away to school in England? Perhaps he could return and take up employment with the Merchant Company.'

'No.' Lee shook his head again and looked at his mother. 'I would rather keep him with me. The last three years were not good for us and the hardship we suffered changed him. There is something wrong with him, something I have yet to define. I have noticed recently a propensity for violence in him, but there is more to it than that. I think it best that he remains with me.'

Lee looked up to the top of the steps at his children and Lin Li, who was examining produce in a fruit vendor's cart. 'Let's join the others, shall we?'

'Very well,' Elanora said as they began walking up the steps through a multitude of pigeons, tourists and hawkers. She had made her decision. 'Regarding Su-lin, I will oversee her education.'

'Thank you, Mother. Lin Li will be delighted.'

'But,' Elanora raised her open palm, 'it will be on my terms – '

'I have the money to pay for it,' Lee hurried to add.

'And that is the first of my terms,' Elanora continued. 'I will pay for all of her education – '

'But – '

'No buts!' she snapped. 'I am Elanora Maria Escaravelho de Ruiz Merchant Brewster, the Merchant Mistress.' She glared, her chin raised imperiously at Lee, but her face softened as she watched him struggling to suppress a smile. 'It's a ridiculously long name, isn't it?' she said, mocking herself. 'Anyway, as I was about to say, I have a position to uphold and will lose great face if I am not seen to undertake the education of my granddaughter, and that includes paying for it. She will one day be a jewel in the Merchant family crown and I must be sure she sparkles accordingly.'

'That's very generous of you, Elanora,' Lee conceded.

'And I will do the same thing at any time for your son, if you wish.' They had reached the fruit vendor's cart and Elanora put an arm around her grandson's shoulders.

'The same what, Grandmother?' the young Jet enquired.

'Perhaps send you to school in England. Would you like that?'

'But what about our school here, Father?' Jet looked at Lee.

'What school?' Elanora was completely lost.

'Why don't we have *yum cha*?' Lee suggested with a look at his son.

'That's a good idea,' Jet said. 'Come along, Su-lin.' He patted his sister on the back. 'You find us a good place for *yum cha*, okay?'

'Don't look so confused, Mother.' Lee indicated that they should follow his wife and children who had headed off back down the cathedral stairs. 'Let's have lunch and I'll tell you about an idea I've had. I believe it may be good for Jet.'

'All right,' Elanora nodded. 'But I haven't got long. I have arranged the company vessel to take me to Kowloon this afternoon. I have important business in Hong Kong that cannot wait.'

龍

'Good day, Katya,' James Merchant said as he stopped at her open office door and focused his gaze directly on her cleavage.

'Good afternoon to you, Mister Merchant,' Katya replied as a shiver of revulsion crept up her spine.

'Meester Mairchant,' James mimicked her Russian accent, as always. 'I love the way you say that. It's sexy.'

'Is there something you wanted, Sir? Mister Wilson is not in his office at the moment.'

'Yes,' James replied. You, he thought, as he leaned casually against the door frame. 'There is something you can do for me. I can't find my bloody secretary, yet again. Could you arrange the company junk for seven-thirty tonight? Have it pick me up at Fenwick Pier.'

'I'm afraid your mother has already booked the vessel for tonight,' Katya informed him. 'She will use it to come to Hong Kong and return to Macau.'

'Oh, really.' James was surprised. His mother rarely used the company junk; she usually travelled on ferries. 'Do you know why she is coming to Hong Kong?'

'She has arranged a business dinner with Mister Wilson,' Katya replied.

'Aaah, I see,' James smiled wickedly.

He was fully aware of the relationship that existed between his mother and Johnnie. Very little went on in Hong Kong that James didn't know about. The affair had been going on for two years, regular as clockwork, in her suite at the Peninsula Hotel. Not that he'd ever cared one way or the other. In fact, he'd been delighted when he'd first heard that Elanora had been cuckolding Richard with a man young enough to be her son, and was even more delighted when he'd heard the lucky gigolo was Johnnie.

'Well,' he continued. 'That's that, I suppose. Could you hire a vessel for me? You know the deal, plenty of good wine, a full buffet dinner, etcetera, etcetera.' He waved his hand gaily. 'I promised a few friends a night of cruising on the harbour.'

'I will arrange something suitable,' Katya said. 'Seven-thirty at Fenwick Pier.'

'By the way.' James tore his eyes from the Russian's breasts and offered her a leering grin. 'I assume you are free, tonight, am I right? Would you like to go sailing with me?'

'Thank you, Mister Merchant, but I cannot.' Katya offered a silent prayer of thanks. 'I must attend the business dinner with your mother and Mister Wilson.'

'Oh,' James said flatly as her answer enfolded him like a wet towel. 'Well, never mind, perhaps some other time, eh?' He made as if to leave, then stopped abruptly. 'You don't happen to know what this little business dinner is all about, do you?'

'No, Sir.' Katya tried to smile, but only managed to look sick. 'I only know I am to take minutes of it for the next company general meeting.'

'Oh, well,' he said breezily, 'I'll ask Johnnie when I see him. *Do'svi'danya*, my little Russian rose,' he finished, and disappeared.

Katya sat at her desk staring blindly at the rosewood surface. Hearing her native tongue spoken by James Merchant had made her skin crawl. The bastard, she thought. He had looked at her as if she was dirt and available any time he wanted her, and she hated him for it. Would she never be free of men like James Merchant?

Faced with the prospect of starvation in war-torn China, she had been driven into a life of prostitution where her youth and beauty had kept her alive. She had hoped, naïvely, that it would not last long. She had prayed that a wealthy client would see that she hated the world she was in and whisk her away to a palace of dreams. But she had watched her pathetic offers of genuine interest and affection fall on stony ground. She had been abused and humiliated by rich arrogant men until she'd lost all hope of salvation and had accepted her lot as one of nature's lost. And then she'd met Johnnie Wilson.

After years of degradation and despondency, Katya Popova now had reason to hope. A decent future seemed a possibility for her and yet once again, just as hope beckoned on her horizon, another callous, arrogant male stood in her path. James Merchant blocked not only her way to honest employment and the independence it could bring, but he also stood between her and the only honest, unselfish man she'd met in years. Katya despised him for it.

龍

Elanora watched Lee's family eating and chatting as they all sat in a small restaurant in the old Sao Lorenqo Quarter of Macau. She bathed in their happiness and their obvious love for each other, but a frown crossed her brow as she thought of the hardship and separation they'd endured in the last ten years.

Lee and Liu Li had withheld nothing from her. She'd learned of their long separations, the dreadful treatment they'd both been subjected to by the Communists, their suffering while being 're-educated' in the mountains of Shansi, and their harrowing escape to Hong Kong.

Both Lee and his wife had strands of grey hair at their temples, she noticed, and they were only in their thirties.

Elanora could only imagine what their daily lives must have been like. Being under constant surveillance and fearing 'renouncement' at any moment by the Party must have been sheer hell for them, she thought.

The family had been guests in her house for the last week and they'd filled the place with love and laughter, enchanting not only Elanora and the servants, but Richard as well. He doted on Jet and Su-lin and talked late into the night with Lee about his life in China. Elanora had not seen him happier in years.

Thank God for Lo Shi-mon, she thought, remembering the man who had trained Lee for so many years in the *way* of *Shaolin*. Thinking of what might have been their fate, had Lee not had such inner strength and wisdom, made her shudder.

'Are you cold, Mother?' Lin Li asked.

'No, my dear,' Elanora assured her daughter-in-law. 'A ghost must have walked nearby.'

'Do you remember a place called Kap Lung, Mother?' Lee asked.

'Kap Lung,' Elanora said. 'Yes, of course, I remember Kap Lung. That was the old monk's retreat up on Tai Mo Shan. I went up there once many years ago with Richard. It was a long low stone hut, with a roof in dreadful need of repair. And it had several stone sheds around it, if I remember correctly. I thought it the loneliest place on earth.'

'That's right,' Lee said. 'It was remote to say the least,' he added, throwing a look to Jet. 'It was the place James and I always camped with Lo Shi-mon when we were children. Remember he used to take us up into the mountains?'

'And I'd meet you both for *yum cha* on Sunday morning in the Place of Five Sighs.' Elanora smiled at the memory. She'd felt like a peasant sitting in that five-way intersection in Kowloon waiting for them, and she'd loved every minute of it. The boys would eat like little pigs and wreak havoc among the tables and chairs, as they'd regaled her with stories of their nights on Tai Mo Shan.

'I loved going to Kap Lung more than anywhere else,'

Lee said. 'The view from so high up on the back of the mountain was breath-taking. I've never forgotten it. You can see practically all of the New Territories, and to the west, Deep Bay, where the pirates used to live.'

'Pirates?' Su-lin asked.

'Oh, yes,' Elanora nodded. 'The pirates of Lau Fau Shan.' She smiled at the memory of the old sea village and The Admiral, The One Eyed Woo, who kept his pirate fleet there many years before. 'It was where Richard caught a criminal called Tiger Paw Chang and destroyed a pirate Admiral's fleet.'

'Do you mean Grandfather Richard, your husband?' Jet was surprised.

'I do indeed, Jet. He was not always as you see him now, you know? You must ask him about his adventures when you return to the house tonight.' Elanora cast a deliberate look at Lee. 'And you must ask him about Kap Lung, my son. You would be surprised by what he could tell you. He has a great knowledge of long-term, territorial leases.'

'I will,' Lee said, but he was puzzled. He remembered James had also associated Richard with Kap Lung. Did Richard Brewster have a lease on the place? Why on earth would he hold a lease on a remote mountain refuge on the slopes of Tai Mo Shan?

'Is anyone living up there?' It was Jet who spoke. 'Or is it empty?'

'I know for certain there is no one there, Jet,' Elanora said. 'Why do you ask?' She looked again at Lee. 'Why are you boys both so interested in an abandoned monks' hovel?'

'I think it would be a good place for the family to live,' Lee said. 'It is a remote ruin, I know, but it could be repaired and the courtyard would serve as a good place for a school of *Shaolin*.'

'Ah, I see.' Elanora deliberately looked away again then turned back and stared straight into Lee's eyes. 'You know it is said to be haunted by dragons, Lee?'

'Dragons?' Su-lin piped up. 'I would like to meet a dragon. What kind of dragons?'

'Golden Dragons,' Elanora answered her granddaughter, but she kept looking at Lee and watched the light of understanding dawn in his eyes. She nodded almost imperceptibly.

So Kap Lung had been used by the Society of Golden Dragons, Lee thought. Elanora would never dare mention the triad society out loud. What had the Dragons used Kap Lung for, he wondered. Probably smuggling. He would consult Richard about the matter.

'Golden dragons!' Su-lin chimed excitedly grabbing her grandmother's arm. 'I would love to meet a golden dragon more than anything. It's sad they cannot be seen.'

Lin Li laughed at her daughter and ruffled her hair affectionately, but she was fascinated by the exchange taking place between Lee and his mother. Lin Li had been told by her husband that a triad society known as the Golden Dragons once existed and that he and Lo Shi-mon had been members of it. Had Elanora been connected to it too? she now wondered.

'Dragons don't exist, Su-lin.' Jet tried to burst her bubble in typical big brother fashion. 'They are mythological beasts,' he said, in what he thought was a very adult voice.

'You are wrong to say they do not exist, Jet,' Su-lin replied. Rather than snap back at Jet like a little sister would, she spoke with the patient tone of a parent. 'Only ignorant people believe in a winged animal that breathes fire. There is no such thing. But dragons do exist,' she nodded. 'They are spirits that live in the air and if they want to interfere in the lives of humans, they manifest themselves in their hearts and minds to carry out their intentions.'

There she goes again, Elanora thought.

'I never told her that,' Lee said to Lin Li. 'Who told you that, Su-lin?'

'No one,' she answered. 'To anyone with a rational mind it is obvious. Consider it, Father. I have seen pictures of dragons and they cannot possibly exist. No animal has the body of a snake, wings like a bird, a dog's head and a lizard's legs.' She giggled at the thought. 'There is nothing like it in all the books I have read about animals. Besides, it is impossible for an animal to breathe fire – that can't happen. Dragons cannot exist as physical things, it is impossible, but they exist in the air. Some are good, some are bad and some of them, I think, may be both.'

Elanora was astounded at the detached logic spoken in such a child-like voice. 'She is possessed,' she said, and the girl's worried mother nodded in agreement.

'I wouldn't worry about it, Mother,' Lee laughed.

'You must stay here in Macau for as long as you wish, but when you leave,' Elanora stood and addressed Lee, 'the girl stays with me, understood?'

'Yes, Mother,' Lin Li said firmly, before Lee could protest.

'Good. It is settled then.' She looked at Lee.

'It is settled,' he nodded, surrendering meekly to three generations of female eyes staring at him, daring his defiance.

'Now, take your children home to Richard. They are better medication for him than all the drugs in China. And ask Richard about Kap Lung.' She looked at her watch. 'I have to leave, my darlings. The company junk will be waiting for me.'

龍

Richard Brewster had seen the Merchant Company junk motor into Macau Harbour an hour earlier. He'd watched through his binoculars as it moored alongside one of the many piers and raised its company flag to tell Elanora it awaited her.

It had taken him fifteen minutes, with the aid of his walking stick, to negotiate the three flights of stairs from his bedroom to the front door and walk down to the vessel. And now he sat on a bollard and watched the activity around him, waiting for his wife to appear.

'Richard!' Elanora called, pushing her way through the throng of people boarding various ferries to Hong Kong, Coloane and other destinations. 'Richard, what on earth do you think you're doing?' she asked as she hurried up to him, flushed from her exertions. 'I sent Lee and the children home to keep you company.'

'It's all right, my love,' he replied waving his walking stick in the general direction of the water. 'I thought I might come down and see you off. I told Ah Po where I was going.'

'Is everything all right?' Elanora's voice was full of concern.

'Of course,' he replied. 'I might be a bit crippled, darling, but I'm hardly at death's door. I think the walk has probably done me good.'

'Well,' she waved at one of the crew from the junk, summoning him to her, 'I'll have one of the men find a rickshaw to take you home.'

'That won't be necessary, Elanora.' Richard struggled to his feet and balanced himself with his stick. 'I walked down here, and I can walk home.'

'But . . .' she began, then stopped, recognising the tone in his voice. She'd not heard such authority for a long time and saw, for a moment, the young Inspector of police she'd fallen in love with so many years before. Richard seemed revitalised somehow, and the flush of colour in his cheeks was not, as she'd first thought, from his exertions, but from somewhere within his being.

She giggled, which shocked her. What must that have sounded like? she wondered. Elanora suddenly felt very foolish and she smiled at him, embarrassed. Suddenly, she felt inordinately happy. 'Would you like to come to Hong Kong and back?' The question just popped out of her mouth, surprising her.

'Are you serious?' Richard asked.

'Yes, why not? I'm having a business dinner with John Wilson at the Peninsula Hotel. Why don't you come, too?'

'I'm hardly dressed to go to dinner at the Peninsula, of all places,' he began. 'I mean – '

'It's only a hotel, Richard, not Buckingham Palace.' She brushed imaginary lint from his shoulder. 'You're wearing a coat and tie. That's perfectly suitable.'

'*Can I help you, Mistress?*' The crewman from the junk stood next to Elanora and saluted Richard. '*Are you well, Blue Star?*'

When Richard had first arrived in Hong Kong in 1925, his English surname Brewster had been mispronounced 'Blewstar' by the Cantonese and in their own language they subsequently named him *Laam Tin*, meaning Blue Star.

'*Blue Star*,' Richard repeated in English. 'No one's called me that in quite a while.'

'Well, what do you say, *Blue Star*?' Elanora said. 'Are you coming or not?'

龍

Katya loved the Peninsula Hotel, it reminded her of Shanghai. Its elegance and old world charm were reminiscent of the grand hotels of the Bund. Chandeliers hung from the foyer ceiling two floors above and in a small alcove on the mezzanine floor a string quartet played the music of Wolfgang Mozart.

She made her way to the dining room and the French *maître d'hôtel*, when he realised whose table she would be a guest at, made a great fuss of her. Before she knew it she was seated with a napkin on her lap, sipping an *apéritif* and cursing herself for being first to arrive.

Sitting alone, she immediately drew the gaze of every man in the room, plus a number of their female companions. Katya's self esteem plummeted, as she tried to dismiss the notion that everyone in the room thought her a *prostituée*. She distracted herself by taking in the architecture, the décor, which included potted palms and beautiful artwork, the silverware and the crystal, then hid her face behind the ridiculously large menu and wished someone would arrive.

'Hiya, Katya. Sorry I'm late.' The soft American drawl was music to her ears.

'Good evening, John,' she replied, placing her menu on the table.

'And you look very beautiful this evening, if I may say so?' Wow was the word that actually came to mind, he thought. She was a knockout.

'Would M'sieur care for an *apéritif*?' the *maître d'* asked.

'I would indeed,' Johnnie replied as he sat next to the girl. 'A whisky and water. No ice, thank you, waiter.'

'It is very kind of you to say I look beautiful,' Katya replied, she hoped demurely, when the waiter had gone. She could not overcome her nervousness. This was the first time she'd ever met him in public and she desperately wanted things to go well. She realised it was only a business meeting, but it was in the most famous hotel in Asia and they would be dining with Elanora Merchant, who was probably just as famous as the hotel.

'The weather today was beautiful was it not?' Katya knew she was babbling, but she went on regardless. 'Autumn is my favourite time of the year in the Far East.'

Johnnie laughed and reached for her hand. 'Katya, honey,' he drawled, 'this is a genuine meeting and you are genuinely employed as a genuine secretary, so be genuine, okay?'

'What?' She hadn't understood. He had said 'jean-yoo-wine' four times. Did he mean 'genuine'?

'Don't let this room throw ya, pardner,' he laughed softly. 'It's just a restaurant. Mind you it's a damn fancy one, I'll grant ya, but it's still just a restaurant.'

'I will try,' Katya managed to answer. She felt such a sudden, strong surge of affection for the American that she thought she was going to be ill. Nobody had ever treated her with such kindness and respect.

'And don't let Elanora throw ya, neither,' he added as his whisky and water appeared. 'She's a mighty impressive woman, but she can get down and dirty with the best of 'em. Believe me, she's got more class than a private railroad car on the Atchison, Topeka and Santa Fe, but the trappin's that come with money don't matter a hoot to her. Elanora's about as basic as you can git, once you git to know her.'

'That accent is appalling, Johnnie,' Katya laughed at him. 'It is the worst I have ever heard. Why do you use it?'

'I only use it when I'm happy, Katya.' He looked into her eyes and she blushed crimson. 'And tonight ain't just business like I said, neither,' he added. 'It's a date. Well, that's how I'm looking at it, anyway, and I hope you will, too.'

'Very well – ' Katya began, but Johnnie cut her short.

'There's Elanora now.' He stood up and waved then sat back down abruptly with a shocked look on his face. 'Well, don't that just beat all?' he said softly.

Katya turned and saw the beautiful Eurasian being escorted through the tables by the *maître d'* with a distinguished, good-looking older man walking with the aid of a stick. People, she noticed, were staring openly and whispering.

'Good evening, John. Good evening, Katya.' Elanora's smile lit up the room. Neither of the two seated could help but notice her eyes. They glowed with happiness.

'Good evening, Captain Wilson.' Richard smiled and extended his hand. 'It's been a while since we last met. It's good to see you again.'

'And it's good to see you, Sir,' Johnnie replied, and he meant it. His eyes went briefly to Elanora's and once again, they said it all.

'And this will be Katya, no doubt?' Richard asked.

Katya extended her hand and Richard Brewster kissed it, but not in the way so many other middle-aged men had done before. Richard Brewster's greeting was brief and courteous in the grand style of an age of gentlemen Katya had thought long gone.

'Would *Madame et Monsieur* care for an *apéritif*?' The *maître d'hôtel* was beside himself with joy. The Merchant Mistress was his property for the evening and Richard Brewster was with her. He had not seen them together for a number of years and their presence would be the talk of the hotel for days to come.

'Thank you, Henri,' Richard Brewster replied. The Frenchman was overwhelmed that the famous *Etoile Bleu*, as the Cantonese referred to him, had remembered his name. 'A bottle of Dom Pérignon, you pick the year.'

'*Certainement, M'sieur,*' the *maître d'* gushed and left them with the menus.

Katya was mesmerised by the famous couple sitting opposite her. They were holding hands like lovers. She knew the story of the beautiful Eurasian woman and her English policeman, she'd heard it a hundred times from the girls in the office. Friends and acquaintances had told her, too, and also wealthy clients who had felt the need to impress upon her the importance of their social standing in the Colony.

She also knew of the affair between Elanora and Johnnie. He'd confessed it one night, after mistakenly calling Katya Elanora, as they'd made love. She wondered whether Richard knew – but if he did, he made no show of it. He was charming and courteous to a fault and contributed regularly and intelligently to the lively conversation that was taking place.

'So you're from Shanghai, Katya?' he asked her.

'Yes.' She nervously fingered the stem of her champagne flute. 'We lived in a house on the Bund. My parents were quite well to do.'

'I visited Shanghai several times in the thirties before the war,' Richard said. 'It was the best city in Asia then. I loved it, especially in the spring and autumn.'

'It was known as the Paris of the Orient,' Elanora added as she squeezed her husband's hand. 'Remember the Royal Palace Hotel, Richard?'

'I certainly do,' he declared and Katya watched his face take on a far away look for just a second. 'We stayed there in the spring. I remember it well.'

And so the evening continued and Katya relaxed into a state of perpetual delight. The cuisine was exceptional, the wine exquisite and the company extraordinary. She basked joyfully in the moments of tenderness and affection shown to her by Johnnie.

Elanora too, was well aware of the attention Johnnie Wilson was paying the girl. Ekatarina Popova will have him eating out of her hand in no time, she thought, and the idea pleased her. The woman was not only beautiful, but she was strong and decisive. Elanora had gleaned as much on their first meeting at the Merchant Company offices. She was just what the doctor ordered; Katya would be a good mate for the young American if she could catch him, and, Elanora smiled, the look on Johnnie's face suggested she was definitely going the right way about it.

Richard was admiring the young couple, too. The girl's breeding and intelligence was obvious, he observed, and to say she was beautiful would be an understatement. He wasn't so old that his gaze hadn't discreetly appraised her voluptuous figure, but each time he'd also glanced to his left and been rewarded with Elanora's timeless beauty, a beauty that seemed to rise above the physical world.

Earlier in the evening he had excused himself from the table and gone to purchase a cigar to have with an after dinner brandy. He knew he could have ordered one from the *maître d'*, but he'd been enjoying the evening so much he decided to stretch his legs; they'd begun to cramp slightly. As he'd returned to the dining room, he'd stopped briefly and observed his wife from a distance. Elanora was simply radiant. He admired the elegant turn of her head, the way she held a champagne flute and how she was always so avidly interested in the person she was conversing with. She was exquisite.

He had not made love to her for many years and as he sat looking at her chatting animatedly to the young couple, he wondered if she'd ever taken a lover. His gaze drifted to Johnnie Wilson. The young American had been infatuated with her when he'd returned to Hong Kong after the war to join up with James. The boy and Elanora had been inseparable at dances and parties held at the Merchant House on the Peak, but if anything had taken place between them, Elanora had never let it be known, by word or deed.

Besides, it didn't matter, Richard decided as he rejoined the table. If anything had happened between his wife and the young fighter pilot, or anyone else for that matter, he had only himself to blame. He'd been wallowing in self pity at the time and in fact had been doing so ever since. At least, that was until a week ago when Lee Kwan had arrived in Macau.

Richard's calves began to ache and he reached down surreptitiously and applied pressure with his fingers to the points on either side of his knees. Lee had shown him how to do it and the effect was remarkable. On the balcony in Macau, the younger man had idly questioned Richard's habitual use of the walking stick, stating that it was not natural to continually support the body in such a way. He explained that Richard's body weight was being dispersed unevenly and the stick was probably doing his knee joints, hips and spine more harm than good. Lee was a master of an art called *shia tzu*, a form of physiotherapy taught to him by Lo Shi-mon, which used finger pressure to certain points on the body and could be self-administered. He had shown Richard pressure points that would relieve his pain and had given him a series of exercises to practise as often as possible.

Lee had also commented, in an off-handed sort of way, which did not invite a reply, that the use of opium would not cure anything, and Richard had felt suitably chastised.

The very next morning, and every morning thereafter, Lee had insisted Richard drink a dreadful tasting herbal concoction which, Lee explained, would assist with pain relief. He also had added, tactfully, that without the drink the exercises would be less beneficial. Richard drank the vile stuff, uncomplaining. He knew precisely what it was: a brew used by Chinese herbalists to ween addicts off opium.

Richard had found the therapy amazing. In only one week he'd experienced more relief than all the doctors in Macau had offered in years. The exercises were simple and designed to stretch muscles that co-ordinated the alignment of his skeleton. And they bloody well work, he thought, as he continued to apply the pressure. He felt the pain noticeably recede.

'Any one for cognac?' he asked as he handed his cigar to the drinks waiter who had arrived with the brandy cart. The man dutifully clipped the Cuban, returned it and stood, lighter at the ready.

'Allow me, darling.' Elanora took the cigar from him. It was an old habit she'd picked up from her first husband, John Merchant. Merchant had been an extremely wealthy Hong Kong businessman and an aficionado of the Cuban cigar, who had insisted Elanora light them for him. To most modern women it would seem a demeaning chore, she knew, but Elanora liked the brief taste of the tobacco on her tongue and continued to enjoy the ritual.

Richard settled back with his cigar as the others renewed the conversation.

'How are you getting on with James and the Company, John? Having any problems?' Elanora said, studying him closely. She could usually tell if anything was wrong by Johnnie's reactions, he was hopeless at hiding his emotions. He didn't flinch, but Katya did – her smile faded slightly and her eyes flashed momentarily. Elanora's heart sank as she guessed Katya's problem instantly. It had to be James, and her opinion of him sank lower than ever. He was a bully and a sexual predator of the worst kind. Katya's wild-eyed glance had confirmed she'd been subjected to his lust.

'No, everything's going along just fine,' Johnnie replied with a careless shrug.

'You know, John, I'm still angry with him for not informing me of Lee's arrival in the Colony,' Elanora said casually and sipped her cognac. 'Do you know precisely when he found out?'

'Yeah, sure. It was the night of the riots in Sham Shui Po, but I already told you that.'

'Your son, Lee Kwan – he rang James' office,' Katya's interjection was purely instinctive. Her feminine mind sensed immediately that Elanora was fishing for information and one glance between them sealed a conspiracy. The two women, like lionesses on the hunt, set about their unsuspecting prey. 'I was there when the phone rang and James asked if it was Lee,' she added. 'Then he asked me to leave.'

'That's right,' Johnnie nodded. 'I came back to James' office as you left.'

'Where had you been?' Elanora asked.

'Well, the office staff and a few clients were having drinks to celebrate Ten Ten Day and James had asked me to take Katya into his office so he could meet her in private.'

'Then James sent you to look for that file.' Katya glanced again at Elanora who gave an almost imperceptible nod of understanding.

'Yeah, that's right,' Johnnie said. 'Then he complained that I had one of his goddamn files on one of the fat cats attending the party. And the file was on his office desk all the goddamn time.'

'So you were alone with James when the call came, Katya?' This time it was Elanora who glanced at Katya. They were on exactly the same wave length.

'Yes.' The girl's face said it all. Her smile was a sick mixture of guilt and relief and Elanora could only imagine what had transpired in the office. 'We were only alone for a couple of minutes when the phone rang. It was Lee on the telephone. I'm sure of it.'

'That's right, I remember Katya coming out of the office,' Johnnie said. 'I walked in as James hung up and his face was as white as a sheet.'

'And that's when he told you Lee was in Hong Kong and he was in trouble?' Elanora wanted to ask him another far more important question, but didn't dare. She was hoping the conversation would provide the answer. Johnnie nodded.

'Then what happened?' Elanora asked.

Richard suddenly became aware of what was going on. His cigar stopped halfway to his mouth as he realised Elanora was up to something. He knew her only too well.

'Aah,' said John, searching his memory. 'Nothing,' he answered decisively. 'We went back out to the drinks party.'

'I see.' Elanora was disappointed. She'd been hoping for more.

'Wait a minute, Johnnie,' Katya encouraged him. 'Didn't you tell me James rang somebody else?'

'Hey,' Johnnie said, snapping his fingers. 'He did.' He placed his brandy balloon on the table and grabbed Katya's hand. 'You're right, honey. He called the Woo twins!' He laughed at the memory and looked at her. 'Remember I told you about those identical twins I met, whose old man was supposed to be a pirate and he couldn't tell them apart so he cut the younger one's earlobe off? You should see these guys, Richard,' he laughed. 'They look like book ends. They are so alike. And their names are,' he slapped his hand on the table, 'get this, Wellington and Napoleon.'

'I've known them since they were babies, John,' Richard

replied. 'I knew their father and your information is correct. He was the most famous pirate in the South China Sea.'

'No kidding?'

'Are you sure it was the Woo twins he spoke to?' Elanora asked. Richard noticed her voice was hollow and her face had suddenly gone pale.

'Oh, yeah,' Johnnie replied. He felt like he'd won some sort of contest. 'He asked the switchboard operator to put him in contact with the Heroes of Waterloo nightclub in Wanchai, then he spoke to at least one of the twins, in Cantonese.'

'Your Cantonese is not very good, Johnnie. Are you sure it was one of the Woo twins he spoke to?' This time it was Katya who asked and Johnnie suddenly felt like a man in a spotlight.

'Am I missing something here?' he asked, unsure of himself. 'Why do I suddenly feel like I'm under cross-examination?'

'Don't be ridiculous, John,' Elanora laughed, but Richard could sense the tension in her.

'It sounds awfully like cross-examination to me, too,' he said. 'Stop harassing the boy.'

'Oh, darling,' Elanora chided, 'I simply wanted to know if it was actually one of the twins James spoke to.'

'Haven't you been listening?' Richard said. 'The conversation was in Cantonese. How in God's name would young John know who James spoke to?'

'Oh, I know,' Johnnie said. 'James told me a day or two later. He said the Woo twins told him where Lee would find his daughter.'

'Well, there you are!' Richard exclaimed. 'Now you know, my dear.' He squeezed Elanora's hand but she didn't respond. She was staring at the far wall and she'd gone pale again. 'Are you all right, Elanora?' he asked.

'What?' She turned to him. 'Oh, yes, I'm just feeling a bit tired, that's all.'

'Then maybe we should call it a night?' Johnnie suggested.

Katya's disappointment was so plain that he whispered in her ear as he leaned down between the chairs to pick up her evening bag. 'Don't worry, it's not over yet.'

Elanora did not miss the exchange and when Johnnie looked at her, she winked surreptitiously and gave him a knowing tilt of her head, making him blush like a schoolboy.

'Thanks,' he said to her, and the word held a thousand meanings.

'You're welcome,' she replied.

'Yes, thank you, Elanora,' Katya added. 'I had a wonderful time.'

They said their final goodbyes at the front doors of the Peninsula.

'You seem happy, Johnnie,' Elanora said softly. 'Hold on to the feeling. It is a rare commodity that people too often take for granted.'

Elanora then took the young Russian by the arm and whispered, 'You helped me tonight and now I will help you. Don't worry any more about James.'

Katya's eyes were filled with gratitude as she squeezed Elanora's hands. 'Nothing bad has happened yet,' she said softly.

'And it won't,' the older woman assured her.

When the young couple had left, Richard declared, 'What a wonderful night.' As they locked arms and walked over to Kowloon Pier, where the company junk waited to take them to Macau, Elanora noticed Richard was carrying his walking stick under his arm.

龍

At the dining room desk in the Peninsula Hotel, the phone rang.

'*Henri* speaking,' the *maître d'hôtel* answered.

'Good evening, Henry.'

'Ah, M'sieur Merchant.' The waiter stiffened at the deliberate mispronunciation of his name. He cupped the phone piece in both hands and glanced about before continuing. 'I am afraid I can tell you nothing, M'sieur. I hovered closely all evening as you requested, but heard nothing out of the ordinary.'

'Think, Henry!' James snapped. He couldn't stand the

pompous Frenchman. 'Someone must have said something.'

'No M'sieur,' the *maître d'* gave a Gallic shrug. 'The conversations I overheard were quite *ennuyeuses* . . . er . . . how do you say? . . . Boring? Yes, boring. They discussed wine, and food and the . . . er . . . signs of the Zodiac.' The last was a lie, but Henri Liselle couldn't help himself. He didn't like James Merchant.

'Is that it?' James sounded peeved, which made Henri smile.

'*Oui, M'sieur*. They enjoyed their meal, they drank cognac, M'sieur Brewster had a cigar and they – '

'Who?'

'Richard Brewster, your mother's husband.'

'*Richard* was there? Are you sure?'

'*Oui, M'sieur*. The one they call *Etoile Bleu, Blue Star*, yes? He was here. It is unusual, *non*?' He hoped the information might be enough to satisfy James.

'It is unusual, *yes*,' James sneered. The French were so in love with their own language, he thought, it was pathetic. 'And you have nothing else to tell me?'

'No, M'sieur.'

'Very well,' James said, and the line went dead.

When Henri hung up he couldn't wipe the smile from his face. He could have mentioned any number of things he'd heard: the Sham Shui Po riots, a telephone call from someone called Lee, the Heroes of Waterloo nightclub and its owners, those dreadful Woo twins who ran the brothels, but he didn't. How dare the insolent English pig think that he would inform on Elanora Merchant. Henri Liselle would rather die then betray the trust of the most gracious and beautiful woman in Asia. Besides, he thought smugly, he earned much more in bribes from Elanora Merchant than James. When it came to espionage, James Merchant wasn't in the same class as his mother.

龍

'You're up to something, Elanora,' Richard said as she joined him on the deck of the Merchant Company junk.

'Am I, darling?' She stood next to him at the railing.

When they'd boarded the company junk, Elanora had gone below and changed into slacks and a blouse while Richard had remained above to enjoy the trip out of the harbour. The moon was full, the autumn night superb and the lights of Hong Kong Island sparkled like diamonds. But the vessel had not headed west towards Macau, it had taken a course straight across the harbour, and by the time she'd joined Richard on deck, the crew was making ready to berth at Fenwick Pier.

'Yes, you are,' Richard said. 'You're up to something all right. Why are we stopping on Hong Kong side?'

'I have to meet someone. It won't take long. You won't even have to disembark.'

'I can only assume this little stop concerns the Woo twins, am I right?'

'What makes you think that?'

'Elanora.' Richard took her hand. 'This is Fenwick Pier, which is one hundred yards from Jaffe Road, which houses the Heroes of Waterloo nightclub, which is owned by the Woo twins. Am I right so far?'

'So?' she asked.

'So,' he said firmly, 'you made it very obvious at dinner that you were interested in a telephone conversation that took place on Ten Ten night between James and somebody who may have been one of the Woo twins.'

Richard paused, letting go of her hand to lean on the railing. He watched as the vessel was tied up and the gangplank was put in place, then he became aware of a solitary figure standing in the shadows on the pier. He noticed too, that the crew of the vessel, having moored it, had disappeared below and the main deck was deserted. On Elanora's instructions no doubt, he thought, and he didn't like it one bit. He was determined to find out what was going on.

'I have to go ashore for five minutes,' Elanora said. 'I won't be long and when I come back – '

'You're not going anywhere, Elanora,' Richard grabbed her wrist, 'until you tell me just what's going on.'

'Richard, you're hurting me!'

'I have a funny feeling something sinister is about to happen,' he said rather harshly. 'We're both too old for intrigue, Elanora. I thought we left all that sort of nonsense behind us, long ago.'

'Richard . . .' she complained.

'Listen to me,' he said in a voice that brooked no defiance. He grabbed her other wrist and drew him to her. 'The Woo twins are synonymous with trouble and when they were mentioned in the same breath as your egomaniacal son James, I began to worry. What's going on?'

'Richard!' Elanora protested. Her wrists were really hurting.

'You will tell me, right now,' he glared at her, 'precisely what is going on, or I'll lock you in your cabin, throw your crew in the drink and sail this bloody ship home by myself.'

'All right!' Elanora felt his grip relax and she pulled free. She rubbed her wrists and glared back at him accusingly, but she knew better than to disobey the Richard Brewster that now stood before her. She'd forgotten the formidable man he had once been. 'I was going to tell you in a few minutes anyway.'

'Tell me now.'

'Lee told me that on the night of the Double Ten celebrations, James had supplied the information that allowed him to find Su-lin.'

'What about it?'

'James told Lee that information had been supplied by the Woo twins.'

'So? What of it?'

'That information couldn't have been supplied by the Woo twins.'

'How can you be sure?'

'The Woo twins were overseas, on business.'

'How do you know that?'

'Because I sent them there.' Elanora turned to the railing and gripped it with both hands. 'They were in Singapore doing a business deal, on my behalf.'

'I see,' Richard nodded slowly. 'Which means James lied about his source of information, and you want to know why, correct?'

'Yes. And there is a person on the pier who may be able to tell me.' Elanora held out her arm and waved at the figure in the shadows, indicating the person should come aboard.

As Richard watched, the figure moved out of the shadows and he was surprised to see it was a young woman, a bar girl, by the look of her.

Tsang Leng-Leng had been told to wait on the pier for the Merchant Mistress, but the Merchant Mistress was now signalling her aboard. She hated boats, but she took off her high heels, ran across the pier, up the gangplank and bowed respectfully to Elanora.

'*Good evening, Miss Tsang,*' Elanora said.

'*Good evening, Mistress.*' Leng-Leng loved the way the Merchant Mistress always called her *Tsang Siu Je*, Miss Tsang. She had done so ever since they'd first met five years before, when Leng-Leng had approached her in the street and begged for help. If it had not been for the Merchant Mistress, the Government would have taken her daughter away.

Elanora had tried to draw Leng-Leng away from prostitution. She'd given her money and arranged work for her, but the girl had returned to the life very quickly. Elanora knew it was the only way the girl could make enough money to keep caring for her child, it was a harsh reality in Hong Kong, so she'd sent Leng-Leng to the Woo twins. If the girl had to be a prostitute she may as well be with them. The twins were decent enough, deep down, and Elanora knew she could trust them. They were her business partners for one thing and they were also terrified of her.

'*This is my husband, Blue Star.*'

'*I am pleased to meet you, Blue Star.*' Leng-Leng had heard stories about this man. His name was honoured by many Chinese in Hong Kong.

'*It is my honour, Miss Tsang.*'

'*You must tell me what you know, then hurry back to your job,*' Elanora said.

'Yes, Mistress. Your son rang the bar on Ten Ten night as you said. The Mama-san confirmed it.'

'Who did he speak to?'

'He spoke to Wu Kai-wah, who was one of the Woo twins' regular customers. Wu Kai-wah was a bad man, a Nationalist criminal. He was the leader of the Brotherhood of Warriors that caused the riots in Sham Shui Po.'

'You said "was", Miss Tsang,' Richard said, 'as if the man is dead.'

'Many people believe he is, Blue Star, and so do I.' The girl had heard whispers that Wu Kai-wah had been disposed of on the orders of the Merchant Company taipan, James Merchant.

'Do you know what happened to him?' Elanora dreaded the answer.

'I will not say what people think.' Leng-Leng looked at Elanora. 'It would be bad joss, Elder Sister.'

'I see.' Elanora nodded as her heart sank. 'When you brand the child . . . ?' She recited the first part of the old saying, inviting its completion.

'Yes, Mistress.' Leng-Leng nodded sadly and looked down at the decking. 'When you brand the child, you brand the mother.'

'Oh, God,' Elanora murmured.

'I am sorry, Merchant Mistress,' the bar girl keened softly. 'I do not believe mothers are responsible for the actions of their children. It is just a stupid old saying.'

'Shhh,' Elanora took the girl in her arms. 'You have done me no wrong. Bad news must be conveyed just as good news is conveyed, true or not true?' The girl nodded in her arms. 'Take this.' Elanora gave the girl a handful of Hong Kong dollars.

'Aaiyaaah,' Leng-Leng gasped. 'I cannot take such a large amount of money.' She tried to hand it back.

'It is for Jenny, your child, Leng-Leng. Make sure she grows up with a good heart. A child with a bad heart is a mother's curse forever.'

When the girl had gone, Elanora gave orders to get under

way for Macau and arranged for tea to be brought to the main cabin.

龍

Elanora sat at a vanity mirror in the main cabin of the junk concentrating far too much on removing her makeup. Their night together, which had begun so wonderfully, had been tempered by the revelations of the bar girl. Prior to Leng-Leng's visit, she'd been enjoying Richard's company so much. He'd seemed so invigorated and cheerful, almost the young lion again, and several times she'd felt his eyes upon her. Could it be that after all these years he was developing a physical interest in her again? she'd wondered. And if so, would she welcome it? Could the sexual side of their marriage be rekindled?

Thoughts of her relationship with Richard pushed the problem of James from her mind. She still loved Richard with all her heart, but how would she react if he touched her? At fifty-four he was still handsome, and a pleasurable shiver ran through her as she thought of his hands touching her. But she quelled any such feelings, knowing the occasion would not arise. She looked at him sitting on the double bed pressing his fingers into the sides of his knees.

'Are your legs giving you trouble?' she asked his reflection in the mirror.

'Yes, they are a bit,' he replied, 'but you know, it's the darnedest thing, Lee showed me these pressure points to push on and gave me some exercises to do and the relief it's giving me is quite extraordinary.'

'That's good.' It was also good that he'd stopped using opium, she thought. It was obvious from the pallor of his skin and the brightness of his eyes. She looked at her watch. 'Why don't you hop into bed for a while? It'll be three hours before we reach Macau. You might get some sleep.'

'What are you going to do?'

'I'll sit in the main salon, I think. I'm not tired at all.' She stood.

'Neither am I,' he said quickly. Elanora stopped and

looked at him, intrigued by the tone of his reply. It was more that of a question than a statement.

'Would you like me to stay with you?'

'Yes, I would,' Richard nodded, 'very much.' Elanora sat and the silence that followed was deafening.

Both suddenly realised they were standing on the brink of a precipice and neither could think of what to say next. Elanora could feel butterflies in her stomach and looking at herself in the vanity mirror didn't help. She could see her breasts rising and falling and foolishly tried to stop them by holding her breath. She could feel the pulses in her neck throbbing and her heart began to pound like a pylon hammer.

Richard was in a similar state, but his problem was far greater. How did he ask a woman, with whom he'd not been intimate for years, to get into bed with him? Despite the fact that Elanora was his wife, he felt he had no right to ask, considering all the time that had elapsed. An even worse thought suddenly gripped him: would he be able to do anything if she did?

Elanora looked at him in the mirror. He was terrified, she could tell, and so was she, but for entirely feminine reasons. The fact that she'd not bathed since the afternoon was all she could think about. She was not prepared for sex. She wanted a silk peignoir, she wanted her favourite perfume. She wanted her makeup back on. She wanted time to prepare, damn it! Then she looked again in the mirror and saw the doubt written all over his face and her heart – and body – cried out for him.

Richard was about to laugh and call the whole thing off, when Elanora stood up. She had her back to him, but was staring at him in the mirror, and the desire in her eyes was evident. He watched her fingers slowly unbutton the silk blouse and peel it back off her shoulders. She let it drop to the floor and without breaking eye contact, reached down and undid her cotton trousers. Letting them slip to the floor too, she stepped out of them, watching him all the while. Then slowly she reached behind her and unclipped her brassiere.

Richard ran his eyes over her back. Her skin was perfect. Her shape was unchanged from the young woman he'd first known. She was exquisite, standing with her arms folded demurely across her breasts and her eyes questioning him? Or were they daring him? he wondered, as he suddenly became aware of his arousal.

'*It has been a long time since you looked at me that way, my lord,*' she whispered softly, shyly, but with a hint of something more in her tone. '*I hope I can still prove worthy of your embraces.*' She turned and took off her silk panties. '*The memories of your body still haunt my waking hours and fill my dreams each night.*' The whispered Cantonese was rhythmic, seductive. '*The thought of your lips caressing my gate of jade is making me wet with desire, my lord.*' She stepped closer to the edge of the bed, and to Richard.

He leaned forward until his nose touched her pubic hair and he inhaled deeply, drawing in the scent of her. His hand went to her hip and Elanora thought she was going to faint. He reached behind to her buttocks and urged her forward as his tongue found her.

Elanora gasped softly, rhythmically, in time with the movement of his tongue until she was on the verge of release. '*Please, lord,*' she gasped, '*take this unworthy woman.*' She placed her hands behind his head and pressed herself to him. '*Take her now, before her heart explodes with the love she has for you.*'

Richard reached up and gripped her shoulders and she fell into his arms.

龍

After what seemed like hours of foreplay he finally entered her.

'Oh, my God,' she gasped, 'oh my God, Johnnie!'

'Yes, Katya,' he said, his lips caressing her throat, 'yes, me too.'

'Oh, please, make it last forever. Make it last forever, Johnnie, my darling.' Katya was on a wild magic carpet ride high over Hong Kong, flying through wisps of cloud with the city lights twinkling below and the moon and stars above her. As Johnnie Wilson thrust harder and faster, the carpet wheeled and soared through the night sky until the sun rose in the east and burst like a huge firecracker. She heard herself crying out as she watched the sparks fall all over the city below, then the carpet slowly descended. It floated through her balcony doors, brushing aside the silk curtains to land gently on her bed.

They lay in each other's arms, gasping for breath, waiting for their racing pulses to subside. Katya ran her hands over Johnnie's back as he kissed her shoulder and throat a thousand times over. Then, finally, with an exhausted grunt, he fell on his back and placed an arm over his eyes.

'Oh, Johnnie,' she sighed happily and leapt off the bed.

'I know,' he panted, 'me too, Katya, me too,' as she disappeared into the bathroom.

Johnnie lay unable to move, looking out at the night sky. Wow, he couldn't stop thinking. He'd never known sex like it. It was incredible.

'That was indescribable,' he called out, laughing as he said it.

'*Mo dak ting,*' she called.

'What?'

'In Cantonese, you say *mo dak ting*,' she replied, laughing. 'It means indescribable.'

'Yeah, well, it was *mo dak ting* all right!'

Johnnie found Katya's cigarettes and lit one. He walked out onto her balcony and looked down on the city below. She had an apartment in a high-rise building on Moorsom Road up near Jardine's Lookout and the view down across the harbour and Kowloon was magnificent.

Yeah, it was *mo dak ting*, all right, he thought. And Ekatarina Popova, his beautiful Russian girl from Shanghai, was *mo dak ting* too. He'd never felt so alive as when he was with her. And he'd never felt so happy either. He considered the thought again and came to the same conclusion. 'Yeah,' he said to himself. 'Happy. She makes me happy.' He looked down at the harbour then yelled, 'I'm happy! She makes me happy, damned happy! What have you got to say to that, Hong Kong?' A ship's horn chose that very second to sound and he laughed. 'Damn right!' he yelled back at it.

'Who are you yelling at?' Katya giggled as she scooted across the floor and jumped into bed.

'A ship,' he answered, stepping back in off the balcony.

'You're crazy,' she laughed.

'Katya.' Johnnie was suddenly serious.

'Yes,' she said, girlishly, pulling the silk sheet tight up under her chin. He didn't respond immediately, so she looked up at him and saw the expression on his face. 'What is it?' she asked, a frown creasing her brow.

'Oh, nothing, forget it,' he replied. 'No, wait a minute, don't forget anything.'

'What?' Katya suddenly felt uneasy.

'What does it mean when someone . . . um . . .' he faltered, '. . . someone special makes you feel happy?'

'Well – ' she began

'It means you're in love, doesn't it?'

Katya stared at him. 'Yes, it does,' she answered softly.

'Katya.'

'Yes?'

'Will you marry me?' Christ, Johnny thought, what are my folks going to say when I tell them I'm marrying a Russky?

'What did you say?' Katya's heart leapt into her throat.

'I said, "Will you marry me?"'

'Is not a joke, right?' Katya stumbled with the English as her mind went chaotically into Russian. 'You don't make joke with me . . . I mean, you're not joking with me are you?'

'Jesus Christ. No!' Johnnie declared loudly. 'I wouldn't joke about something as serious as that. I asked you to marry me!'

'Oh, Johnnie, darling,' Katya began, linguistically confused, her tongue stuck somewhere between Moscow and Shanghai. 'Please you waiting one minute.' She got up on her knees with the silk sheet still beneath her chin. 'You must be careful about this. What will people say if you marry – '

'A former prostitute,' he interrupted. 'Don't play that card,

Katya, it won't work with me.' He moved to the bed and sat down. 'You did what you did to stay alive. I'd have done exactly the same if I was in your position – if I was a girl, that is.' He tried to make light of what he was saying, but Katya began shaking her head. 'Don't say anything yet,' he said quickly. 'Let me finish. The fact you had to lead the life you did for a while doesn't worry me one little bit.'

'Then consider your position with the Merchant Company,' Katya said.

'The only thing that will happen with the Merchant Company is that you'll give up your job to become a housewife.'

'But what will people think?' Katya continued. 'What will James think?'

'I couldn't give a goddamn what James thinks, or what people think, and that includes my parents, by the way. There's only one opinion that matters to me in this town or anywhere else and that's Elanora Merchant's. And she's already as good as told me to marry you!'

'Did she really?' Katya was delighted, and suddenly hopeful.

'Damn right, she did,' Johnnie nodded rapidly. 'You know, she once said to me that I'd find a girl one day who would make me happy. Now that seems like an ordinary thing to say doesn't it? But it's not. Not when you think about it. My momma used to say it too, but I never really understood the simple truth of that statement, because millions of people say it, every day. But I've thought about it a lot recently and I got to thinking about whether or not I'd ever met any girl that truly made me feel that way. And I couldn't think of a single one. That is, until you.'

'Oh, Johnnie.' Katya was feeling dizzy.

'Do I make *you* happy?'

'Yes,' she nodded eagerly.

'Well, to my way of thinkin', honey, if that's the case – '

'You're using that dreadful accent again,' Katya interrupted. 'So you must be happy.'

'Let me finish now, darlin',' he drawled, taking her by the hand. 'The way I see it, what this means is that we're genuinely in love, and people in love get married, right? So I'm gonna ask you little lady, one more time, and I ain't never gonna ask you agin. Will you, Miss Ekatarina Popova, marry me?'

'Are you sure?'

'Dammit girl, I just got through tellin' you – '

'Yes! Yes!' Katya shrieked and threw herself into his arms. 'I will, I will, I will marry you, Johnnie!'

龍

It was eleven o'clock in the morning when Elanora woke up in Richard's bed at the house she'd named *Lung Fa Yuen*, the Dragon's Garden. She'd named it for Richard and, as she stepped out onto the balcony and breathed in the fresh autumn air, she decided she had named it very aptly. She felt wonderful and she spread her arms out as if to embrace the whole of Macau, glittering below in the mid-morning sunlight.

Richard was nowhere to be seen so she went down to the ground floor dining room and found him reading the paper. She adjusted her silk dressing gown as Sally, the kitchen maid, brought in their late breakfast.

'Good morning, my love,' he said upon seeing her enter. 'Still not dressed, I see.'

'Couldn't be bothered.' She stretched lazily, like a cat. 'Where are Lee and the family?'

'They've gone out for *yum cha*. They were waiting for you, but I told them you were sleeping in so they went without you. Su-lin was very disappointed.'

'Goo' morning, Missy,' the girl said in English. 'You loo' very happy today. You have a goo' nigh' las' nigh' I hope so, yes?'

'We had a wonderful night, thank you, Sally.' Elanora looked at Richard as the girl poured them tea. 'Didn't we, darling?'

'What?' Richard looked up and smiled. 'Oh, yes dear, a wonderful night.'

'You obviously made it down the stairs all right, darling. Feeling okay?'

'I tell you, Elanora, those exercises Lee gave me have done wonders for my legs.'

'*And not only the legs you stand on, my lord,*' Elanora murmured in Cantonese. Sally nearly dropped the teapot at this remark and ran back to the kitchen.

'Stupid girl,' Richard muttered and went back to his paper.

Elanora smiled and then helped herself to buttered toast and marmalade. She sat in quiet contemplation for several minutes before broaching the subject she'd rather have not.

'What did you make of the other business last night, Richard?'

He put his newspaper down and put his reading glasses on the dining table before answering.

'Well, I've given it some thought this morning, and it sounds to me like poor old Wu Kai-wah, whoever he was, probably a Nationalist fanatic and a highly paid political agitator, has been conveniently swept off this mortal coil to his next life.' Richard looked at her. 'And your son James probably did the sweeping.'

'I agree,' she turned and, leaning towards him, placed her elbows on the table and cupped her chin in her hands. 'But why, Richard?'

'Well, I'm only surmising, you understand,' he continued, 'but I would say James, for reasons known only to him, had a hand in the Sham Shui Po riots – '

'The Merchant Company has a lot of money tied up in Taiwan at the moment,' Elanora broke in. 'We are building a large hotel in Tai Pei.'

'Well, there you go.' Richard threw his hands in the air. 'The Nationalists wanted a show of strength on Ten Ten Day and bloody James arranged it for them. And,' he pointed a finger at her, 'he would have used that Brotherhood crowd the bar girl mentioned. She said this Wu Kai-wah fellow was the leader of it.'

'Yes!' Elanora declared. She stood up and began pacing backwards and forwards 'And do you know what I believe?'

'I dread to think.' Richard closed his eyes at the thought.

'Lee arrived in Hong Kong on the night before Double Tenth – '

'Lee would never get involved in anything political!' Richard interrupted.

'But he would if the Brotherhood of Warriors kidnapped his daughter.'

'Oh Christ. You're right,' Richard whispered as Sally came back for the breakfast tray.

They waited, sharing anxious looks, desperate to resume their conversation until the girl finished wiping the table.

'Do you want me to get you anything else, Mistress?' the girl asked.

'No,' Elanora smiled. 'You can go now.'

'The women of Tai Kok Tsui village,' Elanora continued when the girl had gone, 'told me it was the Brotherhood that kidnapped Su-lin and Lee said the same thing.'

Richard picked up the teapot and refilled her cup. 'But James would never condone the kidnapping of Su-lin,' he said. 'He might be a complete bastard, but he'd never do that to Lee.'

'I don't think he knew.' Elanora took the fresh cup of tea Richard offered her. 'I think that when Lee rang him asking for help, he was genuinely shocked. Johnnie said he was as white as a sheet, remember?'

'So he rang the Heroes of Waterloo looking for Wu Kai-wah, not the Woo twins.'

'Exactly,' Elanora said. 'Leng-Leng said Wu was a regular there.'

'Could he be related to the Woo twins?' Richard suggested.

'No.' Elanora shook her head. 'His name is Wu as in *wu si* meaning nurse. The twins' name is *Woo*,' she emphasised the different tone, 'which means lake.'

'Right,' Richard nodded as Elanora continued.

'If Lee ever found out that James was even indirectly responsible for the rape of his daughter, there would be hell to pay.'

'I would have loved to have been privy to that telephone conversation,' Richard said. 'I'll bet James tore strips off this Wu fellow.'

'No.' Elanora put her teacup down. 'After half a lifetime in Hong Kong, you still can't think like a Chinese, can you?' She shook her head vigorously. 'James is part Chinese. He would have spoken gently, probably telling the man what a good idea the kidnap had been while he found out where they'd hidden Su-lin. Once he had that information his problem was solved.'

'How do you come to that conclusion?' This time it was Richard who shook his head.

'All he had to do was get rid of Wu Kai-wah, the one man who could connect him directly to the Brotherhood. The others would be taken care of automatically.'

'How, or better still, by whom?'

'Lee Kwan, of course,' Elanora said. 'You do know what Lee Kwan did in Sham Shui Po that night, don't you?'

'He saved my life,' a little voice said.

Elanora froze. She looked at the big armchair in front of the fireplace. It faced towards the hearth, directly away from her. As she stared, Su-lin's face appeared from it.

'What are you doing there?' Elanora tried to sound light and breezy, but failed miserably. 'Are you back from *yum cha* already? Is your father here?' she added, looking around terrified that Lee might have heard their conversation.

'I waited for you, *Ju mo*, to go to *yum cha*, but you didn't come, so I sat here.'

'Come here, girl,' Elanora said firmly.

'Yes, *Ju Mo*.' Su-lin went to her grandmother's open arms.

Elanora took her by both wrists and, holding her at arm's length, looked her straight in the eye. 'Why didn't you reveal yourself when I entered the room?'

'I wanted to hear you speak, Grandmother. You have the most beautiful voice I've ever heard and I need to hear it if I want to sound the same.'

'Did you hear Grandfather Richard and me talking?'

'Yes, Grandmother.'

'How much did you hear?'

'Everything, Grandmother.'

'I see.' Elanora looked at Richard, then smiled sadly at Su-lin as all the wind left her sails. 'Why don't you and I go and have a little talk in the garden, eh?'

'There is no need for that, *Ju Mo*,' the girl replied. 'I will never tell what I heard.'

There it is again, Elanora thought. The look in the girl's eye, the tone of her voice. It's as if I'm talking to my grandmother, not my granddaughter. 'Will you promise me that, Su-lin?'

'Yes, *Ju Mo*,' the girl nodded solemnly.

'You must keep it a secret. There would be terrible trouble between your father and your Uncle James.'

'Two tigers cannot live on one mountain, true or not true?' Su-lin repeated the old Chinese saying that summed the situation up so perfectly.

'That is true, Su-lin,' Elanora replied. 'Your father and Uncle James could not co-exist, if they knew what was in each other's mind.'

'Yes,' the girl nodded. 'They would fight like tigers . . . *Shaolin* tigers.'

BOOK THREE

THE DESCENT

CHAPTER ELEVEN

London, Christmas 1965–66

The girl was truly beautiful and naked, but for a python coiling itself sensuously around her waist and breasts. She was perched on a high backed stool with her long legs crossed demurely, arms raised above her head and the backs of her hands touching. On her fingers were castanets and on her forehead were pasted glass beads, glittering in the rays of light from a mirror ball turning slowly overhead. On a silver chain around her hips a jewel-encrusted dagger sparkled.

Three men approached her, dressed in the skimpiest of loin cloths. The girl paid them no attention as they placed buckets at her feet and began to smear her body, and the python's, with blue paint.

'I am she who has come to you,' the girl intoned. 'I am the instrument of creation and the source of all life. I am the flesh that reflects your shame. I am the placenta and the mucus from whence you slithered, bloodied and wailing.'

The python had by now become annoyed with one of the men painting it blue and it fell to the stage floor with a thud.

'Oh, for fuck's sake!' the girl snapped then, realising she'd dropped out of character, tried valiantly to recover. 'Divorce your minds,' she projected forcefully, 'from the abstracted desire for pure, unsullied, Snow White, fairytale, cardboard cut-out sex. Open yourself to the immensity of the cosmic womb and its tactile joys, sounds and odours.'

The audience of forty or fifty young long-haired students tried to stifle their amusement, but laughed uproariously when one of the young men applying the paint bolted from the stage in obvious terror of the python. Then, the snake, as if sensing audience approval, entwined itself about the girl's legs and forced its head up through her painted thighs, until it appeared like a large blue penis protruding from her groin. It was the *coup de grâce* and the audience lost it completely.

'Right! That's it!' the girl exclaimed as she struggled with the snake. She sprung off the stool, strode to the left of the stage and slung the reptile into the darkened wings of the theatre. 'Reggie!' she screamed.

'What is it?' the frightened assistant stage manager hissed from the wings.

'Put this *fucking* thing in its *fucking* cage and drop the *fucking* curtain!'

The audience fell about on their wooden benches overcome with laughter, as the actress's demands were obeyed.

Nigel Shawbridge sat in the third row wiping his eyes on a sleeve of his duffel coat. 'Oh God,' he groaned to his friend sitting next to him, 'I thought you said this play was supposed to be deeply meaningful and *avant-garde*. Or, what did you call it? Theatre *noir*?'

'That's what this advertises,' Paul Merchant replied, waving a handbill for the play in front of Nigel's nose. 'Here. Read it for yourself. It says, "Our new play, *Organic Matters*, is the visualised erotic energy of the senses and a convulsive densification of imagery", whatever that's supposed to mean. It doesn't say anything about snake charming.'

'Oh, dear,' Nigel sniffed and blew his nose into a handkerchief. 'Well, if the rest is as funny as that bit, it'll transfer to the West End and be the hit comedy of 1966.'

'So near, yet, oh, so far away,' Paul laughed. 'I rather think this basement, in a lane off Oxford Circus, is as close to the West End as it will ever get.' He patted his companion on the knee and smiled.

Nigel's heart skipped a beat. It always did when Paul smiled at him so intimately. He looked again at his friend's face. With jet black hair and a Beatle haircut, Paul was the spitting image of Paul McCartney. When you added the flawless

Eurasian skin and almond eyes inherited from his father, Paul Merchant was just too beautiful to be true.

Nigel couldn't believe that of all the people at Cambridge University, Paul had chosen him as a friend. And the invitation to spend Christmas in London had been an absolute bolt from the blue. He'd never realised Paul held their friendship in such esteem.

'Will they raise the curtain and start again?' Nigel cringed at the stupidity of his question. He'd only spoken to afford another glance at Paul.

'Ha!' Paul hooted. 'You can bet on it. Amateur actors have no shame and even less dignity.' He patted Nigel on the arm and offered a smile that made him more tense than ever.

Why me? Nigel thought yet again. What am I doing spending Christmas in London with Paul Merchant?

In their first year at Cambridge they'd not known one another. Their paths hadn't crossed until a year ago. Nigel was a student of Philosophy and History, and Paul had studied Economics, which he hated, and Chemistry which, Nigel knew, he loved.

It had been a trade off, Paul had told him. His father, James Merchant, the Hong Kong business tycoon, had insisted he study Economics in order to take over the company business one day, but Paul had only agreed if he was allowed to study Chemistry as well. Apparently his father had been furious, but Paul had insisted and got his way. It had meant double the study and effort, but he'd succeeded in gaining bachelor degrees in both subjects at University College in London, and gone on to master both at Cambridge.

And now it's Christmas 1965, Nigel thought sadly. The year had passed so quickly. In January Paul would return to Hong Kong permanently and time would see their friendship fade. But we've still got Christmas. Nigel comforted himself with the thought.

Nigel, overwhelmed, had accepted Paul's offer of Christmas and the New Year in London the moment it was suggested. And now here they were, ensconced in this dreadful little basement, watching the worst excuse for contemporary theatre he could have possibly imagined. He was so excited he could burst.

'Look out,' Paul nudged him. 'Here we go again. If at first you don't succeed . . .'

The curtain rose again and the beautiful girl was back on stage with three other actresses and four actors, all beautiful young things. What they were doing was anyone's guess, but the audience had settled down and seemed engrossed in what was going on. Nigel had absolutely no idea what concept of philosophy they were preaching – and he'd just completed a master's degree in the subject – but Paul was watching avidly, albeit with a grin from ear to ear, so he sat back and let it wash over him.

Three of the actors seemed to be discussing love-making subjectively, from within, sort of, but Nigel could make neither head nor tail of the actual dialogue. Then the entire cast tried to assemble themselves into a pyramid, but the fact that they were all covered in body paint caused them to slip and fall in a tangled heap on the ground.

'I'm having a bit of trouble understanding the underlying theme of the play,' Nigel whispered apologetically, as the cast hastily rearranged itself into a circle. 'I can't seem to get a grip on it.'

'I'd be worried if you could,' Paul replied softly. 'It's a load of utter nonsense, but I've got to sit it out. My sister's in it.'

'Your sister?' Nigel looked at the players. He had never met Georgina Merchant, but Paul had spoken of his twin and he identified the girl immediately. Even smeared in paint and now, for some obscure theatrical reason, wrapped in clear plastic sheeting, the androgynous McCartneyesque beauty the Merchant twins shared was plainly evident.

'That's why we're here,' Paul hissed. 'She's going through her thespian stage, it's all very intense. We're going to meet her after the play for a drink in the Salisbury.'

'Good show.'

'She can be a bit of a handful, but once you get to know her, she's loads of fun. There's a lot more to Georgie than meets the eye, I can tell you. She has a remarkable intellect, quite brilliant in fact. Of course she does her best to hide it. She says it puts off the boys.'

'Will you two shut up?' an irate voice behind them hissed. 'Some of us are trying to watch the play.'

'Surely you mean farce?' Paul answered sarcastically.

'Farce?' the voice spat. 'It's not farce, you ignorant fool. It's new age surrealism.'

'Sorry,' Paul apologised and nudged Nigel in the ribs.

The performance dragged on at a snail's pace to the finale, which consisted of all eight performers entering into a trance-like state from which they intoned a prayer to the signs of the Zodiac. Then they suggestively interacted with each other while smearing jellied eel, raw meat and chicken feathers over their bodies until the lights finally dimmed on a messy, smelly, tangle of bodies and materials. The stage went to black.

龍

'Hell's bells,' Nigel exclaimed as he and Paul burst through the front door of the pub. 'I nearly peed in my pants when that fellow ate the sausage and brought the whole lot back up.'

'And then offered a smell of it to those girls in the front row,' Paul laughed, pointing to a vacant cubicle in the saloon bar. 'And what was it he said? Oh yes, "You can smell yourself," or something, wasn't it?'

'"You can smell your existence,"' Nigel quoted. '"Life is not an airless room. You cannot shy away from the vomit of humanity that surrounds you."'

'That's it!' Paul yelled, and the two laughed uproariously. 'I think I shall take that line to the grave with me.'

'I would, too, and make damn sure I never repeated it.'

'How about you grab that cubicle while I get the beers in?' said Paul. 'Georgie's bringing the cast with her for a drink or two.'

'Right you are.' Nigel dived into the semi-circular seat and used his duffel coat to save space for the others.

'Two pints of ale, please,' Paul ordered.

'Right you are, love,' the barmaid replied in pure Cockney. 'Will that be all, duckie?'

'For the moment, thanks.' Paul placed money on the bar.

The Salisbury pub was crowded, probably, Paul assumed, with after show drinkers, considering they were in the heart of London's West End with its famous theatres.

Paul loved the City of Westminster. He'd spent his teenage years attending the exclusive Westminster School, in the grounds of Westminster Abbey. He'd gained his bachelor degrees at University College, also right in the heart of London, and he knew its streets and lanes well.

'There you go, dearie,' the barmaid said as she placed two pints on the bar.

Paul held the dimple glasses aloft by the handles and made his way back through the thickening crowd to the table.

'This place is certainly a popular venue,' Nigel said as he folded his duffel coat to make room for Paul. 'I suppose you'd have come here often when you were attending University College? It's just up the road, after all.'

'Not really,' Paul replied, sipping his pint. 'I'm not one for the pub and pints, beer and football set. A bit too masculine for my liking.'

'Really?' The remark surprised Nigel. Paul Merchant had been the star half-back for Cambridge University Rugby First XV and a brilliant cricketer as well. He was a natural sportsman and his talent, when combined with his movie star good looks, made him the social target of men and women alike. 'I thought you'd be well in with the rugby fraternity. All those beautiful girls throwing themselves at you.'

'Girls are not my scene, Nige, I thought you might have realised that by now.'

Before Nigel could fully comprehend the confession, a gaggle of gorgeous young men and women forced their way through the drinkers to their table.

'*Nei ho ma, Dai Loh?*' The raucous Cantonese spoken by the beautiful girl standing in front of him jarred Nigel's ears.

'*Ho ho, Sai Mui, ne ne?*' Paul laughed at the confused look on Nigel's face. 'She said, "How are you, Elder Brother?"

and I replied, "Very good, Little Sister, how about you?" I was born five minutes before her, so that makes her my little sister.'

'Was that Chinese?' Nigel managed to ask. He was suddenly confused. Paul had just confessed he was homosexual and now he was speaking in Chinese.

'Nigel Shawbridge, I'd like you to meet my twin sister, Georgina Merchant. Georgie, this is my friend, Nigel.'

'I'm delighted to meet you, Georgina.' Nigel offered his hand.

'You can call me Georgie,' the beautiful girl smiled and shook hands firmly.

'And you can call me Nige.'

To Nigel Shawbridge, Georgina Merchant was the personification of what had been recently termed 'Swinging London'. She stood at least five feet nine in high-heeled knee length leather boots, tan suede mini-skirt and matching waist length battle jacket. The outfit revealed her figure, highlighting her neat waist, pert backside, the line of her back and her incredibly long legs. On her head, atop a mass of long, jet black curly hair she wore a peaked Carnaby cap, Cockney style, tilted to one side in a jaunty fashion.

Ignoring her friends, Georgina threw herself into the cubicle seat and, staring at Nigel, held two fingers in front of her mouth that demanded a cigarette.

'A Campari and soda, darling,' she said loudly, to no one in particular, as Nigel placed a cigarette between her fingers and offered a light.

'With a slice of lemon?' one of her male entourage asked.

'Orange, darling. What else?' Georgina turned again to Nigel. 'So you're my beautiful brother's lover, are you, Nige?'

'Georgie,' Paul growled a warning as Nigel buried his face in his drink.

'I'm so glad he's come out of the closet at last,' Georgina continued. 'The act of physical love, be it with either sex, is so *fucking* important, especially for a man. It exercises the prostate gland, which is essential to avoid incontinence in old age, so I'm told.'

'I'm warning you, Georgie,' Paul said vehemently.

'All right, all right.' Georgina patted her brother's arm. 'I'm sorry, but if I'm going to make a name for myself on the London stage, I have to be seen, and heard, to be outrageous. So, tell me. What did you think of the play?'

'To use your newly adopted vernacular,' Paul smiled tightly, 'it was fucking crap.'

'I know that. I'm not entirely stupid.' She sat upright and took both boys by the arm. 'What I meant was, what did you think of my performance?'

'It stank,' Paul replied bluntly.

'That was the jellied eels and the paint.' She pushed her brother away and turned her full attention on poor Nigel. 'I meant my acting. What did you think of me on stage?'

'I thought,' Nigel said softly, 'you were the most beautiful person I'd ever seen . . . until they painted you.'

'Well,' she exclaimed brightly as her drink was delivered. 'That's a start.'

'And I felt sorry for the snake,' Nigel went on. 'I don't like animals being exploited like that. It's inhumane.'

'That *fucking* snake!' Georgina growled. 'Marcus,' she looked at the young actor who had delivered her drink. 'How many times have I told Teddy – ' she drew breath and squinted angrily at Nigel, ' – Teddy's the writer director of the piece,' she informed him, before turning back to Marcus, 'how many times have I told Teddy that *fucking snake* is not worth the mice it's fed?'

'Hundreds, darling,' Marcus affected with an effeminate wave of his hand. 'But he just won't listen.'

'Exactly,' Georgina gushed. 'Thank you, Marcus.'

'It's the paint,' Marcus continued breathlessly, turning to Paul. 'Satan – that's the snake's name – doesn't like the paint. But Teddy insists he's essential to the opening scene because he's representative of the birth of Man. You know,' he waved his hand in Paul's face, 'the bloody Garden of Eden and the fucking apple or whatever, that Eve bit. Personally I think it's a metaphor for the knob of Adam's dick, but – '

'Yes, thank you, Marcus,' Georgina said archly, but Marcus would not be stopped.

'Anyway, I said to Teddy – ' he went on, sitting down next to Paul.

'Marcus!' Georgina snapped.

'Yes, pet?'

'Fuck off!'

'Ooh,' the young actor gave a moue. 'Snappy, snappy.'

'Paul may be my brother,' Georgina glared at Marcus, 'but he's also my number one fan. Aren't you, darling?'

'Indubitably,' Paul replied and winked at Nigel over the rim of his glass.

'And he's desperate to discuss my performance, so *do* let me get a word in.'

Marcus stood up, miffed, and joined the other cast members who were well on their way to a solid night of drinking.

'So,' Georgina threw looks at both men, 'apart from the suggestion of cruelty to animals, did you find the play wickedly confronting?'

'I'm afraid I'm not qualified to give an opinion,' Nigel replied diplomatically. 'It's my first experience of London fringe theatre. I know it's *avant-garde* and new wave and so on, but not being an *aficionado* of the theatre scene, so to speak . . .' Nigel's voice trailed off as he stared into Georgina's beautiful eyes. She has the same eyes as Paul, he thought, like some sort of jungle animal, some sort of hunting animal. There was a fierce honesty in them. '. . . But I must say, you were terrific,' he finished lamely, then looked to Paul for help.

Georgina smiled and turned to her twin. 'He's absolutely lovely,' she said. 'And he's a gentleman, a rare commodity in Swinging bloody London these days. Oh,' she sighed theatrically and pressed the back of her hand to her forehead, 'why can't I find a gentleman? It's not fair. I'm going to make it a New Year's resolution to search London until I find one. The new year of 1966 will be my Year of the Gentleman.'

'Not in London it won't, little sister,' Paul said.

'And why not?'

'Because you're coming home to Hong Kong with me, that's why not.'

'I don't think so, darling.' She stared at him.

'You finished school in Geneva in October, Georgie,' he continued reasonably, 'and you were supposed to go straight home then. Mother's complaining that you've neither written nor telephoned her for a month and Father has had it up to here with you.' He placed the back of his fingers under his chin. 'I've had him on the phone three nights running and your orders are clear cut, my girl.'

'Really.' Georgina tried to sound defiant, but there was a touch of fear in her eyes.

'I've managed to talk him into letting you stay until the New Year, but that's it.' He shrugged apologetically. 'I fly home to Hong Kong on the sixth of January and, whether you like it or not, so do you. Dear Papa's orders.'

'Well, I won't!' Georgina felt the strange onset of tears, tears of frustration. Her father was dictating her life yet again, and it angered her.

'Don't even contemplate disobeying him, Georgie.' Paul patted her arm affectionately. 'You've had your taste of freedom as far as Father is concerned. Just think yourself lucky he doesn't know about your theatrical aspirations. By, God,' he chuckled, 'if he'd seen you tonight, I dread to think what he'd have done.'

'Probably shot me,' Georgina laughed humourlessly, 'right on stage.'

'And the rest of the cast along with you, I dare say,' Paul added. 'And had you all buried in a pauper's grave.'

'Ha!' Georgina scoffed. 'Then he'd have bought the theatre and turned it into a warehouse.'

'He sounds like a bit of an ogre.' Nigel's remark brought a stare from the siblings. 'I'm sorry,' he stammered, 'I was just thinking out loud.'

'He's a hard man, our father,' Paul said. 'He can be a bit of a martinet.'

'That's putting it mildly,' his twin remarked caustically.

'He made Paul his whipping boy from day one. Nothing he ever did could please Father.' She patted her brother's arm without breaking eye contact with Nigel. 'He was a soft, shy boy with lovely manners, which was probably the first glimmer of his homosexuality showing through . . .'

'Please, Georgie . . .'

'. . . and Father simply didn't see it. He put Paul through the nine chambers of hell trying to make him into a beer swilling, rugby playing thug. Father detests homosexuals, you know? If he knew that you and Paul were – '

'Not now, Georgie,' Paul pleaded. 'We're in London, it's the festive season and you're an outrageous creature of the theatre, remember? And you're in a smash hit in the West End.' He smiled at her. 'So not now, Sis, eh? Let's enjoy the moment?'

'Hear, hear,' Nigel offered raising his pint. 'Here's to *Organic Matters* and its star performer, the outrageous Miss Georgie Merchant.'

'I'll drink to that!' Georgie exclaimed loudly then realised her glass was empty. 'Oh, no, I won't. Wait a minute.'

The two boys watched as she climbed onto the table top and struck a dramatic pose.

'The first man to get me a Campari and soda with a slice of orange,' she declared loudly to all in the bar, 'can have me!'

'Georgie!' Paul was horrified.

'Here you go.' A long arm stretched towards her holding out a Campari complete with a slice of orange, and the gesture brought a huge cheer from the crowded bar.

'Well,' Georgie looked at the man offering the drink and tried to bluff it out. 'Who's a lucky boy then?'

'I'd say I am,' the man replied as she took the glass from him. 'May I help you down from there?'

'You certainly may,' she replied. The man put his hands on her hips, and as he lowered her to the floor, she wrapped her arms about his neck and kissed him full on the mouth.

'Oh, God,' Paul groaned, looking at Nigel. 'Here we go again.'

Having regained the high ground in a game of one-upmanship, Georgie was about to break away when she felt the man's two powerful arms embrace her and the kiss suddenly became the stuff of dreams. As the whole bar howled its approval, she experienced the kiss all the way to her core. The cheers of the crowd receded and Georgie found herself swept away on a sea of bliss. She clung to the stranger, not wanting the kiss to stop. She was not a virgin and she considered herself worldly, but she'd never experienced anything like this before. When at last the stranger relinquished control, she stood panting, staring up at him.

'My name's Jeremy,' he said softly.

'Georgina,' was all she could manage.

'I say, old man,' Paul said. 'Can I have my sister back?'

'Yes, of course,' Jeremy laughed. He took Georgina by the hand and seated her next to her brother.

'Won't you join us?' Paul slid around the circular seat to make more room, as did Georgie, and the man sat.

'The name's Jeremy,' he said reaching across Georgie to shake hands.

'Paul Merchant. This is my friend, Nigel Shawbridge.'

'How do you do?' Nigel replied, shaking Jeremy's hand. 'Would you like a drink? It seems yours has been taken,' he said gesturing at Georgie's Campari. 'I'll get a round in, shall I?'

'Splendid idea, Nige,' Paul said. 'I'll have a pint of Bass. And Jeremy?'

'Whisky thanks. Jameson Irish, no ice.'

'Don't you want another Campari and soda?' Paul asked.

'No.' Jeremy looked at Georgie. 'I don't drink it. I heard you demanding a Campari when you first arrived so I ordered you one. By the time I got to the table, you were standing on it demanding a refill in exchange for your favours. The timing couldn't have been better.'

'Kismet?' Georgie said, looking him straight in the eye.

'I certainly hope so.'

'What brings you to the West End, Jeremy?' Paul asked, as Nigel slid out of the cubicle and headed for the bar. 'Been to the theatre?'

'Yes.'

Georgina, sitting between the two men as they talked across her, was very aware of Jeremy's thigh touching hers. What had happened to her? she wondered. What was it about this man that had engendered such a rush of sensation? She'd never felt anything like it before.

As the two men talked, she tried to get a better look at Jeremy without making her investigation too obvious. He was older than her by about ten years, making him probably thirty odd, she guessed. Tall, about six feet two with a muscular physique, clear olive skin and blond hair, slightly receding. He'll be bald by the time he's forty, she thought. He had a strong face with intelligent blue eyes, but it was his hands that drew her attention. Georgie prided herself on her eye for detail, it was part of the actor's trade, she'd recently decided. And these were not the hands of a working man. They were big and, she had no doubt, powerful, but his palms were soft like those of a professional man, unused to manual labour. And he had the strangest little scars on the knuckles of his thumbs where they joined the hand. Tiny little white scars that ran in straight lines, less than half an inch long. She wondered what on earth could have caused them.

'I went to the opening night in February at the Arts Theatre in Cambridge,' Paul was saying.

'The opening night of what?' Georgina asked, suddenly aware that her fascination with Jeremy's hands had caused her to lose the thread of the conversation.

'Joe Orton's play, *Loot*,' her twin replied. 'Jeremy was saying he likes the kitchen-sink dramatists and I recommended Orton to him.'

'Orton has a nasty and smutty sense of humour, which I don't approve of,' Georgie said. 'And he's repetitive. He can't help himself. If he finds something funny, he repeats it *ad nauseum*.' She looked at Jeremy. 'Give me John Osborne any day, darling, or Shelagh Delaney. Have you seen *Look Back in Anger* or *A Taste of Honey*? They're both far superior examples of the kitchen-sink genre.'

'I've heard of them,' Jeremy replied lamely. 'I'm afraid my knowledge of theatre is limited. In fact, it's nearly non-existent.'

He offered an apologetic look and Georgie's hormones went silly again. God, what's wrong with me? she asked herself. He'll probably turn out to be an oaf, another immature, beer swilling oaf who'll try to grope me in a bloody laneway. She looked at his hands again. Then again, you never know, Georgie my girl. She smiled at him. You just never know.

'Do you like German beer?' she asked him as Nigel placed a whisky on the table and slid in next to Paul.

'Yes, I do. Why do you ask?'

'Well, there's a German beer keller in the Strand off Trafalgar Square that serves freezing cold Lowenbrau and Wiener sausages with mustard and sauerkraut in huge bread rolls. If we hurry we might get there before it closes. What do you say?'

'Sounds good to me,' Jeremy replied enthusiastically. 'But Nigel's just bought me a drink.'

'Don't worry about us,' Paul said. He was rather hoping they'd leave. He'd prefer to be alone with Nigel.

'Then it's settled.' Georgie beckoned Jeremy and they both stood. 'Goodnight, Nigel,' she said. 'It was nice to meet you.'

'And you, Georgie,' he replied. ''Night, Jeremy.'

'Goodnight, Nigel. Paul. It was a pleasure,' Jeremy answered.

Be careful, Little Sister, Paul said quickly in Cantonese.

It is the age of enlightenment, Big Brother. I'm twenty years old and on the pill, Georgie said and winked at him. *I can take care of myself.*

Don't be so sure. He's not the limp-wristed hippy type you're used to, true or not true? He'll eat you for breakfast if you're not careful.

Oh yes, please! Georgie laughed. *I certainly hope so.* She turned to Jeremy. 'Shall we go?' she asked and made her way through the crowd.

'Goodnight, lads,' Jeremy said, then leaned down to Paul's

ear. *'I will take proper care of your sister,'* he whispered clumsily in Cantonese. *'And do not worry, I do not eat breakfast. I eat noodles about eleven o'clock.'*

Georgie heard Paul's roar of laughter from the door and turned back as Jeremy joined her. 'What was that all about?' she asked.

'I tried to down my whisky too fast and spilled it,' he lied, opening the door for her. 'We'd better hurry if we're going to get that beer and sausage.'

Paul and Nigel finished their drinks and left not long after. They made their way slowly from Shaftesbury Avenue to Leicester Square and entered Burton's, one of many over-priced, late night supper clubs in the area. They located a secluded table and Paul ordered vintage champagne to complement crumbed scampi, *pâté de foie gras*, smoked salmon and a platter of English cheeses.

'What's wrong?' he asked, noticing the shocked look on Nigel's face.

'You do realise,' Nigel whispered, after scanning the menu again, 'that what you just ordered will cost about fifty pounds?'

'So? I'm rich, Nige. Get used to it.'

'I'm sorry, Paul. I'm trying, really I am, but what you've just spent on supper represents my entire budget at Cambridge for over a month.' He stared at his companion for some seconds, searching for the right words. 'I come from a working class background and I'm not used to this. I'm uncomfortable with extravagance. I feel as though the waiter will come any minute and ask me to leave. Do you understand?'

'Yes,' Paul nodded.

'I don't have enough money to pay half of the bill. Well, I mean, I do have it . . . in the bank . . . but only just . . .'

'I'll pay the bill, Nige.'

'Yes, I'm sure you will. But that's not the point, is it?'

'Now you've lost me. What is the point?'

'I am not rich,' he stumbled on, 'but I am honest and I have my pride – '

'Sir?' The waiter interrupted, showing Paul the bottle of champagne's label. He opened it, offered a taste for approval, then, after filling their glasses, placed the bottle in an ice bucket and left.

'I'm sorry, Nigel – '

'No,' Nigel interrupted. 'Let me finish. Our friendship is important to me, and when you asked me to come to London to spend Christmas, I was overwhelmed, but I didn't even think about it. I packed a bag and came straight up. You gave me a beautiful room in your grand house in Belgravia and you've been the perfect host. The last three days have been like a dream, and, quite frankly, I've been walking on air, but I'm not rich, I can't afford this lifestyle and – '

'May I ask you a personal question?' Paul leaned forward over the table.

'Yes,' Nigel nodded. 'I suppose so.'

'You *are* homosexual, aren't you?'

'No.' Nigel's face reddened with embarrassment. 'I am not,' he said defensively as he stared at Paul. Then his gaze faltered and he looked away. Tears were welling in his eyes and Paul reached out to take his hand, but Nigel avoided the contact, folding his hands in his lap.

'I think I am, yes,' Nigel said finally. 'But that is not the main issue.'

'Then what is?'

'I have good digs at Cambridge and good colleagues, not what you'd call friends, really, but they respect me. And I had every intention of going on to collect my doctorates and dedicate my life to academia. I was safe in my world of academia, you see? It was cosy and . . . well, yes . . . asexual, but I was content with my lot. That was, until I met you.' He looked again at Paul. 'You've befriended me like no other person ever has and I'm not only flattered, but grateful.'

'My friendship for you is very real, Nige. I'm glad you came up for Christmas.'

'I know,' Nigel sniffed and blew his nose into a handkerchief. 'And I understand the implications more now since you admitted to your own homosexuality in the pub earlier.

I would never have guessed . . . and I must add, I'm not averse to . . . well . . . I mean . . .' He faltered, struggling for the right words, then they came flooding out.

'I haven't been able to stop thinking about our friendship all night, Paul, but we're from entirely different worlds. You're wealthy, charming, completely extroverted and sometimes flamboyant, even. You're athletic, highly intelligent and physically beautiful.' His eyes filled with tears again. 'I'm none of those things. I'm . . . oh God, look at me, blubbering like a child,' he sniffed, then stood. 'Please excuse me a moment, I must regain my composure. I'm embarrassing myself.'

Paul watched him walk out of the restaurant as the waiter arrived with the food.

'Will your friend be returning?' the waiter asked.

'I hope so,' Paul replied. He lit a cigarette and watched the food being placed on the table. Had he made a mistake inviting Nigel to London? He hoped not. He'd considered it very carefully before making the offer and he'd allowed a couple of days for Nigel to settle in and relax.

'Damn it!' he cursed under his breath. After all this time, he'd still underestimated Nigel's sensitivity and it had proven a serious miscalculation. He'd wanted so much for their night out to go well, but, in typical Merchant form, he'd gone at it like a bull at a gate and jeopardised the whole relationship before it had even been properly defined.

Over the preceding year, Paul had decided to come to terms with his sexuality once and for all. After a life of self-enforced heterosexuality, in which several serious affairs with girls had taken place, each one proving more disastrous, he'd arrived at the conclusion that he was fooling no one but himself.

The fact that his father was a homophobic bully had not helped. James Merchant's tirades about homosexuals, which included the use of such distasteful metaphors as 'buggers who bat for the other side' and 'brown-nosed shirt lifters' had seen Paul raised in an atmosphere of dread and loathing for all things homosexual. His father had insisted he learn to fight and excel at every masculine activity ever invented. 'It will prepare you for the evils of boarding school, my boy,' he would declare at any given opportunity. And if Paul ever shed tears, which he did, more and more often as his formative years rolled by, his father was scathingly critical.

Fortunately for Paul, his mother, Katherine, sheltered him from many of the attacks. She monitored her son's behaviour closely and defused potentially dangerous situations by drawing her husband's attention to other more important family matters, imagined or otherwise.

His mother had encouraged in Paul, and his sister, the characteristics that most favoured them. She gave them a love of art and literature, she emphasised the importance of education, she enlivened their imaginations with stories and games, and she gave them kisses at bedtime as she tucked them in. And each day, without fail, she told them they were special and that she loved them dearly. It had been Katherine Merchant alone who had painted the personalities of her children. She, alone, had been responsible for the two beautiful, brilliant and well adjusted young people who now, in turn, coloured her world.

Paul smiled fondly at the memory of his mother. She would understand what he was trying to do and she would be proud of him for the honesty and integrity he was displaying.

'I'm sorry about that,' Nigel said, appearing several minutes later. He sat down and placed his napkin across his lap. 'This looks wonderful.' His smile was forced, brittle, as he waved his hand over the supper spread. 'My God, we'll be lucky to get through it all.'

'Here's to our friendship, Nigel.' Paul raised his glass of champagne.

'Yes,' he replied and they clinked glasses, 'to our friendship.'

'Drink it all,' Paul said after watching him sip tentatively. 'Go on,' he encouraged. 'Drink it down. All of it.'

Nigel did as he was told and watched Paul do likewise then refill their glasses.

'Gosh,' he gasped. 'So that's vintage champagne. Rather more-ish, I must say.'

'Good. Now let's eat like hunting earls, throw the bones to the wolfhounds and let the '53 vintage kick in.'

'Right you are.' Nigel tucked into the feast before them. 'I say, '53 eh? Was that a good year for champagne?'

'I wouldn't have a bally clue, Nige.' Paul laughed, heaping food onto his plate. 'I know Hillary climbed Everest and Queen Elizabeth had her coronation, but just what the grapes of France were doing, one could only guess, probably hanging on the vine awaiting their destiny, waiting to be transformed.' He raised his glass and looked at Nigel. 'Just like us.'

'How so?' Nigel asked through a mouthful of pâté. He raised his glass too, and they clinked and sipped.

'We're hanging on the vine, Nige, you and me. Just like the grapes of Champagne. We're suspended in time waiting, no – hoping – hoping desperately to be picked, pressed and trans-formed into what nature ordained for us.'

'That's a beautiful analogy, Paul.' Nigel stopped eating and looked at his friend. 'But at the same time, it's very sad.'

'Yes,' Paul nodded, 'and there's more. If grapes aren't picked, they rot on the vine and, eventually, they fall to the earth and turn to dust.'

'I don't want to turn to dust.' A look of horror came over Nigel's face. 'My God, what an awful thought.' His eyes held a plea.

'Neither do I.' Paul put his glass on the table and took Nigel's hand. 'When you spoke earlier, you were voicing symptoms of loneliness, a *specific* loneliness. I have suffered that same loneliness, Nigel, but I'm not going to any longer. I decided, when I asked you to spend Christmas with me, that I would not be shackled by it any more. I fell in love with you the moment I laid eyes on you. I think you're brilliant and wonderful and I don't care what anyone thinks anymore, including my father. I'm not going to lock myself away in an asexual environment, as you did. Nor will I be content anymore with the odd clandestine assignation in a rented room above Piccadilly. I want to experience love, with you, and trust, in an honest and open relationship, just like any human being has the right to do, and damn the moral majority.'

A tear ran unhindered down Nigel's cheek.

龍

Georgina Merchant lay in her bed bathed in sweat still recovering from her blissful encounter. She had lost count of the number of orgasms she'd experienced. It seemed, she decided, that the last two hours had been one long uninterrupted orgasm. She'd finally begged for rest and Jeremy, like the only two other men she'd ever slept with, promptly fell asleep. She'd been annoyed on the previous occasions, but she'd not been offended at all this time. She felt happy about it, because it allowed her to examine him.

Jeremy Bent was beautiful, she decided, as she looked at his sleeping form. He was tall and handsome and a thorough gentleman – until he got into bed, that was, then he turned into a monster. But a beautiful monster, she thought, smiling to herself in the moonlit room. A beautiful, brilliant, predatory monster. God, what a lover. She shivered with delight at the memory of their love-making. But then, she'd fallen under his spell before they'd even reached her house in Belgravia.

The beer keller in the Strand had been closed so they'd bought a bag of hot roasted chestnuts from a vendor's cart, sat in Trafalgar Square and discussed the monuments of London. Georgie had taken the bull by the horns and launched into a vivid monologue about London's famous landmarks. She knew all about them and it had taken ten minutes for her to realise she was running off at the mouth, yet again, so, she promptly shut up.

When will you ever learn? she'd asked herself. Good looking girls with brains, as you well know from experience, are anathema to boys.

'Why have you gone quiet all of a sudden?' Jeremy asked. He'd been enjoying her rambling discourse on English architecture and especially her knowledge of Christopher Wren and the building of St Paul's Cathedral.

'I don't want you to think I'm a "brain",' she blurted out, then felt incredibly stupid.

'I think it's wonderful,' he replied. 'Are you an architect?'

'No,' she laughed, embarrassed. 'I'm not qualified in anything really. It's more the fact that I'm nearly qualified in everything. Does that make sense?'

'Where did you go to school?'

'North London Collegiate.'

'Wow,' Jeremy raised an eyebrow, 'very exclusive, I must say.'

'Yes,' she reddened with embarrassment, 'and then *College de Vouraine* near Lake Geneva.'

'The Continent, no less!' He raised both eyebrows. 'Even more exclusive.'

'I can sound like a real know-it-all sometimes.' She wrinkled her nose in apology. 'I had a very broad education in schools that encouraged inquisitiveness. I'm afraid I've studied just about every subject you could name.'

'Philosophy?'

'Yep,' Georgie nodded, 'I'm the full book.'

'Physics?'

'Pretty full there too.'

'Chemistry?'

'No,' she laughed and shook her head. 'I left that one to my brother.'

'Anatomy?' Jeremy stood, and, putting his hand behind her neck, drew her up from where they'd been sitting on the edge of the fountain.

'Yes.'

'Biology?'

'Oh, God, yes,' Georgie breathed, and he kissed her long and deep. She'd been waiting for it. When he put his arms around her, she felt the same rush of emotion she'd experienced in the pub.

He released her and looked into her eyes. 'History?' he asked.

'Yes, I am,' she said dreamily.

'Sorry?'

'I mean, yes.' She quickly recovered herself. 'Yes, I've studied History. Just about all of it. What do you want to know?'

'How about Nelson?' Jeremy gestured upward at the English naval hero atop his column.

'Battle of Trafalgar, 1805. England one, France nil.' *Kiss me again*, she thought.

Laughing, he took her by the hand and they began to walk towards Admiralty Arch.

'Let's see how good you really are. Tell me about Admiralty Arch.'

Georgie explained it in full as they walked under the arch to enter The Mall, and began the long walk towards Buckingham Palace. Jeremy continued to ask questions and Georgie continued to answer them until they'd passed the palace and walked the length of Green Park to Constitution Arch.

'Before you ask,' Georgie said, 'that's Constitution Arch, originally Wellington Arch, and also known as Green Park Arch. It was designed by Decimus Burton and erected in 1828 at Apsley House, which isn't far from here actually. It was transferred to this site in 1883. The statue on top is a chariot, being pulled by four horses. It's known as *The Quadriga*, which is just a fancy name for a chariot with four horses, harnessed abreast, I think.'

'I'm impressed.'

'There's more.' She laughed. 'The original statue on it was of one of the Dukes of Wellington, but it was replaced by *The Quadriga* in 1912. And if you look closely at it in daylight, you'll see a small boy – he's holding the horses' reins. He's the son of some lord or other who sponsored the statue. How's that for nepotism? Have your kid immortalised in bronze, right outside Buckingham Palace, before he's achieved anything more than a dirty nappy.'

They laughed, then Georgie stopped walking and looked at him. 'But the most important thing about this arch is that I live just beyond it, in Belgravia.'

'An expensive part of town,' he remarked, appearing to miss her veiled invitation.

'I own a terrace in Ebury Street. Well, I half own it with my brother, Paul.' She found herself rambling on again. 'Our step-grandfather Richard Brewster gave it to us. It's called Dragon House because it used to be the London townhouse of a company called Dragon Imports, before the war.' She stopped. 'I'm rambling on again, aren't I?'

'It's because you're nervous.'

'Is it?' She wanted to brazen it out, but she knew he was right. She was unsure of her emotions and her hormones were working overtime. She desperately wanted this man to make love to her.

'Yes. You have two options open to you.'

'And what are they?'

'I can take you to your door and kiss you goodnight, or I can take you to your bed and kiss you good morning.'

龍

On the first floor of Dragon House, in the main bedroom, Nigel Shawbridge lay awake as Paul Merchant slept soundly by his side. His gaze wandered around the opulent suite from the four-poster bed they lay in. Everything reeked of wealth. Even in the dark he could make out Chippendale furniture, Dresden china, delicate porcelain figurines and a Turner seascape on the wall which, he could only suppose, was the original. It was unlikely the Merchant family would own a copy of anything.

The previous two nights he'd stayed in the Ebury Street address, Paul had done nothing to indicate anything like this would eventuate – nothing to indicate his desire, or that he was even homosexual. In fact, Paul's admission had come as a complete surprise. Then, in Burton's Supper Club, things had taken a far more serious turn. Nigel's defences had crumbled one by one, and by the time they'd reached the house in Belgravia, his fate had been assured.

Nigel had never dreamed that making love could be so wonderful. His previous experiences had been restricted to rather brutish sessions with older boys at the grammar school he'd attended in Kent, and several unsatisfactory visits to a male brothel in Soho after he'd first arrived at Cambridge. The brothel encounters, in particular, he'd regarded as insalubrious, to say the least. They'd been furtive, grubby, financial affairs which had turned him off the idea of sex altogether, and he'd retreated to his world of dusty academia, vowing never to venture forth again.

Paul had overwhelmed him. From the moment they'd gained the security of the entrance hall, his heady masculinity had been irresistible and Nigel had succumbed like a lamb to the slaughter. Paul had kissed and caressed him until he'd been breathless, then lured him upstairs with whispered promises of more. Nigel had been powerless, unable to resist.

What happens now? he wondered idly. Should he sneak off to the room he'd been provided with, or sleep where he lay? And what will happen in the morning, he wondered. Would there be an awkward silence between them, or a cheerful intimacy? Nigel had no idea. He lay staring at the canopy above the bed, half of him wishing he was back in his digs at Cambridge, and the other half, the newly awakened half, wishing fervently that Paul would wake up and make love to him again.

龍

'I can take you to your door and kiss you goodnight,' Jeremy had said, 'or I can take you to your bed and kiss you good morning.' That's when she'd fallen in love, Georgie decided.

She looked at him sleeping beside her, curled up like a big baby boy, wrapped in a tangle of her silk bed sheets. She couldn't take her eyes off him. But it wasn't sexual desire that made her stare. It was a deep seated need to watch over him until morning came, to see him stretch, and yawn, and wake up to a brand new day.

Georgie rolled onto her side, her face inches from his, and let her eyes roam over his face. It was a strong face, she decided, a handsome face. His nose was slightly too large and his hair was receding a little, but his skin was flawless and his lips, the lips that had driven her wild not an hour before, were perfect. Red and full, she watched as they parted regularly with his breathing.

My God, she thought. I'm in love with him. How could it be possible? They'd only met a matter of hours before, but the thrill she felt looking at him sleeping in her bed was an entirely new sensation to her. It wasn't simply the afterglow of a torrid sexual encounter. Although the encounter, or rather encounters, she corrected herself, had certainly been torrid, she felt tender between her legs and her hips and breasts ached deliciously. No, it wasn't an afterglow, this feeling flowing through her body. It was different, alien, and her female instincts were telling her to tread cautiously. She was in uncharted waters.

Her eyes wandered to his throat, following the gold chain around his neck. It disappeared beneath the sheet, which she carefully pulled aside, and she saw a little pendant, distinctly Chinese in design. How unusual, she thought. Her lover was wearing a piece of Chinese jewellery. It was a sign from the gods that could only mean good *joss*.

Her eyes wandered again, down his body to his hips. She looked at his penis, curled up asleep on his thigh, and she moved down the bed, fascinated. She'd never studied a penis at close quarters before.

'Hello, you,' she whispered, blowing warm air onto it. It reacted, rolling over slightly as if seeking a more comfortable position for sleep. She was mesmerised, and inspected it more closely. She blew softly again. Slowly, it rolled over onto its back and began to grow. Georgie couldn't tear her eyes away. It was as if it knew she was watching, and it grew and grew until it rose from the thigh and stiffened. Then it began to throb, rhythmically.

She moved back up the bed, resting her head on the pillow. 'Oh,' she took a sharp intake of breath. He was awake.

Jeremy was staring at her, a slow smile playing across his lips.

'Now look what you've done,' he whispered.

She was paralysed, unable to break from his gaze. She held her breath in expectation as his arms drew her to him.

Helpless, she rolled automatically onto her back and opened her legs as he rose over her body. Then slowly, he entered her.

The last thing she saw was the pendant, dangling in front of her eyes, before ecstasy overtook her yet again. She heard a voice, then realised it was her own, coming from somewhere far away, whispering, 'I love you. I love you. I love you.'

龍

'Hey! Sleepy head! Wake up!' Nigel heard a voice calling from beyond the mists of sleep. A wet flannel landed on his face, bringing him wide awake, and then Paul followed the flannel, diving on top of him.

'What time is it?' he asked.

'It's early morning and time for a walk.' Paul kissed him on the lips before getting back to his feet. 'Come on, Nige,' he called back over his shoulder as he returned to the bathroom. 'Get up to your room and put on your walking shoes. I'll show you Belgravia. Then we'll go to the train station. The café there does brilliant bacon and egg sandwiches and coffee like you simply wouldn't believe.'

'Have I got time to go to my room and shower?' Nigel sat up and tried to brush his tangled hair with his fingers.

'Yes, but be quick. Here,' Paul said, re-entering the room, 'put this on.' He tossed a towelling bath robe on the bed. 'It'll save you running up the stairs in the buff. Not that it would bother Georgie, but I think she's got old "Jeremy Campari" up in her blasted attic.'

'"Jeremy Campari", that's a good one.' Nigel laughed as he slid out of bed hiding his nakedness with the robe. He pulled it on and knotted the belt as he headed for the door. 'Give me ten minutes,' he said, with a sudden feeling of intense happiness.

'Right you are,' Paul called from the bathroom. 'Ten minutes. Downstairs.'

'Roger Wilco,' Nigel yelled back and pulled Paul's bedroom door closed behind him.

龍

Jeremy Bent awoke and reached sleepily for the beautiful body he'd left dozing next to him, but found only a cold silk sheet. He opened his eyes and squinted. Standing in the French doors that led out onto the roof, she was naked beneath a transparent silk peignoir, and framed by early morning sunlight. The effect was devastating, like a painting from the Dutch Golden Age.

'Good morning,' she said. 'I made breakfast for us. We can eat it in my garden,' she gestured behind her, 'out here on my roof.'

'Aren't I supposed to kiss you good morning?'

'Yes, you are. That's what you said last night.'

'Well, I can't do it if you're way over there.' He held out his arms and she walked over to the edge of the bed. 'You'll have to come closer than that, young lady,' he demanded.

Well, I'll be damned, he thought, as she held her hands together in front of her body, shielding the view of her pubic hair through the diaphanous silk garment, she's embarrassed. Where was the *femme fatale* of last night? he wondered. The girl now standing before him was genuinely unsure of herself.

'I was a bit outrageous last night,' she said shyly. 'And I was very wanton.'

'You certainly were.' He waited for her to continue.

'I hope you don't think that was bad.' She faltered. 'I mean, I hope you don't think badly of me. I've been trying to analyse my behaviour for the last hour. Despite what you may be thinking, it's out of character for me to – '

'Didn't you like what we did?' he interrupted.

'Oh yes,' she replied quickly. 'I think it was wonderful, but – '

'But what?' He reached over putting his hand between her legs, but she grabbed his wrist.

'Don't,' she said, then hastened to add, 'it's not that I don't want you to, but . . .'

'Well, how about that kiss?' She didn't resist as he drew her down beside him.

龍

Armed with the *Times* newspaper, the two young men entered the grand hall of Victoria Railway Station, only a short distance from Ebury Street in Belgravia. Paul secured a table immediately outside the door of the café and, while Nigel separated the sports pages from the editorial, Paul ordered bacon and egg sandwiches and rich espresso coffees.

'Right,' Nigel said, waving parts of the broadsheet aloft. 'We've got the Chelsea Football Club management crisis, an article on Craig Breedlove and his new land speed record, Charles De Gaulle re-elected, the war in Vietnam and the rebellion in Rhodesia. Name your poison.'

'No thanks, Nige. It's all too depressing by half. I think I'll sit for a bit and observe the hoi polloi. I love coming here and doing a spot of people watching.'

'Good idea.'

'I'm far too happy for war and politics at the moment, how about you?'

'Oh, yes,' Nigel replied, but he didn't look at his lover. He made a fuss of folding the newspaper into a neat pile and placing it on the chair next to him.

'You don't sound very sure,' Paul said. 'What's the problem?'

'Last night was wonderful,' Nigel finally looked at him, 'and I'm sure Christmas will be equally so, but – '

'But what, Nige?'

'But what becomes of me . . . of us . . . in the New Year?' Nigel's face was a mask of worry as he looked about to make sure they were not being overheard. 'What happens when you fly off to Hong Kong?'

'Stop it, Nigel,' Paul demanded. 'Correct me if I'm wrong, but I thought we made a commitment of sorts to each other last night. On reflection, I'm damned sure I did.'

'Yes, yes, we did,' Nigel stumbled to reply. 'But in the cold light of day, you know, with the thought of you being half the world away . . .' He ran out of words, looked at his friend and shrugged defensively.

'I told you last night how I feel about you,' Paul said, 'and you responded in kind. I said I love you, Nigel . . .'

'Shhh!' Nigel warned, casting another look around them.

'. . . And you,' he went on, 'repeated that very same phrase. Over and over, if my memory serves me correctly. Am I right?'

'Yes,' Nigel hissed. 'And I meant it.'

'And you'll say it again, I hope, in Hong Kong, when the time is right.'

'Will that really happen?' Nigel asked, suddenly unmindful of those nearby.

'You have my word, Nige. And I *never* renege on a promise. So stop worrying.' Paul stopped talking as their food arrived. 'But we've a rocky road in front of us,' he continued when the waitress had left. 'I have to return to Hong Kong and establish myself, in my own right. I've got plenty of money and there are direct flights five days a week, so I'll arrange for you to visit regularly.'

'I've never been out of England, you know.'

'Well, you'd better get used to the thought, because you'll be doing it a lot starting next year. But in the meantime, you go back to Cambridge and I'll go home to set up an environment we can share. We'll have to be careful at first, but expatriate society in Hong Kong, shallow though it may be, is much more tolerant than English society. I think we've got every show of making a go of it, Nige.'

Conflicting emotions ran through Nigel as he leaned back in his chair and stared at the cavernous roof of Victoria Station. Again, half of him wanted to run home to the safety of his dusty, book-lined digs in Cambridge, but the other half throbbed with nervous expectation as he visualised the two of them living life together in Asia. God, what am I getting myself into? he thought. Then he looked at Paul and his doubts disappeared. 'We'll have a great time, won't we?'

'Yes, we will.' Paul sipped his coffee and smiled, but clouds of doubt had begun to gather in his mind. God, I hope so, he thought.

龍

'The omelette was superb,' Jeremy exclaimed, as George came back out onto the rooftop with a pot of tea. 'The best I've ever eaten.'

They sat at an outdoor table surrounded by potted plants and shrubs, strategically placed to shield them from prying eyes in distant higher windows.

'Where did you get those scars?' Georgie asked, curious again about the tiny white parallel scars running over the knuckles of his thumbs.

'An occupational hazard,' he replied. Georgie suddenly realised with a jolt that she knew practically nothing about the man she was madly and deeply in love with.

'I don't even know what your occupation is,' she laughed. 'You've been in my house all night and for all I know you could be a professional burglar.'

'You've no worries on that front. I'm precisely the opposite, in fact,' he replied reaching over to brush a lock of hair from her eyes.

It was a loving gesture and Georgie delighted in the sweet familiarity of it. She adored him. She was head over heels and her face showed it.

'You're the opposite of a burglar, are you? So, what's that make you, a policeman?'

'Yes.'

'Oh!' Georgie quickly tried to conceal her surprise. She would never have picked him for a policeman. She struggled with an image of him in a London Bobby's uniform. She dismissed the misgivings trying to form in her mind. If she was destined to be the wife of a London Bobby, then so be it, and damn what anybody may think.

'These scars,' he said holding up his thumb knuckles, 'are caused by the recoil of the breech on self-loading handguns. I always make the mistake of holding a semi-automatic with two hands like a revolver and the damned breech cover shoots back and cuts my knuckles.'

A policeman. My God, what will Father say? The thought hit Georgie like a bombshell. Damn him! I'm twenty-one years old, I can do as I like. She smiled at her own defiance. Her mother wouldn't care one iota, and her grandmother had married a police officer, which actually made it a family tradition.

'What are you grinning at?' Jeremy broke into her thoughts.

'I'm sorry, my darling,' she answered. 'I was just thinking of what my father will say when he finds out I'm going to marry one of London's finest.'

'Marry?' Jeremy asked in the strangest tone.

'Oh, no!' Georgina blushed scarlet. 'I mean . . . I was just thinking out loud.'

'Oh, dear.' Now it was Jeremy's turn to blush. 'Look, Georgie, we've got to sort something out – '

'Don't be ridiculous,' she snorted. 'It was just a thought. I mean to say . . . for heaven's sake, I don't even know you.' She suddenly placed a hand over her mouth. 'My God, I don't even know your surname.'

'It's Bent. My name is Jeremy Charles Bent.'

'Bent,' Georgie frowned. 'I know that name.'

'There's something I need to explain to you – '

'How do I know that name?' She looked at him, racking her brain for the answer.

'If you'll just listen to me – '

'I know!' She pointed an index finger in the air and offered him the most beautiful smile. 'It's the name of a Hong Kong police officer. When I was at school in Hong Kong we used to think it was funny. You know, a copper called Bent. We made jokes about it. Inspector Bent is bent, we used to say. Inspector Jeremy is . . . oh no,' the colour drained from her face. She could see Jeremy's Chinese pendant clearly in her mind.

'Please listen – '

'It's you isn't it? You're *that* Jeremy Bent, from the Hong Kong Police.' Her hands went to her mouth as the realisation dawned. 'So you must have known who Paul and I were last night. You'd know all about me. My father and mother, my grandmother – '

'I wanted to say something, but I couldn't seem to find the right moment.' Jeremy reached for her hand, but she recoiled from him.

'How could you?' Georgie got to her feet and glared at

him, the ramifications of their night together beginning to formulate in her brain. 'How dare you?'

'Georgie,' he pleaded.

'So, I'm the latest feather in your cap, am I? And what a feather! Now you can tell all your friends at home you've fucked the daughter of James Merchant, can't you? The snotty rich bitch from up on the Peak. Guess what, boys? I screwed Georgie Merchant till she couldn't sit down!'

'That's enough!' Jeremy stood and glared back at her.

'You can say that again,' she sneered. 'You bastard!'

'If you'll only let me explain. I wanted to tell you last night, but – '

'And you should have!' Tears of anger filled her eyes. 'You should have been honest with me. But that would have spoilt your little conquest, wouldn't it?'

'It wasn't like that,' he snapped.

'Don't lie! It was exactly like that. You planned it down to the last bloody detail, didn't you? The Campari and soda. The chestnuts in Trafalgar Square. The long walk in the moonlight.' A horrified look came on her face. 'I'll bet you even knew where I lived.'

'That's ridiculous.' He reached for her but she slapped at his hands and stepped backwards.

'Do you really see me as some shallow society bimbo? Someone who thinks sex and love and relationships are capricious games? I'm a real person. I'm a good, honest person.'

'I know!' he yelled, his frustration showing.

'You betrayed me!' she screamed. 'You won my trust and betrayed me! And for what? My body? Was I worth it, Jeremy? Was I worth the price of a Campari and soda?'

'Right, that's it!' Jeremy lunged forward and grabbed her by the arms. 'You're going to listen to me,' he roared, then doubled up in pain as she drove her knee into his groin.

'I want you out of my house, right now,' she said looking down at his writhing body on the floor. 'Get your things and leave immediately, or I'll call the police and have you removed.'

'Georgie, please,' he managed to gasp through the pain.

'I will say nothing about last night and I'd strongly advise you to do the same, for your own sake.' She began to stride towards the French doors. 'If you want to continue your career in Hong Kong I'd suggest you heed my advice.' She stopped and turned to him. 'Believe me, the last person on earth you need as an enemy – especially in Hong Kong – is a Merchant.'

CHAPTER TWELVE

Hong Kong, December 1966

The Qantas Boeing 707 had dropped altitude considerably in preparation for landing at Kai Tak Airport and, from her window seat on the starboard side, Kwan Su-lin could see the mansions that dotted the southern side of Victoria Peak and the fishing junk–infested port of Aberdeen. Her excitement mounted as the Peak suddenly gave way to the stunning vista of Hong Kong Harbour. Nestled in the mid-morning sunlight, it glittered like a jewel and Su-lin's hand went to her mouth to stifle a gasp of joy. She was home at last.

The city had changed yet again, just as she had expected it would. Both Kowloon and the island had many more skyscrapers, and the suburbs of Kowloon stretched northward right up to the foothills of the mountains. The harbour remained the same, packed with ships of all kinds, but, she noticed, with an inordinate number of warships. She identified an aircraft carrier, several battleships and many smaller, but no less frightening, grey shapes anchored between Kowloon and the island.

The Vietnam War had escalated rapidly over the last several years and now, in December 1966, half of the US Seventh Fleet lay at anchor in her home town. Letters from her grandmother had described Hong Kong's transformation into 'a city of sin' where no one was safe from the evils of gambling and corruption, and the local population had become slaves to the American dollar. Elanora complained that the soldiers and sailors of America, Australia, New Zealand and other countries contributing troops to the war had chosen Hong Kong as their favourite city for rest and recreation, or 'R&R' as it had become known, and the local population was indulging them with every form of vice.

Thousands of servicemen on leave and desperate for respite from the war were pouring into the city daily. Night-clubs and girlie-bars had proliferated, especially in the tourist areas of Wanchai and Tsim Sha Tsui, and they catered for the soldiers' every whim.

Elanora's letters bemoaned the fact that 'rock and roll' music was the order of the day and dance halls in Mong Kok and Yau Ma Tei, filled with prostitutes and stocked heavily with cheap imported Macau brandy, were nothing less than 'organised temples of lust' as she called them.

The Boeing sailed over Kowloon and leaned hard to star-board, giving Su-lin the most extraordinary view. Not two hundred feet below her she could see people and motor vehicles in the congested streets, so close she felt she could reach down and touch them. Then the plane levelled out as it approached the runway and, on both her left and right, she could see people in the windows of high-rise buildings. She was suddenly terrified – the aircraft was flying straight through the buildings on its way to touching down at Kai Tak.

She saw a highway overpass packed with cars flash beneath her. Then the wheels hit the tarmac and the engines roared in reverse as the plane rushed down the runway that stretched like a needle out into the waters of Kowloon Bay. To her right, she could see Hong Kong Island across the harbour, its hundreds of high buildings glistening in the sunlight, and her grip on the arm rest relaxed. She was home at last.

The smell hit her nostrils as soon as she left the aircraft and began her long walk to Customs and Immigration. Four years in Sydney, Australia, had made her forget how smelly Hong Kong could be to the uninitiated. An open sewer ran into Kowloon Bay right next to the runway and its odour, through the air-conditioning ducts of the airport, was unmistakable.

'Welcome to Hong Kong, Miss Kwan,' the Immigration Officer said in English as he handed back her passport. 'I hope you enjoy your stay in our city.' It was a British passport. The officer had not even bothered to read it. Such was the power of British bureaucracy in Hong Kong, he'd simply stamped it and handed it back.

Su-lin didn't bother to correct his assumption that she was not local. Her grandmother had arranged the British passport for her, probably for an exorbitant amount of money, when she'd left for university four years before and she knew how lucky she was to have it. Su-lin was a *bone fide* English-woman, according to her passport, which also included permanent residency status in Australia.

The little blue book was a treasure most Hong Kong Chinese would kill to possess, for although they'd been born and lived all their lives in the British Crown Colony, British citizenship was unavailable to them. As far as the British, in the United Kingdom at least, were concerned, Chinese were Chinese and would never be considered compatriots.

Su-lin stood waiting for her luggage at the baggage carousel and pondered just how lucky she had been. Her parents had suffered years of political persecution before escaping from China to Hong Kong, where her grandmother, the most powerful woman in the colony, had arranged for Su-lin's education at Hong Kong's best school. Su-lin had been privately tutored and, to earn her grandmother's approval, she'd worked hard to excel. She'd gained her *baccalaureat internationale* at fifteen years of age, a year ahead of her contemporaries and had then been invited to attend Sydney University in Australia. Su-lin had no doubt her grandmother Elanora had a hand in the invitation. She'd completed a degree in medicine and had intended to complete her internship at Sydney's St Vincent's Hospital, but a family tragedy made it imperative she return home.

Su-lin's mother, Lin Li, had been ill for a long time, having never recovered from the hardship she'd suffered in the re-education camp in China years before, and slowly but surely she'd succumbed to tuberculosis. Lee Kwan had not forewarned his daughter of her mother's failing health because he'd wanted her to finish her degree, and so Su-lin graduated with honours, ignorant of the fact that her mother had died on the very same day.

Lin Li died in Lee Kwan's arms, high up on the northern slopes of Tai Mo Shan Mountain in the old monks' retreat, which Lee had secured from Richard Brewster and restored for their residence. Lee Kwan had buried his wife nearby and, according to the letters from Su-lin's brother, Jet, his grief remained inconsolable. Lee Kwan apparently sat each day by her grave and mourned from the depths of his spirit.

It was the reason Su-lin had come home. Her father and brother needed her. She intended to take her mother's place and care for them as befitted a good daughter. Her father had written to her in Sydney and told her to remain and continue her studies, but her internship could wait, she had decided. She had far greater responsibilities – responsibilities to which her mother would have expected her to attend.

Su-Lin's single piece of luggage, a now-battered old suitcase given to her by Richard Brewster, came round on the carousel. She took it and began making her way through the crowded terminal towards the Customs declaration ports.

'*Do you have or not have anything to declare?*' The Customs Officer lifted his eyes from her suitcase and stared at her.

'*Nothing.*' She shook her head.

'*I can search your bag and arrange for your body to be searched,*' the man declared. '*I am told it is a humiliating experience. Or it may not be necessary. The choice is yours.*'

Su-lin stared at him, understanding completely the expression on his face, and contempt rose like bile in her throat. '*Be very careful, Little Brother,*' she said evenly, returning his stare. '*I am not like your compatriots who kow-tow and pay bribes to small time Government officials.*'

'*Are you threatening me?*' The officer grinned maliciously.

'*Do you feel threatened?*' Su-lin knew she should have let the matter drop, but her anger at the man's arrogance was proving difficult to control. How dare he? was all she could think. *'A worm, when it is caught by a bird, understands its fate,'* she said to him. *'It was put on earth to be eaten by the bird, true or not true? Therefore it feels no sense of threat. So why should you?'*

'Are you saying I am a worm?' The man reached with one hand beneath his desk top.

'No. I am saying I am a bird. And before you push the security button I must tell you that my grandmother is waiting for me outside in the arrivals terminal.'

'Your grandmother?' the officer sneered. *'Fuck your grandmother. She can wait.'*

'The Merchant Mistress does not like to be kept waiting, Little Brother.' Su-Lin's statement had a devastating effect. She watched as the colour drained from the man's face. She'd hated using Elanora's name, but in this instance she forgave herself.

'You are the granddaughter of the Merchant Mistress?' the man croaked.

'Yes. And she is waiting to embrace me.'

'Welcome home, Miss Kwan.' The man offered a sickly smile. *'Please follow the white line on the floor. It will take you to the nearest exit.'*

The arrivals terminal was a sea of faces and Su-lin stood searching in vain for her grandmother. Then she saw a uniformed chauffeur holding a white card with her name on it. Next to him stood a beautiful young woman, looking rather impatient, glancing frequently at her watch.

'Georgina!' Su-lin recognised her immediately. Although they'd not seen each other for years, the Merchant twin was unmistakable.

'Su-lin!' Georgina grasped her shoulder. 'Thank God,' she gasped. 'I thought we'd missed you. Grandmother sent me to pick you up. She had to remain in Macau. Richard is ill.'

'Not seriously, I hope?'

'I'm not sure. Elanora was a bit vague on the telephone. Come on.' She indicated for the chauffeur to take Su-lin's suitcase from her. 'We'll talk in the car. You're to stay with us until the weekend, then Grandmother wants you to go to Macau.'

'But I want to go to Kap Lung,' Su-lin said as Georgie took

her arm and began leading her towards the exit. 'I want to see my father and Jet.'

'I'm afraid Grandmother's arranged it all, darling,' Georgina said as they passed through the main doors to the street. 'It's useless to argue with our *Ju Mo*. Just do as you're told, for all our sakes.'

The chauffeur opened the door of the Rolls Royce which was parked illegally immediately outside and Georgie bustled Su-lin into the back seat.

'I just want to see my dad,' Su-lin complained.

'You'll see him soon enough, dear. He knows you're coming. Grandmother had a telephone installed in the retreat at Kap Lung.'

'A telephone?' Su-lin couldn't suppress her surprise. 'Up at Kap Lung?'

'My very word.' Georgie laughed. 'Apparently your father detests it and has wrapped it in a hessian sack to muffle its ring. Anyway, he's sending Jet to Macau on Sunday. He is to take you home on Monday morning.'

'Oh, dear.'

'It's no good complaining, Su-lin. You know *Ju Mo* as well as I do. She always gets her way.' Georgina reached for the bottle of French champagne set in an ice bucket in front of them. 'Let's have a drink.' She took two glasses from the drinks cabinet set into the rear of the front seat.

'I don't drink.'

'If I'm to be your nursemaid for the next two days,' Georgie laughed, ignoring Su-lin's statement, 'the least you can do to make it easy for me is to have a drink.' She filled a glass and thrust it under Su-lin's nose. 'Please?' she begged girlishly. 'Pretty please, for me?'

'All right.' Su-lin gave in graciously. She realised how hard Georgie was trying and surrendered with a smile, but she could sense an underlying sadness in this beautiful girl.

'Goody,' the twin's smile lit up the car. 'Now,' she settled back with her own glass. 'Tell me all about Sydney and university and Australian men, especially the men. Did you fall in love many times?'

Su-lin could only laugh. Georgie was irresistible. Dressed in the latest micro mini-skirt and matching knee length boots, she looked like a model off the cover of an American fashion magazine. They clinked glasses and sipped.

'I'm afraid I had no time for boys.' Su-lin was suddenly aware of her own appearance. She'd worn denim jeans for the flight and her favourite old cardigan. She tried to avoid looking at Georgina's thighs, exposed nearly to the hip, and felt positively dowdy.

'But what about all those bronzed Aussie surfers?' Georgie laughed. 'I've heard they're absolute stallions between the sheets.'

'I wouldn't know about that,' Su-lin said, shyly. 'I visited Bondi Beach many times though, it's not far from the city, only about four or five miles. It's an inner suburb really.'

'And?' Georgie prompted her.

'It's beautiful, probably the most beautiful beach in the world, I shouldn't wonder.'

'But what about the boys?'

'Stop it, Georgie,' Su-lin chided. 'I won't be teased. Tell me about you and the family. You've been home almost a year, according to *Ju Mo*'s letters. What have you been up to?'

'Nothing,' Georgie sighed dramatically. 'Apart from defending myself from moronic young men my father keeps thrusting at me, that is. He's desperate to have me married off.' She took a packet of Viceroy cigarettes from her handbag, removed one and placed it in a ridiculously long cigarette holder. 'Do you think it's too much?' she asked, noticing Su-lin staring at it.

'I don't think you should smoke at all,' Su-lin replied.

'Daarling,' Georgina breathed in high camp exaggeration, 'if it weren't for tobacco and alcohol I'd die of boredom.'

'I don't believe that, Georgina. I remember when we were young, how intelligent you were, even then. You are not the vacuous young society dill you're pretending to be.'

'*Dill*?' Georgina asked. 'And what, pray tell, is a *dill*?'

'It's an Australianism. I think it's short for dilatory. Australians use it in the same way the English use the word twit.'

'Are you calling me a vacuous twit?' Georgina removed the cigarette from the holder and held it in her fingers.

'No,' Su-lin stated flatly. 'I'm saying I remember you being anything *but* a twit. However, you are presenting yourself as one, and I'd like to know why.'

'You certainly don't beat about the bush, do you, cousin?' The Merchant twin stubbed her cigarette out in an ashtray, leaned back in the luxurious leather seat and regarded Su-lin through half closed eyes. Curiously enough, she didn't feel offended by the Chinese girl's enquiry. Su-lin exuded goodness. It seemed to emanate from her like the warmth from a comforting fire. And there was more, something Georgie couldn't quite define.

'I did not mean to be rude,' Su-lin's voice was gentle, almost motherly. 'But I see beyond the affectation, Georgina.' She paused and looked out of the window. 'It is not a sin to be both beautiful *and* intelligent, you know,' she said, watching the passing parade that was Kowloon.

Georgina felt an urgent need to say something intelligent, but she couldn't think what. She racked her brain for a decent subject or at least a witty remark, but her mind was a blank. Do I really appear that facile? she asked herself. The young woman sitting beside her, whom she'd not seen for years, seemed to think as much. A vacuous young society dill, she called me. Is that really how I appear? she wondered. Why did Su-lin's words have such an effect on me? Who is she after all? Just an ordinary woman, merely a cousin, and even that by adoption, whom I haven't seen for years.

Georgie shook her head as she sipped her champagne and she, too, turned away to look out of the window. No, Su-lin was no ordinary woman. There had always been something magnetic about Su-lin, something indefinable that seemed to surround her like a cloud, and now, it was only more pronounced.

They travelled in silence for several minutes, then the two women chose precisely the same moment to turn towards each other. Their eyes locked and Georgina sensed an intense rush of emotion pass into her. It came from this woman sitting next to her, she was sure of it. It washed over her in waves until she wanted nothing more than to be held in Su-lin's arms like a child. The thought embarrassed her and she felt her face redden.

Su-lin smiled. '*Were you shown or not shown the way?*' she asked in Cantonese.

'*The way?*' Georgina replied, puzzled.

'*It does not matter. I believe you can sense it. One day I will explain.*' She took Georgina's hand. 'May I ask you a question?' she said, reverting to English.

'Of course.'

'If there was one person in the world you could emulate, who would it be?' Su-lin asked.

'Grandmother,' Georgie replied without hesitation, and quite shocked herself.

'Yes,' Su-lin nodded. 'I can see her in you.'

'Really?' Georgie felt genuinely flattered.

'Beauty and intelligence can be a formidable combination. And I sense in you the same indomitable spirit. You could do worse than emulate *Ju Mo*.'

'Do you really think I could?'

'What I think doesn't matter. It is what you think that matters.'

'Do you know,' the twin answered with a great sense of positivity, 'I think I probably could if I put my mind to it.'

Georgina suddenly found a new voice and clarity of thought she'd not experienced for a long time. They chatted enthusiastically as the Rolls Royce made its way through the Kowloon traffic on its way to the car ferry which would take them across the harbour to Hong Kong Island.

龍

'*In English, Polly is the name of a bird. A parrot, true or not true?*'

'*Not in this case, Wellington,*' Paul Merchant replied, wishing to heaven that he'd never attempted to explain plastic manufacturing to the Woo twins, especially in Cantonese.

'*But birds do not have fins,*' Napoleon offered. '*Fish have fins, true or not true?*'

'*Paul is going to make a plastic bird with fins,*' Wellington said, then looked at Paul. '*Is that what you mean, Elder Brother?*'

'*No.*' Paul shook his head patiently. '*I said polyolefins. They are a family of plastics.*'

'*Ah,*' Napoleon nodded wisely. '*I understand. You will make a family of plastic birds.*'

'*Will these birds fly, or swim?*' Napoleon asked.

'*They will do both, true or not true, Ah Paul?*' Wellington looked at the flustered young man who was, by now, shaking his head in despair.

'*Ah,*' Napoleon nodded again, with more vigour. '*I understand. It is an excellent idea. A plastic children's toy that can fly like a bird and swim like a fish. It will be very educational. Every child will want one,*' he added hopefully.

The three men stood in a warehouse in the Kowloon suburb of Mong Kok. It was a large building that had once been a bus depot for the Kowloon and New Territories Transport Company, which had gone bust a year previously. It had wide roller doors at each end, both with street access, lots of floor space for machinery and, in one corner of the cavernous building, a small office.

The Woo twins, at Elanora's request, had entered into a partnership with the Merchant twins and had purchased the place to be the base of operations for Paul's plastic manufacturing business. The Woo twins were only too aware of the burgeoning plastic industry and had been more than happy with Elanora's suggestion that they help young Paul and Georgina. Their investment had been a modest one but their business sense told them it would only be a matter of time before it would be returned ten-fold. Paul, Elanora had assured them, was an expert in plastic manufacturing.

'*And you will make these birds with this machine?*' Wellington pointed at the large crate next to him that contained an air compressor the Woos had acquired at Paul's direction.

'*Not exactly.*' Paul sighed. '*That is a compressor. It will link to that machine,*' he explained, pointing to a large boiler, '*which will link to that machine.*' He indicated an even larger air cooling device. '*And that will link to another machine, which will arrive tomorrow.*'

'*And together they will make the plastic birds!*' Napoleon declared triumphantly, pleased with himself for understanding the complicated matter.

'*Excuse my curiosity, can I ask or not ask where you got this air compressor?*' Paul was desperate to steer the course of the conversation away from the chemical properties of plastic.

'*It is better for you not to ask,*' Wellington replied.

'*Definitely better,*' Napoleon agreed.

'*The crate is marked Property of the United States Navy.*' Paul pointed at the brand. '*Should I worry or not worry about it being in our warehouse?*'

'*Not worry,*' Wellington answered.

'*Definitely not worry,*' Napoleon added, sharing a glance with his twin.

'Jesus,' Paul muttered in English.

'Jesus was a Christian,' the elder twin exclaimed, seizing the opportunity Paul's muttered profanity had presented. It would afford him the opportunity to ask an important question without appearing rude.

'And a very good one apparently, Wellington,' Paul said, stifling a laugh. He wondered where on earth the conversation was now headed.

'He is much admired by all *gwai loh*,' Napoleon said, keen to continue the subject. 'Could you make Jesus out of plastic?'

'All *gwai loh* like to have a statue of Jesus,' Wellington went on enthusiastically, 'especially on the cross the Romans nailed him to.'

'And the medallion of the saint called Christopher,' Napoleon chimed. 'Many *gwai loh* like to have this medallion. We could sell many such medallions.'

'And the rosemary beads,' Wellington added. 'Don't forget the rosemary beads.'

'Rosary,' Paul corrected. 'It's rosary beads.'

'Yes,' Wellington said blankly.

'Religious artefacts, eh?' Paul nodded. 'That's a very good idea, gentlemen.' He leaned on the air compressor crate and scratched his chin, considering the matter. 'As a matter of fact, it's a damned good idea.'

Wellington and Napoleon exchanged a knowing look. They had a buyer ready and waiting, but had decided not to tell Paul of the lucrative deal until the manufacturing plant was up and running. It was better, they agreed, not to excite him with the story of Geoffrey Hilditch, thereby allowing him to concentrate on his more immediate endeavours.

Geoffrey Hilditch, a wealthy Irish businessman and frequent patron of the Heroes of Waterloo nightclub, had suggested the idea, in his cups one night at the watering hole. A fanatical Catholic – when he wasn't engaged in all night drinking and fornicating – Hilditch was on the board of directors of the Hong Kong Branch of the Society of Jesus. He had casually remarked that ivory was becoming so scarce that plastic was rapidly replacing it as the material for all Catholic paraphernalia. The Woo twins had listened avidly and then informed him they had just such products already on the production line. Hilditch, a businessman first and foremost, had claimed he'd buy up all they could manufacture and a deal had been struck, dependent upon a satisfactory inspection of the goods before purchase.

'Making the moulds would be simple enough,' Paul said to himself more than the twins, who were grinning at each other like Cheshire cats. 'Then we'd just need to touch them up with a bit of paint, dip them in a light varnish, and Bob's your uncle.'

'I think Jesus is a better idea than the family of birds, Mister Paul?' Napoleon asked hopefully.

'It certainly is,' said the young Merchant with all the seriousness he could muster. 'I think I'll drop the family of birds and go for the range of Christian items. It's a splendid idea.'

'We must leave you with this splendid idea,' Wellington said with a nod to his brother.

'Yes, that is correct,' Naploeon added. 'We must return to our nightclubs in Wanchai to sell happiness to the Seventh Fleet. Is it not amusing, Mister Paul, that we will be taking money from promiscuous American sailors and using it to manufacture statues of Jesus?'

'Ha!' Paul guffawed. 'There's a moral in there somewhere, Napoleon.'

He could not have wished for better partners, he thought, as he watched them walking from the warehouse. He'd had a business plan formulating in his mind which concerned the manufacture of key rings and cigarette containers, but Christian accessories was simply brilliant. And, he smiled, he had a sneaking suspicion the Woos already had a buyer. He knew he'd been manipulated, but it only made him admire the twins even more.

When they had gone, Paul returned to his small office and sat at his second hand desk. The clock on the wall chimed nine and he thought guiltily of his mother and grandmother waiting at Merchant House, hoping for his arrival for dinner. He'd not said yes to the invitation, he'd simply told his mother he'd get there if he could. He had intended to go, but had changed his mind several times since her call that morning, finally deciding not to turn up.

He couldn't possibly return to Merchant House. He'd severed all ties with his father in dramatic fashion several months before and the thought of sitting down to dinner with the tyrant was anathema to him.

Paul had tried for six months to work for his father at the company offices in Ice House Street. His desk had become a mess of shipping timetables, cargo manifests, customs regulations and quarantine inspection orders, and once again he became the object of James Merchant's scathing abuse. Whatever he did was simply not good enough in his father's eyes.

His only respite had been two, all too brief, reunions with Nigel Shawbridge. He'd flown Nigel to Hong Kong for a week in May and another in late July and rented an apartment in Chiangsha Mansions, a rental block in Tsim Sha Tsui, immediately behind the Peninsula Hotel in Kowloon.

The secrecy they'd been required to observe had dimmed their time together, but as Nigel had said to him, anything was better than nothing. Paul had been almost paranoid about their clandestine meetings. He'd never stayed a full night in the flat and had been very masculine and hail-fellow-well-met whenever they'd appeared together in public.

It had been Nigel who had finally given him the courage to confront his father and reveal his plans for a plastics manufacturing plant. 'Explain your idea and offer your father a partnership,' Nigel had said.

In early August, Paul had sought James out at the company offices and asked him for an hour of his time.

'Well, what is it?' James had demanded as he sat behind his enormous rosewood desk.

'I'm no good at the job you've given me, Father.'

'I know,' James had stated flatly. 'You're terrible. You've been a great disappointment to me at every turn.'

'I've tried – ' Paul began.

'No, you haven't,' James interrupted him. 'Tried be damned!' He glowered at his son. 'I don't know what's wrong with you, but I do know one thing. You'll never be able to run this company unless you pull your finger out and show some initiative.'

'I don't want to run the company, Father.'

'But you bloody well will! You are my only son, unfortunately, and that makes you sole heir to the Merchant Company.'

'There's Georgina – '

'Don't be ridiculous!'

'She has a brilliant mind, you know.'

'We are talking about your sister, aren't we?' James sneered facetiously.

'Yes, we are. And she knows the workings of this company inside out. Remember how she always nagged you into bringing her down here to these offices? Every minute she spent here with you she learned something new, and she remembers it all. Georgie could run your whole corporation standing on her ear.' Paul shrugged. 'Mind you, she would never admit it.'

'She's a woman,' James scoffed.

'So is Grandmother, and she's the one who really built this company in the first place.'

'Your sister is a scatter-brained social butterfly,' James snapped, ending the topic with a dismissive wave of his hand. 'You will take over the running of the Merchant Company eventually, whether you like it or not.'

'I'll fail, Father. I'm just not cut out for it.'

'You will not fail.' James placed his palms flat on his desk and glared at his son. 'Johnnie Wilson will hold your hand for the first few years and I'll surround you with experts in every department, so even you can't bugger things up.'

'Uncle Johnnie is another who could take over this company, Father,' Paul said. 'He's been your right hand man for a number of years now and – '

'You're not listening to me, boy!' James' fist crashed onto the desk top. 'This is the Merchant Company, founded by John Merchant, re-established by me, James Merchant, and it will be inherited by you, Paul Merchant. It is a matter of tradition and family honour. I'll not discuss the matter any further.'

'May I discuss the matter I came to see you about?'

'Very well, if you must.' James breathed out heavily and leaned back in his chair.

'I have this idea to start a plastics manufacturing business.'

'You've hinted at this before,' James groaned, 'and I've told you my views on the subject. Plastic is a passing fad. Yes, I know,' he held up his hand for silence as Paul tried to interrupt. 'You believe in it, but I don't. Never have, never will. The Merchant Company is a trading company, a very highly respected trading and shipping company. I will not see it demeaned. Manufacturing cheap plastic toys, like hula-hoops and money boxes, would be regarded by many in this Colony, and abroad I might add, as beneath the station of the Noble House.'

'Father,' Paul continued patiently, 'experiments have shown

that high density polyethylene and chrystalline polypropy-lene can now be produced at very low pressures.'

'That means absolutely nothing to me.' James' tone was dismissive.

'It means there is no need these days for multi-million dollar chemical manufacturing plants set on fifty acres of land. Plastic can now be produced in a small factory at very low cost. It will become a billion dollar business – '

'Let it!' James was losing his patience. 'This company will not put its name to, or be associated with, the manufacture of cheap plastic toys.'

'Then I will not be associated with this company.'

'I beg your pardon?'

'You heard me.'

'If you defy me, I'll destroy you, Paul.' James' voice was full of venom as he glared at his son. 'I don't want you to be in any doubt about that.'

Paul's eyes locked with his father's for several seconds before he replied. 'Do you despise me that much?'

'Very well,' James nodded slowly. 'If you must know . . . yes.'

'And yet you're willing to have me inherit the company?'

'You still don't understand, do you?'

'I'm afraid not.' Paul shook his head.

'I have created a dynasty here in Hong Kong. The Merchant Company is the flagship of this Colony and it will live on as a testament to the name of Merchant.' James stood, came out from behind the desk and circled Paul like a predator. 'And as much as I abhor the idea, you will, and I stress the word *will*, accept the onus of responsibility that comes with your name.' He stopped, standing directly behind Paul, and spoke to the back of his head. 'You will nurture the company and see that it prospers during the years of your reign and then, you will hand it on to your first born son. That is your destiny, Paul. It is carved in stone.'

James moved around in front of his son. He sat on the edge of his desk and glared defiantly as Paul stared back at him. 'Now, tell me,' he murmured. 'Just which part of your destiny do you still not understand?'

'The part – ' Paul began softly.

'Speak up!' James demanded. 'I can't hear you.'

'The part,' Paul repeated loudly, 'that says I should spend the rest of my life maintaining a shrine to the memory of a man who despises me.'

James' open handed blow struck Paul on the side of the head and sent him reeling off the chair onto the floor, where he lay staring up at his father.

'You asked for that,' James said.

'No, I didn't.' Paul stood and walked to the door. 'We won't be seeing each other again. I have a life to live and I intend to get on with it. I'm going to start my own company and to hell with you!'

'There is only room for one Merchant company in Hong Kong.' James pointed his finger at his son. 'If you walk out that door, I'll destroy you. Don't ever say you weren't warned.'

'I was warned years ago,' Paul replied as he opened the door. 'By my own mother, would you believe?'

Sitting at his desk in the darkened office of the warehouse, Paul now shuddered at the memory of that fateful meeting with his father. He picked up his wallet from his desk and opened it, and a photograph of Nigel Shawbridge smiled back at him.

'God, I wish you were here,' he said softly.

龍

'Oh, El,' Katherine Merchant sighed as she opened the door to her mother-in-law. 'It was so good of you to come,' she said, ushering Elanora into the main foyer of the Merchant House.

'I couldn't wait another moment to see Su-lin,' Elanora replied as the two women brushed cheeks in a greeting. 'How is she?'

'Your timing is spot on, I think,' Katherine said. 'I'm fairly sure our new young doctor is quite Georgina-ed out, although she's too well-mannered to say so.'

'Ha,' Elanora laughed. 'I'm sure Georgie means well. Are they here?'

'Yes.' Katherine ushered her into the downstairs drawing room. 'They're upstairs in Georgie's room talking.' She offered a slightly puzzled look to her mother-in-law. 'Su-lin seems to have had a profound effect on my daughter.'

'Su-lin has a profound effect on everyone. She's a remarkable young woman.'

'Well, I hope they see more of each other. Georgina's talking like an adult at last and I'm quite sure it is because of Su-lin.' Katherine tugged a bell cord to summon a maid. 'Would you care for some tea? James rang to say he'd be late for dinner,' she shrugged apologetically. 'It's Friday night; he's always late on Friday nights. So, we've got time on our hands.'

'I'd rather a hefty glass of whisky, my dear,' Elanora replied. 'I caught the ferry from Macau this afternoon, dropped my things off at the Peninsula and caught the ferry to Hong Kong side.'

'You could have a room here, you know.'

'No, thank you.' Elanora's response was very definite. 'A large whisky will suffice.'

'Of course,' Katherine replied as the maid entered. 'Ji Li, a whisky for the Merchant Mistress. Make yourself comfortable, El, I won't be a moment. I'll go and tell the girls you're here.' She turned at the door. 'Take a moment to relax. Believe me, you'll need all the energy you can muster.'

'I can't wait.' Elanora's face shone with anticipation.

When Katherine had gone, Elanora looked around the room that had once been her study and office. The years had gone by so swiftly, she thought. It was in this house that she'd first met Richard Brewster, the love of her life.

Richard. Her mind went to him lying sick in Macau. Time and his war wounds had finally taken their toll and she knew he wouldn't recover from the pneumonia he was suffering. His lungs were failing and the doctors had told her to expect the worst. Six months they'd given him. She would lose the only man she had ever truly loved in six months.

The last ten years she and Richard had spent together had been the most fulfilling she had ever known and she would be forever grateful, to Lee particularly, for creating them.

Thanks to him, Richard had never again resorted to opium and he'd maintained the physical exercises Lee had given him and, until a year ago, had not even required his walking stick. But the horrors of war and internment had done their damage to Richard years before.

James was also to blame for Richard's decline over the past several years. He'd refashioned the *Gaam Lung Tong* into a ruthless business cartel, a collective of the most formidable *taipans* in Hong Kong, and Richard had witnessed its development with increasing sadness.

Elanora had watched too. James' *Gaam Lung Tong* was nothing like the old Society of Dragons she had known in the 1920s and '30s. That society, or triad as some called it, had been created as a fortress for survival by desperate men in desperate times. Yes, Elanora had to admit, they had done some terrible things and had become rich along the way, but at its most basic, the Dragons had been a benevolent organisation. It had been an institution peopled by policemen of all ranks and it had been of great assistance to many of them in times of trouble.

This was not the case with James, and the greedy, avaricious rabble he'd gathered around him. They used the name *Gaam Lung Tong* in a way that disgusted her. The making of money was their only aim and they didn't care who they trod on, or ruined, or killed, to get what they wanted.

This above all else, Elanora knew, had brought Richard to the state he was now in. Quite simply, his heart was broken and soon he would die.

It would be Christmas in two weeks and it would be Richard's last, so she was determined to make it wonderful for him. She would surround him with those he regarded as his grandchildren. It was the reason she'd allowed Su-lin to return from Sydney. Richard adored Su-lin and her brother, Jet, as he adored the twins, and Elanora was determined to have them all in Macau for the celebrations. It was why she'd chosen tonight to come to Hong Kong. She'd been invited, at very short notice, to dinner by Katherine, and would use the opportunity to tell them all of her plans.

She'd warned her son James, in no uncertain terms, not to interfere with her Christmas arrangements. She knew he would, if he thought he could get away with it, because he despised Richard for failing to join him in restoring the company business, and for refusing to help restore the *Gaam Lung Tong*.

And James has restored both, she thought, as the maid entered with her whisky.

'*Mistress,*' the girl whispered reverently handing Elanora the glass.

'*Thank you, Ji Li,*' Elanora replied and watched the girl leave.

Yes, she thought as she rose and crossed to the window. James has restored both. He was a brilliant businessman and he'd made himself, and the Merchant Company, the most powerful force in Hong Kong. She looked out over the gardens in the front of the house, pleased to see that Katherine had kept them immaculate.

He'd restored the Society of Golden Dragons too. The *Gaam Lung Tong* was alive and well. Although he'd tried to keep its restoration secret, nothing escaped the spies employed by Elanora. It was a business cartel now, far more than a simple triad. It was a financial pressure group made up of Hong Kong businessmen and James was its leader. He had the whole town under his thumb and ruled it ruthlessly. Nothing of any financial importance happened in Hong Kong without James' prior approval.

'*Ju Mo!*' Su-lin shrieked, and Elanora turned, only to be enveloped in her granddaughter's arms. Georgina, who was one pace behind Su-lin, rescued the glass of whisky from Elanora's hand and placed it on the piano.

'My darlings!' Elanora exclaimed, including Georgina into her embrace. 'How wonderful to have my two darling girls together.' She smiled radiantly at Katherine who stood at the open door. 'My *three* darling girls,' she added.

'We've had the best time, *Ju Mo*,' Georgie said, breaking from the embrace and sipping Elanora's whisky before handing it back to her. 'Haven't we, Su-lin? We've *yum cha*-ed and shopped until we dropped, in between walking and talking, for two whole days without taking a breath.'

'Really,' Elanora said, holding Su-lin at arm's length.

'Yes,' Su-lin replied and gave Elanora the most beautiful smile. 'Georgie's been wonderful.'

'Well, I'm afraid you two must be parted for a while.' She smiled at Su-lin. 'You will return to Macau with me tomorrow. We have things to discuss.'

'Yes, *Ju Mo*,' Su-lin nodded eagerly.

'Can I come too?'

'No, Georgie,' Elanora shook her head.

'Oh, please, *Ju Mo*? I won't get in the way.'

'I said no, Georgie,' Elanora replied firmly, putting an end to the matter. 'Su-lin did not return to Hong Kong to become your personal companion. She has family matters to attend to that cannot wait. Her father needs her up at Kap Lung.'

'Why don't we order drinks and have our own little party before dinner?' Katherine suggested as she pulled the bell cord. 'We four haven't been in the same room for years. We've got lots of catching up to do, and Su-lin can tell us all about Australia.'

'Will Paul be coming to dinner?' Georgie asked with wide eyed innocence, but her glance at Elanora was anything but naïve.

'I invited him, dear,' Katherine replied, fussing with the cushions on the couch.

'Did he accept?' Georgie gave Elanora another knowing look.

'Not exactly,' Katherine said a little too brightly, as the maid appeared to take their orders. 'But I'm sure he'll be here. I've set a place for him.'

'I'm sure he'll be here, too,' Elanora said taking control. 'Now, girls, what shall you have to drink?'

龍

The large grandfather clock in the main foyer struck nine o'clock as James Merchant entered the dining room.

'Just made it,' he joked, tapping his gold Rolex watch with

his index finger. 'Hello, darling,' he said, kissing his wife automatically on the cheek. He made his way around the long table to greet Georgina and his mother, who were sitting side by side.

'Good evening, Daddy,' Georgina said, a little too sweetly.

'Good evening, darling,' he replied, kissing her on the cheek. 'And Mother,' he pecked her, too, 'how nice to see you at Merchant House. It's been a long time. And Su-lin. Bless my soul,' he said, making a show of moving right around the other side of the table to kiss her. 'I haven't seen you since you were a young girl.'

'You would have if you'd found time to come home,' Georgina commented archly. 'She's been here for two days, Daddy.' In a matter of only forty-eight hours Georgina had re-discovered her childhood cousin, and had decided they were going to be best friends, for life.

'Good evening, Uncle.' Su-lin saw the flash of anger in James' eyes as she accepted his lips against her cheek. 'It's good to be home.'

'And you're a doctor, so I hear.' James tried to sound jovial as he sat and placed his napkin across his lap. He was acutely aware of the empty seat between him and Su-lin, guessing immediately that the setting was for Paul.

'Not quite,' she replied. 'I've only graduated with a degree in medicine. I've got two years of internship before I can hang up my shingle.'

'*Do you still follow the* way *of Shaolin?*' James had noticed the calluses on her knuckles.

'*I am a humble disciple, Uncle,*' she replied.

'Yes,' he looked into her eyes, 'I'll just bet you are.' As an exponent of the art, James could sense her power from where he was sitting. She exuded the force of *Shaolin*, but there was something else, something in her eyes. Was it anger? Malevolence? Whatever it was, she was trying to shield it from him, but it was strong, too strong for her to hide completely.

The exchange in Cantonese intrigued Georgina. Her father had said, 'the way of Shaolin'. She looked at Su-lin. Did he mean the *'way'* that Su-lin had talked of during their ride from the airport? Surely he must.

She glanced at her cousin's hands, noticing again the callused knuckles. Vague memories came back to her of Su-lin as a little girl, spinning through the air as the *kung fu* fighters did, and she remembered her uncle Lee Kwan admonishing his daughter for showing off.

Georgina had watched her father practise *Shaolin kung fu* many times during her youth. It had been thrilling in its balletic complexity, but it had always frightened her. And Su-lin had just admitted she was 'a humble disciple', as she'd put it. Was it possible that this shy, softly spoken little doctor sitting opposite her could be a skilled exponent of such a violent and dangerous art? Impossible, she thought, looking across the table at Su-lin. She could not imagine the girl hurting anyone, she radiated goodness. Or was there more to *Shaolin* than mere fighting techniques? A gentle side to the art perhaps? Something to do with healing? Su-lin was, after all, a doctor of medicine.

Georgina remembered the episode in the car when their eyes had locked. The sudden, inexplicable, happiness she'd felt. Could that be part of *Shaolin*, too? But of one thing she was certain. If there *was* a gentle side to *Shaolin*, then it was a side that her father certainly did not possess.

'Tell me, darling,' James spoke to Katherine, 'are we expecting anyone else?' He indicated the vacant setting on his right.

'I invited Paul,' his wife replied glancing at Elanora. 'I thought it might be nice for Elanora if all four of us were here as a family. And, of course, Su-lin hasn't seen him for years.'

'Marvellous, marvellous,' James replied expansively, but his eyes told a different story. 'What a good idea.' He looked at his wife. 'So, where is he then, this errant son of mine?'

'I'm sure he'll be along shortly,' Katherine said with a false smile. 'Shall we begin?' She rang a small bell. Two maids entered and began serving.

Katherine was beginning to feel ill at ease. Inviting Paul had been a stupid mistake, but she'd so wanted her family to be together for Elanora's sake. Now, quite abruptly, she realised her error and began to pray fervently that her son would not arrive.

Katherine looked in turn at James and Georgina, both smiling and playing the happy family to perfection, but she knew it wouldn't last. The two fought like cat and dog at every given opportunity. Georgina despised her father for the tyrant that he was, and particularly for the way he'd treated her twin brother over the years, and she had a temper to match James'. I've put them in the same room, and in front of Elanora, who was revisiting Merchant House for the first time in years, Katherine thought, horrified. How could I have been so utterly stupid?

She looked again at James seated at the head of the table and shuddered with revulsion. Their marriage was a complete sham. The love she had felt for him had disappeared long ago. He had not touched her in years and an unspoken agreement seemed to have been reached wherein they pretended to be a happily married couple, simply for appearance's sake. She knew he had several mistresses in town that he kept in apartments and visited regularly, but she no longer cared enough to raise the issue. Katherine now lived only for her twins, Paul and Georgina.

James maintained the conversation as the dinner proceeded. He could be charming and witty when he chose to be, a brilliant conversationalist. He steered the talk between matters Australian, which he directed at Su-lin, and his latest Merchant Company project, a new block of high-rise apartments to be built in Kowloon. But when the clock chimed a quarter to ten and Paul had not arrived, he couldn't resist showing his irritation.

'Well, so much for us being here as a family,' he said loudly and glared at Katherine. 'I'm sorry, Mother,' he looked at Elanora, 'but I'm afraid your grandson – '

'Don't start, Daddy,' Georgina interrupted. She was fiercely protective of her twin brother and was not remotely afraid of her father. 'Paul's done nothing wrong in anyone's eyes but yours.'

'Georgie darling,' Katherine began. 'I don't think Su-lin will be interested in – '

'Nothing wrong, Georgina?' James' pent up anger finally burst forth. 'He's a snivelling little cur! – '

'Please, James?' Katherine begged, but there was little conviction in her voice. Her worst fears were about to be realised. There would be no stopping either father or daughter now.

'Paul has started a new business and left Daddy's employ.' Georgina spoke directly to Su-lin. 'He's gone into plastics manufacturing, at which he's an expert, I might add, and Daddy doesn't like it. Do you, Daddy?'

'It's got nothing to do with me liking it or not!' James threw his napkin on the table and picked up his drink. 'It was the underhanded way he went about it that infuriated me.'

'Underhanded! ' Georgina declared vociferously. 'He offered you first option. And now he's invested his own money and is going it alone.'

'His own money?' James sneered. 'He's never earned a single, solitary dollar in his whole life! Don't you mean his inheritance?'

'All right! He's invested part of his inheritance,' Georgina roared back. 'And part of mine, too, as you well know.'

'And we all know where you both got that from, don't we?' James looked accusingly at Katherine and then Elanora.

'It's Mother's money to do with as she pleases,' Georgina stated flatly.

'It was *my* money,' James responded through gritted teeth, 'from the sale of this very house, which your grandmother saw fit to return to your mother.' He scowled at Katherine as if it were all her fault.

'Mother's money did not *only* come from Grandmother!' Georgina shouted. 'The rest is from Grand-uncle Billings' estate in England, which you can lay no claim to.'

'Be that as it may!' James roared. 'Paul's gone into business and – '

'And you're doing everything in your power to see him fail!' Georgina cut him off.

'I beg your pardon?'

'Your business cronies, in that stupid Dragons club you're so secretive about, have placed barriers in front of him at every turn.'

'You're talking utter nonsense!'

'Oh, please, don't,' Katherine began.

'For God's sake, don't beg, Mother,' Georgina said. 'Stand up to him for once.'

'How dare you speak to your mother like that!' James spat at his daughter.

'I learned it from you!'

As James and Georgina, now both on their feet, squared off across the table top, Elanora stared vacantly at the plate in front of her, listening to her family implode. What have I created? she thought. She looked at her son now hurling accusations of family betrayal at his wife and daughter. He was raving like a man possessed. He's mad, was all she could think. As her eyes moved down to her lap she realised she was wringing her napkin in her hands. He's capable of anything.

She looked up at Georgina screaming counter-accusations, defending her brother, and now her mother. She's so beautiful, Elanora thought, and so smart, but she's got the same fire in her as her father. And James will destroy her, just like he's destroyed everyone who has tried to love him.

She looked at Katherine, who was weeping into a handkerchief now. She'd been just like Georgina, beautiful, intelligent and loving. She'd given her heart and soul to James and he'd broken her. He'd turned her from a sparkling, witty, young girl into a timorous, indecisive mess. A weak woman, who could only sit and cry as her husband yelled abuse at her. Then she looked at Su-Lin sitting serenely, her eyes closed, opposite. The girl could be sitting in contemplative solitude in a garden, Elanora thought, then Su-Lin opened her eyes and stared directly at James. Elanora was shocked by the girl's malevolent expression.

'And as for *you*, Mother – ' James rounded on Elanora, demanding her attention.

'You leave my grandmother out of this!' Georgina shouted wildly.

'Su-lin, gather your things together, we're leaving. You will stay at the Peninsula with me.' Elanora's command caused a hiatus. Silence reigned as she stood and walked to the dining room door. Su-lin followed quickly and hurried away to her room, desperate to be gone from the house.

'Mother.' There was a warning tone in James' voice.

'Don't call me that!' Elanora's voice cut like a knife. 'You are not my son. You disgust me.' Her eyes glowered at him.

'You don't mean that.' James' voice was warm, placatory. 'Come back and sit down. This is nothing, just a family discussion. It's the first time we've been together in the family home for – '

'Home?' Elanora cut him off. 'This is not a home, it's an evil place. A loveless shell. I should have known better than to ever return to this house. Your father, John Merchant, built it as a shrine to his success, but in reality he built a cage. A bird cage with me as its phoenix in residence. He hoped to impress people by filling it with works of art, but he only succeeded in filling it with sadness. And now it's filled with hate. And you, James, have made it so.' She looked at the two women and her tone softened. 'From tomorrow I will be in Macau, if you need me, girls.' She glared again at James. 'I'm sure you will. Goodnight.'

As Elanora left, Georgina looked contemptuously at her father, threw her napkin on the table and followed her grandmother from the room.

James went to the sideboard and poured himself a hefty measure of cognac. He crossed to the enormous fireplace and swilled the liquid in its balloon, staring up at the portrait of his mother.

'Damn you, Elanora,' he muttered softly, then turned to the forlorn figure of his wife, still seated at the table. 'Well,' he said, 'that was a fiasco, to say the least. I hope you're satisfied, Katherine?'

'Me? I didn't do anything.'

'You're right,' he said, hatred evident in his voice. 'But then you never do, do you?'

'What did you expect me to do?'

'Control your daughter, for one thing.'

'Georgie was just standing up for her brother as she always does.' Katherine blew her nose and looked at him. 'You started it. You behaved appallingly.'

'And can you blame me? When my daughter started airing the family's dirty linen in front of Su-Lin . . .' James began to pace in front of the fireplace. 'It was humiliating. My own flesh and blood admitting she betrayed me – '

'Georgie didn't betray you!' Katherine cried. 'She merely invested her own money in a small business venture with Paul.'

'That was *my* money!' James smashed his fist against the mantlepiece. 'I gave it to Elanora in exchange for this house and for some inexplicable reason she gave it to you!'

'And I gave part of it to the children, along with part of my inheritance from Uncle Herbert.' Katherine stood and held her hands out, appealing. 'What's wrong with that? They're young and adventurous and they've started their own business. You should be proud of them. Paul is a clever young man – '

'Paul is a homosexual!' James shouted, then stood glaring at his wife as silence engulfed them, only to be shattered seconds later by the huge grandfather clock chiming ten o'clock.

'Good God.' Katherine let her arms fall to her sides. 'So this is what it's all about? Paul's homosexuality? I should have known.'

'You mean, you know?' It was James' turn to be shocked.

'Of course I know,' she declared, 'I've always known. I'm his mother.'

'Why didn't you tell me?'

'Because you would have killed him.'

'Ha,' James scoffed. 'Don't be ridiculous.'

'I'm not being ridiculous, James.' Katherine sat down at the table and sighed. 'When he was a little boy, I hoped and prayed you would have the sensibility and sensitivity to recognise it. But, of course, you didn't. So I kept it a secret from you until he was old enough to go to school in England.'

'You should have told me.'

'Told you?' Katherine shook her head. 'Told the great James Merchant that his son and heir had all the hallmarks of being homosexual? You would have killed him,' she nodded grimly. 'I know you, James. You would have drowned him in a sack like an unwanted kitten, or broken his neck, as a fisherman does a netted bird.'

'Now you're really talking nonsense.' James took a cigar from the humidor on the sideboard and made a show of lighting it.

As Katherine watched him, an overwhelming sadness at the years of their loveless marriage overcame her. When they had first met, she had loved him with every fibre of her being. She would gladly have died for him. But he had never fully loved her in return, and when the twins had been born, they'd suffered the same fate.

Finally she spoke, quietly at first, then with passion and anger. 'You were the worst father Paul could ever have had and still he loved you. You pushed him and bullied him every single day of his young life. I remember vividly the countless times you called him a sissy, or a nancy boy, and the pain and hurt in his eyes as he tried to live up to your expectations. I couldn't wait for the day he was old enough to go to England, even though it meant losing him, because it was his only chance to escape from a father who detested him.'

'He's been flying his lover in from London, you know?' James acted as if he'd not heard her diatribe. 'He's a fellow called Nigel Shawbridge. They were at university together, apparently.'

'Have you been spying on him?' Katherine was appalled. 'Your own son?'

'It may have escaped you, Katherine, but according to the laws of Great Britain and, indeed, Hong Kong, engaging in a homosexual act is a criminal offence, punishable by imprisonment.'

'How could you?'

'Can you forget your son for one minute,' James snapped, 'and imagine the damage that would befall the Merchant Company if its heir apparent were to be dragged through the courts and branded, not only a criminal, but a bloody shirt-lifter to boot?'

'I refuse to listen to any more of this.' Katherine rose and walked towards the door. 'You're mad, James. Completely mad.'

He moved swiftly to intercept her, grabbing her roughly by the throat. 'You'll listen all right,' he snarled and forced her to sit at his end of the table. 'He is no son of mine. I intend to put a stop to his new business venture and his disgusting personal behaviour once and for all.'

'Don't you dare harm him!' Katherine broke free of his grasp. 'Or I'll – '

'Or you'll what, Katherine?' James brought his face within an inch of hers. 'You will do nothing, do you hear me?'

'Stop it,' Katherine wailed, 'you're frightening me.'

'That is my intention. You betrayed me, Katherine, and I will not tolerate betrayal from anyone, especially my own wife.'

'If that's how you feel, then I'll leave you.' Katherine tried to sound determined, but she was truly afraid of her husband.

'Ha! You pathetic bitch,' he sneered. 'Listen carefully. You will continue to play the part of loyal wife and mother. And you will discuss nothing of what has transpired between us, not with the twins or anyone else, is that clear? And if you, or my mother, so much as raise a finger to help them, I'll crush the lot of you.'

龍

Elanora rose very early on Sunday morning. She and Su-lin had not stayed in Hong Kong. Elanora had called the company junk and sailed home to Macau.

She went immediately to Richard's room, but he was sleeping peacefully, so she closed the door quietly and made her way downstairs. As she reached the ground floor, her maid, Sally, still in pyjamas, burst through the kitchen doors, her face as white as a sheet.

'*Mistress!*' Sally cried. '*Come quickly.*'

'*What is the matter?*'

'*Young Mistress Su-lin has taken her life.*'

'*What?*' Elanora gasped. '*Where is she?*'

'*In the garden,*' the maid wailed. '*She has hanged herself.*'

Elanora pushed past the hysterical girl and ran through the kitchen and out of the rear door into the garden. There, hanging from a rope attached to a branch of the huge mulberry tree in the corner of the yard, hung the still form of Su-lin.

'Oh, my God, no!' Elanora screamed as she ran towards her granddaughter. She stopped in front of the body and reached up to touch Su-Lin's hand.

Suddenly Su-lin's eyes opened and her hands came up from her sides, grabbing the noose encircling her neck. Her arms took her weight and she removed her head from the noose and dropped to the ground.

'I am so sorry,' she said. 'I – '

'*Aaaiiyaah!*' Her grandmother wailed in high pitched Cantonese fashion. She leapt away from the girl and staggered to a bench seat beneath the tree and sat, holding her face in her hands.

'I am so sorry, *Ju Mo*,' Su-lin said as she sat and took her grandmother in her arms.

'How could you even contemplate such a thing?' Elanora cried. 'Are you so unhappy? Is it because of the death of your mother?'

'*Ju Mo*, calm down.'

'You scared me half to death! You stupid girl!'

'I'm sorry.'

Elanora watched, horrified, as Su-lin returned to the noose, drew herself up by the arms, re-inserted her head and let go. She hung suspended again, her entire bodyweight supported by her neck muscles. Then she released herself and dropped to the ground.

'It is simply an exercise, Grandmother.'

'How can you do that?' an amazed Elanora asked.

'I didn't mean to upset – '

'No, no!' Elanora pointed at the noose. 'That! What you actually did!'

'By using *chi*, Grandmother. It is a form of energy that exists within the body. When control of it is mastered, it becomes a source of great power, giving the body added resistance to blows, and greater force in attack. It is accomplished with specific breathing techniques.'

'Did your wretched father teach you that?' Elanora's fleeting relief at her granddaughter's physical and mental well-being was now swiftly replaced by irritation. 'Is it part of this damned *Shaolin* business he has raised you with?'

'It is the most advanced and powerful discipline in the arts of *Shaolin*. There are very few who ever master it.'

'Is this what your father calls the *way*?'

'No,' Su-lin shook her head. 'I cannot really explain what the *way* is. It is . . .' she struggled for a word, '. . . acceptance, perhaps.'

'Of what?'

'Acceptance of what is.' Su-lin shrugged. 'Discussing the *way* is futile. The *way* is intangible. Have you ever found yourself with a piece of paper in your hand that you wish to dispose of? Your eyes seek the waste paper bin and you make the decision to throw it. Once you have made the decision it becomes a matter of chance as to whether you will be successful. Sometimes you throw accurately and sometimes you miss. But,' Su-lin pointed her finger skyward, 'sometimes you don't think about it at all – you just throw it and, invariably, on those special occasions, the paper finds the bin. That is as close as I can come to explaining the *way*. It is a state in which you never miss.'

'And you need *chi* for that?'

'No,' Su-lin laughed. '*Chi* is part of the physical side of *Shaolin*. The part that takes you to the highest level in combat.'

Su-Lin went to the garden and picked up two flat stones. She placed them on the ground in front of the tree and used them as platforms for her fingertips as she sprung into a handstand and came to rest with her heels against the tree trunk. 'Watch, *Ju Mo*,' she said.

Elanora watched as the girl retracted three fingers on each hand until only thumbs and index fingers supported her weight. Then she retracted her thumbs and remained upside down, supporting herself upon only her index fingers, then dropped again to her feet.

'I believe I am probably the only woman in the world who can do that.' There was no boast in her voice, it was a simple statement of fact. 'And probably that, too,' she pointed to the noose. 'It is because I have learned to control *chi*.' She sat next to Elanora and smiled.

'My maid thinks you chose to join your ancestors,' Elanora chided. 'You've frightened her witless. You should have warned us.'

'I'm sorry, *Ju Mo*.'

'Your father once told me that you would be a great exponent of *Shaolin*.'

'At first I practised the arts to please him. The exercises were just a game that Jet and I played with my father, just as other families play games together for amusement. Then, slowly, I began to realise that the physical disciplines of *Shaolin*, combined with the mental disciplines, gave me the ability to look at life and my existence differently. Together, they have helped me to form a philosophy.'

'You have your own philosophy?'

'Of course. Doesn't everyone?'

'Well,' Elanora replied. 'Yes, I suppose they do.'

'I have gathered knowledge, I have formed opinions, and I use those opinions to assist me in negotiating a path through the forest of life.'

'The forest of life?' Elanora's tone was superior, and slightly cynical. She hated the way she'd sounded, but she felt beseiged. She was supposed to be the grandmother, the one who offered wisdom and advice, but Su-lin made her feel inadequate.

'Do not look so confused, *Ju Mo*,' the girl laughed. 'The forest of life is an expression my father uses often. When I was sent to the Ba-yi School in Peking, my Communist teachers tried to discourage me from forming my own opinions, but I refused and went on a hunger strike.'

'My God,' Elanora said softly.

'Eventually, because I was a General's daughter, they left me alone, and I realised then how valuable my father's instruction had been. I had been subjected to the will of others who ordered me to follow a path I did not wish to follow. I resisted, passively, and in doing so, I learned the true meaning of *Shaolin* philosophy.'

'Which is?' Elanora asked.

'Understand that which surrounds you, form your own opinions and walk the path of least resistance.'

'Through the forest of life.' Elanora was once again annoyed by her own cynical tone.

'Yes. My father describes life as a forest we all must walk through and the easiest way to do it is to take the path of least resistance. Step around the trees, stoop beneath the branches and make sure the earth is firm wherever you place your feet. Be considerate of the life that surrounds you and be aware of the elements, for they cannot be controlled and will, at times, govern your direction.'

'That sounds awfully like Taoism to me,' Elanora said.

'It probably is, for all I know. I've never studied it. The first *Shaolin* masters were Buddhists and I believe followed the Tao, which, funnily enough, means the *way*. But what does it matter? The words I spoke are my father's words. Whether they coincide with the beliefs of others is incidental. There is nothing new in philosophy, *Ju Mo*.'

'So, what are your beliefs, *sai lui*?' Elanora used the expression 'little girl' fondly.

'I have no beliefs. I have only opinions, which of course, are subject to change. Each day of life brings new knowledge, and new knowledge can alter opinions. I am simply me, Grandmother, a pupil of *Shaolin*, walking through the forest of life.'

'And what do you expect to find on the other side of the forest?'

'Ha!' Su-lin stood up and stretched, then threw herself into a run, circling the lawn. 'Who knows, *Ju Mo*,' she cried, somersaulting through the air with a twist and landing on her feet on the grass facing Elanora. 'Probably another forest. It is not important. It is the walk that matters.'

Elanora watched the girl move fluidly back and forth across the small stretch of lawn. It was like watching a beautiful animal. Su-lin struck the air rapidly with her fists and the force of her movements caused her silk sleeves to crack, like claps of thunder, Elanora thought, or the sound a sail makes when it flaps in a freshening breeze.

Her granddaughter was proving, yet again, the most remarkable female she'd ever met. Su-lin had always seemed wise beyond her years. And beyond mine, Elanora thought with a smile. The girl's explanation of the *way* had been quite profound. Or had it been?

Elanora's western half had taken Su-lin's philosophy with a grain of salt. She was used to the clichés intended to promote the mystique of *kung fu*. Most of them were facile statements, easily interpreted and discarded for what they were: pretentious, quasi-oriental rubbish, in her opinion. But the eastern half of Elanora sensed something very real in Su-lin. Something special. Su-lin had a complete lack of artifice. What she preached had a ring of sincerity to it that was difficult to deny.

Has she learned that basic truth that *Shaolin* promises? Elanora wondered. Does she possess the real knowledge of those ancient arts; the mystical 'magic' supposedly possessed by the old masters? Her western brain knew that magic did not exist, but her oriental mind suspected that it did. The dichotomy intrigued Elanora.

'Speaking of walking,' Su-lin said, concluding her exercises, 'why don't we walk down to the Old Quarter this morning and find some *yum cha*? I'm starving.'

'That's a wonderful idea,' Elanora said, taking her granddaughter by the arm. 'We have much to discuss. What better way to discuss it than over *yum cha*?'

CHAPTER THIRTEEN

Christmas 1966 came and went for Elanora and Richard, locked behind the stone walls of *Lung Fa Yuen*, and under threat, as a new and dangerous political phenomenon sweeping across China finally reached the streets of Macau.

A book called *The Quotations from Chairman Mao Tse-tung*, better known as *The Little Red Book*, had been published in 1964. It contained hundreds of excerpts from Mao's writings and speeches on Communist philosophy and within two years, thousands of youths had left their schools and jobs to join the political tidal wave that became known as the Cultural Revolution.

The young zealots, known as the Red Guards, quoting Chairman Mao's slogans and mottos, ruthlessly attacked the bourgeoisie, the bureaucrats, intellectuals and non-revolutionary industry. They opposed revisionism, careerism and every other thinkable transgression against Marxist-Leninism and the movement spread like wildfire across China, bringing the country to the brink of anarchy.

During the Christmas of 1966 it finally reached the tiny colony of Portuguese Macau. Carrying their *Little Red Books*, violent groups of Red Guards wrought havoc in Macau, rioting and destroying public property.

Elanora remained in Macau amid the ever worsening political situation, hovering over Richard as his health deteriorated with each passing day. Georgina went to Singapore, James Merchant left home altogether, and Paul disappeared into Kowloon. The Merchant family remained divided, its open wounds weeping in the cold Christmas days of winter.

In late January of 1967, Georgina sought out her twin brother in Kowloon. 'You can't stay here, old girl.' Paul indicated his small apartment by spreading his arms. 'There's barely room to swing a cat.'

'Katya said I could stay with her and Uncle Johnnie,' Georgina said, 'but I'd be imposing upon them, Paul. They've done enough for me already – after all, I've just spent Christmas and New Year with them in Singapore.'

'What about Macau?'

'Are you serious?' Georgina exclaimed. 'Haven't you read the newspapers?'

'I heard there was some trouble before Christmas, but it's not bad is it?'

'The Cultural Revolution has stepped over the international border, brother. The Red Guards have started playing their nasty games with the Portuguese. Elanora thinks it's only a matter of time before they try it on with the British here in Hong Kong. She absolutely refused to let me come. Not only that, but Grandfather's no better – his health's deteriorating every day.'

'Well, you'll just have to go home,' Paul said.

'I couldn't!'

'Apparently Father hasn't been there since before Christmas.'

'Really?'

'Oh, yes,' Paul nodded. 'He walked out on Mother and is living with one or another of his mistresses on Hong Kong side somewhere. And Mother, I'm sure, could do with your company.'

'Are you sure I can't stay with you?' Georgie pleaded.

'Look at the place, Georgie,' he replied. 'There's only one bedroom and besides, there's Nigel. He's coming over for a visit.'

'All right.' Georgina resigned herself to her fate. 'I'll go home to Merchant House, but if so much as Father's shadow appears on the driveway, I'll be back here on your doorstep faster than you can say Jack Robinson.'

'You've got a deal, *Sai Mui*,' Paul laughed. 'Now, would you like a cup of tea? Or perhaps something a little stronger?'

'You know me, *Dai Loh*, Campari and soda?'

'I don't have any oranges, sis.'

'No matter. Beggars can't be choosers.' Georgina followed her brother into his tiny kitchen and leaned against the refrigerator watching him prepare her drink. 'Have you seen much of Mother, Paul?'

'No,' he replied guiltily, 'but she understands. She knows what I'm up against with Father. I daren't take my eye off the ball. Any obstacle he can throw in my way he does so with a vengeance.' He nudged her aside and opened the refrigerator. 'You'll want ice, I presume?'

'Yes please.'

Paul took an ice tray from the freezer and set about bashing it on the kitchen sink.

'How is Mother holding up?' she asked.

'Well, Father has abandoned her financially, so she's now living on her own money. We can't expect anything more from her.'

'Oh, dear.' Georgina extended her glass and he dropped several ice cubes into it.

'Yes.' Paul turned and stared at her. 'We're almost broke, you know. Father's interfering minions have forced me to pay out twice the amount I allowed in our budget for raw materials.'

'What about the Woo twins? Can't they chip in?'

'I'm afraid not, I've already asked them. I think they're beginning to get the jitters. But I've got a trump card up my sleeve.'

'I trust it's the Ace of Hearts,' Georgie said, thinking levity might ease the sinking feeling in her stomach.

'It's better than that, thanks be to the Woo twins,' Paul said, pouring himself a whisky. 'It's an order for one hundred thousand statues of Jesus on the cross and fifty thousand St Christopher medallions. I can knock them out in two weeks and get our heads back above water.'

'Providing Father doesn't throw any more spanners in the works?'

'Yes.' Paul smiled grimly. 'Here's hoping,' he said and raised his whisky before taking a long swallow.

'Well,' his twin turned and walked back into the small lounge room, 'on a more positive note, when is Nigel due in our fair Colony?'

'Friday evening,' he said following her. 'And I can't wait.'

'It's the real thing for you, isn't it?' She sat on the sofa.

'Yes, it is.' Paul threw himself into the apartment's one and only chair. 'I love him.'

'I envy you, brother,' she sighed.

'And what about you, sister, any love on your horizon?'

'Not even a far distant sail,' Georgie laughed.

'What about that handsome fellow you met in London? The fellow who turned out to be the Chief Inspector from right here in Honkers. What was his name?'

'Jeremy Bent,' Georgina said flatly.

'Yes. That's him. Nige and I call him Jeremy Campari.'

'Very funny.' She wrinkled her nose at him. 'He was nothing more than a one night stand.'

'Don't give me that, old girl,' Paul scoffed. 'I'm your twin, remember? You fell in love with him the minute he kissed you. I felt it myself. The feeling was so strong I nearly kissed him too. I felt sure you would have looked him up here in Hong Kong.'

'If you want the truth,' she raised her chin imperiously, 'I hate him.'

'Oh, please,' he pulled a face. 'Just because he failed to tell you he was a Hong Kong copper? That's silly, sis.'

'I'd rather not discuss him, if you don't mind.'

'All right, all right.' Paul could sense her turmoil.

Georgina had been unable to forget Jeremy Bent and her heart had skipped a beat at the mention of his name. She'd seen him only once in the past year and that had been on the Star Ferry. Unfortunately, the ferry he'd been on had been going to Hong Kong side and she'd been on one heading for Kowloon. They'd stared at each other as the ferries passed, not fifty yards apart. Jeremy had waved, but she'd ignored him, turning away from the railing and taking a seat.

'Will you stay and have dinner with me, Georgie? Then

you can take a taxi to the Star Ferry and another to Merchant House. Mother will be delighted to see you.'

'That would be nice,' Georgina replied, keenly aware, yet again, of the emotions aroused in her by the mere mention of Jeremy Bent. 'And you can tell me all about Nigel and everything else over a glass of wine.'

'I haven't got any wine,' Paul laughed. 'We're broke, remember?'

'Never mind,' Georgie smiled lovingly. 'Campari will suffice and we'll put our faith in Jesus and St Christopher to get us through.'

龍

'It's just wonderful, Paul,' Nigel Shawbridge exclaimed as he stood, hands on hips, taking in the interior of the converted bus depot Paul Merchant had transformed into his plastics factory.

It was early on Saturday evening and Paul had insisted Nigel, who had flown in the previous evening, see the place before they dined.

'Pretty impressive if I do say so myself, Nige.' Paul beamed.

'And I just love the company name, Gemini Holdings.'

'That was Georgina's idea. What with us being twins and partners with the Woo twins, she insisted it could be nothing else.'

'Well, I think she's brilliant. You're so lucky to have her as your sister.'

'Yes, she's a good stick all right.' Paul looked at Nigel. 'You know this set up cost us a bundle, don't you?'

'Now, now,' Nigel chided. 'No negativity. Gemini Holdings will be an enormous success.'

'Well, the good news is it's ready to go, Nige. A month before schedule.'

'Really?'

'Absolutely. We begin production next Monday morning, the 6th of February, 1967. An auspicious date too, I might add, according to the *fung sui* man.'

'Who?' Nigel asked, nonplussed.

'The *fung sui* man.' Paul laughed. 'Have you never heard of *fung sui*, or *feng shui*, as they say in Mandarin? Literally translated *fung sui* means wind and water, but there's a whole lot more involved I can tell you.' He put his arm around Nigel's shoulder. 'We've got a while before we dine. Come into the office and I'll make you a cup of tea and explain one of the Orient's greatest mysteries.'

'Is this foong soy business you're talking about based on the art of geomancy?' Nigel sat on an old armchair Paul had acquired as office furniture and put his feet up on the desk.

'I suppose you could describe it, loosely, as similar to medieval geomancy,' Paul said as he wiped two cups with a tea towel. 'But it's far more complicated than simply making predictions based on lines drawn on the ground, or a hand-ful of dirt thrown in the air. To the Chinese, *fung sui* is a science based on finding harmony and balance with the forces of nature.'

'And just how do they go about that?' Nigel produced a packet of cigarettes from his pocket and proceeded to light up.

'They believe that energy, or *chi* as they call it, is in and around everyone and everything and – '

'That's not as silly as it sounds,' Nigel interrupted. He blew a puff of smoke onto the match he was holding, extinguish-ing it. 'Philosophically speaking I find myself coming to the same conclusion of late.'

'Well, the Chinese concluded it some time ago. Four thousand years ago to be precise,' Paul laughed as he spooned tea leaves into a pot. 'Anyway, *fung sui* men, or geo-mancers if you like, play a pretty important role in Chinese society. They are hired to enter a building or dwelling and, by using a compass and a circular plate with symbols on it, which they call the Dial of Hope, they determine what the *chi* is doing and tell you how to take advantage of it.'

'So you've had this place foong soyed have you?'

'It was the first thing I did.' Paul tossed a packet of biscuits into Nigel's lap. 'Be a good chap and open those will you,' he said, picking up the electric kettle. 'I'll just get some water.'

Nigel grappled with the biscuit packaging as Paul left the office. He tugged violently at the cellophane wrapping, then cursed under his breath as the biscuits spilled all over the floor.

'Sorry,' he said, busy picking them up as Paul returned.

'Not to worry.' Paul ruffled his lover's hair with his free hand as he passed. 'Just put them on the table. No harm done.' He put the kettle on the sideboard, plugged it in and flicked the switch.

The explosion that followed blew the windows out of the small office and Paul and Nigel were engulfed in a ball of flame. Bottles of chemicals outside on the warehouse floor exploded in the heat of the blast and within minutes the whole factory was a raging inferno.

龍

The following morning, Katherine Merchant slammed the telephone into its cradle and, terrified, stared at her daughter.

'Well?' Georgina asked.

'They can't find him.' Katherine sat on the sofa in the drawing room of Merchant House and locked her fingers together in a vice-like grip. 'No one's seen him since the fire was reported.'

'He wouldn't have been working at the factory, Mother, not at that hour.' Georgie tried to keep the pain out of her own voice. 'And not on a Saturday night in any case.'

'Then where is he?'

'Have you tried Grandmother's house in Macau? He may have been concerned for her, what with the riots and everything else.'

'Of course,' Katherine snapped. 'She was the first person I rang.'

'Well, don't start getting worked up,' Georgina began, then fell silent, dreading the news of her twin that she knew would come. Then she looked up and saw her father standing in the doorway, his face as white as a sheet.

'What are you doing here?' Katherine whispered. 'Oh God, is it Paul?'

'I've got some bad news, I'm afraid,' James replied.

'Is it Paul?' Katherine managed to ask again.

James Merchant nodded. 'Two bodies were found in the factory. The police are quite sure one is Paul's.'

'Oh, God no,' Katherine wailed, placing her hand over her mouth. 'Oh no. Oh God no.' She stood and walked from the room.

Georgina kept her emotions in check. She'd known Paul was dead since the previous evening, even before the report of the factory fire. She'd been alone on the garden terrace when an unreasoning sense of terror had consumed her. She had felt her twin dying. She had felt his agony and sensed his spirit, in its distress, calling to her. And then an image of her father's face had appeared before her and she'd collapsed, unconscious on the cold stone flagging. She had no idea how long she'd lain there, but she awoke with a splitting headache and a lump on her head and had put herself to bed.

The visions had reoccurred during the night. Three times she'd awoken from fitful sleep to see Paul's face. Her twin seemed to be calling for help and then her father's face had appeared. When she finally arose, not long after daybreak, and had been informed of the factory fire, she knew that Paul was dead and that James was in some way connected with his death.

Father and daughter stared at each other. The animosity in Georgie was palpable.

'What's the matter with you? I just told you your brother is dead.' James spoke.

Georgina continued to stare as her hands closed into fists.

'Why are you staring at me?' James demanded defensively.

'You did it,' she whispered.

'I beg your pardon, young lady?'

'You did it,' she repeated. 'You burnt down our factory.'

'Don't be ridiculous,' James snapped dismissively.

'You did it!' Georgina's voice rose an octave in accusation.

'No hysterics, Georgina, please,' James said firmly. 'Think of your mother.'

'*You did it!*' she screamed with all the power she could muster.

'Shut up!' James moved quickly across the room towards her.

'You killed my brother, I know you did. He told me!'

'Shut up, I said!' He slapped his daughter across the face. 'You have no idea what you're talking about.'

Seconds passed as Georgina held the side of her face, gazing with hatred into her father's eyes. 'What are you going to do now? Am I next? Do you intend to kill me, too?' she whispered.

'You're talking nonsense,' James said.

'Oh no, I'm not!' Georgina shouted. 'Twins sense things! I was in that fire with my brother. I felt him die. And do you know what I saw in those flames? *Your face!*'

'You don't know what you're saying, Georgina. You're hysterical.' James took her by the arm but she pulled away and ran to the open doors.

'That is the last contact you'll ever have with me,' she spat, her eyes wild as she spun back towards him.

'Get out of this house!' James thundered.

'This is my mother's house, not yours! But don't worry, after I've made sure Mother is all right, I'll leave. And not only this house, but Hong Kong.'

'And good riddance is all I have to say.'

'You disgust me!' Georgina trembled with rage. 'Don't worry,' she sneered. 'I won't say anything to the police for my mother's sake and, besides, I have no proof, but I know what you did. I know it in here.' She thumped her chest with a fist. 'And I'll *never* forget. I'll get you one day, you mark my words . . . I'll get you, you bastard!'

James watched the girl run across the huge entrance hall, past the elephant fountain and disappear. He heard her running up the stairs as he stood regarding himself in the large wall mirror in the study.

'It was an accident,' he whispered to his mirror image. 'The boy's death was an unfortunate accident.'

James walked out into the dimly lit hall, took his hat from the hat stand by the front doors, let himself out and closed the door quietly behind him.

In the rear of the main hall, at the doors that led into the ground floor ballroom, Katherine Merchant stood in the shadows. She watched James cross the hall and exit.

Even standing some distance away, she'd heard most of Georgina's accusations. She had always been aware of the special bond between her twins. Ever since they were babies, if one cried the other cried, it didn't matter how far apart they were. If one was injured, the other sensed their sibling's distress, and they both experienced the pain. And if one were to die, Katherine knew beyond all doubt that the other would know.

'And if she doesn't get you, James,' Katherine swore softly in the darkness, 'you can rest assured, I will.'

龍

Elanora placed an afternoon tea tray on Richard's lap, helped him to a sitting position and plumped his pillows.

'Is everything all right, Elanora? You look as if you've been crying. It's not those damned Red Guards rioting again, is it?'

'No. It's just a touch of hay fever, darling,' she replied, wiping her eyes with a handkerchief. 'Will you excuse me if I don't sit with you this afternoon? I've got a hundred and one things to do.'

'Of course, my dear.' Richard knew, as he watched her leave that something was wrong, but he decided if Elanora wished to keep it to herself for the moment, then so be it. She would tell him in her own good time.

Elanora sat in the downstairs drawing room and stared into the empty fireplace. Paul. Dead. Her beautiful grandson burnt to death. How was she going to break the news to Richard? Another body had been found in the ashes and Elanora was in no doubt of its identity.

She had been informed on Friday night that Nigel Shaw-bridge had entered Hong Kong. She'd known for some time of the affair between the two young men and had made arrangements with her spies in Hong Kong Immigration to always be informed of his entry into the Colony.

'Paul,' she whispered sorrowfully. 'My darling Paul.' He

would have taken his friend – Elanora refused to contemplate the word lover – to see his new factory premises and they'd been unable to escape the fire. Elanora was a creature of her time and try as she might, she'd never been comfortable with the fact that her grandson had been a practising homosexual. Nature had played one of its cruel tricks, she'd decided, but she had never allowed it to colour her feelings for her grandson. She had loved Paul deeply.

And now he's gone, she thought. Just like that, in a tragic accident. But was it an accident? Her mind screamed the question as it replayed a brief conversation she'd had with Johnnie Wilson several weeks before. Apparently, at a meeting of the Golden Dragons financial clique, James had declared war on his own son. Oh God, she pleaded silently, surely not even James would go so far as to murder his own son? But as much as her mind tried to deny it, her heart insisted otherwise.

Georgina had rung her with the news of Paul's death and in the same breath had vehemently insisted the same thing. 'It was Father's doing,' Georgina had cried down the phone line. 'I know it, *Ju Mo*. He told Paul he'd destroy him if he attempted to start his own business, and I believe he's done just that. He killed his own son, *Ju Mo*. Perhaps he didn't mean for Paul to be at the factory, but I just know he had that factory destroyed and that amounts to the same thing.'

Elanora had chided her granddaughter, telling her she was upset and that she was saying things she'd regret, but now the seed of doubt had been sown and she could not remove it.

龍

That same Sunday morning, in the office one floor above the Heroes of Waterloo nightclub, Wellington and Napoleon Woo sat counting the takings from their various girlie-bars for Friday and Saturday night.

'It is joss, Wellington, bad joss. The worst joss. James Merchant's madness has cost us a considerable amount of money.'

'Would you like me to send him a bill to cover our losses?'

'Aaaiiiyaahh!' Napoleon exclaimed. 'Are you crazy? He would kill us, like he killed his own son.'

'I was making a joke.'

'Do you think or not think now would be a good time for us to go to Singapore?' Napoleon asked his brother. 'We could see Jenny,' he added, referring to their adopted daughter attending boarding school in Singapore. 'Besides, it is high time we checked on our business interests in the City of the Lion, true or not true?'

'Calm your fears, Little Brother,' Wellington replied to his twin, younger by ten minutes. 'James Merchant will be angry with us for engaging in business with his twin children, but he will take no action against us. We are small fish, once again caught up in the business of the Merchant family. How were we to know he disliked his own son?'

'True,' Napoleon nodded as he went to the safe and deposited a large amount of cash. 'But there is always the danger that in his madness he might not consider that point relevant, true or not true?'

'If he approaches us we must tell him the truth – that it was the Merchant Mistress who suggested we go into partnership with his children. We believed he knew of the arrangement and if he disapproved, he should have told us. How were we to know?'

'That is a good idea, Elder Brother,' Napoleon said, 'but I think we should tell him from Singapore. Good or not good?'

'Good.' Wellington stood up and handed his twin another large roll of bank notes. 'The long distance telephone is a wonderful device. Buy two air tickets to Singapore.'

龍

Katya Wilson stood at the balcony doors of her flat staring blindly at the harbour below, tears running silently down her cheeks.

'I see you've heard the news,' Johnnie Wilson said as he walked up behind her and enfolded her in his arms.

'Yes,' Katya nodded. 'That lovely boy. Such a tragic

accident.' She turned and buried her head in Johnnie's shoulder. 'He was so young. Just a baby.'

'Twenty-one,' Johnnie heard himself reply as he stared out across the harbour at Kowloon.

'I must ring Katherine and poor Georgie, they'll be heartbroken. I am their friend and I must go to them.'

'I wouldn't do that right at this moment, Kat,' Johnnie warned.

'Why not?' Katya lifted her head back and looked at him.

'It's only servant's chatter, but from what I hear, all hell's broken loose up at Merchant House.'

'What has happened?'

'Georgina apparently accused her father of having something to do with the fire.'

'What?' Katya gasped. 'That is a terrible thing to say. I cannot say I like James, he is an unscrupulous man, yes? But . . .' Katya searched her husband's eyes. She had told Johnnie of James' lecherous behaviour towards her, but since their marriage he'd treated her with cool disdain, knowing she was now beyond his reach. The man was a complete bastard, she knew, but would he actually kill his own son? 'It could not possibly be true, could it?'

'Of course not.' Johnnie tried to chuckle but it came out like a cough. Christ Almighty, he thought, I hope not. His mind suddenly filled with a vision of Dickie Beckham lying in an aircraft mechanic's pit with his neck broken and he shuddered involuntarily.

Johnnie Wilson had been witness to James' anger when he'd heard of the formal creation of Gemini Holdings, several months before.

'There's only room in town for one Merchant company,' James had stated vociferously at a meeting of the clandestine financial group called the Golden Dragons, of which Johnnie was a reluctant member. 'I warned Paul of the consequences, but it seems he's chosen to ignore me,' he'd said to the gathering of well known financiers. 'Find out who's supplying him with raw stock and buy them off. Make contact with anyone working for him and advise them to seek alternative employment. I want his legs chopped out from under him.'

'But he is your son – ' Francis Kwok, a well known private banker had protested.

'No son of mine will compete with me on Hong Kong soil!' James had snapped, glaring at the Chinese financier. 'I want him shut down.'

Johnnie Wilson had listened, horrified, as James Merchant, his face twisted in anger, had ordered the destruction of his own son's company. But destruction of a company was one thing, Johnnie reasoned. Arson and murder were other things entirely. Surely even James wouldn't go that far?

His thoughts were shattered by the sound of the front door chimes. He and Katya went arm in arm to answer it.

'Hello Uncle John, Katya,' Georgina said as the door opened. 'I'm back. Would you mind putting me up for a night or two?'

Katya took the girl in her arms and the tears started in earnest.

龍

James Merchant sat in the darkening apartment and sipped at his whisky. He eased himself back into the big leather armchair and loosened his tie, wondering where the Ping sisters were. Probably playing mahjong, he thought. Both girls were inveterate gamblers and bad ones to boot. Their gambling debts cost him a small fortune each month, but he considered them worth it. They were a pair of flawless Chinese beauties and sexual hellcats in the bedroom.

He wasn't angered by their absence. He hadn't rung to tell them of his arrival and it was Sunday after all, the afternoon they usually spent gambling. In fact, he was quite content to be alone in the apartment. It would give him time to re-evaluate the situation now confronting him.

He thought of his son's charred remains, now no doubt lying in the Hong Kong Mortuary. He hadn't meant for Paul to die, but the thought of him and Nigel Shawbridge, also now a pile of ashes, lying side by side in the morgue didn't upset him. Paul would never have managed the Merchant Company properly and would most certainly have never produced an heir to succeed him, not given his disgusting sexual proclivities.

His mind travelled back less than an hour to the startled look on the face of Sean Poots as he'd intercepted him sneaking down the back fire escape of the Mission to Seamen's hostel into Walking Stick Lane. James had kicked the suitcase from the man's hand and slammed him against the wall.

'And just where do you think you're going?' James had said as he'd grabbed the former IRA man by the throat. It had been a mistake to engage the drunken Irishman to destroy the factory.

'I was just – ' Poots choked as the fingers tightened around his neck.

'I thought I made it perfectly clear to you that no one was to be hurt?'

'But . . . but . . .' Poots had spluttered.

'You used a manual detonation device, you bloody moron!'

'Please – ' the man managed to gasp.

'Didn't it occur to that bog-Irish brain of yours,' James snarled, his anger surging as he pushed the man into a doorway, 'that someone had to flick a switch in order to set off the bloody bomb?'

Sean Poots heard the click of the flick-knife as it sprang open and struggled desperately to free himself from the vicelike grip around his throat. He tried in vain to wrestle with James' free hand and then he felt the blade enter his stomach.

James pushed upward with all of his strength and Sean Poots stiffened in death as the knife reached his heart.

'Good riddance,' James muttered now as he sipped his whisky. He took the envelope, containing five thousand English pounds that he'd retrieved from Sean Poots' lifeless body, and threw it onto the coffee table beside the armchair. He sighed, content in the knowledge that he was in the clear. People could think what they liked, but no one could connect him with the fire or the deaths. Poots had been his only connection with the crime and his body was already being disposed of.

A frown creased his brow momentarily as he thought of his family. Damn them all, he decided. They could accuse him until Judgement Day, but none of them could prove a thing. He'd warned Paul, hadn't he? He'd given him every opportunity to get shot of his stupid ideas and toe the line. And he had definitely never meant to hurt the boy, or his damned lover. It had been an accident, pure and simple.

He thought of his daughter screaming accusations at him. Well, damn her too, he thought. Everything he'd ever tried to do for Georgina, she'd rebelled at. And Katherine had been no help. Bloody Katherine. She had slowly but surely turned the twins against him. It had started when they were children. She'd never allowed him the opportunity to exert his influence over them. He remembered vividly her over-protective attitude towards Paul in particular, rushing him off to his room whenever he'd admonished him. No wonder the boy had become a homosexual.

James rose and crossed to the windows. He opened the venetian blinds and looked down on the harbour, now a blaze of lights, as dusk deepened to darkness. Dear old Honkers, he smiled, the capitalists' capital of the world and I practically own it. And I bought it with Communist money. The thought made him snort with laughter, causing the ice to rattle in the glass of whisky he held against his chest.

The money he'd received from the Russians had bank-rolled him at a time when everyone else was going broke and he'd seized his opportunity with both hands. He'd risked his life in two wars and would have returned to Hong Kong with practically nothing to show for it had it not been for the theft of that Sabre jet. He'd restored the Merchant Company to its former glory and put his ungrateful family right back in the lap of luxury. And how had they repaid him?

If Paul had only listened to reason, none of James' recent actions would have been necessary. But it had been Katherine who'd started the whole mess, hadn't it? She'd given the start-up capital to her son and urged him to go against his father's wishes. And Georgina had joined in the fiasco by insisting half the investment capital be hers. They were as much to blame as he was for the dreadful mess that had eventuated. And then, of course, James thought bitterly, there was his own mother.

Elanora had conspired with Katherine, James was sure of it. She'd not only actively encouraged Paul in his disastrous venture, but had also engaged the Woo twins as his partners. Yes, he thought as he returned to his armchair, his mother was just as much to blame as anyone else. Elanora was the hub of the wheel on which they all revolved. It had been a conspiracy from the outset, led by Elanora, in which his whole family, and the Woo twins, had worked against him.

He'd thought long and hard about admonishing the Woo twins, but had decided against it. They were too deeply enmeshed in Merchant Company businesses to alienate, but there would come a time when he would do more than admonish them, he'd return their treachery in kind. Every dog has his day, gentlemen, James thought, and smiled in the darkness in anticipation of the event.

His thoughts were interrupted by the sound of the apartment door being opened and excited giggling as the Ping sisters came down the hallway.

'James,' they cooed collectively upon seeing him. They dropped their purses and several shopping bags and rushed to his side.

'*What a wonderful surprise,*' Elsie exclaimed as her eyes fell on the open envelope packed with bank notes lying on the coffee table.

'*We were not expecting you,*' her sister Theresa added, as she too, spied the money.

James didn't bother to answer as they fawned over him. He was in one of his castles and two of his subjects were in attendance. He grabbed Elsie by the throat and kissed her roughly before releasing her.

'*Have you missed us that much, lord?*' Elsie loved being manhandled by James Merchant. She could practically smell his lust and it excited her instantly, but she couldn't resist picking up the envelope.

'*Put it down,*' James said softly, watching as she complied with a grin. '*You have to earn it first.*'

'*Do you want or not want another drink, my lord?*' Theresa offered.

'*No,*' James replied. '*Run me a bath. I'll be staying here tonight and I'll need you both to satisfy me.*'

'*Aah,*' Elsie purred. '*Your lust for the Ping sisters is aroused, true or not true, my lord?*' She ran her hand over the front of his trousers.

'*I will fill the bath tub,*' Theresa said, lifting her skirt and rubbing her hand over her mound, '*while my sister plays the flute for you, my lord.*'

Elsie needed no second bidding as she undid James' trousers, took out the *flute* her sister had been referring to and caressed it with her lips. '*Tonight we shall burn for you, lord,*' she whispered, as her eyes drifted again to the envelope on the coffee table, '*and tomorrow you shall find us as ashes.*'

龍

The first rays of the Monday sun crept slowly but surely over the top of Tai Mo Shan, the highest peak of the Kowloon Mountains, and flashed brilliant gold on the surface of a rock pool beneath a small waterfall, then rushed to light up the ancient stone walls of the retreat known as Kap Lung.

Ten years before, Lee Kwan had moved his family to Kap Lung, a broken down, deserted monks' retreat, high on the northern side of Tai Mo Shan. Together with his son, Jet, he had restored the roof of the long, low stone hut and made it habitable. He'd repaired the barn and animal enclosure and cleaned and reset each and every stone in the courtyard that separated the buildings to create a smooth, even surface on which to practise the arts of *Shaolin*. Then he'd built a dam beneath the waterfall and created a pool some twenty yards wide, which served as a source of fresh water.

'You are not practising, Su-lin,' Lee Kwan said, shielding his eyes from the winter sunlight reflecting off the surface of the pool. He saw his daughter sitting on a rock, idly dangling her feet in the cold water. 'Do you mourn for Paul Merchant?'

'Yes, Father,' she replied. 'But my real grief is for your mother and Georgina and Katherine.'

'And do you not grieve for the father, James Merchant?' he asked, coming to a halt behind her and gazing at their reflections in the still water.

The fact that Su-lin did not reply gave him cause for concern. He could feel the anger emanating from her and wondered at its origin. 'I can sense that you are experiencing more than grief, daughter,' Lee said. 'What else is it that troubles you?'

'It is nothing, Father.'

'Anger can never be described as nothing, Su-lin, and it is anger that I sense. And, perhaps, fear? Unburden yourself by explaining the problem that is so obviously troubling you.'

Su-lin had felt her father's approach and had tried desperately to quell the emotions that burnt within her. She knew he would sense her agitation, but the feelings had been too strong for her to control.

The night before, the phone had rung in the retreat. Although her father kept the despised instrument, installed by Elanora, wrapped in a hessian sack, she'd heard it nonetheless and answered. Georgina's distraught voice had called down the line. Her brother, Paul, had been killed in a fire, she'd cried, and before Su-lin could calm her, she'd further claimed that her father, James, had been responsible. Su-lin had listened with growing unease as Georgina had recounted her fears and dismay. Then, when the girl had finally fallen silent, Su-lin had talked with her long into the night, slowly but surely calming her down.

'I must go to Paul Merchant's funeral, Father,' Su-lin said. 'Georgina is in need of my friendship.'

'That is not a cause for anger.'

'It is not only anger I feel.' She looked up at her father. 'It is fear, too.'

'Fear is not an emotion, daughter – '

'Yes, I know,' Su-lin interrupted. She stood and began reciting her father's axiom. 'Fear is the warning bell of the human alarm system. Its purpose is two-fold. It alerts the mind to danger and prepares the body to respond. After that it should be dispelled. Logic alone must decide the course of action.'

'Word perfect,' Lee replied, 'but what good is the definition if you do not abide by it?'

Su-lin threw a small stone she'd been holding into the pool and stood watching the ripple effect it created. 'I hold no fear for myself,' she said finally. 'My fear is for Georgina,' she turned to her father, 'and perhaps others in the family.'

'This problem, it arose from the telephone call last night, is this not so?'

'Yes.'

'And it obviously concerns the Merchant family?'

'Yes,' she sighed, placing a hand on his shoulder. She knew him too well. He would gently cross-examine her until he boxed her into a corner. The time had come to tell him everything, and that included betraying the trust of her grandmother, who had sworn her to secrecy so many years before, in Macau.

龍

Paul Merchant's funeral was a very private affair. Katherine and Georgina cast his ashes into the wind and watched them scatter across the slopes of Victoria Peak while, standing behind them like black gravestones beneath a cold overcast sky, a small group of family and friends mourned his departure.

James Merchant stood apart from the group of mourners and left immediately the ashes were cast. He was followed not long after by others, including John and Katya Wilson. All desperate to put the dreadful episode of Paul's death behind them, they walked the path worn between the low tangled vegetation that led to the car park.

Finally, as rain clouds threatened to engulf the Peak, Jet Kwan escorted his grandmother Elanora away and they were followed by Georgina and a weeping Katherine. Su-lin stood alone, staring out over Lamma Island towards the South China Sea.

Memories flitted through her mind as the chill wind whipped at her black dress and shawl. She held her hair away from her eyes and, as light rain began to fall, she saw in the mist a vision of herself, playing with Paul and Georgina in the gardens of Merchant House. She saw, too, her grandmother and Katherine sharing tea on the balcony and Richard Brewster, hobbling along, trying to play football on the carefully manicured lawns with Jet and the house servants.

What had become of her lovely family? she wondered. They had been united in their happiness and good fortune. As recently as four years ago, before she'd left for Australia, they'd been together in Macau sharing Christmas and New Year, exchanging presents and caring for one another. What had happened to shatter the idyll? What had torn them apart?

The question is not what, it is who, she thought, and the answer came immediately to mind. James Merchant had torn them apart. James Merchant had destroyed his family, as surely as night follows day.

龍

Su-lin had arrived on Hong Kong Island from Kap Lung the previous day and had spent the night with Georgina, as a guest of the Wilsons. Dinner had been a sombre affair and Katya had made sure it concluded early. With the subtle manipulation of Johnnie, she had arranged for the girls to be alone.

They had sat on single beds and faced each other in the guest room they were to share, Su-lin with her hands locked in her lap and Georgina hugging a pillow against her chest.

'My father has torn this family apart, Su-lin,' Georgie had stated flatly. 'I never realised what he was up to until recently. Paul and I spent years at boarding school and in our absence my parents' relationship deteriorated more and more with every passing year.'

'That is no fault of yours, Georgie.'

'Oh, I know,' she smiled sadly. 'But I can't help but wonder – if we had been here, Paul and I, that is – would it have made a difference?'

'My father says that a marriage needs three elements: love, trust and friendship. And of the three, friendship is the ultimate attainment, because true friends never part.'

'Well, there was certainly love between them at some stage, I'm sure,' Georgie said, 'and I suppose trust along the way. But you know, now that I think about it, I can never remember seeing my parents as friends. They always seemed more like business partners. Isn't that strange?'

Su-lin let the beautiful young girl talk, aware that it was the beginning of Georgie's grieving process. She spoke sporadically, leaping from one subject to another, happier times, trips to Macau, her school days in Europe, her grandmother, her friends, then, finally, her twin, and her tears began to flow.

Su-lin moved to sit next to her and took the weeping young woman into her arms. She murmured words of condolence and hope until, after what seemed like an eternity, silence filled the room, broken only by the grieving girl's occasional sobs.

Eventually Georgie sat up straight, put the pillow she'd been hugging behind her, wiped her cheeks and looked directly into Su-lin's eyes. 'My father is responsible for Paul's death, you know,' she said. 'I'm quite sure of it.'

'You told me as much on the phone when you called Kap Lung.' Su-lin stood and sat back on her own bed. 'As I said then, it is a dreadful accusation, Georgina.' She leaned forward and took Georgina's hands in her own before continuing. 'And it is pure supposition on your part.'

'I'm aware of that,' Georgie sniffed, wiping her eyes on her sleeve. 'I have no proof, but I know it is true. And I'm sure my mother and *Ju Mo* are of the same opinion.'

'Has your mother said this?'

'No,' Georgina snorted humourlessly. 'Mother has done nothing but weep.'

'What has *Ju Mo* said?'

'The same as you.' Georgina stood and crossed to her

suitcase in search of a handkerchief. 'Grandmother said I should calm down and not say things I might regret.'

'It is good advice, Georgina.' Su-lin leaned forward, put her head on her knees, wrapped her arms around her legs, and watched the girl rummage through her suitcase. 'As you've admitted yourself, you have no evidence that your father did anything at all.'

'I know what my father did!' Georgina snapped. She stood up from her suitcase and blew her nose into a handkerchief. 'I'd bet my life that factory fire was no accident. The police said it started with an explosion, a very large explosion, and accidental fires don't start like that. They're usually the result of an electrical fault or a careless match, or whatever.' She shook her head as if to clear her thoughts and returned to sit on her bed. 'There was definitely an explosion. It was even reported in the *South China Morning Post*. A witness said there was a very loud bang and the factory was a blazing inferno in a matter of minutes. That doesn't sound like an accidental fire to me.'

'No. I suppose it doesn't, when you explain it like that.' Su-lin knew only too well what James Merchant was capable of – she'd experienced it herself as a child with her abduction and rape, but she'd had proof. Georgina's case was one of pure supposition. The girl was utterly convinced, to the point of paranoia, despite not even a shred of evidence, of her father's involvement in her brother's death. 'Are the police investigating the matter?'

'Of course not.' Georgina gave a high pitched laugh. 'Haven't you read the newspapers?' She got up and began pacing the bedroom floor. 'Apparently they're already satisfied the fire was an accident, after only two days. Can you believe that? And that makes me all the more certain that my father did it. He's used his money and influence to have the case closed. I'm absolutely convinced of it.'

'You do realise that you can never say any of these things in public, don't you?'

'I'm not that stupid, Su-lin,' Georgina scoffed. 'I know what my father is capable of. He'd probably demand that I be examined medically and I'd finish up in Castle Hill Mental Hospital.'

'What are you going to do?'

'What *can* I do?' Georgina stopped pacing and stared at her cousin. 'I know what I'd like to do. I'd like to make my father suffer the same horrific death as my brother!'

'That is foolish talk,' Su-lin warned as Georgina continued her pacing.

'At the moment perhaps,' Georgie agreed, nodding her head rapidly, 'but one day I'll have my revenge, Su-lin. I'll repay my father for all of the misery he has brought on my family. I'll repay him for the way he's treated me, for the way he's treated my mother, for the way he's treated *Ju Mo* and Richard, and all the other people he's trampled on. And most of all, I'll repay him for what he did to Paul.'

'Your hatred is strong, Georgina,' Su-lin said softly, 'and hatred is a dangerous human trait. Be sure it does not destroy you.'

'Don't you worry about me, cousin.' Georgina stopped and smiled.

'I cannot help but worry,' Su-lin replied. She was startled by Georgina's gaze. Her eyes were bright, unnaturally bright, they gleamed with an animal ferocity which, as Su-lin watched, turned to feline cunning.

'I'm going away,' Georgie said, as she sat on Su-lin's bed. 'Straight after Paul's funeral tomorrow, I'm going to Singapore.'

'Singapore?'

'Yes, it was Grandmother's idea.' Georgie smiled again and the gleam faded from her eyes. 'She's worried about me, too. She knows I can't stay at Merchant House and she said my presence in Hong Kong will only lead to more trouble, so she's offered me a job in Singapore.'

'What sort of job?' Thank God for *Ju Mo*, Su-lin thought. Elanora had obviously sensed Georgie's paranoia too, and had taken steps.

'For the first six months I'll be working at Raffles Hotel, studying hotel management. After that, I'm to work as a manager in *Ju Mo*'s hotel.

'Grandmother owns a hotel in Singapore?' Su-lin was genuinely surprised.

'Elanora's spent the last five years transferring her business interests to Singapore. She now has a lot of her money tied up there, and I know why. It's because she doesn't trust my father any more than I do.'

'Forget your father,' Su-lin said earnestly, getting up onto her knees and placing her hands on Georgina's shoulders. 'Forget this whole horrible time,' she commanded. '*Ju Mo* has presented you with a wonderful opportunity. Go to Singapore and make a new life for yourself.'

'That is my intention, but . . . I'll never forget,' Georgie replied as a wonderfully warm sensation flowed through her body. She began to relax as Su-lin's expert fingers located the pressure points and her concentration turned to small objects in the room, like the mat on the floor and then a watercolour of Japan's Mount Fuji on the wall. What had she been angry about? She tried to remember but her mind refused to focus. It was being led somewhere against her will, but she couldn't seem to care.

Su-lin was talking to her, but her voice was somehow distant and she sensed the conversation was of little importance anyway. Her cousin would not be offended if she didn't pay attention. The beautiful sensation seemed to go on forever and then Su-lin was standing at the open doorway saying something.

'What?' Georgina heard herself ask.

'I said let's go into the kitchen and make a hot drink. It will make us sleep.'

'Yes, let's,' Georgie said. She stood and seemed to glide through the doorway into the corridor and float towards the kitchen. She could sense her cousin following and she felt a wonderful feeling of security envelop her.

龍

On the Friday morning after Paul's funeral James Merchant sat in the company offices in Ice House Street, picked up his desk clock and savoured the fact that he had no appointments for an entire hour. At first, the rarity of such an occasion amused him, but the more consideration he gave to it, the more irritated he became.

What good to man or beast was one solitary hour? What could one do in sixty minutes that would be of any benefit? Three thousand, six hundred seconds was too little time to do anything of any consequence and yet, too much time to waste on trivialities. Which idiot, he thought, had been the first person to decide that one twenty-fourth of a day should be the quintessential measurement for the existence of the world? Why hadn't the idiot, whoever he was, made it metric? Ten seconds in a minute, one hundred minutes in an hour, one thousand hours in a day all seemed much more practical, didn't it? Or did it?

'Excuse me, Mister Merchant?'

'What?' James nearly flew out of the chair when his secretary opened the door. He looked at the clock in his hand and realised he'd wasted twenty-three minutes of his free hour. 'Shit!' he exclaimed and threw the offending time-piece across the room. 'What is it, Marie?'

'There is a coolie here who insists on seeing you. I've called Security, but – '

'Hello, James?'

'Lee,' he exclaimed as his brother stepped past the horrified secretary. 'Tell Security not to bother, Marie. That will be all,' he ordered the young woman. Then, as she left, he moved around the desk towards Lee Kwan, his hand extended.

'I wish to speak with you,' Lee said, as he shook his brother's hand.

'After ten years, I should bloody hope so.' Had it really been that long? James thought. After Ten Ten Day 1956, he remembered, they'd gone to the old Walled City and spent the day together, laughing and recalling their youth. Christ, he thought again, ten years. James offered him a seat, but Lee declined the invitation with a shake of his head. 'How wonderful it is to see you. It's about time you came down off that mountain. I don't know how you stand it.'

James moved back behind his desk and sat down. He

observed his brother standing in the middle of the room and his heart sank as he took in the poor clothes, bare feet and ridiculous conical bamboo coolie's hat. 'You look bloody awful, Lee,' he said. 'Are they the only clothes you've got?'

'They are clean, are they not?' Lee took off his bamboo hat and brushed his hair with his hand.

'That's not what I meant and you know it,' James replied. 'And I suppose you walked all the way here from Kap Lung?'

'Yes,' Lee nodded lazily, as his fingers played with the small dragon medallion set on a chain around his neck.

'Don't tell me you've still got that medallion?' James laughed.

'Certainly,' Lee replied, 'haven't you?'

'No.' James shrugged. 'I gave mine away to a little kid in London, during the war.'

'Well, it was a long time ago that we received them.' Lee continued fiddling with the medallion.

'Yes, it was,' James nodded. 'Nineteen thirty-three to be exact, and we were only thirteen.'

'Yes. A very long time ago.'

James couldn't help the uneasy feeling that was creeping over him. Lee Kwan seemed remote. There was a coldness about him.

'So, what brings you down to Hong Kong after all this time, *Sai Loh*?'

'I came here to find out the truth, James.'

'The truth?' James felt a chill creep up his spine. Lee had a look in his eye, the like of which James had not seen before. 'The truth about what?' he asked, hoping it had nothing to do with the circumstances surrounding Paul's death.

'Double Ten Day, 1956,' Lee said.

'Double Ten Day, 1956,' James repeated, stalling for time to think. He knows something, James thought. Somebody's told him something about the bloody Brotherhood of Warriors and the riots in Sham Shui Po. Christ, he thought, has he heard I was involved? After all this time, could he have found out anything? Tread carefully, James, he warned himself.

'It was the day after I arrived in Hong Kong,' Lee said. 'The day Su-lin was kidnapped and raped. Surely you remember?'

'Of course I remember,' James replied carefully. Beneath his desk, he slipped his feet out of his shoes. 'How could anyone forget that night?'

'Su-lin forgot it, or rather, she erased it from her memory when she realised it would serve no purpose to remember it.'

'She is a remarkable young woman, Lee.' James watched as Lee dropped his bamboo hat onto a chair.

'Are you preparing for combat, James?' The eyes of the two brothers locked.

'That's where this conversation will lead, if it continues,' James replied, getting to his feet.

'There is no need for it to continue,' Lee said quietly, picking his hat up. 'You have answered my question already,' he said, and turned to leave.

'Now wait just one damned minute, will you?' James snapped, and sat back down behind his desk. Lee turned slowly to face him. James knew it was of no use to lie. 'I wanted to tell you at the time – '

'You should have.'

'It was never my intention for anything to happen to Su-lin that night. I didn't even know they'd kidnapped her until you rang me.'

'If you wanted me to be involved as a Nationalist figure-head in the Sham Shui Po riots, you only needed to ask me.' Lee sat down, placed his hat on his lap and looked at his brother. 'I would have declined, but – '

'I didn't want you involved in anything!' James gave an exasperated shrug. 'The bloody Brotherhood of Warriors acted on their own in that one. They heard the great, bloody Shanghai Dragon, or whatever it is they call you, had arrived in Hong Kong and they wanted you involved. It had nothing to do with me.'

'Be careful, James, or you will absolve yourself from blame entirely.' Lee's remark dripped sarcasm.

'Not entirely, *Sai Loh*!' James snapped in retaliation. 'My company had a lot of money tied up in Taiwan at the time and the powers that be on that island intimated to me that it would be a good idea if I assisted the Hong Kong National-ists in their endeavours.'

'So, for the sake of making money, you assisted a group of political fanatics to stage a riot.' Lee shook his head. 'Your lust for wealth and power disgusts me. Sixty-two people died on Ten Ten Day, James. Hundreds more were injured or lost their homes. Su-lin was kidnapped and raped – '

'I told you that was not my fault!' James yelled, rising to his feet.

'Which was not your fault?' Lee said as he too, stood. 'The deaths, the injuries, or the kidnap and rape?'

'None of them!' James moved around his desk and stood not three feet from Lee. 'And who are you to come here and accuse me? Captain Lee Kwan, the Dragon of Shanghai? Ha! Don't make me laugh,' James sneered. 'For twenty years you were a paid soldier, which amounts to nothing more than a professional killer. So you chose to run away and live on a mountain, so what? It doesn't alter the fact that you killed for money, just as I've done.'

'That is true,' Lee nodded, 'but I stopped a long time ago, unlike you.'

James looked his brother in the eye, but his gaze faltered. He's heard something about Paul's death, James thought. Something that has made him leave his precious mountain.

'And just what is that remark supposed to imply, Lee?' he asked carefully. He'd heard something very recently, but what? And who had said it? Georgina? Elanora? Or did he know about Sean Poots? No, he couldn't possibly know about the Irishman. It could only have been Georgina's hys-terical accusations via Su-lin, James decided.

'Did you cause your son's death?'

'Ha!' James' laugh was scornful. 'You've been listening to Georgina, no doubt.'

'I came to find out the truth,' Lee said flatly, 'for my own sake. For the sake of our friendship. Did you have anything to do with your son's death?'

'Be careful, *Sai Loh*,' James warned. 'My daughter is an empty-headed hysteric who, if she doesn't keep her mouth shut, is going to find herself in serious trouble. What happened to Paul was an accident.'

Lee began to shake his head. 'Like what happened to Su-lin was an accident?'

'I did not kill my son!' James roared.

'Your denial comes too late, James.' Lee crossed to the door. 'Besides,' he stopped and turned, 'the truth is written all over your face. You never could lie to me.'

'You bastard!' James yelled. 'Don't you dare walk out on me!' As Lee's hand reached to open the office door, James flew after him and grabbed his shoulder. In an instant he was flat on his back on the floor, with Lee standing over him.

'You are no match for me, *Sai Loh*,' Lee said gravely and the words, Little Brother, were not lost on James. 'The *way* is weak in you. It always was, because you never sought to understand it.'

'Get out!' James hissed angrily, but he remained where he lay.

'You killed your own flesh and blood.' Lee's upper lip curled into an expression of utter loathing. 'The darkness has finally taken you. You are lost, James. Our brotherhood is ended.' Lee shook his head and left, closing the door gently behind him.

It was several minutes before James burst out of his office and roared at his startled secretary, who cowered at her desk.

'Marie! Find my daughter, Georgina, and get her in here immediately.'

'She's gone, James,' Johnnie Wilson answered. He stood in the reception area staring, open-mouthed, at his dishevelled boss.

'What do you mean, she's gone? Gone where?'

'I thought you knew,' Johnnie replied.

'Knew what?' James demanded.

'Georgie flew to Singapore, this morning.'

BOOK FOUR

THE DARKNESS

CHAPTER FOURTEEN

Hong Kong, 1967

The copperplate handwriting first drew James' eye to the letter lying on his secretary's desk among the other mail. He picked it up to admire the old fashioned flowing style and noticed it was addressed to him, care of the Merchant Company, Ice House Street, Hong Kong Island, Hong Kong. It was postmarked 17 May 1967, Yorkshire, England.

'Good morning, *taipan*,' one of his young Chinese executives called as he passed.

'Mmmm,' James murmured absently as he entered his office, still fascinated by the old world handwriting. He threw his briefcase on a sofa, sat at his desk and with a silver letter opener, slit the envelope and began to read.

Dear Sir,

I trust this letter finds you well. I am writing firstly to ascertain the health of your step-father Richard Brewster. I wrote to him six months ago at his last known address, Merchant House on Victoria Peak, but have received no reply to my correspondence. I find myself in fear for his well-being. God grant I am wrong.

I was a serving officer in the Hong Kong Police before World War II and met you on several occasions, the most notable being the night of your induction into a certain society of which I was one of the Honoured First Five and about which I shall commit nothing more to paper for reasons you will surely understand.

I find myself fallen upon hard times and in need of assistance. As one of the First Five, I attended a meeting in Hong Kong in December 1941, where I was informed that the remains of 'the four who came from foreign cities' had been placed in a Swiss bank for safekeeping two years prior in 1939. I was wondering if they had ever been redeemed. If Richard is no longer alive, as I fear may be the case, then it is quite probable you and I are the only ones who remain of the seven with the knowledge to redeem.

Might I request that you inform me, first and foremost, of your step-father's well-being as he was truly my greatest friend. Furthermore, if the redemption has occurred, which I believe would be the case after all these years, could you find it in your heart to grant me a small sum, or perhaps an annuity from that old Dragon Imports account, to alleviate my circumstances.

My needs are few, Sir, but my situation is dire.

I await your reply with trepidation,

Terrence Delaney

'Good God,' James declared aloud, as he placed the letter on his desk. 'Terrence Delaney. I thought he was dead.'

James remembered Terrence Delaney: a tall, brusque, heavy drinking Yorkshireman with deep, haunted eyes. Delaney had been a war hero who'd served in World War I on the battlefields of France, or so he'd been told. And he'd been one of the four policemen Richard Brewster had chosen to form the illegal triad known as the Society of Golden Dragons.

He remembered that night vividly. He and Lee had been branded, each on a shoulder. The scar left by the iron was a snarling dragon, which now tingled. He scratched it absent-mindedly.

James rose from the chair and moved towards the pot of coffee, always delivered when his secretary noticed his arrival, then stopped and stared vacantly at a framed oil painting of the harbour hanging by the door.

'A meeting of the Honoured First Five in December 1941,'

he said softly. He crossed to the bar and poured himself coffee. What on earth had that meeting been about? December 1941 had been the month Hong Kong had fallen. James had been in England serving in the R.A.F. when the Colonial Forces had surrendered to the invading Japanese on Christmas Day 1941. So what had the Honoured First Five been up to then, apart from fighting the Japs?

He returned to his desk and picked up the letter. 'I was informed,' he read aloud, 'that the remains of the four who came from foreign cities had been placed in a Swiss bank for safekeeping.' He scratched his chin. 'Jesus Christ!' he muttered, incredulous. 'The statues. Delaney means the golden dragons.'

His mind rushed back over the years recalling a sequence of questions and answers that he had been required to memorise which had contained the words 'from the four foreign cities'. It was a direct reference to the four golden statues. James remembered them vividly. They had stood three feet high and were made of solid gold. They had been manufactured by wealthy Chinese expatriates living in four foreign cities, Honolulu, San Francisco, Tokyo and Sydney.

Because of World War I, all foreign aid had been suspended to Sun Yat-sen and his Nationalist Army in China, so his foreign supporters had sent the statues instead of money. The statues had been stolen and for years had lain on the bottom of Tatong Channel in Hong Kong, until finally, they had fallen into the hands of Richard Brewster.

With excitement rising from the pit of his stomach, James looked at the letter again. 'The remains of the four who came from foreign cities,' it read. But what remains? James asked himself. There were no remains. The solid gold statues had been melted down and exchanged for money, which had been invested to support the illegal society.

Unless, James' mind reasoned, not all of the money had been invested. Or, indeed, not all of the gold had been converted to cash. There was a thought. Perhaps Richard had put some of it in a Swiss bank? Set it aside for a rainy day? It would be typical of Richard Brewster; he had been a clever bastard in his time. James nodded, chewing his lip as his brain processed the conundrum Delaney's letter presented.

James decided to have Johnnie Wilson do a bit of bank account snooping. Delaney's letter even gave the account name, Dragon Imports, so it shouldn't be too hard to locate.

'But as for you, Terrence, old boy,' James said as he rose from his seat, 'I'm afraid you miss out, whichever way it goes. Whatever money, or gold bullion, is in Switzerland will be mine alone. That's the way the fortune cookie crumbles.'

He laughed at his own joke as he screwed the letter up, dropped it in the waste paper basket and headed for the door.

龍

Jeremy Bent roamed the sumptuous hotel suite examining every single feature but, try as he might, he could not find a single fault. Well, he thought, at least nothing worth complaining about. Jeremy desperately needed to find something legitimately wrong.

'Bugger it,' he muttered as he looked at his watch. His carefully conceived plan required him to complain at precisely eight a.m. and it was now seven forty-five. Things were going pear-shaped. 'And I haven't even had breakfast,' he moaned.

He searched the rooms again but found absolutely nothing broken, dirty, or out of place. The whole suite was not only enormous, he decided, but immaculate. Sick and tired of searching, he threw his fifteen stone into a cane chair, intent on devising an alternative strategy. It collapsed beneath him.

'Thank Christ for that!' he declared as he got up off the floor, rubbing his elbow. He went to the bathroom and finished grooming the image he saw in the mirror. Satisfied with his efforts, he returned to the bedroom, picked up his dirty singlet and threw it in his suitcase, then he sat on the bed staring at the house phone, waiting for his new Seiko watch to sound its alarm at precisely eight o'clock.

Just as he'd decided his new watch might be broken, the alarm went off. He grabbed the phone, dialled nine and began tapping his foot impatiently.

'Good morning. Reception,' a pleasant female voice answered.

'Yes. Right,' Jeremy began hesitantly. 'Now look here,' he said. 'It's suite 201 here.'

'Yes, Sir, I know,' the receptionist replied.

'Well, good.' Jeremy stumbled on. 'So you know, do you?'

'Yes, Sir. Your room number lights up on the switchboard,' the girl said sweetly.

'The number lights up, does it? Well, that's a start.' He was not a complainer, he suddenly realised. He'd never complained about anything much in his life and now that he had to, he was finding it difficult.

'Yes, Sir. It is a good start,' the girl answered. 'How may I help you?'

'Well . . . it simply isn't good enough . . . is it?'

'What isn't, Sir?'

'The chair . . . in my room.'

'Would you like it replaced? If it's not suitable I'll have housekeeping replace it immediately, Sir.'

'No, no, no,' he said. 'You don't understand.'

'That is true, Sir. I don't.'

'Look, do you speak *Gwang Dung wah*?'

'Of course, Sir.'

'Oh.' Jeremy had immediate second thoughts, because his Cantonese was dreadful and invariably got him into trouble. 'Fluently?'

'Yes, Sir. I am Cantonese.'

'Oh, well, never mind.' He was getting himself into an awful mess. 'The problem is, I sat on the chair and it broke.'

'Oh dear, Sir,' the girl said sincerely. 'Are you hurt? Do you wish me to call a doctor?'

'No, no, no, no,' Jeremy said rapidly. 'I don't want to see a doctor, I want to see the manager. The one who starts work now, at eight o'clock.'

'Very well, Sir,' the receptionist said. 'I shall send the Day Duty Manager to your suite immediately.'

'Thank you,' Jeremy replied. 'I'm sorry about the complaint. And I do hope I didn't sound too stern for you?'

'Oh, no, Sir. Your voice is very firm and manly, but it has a gentleness to it that is also pleasing to the ear. I shall send the manager straightaway. Will that be all?'

'Yes, thank you,' he said, puzzled, as the girl hung up.

He stood and frowned. 'Firm and manly?' He posed the question to his image in the cupboard mirror opposite where he sat. 'With a gentleness that's pleasing to the ear?' He gave the description some more consideration. 'Jesus.'

With the complaint made and the manager on the way to the suite, Jeremy went to the bathroom and straightened the items on the vanity, then picked up the towel he'd used and hung it neatly on the rail. Satisfied, he went back into the bedroom and looked again to make sure it too, was tidy, then he adjusted his clothes in front of the mirror.

'You're looking good, Inspector Bent,' he said standing to attention. 'Bloody good. You're a fine specimen of a man.'

The doorbell rang. 'Right, this is it,' he declared. He strode to the door and flung it open.

'Jeremy!' the manager exclaimed.

'Hello, Georgina.'

'What are you doing here?'

'I'm your guest.'

The inanity of the remark, coupled with the stupid grin on his face, made Georgie's blood boil. She glowered at him. 'Is this some sort of bloody joke?'

'No.'

'According to the hotel register, this suite is occupied by a Mister Salisbury.'

'Ah,' Jeremy raised his hand defensively, 'that bit's a joke. You know, seeing as how we met in the Salisbury pub in London.'

'Well, I don't find it amusing.' Georgie spun on her heel and walked away up the corridor.

'Are you the Duty Manager?' Jeremy called after her.

Georgina stopped in her tracks. 'You obviously know damned well I am,' she called over her shoulder.

'Well,' he called back, 'I've got a complaint to make.'

Georgina closed her eyes and clenched her fists, before

turning and striding back to the door. She stood, legs akimbo, placed her hands on her hips, and glared at him. 'Very well, *Mister Salisbury*, tell me, what's the problem?'

'You'll have to come inside.' He stood back and gestured for her to enter the suite.

Georgina gave a resigned look and stepped past him. She moved through the lounge-dining room into the bedroom, saw the broken chair, then swung back to look at him. 'Is this it?'

'I sat on it and it broke,' he offered.

'Were you injured, Sir?'

'No, only my elbow is a bit sore.' He rubbed it as if to confirm his statement.

'What a pity.' Georgina's sarcastic smile said it all.

'But the point is, I could have hurt myself, isn't that so?'

'It certainly is.' Her reply was very formal. 'On behalf of Raffles Hotel I would like to apologise sincerely for any inconvenience or injury you've incurred – '

'Oh, cut it out, Georgie – ' Jeremy's interruption failed.

'If Sir would care to see a doctor, I can arrange it,' she continued, 'or, if Sir would care to check out immediately, I can assure him that no payment for accommodation, meals, or services will be necessary. His stay at our establishment will be free, courtesy of the management.'

'Georgie – '

'Now, if Sir will excuse me, I have work to do.'

Jeremy beat her to the front door, closed it and leaned his back against it.

'Get out of my way, Jeremy.'

'Give me a chance, Georgie, please?' He held his hands out as a plea. 'I came all the way to Singapore to see you. I didn't want to knock on your office door, or embarrass you by attracting your attention in the foyer. I didn't know what else to do except wait until you started work, then make a complaint, knowing you'd have to come to the room.' Jeremy paused and tried to smile. 'Please, hear me out?'

'I'm listening,' she said, crossing her arms over her chest and moving her weight onto one heel. 'Get on with it.'

'I saw you on the Star Ferry a few months ago,' he began.

'Did you?' she replied, remembering the incident vividly. 'I didn't see you, I'm afraid.'

'No, well, you were on a ferry going to Kowloon and I was on one going to Hong Kong side. I was standing at the rail and so were you. I felt sure you'd seen me.'

'Well, I didn't.'

'I waved.'

'Did you?' Damn it, she thought. He's trying really hard and his blue eyes are beautiful. Why did this man have such an effect on her? They hadn't spoken for at least a year, not since the morning she'd thrown him out of her house in London. But she felt her anger subsiding as she looked into his eyes again. The sincerity she saw there forced her to look away. He was getting to her.

'And I went to your brother's funeral up on the Peak, but there was only close family there, so I just sat in the car for a while and left. He was a nice fellow, Paul, even though I only met him the once. I liked him straightaway. You have my sympathy.'

'Thank you.' He's gorgeous, she thought, despising herself as her defences began to crumble.

'I've wanted to see you for such a long time.'

'Have you, really?' Images of their naked forms locked together in her bed in London flashed through her brain. She felt her body begin to melt.

'Oh, yes.'

'This suite will cost you a month's pay you realise, don't you?'

'I wouldn't care if it cost me my life.'

That did it. Georgina threw herself into his arms.

龍

Elanora leaned over her husband and wiped his fevered brow with a damp cloth. I'm going to lose him, she thought. And I'm going to have to remain in this world without him. When I eat, or walk the streets, or take the ferry to Hong Kong, I'll be moving through the world alone. Will I be able to bear it? Will I adjust to a world without Richard?

She placed the cloth in the bowl of water by his bed and got to her feet. She looked about his room as anxiety increased its grip on her mind. She took his dressing gown from the chair it hung on and went into his dressing room. Once inside, the smell of her man overtook her. She buried her head in the clothes that hung in neat rows on either side of the room. She inhaled deeply, taking in the familiar scent of him, then drifted idly about picking up various personal items. Leather, cotton, aftershave fragrances, shoe polish, shaving cream, all things male that were the world of Richard Brewster surrounded her. The different aromas assailed her senses until tears welled up in her eyes and she left the room.

She looked at Richard lying peacefully asleep, then moved to the window and looked down at the Macau seafront. She shook her head, unable to focus her thoughts. She could not begin to contemplate what life would be like without Richard Brewster.

'Mistress,' Sally the maid cried as she burst into the room.

'Shhh!' Elanora rasped angrily. 'The master is sleeping. If he wakes you will be sorry, girl. What is it?'

'Your son,' the girl whispered.

'Lee Kwan?'

'No, Missy. Master James. He is in the study downstairs.'

'Tell him to get out – no wait, tell him stay there. I'll be down directly.'

James in Macau? The thought unnerved her. What in God's name could he possibly want? He was the last person she needed to see. She looked again at the sleeping form of Richard before closing the door quietly behind her.

'Hello, Mother,' he said as she entered the study. He'd been leaning against the fireplace, idly examining a seashell he'd picked up from the mantlepiece. He returned it to its rightful place and moved to her side, kissing her on the cheek.

'What do you want?' Elanora's voice was cold, dispassionate.

'What makes you automatically assume that I want something?'

'You would not be here otherwise,' she replied, taking a seat at the table.

James laughed, trying to evince an air of good intention. 'Is it impossible to believe I may have come here simply to enquire after Richard's well-being?'

'Yes.'

'All right.' The smile disappeared from his face. 'If that's the way it must be, so be it.'

'Why are you here, James?'

'I need to speak to Richard.'

'You can't.'

'Why not?'

'Because he's ill.'

'Oh, God,' James groaned. 'Richard has been ill since the war, Mother,' he declared. 'I just want to talk to him.'

'What about?'

'Nothing you'd be aware of,' he said, then a thought struck him. 'Or would you?'

'Try me,' she replied. Angry as she was, Elanora's curiosity was aroused. What question would drag James all the way from Hong Kong to Macau in search of the answer? Perhaps, if the question was simple, she could answer it and get rid of him, and, if the question was of any consequence, she'd be better off knowing it than remaining in the dark.

'All right.' James sat down and smiled, but it was not the smile of a son for his mother. 'Just over a week ago I received a letter from Terrence Delaney. Do you remember him?'

'Yes, vaguely,' she lied. Delaney, she knew, had written to Richard the previous year. The letter had been a brief enquiry after Richard's well-being, but Richard had decided not to answer. He knew by then he had little time left and the news would have been cold comfort to Delaney. Richard had been firm in the opinion that the days of his Golden Dragons were better off left in the shadows of the past.

'Vaguely?' James gave a dubious look. 'Even I remember him and I was only a boy.'

She'd known Delaney well and liked him, but she was determined to contribute nothing until she knew what James wanted. 'He was a Yorkshireman,' she said. 'A friend of Richard's.'

'A friend?' Richard scoffed. 'Oh, please, he was more than a friend, Mother. Delaney was one of the principal office bearers in the Society of Golden Dragons.'

'Was he?' Elanora replied evenly, but the mention of the triad society unsettled her.

'Yes, he was,' James replied, giving his mother a doubtful look. 'Delaney was one of the First Five. Surely you knew that?'

'I took no interest in those affairs.'

'Oh, come now, Mother.' He raised an eyebrow. 'We both know that's not true.'

'It *is* true,' Elanora snapped. 'And as far as I am concerned those days are best forgotten.'

'Mmmm,' James chuckled. 'The bad old days, eh?'

'Exactly. Now, can you get on with it?'

'Certainly. It appears a bank account was opened at the Bank Suisse in Geneva, before the war. The account was in the name of Dragon Imports, the international front for the Society of Golden Dragons.'

'Delaney told you that, did he?' She tried to sound casual, disinterested.

'Yes, he did,' James smiled lazily. He was enjoying the game of cat and mouse. 'But there was a lot more he didn't tell me. So, I did a bit of snooping and found out the account is still active.'

'Is it just?' Elanora tried valiantly to maintain an air of nonchalance.

'And what's more,' James paused, staring at his mother, gauging her reaction, 'it seems the account is separately insured.'

'Really?' Elanora's apprehension was growing with his every word. 'And what does that mean?' She knew precisely what it meant, but the fact that James knew terrified her.

'Let's stop playing games, Elanora.' His voice now had a sinister edge. 'You know as well as I do what it means. Your knowledge of bank procedures is second to none, but I'll refresh your memory, shall I? When a bank decides to individually insure an account, it means it's worth more than the bloody building that houses it.' He looked into her eyes again, searching for any signs of worry, or fear. 'Whatever is being held in that bank,' he said slowly, 'must be worth a king's ransom.'

'How did you find all this out?' Elanora stalled for time as her mind struggled to analyse their conversation. How much did he know? she wondered. And what was he intending to do?

'You don't really expect me to answer that, do you?' He smiled coldly.

'No.' She already knew the answer. Johnnie Wilson, she thought, Hong Kong's greatest industrial spy. Over the previous ten years, Johnnie had developed a network of agents in Geneva and other financial cities in Europe that his own American CIA would be proud of.

'I believe I may have authority to open that account, but the trouble is, the account is escrowed. To open it, apparently, I need to know the answers to a series of questions.' He smiled at her again. 'You don't happen to know them by any chance, do you?'

'Of course not,' she lied again. She not only knew about the deposit box and how to gain access to it, she also knew what it contained.

'Are you sure?' He looked at her.

'I'm positive.' She stared right back at him. 'I don't know any of these questions or answers you're looking for. I didn't even know about the account. It's the first I've heard of it.'

'Then I'll have to ask Richard.'

'No!' Elanora held a commanding hand up. 'Richard's very sick. He is beyond speech, but that is beside the point as far as you're concerned.' Elanora glared at her son. 'I would not allow you to speak to him under any circumstances.'

'But I must speak with him, Mother.' James stood and his tone carried a warning. 'I need to know what's in that account.'

'Don't you dare make demands in my house!' Elanora also

rose to her feet but James ignored her and made his way through the study doors towards the stairway in the foyer.

'Where do you think you're going?' She reached the stairs in time and grabbed him by the arm.

'I intend him no harm, Mother,' James said, 'but I must see him.' Then, breaking free of her grip, he took the stairs three at a time.

'Sally!' Elanora screamed.

'Yes, Missy?' The girl had been standing in the hallway, terrified by the exchange.

'Call the police.'

Elanora went after him as fast as she could, but he reached the top floor well ahead of her. Fortunately, he went to the wrong room and she caught up with him at Richard's door.

'How dare you come into my house like this!' she screamed as he crossed the corridor. The two of them burst into Richard's room.

James was truly shocked at Richard's appearance. He stood staring at the shell of the man he'd known, unable to believe the change. Richard was no more than skin and bone. There was nothing left of him.

'He's dying,' Elanora said quietly.

'Richard?' James moved closer to the bed.

'He's dying, damn you!' Elanora cursed.

'Richard, can you hear me?' James touched the man's shoulder. Richard's eyes opened and stared blankly at the ceiling. 'Richard, there's a bank account in Switzerland – ' he began, but Richard's eyes closed. 'Richard!' James shook the body roughly. 'Wake up, man!'

The sight of her husband being shaken was the last straw for Elanora. She grabbed her son by the coat sleeve. 'Leave him alone!' she shrieked like a banshee. 'Leave him alone and get out of my house!'

'Stop it, Mother!' James pushed her roughly and she fell to the floor behind him.

'I'll have you gaoled for this,' she hissed from where she lay. 'The police will arrive soon and I'll have you gaoled, do you hear me?'

James looked at her lying on the floor, then, with another glance at the comatose form of his step-father, he turned and left the room.

Elanora struggled to her feet and went to the bed. Richard's eyes were closed and his breathing was shallow and irregular. 'Oh, my darling,' she wept. 'Oh, my precious darling. Did he hurt you?' Richard groaned, it was barely audible.

'Shhh, my darling,' Elanora whispered, stroking his brow. 'He's gone now.'

'Listen.' The sound of his cracked voice shocked her.

'Oh, Richard, I thought I would never hear you again.'

'James . . .' Richard began.

'Yes, he was here, but don't worry. He's gone now. Rest, my love.'

'Warn . . .' Richard whispered and, with what strength he had left, he seized her wrist. 'Warn Lee,' he managed to say, as he heard voices calling him from far away.

'Hush, my darling.'

'Elanora,' he whispered as the voices came nearer. 'I love . . .' His eyes closed.

'No! No, Richard,' she sobbed, all thoughts of Lee disappearing. 'Come back, my darling. Don't leave me. Please don't leave me!'

龍

Johnnie Wilson stood on the Star Ferry concourse on Hong Kong side. In the gathering twilight, he watched disembarked passengers coming out of the terminal. Occasionally his eyes wandered to the harbour waters, where the ubiquitous warships, dark and dangerous shadows, lay at anchor. The Vietnam War was raging to the south and the newspapers were claiming there was no end to it in sight.

Although it was Sunday, Johnnie had to work, so Katya had gone shopping with friends in Kowloon City Markets. She'd called him at the office and suggested he meet her at the ferry and take her to dinner. He stood waiting patiently for her to arrive.

He watched people scurrying this way and that in their efforts to get home. Taxi drivers honked their horns, urging others in front of them on the rank to get a move on, while red double-decker buses and yellow minibuses spewed exhaust fumes as they nudged slowly, like cattle, through the island's busiest bus terminus.

Johnnie flinched suddenly. To his left several long strings of fire-crackers exploded, rattling off like machine-gun fire. A contingent of Red Guards, twenty or thirty of them, some barely into their teens, were shouting and waving red flags. They wore red handkerchiefs around their necks and held Mao's *Little Red Book* aloft for all to see. One young guard was holding a sign which read 'Overthrow British Fascism, Imperialism and tirenny'. Johnnie noted the misspelling and the fact that the young guard's bright red T-shirt had the words 'Manchester United FC' emblazoned across it.

Political thuggery was the same anywhere in the world, Johnnie thought, as he watched the young Communists making a nuisance of themselves, jostling people as they attempted to pass by. The Red Guards, from what he'd seen so far, were no different to extremists anywhere. Half of them were probably illiterate and had learned, parrot-fashion, the quotations they were shouting in people's faces. But like it or not, he decided, the Red Guards were the ugly political face of Maoist China and they were creating serious trouble in the Colony.

Johnnie had witnessed the civil unrest in 1956, but although there had been rioting and even deaths, it had been clumsily orchestrated by Nationalist fanatics in Hong Kong, not really by the Government in Taiwan, and the whole affair had only lasted a few days. This time however, the Chinese Communist Party in Hong Kong, with the apparent approval of Peking, was not only identifying itself with the demonstrations and riots, it was planning and organising them.

The troubles had started in the previous month of May, in a plastic flower factory of all places, in Kowloon. A labour union with justifiable grievances had called a strike against the factory and the workers had marched off the job.

Members of the union waving Mao's books and reciting his quotations had picketed the factory entrance. Hong Kong's Communist Party cadres, after taking several days to become aware of the situation, had finally realised they had a situation they could exploit. They'd picked up the workers' rallying cry and had hurried their members, led by several professional agitators, to join the striking employees in the street. The police had finally attended and a riot had been the inevitable result.

But this time, Johnnnie thought as he watched the young thugs' performance, unlike 1956, the trouble had been going on for six weeks and there appeared no end to it in sight. Demonstrations that deteriorated into riots were being staged all over the Colony. Bombs were being exploded in the streets, cars were being set alight and people had been kidnapped, even murdered. The Hong Kong Police were stretched to their limits and warnings by the Governor of possible military intervention had no effect. There will be no quick fix, Johnnie thought, shaking his head sadly. The 'People's War', as the Communists were calling it, with its labour strikes, riots and psychological scare tactics, had come to Hong Kong.

'Darling,' Katya called. She skipped between two taxis and ran to him.

'Hi, honey.' He accepted a kiss on the cheek as she arrived, breathless, on the footpath. 'Come on,' he said, nodding his head in the direction of the group of young Communists as he took her by the elbow. 'Let's get out of here, pronto.'

'Where are we going?' Katya skipped to keep up with him as they walked past City Hall.

'I thought, maybe, the Hilton?' Johnnie tucked her arm beneath his as they crossed Connaught Road Central.

'Johnnie, slow down,' Katya complained when they'd reached the opposite footpath.

'I'm sorry, honey.' He stopped and smiled at her. 'It's just that those Red Guards spook me.'

'Me, too,' she replied as they resumed walking. 'There was more trouble in Kowloon City today. A mob smashed the windows in some shops and the police attacked them.'

'The police don't attack people, Katya,' he smiled, 'they intervene.'

'Not this time,' she panted, struggling to keep pace again in her high heels. 'I heard the young English Inspector yell, "Right lads, that's it. Get them," and the police attacked.'

'And it's only gonna get worse, honey,' Johnnie said grimly. 'We might have to think seriously about getting out of town, until things sort themselves out.'

'Really?'

'Yeah, really,' he nodded, squeezing her arm against his side.

They walked up narrow Jackson Road and turned left into Chater Road where the bright lights of the Hilton Hotel beckoned.

Katya loved the foyer of the Hilton. For some strange reason it always made her feel happy and simply stepping into the cool air-conditioned atmosphere was enough to lift her spirits. The chandelier overhead, tastefully lit glass wall panels and the enormous floral arrangement, always on display on a central table, inevitably made her think of Christmas. She had absolutely no idea why.

'Oh, damn it,' Johnnie cursed as he felt the telegram in his coat pocket. 'Will you excuse me for one minute, darling? I've got to ring James.'

He left her admiring the flowers and went to reception. A young woman placed a telephone on the desk at his request as he took out the telegram and examined it again.

'To John Wilson' it read, 'from Alexi Duval, Duval & Associates, Geneva Switzerland. Further information on your enquiry STOP Just received notification of a caveat placed on the original instructions of 1939 STOP Caveat dated 1948 states shoulder brand identification changed to medallion to gain access to account STOP Drawing and description of medallion held by Bank Suisse STOP Acquisition of drawing or facsimile impossible END'.

Johnnie folded the telegram, put it in his pocket and dialled the office only to be told James was unavailable.

'Where is he, Marie?'

'I do not know, Mister Wilson,' James Merchant's secretary replied. 'I have not seen him since this morning. He went to Macau and he has not called to let me know his whereabouts.'

'Well, if he calls, tell him I've got some more information from Geneva. I'm dining at the Hilton until around nine o'clock then I'll be home for the rest of the evening.'

'Is the matter urgent?' she asked. 'If it is, I will try to find him, although,' she hesitated, 'it is Sunday night.'

'No,' Johnnie assured her. 'Don't bother, Marie, thanks. I'll talk to him tomorrow.'

He put the receiver down and stood scratching his chin. A week earlier, James had instructed him to locate an old Swiss bank account. Johnnie had told him it would be expensive, but James had not cared. He'd been pretty worked up about it and had told Johnnie to use every Swiss contact he had if necessary to get the information.

Alexi Duval, for a lot of money, had discovered that an account with the name Dragon Imports had been opened at Banque Suisse in July 1939, but was escrowed. And furthermore, and most fascinating to Johnnie, was that the account was separately insured by Banque Suisse. With all his dealings with bankers in Switzerland over the previous ten years, he'd known of very few incidents where a bank had insured a single account separately against loss. Whatever the account contained, it would be of incredible value. No wonder James had been so hot to locate it.

Alexi's informant had also said that a list of seven people could gain access to the account. Five were named and could simply identify themselves, but another two could access the account by showing a specific brand on either their right, or left, shoulder. Then a series of questions must be answered before the account would be opened. James had a brand on his shoulder, a scar in the shape of a dragon. Johnnie had seen it many times over the years.

It was all very intriguing stuff, Johnnie thought, as he went to join Katya. What was being held in escrow, in that deposit box in Geneva? James had divulged nothing when he'd been given Alexi Duval's information, but his excitement had been obvious. 'Well done, Johnnie,' was all he'd said. 'Keep snooping and find out whatever else you can.'

Well, I have more information, James, Johnnie thought. But you're nowhere to be found, so it will just have to wait.

'Did you get him?' Katya asked when he joined her.

'Nope,' he shrugged. 'If he doesn't bother to let people know where he is, he can go to hell.'

'I think he should go there anyway.'

'Ha!' Johnnie guffawed, drawing several looks. 'At least then people would know where to find him.' He took her by the arm. 'Come on, baby, let's eat. I'm starved.'

龍

'My grandmother?' Georgina sat bolt upright in bed.

'Yes.' Jeremy sat up beside her. 'I met her in Hong Kong last week.'

'My grandmother sent you here?'

'Yes. You didn't seriously think I could afford a suite at Raffles on my salary, did you?'

'You said you wouldn't care if it cost you your life!' Georgina exclaimed loudly.

'Shhh,' he hushed. 'It's four in the morning. The last thing we need is for the night manager to answer a complaint and find *you* here.' He placed his hand on her naked shoulder. 'You look beautiful bathed in moonlight,' he murmured.

'Oh, shut up!' She looked at him. 'You bastard! That is the only word to describe you, Jeremy.' Georgina leapt out of bed and began searching for her clothes. 'You conned my grandmother into paying for your trip to Singapore. How could you?'

'No, no, wait a minute.' He flew out of bed and took her by the arm. 'You're jumping to conclusions again, just like last time in London.'

'Oh, I'm jumping to conclusions, am I?' She stopped struggling and faced him. 'You lied to me in London, did you not?'

'It wasn't a lie, it was merely . . . an omission,' he said defensively.

'Call it what you like,' she said fiercely, breaking away from him. 'The fact remains you were dishonest. It was a deliberate ploy to get into these.' She picked up her silk panties and thrust them at him.

'Oh God,' he groaned and clasping her fist and the panties in his hands, he buried his face in them. 'I could spend my whole life with my face jammed in your knickers.'

Georgina stared at him, baring her teeth until her nose wrinkled. 'You are disgusting.'

'I was going to tell you about your grandmother,' he said huskily, 'but when I saw you . . . you know . . . angry like you were . . . and . . . well . . . all I could think of was these.' He thrust his face back into her panties, inhaled and fell back on the bed.

He's a bastard, Georgina thought as she stood grinning down at him, but a loveable one.

'I would walk over burning coals for you, Georgie,' he murmured. 'I would search this mighty globe to find you the perfect rose. I will go to my death with an image of your smiling form shimmering before my eyes.'

'You really are a bastard, Jeremy Bent,' she whispered, grinning into the darkness.

'Well?' Jeremy sat upright.

'Well what?' Georgie shivered.

'You have three options.'

'And what might they be?'

'You can get dressed and walk out in high dudgeon, or you can lie quietly with me and let me explain,' he said and fell silent.

'That's only two,' she said softly. 'What's the third option?'

'It's dependent upon which of the first two you choose.'

Georgina walked around to the side of the bed, climbed onto it and lay on her back with her head on the pillow.

'Good choice.' He moved up and lay beside her.

'It wasn't very difficult,' she whispered.

'I'm glad.' He reached for her hand and they lapsed into silence.

'So?' Georgie said finally.

'Right. Well, it's like this.' Jeremy took a deep breath and began. 'I was on PP Detail –

'Pee-pee what?'

'Personal Protection Detail.'

'Oh, right you are,' Georgie giggled. 'I thought you were being smutty again.'

'I was under orders to guard a VIP at the International Human Rights Dinner. It was at the Mandarin Hotel a couple of days ago and I was introduced to your mother and grandmothe – '

'Was my father there?'

'No, he wasn't,' Jeremy squeezed her hand, 'and stop interrupting. Anyway, as the evening wore on I got up the nerve to ask your grandmother how you were and, one thing led to another, and she paid for me to come to Singapore. And . . . ah . . . that's about the strength of it.'

'Jeremy!' Georgina spun her body and punched him in the ribs.

'All right,' he grunted, 'there's a bit more to it. She's a remarkable woman, the Merchant Mistress – '

'You can say that again.'

'Before I knew it, she had me pouring my heart out. I told her about London – '

'Not in detail, I hope?'

'Don't be ridiculous,' Jeremy snorted. 'I told her I loved you, Georgie.' Jeremy turned towards her. 'I told her I've wanted you so much that I haven't been able to eat properly, or sleep at night. I told her that all I ever thought about was you.'

'You didn't,' she whispered in the darkness. 'What did she say?'

'She told me you were here in Singapore and insisted I get the next plane out of Hong Kong.'

'Really?'

'Absolutely,' he said, then his body began to shake with laughter.

'What's so funny?' Georgie demanded.

'I told her I couldn't – "A", because I had to work and, "B", because I couldn't afford it.' He stopped laughing at the thought of Elanora's response. 'It didn't go down well with her.'

'What did she do?'

'She got up, walked out and came back a few minutes later with the Commissioner of Police, who didn't look happy. But yesterday morning I was put on a plane to Singapore.'

'That's my grandmother,' Georgie declared. 'And I suppose she told you to tell me that if I didn't fall into your arms, she'd come down here and see to it herself, am I right?'

'No, all she said to tell you is, "love is a many splendoured thing". I have no idea what that means.'

'I do. It's the title of my grandmother's favourite book,' Georgie explained. 'It was written by Han Suyin; she was a doctor in Hong Kong. You must have heard of it. They made a film of it with William Holden and Jennifer Jones.'

'Nope,' Jeremy shook his head on the pillow. 'What's the significance?'

'It's just a love story,' Georgie shrugged, embarrassed. 'And Elanora's always had this thing about the song from the movie. She makes me play it for her on the piano every single time I go to visit her.'

'How's it go?'

'I don't know the words. It's about two lovers who meet and kiss high on a windy hill.'

'And their world stood still.'

'So you *do* know it?' Georgie murmured. She rolled onto his chest and draped a leg over his thigh. 'You really *are* a bastard, Jeremy Bent.' She smiled in the moonlight and kissed him and her world, too, suddenly stood still.

龍

James lay face down on the table as the little Thai girl walked up his back, her toes digging into his muscles searching for knotted sinews. Another girl worked on his feet, her tiny hands, as strong as a plumber's, digging into his soles then wrenching his toes, one by one. They were experts in Thai massage. His mind drifted, as pleasure mingled with pain, until he was unsure of where he was or what was happening to his body.

Dragon Imports and seven people, he thought idly. It hadn't been difficult to figure out. The first five would have to be exactly that – the First Five: Richard Brewster, Robert McCraw, Malcolm Linden, Lo Shi-mon and Terrence Delaney, the five police officers who had formed the *Gaam Lung Tong* in 1925. And the two who must identify themselves by a brand on their left or right shoulder could only mean the Dragons of Shaolin: he and Lee Kwan.

'Over,' one of the girls said softly as they pushed at his shoulder and hip. James rolled onto his back and four hands applied oil to his feet and arms, before continuing their sensuous work.

Any one of seven men, he thought, were authorised to answer a series of questions in order to gain access to the account. And the seven were all members of the Society of Golden Dragons. What did one do to gain entry to the world of the Golden Dragons? One answered a series of questions. It was all too easy, James smiled, pleased with himself.

'You like?' one of the girls whispered in his ear, misinterpreting his smile as one of sensual contentment.

'Mmmm,' James groaned from deep within his chest as his memory flew to the lawns of Merchant House in 1933. He and Lee Kwan sat on the lawn facing Lo Shi-mon, their teacher. Their conversation had been in Cantonese.

'*To gain entry to the world of the Golden Dragons, what must you do?*' Lo had asked.

'*Knock three times,*' James had replied wearily. He and Lee were desperate to go and play, but Lo Shi-mon always made them repeat the same formula.

'*Correct. First, you must knock three times,*' Lo had taught them. '*Then you will answer the questions that are asked of you. You must commit them to memory forever.*'

'*We already have, Teacher,*' Lee had groaned.

'*Then show me,*' Lo had demanded. '*Speak to your brother.*'

'*Your heart is what colour?*' Lee had begun.

'*My heart is blue,*' James had answered.

'*Your soul is what colour?*'

'*My soul is golden.*'

'*Your master is who?*'

'*The Golden Dragon.*'

'*He has how many brothers?*'

'*Four.*'

'*His brothers came from where to here?*'

'*From the four foreign cities.*'

'*They brought what with them?*'

'*They brought the truth.*'

'*And their eyes are which colours?*'

'*Red, blue, green and white,*' James had finished and Lo Shi-mon had allowed them to go and play.

Too easy, James thought again and winced as fingers dug into his calves. All he had to do was go to Geneva and collect his prize. But what *is* the prize? he wondered. 'The remains of the four who came from foreign cities,' Delaney's letter had said. The remains of the statues must surely be gold, he thought, but the statues had been melted down and converted to cash. Damn it, he cursed silently, what in hell was in that account that had made the bank insure it?

He felt a tingle of excitement rise in his abdomen and it was not merely the thought of what lay in the account that provoked it. One of the Thai girls had reached his thigh with her masterful hands. She forced her palms up the sides of his leg and the fingers of one hand probed firmly into his groin, which caused a stirring of his member.

The girls muttered to one another in Thai and began giggling.

The girl massaging his groin climbed onto the table and placed a leg either side of his hips. He felt the lips of her vulva rubbing along his shaft.

'Ooh,' the girl massaging his upper arm gasped, as she discovered the scar of the dragon on his shoulder. She muttered to her partner in Thai.

'My friend ask if you are a dragon?' The girl sitting above

him asked as she manoeuvred her entrance over the tip of his penis.

'Yes,' James opened his eyes and stared at the tiny Thai girl as she slid onto him. She moved expertly, contracting the muscles of her vagina to heighten his pleasure. He placed his hands on her hips and moved her up and down until she began to gasp.

His orgasm arrived quickly and he spent himself, but he didn't stop using her. Like her partner, she was an expert at her trade and James knew they faked orgasms to heighten the effect of the massage on their customers, but he could sense his show of strength had surprised the girl and she was experiencing sexual enjoyment. She's losing it, he thought, and it amused him to watch her fighting for control.

'I am a big dragon, yes, little one?' He pushed his hips up to meet her quickening thrusts.

'Yes,' the girl gasped. She continued to keep her head down, refusing to look at him, and her long black hair brushed rhythmically over his chest as her orgasm approached.

'Look at me.' He could feel her stomach muscles contracting. 'Look at me,' he demanded. 'Look into the eyes of the dragon!'

The tiny girl's head came up and her eyes locked onto him as the orgasm struck. She bared her teeth and her eyes took on a fierce gleam.

'Look into the eyes of the dragon,' he said, this time to himself, when the girl had fallen silent, her head resting on his chest. Then he began to laugh. 'That's it!' he roared frightening the wits out of her. 'Red, blue, green and white!' He lifted her up like a child and dropped her onto the floor. 'The eyes!' It was so obvious to him now.

James sat bolt upright. The answer had been there all along, in the recognition code, but he'd recited it so many times it had become like a song, the words didn't register any more.

He remembered vividly the four magnificent statues he'd seen as a boy of thirteen. The eyes had been massive gemstones, two of ruby, two sapphire, two emerald and two of diamonds. He remembered them now. He could see them, gleaming in the soft candlelight.

'The *eyes* are the remains of the dragons!'

CHAPTER FIFTEEN

Father Raphael walked down the path from the grave and stopped beneath the one and only tree on the hillside of the island of Coloane. He stood gazing out over the vista of the Pearl River Estuary and, to his left, he could see in the distance the tiny city of Macau, with its skyline dominated by the façade of the Church of Sao Paulo. Directly before him to the east, the morning sun glittered on the waters of the South China Sea so brightly that he was forced to shade his eyes.

The warm summer breeze tugged at his cassock, as if urging him to look back up towards the grave of Richard Brewster. There, against a backdrop of azure blue sky, Elanora and Lee Kwan stood, holding hands, speaking earnestly. He couldn't hear what they were saying, but his old bones knew there was trouble in the Merchant family.

What had happened, the old Jesuit wondered, to cause Elanora to refuse attendance at the funeral to everyone? Half the Colony of Hong Kong would have attended Richard Brewster's funeral, had they been allowed. The hillside of Coloane would have been packed with people, but not even family members had been allowed to attend. Raphael shook his head, as he shaded his eyes and looked again at the couple by the grave. Another drama in the life of the all-powerful Merchant family was no doubt unfolding, but he had no idea what it concerned. And he knew better than to ask. Elanora had said nothing to him, but the worry in her eyes had betrayed her.

'Your arrival is timely,' Elanora said to Lee. 'I was going to send for you today.'

'*What is the matter?*' He sensed her anxiety.

'*I have need of you, son. I need to talk to you and tell you of the troubles that burden me.*' Elanora looked at Father Raphael down the hill out of earshot, but she lowered her voice nonetheless. '*I need to talk of dragons, understand or not understand?*'

'*Understand,*' Lee replied as a feeling of uneasiness crept over him. '*But why should we talk about dragons, Mother?*' He indicated the open grave beside him. '*The last dragon is dead. His remains will lie undisturbed in the ground at our feet, true or not true?*'

'*True, Lee.*' Elanora looked him in the eye. '*But the remains of other dragons are being disturbed.*'

'*Other dragons?*'

'*Yes, Golden Dragons. That is why we must talk.*'

'*Is it James?*'

'*Of course!*' Elanora gave a shrug of resignation. '*Who else would it be? Come.*' She took his arm. '*Help me down the hill. My boat is waiting to take us across to Macau. We will discuss it at Dragon's Garden.*' She laughed humourlessly as she uttered the name she had given to the house of Richard Brewster, and looked one last time at the grave. 'How appropriate,' she whispered in English. 'Wouldn't you say so, Richard, my love?'

龍

The Hotel Beau-Rivage on the Quai du Mont-Blanc in Geneva was a classic reminder of the opulence nineteenth century Switzerland afforded the wealthy, with its chandeliered suites, its classic French restaurant, and its afternoon teas in *L'Atrium*, a grand foyer with magnificent marble columns and a soaring ceiling.

James Merchant walked through *L'Atrium* and down a set of steps guarded by polished bronze battle horses, rearing fearfully at some perceived horror. He stepped out of the doors onto the Quai du Mont-Blanc and filled his lungs with fresh morning air. Immediately before him, through the masts of cruise ships that lined the *quai*, was the grand view of Lake Geneva where it met the Rhone.

The previous day he'd called Charles Middleditch, the Merchant Company's permanent pilot, and told him to fuel up the company's Lear 24 jet. Then, without telling anyone, they'd taken off. The route had been an arduous one, over Vietnam and Thailand with a re-fuel in New Delhi, then on to Geneva.

Once in Geneva, he'd instructed Middleditch to re-fuel the Lear and take twenty-four hours off, but to remain close by for a quick departure. James was taking nothing for granted. He had a precise plan.

The city of Geneva was split by the great Rhone River with the Old Town, *Vieille Ville*, on the south side. It was to the Old Town that James now headed.

He knew the city well, having been there numerous times on business. He considered it efficient, clean and, most importantly, safe, which to James, meant it was ruled by money. There were no poor people in the Old Town of Geneva, he mused, as he walked down the *quai* to the Pont du Mont-Blanc. If indeed the city did have any poor people they kept them well hidden, probably in some wretched outer suburb, he decided.

Despite an excellent public transport system, and the fact he had a car at his disposal, he'd chosen to walk to the bank. The ease and pleasure of walking in the Old Town made a car unnecessary, even a nuisance.

He crossed Pont du Mont-Blanc, the bridge that marked the point at which the Rhone met Lake Geneva, paused to take in the view, then strode happily into the Old Town and down Place Longemalle.

James had left Hong Kong without telling a soul where he was going. He felt like a child going to a sweet shop, a very expensive sweet shop. He smiled as he pictured himself choosing brightly coloured gemstones from a glass jar, instead of mixed treats.

'They must be worth a bloody fortune,' he said aloud. And good old Johnnie Wilson had given him not only the address of the sweet shop, but the knowledge he needed to open the jar.

As he walked, he thought of Richard. Bad *joss*, his mind whispered, bad *joss*. It had been a mistake to go to Macau, he now realised, but damn it, he cursed, he'd just been tying up loose ends. How was he to know Richard was so close to death? The fool had complained for years of being at death's doorstep, crying wolf at every opportunity. All I wanted to do was ask him a couple of questions. How was I to know he'd drop off the bloody perch the minute I arrived? But it was bad *joss*, nonetheless.

Thank Christ Elanora had not followed up her threat of making an issue of it with the Macau Police, he thought, as he came to the Place du Bourg-de-Four and glanced disinterestedly at the magnificent Cathédrale St Pierre. Mind you, the following morning the bitch had made it pretty obvious to the family that his visit had contributed to Richard's demise. Katherine hadn't been able to disguise her joy when she'd rung to tell him he was not to attend the funeral. And then, Elanora had held the funeral service alone. Incredible! He shook his head. No one had been allowed to attend, including Katherine and Georgina. Absurd.

But look on the bright side, James, he encouraged himself as he continued on down the Rue de Saint-Léger alongside Parc des Bastions, ignoring entirely its beautiful trees, manicured lawns and gardens, it allowed you to leave Hong Kong straightaway, didn't it?

Finally, he turned into the Boulevard des Philosophes and entered the Banque Suisse Genève. Ah, money, he thought and smiled happily as he presented himself at the enquiry counter. The place reeked of money. Switzerland reeked of money. That was why he liked it so much.

'*Bonjour, M'sieur.*' An attractive woman approached him.

'Good morning,' he replied. Early thirties, James guessed, appraising her, blonde, damned good looking. 'I'm here to close an existing account.' He handed her a slip of paper containing the account name and number.

'This must be a very old account, M'sieur,' she said after

reading the details. 'The account number has only six numerals.'

'That's right, it was opened before the war and I want to close it.'

'If you will wait a moment, Sir.' She went to a desk and showed the man seated there the slip of paper. It seemed to arouse his interest. He took off his glasses and stared at James before getting up and disappearing through a doorway behind him.

'You will not be kept long, M'sieur,' the woman said, returning to the counter.

'*Comment vous, appelez-vous?*'

'My name is Jeanne Marceau, M'sieur.' Her smile revealed a set of perfect teeth through lush, red lips.

'Mine is James Merchant.'

'How do you do, M'sieur Merchant.'

'I do very well, actually. In fact you might say today, particularly, the world is my oyster.' He deliberately lowered his gaze to her breasts. '*Avez-vous un mari?*'

'No, M'sieur.' The question did not seem to phase her one bit. 'I do not have a husband.' She looked at him knowingly, then pretended to straighten a pile of sales pamphlets on the counter.

James was just about to ask her to have dinner with him when the man with James' slip of paper re-appeared, followed by a second man, older, and obviously his superior. They approached him, almost running in their haste.

'*Bonjour, M'sieur,*' the second man said. 'You wish to enquire about this account?' The man waved the piece of paper at him.

'That's correct.'

'Do you have identification?'

'I don't believe I need any identification except what is on my shoulder, M'sieur,' James tapped his left shoulder with his fingers, 'but I brought some just in case.' James placed his passport on the counter.

The man inspected it closely. 'Does M'sieur speak *chinois*? he asked without taking his eyes from James' passport.

'Yes. I speak fluent Cantonese.'

'Good. It is a specific requirement.'

'I know,' James replied, looking at the girl. Was that an invitation in her eyes? 'Now might I suggest we get on with it?'

Jeanne Marceau stared straight back, appraising the Englishman. So this is James Merchant, she thought. Good looking, mid-forties and bold, with the air of casual confidence exuded only by the very rich. James Merchant was sexy, very sexy, but not to be trusted.

The man looked up and a smile broke through his usually inflexible financial façade. 'I am Felix Foveaux, General Manager.' He extended his hand and James shook it. 'If you would care to come into my office, the two of us can discuss the account you are enquiring about, in private. It is rather an important account, as I'm sure M'sieur must know?'

Yes, I know,' James smiled back at him. 'It has a separate insurance cover, *n'est-ce pas*?'

'*Oui.* That is correct, M'sieur. As I said, it is a very important account.'

'Excellent,' James exclaimed heartily. 'Then it's Swiss coffee and strudel for three in your office, Monsieur Foveaux.' He was on top of the world, enjoying himself immensely.

'For three, M'sieur?' The man was perplexed.

'Yes.' James looked again at the woman. 'Mademoiselle Marceau and I are old friends,' he lied. 'I'd like her to be present.' He was feeling lucky, a fortune in gems and now, the attentions of a beautiful woman. He winked at Jeanne.

'Certainly,' the manager replied, terrified of offending. 'Jeanne?' He turned to the woman.

'*Oui, M'sieur Foveaux?*' She had a hand over her mouth to suppress the laughter that was threatening to escape.

'Coffee and strudel for three, in my office, *s'il vous plaît*?'

'*Oui, M'sieur Foveaux.*'

'Right. It's settled then.' James beamed at the girl. 'And perhaps later we can have dinner and talk about old times?'

'Certainly, James,' she replied from behind her hand. 'How is your mother?'

'The old girl's in French Polynesia, Tahiti to be exact, brought low by a dose of dengue fever, but at least the syphilis is under control.'

The bank manager's jaw dropped open and Jeanne Marceau spun on her heel and fled before she lost her composure altogether.

龍

'Today is Wednesday,' Lee said. 'James came here on Sunday, right?'

'That's correct,' Elanora replied.

Mother and son had returned from the island of Coloane and now sat in the back courtyard of Dragon House in Macau, beneath the same tree from which Su-lin had 'hanged' herself. The two fell silent as Sally served them tea and biscuits and, sensing the urgency in the air, hurriedly withdrew to the kitchen.

'And no one's seen hide nor hair of him since?'

'Not so much as his shadow,' Elanora replied as she watched the maid disappear through the kitchen door.

'Do you know where he is, Mother?'

'I could hazard a wild guess.' Her sarcasm was obvious.

'Geneva?'

'Of course.'

'When did Richard open this bank account?' Lee asked as he sipped his cup of tea.

'He didn't, I did.'

'You?' He was surprised.

'Yes. It was in late July 1939, just before the war broke out in Europe. Richard had the dragons' eyes with him in London and he arranged for me to take them to Geneva, with an escort of course – an enormous bodyguard – but still . . .' She shuddered at the memory of her trip to Switzerland. 'I carried those damned eyes on the train with me. A fortune in gems sitting in my handbag, would you believe? I was terrified of being robbed, escort or no escort. It was a very harrowing experience.'

'Why Switzerland? Why didn't Richard secure them in the Bank of England?'

'Because war was imminent and, for all we knew, the Bank of England could well have become the Bank of Germany in a matter of months.'

'It's strange.' Lee placed his empty cup on the small garden table. 'Richard never told me about the account. Not that I would have cared, but – '

'How could he tell you?' Elanora interrupted. 'You were up to your neck in a game of Chinese espionage. By the time the others in the society were told it was December 1941, only days before the Battle of Hong Kong. The British surrendered on Christmas Day, Richard was interned in Stanley Prison Camp and you escaped to China, where, I might add, you remained for fifteen years with barely a word to those who loved you.' Her tone was accusatory.

'I had my own family to look after by then,' he replied, not rising to her accusation. 'But I've been back in Hong Kong for ten years now, and still he never told me.'

'He never told James either.' Elanora's expression was more smirk than smile. 'And when he survived the war, Richard decided not to tell you because he knew the eyes would mean nothing to you. He didn't tell James because he simply didn't want him to have them.'

'Why didn't Richard go to Switzerland and get them back himself? They must be worth a fortune.' Lee watched in silence as Elanora refilled his cup from the pot of tea.

'After the war, when I returned to Hong Kong,' she continued, 'Richard was a broken mess. The last thing he needed was another bout of empire building. We still had money, more than enough, in fact. Richard sold Hallowdeen, his family home in Surrey. And I had accounts and investments in Australia and in Britain, and we had Merchant House. We were hardly destitute. So I nursed Richard back to health only to have James come home and drive us insane with his single-minded desire to restore the family fortunes.'

'James wanted to restore the Merchant Company, I know that.'

She put the pot down and locked her fingers in her lap. 'Yes, but, more importantly, he wanted to restore the Golden

Dragons Society. When Richard showed no interest, they began to fight. Over the ensuing years the situation between them became intolerable. James accused Richard of being weak and a coward. It was horrible.' She sat still lost for a moment in her memories.

'Go on, Mother,' Lee urged.

'I never thought I'd be happy to see a war break out again, but when Korea happened and James rejoined the Royal Air Force, what followed was two years of bliss. We lived in Merchant House with Katherine and the twins, and Richard was happy for a time.'

'But then James came home.'

'Yes,' she nodded. 'And all of a sudden he had money. A *lot* of money, at a time when most Hong Kong businesses were struggling to survive, because of the trade embargo placed on China by the United Nations.'

Lee stared guiltily at the ground. He knew only too well how James had acquired his initial wealth and he dreaded the thought of Elanora's reaction should she discover the truth.

'James bought while others sold.' Elanora shook her head, incredulous. 'He acquired companies and property all over the Colony and then proceeded to make a fortune. And in doing so, he destroyed people and families he'd known since he was a child, never once showing the slightest twinge of remorse.'

'Mercy was never one of his strong points, I'm afraid.' Lee tried to make a joke of the line, but failed miserably.

Elanora stared at him for several moments. 'Are you all right?' she asked.

'Yes, of course. Why?' He looked away.

'You seem . . . I don't know . . . nervous.'

'I'm fine.'

Her gaze remained focused upon him and she raised an eyebrow. 'Do you remember Ho Man-lai?'

'No.'

Lee's reply was a little too quick, Elanora thought. 'Are you sure?' Her voice accused him. He was hiding something from her, she knew it instantly. 'You and James played with him when you were little boys at Merchant House. Surely you remember Ho Man-lai. You three were inseparable.'

'It was a long time ago, Mother.' Lee felt sick. He couldn't look her in the eye.

'You're lying,' she said. 'You just lied to me.'

'Perhaps I do remember . . .' he began hesitantly.

'He became the Hong Kong boss of the Chinese Secret Service during the Korean War.'

'Yes, I know.'

'You have never lied to me before, Lee.'

'No, Mother.' He felt ashamed. The woman sitting beside him had given him everything a heart could give and he had deceived her.

'James was mixed up with Ho Man-lai in some sort of racket,' Elanora continued, relentless. 'They were as thick as thieves during that war. Do you know what they were up to?'

'Yes.' Lee's answer was followed by a deep sigh. Never in his life had he been able to maintain his composure when being cross-examined by Elanora.

'Where did James get all that money, Lee?' It was not a question, it was a command.

'He sold a plane.'

'What sort of plane?'

'A jet fighter.'

'Don't be ridiculous,' she snapped.

'I am not being ridiculous, Mother.' Lee now couldn't wait to unburden himself of the secret. 'James stole an F-86 Sabre jet fighter from the United States Air Force and sold it to the Russians.' He looked at her forlornly. 'For a million dollars. And I helped him.'

'Good God.' Elanora sat stock still as the implications of his statement took root. James had committed treason. Her son was a traitor. But the shock of the revelation wore off as quickly as it had set in. Why am I not surprised? she thought. James was capable of anything, including the murder of his own son. She closed her eyes, breathed in deeply and exhaled. 'Well,' she said finally, 'you'd better tell me about it.'

Lee felt like a guilty child as he confessed to his mother.

He told her the story of the Korean War deals from day one when he'd been approached by James, via the Woo twins, to buy stolen US Army radios, to the deal with the KGB and the theft of the jet.

'I was the go-between,' he finished. 'I arranged the deal between James and the KGB. I am as guilty as he is, Mother.' He sat in silence awaiting Elanora's verdict.

'You were a General in the PLA, were you not?' Elanora's thoughts moved swiftly.

'Yes, but – '

'Then your actions cannot be questioned.' She spoke forcefully, needing to nip in the bud any feelings of guilt or recrimination he might be feeling. James no longer held a place in her heart, but Lee did, now more than ever. 'You were acting in the best interests of the country you were serving. Besides, had you refused to assist the KGB, you wouldn't be here now.'

'It's not that simple.'

'Yes, it is! Your wife and children were under house arrest in Peking. Lin Li told me herself, so don't give me any maudlin rubbish about guilt. You have nothing to feel guilty about.' Elanora gave him a withering look. 'Anyway, we have a more pressing problem at hand.'

'The eyes of the dragons.'

'Yes. Now that James knows about those damned eyes he'll stop at nothing until he has them.'

'He may well have them already.'

'No, he hasn't,' Elanora shook her head emphatically. 'I would know if he did.'

龍

James placed his knife and fork on the empty plate in front of him, wiped his mouth with a napkin and forced himself to smile at his dinner companion.

'The meal was beautiful,' Jeanne Marceau smiled back, 'as is the wine.'

James picked up his glass, sipped at the beautiful red wine of Bordeaux and allowed his gaze to caress the body of

Jeanne Marceau as he thought back over the events of the day.

Felix Foveaux, the General Manager, had arranged for two Cantonese gentlemen to attend the bank that afternoon and James had guessed correctly regarding the questions he would be asked.

One of the Cantonese had knocked three times on the table.

'*Your heart is what colour?*' the second Cantonese had asked him and James' pulse had gone through the roof. It *was* the recognition code of the old triad.

'*My heart is blue,*' James had replied.

'*Your soul is what colour?*'

'*My soul is golden.*'

'*Your master is who?*'

'*The Golden Dragon.*'

'*He has how many brothers?*'

'*Four.*'

'*His brothers came from where to here?*'

'*From the four foreign cities.*'

'*They brought what with them?*'

'*They brought the truth.*'

'*And their eyes are which colours?*'

'*Red, blue, green and white,*' James had answered the final question and smiled. 'Is that it?' he'd asked, looking towards Felix Foveaux.

'There are four more questions, Mister Merchant,' one of the Cantonese had said.

'Four more?' James had suddenly felt uneasy.

'Four more questions must be answered by the claimants.'

'Oh yes? And what are they?'

'*What was the gift of Lo Shi-mon?*' he was asked in Cantonese.

'*Gift?*' Damn it, he'd cursed silently.

'*That is the question.*'

The gift of Lo Shi-mon? James racked his brains for the answer. What bloody gift? What had Lo Shi-mon given to him? Nothing. Had Lo given a gift to Richard? Or the society? Then the answer hit him like a thunderbolt. He had been the gift. He and Lee had been Lo Shi-mon's gift. Lo had trained them in the arts of *Shaolin* and presented them as the Dragons of Shaolin. *'Lee and I were the gifts!'* he'd exclaimed.

'That is not the correct answer,' Foveaux had said watching one of the Cantonese shake his head.

'No, I know,' James had said quickly then looked at the two Cantonese. *'The answer is the Dragons of Shaolin.'* He'd watched nervously as one of the men had turned to Foveaux and nodded.

'Very good, M'sieur,' Foveaux had said. 'You may continue.'

'Why do they face north, shoulder to shoulder?'

'To conceal their identity,' James had answered immediately. Both he and Lee had been branded, James on the left shoulder and Lee on the right. When they faced north the brands were concealed as their shoulders lay against each other.

The tension in the room had been palpable. One of the Cantonese had again confirmed his answer was correct with a nod to Foveaux. Two more questions, James remembered thinking, two more questions.

'Why do they face south?'

'To defend the Noble House.' James had known that one all right. When they revealed their brands to the world, it meant they were going to kill. And the two Cantonese knew it too. They were suddenly frightened.

'And what is their gift?'

All the tension had left James. When he or Lee killed for the society, they were given a tiny statue, a little dragon carved from gold, to leave next to the corpse. He'd looked at the two Cantonese and they'd been distinctly uncomfortable. They'd realised they were speaking to a member of a triad, and not just a triad member, but an assassin. *'A little dragon carved from gold,'* he'd said slowly and ominously.

Both of the Cantonese had stood up. They'd confirmed to Foveaux that James had answered the questions satisfactorily, and had been desperate to be out of the room.

'You have answered correctly, M'sieur Merchant,' Foveaux had said. 'It only remains for you to produce the identification you must present and we'll go to the vault.'

'What identification?' James had had no idea what he meant.

'The conditions of the account say you must produce something before you can have access to the deposit box.'

The uneasy feeling had returned momentarily, then James had laughed. 'Oh, yes,' he'd said. 'Of course.' He'd removed his sport jacket, undone his shirt and revealed the scar of the snarling dragon on his left shoulder.

'I'm afraid that's not the identification required, M'sieur.' Foveaux had said and coughed nervously into his hand.

'It has to be,' James had replied, desperation creeping into his voice.

'No, Sir.' Foveaux shook his head.

'Then what is it?' James had demanded.

'I'm afraid I cannot tell you, M'sieur Merchant. It is for you to know.'

James' blood had begun to boil. He'd wanted to kill Foveaux where he stood, but he'd managed to control himself until he'd left the bank.

Even now, as he looked at his dinner companion, his blood was still boiling. He still felt the urge to kill, but he would assuage his desire in an equally pleasurable way. He'd been that way all his life; whenever his blood lust was aroused he'd either killed, or used women to release his hostility. He reached across the table and took Jeanne Marceau's hand.

'For a man who didn't get what he wanted,' she looked at her hand in his, 'you don't seem unduly disappointed.'

'What makes you think I didn't get what I wanted?'

'You didn't gain access to your account.' She ignored the double entendre.

'I don't suppose you know what I have to produce to open that account, do you, Jeanne?'

'No,' she shook her head and laughed. 'Oh, you are a devil, James. The details of that account are not available to unimportant people like me.'

'If you could find out,' he murmured, stroking her fingers, 'you'd save me a trip to London.'

'Stop it, James,' she said, but did not withdraw her hand.

'It was only a suggestion.'

Jeanne Marceau stared at him. 'Did you invite me here tonight to bribe me, or bed me?'

'Which would you prefer?' He stared right back at her.

'Well, put it this way,' her faced softened into a half smile, 'you will be wasting your time if you try to bribe me.'

龍

It was Thursday afternoon when Johnnie Wilson placed the telephone call to Macau, only to be told the Merchant Mistress was not at home and was not expected back until the following morning.

'*She went where from Macau?*' he asked clumsily in Cantonese.

'*Hong Kong,*' Sally the maid answered. Then, in typical Cantonese fashion, satisfied the caller had the information required, she hung up.

'Your Cantonese gets worse with each passing year, Johnnie,' Elanora said as she closed his office door behind her.

'Elanora!' he exclaimed, getting up and circling his desk to greet her. 'You must be psychic. I was just trying to call you.'

'So I gathered.' She accepted his peck on her cheek. 'I couldn't help but overhear your appalling tones.'

'I'm afraid I ain't never gonna git the hang of the old *Gwang Doong waaah,*' he drawled in his worst Texas accent, knowing how much it amused her. He guided her to a seat, returned to his desk and sat beaming at her. 'It's good to see you, Missy.' He still used his pet name for her on the rare occasions they were alone. 'Damn it, but your eyes light up my day.'

'Texan flattery will get you nowhere, Mr Wilson,' she smiled weakly, 'but don't stop. I could do with a little more laughter in my life at the moment.'

'Yes,' Johnnie's smile faded. 'I just bet you could. I was so sorry to hear about Richard.'

'Thank you. He'd been ill for a long while.'

'Katya and I sent flowers. Did you get them?'

'Yes, they arrived, thank you both.' Elanora put her hand-bag on the floor and sat back, her hands resting in her lap. The ferry trip from Macau had tired her. 'So how is your gorgeous Russian? Still as beautiful as ever?'

'Yes, she's well. She was disappointed that the funeral was closed to outsiders. She liked Richard a lot and wanted to say a last farewell to him – as did I.'

'It wasn't only closed to outsiders, Johnnie.' Elanora looked directly at him. 'It was closed to everyone.'

'Yeah.' He shifted uneasily in his seat. 'I know that. Katherine told us.'

'And did she explain why?'

'She couldn't. Why did you do it, Missy?'

'Because I was afraid the funeral would disintegrate into a family war. Can you imagine James and Georgina on opposite sides of the grave?'

'It doesn't bear thinking about.' Johnnie shook his head. 'They would have finished up in it, on the coffin, trying to kill each other.'

'Precisely. That's why I did what I did,' Elanora sniffed. 'Aren't you going to offer me a cup of something?'

'Oh, I'm sorry. How rude of me. It's just that you appeared so suddenly, right after I'd tried to call you. Would you like tea or coffee?' He reached for the intercom.

'English tea would be lovely, thank you.'

'Twiggy,' he said into the machine. 'A pot of English tea please.'

'Yes, Mister Wilson,' the voice of his secretary replied.

'Twiggy?' Elanora said taking off her gloves.

'Yeah,' he shrugged. 'After some skinny English model. When she first started working for me her name was Barbara, but she's changed it several times since then.'

'All young Cantonese women change the English Christian names they give themselves. It means no more to them than changing their hairstyle or shoes to the latest fashion.'

'It drives me insane,' Johnnie laughed. 'Barbara – Evelyn –

Virginia – now Twiggy . . . out there,' he waved vaguely towards his outer office, 'has worked for me for three years and I have to keep writing her current name on my desk blotter.'

'It's one of the vagaries of Hong Kong life, I'm afraid.' Elanora smiled fondly. 'But you're an old China hand, Johnnie. Surely you must be used to the place by now?'

'Yeah, I suppose so.' He stood, crossed to the window and gazed out over Ice House Street towards the Star Ferry terminal. 'I love this city, you know?' He turned to her. 'It took a bit of getting used to, but I love it.'

'And after, what is it, thirteen years . . . ?'

'Fourteen. Goin' on fifteen,' Johnnie corrected.

'. . . Nearly fifteen years, you know it so well.'

'Oh, yeah,' he nodded as his secretary entered the room with the pot of tea on a tray. 'Just leave it on the desk thanks, Twiggy.' The girl did so and left. 'Shall I be Mother?' he asked, picking up the teapot.

'That phrase is so English,' she laughed. 'You've been in this town far too long.'

'Like I said, nearly fifteen years. I'm damn near more English than American.'

'You'd know practically everyone worth knowing in this town by now, I suppose?'

'I guess I would,' Johnnie replied, enjoying the easy conversation immensely. He adored Elanora Merchant and the chance to sit and while away some time with the elegant, aging beauty made him feel ridiculously happy.

'All the prominent citizens?'

'Yep,' he nodded, offering her a tray of biscuits. 'Ginger snaps, my favourite.'

'No, thank you. And you and James would know all the company directors?'

'All those of any importance.' Johnnie slumped in his seat and sank his teeth into a biscuit.

'And all the bankers, of course?'

'For sure,' he nodded. 'I know them all. Every single one of them.'

'Like you know all the bankers in Geneva?'

'Yeah, you could say that,' he said cheerily, then suddenly stopped chewing, mid-mouthful. He squinted at her. 'Why do you ask?'

'No particular reason,' she shrugged.

'Don't give me that. You've got your inscrutable oriental face on.'

'What?' She raised an eyebrow.

'And don't "what" me, Elanora. I know that face.' He put his half eaten biscuit on the desk and pointed his finger at her accusingly. 'I know you, Missy. You're doing it again.'

'I don't know what you're talking about.'

'Yes, you do.' He leaned towards her wagging the finger. 'You do the inscrutable face thing like you're thinking about nothing, but your mind – ha! – your mind is doing things!'

'You're speaking gibberish, John.'

'And don't use that mother tone, like you do. That's just another part of the trick.'

'Why were you trying to ring me today?'

'I won't tell you,' Johnnie snapped like an aggressive child. He picked up the remains of the biscuit, bit into it and began chewing furiously.

'Was it about James being in Geneva?'

'How did you know James was in Geneva?'

'You just said he was.'

'Did I?' Johnnie was suddenly unsure of just what he had said. 'I didn't say that. Didn't you say that?'

'Ooh!' Elanora sounded exasperated. 'We just mentioned James and Geneva in the same breath, so I assumed that's where he is.'

'Did we? Who mentioned him?'

Elanora gave him a puzzled look. 'Now you're confusing *me*. He *is* in Geneva, isn't he?'

'Yes, of course he is.' Johnnie tried to sound composed. 'I mean . . . I'm not sure I should tell you.'

'Well, will you tell me when he left Hong Kong?'

'Monday. He's been missing since then. I know, because

I've got some information he wanted rather urgently and I couldn't find him. He took the company jet.'

'He took the Lear?'

'Yeah, the Lear-24 landed in Geneva. I'm automatically informed whenever the jet is used, but wait . . .' He looked at her. 'Ha!' he laughed and shook his head. 'Wait a minute, wait a minute.' He stood and returned to the window before looking back. 'I'm a graduate of West Point Military Academy. I have a degree from Oxford University in England. I'm not stupid, Elanora.'

'I know that, John,' she answered demurely. 'You're a wonderful, intelligent, human being.'

'Nobody else in the world can do that to me, you know?' He sighed, exasperated.

'Do what?'

'You know what! The sudden, unexpected appearance,' he gestured with his hands towards the door as he returned to his desk and sat down. 'The cup of tea, then the cosy fireside chat that turns into an interrogation . . .' He leaned his elbows on the desk and rested his chin in his hands. 'You know what I mean, don't you?'

'Yes.'

'Okay, just so long as you know that I know.' He smiled at her. 'Whaddya wanna know?'

'What is James doing in Geneva?'

'He's not in Geneva.'

'You said the jet is in Geneva.'

'No, I said it landed in Geneva. As of one hour ago, according to Charles Middleditch, the company's pilot, the Lear-24 is in London.'

'Oh, my God.' Elanora felt suddenly ill. 'London, of course!'

Johnnie frowned. 'I think we'd both better lay our cards on the table, Missy. Maybe, between us, we can figure out just what in hell that boy of yours is up to.'

龍

James Merchant left Charles Middleditch looking after the aircraft and caught a cab into London. He checked into his favourite hotel, '22 Jermyn Street', its actual address. It was in St James, not fifty yards from Regent Street and Piccadilly Circus, right in the middle of the West End. He used it on the occasions he visited London, rather than the house in Belgravia, once the property of the Golden Dragons Society, but now, since Paul's death, owned entirely by Georgina.

Georgina, he thought, as he entered the single doorway of the hotel and walked up the narrow passage to the porter's station, my recalcitrant daughter, who is now cooling her heels as a hotel manager in Singapore. Well, good riddance, he thought.

Her job was, he knew, courtesy of the girl's interfering grandmother. Georgie a hotel manager? Good God. The thought was laughable. The Georgie he knew was incapable of managing her own life, let alone a hotel.

'Hello again, Mister Merchant,' a young woman said in a lilting Irish brogue.

'Hello to you, Annie,' he replied as she handed him the key to his regular suite of rooms.

'This arrived for you just an hour ago.'

He pocketed the telegram she handed to him. 'Assistant Manager now, I see,' he smiled, indicating the badge on her lapel.

'Yes, Sir,' she laughed. 'Goin' up in the world, you might say.'

'Well, good for you.' He thought again of Georgie as he got into the small elevator, pushed his floor button, then deliberately held the lift door open. 'Annie?' he called to the girl.

'Yes, Sir?' Her head appeared at the lift door.

'Do you enjoy it?'

'And what might that be exactly, Mister Merchant?' Her smile held no warmth, it was fixed, professional.

The young woman was nobody's fool. She was no doubt propositioned occasionally by the hotel's wealthy clients, James decided, and had developed a firm, yet polite rebuff that began with the sentence she'd just uttered. 'Being an Assistant Manager, I mean.'

'I do, Sir.' She smiled legitimately, realising his enquiry had been genuine. 'It's fascinating work and I get to meet people from all over the world. Like yourself, Sir. You being from Hong Kong and all.'

'Well, keep up the good work, my dear.' James pushed his floor button again. 'Who knows, one day you may end up running the place.'

'Oh, I don't think there's much chance of that, Mister Merchant.' She restrained the lift door momentarily. 'I'm still only a woman, after all.'

'Isn't the Swinging Sixties supposed to change all that? You know, women's liberation, that sort of thing?'

'Make no mistake, Sir,' the young woman released the door. 'It's a man's world we live in and that's the truth of it.'

James caught a final glimpse of her face as the lift doors closed. She wore that same mystic smile worn by Da Vinci's Mona Lisa. That expression which seemed to say, I know something you don't know, but don't bother asking me what it is, because although it's a truism to the female mind, you as a man would find it incomprehensible.

'Women,' he muttered as the lift door opened at his floor. He made his way along the corridor and opened the door to his suite.

The set of rooms was of another world. Turn of the century London was suddenly all about him, Victorian and Edwardian furniture pieces, lush carpets and wallpaper, gaslight fittings, floral decorations, hunting scenes and heavy brocades. He dumped his overnight case on the bed and made his way to the well stocked bar in the living room.

'Well done "22",' he exclaimed upon seeing the bottle of Royal House Scottish whisky on the table next to a bowl overflowing with fresh fruit. It was his favourite drink, a highland blend that was difficult to acquire. The card tied to the neck of the bottle read simply, 'Welcome back Mr. Merchant.' He made a mental note to leave a large gratuity when he checked out. It was the thoughtful, personal touches like that, when added to the normal high standards the hotel maintained, that made 22 Jermyn Street a really special place.

'Special? No. Unique,' James added, pouring himself a drink. He took the telegram from his pocket. It was from Johnnie, he noted. He sat down and read, taking a swig of the whisky. Then he put down his glass. 'Caveat dated 1948 . . .' he read the facts out loud, '. . . The last on the list . . . must present a medallion as identification . . . A medallion? What bloody medallion?'

James got up, glass in hand, and slowly paced the floor. He stopped and gazed out of the window into Jermyn Street. And what was the significance of 1948? And why had Richard placed a caveat on the account that year? Then the answer hit him like a bolt from the blue. 'Well, I'll be damned,' he murmured out loud, as the pieces of the puzzle fell into place. 'The medallions, of course.'

When he and Lee had left Hong Kong to attend school in England, Richard Brewster had given them each a small medallion on a gold chain as a parting gift. Identical, and no bigger than a sixpence, the medallions had been made of silver. A golden dragon had been embossed on each, the dragon breathing fire, a tiny pearl seated in the flames coming from its mouth.

'And I gave mine away,' he groaned.

James' mind flew back to 1941. The London Blitz. A street of terrace houses in Battersea. Every house a blazing inferno. A little boy, alone, standing in that street of flames. It was the only genuine act of kindness James Merchant had ever knowingly committed. The little boy had been terrified. His family had been burnt to death in that street and James had taken the child to a refuge run by the Sisters of Mercy.

'And I gave him the bloody medallion!' He laughed at the irony of it. 'I gave an orphan the key to a fortune in precious stones!'

It all came back to him now. He remembered vividly a blazing row he'd had with Richard on the balcony at Merchant House during which Richard had asked if he still had his medallion. James had taken great pleasure in telling him that he'd given it away.

So, he thought, the caveat had been Richard's way of

taking his revenge. He put it in place knowing I didn't have the medallion. 'But you were too smart for your own good, Richard.' James slapped his knee, delighted. 'I don't need your precious medallion after all, old sport. I've got Delaney, and as one of the First Five, he doesn't need a bloody medallion to get the gems.'

He picked up the phone and made a local call. He allowed the number to ring three times, then hung up, and redialled it.

'*Wei?*' The male voice was typically Cantonese, sharp and aggressive.

'*This is Mister Merchant speaking.*'

'*Ah, but how can I be sure that is true?*'

'*Because I just dialled your number and let it ring three times, then dialled again.*'

'*But how can I be sure it was you who rang and hung up?*'

'*Because that was the pre-arranged signal we agreed upon.*'

'*I never agreed to a pre-arranged signal.*'

James took a deep breath and sighed slowly before continuing. '*I am speaking to Jimmy Fong, true or not true?*'

'*Not true, I am Mister Fong's assistant.*'

'*Where is Mister Fong at this moment?*'

'*He's sitting next to me smoking a cigarette.*'

'*Then put him on the fucking phone, you useless piece of dog shit!*' James roared.

'*Wei?*' another voice asked.

'Don't you start, Jimmy,' James snapped. 'The last thing I need at the moment is the merry-go-round of Cantonese logic. We'll speak English if you don't mind.'

'Okey-dokey, Boss,' Jimmy Fong replied cheerily. The last thing *he* needed was a run in with the Merchant *taipan*. He'd been a Merchant Company operative in London for many years and knew better than to rub James Merchant the wrong way.

'Who's the idiot who answered the phone?'

'My nephew, Boss.' Jimmy Fong took a moment to slap his dead brother's son across the side of the head. 'He's a good kid, but young, you know?'

'Well, if you want him to grow any older, keep him away from me. *Understand or not understand?*'

'Understand, Boss.'

'Okay. Have you done what I requested?'

'Yes, Boss.' Jimmy Fong looked at Terrence Delaney, slumped in a chair opposite him. 'The merchandise is sitting right in front of me.'

'What condition is it in?'

'Fair to middlin', I'd say, Boss.' After years in London, Jimmy's accent wandered disastrously between Cantonese and Cockney. 'Mind you, what wiv it bein' an antique an' all, I couldn't guarantee it's got a long and happy life in front of it, if you know what I mean? And it smells like a bleedin' brewery.'

'Will it survive two hours in an aeroplane and a good day's work?'

'No worries, *taipan*. It should do that in a doddle.'

'Do you know Captain Middleditch, the Merchant Company pilot?'

'I most certainly do, Boss. I've dealt with him several times.'

'Good. He's expecting the cargo tomorrow morning, early.'

'Consider it done, Mister Merchant.'

'What about Customs?'

'All fixed. Immigration, too.' Jimmy winked at his nephew as he spoke reassuringly to his big boss. As Manager of an air catering service at Heathrow, Jimmy Fong had no trouble moving property, and people, in and out of England without interference from British Customs and Immigration. 'As the sayin' goes, Boss – you can't go wrong, if you deal with Fong.'

'You've done well, Jimmy boy,' James said. *'May you sire one hundred sons.'*

'All born with two heads so I waste my wealth buying hats for them.' Jimmy laughed, concluding the old Cantonese jibe. 'And the same to you, *taipan*.'

James hung up, well satisfied. He would soon have his fortune. Only Lee Kwan could thwart him now. He knew Lee still had his medallion, he'd seen it around his neck not long ago, but he also knew that Lee would not leave his mountain retreat to fly to Geneva. Not even for Elanora. Fortunes meant nothing to Lee.

He helped himself to another whisky and toasted the fact that in twenty-four hours Terrence Delaney would personally recover the eyes of the dragons, before he joined his Yorkshire ancestors in that great big coalmine in the sky.

龍

Elanora stirred from sleep. In her half awakened state she reached for Richard. She had been dreaming of him, a curious dream in which they were alone together on a tropical island after the shipwreck of the Merchant Company junk. They were making love on the beach when the bow of an enormous ocean liner ground into the sand casting a shadow over them, and when she'd looked up James' face had been leering at them from over the bow.

No tears came as she stared at the ornate moulded ceiling. She'd been prepared for the parting. In the preceding six months they'd talked at length about their lives together, their happiness, their achievements, their losses and regrets. They had shared a great love.

She rolled onto her side and fluffed her pillow. The face of Richard smiled at her from his picture, which she kept on the bedside table, and a groan escaped her lips as the terrible truth struck yet again. She began to cry, silently, the tears flowing freely onto her pillow as her heart ached anew. He's been dead only six days, she thought. I buried him on Wednesday and have spent the days since tracking James' whereabouts and worrying about that accursed bank account in Switzerland.

The mere thought of James made her fly out of bed and she stormed into the bathroom and turned on the shower taps with violent twists of her wrists. Damn him to hell, she cursed silently as she stripped off her nightgown.

She showered and dressed quickly. Damn him, she cursed again as she descended the stairs. She knew James was not directly responsible for Richard's death, but the way he had burst into his bedroom and seized him had certainly hastened the matter. At that precise moment, she decided, had she had the chance, she would have killed him. She most definitely would have killed her own son. The irony of the thought didn't escape her. 'Like mother, like son,' she laughed humourlessly.

As she reached the bottom of the stairs, she noticed the front door was open and her beloved Lee was sitting on the outside steps. She had asked him to remain with her since the funeral. He was gazing contentedly down the cobbled street to where it curved away onto the Praia Grande and wharves below her house.

'Lee, darling,' she called and he stood and smiled. 'What are you doing out there?'

'Good morning, Elanora.' He waved his hand vaguely in the direction of the street. 'I was wondering how many men, and how long it took them, to place all these cobbles side by side so neatly, to form the street. Or was it only one man's achievement?'

'Cobbles?' Elanora asked, stepping through the front door to stand beside him. 'Isn't the word cobble-stones?'

'No, it isn't. That question occurred to me as I sat here, so I used Richard's new Oxford Illustrated Dictionary and looked it up. It says, "cobble, a water-rounded stone, larger than a pebble and smaller than a boulder."'

'Well, you learn something new every day.' She smiled at him wanly.

'Then I wondered if you had learned anything new from your Mister Wilson, yesterday.'

Elanora's smile disappeared. 'Come into the parlour and I'll tell you what I found out.' She turned and entered the house. 'Sally?' she called loudly.

'Yes, Missy?' The girl appeared from nowhere.

'English tea for two in the front room, and some toast and marmalade.'

'Is already prepared, Missy,' Sally replied, and disappeared again.

When they were seated, Elanora gazed at the fireplace wondering where to begin. Her meeting the previous day in Hong Kong with Johnnie had realised her worst fears.

'James is way ahead of me,' she began. 'He flew out of Hong Kong on Monday night in the Company jet.'

'Your company has its own aircraft?' Lee was impressed.

'Yes, a Lear-24. According to Johnnie Wilson it landed in Geneva on Wednesday.'

'The day of Richard's burial.' Lee shook his head. 'Bad *joss*.'

'I've been complacent. I should have sent you to Geneva as soon as I knew what he was up to. You could have presented your medallion and retrieved the stones – '

'I would not have gone, Elanora.' Lee looked at his mother and smiled gently.

'Why not?' She was surprised by his remark.

'This,' he replied, opening the neck of his tunic to expose the little medallion hanging around his neck, 'has been around my neck since I was thirteen years old. It was a personal gift to me from Richard Brewster and as such, it means more to me than all the precious stones in the world.'

'You don't have to exchange it, Lee, you merely have to present it to redeem the stones.'

'But I don't want them.'

'Don't talk nonsense,' Elanora chided as Sally placed their breakfast before them. She left quickly.

'What would I do with them, Mother? Decorate the door of my house? Attach them to the harness of my old oxen? To me they would be pretty coloured stones that catch the light. Worthless baubles to be given to a child as playthings.'

'Now you're being silly.' Elanora poured tea for them both. 'They're worth a fortune.'

'To you, perhaps, or to James, but not to me.'

'Then what about your children?' She waved a small porcelain pot at him. 'Milk?' she asked.

'Yes, thank you.' Lee offered his cup to her. 'The gaining of wealth is no different to the gaining of wisdom, Mother. It takes time, and during that time, the person involved learns to handle it. My children are healthy and intelligent. If at some stage they wish to be wealthy, I'm sure they are both capable of becoming so, but I will not thrust sudden wealth upon them.'

'Would you rather James got hold of them?' Elanora slammed the teapot onto the table, stood and began to pace the floor, wringing her hands.

'But he can't get hold of them. Isn't that why Richard placed the caveat on the account? He knew James didn't have his medallion.'

'He doesn't need his medallion!' She stopped and gripped the back of her chair. 'According to Johnnie Wilson, James landed in London yesterday.'

'I'm confused.' Lee shook his head. 'Why would he go to London?'

'Terrence Delaney is in London.'

CHAPTER SIXTEEN

Panic seized him. He was alone in the trench. All of his men had deserted their posts. He chanced a peek over the sand-bags and saw it, a cloud of smoke. Chlorine gas. He fumbled putting on his gas mask, knowing it would do him little good. Oh God, he prayed, not again. He'd been a victim of chlorine gas at Verdun and now it was going to get him again at the Somme.

He stumbled along the trench to the Command Station and fell through the door, but it was not as he remembered it. There were no officers, no beds, no map table. Instead it appeared to be the entrance of a tunnel. He staggered along it. It was dark and dank. Strange, he thought, the air smelled of the sea. And suddenly he broke out into the light of day.

He was on Victoria Peak. What on earth is going on? his mind screamed as his eyes took in the vista of Hong Kong lying below. He tripped and began to roll, over and over down the hill, until he came to a stop on a small beach.

'Over here,' a man called, and he recognised the voice of Richard Brewster. He looked up and saw Richard in a small sailing boat, out in the water. Seated in it were his old friends, Robert McCraw, Malcolm Linden and Lo Shi-mon. They were waving, urging him to join them. He waded into the water and was pulled on board by Richard.

'The Famous First Five, together again.' Robert McCraw slapped him on the back. 'It's good to see you, laddie,' the big Scot growled happily. 'The Golden Dragons re-united. We thought you weren't going to make it.'

'We've no time to lose, men,' Richard shouted, pointing skyward.

Terrence Delaney looked up. In the sky, a massive black dragon circled, screaming its wrath, breathing fire in great gusts.

'It's James Merchant!' Lo Shi-mon yelled. 'Richard's step-son.'

'Elanora's boy?' Terrence asked.

'Yes, but his heart is black,' Lo said. 'He is no longer one of us.'

'But don't worry, old man,' Malcolm Linden laughed. 'He can't see us.'

'These are what he's after,' Richard called out, holding up two huge gemstones, one in each hand. 'I've got his eyes. Here,' he threw them to Terrence, 'look after them for me, will you? Guard them with your life. If he gets hold of them, we're all done for, man.'

Delaney looked at the gemstones he was holding. They were massive, and as he watched, they turned from ruby red to sapphire blue, then to emerald green.

'Terrence, look out!' someone shouted.

He looked up and saw the huge black dragon descending, its claws opened wide, getting closer and closer. The boat rocked violently.

Terrence Delaney awoke from his nightmare only to assume he was in another. He was belted into a leather seat in some sort of aircraft. It seemed to be hurtling through the clouds at an incredible speed. His hands were trembling and sweat poured from his brow. What in God's name is going on? he thought, terrified. He locked his fingers, trying to stop the shaking, then searched his pockets for the flask of whisky he always carried, but it was nowhere to be found.

Images flickered through his mind. You remember me, don't you, Terrence? an English face asked him. No whisky for you, a Chinese face flashed, laughing at him. You are *yum joi jau*, another younger Chinese laughed. *Yum joi jau?* Delaney remembered it meant drunk in Cantonese. Geneva . . . the English face returned . . . Geneva . . . You'll get whisky in Geneva . . . Redeem the stones . . . you'll get all the whisky you can drink, old boy.

Terrence tried to remember. Two Chinese had bought him a drink in the Tallow Tavern in South London. He'd been drinking on his own, as usual, when the two men had entered the bar.

'*Nei ho ma?*' one had asked him.

'I'm fine, thank you,' he had answered.

'Hey, you understand Cantonese. What say I buy you a drink, guv'ner?' The Chinese had spoken in an appalling half Cockney, half Cantonese accent.

Terrence Delaney blinked rapidly, trying to clear his brain. Three faces of the Englishman returned simultaneously. 'I'm James', they shouted at him, 'James Merchant. Elanora's boy.' The voice echoed, rattling around inside his head.

'Hello, Terrence.' Delaney looked up. The Englishman was standing in front of him. 'I'm James Merchant,' the man said. 'I suppose you must be a bit confused, old man?'

'You haven't seen a flask of whisky, have you?' Delaney asked in his heavy Yorkshire way.

'You mean this?' The man withdrew Delaney's flask from behind his back and waved it about but when Delaney reached for it, he once again hid it behind him. 'I'm afraid there won't be any whisky for you until we get to Geneva, my friend.'

'Geneva?' Delaney was utterly confused. 'What are you on about? Geneva?'

'You were Shanghai-ed, Terrence,' James Merchant said. 'I'm sorry about the Mickey Finn you were given, but I've got to get you to Switzerland.'

'Mickey Finn?' So that's what happened, Delaney thought. The bloody Chinese had spiked his drink. No wonder he couldn't remember anything.

'That's right,' James Merchant smiled humourlessly. 'I tried talking to you earlier, but you drifted off.'

Terrence Delaney was suddenly afraid. In his lifetime he had met and dealt with many men, good and bad. And this one was bad. He recalled James Merchant as a thirteen-year-old boy; even then, he'd had the eyes of a killer. The boy and his adopted brother had been trained by Lo Shi-mon as assassins, to be unleashed like wild dogs on the enemies of the Golden Dragon Society. Terrence knew, beyond all doubt, that he would never see England again.

'It saved time and explanations, Terrence.' James sat down next to him. 'You wrote to me in Hong Kong, remember? The eyes of the dragons?'

'Aye. You're Brewster's young step-son, aren't you?'

'That's right. And you're the last of the Famous First Five. I'm taking you to Geneva where you will attend a meeting, with me, in the Banque Suisse Genève.'

'To redeem the eyes of the golden dragons?'

'That's correct.'

'And if I don't?'

James' laugh was cold, cruel. 'Don't even consider disobeying me.' He stood and leaned into Terrence's face. 'If you try, I'll kill you. It's as simple as that. And your death will not be quick.'

Terrified as he was, Delaney spied his flask in James' hand and reached for it. 'Just one sip,' he pleaded. 'Just to steady my nerves. I don't like flying.'

'Sorry,' James shook his head.

'But you don't understand, lad,' Delaney began. 'I need a drink badly. Just one.'

James stood upright and walked towards the cockpit door. 'Not until we've concluded our business to my satisfaction, old man.' He stopped and waved the flask at Delaney, mocking him. 'After that you can have all the whisky in the world. As a matter of fact, I'll buy it for you,' he finished, and went through into the cockpit, closing the door behind him.

'I won't ask what we're doing flying an ancient alcoholic to Geneva,' Charles Middleditch said as James seated himself in the co-pilot's seat.

'Good. It's better that you don't,' James replied.

'How is the poor old sot? Still sleeping soundly?'

'No. Unfortunately he's awake and none too happy.' James replaced his headset. 'How are we doing, Charles?'

'We're cruising at thirty-nine thousand feet and thirty minutes out of Geneva. We should be thinking about our descent soon.'

In the cabin, Delaney gripped the arms of his seat. He was sweating heavily and his whole body trembled. He recognised the onset of *delirium tremens* and began to panic.

'Sweet Mother Mary,' he groaned, casting a glance out of the window. The ground was miles below. I'm in a flying coffin, he thought, a cigar tube rocketing through the sky. His fear of flying was made even worse by the imaginary spiders now crawling over his arms. He brushed at them feebly and started to whimper as the demons inside him began to scream for alcohol.

'Why in God's name did you ever write that letter?' he heard Richard's voice ask him.

'Richard?' Delaney looked about frantically, tossing his head from side to side as cramps began to grip his stomach. 'Richard, old friend,' he called. 'Thank heavens you're here. I can't get up.'

'Och, laddie,' he heard Robert McCraw call to him. 'What have you done, Terrence? You've alerted that black-hearted bastard to the whereabouts of the eyes.'

'I just needed a few pounds to tide me over, lads,' Delaney cried as the pain bit into his stomach. 'I thought you were still alive, Richard. I just wanted . . . Aargh!' He doubled over in the seat as the cramps seized his torso.

Along with his withdrawal symptoms, whatever his kidnappers had put into his drink was now having its secondary effect. Vomit suddenly spewed from him, splattering all over his lap. He placed his hand over his mouth and when he removed it, he saw gobs of blood dripping through his fingers.

'Richard,' he gasped, 'where are you, man? Help me. I'm gut-ripped, Richard. For the love of God, if you are my friends, help me!'

'You've betrayed us, Terry,' Malcom Linden's voice intoned.

'Malcolm,' Delaney cried out. He twisted his head searching for his former police colleague. 'Malcolm, please? I didn't mean to betray anyone.'

'The boy I trained is evil.' It was the voice of Lo Shi-mon. 'You have made it possible for him to redeem the eyes of the golden dragons.'

Delaney fumbled with the strap restraining him. His fingers found the seat belt release and it snapped open. He got to his feet, wincing with the effort and stared frantically about the cabin.

'You must escape before James comes back,' a voice called. 'He mustn't get hold of the dragons' eyes.'

'He's right, Terrence.' It was Richard's voice now. 'Get out! He'll kill you when he gets the eyes.'

'But we're miles above the earth, lads!' Delaney screamed. The intensity of the pain in his gut was almost paralysing him.

'You're a dragon, laddie!' It was Robbie McCraw now. 'You can fly! Come outside and fly with us, man!'

In the cockpit, as James changed the transponder frequency to contact Geneva, a red light began flashing on the instrument panel.

'That's odd,' Middleditch remarked. 'The cabin door's disarmed.'

'Get back there and see what's going on,' James ordered.

In the cabin, Delaney heaved with all his strength against the disarmed door, praying for it to open. 'It won't budge, lads,' he cried. He stood and gazed madly about. Then, moving to the compartment at the rear of the cabin he found what he was looking for. Behind the rear bulkhead on the wall above the spare oxygen bottles, emergency equipment and fire extinguishers he saw a large pick and blade axe. He seized the handle and ripped the axe from its wall mounting.

Charles Middleditch opened the cockpit door to find the main cabin empty. The old fellow must be in the toilet, he assumed. Closing the cockpit door, he started for the rear of the plane, intent on checking the cabin door, only to be suddenly confronted by the sight of the giant drunk, staggering into the main cabin, wielding the aircraft's emergency escape axe.

'Good God!' Middleditch held his hands up defensively,

but he was no coward. He took several steps towards the man. 'What do you think you're doing?'

'Hurry, Terrence!' voices called from outside the plane. Delaney could see his friends through the windows. They were dragons, flying alongside the aircraft, urging him to join them.

The big Yorkshireman roared and swung the weapon with all his might. The pick and head of the axe smashed the window. Cabin pressure did the rest.

'Nooo!' Charles Middleditch screamed. The roar inside the cabin shattered his eardrums. As emergency oxygen masks dropped from the ceiling, he saw the big man sucked through the huge hole that had once been a window. Then he felt himself flying through the air and out of the fuselage, into the stratosphere.

In the cockpit, as the aircraft shook violently, James fought with all his strength to gain control. Forty seconds, he thought. Forty seconds to get oxygen and avoid blacking out. What in Christ's name had happened? A tremendous roar filled his ears and water vapour, like smoke, filled the cockpit. Maps and papers flew all about him and a warning 'beep-beep' sounded, alerting him that aircraft decompression was rapid.

James' fear was momentary. Even as he reached for his oxygen mask and strapped it on, his breathing slowed and his heart rate began to drop. His body prepared for action. His *Shaolin* mind whispered its soothing message. *Relax,* he heard his teacher's voice whisper inside his head. *Let your mind take control of your body. Use your senses, detect the threat, choose the correct response, strike, withdraw, defend. Relax, Little Brother. Analyse and respond.* He felt a soft, sensual thrill as his body relaxed more and more, until the aircraft became an extension of his being. His body became a conductor of impulses from the brain to his hands and feet.

James reached for the jet's thrust levers and closed them down, then deployed the speed brakes and lowered the nose of the aircraft. Maximum safe rate of descent, he thought calmly. Make it safe, James, don't descend too fast. Get down to twelve thousand feet and level out.

He reached for the transponder and selected the correct frequency to alert Geneva Air Traffic Control. 'Geneva, Geneva, this is Lear-24 Victor Foxtrot Alpha 116. I have left thirty-nine thousand feet. I am on emergency descent to twelve thousand feet. I am south bound in Upper Green Four. Over.'

'VFA-116, this is Geneva Control, copied. You have left thirty-nine thousand feet on emergency descent to twelve thousand feet. South bound in Upper Green Four. Switch now to emergency frequency 121.5. Over.'

'Roger, Geneva. Switching frequencies. Out.' James complied, then let his eyes rove quickly over the instrument panel as the cockpit moisture began to lessen. Apart from rapid depressurisation, the aircraft seemed mechanically sound.

On frequency 121.5 MHz James began a commentary as the aircraft dropped through thirty thousand feet, alerting any aircraft in his flight quadrant of Upper Green Four to his situation and altitude. Through the clearing atmosphere in the cockpit, his eyes searched the skies and he flexed his hands and feet preparing for any evasive action.

He was also acutely aware that he was descending rapidly somewhere over the Rhone Alps. 'Don't hit a mountain, James,' he muttered between transmissions. 'No other aircraft and no mountains. Just get down to twelve thousand feet and level out. Worry about where you are after that.'

龍

'Good morning, Mr Bent,' Georgie stated brightly as she stepped from the thatched hut onto its small verandah.

'Good morning, Mrs Bent,' Jeremy replied. Lifting his hat from over his eyes, he gazed up from the deckchair at his wife of twenty-four hours. Nude from the waist up and wrapped in a sarong knotted at the hip she could not have looked more beautiful. 'You're practically naked, you shameless hussy,' he said.

'We're in the middle of nowhere,' Georgie exclaimed, throwing her leg over his body and sitting directly astride his hips. 'And besides, it's perfectly all right for a woman to appear naked in front of her husband, isn't it? Unless of course, you'd rather I didn't.' She moved to get off him.

'No, no.' He pulled her back down by her hips. 'Stay where you are and we'll talk about the first thing that pops up.'

'Don't be crude.' Georgie grinned. Wriggling out of his grasp she got to her feet. 'Can't you think of anything but sex?'

'Not off hand, no,' Jeremy replied.

'What about breakfast? Have you thought of that?'

'I was thinking of it when you sat on my lap.' He stood up and took her in his arms. 'Why don't we go back to bed and then have breakfast?'

They kissed long and deep then Georgie broke free and took several paces backwards. 'Oh no,' she cried happily. 'If you expect to have me on the hour every hour, as you seem to have done since we left the Registry Office, then you'd better feed me, or I'll be no good to you at all.'

'Well, it just so happens,' Jeremy took her by the hand, 'I've arranged a wonderful Thai breakfast for you down on the beach. Come on.'

The newly-weds walked hand in hand through palm trees down to the beach, not fifty yards from their front door, blissfully unaware that a world outside their own even existed.

Unbeknown to anyone, they'd married in Singapore the previous morning. A deeply meaningful conversation the night before had been the trigger. Jeremy had arrived in Singapore from Hong Kong with five days' leave. He'd arranged it because of concern for Georgina. Her grandmother had flatly refused her attendance at Richard Brewster's funeral, insisting she remain in Singapore. Georgie, unable to understand why, had been deeply hurt. The fact that no one in the Colony including her mother had been invited meant nothing to her. Georgie had been so depressed and angry with her entire family that Jeremy had applied for emergency leave.

He'd spent the night with her at Raffles in a room she'd arranged for him free of charge, and between extended bouts of love-making he'd proposed. The vehemence of her response had shocked him.

'Yes!' she'd answered, throwing her arms around his neck. 'Yes, yes, yes! Let's get married tomorrow.'

'Tomorrow?' He'd been truly shocked.

'Yes, tomorrow. We'll bribe somebody to cut through the red tape. This is Singapore.'

'But what about your family? Your mother, your grand-mother – '

'Damn them! As far as I'm concerned it's no business of my parents who I marry, or when. And as for *Ju Mo*, well, if she sees fit to bar me from my own grandfather's funeral, then I'll bar her from my wedding.' Her eyes expressed a cunning gleam as the thought took hold. 'That's exactly what I'll do. It'll teach them all a lesson.'

'Whoa!' Jeremy had exclaimed, hands held high. 'Don't you think you might be going off half cocked?'

'My family,' she'd declared vehemently, 'or what's left of it, can go to hell. I'll start my own family with you, the man I love. We'll have babies, lots of them, and I'll make sure we're always together and happy.'

'Oh dear, Georgina,' Jeremy had muttered. 'Shouldn't we give it a little more thought?'

He imagined the furore a sudden elopement would cause, not only with her family, but also with his superiors in the Hong Kong Police Force. His Commissioner would castrate him, probably at the screaming insistence of Elanora Merchant, or her psycho son James. Christ, what a family, he thought. 'It's a big step,' he'd finished lamely. 'We need time to settle in to the idea and – '

'Hold on, sport!' She'd hit him in the chest with the flat of her hand. 'Are you serious about wanting to marry me?'

'Of course I am. I love you, but Hong Kong's in a state of emergency. There are riots and bombings almost daily. We're practically at war with China. For God's sake, Georgie, I've only got five days off – '

'It's now or never, *sport*!' She'd spat the word.

And that had been it. They'd been married at nine o'clock the previous morning at the Singapore Registry Office and flown to Koh Samui, a small island in the Gulf of Thailand, for a three-day honeymoon.

On the beach, a small wooden table and two chairs awaited them. Jeremy sat her down with some ceremony and Durien, a pretty middle-aged Thai woman from the nearby village of Baan Taling Nam, served them glasses of fresh orange juice.

Georgie sipped her drink, taking in the exotic tropical surroundings, the long deserted strip of sand, the tall palms leaning out over the beach, and the aqua blue water. It was paradise. 'How did you know about this place?'

'The expatriate Hong Kong Police Inspectors know all the good places in Asia,' he explained. 'When their holidays arrive none of them can be bothered going home to the UK or Australia, or wherever in the Commonwealth they're from, so they explore countries closer to home. Paul Tarrant, a mate of mine, found this place last year and has never stopped raving about it.'

They'd flown in from Singapore in an old propeller driven aircraft, landing at Cha Weng Airstrip on the north of the island and then travelled by four-wheel drive to the southern end and the little village of Baan Taling Nam. Tarrant had told Jeremy to locate a woman in the village called Durien Phumkumpol who would arrange their food and accommodation.

'Baan Taling Nam has such a romantic ring to it, don't you think?' Georgie babbled gaily as the pretty Thai lady served them mangoes and papayas, with fresh limes to squeeze over the fruit. 'It's like that island in the movie *South Pacific*, isn't it?'

'Bali H'ai?'

'Yes that's it, Bali H'ai. It's just like Bali H'ai. Oh, Jeremy.' She reached over and squeezed his hand. 'I'm so happy.'

'So am I,' he replied, looking at her. Georgie sat, totally at ease with her breasts exposed and a flower planted in her long hair. He could never remember seeing a more beautiful, or more erotic, sight in his life. Against tiny islands jutting out of the water a mile off shore behind her, Georgie looked like the girls in travel magazine pictures, wild, free, sensual and breathtakingly beautiful.

'Don't you wish we could stay here forever, Jeremy?'

'Yes,' he answered, thinking of the reception he'd get when he returned to Hong Kong. Practically everyone there, policemen or otherwise, he thought, would have good reason to castrate him. 'By the way, you are going to return to Hong Kong and live with me, aren't you?'

'Oh,' Georgie stopped eating and looked at him. 'I hadn't thought of that,' she said and returned to her mango.

'Well, you are – aren't you?' He stared at her, but she didn't respond.

'I'll have to give it some thought,' she mumbled through a mouthful of fruit.

'What's there to think about? We're married.'

'Well, I know that, silly,' she laughed.

'Georgie.' Jeremy's voice carried a warning.

'Let's go back to the hut and make love, shall we?'

'Georgie!'

'Why do we have to worry about a stupid thing like that?' She put her mango down and gazed out over the sea. 'I mean, we're on our honeymoon. Let's not spoil it by worrying about trivialities.'

'*Trivialities*? Look at me, Georgina!' She didn't move. 'Georgie! Look at me!'

'What?' she sighed, turning towards him.

'What am I going to tell everybody?'

'Don't tell them anything.'

'That's preposterous!'

'Why?' Georgina warmed to her idea. 'My father will be furious if he finds out, and Grandmother will probably insist on your dismissal from the Police Force, at the very least, for daring to elope.'

'She wouldn't do that would she?' Jeremy's face was ashen. 'She likes me.'

'Weeell, maybe not, but my father would definitely do something stupid. Let's face it, you're probably better off keeping your mouth shut.'

'But we're married!'

'Yesterday you were quite happy to come and visit me in Singapore and get free sex.'

'Free sex? That's a terrible thing to say,' Jeremy began.

Durien Phumkumpol placed a boiled egg in front of him. 'Is it not better to keep your mouth shut and get free sex,' she asked, 'than to open your mouth and get into trouble?'

'If you don't mind, Durien,' Jeremy replied sharply, 'this happens to be a private conversation.'

'Then why are you talking so loud? In Thailand, if people talk so loud it is because they are seeking the opinions of others.'

'Durien's right, Jeremy.' Georgie patted his hand. 'Isn't it better for us to keep our little secret rather than for you to go off and get yourself into hot water?'

'You're exaggerating things a little, aren't you?'

'No.' Georgina shook her head. 'I'm serious. My father is a tyrant. In fact, it was probably rather stupid for us to have married without his knowledge. He'll be absolutely furious.'

'Well, it's a bit late to be saying that now, isn't it?'

'No. I would have married you anyway, with or without his consent. But it might be better if we keep it a secret for a while.'

'This conversation is not happening,' Jeremy declared placing his hand on his forehead.

'It would only be for a while, my love,' Georgie assured him.

'Oh, yes?' he asked sarcastically. 'And how long, might I ask, is a while?'

'Um,' she grinned cheekily, 'a year?'

'A year!'

'Just until I finish my course in business administration. During that year you'll get free sex upon request. Whenever you have the slightest urge you can fly to Singapore, or I'll fly to Hong Kong and meet you in secret – '

'A year!' Jeremy couldn't believe what was happening.

'I'll treat you like a king,' she went on, 'I'll learn every position in the Karma Sutra. I'll beg you to take me. I'll moan and whisper in your ear the way you like it. And tell you that you're a god and I can't live without your massive shaft being embedded in me, up to the hilt. I'll do it in public places, on buses, in cinemas . . . even in church . . .'

'You're talking like a tart,' he laughed.

'I know,' she laughed with him. 'Aren't you lucky?'

'God, I love you.' He called it out loud. 'Did you hear that, Mrs Phumkumpol? I love my wife so much I'd die for her, right this minute if necessary.'

'You don't have to die,' Durien called from her little food hut. 'You only must keep your mouth shut.'

When Jeremy looked back at his wife she was smiling, and the look in her eyes left no doubt that his feelings were reciprocated.

'I'm yours, Jeremy,' she said. 'I'm yours forever and always.' She reached across the table and stroked his cheek lovingly. 'Just give me a year? One year?'

He nodded slowly. 'As long as you're mine,' he whispered taking her hand, 'nothing else matters.'

'You foolish boy,' she whispered back, 'I've been yours ever since you kissed me in the Salisbury pub.'

When Mrs Phumkumpol returned to the table and cleared away their plates, the man began talking about London and his family, but she knew such conversation would not last long. The girl was staring into his eyes and her expression was of such animal intensity that Durien decided it was time she disappeared.

'God, I'm hot all of a sudden,' Georgie exclaimed. She ran her hands through her hair and stared at him through half closed eyes.

'Yes,' he answered. 'It is getting hot. We'd better find some shade.'

'I didn't mean that kind of hot,' she said huskily.

'I know.' He brushed a lock of hair from her eyes. 'Why don't I take you back to the hut?'

Durien Phumkumpol smiled knowingly as she watched the young Englishman carry his woman through the trees towards the hut.

龍

'VFA-116, we have you, visual,' Geneva tower called through James' headset.

'Roger Geneva,' James responded. 'Flight systems seem to be A-okay and indicators suggest my landing gear is down and locked. Request fly past for visual confirmation.'

'Roger to that, VFA-116.'

James flew the Lear-24 across the airport and circled to land.

'VFA-116 from Geneva tower, there is a large hole amidships on the port side, but all else appears normal. We confirm your landing gear is down. You are cleared for emergency landing on runway 27 Right. Wind at two hundred and sixty degrees and five knots.'

'Roger Wilco, Geneva Tower. I'm landing on 27 Right as advised.'

The touchdown proved uneventful and James stopped the plane at the end of the runway, turned into the first taxi way, then shut down the engines. As he leaned back in his seat and removed his headset, he heard fire trucks and emergency vehicles approaching, sirens and horns blaring.

He breathed a sigh of relief. He'd been bloody lucky, he thought. Christ alone knew what had gone on in the cabin. He unbuckled and got out of his seat, then opened the cockpit door and entered the main cabin. The scene that confronted him left little to his imagination. Yellow oxygen masks dangled from the ceiling panels and one of the windows on the port side was completely gone, replaced by a gaping hole.

A quick search proved what he'd suspected. Delaney and Middleditch were not on board. He observed, as he walked past the cabin exit door, that it was indeed disarmed, but unopened. Then he noticed that the emergency escape axe was missing from its wall mountings on the rear bulkhead.

The old man had smashed the window, James said to himself, incredulously. In a fit of drunken insanity the crazy fool had wanted to get out of the aircraft. He'd probably tried the door and failed, so he'd driven the escape axe through the window and the two men had been sucked through it like dust through a vacuum cleaner, out into the freezing high altitude air.

The exit door suddenly opened and firemen were simultaneously looking at him through both the open doorway and the hole in the side of the plane.

'*Zu ist okay, ja?*' the man at the door asked.

'Yes,' James answered. 'I'm fine.'

'*Mein Gott!*' another exclaimed as he climbed through the hole from the wing and looked at the carnage wrought by the depressurisation. 'What happened?' he asked in English.

'I haven't the foggiest idea,' James replied. He already had his story worked out. 'There were no passengers, only the Captain and me. A warning light in the cockpit alerted us the cabin door was disarmed. My Captain – Captain Charles Middleditch – came back into the cabin to investigate and suddenly the plane began to depressurise. I couldn't even begin to guess what happened. I managed to land the aircraft and then came back to find this mess.' He gestured about him.

'You will be required to speak with the Civil Aviation Authorities, Mr . . . ?'

'Merchant. James Merchant.'

'The Crash Investigation Unit Officers will need a statement from you.'

'I understand.' James sat wearily in one of the leather seats.

'I'm sorry, Sir,' the fireman said, 'but you must leave the aircraft at once. It is regulations. I must clear it of all passengers and crew, before I can report to the Air Traffic Control Tower that the plane is safe.' He indicated the cabin door with his arm.

'That's okay,' James replied. He stood and went to the doorway.

'Before you go, Mr Merchant . . .' the fireman called.

'Yes. What is it?'

'For my report, can you please tell me who owns this aircraft?'

'I do. That is to say, it's owned by the Merchant Company

of Hong Kong, of which I am the Chairman of the Board of Directors.'

It was enough. By that evening it was world news.

龍

'Hong Kong Millionaire in Midair Mystery' screamed the headline in Geneva's evening newspaper. 'Millionaire Hong Kong business tycoon, James Merchant,' James read on, 'piloted his own aircraft in an emergency landing today at Geneva Airport. Mystery surrounds the incident, but un-confirmed reports say the aircraft, owned by the Merchant Company of Hong Kong, has been impounded by Civil Aviation Authorities pending further investigation.'

'Damn it!' James threw the newspaper onto the table of his suite in the Hotel Beau-Rivage. Now everyone in the world would know where he was, including Elanora, and she would know what he was up to. What will she do, he wondered?

'And all because of a drunk!' He strode into the bedroom cursing the day he'd ever heard the name Terrence Delaney. He'd wasted a great deal of time and money to get the eyes of the dragons and the drunken old fool had destroyed his plan with one swipe of an axe.

'And not only the plan, but my bloody plane as well,' he grumbled at his reflection in the mirror as he straightened his bow tie. 'A half a million dollars' worth of aircraft!' The thing was stuffed, completely stuffed. There would be no structural damage and the window could be replaced, but it would never again be worth anywhere near what he'd paid for it.

As he was putting on his white dinner jacket he finally remembered the pilot. Yes, let's not forget good old Charles Middleditch, he thought, a Company man to the end. Died in the line of duty. Must send a message of condolence to his family, and a wreath. Good touch, yes, a wreath to the bereaved family. Did he have a family? James made a mental note to find out.

He returned to the living room, picked up his wallet and room key and gave himself a final inspection in the wall mirror. He looked good for his forty-eight years, he decided, and to justify his decision, he reminded himself of the thirty-two year old woman who would shortly be arriving downstairs to dine with him.

Jeanne Marceau, the gorgeous blonde bank officer, had called him that afternoon. She'd sounded quite relieved when she heard his voice on the telephone, and when he'd suggested dinner she'd readily agreed.

He looked at his watch, eight twenty-four p.m. precisely, six minutes from his rendezvous. James didn't believe in the stupid middle-class idea of being fashionably late. He'd arrive at exactly the appointed hour and wine and dine the woman, then bed her.

Another image of Terrence Delaney flashed through his mind. He'd been thwarted by fate yet again but, unlike the war years when he'd been able to kill someone in order to release his pent up hostility, this time he would have to employ the body of Jeanne Marceau to assuage his anger. He'd used her two nights before and she'd met him stroke for stroke.

Jeanne Marceau had proven to be one of the most accomplished lovers he'd ever had. She appeared to love sex to the point of depravity. In fact, he wondered, thinking of their last night together, just who had had whom? Well, my little Swiss miss, he mused, opening the door, let's see who has whom tonight.

James walked across *L'Atrium* and entered the hotel's restaurant at precisely eight-thirty p.m.

'*Bonsoir, M'sieur Merchant,*' the *maître d'hôtel* said.

'Good evening to you, too, Alain. I'm to dine at eight-thirty with – '

'Mademoiselle Marceau, I know,' the *maître d'* interrupted with a slight bow and a wave of his arm in the direction of the far corner of the room. 'She is here already, M'sieur. She awaits you at a small cubicle I, myself, have set aside for you personally, where you may be assured of privacy.'

'*Merci, Alain,*' James replied and followed the tall skinny man through the tables of diners.

'Good evening, James.' Jeanne Marceau smiled up at him.

'Good evening, Jeanne.' Christ, she looks good enough to

eat, he thought as he slid into the booth next to her. 'May I say you are looking exceptionally beautiful this evening.'

'*Merci, M'sieur, et toi aussi,*' she said huskily returning the compliment and leaving James in no doubt her libido was in much the same state as his.

'I've missed you,' he said, as the *maître d'* placed a napkin over his lap.

'It's only been forty-eight hours since we parted,' Jeanne replied.

'Yes, I realise that, but – '

'Would M'sieur care for an *apéritif*?' The *maître d'* interrupted, drawing a frown from James. '*Pardonnez-moi, M'sieur Merchant,*' he recovered quickly, 'I only wish to see you comfortably ensconced with your companion.'

'*Moët et Chandon.*'

'Any particular year, M'sieur?'

'No, you choose,' James snapped and the *maître d'* scurried off. He turned his attention back to Jeanne, who was grinning at the exchange.

'You were saying you missed me,' she said.

'Ah, yes. I wanted to take you to London with me yesterday, you know.'

'Well, thank God you didn't.' Her smile faded. 'Or you would now be dining alone, *n'est-ce pas*?'

'Yes,' James winced. 'Of course. I see your point.'

'I was so worried for you when I heard the news on television. That is why I called this hotel. I am very fond of you, James.' She placed her hand over his.

'And I of you,' he replied, squeezing it.

'I have not been able to stop thinking about you since our last meeting. I believed I would never see you again. And when I heard there was an accident with a plane and I heard your name mentioned, I nearly died.'

'Well,' he chuckled, 'so did I.'

'It must have been exciting, yes?'

As she leaned forward, James noticed a strange gleam in her eyes. She's turned on, he thought, titillated by danger, as he'd found many women were.

'So tell me what happened, James,' she asked, a little breathlessly.

'I shouldn't really talk about it. I've got to make a statement to the Crash Investigators tomorrow morning at eleven o'clock.'

'But surely you can tell me?' Her eyes widened. 'I am your lover.'

'Well, I've really got no idea.' He shook his head. 'The cabin door disarmed somehow. I sent my pilot back to see what was wrong and something terrible happened, but I've no idea what. It simply defies explanation.'

'They say on the radio that there is a big hole in your aircraft.'

'That's right, a *very* big hole. My pilot unfortunately got sucked through it. It's the only possible explanation.'

'Out into the sky, yes?' Jeanne placed her hand over her mouth. 'But how could that happen? Aeroplanes do not just burst like American bubble gum, do they?'

'Well, I've got a theory,' James began, 'but I really shouldn't tell you until I've spoken to the investigators tomorrow.'

'Oh, please!' Jeanne implored him. 'I'm a bank clerk, James, I do not live a very exciting life. Tell me your theory, please?' She smiled seductively and her hands disappeared beneath the table. 'You might find it well worth your while.' This last statement was followed by a sexy intake of breath.

'Is that so?' The woman's libido was extraordinary. 'Well, it's just a theory, you understand?'

'Yes, of course.' Jeanne wriggled in her seat. 'Tell me, quickly!'

'When I landed and checked the aircraft, I noticed the emergency axe was missing from its mounting on the rear bulkhead wall – '

'An axe,' Jeanne gasped. '*Oh, mon Dieu!*'

'I think there was another person on board the plane – '

'A criminal?'

'Well, a stowaway, at least.'

'And he had the axe and was going to hijack the plane!' She moved around the booth until their thighs were touching, then grabbed his leg. 'Tell me!'

'I believe Charles, my pilot, confronted the man and somehow the window was smashed, probably by the swinging axe. Do you know what happens in a pressurised cabin when the fuselage is pierced?'

'No.' Her eyes were glowing. 'Tell me . . . no . . . wait,' she hissed.

The *maître d'* had returned. After receiving James' approval, he opened the bottle and poured the champagne.

'Go on,' Jeanne urged as he left.

'When the axe pierced the fuselage, the effect would have been devastating,' he said.

'Tell me about the men?' James could feel her hip moving rhythmically against his leg. 'What happened to the men?'

'The men would have screamed as their eardrums were smashed, and then they would have been sucked out of the aircraft – '

'And they would have screamed all the way down. *Mon Dieu*!' She shifted on her seat and James noticed that her face had gone decidedly red.

'This is becoming rather more than a story to you, isn't it?'

'You must tell me all of what happened.' Her eyes blazed at him. 'Please?'

'Considering the effect it has on you,' he grinned lasciviously, 'I'd be a fool not to.'

'But tell me upstairs. Quickly. I want you inside me, James.'

'Would M'sieur care to order?' It was the *maître d'*.

'No,' James said decisively, looking straight at Jeanne. 'Mademoiselle Marceau and I have business to attend to that can't wait. What time do you serve supper?'

'Until two a.m., M'sieur.'

'Good.' He stood and offered a smiling Jeanne Marceau his hand. 'We may, or may not, return.'

龍

It was Sunday morning before the news of James' emergency landing and the apparent death of Charles Middleditch were reported on Hong Kong's Pearl TV network.

Johnnie and Katya Wilson heard the news flash and rushed in from their balcony breakfast to watch the story unfold.

'Charles, dead?' Katya exclaimed, shocked. 'How could it happen?'

'He's mad,' Johnnie said as he pointed the remote and switched off the set. 'The guy's fucking crazy, Katya.'

'Who?'

'James fucking Merchant! It's not only Charlie Middleditch who's missing.' He remembered Elanora's visit to his office. 'They had another guy on that plane, I'd bet my life on it. A guy called Delaney.'

'I don't understand,' Katya said, picking up the remote and turning the television back on. 'The news didn't say anything about another man.'

'And to top it all off, he's gonna lose his company and take us all crashing down along with him. I've got to ring Elanora.' Johnnie crossed towards the telephone in the hall. 'I'll explain in a minute,' he called back to her.

Katya stared at the image of the young woman on the screen as she repeated the scrappy information, obviously thrown together from various other news media reports. James had landed the company jet in Geneva which had a large hole in the fuselage. The Captain of the aircraft was missing, believed lost in midair, but there was no mention of anyone else being on board the aircraft.

'Jesus, dammit to hell! The line's busy,' Johnnie said returning to watch the report.

'They are saying only two men were on the plane and Charles is missing.' Katya sat in a lounge chair, deeply shocked by the apparent death of the Merchant Company pilot.

'Honey, I've got to go.' Johnnie went to the table and picked up his car keys. 'I've got to get into the office. There'll be news people breaking the doors down for a story. I'll have to draft an official media statement.' He returned and kissed her on the cheek. 'I'll tell you about it later,' he said heading for the door. 'Oh.' He stopped and turned. 'If Elanora calls tell her I'm on my way to the office and I'll ring her from there.'

'Darling, wait . . .' Katya called, but the door closed and he was gone.

龍

In the suite of rooms at the Hotel Beau-Rivage, Jeanne Marceau lay awake, staring at the ceiling. A light breeze drifted through the window, stirring the silk curtains, throwing a ray of moonlight across the room. She looked at her watch. It was three a.m. Then she looked again at the sleeping form of James Merchant before slipping out of bed and crossing to the double doors that led to the living room.

Closing the doors behind her, she quickly gathered her clothing from around the room, remembering the way she'd so brazenly stripped for him when they'd reached his suite. She had done so intentionally, leaving her clothes in the living room, in order to make good her escape. She dressed as fast as she could. Then, after checking her appearance in the large wall mirror, she quietly slipped out of the front door and headed for the elevators.

龍

It was just after midday when the telephone rang in Macau. Elanora had seen the news reports on television and was pacing the floor, waiting impatiently, but the shrill noise still succeeded in startling her.

'Hello?' she said quickly.

'Madame Merchant?' the caller asked.

'Jeanne? Is that you?'

'Oui, Madame.'

'Thank God, you've called.' Elanora sat on the chair by the telephone table. 'Let's have it, my girl. What did you find out?'

'You were right, Madame Merchant, there was another person on the plane.'

'I knew it. Thank you, Jeanne, you have done well.

'Merci, Madame.' She was always polite to the bank's top clients, especially those she spied for. 'But there is more, Madame.'

'Tell me all you know.'

Several minutes later, Elanora hung up, and in her apartment in Geneva, Jeanne Marceau replaced the handpiece with a feeling of satisfaction. It had been worthwhile. Payment would be made in the prompt and customary manner. Elanora Merchant was always reliable.

'Marie-Louise,' she called to her lover in the kitchen. 'How does a few days of sunbathing in Monte Carlo appeal to you?'

She was answered by a delighted squeal as her girlfriend rushed into the living room and descended upon her.

龍

Jet Kwan eased the yoke from his shoulders and emptied the two buckets of water he'd carried from the dam into the water tank behind the main house. He was angry. Why could they not install plumbing like normal people? Why was his father so resistant to change? Even the poorest people in the housing estates of Kowloon had access to tap water.

For ten years Jet had been a faithful student at his father's retreat, cleaning, scrubbing and polishing everything from the furniture to pots and pans – even the stone flagging in the central courtyard. Then, in between the meaningless chores, he instructed several village children in the most rudimentary forms of *Shaolin* in return for rice, vegetables and meat.

My sister, he thought on the other hand, *has had years of experience living and training in Australia. She is the lucky one. She took* Ju Mo's *offer and went abroad, as I should have done, and now she is a medical doctor working at the Kowloon Hospital.*

He could count on one hand the number of times he'd been allowed to venture into Kowloon alone, and on the occasions he'd dared to complain, his father insisted the 'real' world was right here in Kap Lung. The 'outside' world, he was told, was a world full of vice and corruption, where humans were no better than animals and greed, avarice and material gluttony abounded. Inner peace and harmony, he was informed, could only be found in hard work, and the contemplation of the nature of the world.

But how can I contemplate the nature of things I have yet to perceive? The very idea is ridiculous, he thought. I am twenty-eight years old and I've yet to see any of the world I'm expected to contemplate. I am twenty-eight years old and I am living the life of a *Shaolin* monk and yet I am no such thing. I am twenty-eight years old and have yet even to touch a woman intimately.

He heard the telephone ring and smiled grimly. The telephone, he thought, was the only instrument of modern technology his father had allowed at the Kap Lung School. His grandmother had insisted on its installation and his father had finally capitulated.

He entered the house and removed the hessian sack his father insisted it remain wrapped in.

'Hello,' he snapped into the handset.

'*Jet, it is your grandmother, I need to speak to your father urgently.*'

'So do I, Grandmother,' he grumbled. 'So do I.'

'*It is urgent, Jet,*' she insisted.

'*Please wait, Grandmother.*'

Jet found his father in the small blacksmith's hut vigorously pumping the forge bellows.

'*Father.*'

'Not now, Jet,' Lee answered. '*I must replace the shoes on our old ox before –* '

'It is Grandmother,' the boy interrupted. Jet Kwan hated calling his father to the telephone, knowing how much he detested the instrument. If it had been anyone other than his grandmother making the demand he would have refused point blank. '*She wishes to talk to you on the telephone. She is very insistent, Father.*'

Jet watched his father walk across the long, rectangular courtyard and disappear into the house. I must try to talk to him, he thought. I must try to tell him of my discontent. I have lost the inner peace I once knew. Now I have nothing but inner turmoil and if I do not escape, I'll go mad.

'*Mother,*' Lee said, placing the handset to his ear.

'*Lee. You must go to Geneva at once.*' Elanora spoke rapidly.

'*Calm down, Elanora,*' he answered gently. '*Tell me what has transpired?*'

'*We have a window of opportunity. It is a small window, but a window nonetheless. We must act quickly.*'

Lee listened patiently as Elanora recounted her story.

'*What James has done is abhorrent,*' he said when she'd finished, '*but I have told you already, I will not go to Geneva. I have explained why.*'

'*But Terrence Delaney is dead, understand or not understand? James cannot get the stones. He is to fly back from Geneva tonight. If you leave now you can thwart him.*'

'*The stones are of no interest to me, Mother. They are bad joss.*'

'*Throw them in the ocean for all I care, but you must go and redeem them.*'

'*I will not,*' Lee said firmly.

'*Then give the medallion to me.*'

'*To you?*'

'*Yes!*' Elanora said desperately. '*The caveat Richard placed on the account does not specify who should present the medallion. It merely states that a sixth or seventh unnamed person can present the medallion after answering a series of questions. I know the answers. I can go, understand or not understand? I can redeem the eyes myself.*'

'*Are you desperate for money, Mother? Or is it simply that you don't want James to have the eyes?*' Lee was deeply disappointed in her.

'*Yes, that's right. I need money, my son. Please, I beg you, give me the medallion.*'

She's lying, he thought. But why? Then he understood, and his shame was monumental. Elanora didn't want the eyes at all. She only wanted the medallion. She wanted it because she knew James would kill whoever had it in their possession.

'*Lee? Are you still there?*'

'*Yes, Mother.*' He touched the gold chain around his neck. She is prepared to die for me, he thought, and a deep sorrow descended upon him.

'*Give me the medallion, please,*' she begged.

'*I cannot, Elanora.*' He felt a breeze rush through the doorway and the little ornament suddenly went cold against his chest.

'*Two tigers cannot live on one mountain, understand or not understand?*' He could hear the fear in her voice now. '*James is coming for it, Lee. He is insane. He will kill you to get it. Please give it to me.*'

'*The wheel of life turns for us all, Elanora.*'

'*Don't do this, my son,*' Elanora begged. '*Please, for my sake? For the sake of your children? Please!*'

'*I am sorry, Mother,*' he said softly, and replaced the handset in its cradle.

CHAPTER SEVENTEEN

The heat of mid-July hit Jeremy Bent like a furnace blast as he stepped through the arrivals door at Hong Kong's Kai Tak Airport. The temperature, coupled with the high humidity, soon had his clothes wringing wet.

He saw his police Land Rover parked directly opposite and his driver, who'd been leaning against the bonnet smoking, quickly snapped to attention upon spying his Divisional Inspector. The young constable threw his cigarette butt into the gutter and almost leapt across the road to take Jeremy's suitcase from him.

'Ah Sir,' he said cheerfully in Chinglish, the language perfected over the years by the Hong Kong Police. '*Lei yau* good time in Sing-a-pore?' He almost sang the sentence. 'You find the *leng lui* and have the good time, yes?'

'Yes,' Jeremy chuckled, 'I found the beautiful girl and had the good time.'

'She the *gwai lui* or the *tong lui*?'

'She is an English girl, not Chinese.' Georgina was in fact one-eighth part Chinese, Jeremy thought, but to open a conversation on that topic, in Chinglish, would be worse than discussing Newton's Laws of Gravity. He opened the rear door of the Land Rover, threw in his hand luggage and got into the front passenger's seat.

The young policeman slammed the rear door and got into the driver's seat. 'This *gwai lui*, she have the good blest I fink, yes?'

'The word is "breasts", Constable Ho,' Jeremy replied, fully aware that the young officer was practising his English, for without it he'd stand little chance of promotion. 'It's plural, and yes, she has fabulous breasts.'

'Fa-bu-lous,' the Constable enunciated as he started the vehicle. 'I do not know this word, Ah Sir. Fa-bu-lous,' he repeated taking great care to pronounce the 'l' correctly. 'What it mean?'

'*Mo dak ting,*' Jeremy translated.

'*Waaaah,*' the young driver exclaimed. Roughly translated, *mo dak ting* meant indescribable. He swung the Land Rover into traffic with the reckless abandon all police drivers seem obliged to employ. 'Your *gwai lui*, she have the blest what is *mo dak ting*. Fa-bu-lous.'

'Yes,' Jeremy said firmly. 'But if you don't mind I'd rather not have any further discussion of my wife's breasts.'

'She is your *tai tai*?' the Constable exclaimed. 'She is your wife, Ah Sir, *hai m hai ah*?'

'*M hai!*' Jeremy gave himself a mental kick in the backside as a vision of James Merchant appeared before him waving a shotgun. 'Not true, she is definitely not my *tai tai*. She was just a *gwai lui* I met in Singapore. Now shut up and take me to Mong Kok *Chai Gwoon*.'

'You no go to Mong Kok Police Station, Ah Sir,' the driver replied with a definite shake of his head.

'*Dim gai?*'

'I don't know why, Ah Sir.' The constable took an envelope from the dashboard and handed it to Jeremy. 'This letter will tell you why. All your fings are packed in the rear compartment. All your uniforms, Ah Sir.'

'My uniforms? What's going on?'

'I only know I take you to Sha Tau Kok *Chai Gwoon*, Mista Bent.'

'Sha Tau Kok? Up on the border?'

'Yes, Ah Sir. I fink you maybe are transferred there, Ah Sir. There is *ma faan* yesterday at Sha Tau Kok.'

'Trouble? What sort of trouble?'

'The *kung yan*, they open fire yesterday,' the driver explained as he turned onto the main road to the New Territories.

'The workers opened fire? Are you saying the Chinese opened fire across the border?'

'Yes, *Dai Loh*. The *kung yan* open fire on Sha Tau Kok *Chai Gwoon*. They kill five policemen yesterday.'

Jeremy ripped open the letter and read it quickly. The Constable was right. He'd been transferred, effective immediately, from Mong Kok in Kowloon District to Sha Tau Kok in the New Territories. As he read on a feeling of deep unease spread through him. He put the letter back in its envelope and stared out of the window, his uneasiness now replaced by cold fear.

He could not believe that the situation in Hong Kong could have deteriorated further in only five days. But there it was, in black and white. The Colony had been declared a state of emergency when he'd left, but now it sounded like it was on the brink of war.

Strictly speaking, he decided, the 'border incident', as the letter so blithely referred to the murder of the five policemen, could be construed by the British Government as an act of war. The tone of his transfer order suggested that the Hong Kong Government was going to play the incident down, but it also suggested that if any further incidents occurred, there could be an international confrontation.

And I'll be sitting right in the middle of it! he thought. Christ. At this moment I am being driven to the hottest spot on the entire planet. And I just got married. A vision of Georgina on the beach at Baan Taling Nam with her breasts exposed filled his mind.

He looked at his driver. 'Do you think there will be any more *ma faan* at Sha Tau Kok?'

'Yes.' The Constable nodded without taking his eyes off the road. '*Ho daai laan ma faan!*' He nodded again. 'How you say in English? Big fucking trouble. But better you should say big shooting trouble. They will not do the fucking like with the woman, they will do the shooting like with the gun, I fink!'

They drove on in silence, each policeman alone with his thoughts. Jeremy considered their situation. There was no worse feeling for a police officer of whatever rank than uncertainty. That was why command and control were the very essence of policing. Not knowing the extent of a situation, and therefore not being able to at least guess at a probable outcome, made men nervous and uneasy, and it was particularly so with policing. For police officers, a clear understanding of a situation and a clear set of orders to follow were all that were required to weigh the probability of a successful outcome in their favour, but a lack of either element in the equation could mean failure. And failure to a police officer could mean death.

Such were the thoughts that occupied the two men as they drove north into the New Territories beyond the Kowloon Mountains. Jeremy had the constable stop in the town of Tai Po and he bought them both a meal in a small roadside shop. Then they continued north, crawling inexorably closer and closer to the Shum Chun River, the small watercourse, almost a creek in places, that constituted the border between the British Crown Colony of Hong Kong and the Peoples' Republic of China.

They drove through the town of Fan Ling, now a temporary home to the hastily formed Anti-riot Squads, and the place was a hive of activity. The town and its inhabitants fed off the operations of the new unit, supplying it with many of its requirements from food to mosquito netting. Today, to Jeremy at least, it seemed as if everyone in the area was working overtime. Police vehicles scurried here and there, their horns angrily demanding right of way over hawkers' carts, food and medical supply trucks and people. The police force was getting ready for any possibility and the increased local activity was the result, Jeremy assumed, of what had occurred yesterday, in the border village that lay not five miles ahead of him.

About one mile short of Sha Tau Kok they came to a road block and, what appeared to Jeremy, to be some sort of temporary command post. There was a number of police trucks and Land Rovers parked strategically in a square formation for protection and several riot platoons were standing in the middle of the square, mingling with Gurkhas.

Jeremy had worked with the Gurkha Regiments on many occasions in the past; in his opinion they were the finest soldiers in the British Army and the very sight of them cheered him no end. He saw, too, one of their officers, a Major, and recognised him immediately. He was talking to another, younger police officer.

'Let me out here, Constable,' he ordered. 'Take my gear up to the station, then you can return to Kowloon.' He got out of the vehicle.

'Well, well,' the other officer called as he caught sight of Jeremy, 'you must be the new Chief Inspector, come to save us all from the Chinese hordes. I'm Inspector Geoffrey Stevens, Sir. How do you do?' he said extending his hand.

Jeremy shook it, but Stevens' flippant remark had annoyed him. 'Mr Stevens, what in God's name went on yesterday?'

'Just a minute, Sir,' Stevens said. He indicated the Gurkha officer. 'Do you know Major Bronte?'

'Yes, I do.' He shook hands with Anthony Bronte. 'How are you, Tony?'

'A bit shaken up if you must know, Jeremy. We could very well be on the brink of bloody war and no one seems to have a blasted handle on it.'

'Is that so?' Jeremy's gloom returned.

'He's not wrong, Sir,' Stevens said nodding rapidly. 'The village,' he indicated north towards the border with his thumb, 'turned into World War III yesterday. The bloody Red Chinese opened fire on Sha Tau Kok Station.'

'Are you sure it was the Chinese Army?'

'No, we're not,' Tony Bronte chimed in. 'No one is, and that's the problem. No one actually got a look at any of the snipers. They opened fire from less than one hundred yards, but they were well concealed and the firing was sporadic, not really co-ordinated, if you know what I mean.'

'Well, no, I don't,' Jeremy admitted. 'Not exactly.'

'Well I'm of the opinion,' Major Bronte continued, 'that they weren't PLA soldiers. I mean, if they were, they would have maintained constant fire, you know? They'd have kept up some sort of sustained attack in order to seize the post, as a first step in taking the Colony. And I can't see the point in it, really. I mean, if the Chinese Government wanted to take Hong Kong they could do it with a bloody telephone call. There's no need for them to shoot anyone, is there?'

'No.' Jeremy shook his head. 'I see your point.'

'Well, I'm having none of it,' Geoff Stevens said angrily. He lit a cigarette and Jeremy noticed his hands were shaking. 'For all we know bloody Peking may have half the bloody PLA lined up, out of sight on the other side of the border.'

'And there's my point,' Tony Bronte said. 'Two different opinions and no evidence. Young Stevens and I are no different to the powers that be in London. No one at home seems able to make up their minds on what occurred, let alone what anyone should do about it. We've had no orders, no instructions of any kind. Everyone above the rank of Major seems to be fence sitting, if you get my point.'

'Well, there's nothing new in that, is there?' Jeremy's comment brought a laugh from the Gurkha officer, but the young Inspector Geoffrey Stevens looked blankly at the horizon and puffed rapidly on his cigarette.

'Inspector,' Jeremy called him back to the present, 'were you up there yesterday?'

'No, thank Christ,' Stevens muttered. 'I was at Man Kam To Station, on relief duty.'

'What happened? Do you know?'

'They shot the blazing daylights out of the place.' Stevens dropped his cigarette and extinguished it with his boot. 'That's what happened. Five rank and file were killed.'

'No officers?'

'No, praise God!' Stevens laughed mirthlessly. 'There are only two of us, the Senior Divisional Inspector and me.'

'And where's the SDI now?'

'He's been called into HQ on Hong Kong Island, supposedly to offer advice to the Joint Army Police Intelligence Committee, half his luck.'

Jeremy watched the boy, for that's all Stevens was, as he lit another cigarette and glanced about nervously. 'You're his replacement, from what I can gather,' Stevens said, seeming to make the statement as an afterthought. 'Somebody at HQ must have it in for you.'

'So you're the Senior Officer at Sha Tau Kok today?'

'Not now.' Stevens gave a mock salute. 'You're here, and you're bloody welcome to it.'

'What are you doing down here at the road block?' Jeremy asked.

'I came down for a smoke.' Stevens leaned against a vehicle. 'A bit of a breather, so to speak.'

'And who's in charge at the station?' James ground out through clenched teeth.

'The Station Sergeant's there and – '

'Stand to attention when you address a Senior Officer!' Jeremy roared the order.

'Sir!' Stevens snapped to attention.

'Now, you listen to me, Inspector,' Jeremy snarled. 'Five men died in that station yesterday. Am I to understand that you've left the others alone with their fear and grief, worried sick that it might be their turn today, to come down here and have a cigarette?' He could hardly contain his fury.

'No, I mean – '

'What's going on over the border at the moment? Do you have any idea? How do you know the station isn't under fire at this very minute?'

'Because the station is crawling with – '

'*Not another word!* You get back to your post right now, Inspector, do you hear me?!' Jeremy leaned into the young man's face. 'You get up there immediately and at least *try* to give the impression that *someone* is in command of the situation! I'll be fifteen minutes behind you.'

'Yes, Sir!' Stevens saluted and then stood stock still, waiting.

'A salute is a sign of respect.' Jeremy lowered his voice to a sneering whisper. 'You don't seriously expect me to return it, do you?'

'No, Sir.' Stevens lowered his arm to his side.

'Now move!' Jeremy roared.

'I'm sorry about that,' Jeremy said to an embarrassed Major Bronte, when the young man had gone. 'Some of the recruits we get these days . . .' he finished lamely and shrugged.

'He's got the jitters,' Bronte said, watching the young Inspector depart. 'You may well have a problem on your hands with him.' He turned to Jeremy and sniffed disdainfully. 'We don't have that sort of problem in the Gurkhas Regiments.'

'No, indeed.' Jeremy decided he'd talk to the lad as soon as he had an opportunity. 'As a matter of fact,' he said, keen to change the subject, 'I'm rather glad your lot is here. Can I rely on you if the proverbial hits the fan again?'

'Of course,' the Major said stiffly. 'If I hear so much as a gunshot, my men will be all over your station like grey paint on a battleship.' His face then softened. 'Mind you, if fifty Communist divisions are pouring over the border when we get there, I'd say we'd be of little help.'

'Well,' Jeremy smiled and offered his hand, 'come anyway.'

'We'll be there,' Tony Bronte nodded, shaking hands. 'Good luck.'

Jeremy's arrival at the station went unheralded and he was appalled. He was not even wearing his uniform and yet he'd been allowed not only to approach the gate without being challenged, but had actually walked right into the Charge Room without being noticed.

He leaned over the Charge Room counter and saw a young Constable busily scrubbing the floor. 'Where is your Inspector?' he asked.

'*Mei ah wah?*' the young man said, leaping to his feet.

'I said,' Jeremy replied loudly, '*Lei ge Bong Baan hai bin do ah?*'

Before the startled young man could answer, another voice intervened. 'Inspector is not here. I am the Station Sergeant. Can I help you?'

Jeremy spun round to see a stocky, balding Chinese aiming a Colt revolver at him. 'What's your name, Sergeant?'

'I think,' the man replied, 'you must tell me your name first.'

Jeremy smiled. 'Well done, Sergeant, it's good to see someone around here is on the ball.' He reached carefully into his pocket and withdrew his wallet. He opened it and showed the man his Hong Kong Police Warrant Card. 'I'm your new boss. My name is Bent. Chief Inspector Jeremy Bent.'

The man inspected Jeremy's picture on his ID and the relief that flooded his face was obvious. He put his revolver into its holster and saluted. 'Station Sergeant Fong, Ah Sir. I am very happy you are here. It is good for HQ to send a Chief *Bong Baan* to Sha Tau Kok. Since yesterday we only have the baby *Bong Baan*.'

'And where is our baby *Bong Baan* at the moment?'

'Inspector Stevens, he has gone on a border inspection with all the *Geng Si*.'

'There are Superintendents here?' Jeremy felt a cold shiver run down his spine. Of course, he cursed himself, the place would be crawling with Senior Officers by now. That's obviously what young Stevens had attempted to tell him when he'd dressed him down in front of the Gurkha Major.

'Yes, Sir. They all come from Hong Kong and Kowloon to make what they call the evaluation of the situation, I think.'

'Jesus, how many of them?'

'*Ho do*, Ah Sir. Very many.'

'Are any still here?'

'One man is still here, but he is not Hong Kong Police. He is from the Government, I think. He has been looking at the village through the binoculars.'

'Right. I'd better get into uniform first, then have a chat with this fellow.'

'It is good to wear the uniform, Ah Sir. If the men see your *saam laap*,' he tapped his shoulder with three fingers emulating the three pips worn on the shoulder by Chief Inspectors, 'they will be very happy. They will like to have a Chief Inspector as officer in charge.'

'Well said, Sergeant,' he nodded. 'I'll get into uniform straightaway. We'll do a station inspection and hopefully run into this Government chap.'

The station inspection revealed to Jeremy the true extent of what had occurred the day previously. There were bullet holes everywhere, windows had been shot out and there were bloodstains inside, and out in the courtyard.

'I want the bloodstains cleaned up, Sergeant Fong,' he said.

'A detail has already started, Ah Sir,' the stocky Sergeant assured him.

'And I want the lookouts replaced every two hours. But I want this station secured first. When the *Geng Si* come back, I want them properly challenged before they're allowed to set foot in this place, *understand or not understand*?'

'Yes, Sir.' Sergeant Fong saluted smartly.

'Very well.' Jeremy returned the salute. He was about to issue further orders when a man in a grey suit entered the room.

'Excuse me,' the man said in a very British accent. 'Would you by any chance be Chief Inspector Bent?'

'I am. Carry on, Sergeant.'

'Yes, Sir,' Fong replied and left the room.

'My name is Maynard Pottinger.'

'And your business here, Mr Pottinger, is . . . ?'

'Please, call me Maynard. My business, if that's the right word for it, is to act as a go-between. I'm employed by the Ministry of Foreign Affairs in London. I came to Hong Kong last month to act in an advisory capacity to the Governor, but now I find myself having to report not only to him, but to my superiors in London as well.'

'Well perhaps you could advise me, too,' Jeremy smiled. 'I have absolutely no idea what transpired here yesterday. Would you care for a chat in my office? That is, if I can find it. I was only transferred here this morning.'

'Yes, I know,' Pottinger replied. 'Recommended by the District Police Commander Kowloon, no less.'

'The DPC Kowloon, eh?' Jeremy raised an eyebrow. 'Old Robbity Bob Mulvaine. I knew he didn't like me.'

'On the contrary,' Pottinger replied, as he followed Jeremy in search of his office, 'he said you were a damned fine officer. Said you could be relied upon to remain calm in a flap.'

Jeremy found what he assumed was the office of the officer in charge and when they were seated, he spoke very directly. 'Is there going to be a war between us and China?'

'A war? Good God, no,' Pottinger chuckled. 'Without going into the specifics of yesterday's little incident – '

'Yesterday's *little incident*?' Jeremy interrupted. His voice was cold. 'Five of my police colleagues were murdered in yesterday's *little incident*, Mr Pottinger.'

'Yes,' the man muttered, reacting to Jeremy's tone. 'Yes, I'm awfully sorry. That must have sounded terribly off-hand. It's the way we tend to speak in my business. I do apologise.'

'And precisely what is your business? Are you MI5 or MI6?'

'Oh, no,' Pottinger chuckled, 'nothing quite so grand. I'm not a spy, Chief Inspector. I'm simply Foreign Office.' He shrugged. 'I'm a political analyst, for want of a better description.'

'Very well. Your apology is accepted. Please continue.'

'Well, the horrific events of yesterday will probably go a long way towards easing the problem between us and them.' He pointed northward towards Mainland China. 'You see, the Chinese Government in Peking has long thought that there is an invasion pact existing between Britain and the United States of America.'

'And is there?'

'To be perfectly honest with you, I don't know. But that's the whole point, you see? Neither do the Chinese.'

'Mr Pottinger.' Jeremy stood up and moved to the window where he looked cautiously out over the small village of Sha Tau Kok and the plains of Communist China beyond. 'Don't give me obtuse political rhetoric. I'm not the Governor of Hong Kong. I'm a simple policeman with a job to do. I've never been stationed on the border before and I'd like to know if I'm to be the first casualty in a bloody war with the PLA. Just tell me what you think will happen next.'

'Nothing,' Pottinger replied and gazed at a military map on the wall.

Jeremy looked at him. 'Nothing?'

'Precisely.' He smiled at Jeremy. 'In my opinion, the murder of those five men yesterday was not an act ordered by Peking, nor was it an act of the Red Guards, as stupid as they are. It was engineered by hard-core Maoist fanatics from inside Hong Kong.'

'From inside Hong Kong, you say?' Jeremy returned to the desk and sat down. 'Do go on.'

'I'll keep it simple, shall I?' Pottinger stood and scratched his chin, then moved to examine the wall map more closely. 'In a nutshell, Hong Kong's Maoists went much too far yesterday. Peking will not come to their aid. Peking will drop them like a hot potato.

'When Hong Kong's riots first erupted in May,' Pottinger continued, 'the residents of the Colony thought, as indeed did people abroad, that it was a momentary aberration, a simple reflection of the political upheaval taking place on the Mainland. In short, they thought it was a flash in the pan and that business would quickly resume as usual.

'You see,' he sat down opposite Jeremy, 'China and Hong Kong have always co-existed peacefully, and the reason is not one of altruism; it's purely financial. Since 1949 the Communists in Hong Kong, who make up half of the population, I might point out, have built up a network of more than five hundred businesses and banks in the Colony. Each year, these enterprises pour more than five hundred million dollars into the Communists' most important economic organisation in the Colony, the Bank of China. The bank in turn transmits each year, to Peking, more than half of China's foreign exchange. Are you following me so far, Chief Inspector?'

'Yes,' Jeremy replied. 'I'm with you.'

'Good. Now you must ask yourself, why did the Communists take to the streets this spring and risk killing the goose that lays their golden eggs?'

'Tell me.' Jeremy put his elbows on the desk and rested his chin in his hands.

'The political turmoil inside Mainland China has been brought about by the actions of none other than the egomaniacal Mao Tse-tung himself. The rampant thuggery of the Red Guards and the persecution of whole classes of people inspired Hong Kong's Maoists to indulge in their own political thuggery in capitalist Hong Kong, to show their beloved Chairman how fervently their political ardour burns.

'Well, of course Chairman Mao smiled benevolently on these fanatics who live in his foreign piggy bank, believing it was high time the British learned just how powerful China has become. But my opinion is that yesterday's actions by Hong Kong's Maoists went too far, even for Chairman Mao's liking. He and his ministers are now faced with not only the possibility of severed diplomatic relations with Great Britain, but even worse – the loss of five hundred million dollars a year in foreign exchange.'

'So what you're suggesting is, things will cool down. Am I right?' Jeremy had picked up a ruler and was now tapping it absent-mindedly on the desk.

'Precisely,' Pottinger nodded. 'You see, by nature the Chinese are capitalists to the core and this is especially so of the wealthy Hong Kong business clique. The Cantonese are genetically programmed to make money.' He smiled at his little joke. 'Communism is by definition anathema to them; it means the sharing of a nation's wealth equally and that very principle goes against the Cantonese psychological make up.'

'And yet you say they give half of their money to Peking, annually, through the Bank of China.'

'Correct,' Pottinger raised his forefinger and gave a wry smile, 'but don't forget, they keep the other half.'

'Ah, yes. Of course.' Jeremy dropped the ruler on the desk. 'So, they pay Peking a fee of fifty per cent to keep their little capitalist enclave alive?'

'Precisely. And like their masters in Peking, they want it to remain alive. But,' Maynard Pottinger stood, 'one or two genuine Maoist fanatics in Hong Kong put it all at risk yesterday, with an idiotic plot that fooled no one, especially Peking. And my guess is they'll be put back in their proper place today, you mark my words.'

Pottinger walked to the door and was nearly bowled over by the breathless entrance of Geoffrey Stevens. 'Excuse me,' he gasped, stopping in front of Jeremy's desk. 'Sir, I've got a load of brass hats in the Charge Room and no tea. What should I do?'

'You see, Mr Bent?' Pottinger remarked. 'Tea. It has solved the British Empire's problems since time immemorial. Things are returning to normal already.' He offered two fingers in a mock salute. 'I must get back to Honkers. Probably won't see you again. Hope my assessment of the situation is of assistance to you.'

龍

Johnnie Wilson drove through Wanchai on his way to Central and the offices of the Merchant Company in Ice House Street. It was eight o'clock on Monday morning and usually the streets would be packed with people beginning a new week, but today it was not the case. The streets were practically deserted. Apart from several groups of Urban Services workers, cleaning up the mess, and the ubiquitous grey police Land Rovers of the police Anti-riot Squads, there was no one to be seen. All the shops were closed and the trams that usually blocked traffic on Hennessey Road had vanished.

He drove past several burnt out cars and another overturned and still smouldering, the result of the Wanchai riots the previous day. On that Sunday, after preparing the press release regarding James and the aircraft, Johnnie'd had to drive right around the island in order to avoid the demonstrations and get home to Katya.

Hong Kong was in its death throes and Johnnie had decided to pack up his belongings and take his wife away. Where he didn't know, but leave they would, because to stay was simply asking for trouble. His fear had been justified by the headline in the *South China Morning Post*. He looked again at the newspaper on the car seat beside him: 'FIVE MURDERED AT SHA TAU KOK'. Five policemen were dead and the Colony was in mortal fear of invasion by the PLA. The Government had not seen fit to release the news of the murders until this morning, given the rioting in the streets of Wanchai and the panic it could have provoked, but it had proven to be the final straw for Johnnie Wilson.

Elanora had tried to allay his fears about Hong Kong's future on the phone the previous day. He'd called her from his office as the riots were taking place in Hennessey Road and they'd discussed the deepening crisis Hong Kong faced. The Colony was a powder keg in danger of exploding and there were also unconfirmed reports making the rounds about some sort of trouble on the border.

Elanora declared she'd never known anything quite like it, but had suggested that the Colony had faced problems with China before and had always been able to come to some sort of agreement. But Johnnie had not been convinced and when she'd finally attempted to discuss James and the gemstones, he'd listened politely but it had seemed irrelevant, given the current situation.

And now, this morning, the newspapers were filled with the incident on the border at Sha Tau Kok. Even the riots in Wanchai, which had seen two people killed and countless others injured on both sides, had only made the second page, and James' little incident with the Merchant Company jet had been reduced to a single paragraph on page four.

Johnnie got out of his car in the car park beneath the Merchant Company building and took the elevator to the top floor. He went to his office and no sooner had he thrown his coat over his chair than Twiggy, his secretary, entered, her hands full of telex messages.

'Mister Wilson, these messages have come from all over the world. Investors are worried about the situation in Hong Kong and they all want answers.'

'Well, I don't have any answers,' Johnnie snapped, causing an immediate quiver from Twiggy's bottom lip. 'I'm sorry,' he apologised immediately. 'I didn't mean to yell at you, but until someone in the Government makes some sort of statement, I can't reply to those messages.' He patted her on the shoulder. 'Be a good girl and get me a coffee, will you, then give everyone the same answer – '

'What answer?' Twiggy snapped as tears filled her eyes. 'The *taipan* won't give me an answer either.'

'James is here?'

'Yes. He is in his office. He yelled at me, too.'

If Twiggy expected any comfort it was not forthcoming. Johnnie flew out of his office and disappeared.

'Johnnie, my lad,' James declared as the American arrived in front of his desk.

'Where the fuck have you been?' demanded Johnnie, angrily.

'Now, Johnnie – '

'Have you seen what's been going on out there?' Johnnie said pointing to the window. 'This Colony is in deep shit, James, and you take off for a week on a fucking treasure hunt?'

James eyed Johnnie suspiciously. 'You seem very well informed.'

'What's it matter now?' Johnnie yelled.

'Elanora,' James nodded. 'I should have guessed. You two have no secrets from each other do you? You know what I think – '

'I don't give a flying fuck what you think!' Johnnie shouted him down. 'While you've been off on your wild goose chase, in which, I might add, you made the world news by not only destroying the Lear-24, but managing to kill Charlie Middleditch, this place has turned into a fucking nightmare.'

'Just how much do you know,' James stood up behind his desk and walked around to the American, 'about my, what did you call it? My "wild goose chase"?' They stood toe to toe, glaring at each other.

'You're behaving like a fool, James.' Johnnie broke eye contact and sat in a large leather chair. He shook his head and laughed softly. 'In the last two months, while you've been busy leaving your wife, destroying your family, fucking every whore in Kowloon and chasing after precious stones that may or may not even exist,' he waved his hands in the air, 'have you noticed what the stock markets have been doing?'

'You seem intent on telling me,' James said, sitting on the desk. It seemed that even Johnnie had turned against him, too. 'Go on.'

'They started to drop. Slowly at first, I must admit, but over the last week while you've been off treasure hunting, things got a little more serious until, by midnight last night, shares in the Merchant Company and all of its subsidiaries have dropped between five and nine per cent.'

'What?' James was genuinely alarmed.

'Oh, yeah,' Johnnie drawled sarcastically in his worst Texan accent. 'This last week has been a doozie. And, with the goddamn gunfight at the OK Corral on the border, they've probably dropped as much again. We're looking at a fucking meltdown of somewhere between fifteen and twenty per cent here, Jimbo. We're staring into the face of a fucking crash!'

'Christ.' James' face was ashen.

'And he ain't gonna help you. You either convince your shareholders, both here and in London and New York, that Hong Kong is not facing a takeover by the People's Republic of China, or you, old buddy, are facing financial ruin.' Johnnie leapt to his feet. 'Do I have your fucking attention now, Wing Commander?'

'Yes!' James roared back. 'All right.' He crossed to the window and stared at the harbour. Nothing and no one would destroy his company. He made the vow silently. He would survive. He was James Merchant, *taipan*, and he would weather all they could throw at him. And 'they' included his mother and the devious bastard whom he'd once called his friend, Johnnie Wilson.

Johnnie felt a sudden and inexplicable surge of sympathy for James. 'You've been looking through your gunsights concentrating on a target that just wasn't there, Jimbo.' He crossed to the window and put his arm around James' shoulders. 'And now you've got Mig-15s all over your tail. I think it's about time you listened to your wingman, don't you?'

'I don't need sympathy,' James said coldly. Shrugging Johnnie's arm off, he returned to his desk. 'Especially from a man who has been conspiring with my mother to bring about my downfall.'

'Am I hearin' you right, pardner?' Johnnie stepped away from the window. On his face was a look of utter disbelief.

'She was your mistress,' James sneered, 'and now she's your co-conspirator in a coup designed to unseat me from the Company chairmanship.'

'You're out of your mind, James.'

'Am I?' He smirked. 'You were both no doubt aware that the share prices were falling and obviously decided not to tell me.'

'How could I tell you? I couldn't find you!' Johnnie approached the desk and leaned over it. 'First, you took off for Geneva without telling anyone, then you were in London and then back in Geneva again. I tried to contact you, James, but you didn't want to know about it!'

'Get out of my office,' James said flatly, pure malice in his eyes.

Johnnie stood erect and looked at the friend he'd known for fifteen years. 'I'll not only get out of your office,' he said coolly, 'I'll get out of your life altogether.' He walked to the door and opened it. 'You're insane, James.'

'Better still . . .' James reached into his desk drawer and withdrew a silver-plated Colt .45 automatic. He aimed it squarely at Johnnie. 'I'd advise you to get out of Hong Kong altogether, John. I deal swiftly with those I can't trust. You of all people ought to know that.'

'Well, now, don't that just beat all,' the Texan drawled, pointing at the gleaming silver weapon. Then he left, closing the door softly behind him.

James continued to point the handgun at the door, then placed it gently on the desk. It lay there, shining brightly in the light from the windows. The inscription was clear: 'TO JAMES, IN CASE YOU HIT THE DECK, FROM JOHNNIE. KOREA, 1951.'

龍

The following day at the Extraordinary Chairman's Meeting called by James, Elanora voted in favour of the Merchant

Company Financial Defensive Strategy he'd put forward to the board of directors. It was quite brilliant in its simplicity.

When Johnnie had left, James had worked all day and most of the night, moving through the world's time zones by telephone, wheeling and dealing, making pledges and calling in every favour he'd had up his sleeve. Finally, he'd stopped the bleeding and prepared the strategy, which the board had accepted, with Johnnie Wilson noticeably absent, by a vote of five to four.

'Mother,' James called as the meeting came to an end and he saw her heading out the door. 'Might I have a word?'

'We have nothing to say to each other,' she replied as he caught up with her, 'unless you want to formally terminate our relationship, but then, you need a gun to do that don't you?'

'So you've heard?'

'Katya rang to say goodbye. They're leaving for the United States tonight.'

'I wanted to say thank you for voting for my proposal.' He attempted a smile.

'Stop it!' she hissed, drawing the attention of the last board members leaving the room. 'You disgust me,' she said when they'd gone. 'Don't think I don't know what you've been up to. And now you've got the death of Charles Middleditch on your hands.'

'It was an accident.'

'Not to mention Terrence Delaney!'

James froze momentarily, then seized the boardroom doors and pulled them shut. 'What are you talking about?'

'I know what happened on that aircraft.'

'Be very careful what you say, Mother.'

'Don't threaten me, James.' Elanora raised her chin defiantly. 'If you'd paid a little more attention to the Company's share transactions over the last several weeks, you'd know that you're in no position to threaten anyone, especially me.'

'What are you saying?'

'While you've been in Europe making a fool of yourself, I, and to a lesser extent Katherine, have been buying Company shares as frantically as others have been selling them.'

'How many do you hold?' James felt a cold hand seize his stomach.

'Oh, don't worry,' Elanora said sweetly, 'not enough to unseat you as Chairman.' Then she watched, delighted as the frown eased on his brow, before driving the stake into his heart. 'That was, until this morning. I bought Johnnie Wilson's portfolio, which means as the principal stockholder, I've got you over the proverbial barrel.'

'You bitch!' Fury flooded through him.

'I must say, James, for a moment there we were on rather thin financial ice,' she laughed derisively, 'but thanks to the pledges you made to my brokers in London and New York and the brilliant proposal you put forward to the board, it looks as if I'll be wealthier than I've ever been in my entire life.'

'You won't get away with this, Elanora.'

'I already have!' She glared at him. 'And don't bother worrying Katherine with your troubles, all her stock has been notarised and pledged to your daughter.'

'What?'

'That's right. Georgina will supplant you as *taipan* when the time is right. Until then I'll allow you to retain the chairmanship as my puppet of course, on one condition.'

'And what is that?'

'Keep well away from Tai Mo Shan.'

'Why would I want to go to Tai Mo Shan?' James acted the innocent.

'Stop playing games!' Elanora hissed. 'If you go anywhere near Lee, I'll dismiss you from the board and let all of Hong Kong know how two women outsmarted you. *You will lose great face, understand or not understand, ah? I will humiliate you.* Now get out of my way.' She brushed past him and opened the doors, drawing looks from secretaries and board members alike as they milled around in the foyer, and strode triumphantly towards the elevators.

She pushed the button, then turned to James, who was standing open-mouthed in the boardroom doorway. '*When a man holds a candle, Little Brother,*' she called in Cantonese, *'he must not become transfixed by the flame, or the wax will burn his fingers, understand or not understand?'* The elevator arrived, and Elanora smiled thinly at James. Then she disappeared.

'What are you staring at?' James' outburst caused a flurry of activity – secretaries disappeared, and those board members who had remained chatting headed for the nearest exits. But they did so delighted by the knowledge that James Merchant was visibly upset and it was the Merchant Mistress, whom they adored, who had upset him.

James took an umbrella from the stand in his office and left the building. He told no one where he was going because he had no idea himself. He just needed to walk, to breathe some air and think – yes, think. He was far from defeated, despite what his gloating mother might believe. He was James Merchant, *taipan*, and he was far from defeated. He merely needed to formulate a plan of action, then go after his enemies, one by one.

Before he'd realised where he was going, he found himself in Central Square. He bought a bag of breadcrumbs from an old woman and sat feeding the perennial flock of pigeons that made the square their home. Their cooing, as they gathered in front of his legs greedily jostling each other for the morsels, had a calming effect on him. He felt his mind and body relax and his brain began its devious calculations.

Elanora came first to mind. The treacherous bitch, she would get what was coming to her. Then Johnnie Wilson, the one man he thought he could trust, came wandering into his mind's eye. The bastard, James thought. He'd sold his shares in the Company to Elanora, shares James had given to him. Well, so much for friendship. Johnnie would keep. James would have the last laugh eventually, even if he had to go to Texas and wring the bastard's neck.

And who else had conspired against him? Katherine, of course, she'd be in anything to hurt him. The Woo twins? They held shares in many of the subsidiary companies. Yes, he nodded as he sprinkled more breadcrumbs on the ground, the Woo twins had always been particularly fond of Elanora.

Perhaps she'd slept with them too? At the same time probably. The thought made him smile. He wouldn't be at all surprised, the perfidious fucking slut.

Who else? he asked himself as he stood, emptying out the last of the breadcrumbs and tossing the bag into a bin. Georgina? Had she known what her mother and grandmother were up to? And she was to become Chairman of the Company. Well, that didn't matter, she'd be the easiest to defeat.

He strode purposefully eastward, away from the business district of Central, past H.M.S. Tamar, the British Naval Base, and on towards Wanchai. And as he walked, his paranoia deepened, until the list became endless. Former friends and business associates he'd not spoken to in years suddenly became his enemies. And they would suffer for their disloyalty, he decided. With his mind spinning a web of hate in which to entrap his victims, he walked on until he found himself standing on Fenwick Pier staring across at Kowloon.

'*One dollar?*' A voice interrupted his thoughts.

He looked down at a dishevelled beggar. The old mendicant was filthy. Dressed in rags with a mat of thick black hair hanging down to his elbows, he sat cross-legged on the pier's edge with his hand outstretched.

'*You want money do you, old man?*' James asked in Cantonese. '*Well, so do I,*' he snapped, poking the man with his umbrella. '*Why don't you fuck off before I throw you into the harbour?*'

'*Chi sin gwai loh,*' the old beggar declared. He got hurriedly to his feet and moved away.

'*I'm not a crazy foreign devil, you old fool!*' James yelled after him. '*I am Chinese like you, but unlike you I'm the big boss of Hong Kong. I own this city.*' Then he cursed inwardly. 'Well, I used to own this city,' he murmured in English.

It began to rain, gently at first, but typical of Hong Kong summer rain, it soon became a deluge. James put his umbrella up and began walking aimlessly along the harbour's edge, in the direction he'd come from.

He'd been stupid in the extreme. Elanora had been right with her parting shot. He'd let his eyes become transfixed by the candle flame and he'd got his fingers burnt. He'd been so intent on getting the eyes of the dragons that he'd ignored his entire financial empire and it had almost all gone up in a puff of smoke.

He stopped walking and looked out over the harbour waters, his gaze eventually rising to the distant Kowloon Mountains, and his jumbled thoughts slowly fell into place like an enormous jigsaw puzzle. Gau Loong Shan, the Mountains of the Nine Dragons. James smiled. Just when things look their darkest . . . He'd returned to Hong Kong from Geneva resigned to the idea that the stones were not meant to be his. He'd decided enough was enough. But that had been yesterday. He hadn't needed money yesterday. Nor had he been threatened yesterday.

Elanora's words fuelled his anger as he walked on. All I need is the stones and I can own this city again, he thought. His gaze returned to Gau Loong Shan, his eyes homing in on Tai Mo Shan, the mountain that was home to Lee Kwan. Getting the medallion from Lee Kwan would be no easy task. James' interest in *Shaolin* had faded over the last few years, until he now no longer even practised the art. In a fair fight, Lee would defeat him easily. But who said it had to be fair? And what would the death of Lee do to Elanora? James stopped and laughed out loud, drawing odd looks from passers by. It would destroy her! It would break her heart!

He looked again at the distant mountains. *'It is you or me, Little Brother,'* he whispered. *'Two tigers cannot live on one mountain.'*

CHAPTER EIGHTEEN

J et Kwan sat on the front steps of the long stone hut and remembered the day he had first arrived at Kap Lung with his parents. His father had secured the long-term lease on the place, which had been held by none other than his grandfather Richard Brewster. Richard arranged for Lee to purchase the lease in 1956, making him the occupier until the New Territories lease from China expired in 1997. Together with his parents, Jet had worked hard to make the place habitable and it had been the family's home ever since.

He let his eyes wander. Before him lay the old stone courtyard on which he had practised his *Shaolin* drills since his family had first arrived from China over ten years before. He could recall the shape of each stone, because he'd swept and washed them so many times.

To his left stood another stone hut which housed his father's students – that is, when he decided to accept one, which was not often. At other times it had given shelter to the lost, and to the occasional pilgrim who'd happened to wander across the mountain.

To his right, the courtyard opened onto the hillside where he could just see the pool his father had created. His father had built a dam of stones to capture the water that, at certain times of the year, cascaded down from the mountain top. At the moment it was running freely, the result of recent monsoonal rains.

Directly opposite him was the stable, home to *Fei Jui*, their old ox, but it was empty as usual. Fat Boy had an adventurous spirit and liked to wander over the mountainside when not required to work. Jet had often been sent to find the inquisitive beast and bring him home to face his responsibilities, only to find that upon their return, his father had, whenever it had been physically possible, done Fat Boy's work for him. Lee Kwan would then spend the next hour criticising the old ox for his wanderlust while feeding him handfuls of loam sprinkled with sugar water.

Next to the stable stood the forge, where his father was at that moment working tirelessly to straighten a cart axle for a man from the village in the valley below. His father would accept no payment for his labour – that was his father's way.

Jet sat, trying desperately to capture what he hoped would be fond memories in his mind, because he was leaving Kap Lung that very day, to seek his fortune. He had not, as yet, told his father of his imminent departure. He'd had the conversation with Lee Kwan several hundred times in his mind, but now the moment of truth had arrived he was feeling a little apprehensive.

He'd called Su-lin at the hospital in Kowloon, using the telephone without his father's knowledge, and discussed the matter with her. She had agreed he should go, telling him he must follow his heart. She'd also assured him that his father would understand, but as Jet looked across at Lee, sweating in the forge, his anxiety about the impending conversation returned.

Finally, he stood and walked across the courtyard. He stopped at the entrance to the forge and called tentatively. *'Father?'*

'What is it, Jet?' Lee asked, dropping his hammer and turning to his son.

'I must talk with you,' he said stepping inside.

'I was hoping you would,' Lee said softly, *'before you left.'*

'What?'

'You have decided to leave Kap Lung, true or not true?'

'Not true – ' he began, then stopped. *'How did you know?'*

'I have been expecting it for some time now.' Lee picked up a cloth from the forge rail and dipped it into a large drum of water. He rinsed it and wiped his face and chest of sweat,

before continuing. '*I have watched you, Jet. Your discontent has become more obvious with each passing day. You have shown no interest in your work –* '

'*What work?*' Jet exclaimed. '*I do menial tasks, Father. Tasks fit only for children and old men. I live the life of a servant. You won't even let me teach, unless it is to instruct little children from the village below.*'

'*It was you who chose this work, Jet, true or not true?*' Lee stared directly at his son. '*You could have gone abroad and attended school. Your grandmother offered both you and your sister the chance. Su-lin chose to go to Australia and study medicine, but you chose to come to Kap Lung with me and set up this place.*' Lee gestured around them. '*Do you now regret your decision?*'

'*I was seventeen years old. You told me the world was a bad place and I would be better off remaining with you. You made the decision for me. And you have kept me here for ten years as your servant.*'

'*Perhaps you are right.*' Lee had been waiting for the day when Jet would break the bonds that tied him to Kap Lung and take off into the world at large. His hopes for the boy had been fading for some years. Jet would never understand the *way*. He simply didn't have the intelligence. '*I hoped you would find happiness in Kap Lung.*'

'*We live like monks here,*' Jet complained. '*I want to see the world.*'

'*You may not like what you see.*'

'*But surely that is for me to decide, Father?*'

'*You could remain here with me, Jet,*' Lee said softly, '*at least until the summer has gone. We will then discuss your desire and –* '

'*No!*' Jet stepped several paces back into the courtyard, his voice raised in protest. '*This time you will not have your way, old man!*'

'*Calm your mind, Jet. Anger is a foolish emotion.*' And one you have never learned to control, Lee thought.

'*If I remain as you suggest, you will only use your persuasive techniques to make me stay here forever.*' It was true.

His father was a master of argument. His gentle voice caressed and his tongue dripped logic until resistance became a futile exercise.

'*So your mind is made up?*'

'*Yes!*' Jet ran across the stone flagging to the long hut and grabbed his meagre bag of belongings from behind the door. He waved it at Lee and yelled across the yard. '*I am going, old man, and you will not stop me.*'

Lee stared at his son for some seconds, then he turned and picked up his hammer. He tapped it several times on the anvil and continued with his work.

'*I am leaving!*' Jet yelled. '*I have to go.*' But the only answer was the noise of hammer blows. He stared at the form of his father bent over the anvil, and then, with a shrug of his shoulders, he set off down the mountain.

At the Rest Rock, some half mile down the steep mountain track, Jet turned and looked back one last time. He saw the smoke rising from the forge chimney and he raised his hand in farewell.

'*Goodbye, old man,*' he called, but a mountain breeze swept his words away.

龍

That same morning, James Merchant walked off the Star Ferry at Kowloon terminal and disappeared into the mass of humanity in Nathan Road. He was dressed as a coolie, in black pyjama-like clothes, rubber-soled cotton slippers and a conical peasant's hat. Over his shoulder he carried a knapsack containing a bottle of drinking water, an apple, some dry biscuits and cheese, one hundred thousand dollars in cash and his silver-plated Colt .45 automatic handgun.

It was barely eight o'clock in the morning as he strolled in leisurely fashion up the wide boulevard towards Mong Kok, where he would take public transport to the New Territories. He enjoyed the anonymity afforded by his disguise. People barely gave him a second glance as he stopped occasionally to watch them opening shops and dressing the footpath with their wares.

He loved the Cantonese and he understood them. Even the Colony's state of emergency would not stop them from trading. They were totally consumed with the business of making money and to James that was the ultimate endeavour. He'd controlled several fortunes in his life, and had tasted the sweet juice of success these struggling merchants sought.

He smiled at the irony of it all as he passed a small green park. For the first time in his life he was actually poor, he thought, by his standards, anyway. His mother had outsmarted him. She'd supplanted him, while his back was turned, as powerbroker in his very own company. Hate mingled with genuine admiration for Elanora as he pictured her again, standing at the elevators, her chin raised defiantly, glaring at him.

Well, she's had her moment, he thought grimly. By tonight I'll have Lee's medallion and then we'll see who has the last laugh.

龍

'Excuse me, Ah Sir?'

'Come in, Sergeant.'

Jeremy put his pen down and rubbed his eyes. He was in the process of writing a Situation Report for the Joint Army Police Intelligence Committee, attempting to forecast events at Sha Tau Kok over the ensuing weeks, a report which he considered a waste of time.

'Kowloon Command say the villagers can do *kung fu*.'

'Excellent.' Jeremy was always amused by the Cantonese term *kung fu*. It meant 'work', but pronounced with different tones it meant 'fighting', as in the martial arts.

'Is good news, Sir, *hai m hai ah*?'

'*Hai, Sa jin*, it is very good news. Let's hope the villagers do *kung fu* and not *kung fu*, *hai m hai ah*?'

'*Hai, Bong Baan*. You make the joke, Ah Sir, right? It is very funny.' The Sergeant obviously understood the play on words, but nevertheless his face remained expressionless.

Jeremy was reminded for the umpteenth time of the vast gap between the two cultures that shared Hong Kong. 'East is east and west is west, eh, Sergeant,' he murmured, not expecting an answer.

'East okay and west okay,' the Sergeant responded earnestly. 'No trouble there, Ah Sir. East and west you only have the water. Deep Bay is west and Mirs Bay – '

'Yes, all right, Sergeant. That's not what I meant exactly – '

'North and south are have the trouble, I think so.' He nodded decisively. 'North is the Communists and south is Hong Kong.'

'Thank you for correcting me, Sergeant Fong,' Jeremy said, putting an end to the topic. He'd been in Hong Kong far too long to get caught in a conversation wherein Chinese logic was used in English. He stood and stretched his limbs, then crossed to the window that looked down over Sha Tau Kok. He could see villagers already opening shops and setting up stalls in the tiny main street below. 'News carries fast I see, Sergeant Fong?'

'I already send the news to the people, Ah Sir. They are very happy.'

'Yes, I can see that.' More people were pouring into the tiny lane as he spoke.

A curfew had been placed on the village the previous Saturday night, after the shootings. Jeremy had realised the military necessity of the curfew, but over the last three or four days, it had become more and more apparent to him that Maynard Pottinger's appraisal of the situation had been right on the money. There would be no more trouble. The shootings had been an isolated incident.

As a result, the previous night he'd requested the curfew be lifted immediately, his reason being that the villagers of Sha Tau Kok would cause more trouble than the PLA itself if they were denied any longer the right to resume their daily business. To the Cantonese, business was life.

The Sergeant remained impassive. 'Maybe you should tell me, Ah Sir, to tell the *bibi jai Bong Baan* that you say to make the Village Patrol?'

'You're a wise fish, Sergeant,' Jeremy chuckled, turning from the window. 'I'll tell you what, I've had an idea. You tell the baby boy Inspector I wish him to make a Village Patrol.'

'That is a very good idea, Sir.' This time the Cantonese Sergeant was well aware of the humour in the situation. His eyes twinkled, but his expression remained inscrutable.

'The sooner things get back to normal around here, the better, *hai m hai ah?*'

'*Hai, Bong Baan.* And I think it is good for Inspector Stevens to do the Village Patrol.'

'Oh? You do, do you?'

'I think he is a little bit *mong cha cha*, Ah Sir.'

'*Mong cha cha?*' Jeremy was surprised at the Sergeant's boldness in making a personal observation about his Senior Officer. And he knew better than to ignore it. The Sergeant was obviously trying to tell him something. '*Mong cha cha*,' he repeated. 'Are you suggesting that Inspector Stevens is *chi sin?*'

'No, Sir,' Fong exclaimed, frightened he'd gone too far. '*Chi sin* means crazy. Mister Stevens is different to *chi sin*, he is *mong cha cha*, how you say . . . er . . .' he tapped his head with his forefinger. 'Confused?'

'Confused?' Jeremy was well aware of the Cantonese slang phrase, *mong cha cha*, but such are the vagaries of Cantonese that it could mean anything from confused, to dizzy, to halucinatory or even stark raving mad. 'Just confused?'

'Yes, Sir.' Sergeant Fong had meant much more, but he, too, was at the mercy of translation between two entirely different languages and he decided for his own sake to take it no further.

'Well, get him out on a patrol and get some fresh air into his lungs. And send two PCs with him.'

'Yes, Sir.' Fong saluted and headed for the door.

'And you go, too,' Jeremy added, 'just to keep an eye on things.'

'Yes, Sir,' the Sergeant called from the hallway.

龍

Jet Lee sat in the small tea house in the village of Kap Lung and stared disconsolately up at the side of Tai Mo Shan, which he'd just descended. He imagined for one moment he could still hear his father's hammer blows ringing out from the forge.

He'd done it. He'd escaped his father's clutches at long last and was determined never to return. Well, perhaps he would return some day, he thought, but regarding his immediate future, living the life of a hermit cut off from the outside world was not for him. No more daily grind for him. No more scrubbing, washing and polishing. Oh no, never again. He was free at last. He would drink his fill of life and perhaps, one day, he might return to pay his respects and impress his father with his wealth and fine clothes.

Jet's gloom deepened as he imagined Lee Kwan's response to such ostentation. His father would point him out to Fat Boy the ox and loudly expose him as a fool. He sipped his tea and looked at the old men playing checkers at the next table, then reached into his meagre bag of belongings and took out a packet of Viceroy cigarettes. He'd acquired the habit several months ago during one of his rare trips to Kowloon. It had been a small form of rebellion. He'd never let his father see him smoking, of course. He'd made sure to do it well away from the house, beyond the dam.

Soh Ti-pei, the shop owner's daughter, knew the good looking young man from the mountain. He had been to the tea house several times over the years. He was Jet Kwan, son of Lee Kwan, the *Shaolin* master of Tai Mo Shan. She served him another pot of jasmine tea, and a sticky bun which was courtesy of her father she told him, but in truth she'd stolen it.

'*A sticky bun,*' Jet said. '*I rarely get to eat such delicacies.*'
'*It is a gift from our humble house, Mr Kwan,*' she replied.
'*Please thank your father for me.*'
'*I will,*' she smiled cheekily, '*when he returns from the city.*'
'*Oh, I see.*' Jet smiled, joining in the conspiracy. '*So it is you I must thank.*'

She is playing with me, he thought. His sister, Su-lin, had told him many times that he was handsome and girls would pay him lots of attention, but he'd rarely had the opportunity to experience it. And now, confronted with the situation, he had little idea what to do next.

His embarrassment was short-lived, curtailed by another man who came to the shop and sat at a table. Ti-pei went off to serve him and Jet watched her firm bottom as it sashayed away from him. He would have many women, he thought. He would make up for lost time by learning the art of love-making and wooing every girl he came across. He would have a good life.

He lit a cigarette and puffed on it, then leaned back in his bamboo chair and struck what he hoped was a manly and enticing pose, but his thoughts of Ti-pei disappeared as his attention was drawn to the man who had recently arrived. The stranger kept his bamboo hat at a low angle and Jet had trouble seeing his face, but he could not help feeling that he knew this man.

Damn it! James cursed silently as he recognised his nephew, Jet Kwan, sitting immediately opposite him, leaning in his chair puffing clumsily on a cigarette. The boy was staring at him. There was no escaping recognition. He lifted the brim of his hat and smiled.

'Uncle James,' Jet exclaimed, jumping up and crossing to the table, 'what are you doing here?' He gave his uncle a strange look. 'And dressed like a coolie.'

'Hello, Jet. Sit with me and drink some tea?'

'The last person I expected to meet on the first day of my journey is you, Uncle.'

'Your journey?' James was not remotely interested in Jet's journey or anything else about the boy for that matter, but he had to make conversation.

'The rest of my life, Uncle,' Jet explained. 'I have left Kap Lung forever. I am going to Kowloon to seek my fortune.'

'Really?' Christ, James thought, the boy's a case of arrested development. He must be well into his twenties. He'll last ten minutes in Kowloon. 'Do you have somewhere specific to go?'

'I will stay with my sister, Su-lin. She is a doctor at the hospital and has her own flat in Ho Man Tin, near the rail-way station.'

'I see.' James could imagine how happy that would make Su-lin. Having the oaf in her life night and day would drive her insane. *'And what are you going to do to earn a living?'*

'Well,' Jet leaned in conspiratorially, *'don't tell Father, but I'm going to teach Shaolin kung fu. There are no teachers of Shaolin in Kowloon, or all of Hong Kong for that matter.'*

'The arts of Shaolin should not be taught to the ignorant. They are the last pure forms of warrior-monk culture. Your father will be furious when he finds out.'

'How will he find out?' the idiot grinned gleefully. *'He never leaves his mountain.'*

Ti-pei arrived with a pot of tea for James. She placed it on the table and poured him a cup.

'Would you like or not like to drink tea with me, nephew?' James asked again.

'Like. Thank you.' Jet looked up at the girl. *'Ti-pei, this is my uncle, he is the number one taipan in all of Hong Kong.'*

'How do you do?' Ti-pei looked at the unkempt stranger and wanted to accuse the young man of lying, but she would never offend one of her father's customers; he would kill her if he found out. Besides, she didn't want to offend the boy from the mountain either, she'd had her eye on him for some time. It is a pity, she thought, that he is so poor. He would make a good husband if he had money.

'I am very well, Ti-pei,' James replied and waited for the girl to leave. He could have hit Jet for introducing him. The last thing he needed was to be remembered by witnesses as a visitor to Kap Lung village, and especially today.

He already had the problem of Jet on his hands. If he found it necessary to eradicate Lee, an event he hoped would not be necessary, he would then have to eradicate Jet, and now little Ti-pei would need to be added to the list. He could not possibly leave anyone who could bear witness to his arrival in the New Territories. Should he kill them now? he wondered. No, too many people about. He would have no trouble finding them if he needed to. He would see what transpired on the mountain first.

'Are you on your way to visit my father?'

'Yes,' James answered tartly. Why else, he wanted to scream, would I be in a remote village in the New Territories, dressed like this? The young man's cheerful yet rather stupid demeanour irritated him, but he managed to contain his anger. *That is why I am dressed this way. I did not want to be recognised.*

Father will be pleased to see you. Jet twisted his head as he spoke, watching Ti-pei moving around the verandah of the tea house. *He never gets visitors, apart from the odd pilgrim wandering on the mountain.*

She is beautiful, Jet.

Who? The young man's face turned bright red.

Ti-pei, of course. James smiled. *She is young, firm and ripe for a young man. Will you bed her before you continue your journey?*

Well, I would like to, Uncle, but – '

You have no experience with women, true or not true?

True, Uncle. Jet nodded.

Do not let your inexperience destroy your desire, nephew. James took a twenty dollar note from his pocket and handed it to Jet. *When I am gone, take the girl by the arm and tell her you have something for her. Then steer her behind the building and offer her the money.*

Will that work, Uncle?

It never fails, my boy. That is more money than Ti-pei has ever seen.

Thank you, Uncle James.

Money is all you need in life, Jet. James caught his eye. *You can have anything you want if you have money.*

I will remember what you have told me, Honourable Uncle. Jet bowed his head slightly.

Well, I must go, James said, getting to his feet. *I have business with your father.* That's got rid of the idiot, he thought. The boy's testosterone and the girl's good looks will do the rest, while I get on with my mission.

Yes, Uncle. Perhaps I will see you in Hong Kong one day?

Of course, why not? James smiled to himself as he thought in Cantonese, *Not as long as your arsehole points to the ground, nephew.* How incredible, he was thinking like a peasant. Am I that much Cantonese? he wondered. Just one day in a coolie's clothing and I've become one of them.

Jet watched his uncle leave and take the track that would lead to his father's house. What are you up to, Uncle James? he wondered. What has made you enter the world of peasants? What is there at Kap Lung compound that makes you take such an arduous journey?

'Goodbye, Uncle James,' he called and received a perfunctory backhand wave in return.

龍

Inspector Geoffrey Stevens walked through the narrow main street of Sha Tau Kok with a feeling of dread. It had been only three days since five men had been shot and he was sure the Communists were watching him at that very moment. Each step he took could well be his last. He imagined the bullet spinning through the air and striking him in the chest. Everyone and anyone was his enemy.

He wished he'd never come to the infernal place. He wished he'd never even heard of the Hong Kong Police. He wished he was back home in Gloucester drinking pints of ale with his friends. They'd tried to talk him out of joining, but he'd had to prove them wrong.

The previous Friday evening he'd written his letter of resignation from the force, but Saturday's massacre had put the kybosh on that. He couldn't possibly resign now; he'd be seen as a coward deserting his post just when things looked blackest. He was stuck in the most dangerous place on earth and knew without doubt that his days were numbered. The Communists would get him for sure.

As he patrolled the street, the various hawker stalls and tiny shops seemed to him like the gullet of a giant snake and he was being swallowed down it. The merchants and their women seemed to stare at him and even the children he passed stopped their play and stared silently at his back. He knew it. He had no need to turn around and catch them out. He could feel their malevolent stares burning into his shoulderblades.

Station Sergeant Fong walked several paces behind, watching his young Inspector with concern. The *Bong Baan* was agitated and Fong could understand why, but there was something more than natural nervousness going on in the mind of Inspector Stevens. Not five minutes before, Fong had seen the young man surreptitiously undo the flap button on his holster and finger the butt of his revolver.

Go and fuck your mother, he'd cursed silently. That was all he needed at the moment, a baby Inspector losing his wits. Inspector Stevens was seriously *mong cha cha.*

'Good morning, Sergeant Fong,' a sweet voice called.

Fong turned and saw the rice vendor's daughter smiling at him. She was a pretty woman and would make delicious entertainment for him in the not too distant future. He was about to return her greeting when he heard his Inspector.

'Get away from me!' Stevens yelled.

Fong looked and saw the idiot pointing his service revolver at a hawker woman. He ran up to the man and grabbed his wrist. 'What is wrong, Ah Sir?' he asked carefully.

'She's got a gun!' Stevens gasped and Fong could feel the young man's body trembling.

'No, Sir,' he replied. 'Look.' He grabbed the old woman's hand and held it up to reveal she was holding a dried fish. 'It is just a fish, Ah Sir,' he said softly.

'*What's the matter with the scrawny cunt eater?*' the woman yelled.

'*He thought you had a gun,*' Fong replied.

'*A gun!*' she shrieked. '*What would I be doing with a gun?*'

'*I have shown him he was mistaken,*' Fong said. '*Now get about your business and stop waving that fish about.*'

'*Is his penis connected to his forehead?*' The woman was not going to be silenced. '*What kind of a useless dog fucker would mistake a fish for a gun?*' She screamed the question, waving the fish above her head for all to see. '*Only an arse licking Englishman would think this,*' she pointed at the fish she held aloft, '*was a gun.*'

'*That's enough out of you,*' Fong growled as people began to gather around, laughing.

'Sergeant!' Stevens yelled. 'Place this woman under arrest.'

'Ooh, no, Sir,' Fong pleaded. 'She is only a stupid old woman. We must not arrest her. There will be big trouble.'

'*What's he on about now?*' the woman demanded.

'*He wants Fong to arrest you,*' someone in the crowd translated.

'*What for?*' she shrieked.

'*It would be better if you shut up,*' the Sergeant pleaded.

'*You are the result of unnatural copulation,*' she screamed directly at Stevens, '*probably between a dog and a monkey, by the look of you.*' She thrust the fish in his face. '*This is a fish, you useless excuse for a pig's cunt!*'

Geoffrey Stevens' eyes widened in terror as the crazy old hag thrust into his face what he perceived in his madness to be a firearm. He broke free of Fong's grip and fired twice, hitting the old woman in the chest.

龍

'*Take me to Kowloon with you,*' Ti-pei gasped as Jet thrust into her.

'*I have never felt anything like this,*' he moaned.

They were on her small bed in the rear of the shop. He'd lost his virginity ten minutes before and was now embarking on his second journey into the body of a woman. The feeling was indescribable. Why had he waited half his life to experience such delicious joy?

'*Take me to Kowloon with you, Jet,*' the girl moaned under him.

'*Indescribable,*' he cried out as he ejaculated. '*It is truly the most exquisite feeling I have ever known in my whole life.*'

He groaned as he withdrew and lay beside the girl. But as his breathing slowed, he found himself thinking, what does my father have that would make Uncle James climb a mountain?

龍

James paused for breath. He hadn't realised he was so out of condition. He could see the compound of Kap Lung above him, not a half mile distant. As he filled his lungs with air, he leaned against a large rock and took in the magnificent view of the New Territories behind him. To the north, from where he stood he could see practically to the border. To his left he could see Deep Bay and to his right, all the way over to Mirs Bay in the east.

It was little wonder that a man like Lee loved living up here, he thought. But then could you call the life of an aesthete *living*? James could no more entertain thoughts of living without women and money and luxurious surroundings than he could imagine living the life of a coolie on the Kowloon docks. It was all well and good to have a philosophy of peace and the simple beauty to be found in nature, but not all the time, surely? James had had enough of the view already.

He looked back down the track he'd walked. There was no one on it for as far as he could see. He glanced up at the smoke rising from the buildings at Kap Lung, then opened his bag and took out his Colt .45. He was about to talk to a dragon, a very dangerous dragon, and he had no intention of being caught unawares. He cocked the weapon, slipped the safety catch on and put it back in his knapsack. Then, with his sleeve, he wiped the sweat from his brow and continued the climb.

Up in the forge at Kap Lung, Lee Kwan watched the figure walking up the track. He fondled the small medallion on the chain around his neck. So, it has come to this, Little Brother, he thought. His heart began to ache and he felt a deep sadness invade his spirit.

He pumped the bellows on the forge and watched the coals burn brighter, then picked up the file he'd been using and continued with his work.

'Hello, James,' he said eventually. He did not bother turning around.

'How did you know it was me?' James replied, easing his knapsack from his back until it hung from his shoulder by one strap.

'I saw you pause at the Rest Rock.'

'The Rest Rock?'

'The large stone you leaned upon to catch your breath. It is about half a mile down the hill.' Lee put down the file and turned towards his brother. 'It's what my wife, Lin Li, called it, when we first came to live here.' He wiped his naked torso with a damp cloth. 'The children have called it that ever since.'

'You could tell who I was? Even dressed like this?' James was impressed. 'And from half a mile away?'

'I knew you were on the mountain for a long time before I saw you.'

The remark sent a chill down James' spine. 'Before you saw me?'

'It was only a feeling,' Lee shrugged, 'but it proved to be true, so who can say? Perhaps I did know.'

'Don't start that *Shaolin way* rubbish with me, Little Brother.' James took his water bottle from the knapsack and drank greedily. 'I won't beat about the bush, Lee,' he said putting the bottle back in the bag. 'You know why I'm here, don't you?'

'To secure that which you require to continue your life, no matter what the cost.'

'Philosophy is wasted on me, Lee,' James sneered. 'Are you going to give me the medallion?'

'No.' Lee shook his head sadly.

'I have no intention of remaining on this desolate hillside any longer than I have to, Lee.' James patted the knapsack. 'There's enough money in here to help you turn this place into something special. A real retreat and a fine school of *Shaolin*. It would be the only one outside China.'

'You will never understand, will you? I have no need of money.'

'I have to have that medallion.' He stared transfixed at Lee's neck. He could see the medallion gleaming against Lee's bare torso. 'You don't understand. I'd honestly given up on it. I was going to forget the whole business, but Elanora betrayed me while I was away – ' He could hear the sense of desperation creeping into his voice.

'Elanora would never betray anyone, James. Not even you.'

'She bought the Merchant Company behind my back!'

'Have you ever thought that she may have done so for your own good?'

'Stop it!' James yelled, his face reddening as he felt himself losing control. Visions of Elanora and Katherine filled his mind. They were laughing at him. 'Take the money I'm offering you and give me the medallion!'

'It was a gift from Richard. I will not part with it.'

'But it's the only way I can fight back! Don't you understand? It's worth a fortune!'

'To me it is priceless. I will never part with it.'

'Then I'm sorry, Lee.' James reached into his knapsack. 'I'm not going to fight you for it, because I know I'd lose. And I don't like losing.'

James wrapped his hand around the automatic and released the safety catch. Not daring to withdraw the weapon from its concealment, for fear that Lee would be on him in a second, he fired twice through the bottom of the knapsack.

The .45 calibre bullets hit Lee in the lung and stomach. He grunted at the force of the blows, staggered backwards and fell, disappearing from sight behind the forge.

It's done, James thought with a mixture of exhilaration and relief, and then a sense of shock at how easy it had been.

Then, to his horror and amazement, he saw Lee rise to his feet from behind the forge. And Jesus Christ, the man was smiling. Dear God, James thought. Is he bullet proof? Then he saw Lee's left hand clasp his abdomen as blood pumped from the wound, flooding his trousers.

'Have no fear, James.' Blood bubbled through Lee's lips as he spoke. 'You have succeeded. The wounds are fatal.'

The words were clear and distinct, but they seemed to come from another place, and James' world slowed down, as if moments had become minutes. He watched, stunned, as Lee leaned on the forge's edge, his hand moving inexorably towards his neck. James knew his brother's intention, but his finger had frozen on the trigger of the Colt. He knew he must pull the trigger, but the scene taking place before his eyes seemed somehow ordained. There was nothing he could do to stop it.

He stared in horrified fascination as Lee's hand enclosed the medallion and he saw the chain snap as it was jerked from his neck. The little gold links seemed to tumble through the air like tiny fireflies, twinkling in the glow from the coals.

For what seemed an eternity he watched, mesmerised, unable to move a muscle. Lee opened his fingers and, in the palm of his hand, the silver and gold disc gleamed defiantly. Through the shimmering heat from the forge, the tiny medallion seemed to grow in size one thousand times. The dragon on it stopped its play, as if aware that someone was watching. It seized the pearl, its source of power and right of entry into heaven, and clenched it in its claws. Then it slowly turned its head and stared at James, its eyes glowing with anger at the mere mortal who dared to intrude. Then it roared. The sound it made was one of pure hatred and flames blasted from its nostrils, filling James' vision.

James shook his head and watched Lee's arm slowly extend further out over the roaring forge, flames licking at the medallion, now returned to normal size, sitting in the palm of his hand.

No! James wanted to yell, as the smell of Lee's burning flesh reached his nostrils. Desperately he tried to pull the trigger, but he was paralysed.

'This time you will lose, James.' Lee seemed impervious to the pain. 'More than a fortune. More than you will ever know.' Lee tilted his hand and the tiny medallion and chain fell onto the coals and disappeared in one fiery instant, consumed by the ferocious heat.

The sound of his brother's voice broke the spell.

'You bastard!' James screamed, and he fired the handgun until the magazine was empty.

龍

Jeremy heard the sound of gunfire from his office. He leapt to his feet and looked out of his window down into Sha Tau

Kok. The street was bedlam. People were screaming and rushing about. He spun and ran for the Charge Room as fast as he could.

'Give me a revolver,' he said to the young Charge Room Constable, whose face was ashen. The boy fumbled under the counter and produced a Colt .38 and six rounds of ammunition.

'Ring HQ Kowloon and HQ Hong Kong,' he ordered as he loaded the weapon. 'Tell them there is gunfire at Sha Tau Kok. And get a message down to Major Bronte with the Gurkhas.'

With that he ran into the rear compound and made for the main gate.

Geoffrey Stevens was out of his mind with fear. He saw what he believed to be PLA soldiers all around him, not villagers and tradespeople ducking for cover. All he knew was that the Communists were invading Hong Kong and he was going to be the first to die. Panicking, he shot a man in the leg and began running east up the street to where it met the main road coming down from the police station, at the actual border crossing.

Two PLA border guards saw Geoffrey Stevens coming towards them, pistol in hand. They looked at each other and drew the AK-47s from their shoulders. Both took aim at him, but were then distracted by another English policeman, running down the hill from Sha Tau Kok Station and he, too, was brandishing a revolver. Could it be possible, they thought, that the Hong Kong Police were invading the Motherland of China? The idea was crazy. But then, so were Westerners as far as the Chinese were concerned.

The chasing crowd caught Geoffrey Stevens just as Jeremy got to him. People were hitting both policemen with sticks, stones and anything else they could lay their hands on.

'What in God's name's wrong with you, Stevens?' Jeremy had no idea what had occurred. Suddenly, he was being attacked, and the two of them fell to the ground. A dozen villagers threw themselves on top of them.

'This foreign devil killed a fisherwoman,' one villager yelled to the border guards.

'Get off me!' the delusional young Inspector screamed, firing his weapon again and again, until it was empty.

Station Sergeant Fong reached the mass of tangled arms and legs knowing that both his Inspectors were somewhere underneath. He grabbed one of the villagers by the scruff of the neck and pulled him away, at the same time firing his revolver into the air.

The border guards watched, not knowing what was going on, but slowly realising it had nothing to do with China.

The shots from Fong's weapon brought some semblance of order to the situation and slowly, the melee disentangled itself. One villager had been shot in the leg and another stared at a hole in his hand as blood poured from it onto the ground. Geoffrey Stevens got to his feet screaming wildly and Fong smacked him over the head with his pistol butt, knocking him unconscious.

The Sergeant noticed an eerie silence had fallen over those around him. He looked down and saw Jeremy Bent, lying on the street staring blindly up at him. The baby *Bong Baan*'s bullets had left a hole in his neck and another in his chest, and beneath his head a large pool of blood was rapidly forming.

龍

James Merchant staggered into the courtyard. He'd watched his last hope of salvation disintegrate before his eyes in the ferocious heat of the forge. And he'd murdered his adopted brother. He'd ruined his life in one moment of madness.

He took a deep breath and exhaled forcefully. But he was alive wasn't he? And Lee, the master of *Shaolin*, was dead. So much for your *way*, Little Brother, he thought as a feeling of triumph swept through him. So much for your blind belief in the powers of *Shaolin*, eh? Where were they when the bullets hit you?

But then he remembered Lee's hand over the forge and the smell of his flesh burning. He must have felt pain, James thought, his hand had actually caught fire. But he'd never flinched. Lee had slowly and deliberately tilted his hand and let the medallion fall to its fiery fate. And James had watched, powerless to stop him, even as his own fate was decided in the heat of that forge. Without the medallion he was finished. Elanora had won.

But he was alive, he thought. Damn the medallion. He was alive and, ultimately, that was all that mattered. He would find another solution, win back all that was rightfully his and destroy Elanora along the way. He was James Merchant, *taipan*.

'*You were wrong, Little Brother,*' he called aloud and began to laugh. '*I lost nothing, only a piece of jewellery, while you,*' he raised his arms to the sky and turned in a circle, experiencing the sweet taste of victory, '*you lost your life.*'

The first arrow hit him in the chest and pierced his lung. The shock of the assault caught him totally unawares and he gazed, stupefied, at the feathered shaft protruding from his body.

The second arrow hit him directly in the heart and his last view of life was that of his nephew Jet Kwan standing outside the door of the house, threading another arrow into his bow and letting fly. James Merchant died, unaware of the third arrow entering his temple.

EPILOGUE

Nineteen sixty-seven, the year of the Fire Goat, proved to be just that, a year of fire, and pain and death. Hong Kong had been brought to its knees by strikes, rioting and acts of terrorism, the violence of which had not been seen since the Japanese invasion during World War II.

And so it was that 1967, the year of the Fire Goat, passed into 1968, the year of the Earth Monkey. On a Sunday morning in the humid heat of July, Georgina returned from her home in Singapore to Merchant House, high on the side of Victoria Peak.

The Merchant Corporation Rolls Royce, which picked her up from Kai Tak Airport, rolled almost silently through the streets of Kowloon. Georgina saw no evidence of the violence of the previous year. Hong Kong, as she knew it would, had survived, and everywhere she looked it was business as usual. Commerce, once again, ruled supreme.

The most remarkable aspect of 1967, in Georgie's opinion, had been the improvised brilliance of the normally lethargic British Colonial Government. Communist strikes, propaganda and riots had been countered at every turn. Using the standard press release phrase, 'The government, with deep regret . . .' as a precursor to every act in retaliation, the British had separated the hard-core Maoists from the supporters they so desperately needed, Hong Kong's Cantonese business leaders.

Instead of the Communists acting and the government reacting, the British, she realised in hindsight, had very cleverly allowed the Communists to act, then waited patiently for the public to demand action. Only then had they moved against the Maoists to the unbridled joy of Hong Kong's money-mad Cantonese.

But it was on the Kowloon–Hong Kong Island car ferry that Georgie finally realised how much she'd missed her home town. The panoramic island was breath-taking when it was viewed from the harbour and Georgina's heart went out to the sheer beauty of it.

The drive from the ferry to the Peak had much the same effect on her and when the Rolls pulled up at the front doors of the mansion and Georgina stepped into the waiting arms of her mother, she felt sure her heart was going to burst.

'I've missed you so much,' Katherine whispered.

'You only saw me two weeks ago,' Georgina replied, 'on your fifth trip to Singapore in the last year.'

'It doesn't matter. I've still missed you. This house has missed you.'

'I never thought I'd see this place again,' Georgina said when they'd broken their embrace.

'Why ever not?' Katherine Merchant raised her eyebrows. 'You own it.'

'No, thanks,' Georgie shuddered. 'It's all yours, Mother, I don't want it.'

'Don't be silly, girl,' her mother chided. 'You're to become the Chairman of the Merchant Corporation. You'll be expected to live here. Everyone in Hong Kong will expect it.'

'Well, they're in for a rude shock, aren't they?' Georgina took the first couple of steps up towards the main doors, then turned to her mother. 'In fact, they're in for a series of shocks.'

'What do you mean?' Katherine joined her.

'I'm here in Hong Kong to attend a ceremony at the cemetery in Sha Tau Kok, to honour the memory of my husband and the other men who died there, last year.'

'Yes, I know dear.' Katherine took her by the arm and they continued up the steps. 'But after that – '

'After that, Mother, I'm returning to Singapore.'

'What?' This time it was Katherine who stopped dead in her tracks. She stared uncomprehendingly at her daughter. 'But . . . but . . . what about the Merchant Corporation? Elanora and I went to so much trouble. We allowed you a year to grieve. You're the principal shareholder. You have to be here. The other shareholders will demand it.'

'I'm sure they will, Mother,' Georgie said with a hint of distaste.

The death, under strange circumstances, of James Merchant had caused a serious flutter on the Hong Kong Stock Exchange, but when it was revealed that his share holdings in the Merchant Company were almost non-existent, the corporation had weathered the storm. And in October, when it was announced that the American John Wilson had been recalled to take over the helm as the new Chief Executive Officer, the markets reacted favourably.

'Johnnie Wilson's doing a fine job by all accounts. Why do I have to be here?'

'You just . . . well . . . you just have to be,' Katherine stammered.

'My home is in Singapore, Mother,' Georgie said firmly. 'I have a nice house there, and friends. I'm happy living in Singapore and that's where I'll continue to live.'

Katherine saw the flash of fire in her daughter's eyes and it reminded her instantly of James Merchant. The arrogant tilt of the head and the movement of the muscles in her jaw were so reminiscent of her dead husband they caused her to shiver.

'Oh, my goodness,' Katherine murmured. 'Whatever will your grandmother say? Elanora's expecting you to stay here and run an empire, not run home to Singapore.'

'She'll understand,' Georgie replied dismissively. 'I'll think of something to tell her.'

'Well, I'd think quickly if I were you, darling,' Katherine said in her most motherly tone.

'What do you mean?'

'She's here.' Katherine pointed at the front doors then began walking towards them. 'She's waiting for you on the upstairs balcony.' She stopped at the doors and turned to look back at her ashen faced daughter. 'What's the matter, dear?' She tilted her head and smiled sweetly. 'Cat got your tongue?'

Georgina swept in haughty fashion past her mother only to be greeted in the main hall of the mansion by twenty smiling servants, lined up in an avenue of welcome. They were silent and nervous, casting glances everywhere but directly at her. To the household staff Georgina Merchant was the new Merchant Mistress and the new *taipan* of their Noble House.

It had been rumoured that Georgina Merchant had been secretly married to the English Chief Inspector of Police killed in a second shooting incident at Sha Tau Kok. Apparently, upon her arrival in Hong Kong the previous year from Singapore to attend the funerals of her father and uncle, she'd seen a newspaper report of the death of Jeremy Bent, and had fainted in the terminal at Kai Tak Airport.

But rumours, as the people of Hong Kong knew, and especially household staff, had always surrounded the Noble House of Merchant. Who was to know the truth? Rumours were the badges of fame, *hai m hai ah*? Rumours of theft and corruption had enveloped John Merchant, the original *taipan*, true or not true? Rumours of secret societies and even murder had surrounded Richard Brewster, true or not true? And stories of benevolence and indeed, revenge, had always clung tenaciously to the skirts of the Merchant Mistress, had they not? Who knew the truth? some asked. And who knew the lies? others whispered.

The only noise to be heard was the tinkling of water in the enormous fountain that dominated the main foyer, as it cascaded from the trunks of four elephants. Ah Po, the long standing house *amah* and former nanny to Georgina and Paul, was first to break the tension.

'You come home to be the new *taipan*, Missy?' the old woman began, then collapsed into a fit of histrionic wailing.

Georgina hugged the old woman and greeted many of the others with warm handshakes until finally she'd crossed the hall and found herself staring at the grand staircase leading to the upper floor, and Elanora.

'Come along, Georgie,' Katherine seized her by the arm. 'We mustn't keep *Ju Mo* waiting.'

My God, how she's aged, was the first thought to strike Georgina as she stood and looked along the balcony at her grandmother. The last time she'd seen her had been at the funerals of James and Lee Kwan.

James Merchant's body had been cremated by his embarrassed family, his remains hastily spread on Victoria Peak and the entire matter soon forgotten by a population hell bent on recovering its prosperity from the ashes of 1967. All that concerned the business community of Hong Kong was, who would run the Merchant Company? When John Wilson was appointed CEO in October, James Merchant became a distant memory, and an unfavourable one at that. It seemed no one had liked him.

The death of Lee Kwan Man Hop had been another matter. To a great many Chinese he was the Dragon of Shanghai, and to many others, the Angel of Nanking. His traditional burial on a hillside of Tai Mo Shan had been attended by hundreds of mourners. They'd braved the summer sun and the arduous climb to pay their respects, and among them had been the Merchant Mistress and her granddaughter Georgina.

The most famous woman in Hong Kong and her now equally famous offspring, Georgina Merchant – rumoured to be the principal shareholder in the newly created Merchant Corporation – had stood, hand in hand with Jet Kwan and Doctor Kwan Su-lin, at the ceremony to honour the passing of their father.

The old woman whom Georgina was now observing, sat at a table with a tea set in front of her, looking out over the harbour below. She's gone grey, in only one year, Georgie thought. Her beautiful jet black hair has finally gone grey.

Events in the Year of the Fire Goat had conspired against Elanora. She had managed to save the Merchant Company, but she'd been robbed of her husband, her son, her grandson and her beloved Lee Kwan. Lee's murder in particular had been the final straw. She'd turned grey overnight as grief nearly destroyed her.

But she survived, Georgina thought, her heart swelling with pride, despite the efforts of her black-hearted son James.

James' death, which had been discussed *ad infinitum* at dinner parties and gentlemen's clubs with knowing looks and the odd raised eyebrow, had gained little recognition in the Colony's press. Rumours abounded regarding what had taken place on Tai Mo Shan at the Kap Lung retreat, but the newspapers simply reported the facts offered by the Hong Kong Police.

To the investigating officers it had obviously been a murder, but just who had murdered whom could not be resolved. There were no witnesses to the incident. The circumstantial evidence suggested James had gone to Kap Lung and a confrontation had arisen between him and his adopted brother, the *Shaolin* master and Chinese war hero, Lee Kwan Man Hop. James Merchant's body had been found in the courtyard with an empty .45 calibre Colt in its hand and Lee Kwan's had been found in the forge with a bow and empty quiver lying next to it.

Nine bullets had pierced the body of Lee Kwan and three arrows had been found embedded in the corpse of James Merchant. That they had killed each other had not been in doubt; however, it could not be ascertained in what chronological order of events the wounds had been sustained.

Two witnesses had given evidence at the coronial enquiry. Jet Kwan, the son of the deceased *Shaolin* master, stated he had left Kap Lung retreat early that morning and gone to the village in the valley below. He had picked up his long-time fiancée, Miss Soh Ti-pei, and together they'd gone to Kowloon. Miss Soh corroborated Jet Kwan's story, but neither witness could shed any further light upon the incident. Owing to a dismal lack of other evidence, the coroner had had no alternative but to close the case, with the rather strange finding of 'death by misadventure'.

Elanora still has her straight back and the elegant tilt of her head, though, Georgina thought. The Merchant Mistress was still an impressive picture of grace, dignity and timeless beauty.

'Ju Mo,' Georgie called and hurried along the balcony.

'My darling girl,' Elanora exclaimed holding her arms out. 'Oh, how I've missed you,' she said, as her grandaughter fell to her knees and entered her embrace. 'My darling, darling Georgina.'

'And I, you, *Ju Mo,'* the girl sobbed. Georgie had not realised how much until she'd entered her grandmother's embrace and been assailed by the delicate perfume she remembered so well.

'Sit,' Elanora commanded, relinquishing the girl. 'Sit and take tea with me. We have so much to discuss, I don't know where to begin.' She swivelled her head. 'Where's Katherine?'

'Mother thought it best to leave us alone for a while.' Georgina took a seat and poured them tea. 'I have something to tell you, *Ju Mo.'*

'Later, dear,' Elanora replied dismissively. 'First things first. I've arranged several meetings for you the day after tomorrow, two of which you can avoid if you wish, but the meeting at ten o'clock on Tuesday morning with Johnnie Wilson is a must.'

'But, *Ju Mo* – '

'Hush, girl!' Elanora silenced her with an imperious wave of her hand. 'Do you know the meaning of the phrase corporate raider?'

'Of course.'

'Well, never mind,' Elanora carried on heedless of her granddaughter's answer. 'It's a new phrase that has crept into the lexicon of company business over recent years. I don't like the phrase myself, but it is an accurate description of the unmindful and reckless predators who seem to haunt the world's stock exchanges of late.'

'Ju Mo.' Georgina placed her hand on Elanora's arm. 'I'm here for the ceremony at Sha Tau Kok tomorrow and then – '

'Of course you are, my love, the memorial service for Jeremy and those other young policemen. That's why I've arranged the meetings for Tuesday.'

'I'm flying home to Singapore on Tuesday, *Ju Mo.'* Georgina held her breath, watching her grandmother stare out at the distant Kowloon Mountains. 'Did you hear me, Grandmother?'

'Oh, I heard you all right!' Elanora's voice cracked like a whip.

'I'm flying home to – '

'Your home is here, Georgina!' It was not an observation, it was a command. Elanora realised she had a fight on her hands and it was a fight she must win. She turned and tilted her head slightly, glowering at her granddaughter. 'Don't you dare to even contemplate backing away from your responsibilities, my girl!'

'But, *Ju Mo*.' Georgina was taken aback by Elanora's vehemence.

'I thought it might come to this,' the older woman continued. 'My heart ached for you last year. No woman should have her first love snatched away in such a tragic fashion. So I let you return alone to Singapore to deal with your grief, but it seems I made a mistake. You have forgotten who you are. *Diu lei lo mo!*' She cursed in gutter Cantonese. 'I knew it would come to this!' Elanora smashed her fist onto the table top, rattling the porcelain tea set.

Georgina flinched. She had never seen Elanora so angry. And had she heard correctly? Did her grandmother actually say, '*Go and fuck your mother*'? The filthy language shocked her even more than the violent physical display.

'Who do you think you are?' Elanora glared at her. 'You are not some impoverished peasant from the rice paddies, nor are you one of those vacuous middle class social butterflies this Colony abounds with. You are Georgina Merchant.'

'My name is Bent!' It was Georgina's turn to glare. 'Georgina Bent!'

'So be it!' Elanora snapped back. 'Call yourself what you will! Although, I'd prefer you used the family name for business purposes.' She dismissed the retaliation with an imperious wave of her hand, crushing the girl's bravado with it. 'Your name doesn't matter, do you hear me? But your position does. You are the heir apparent to the Noble House of Merchant. You will inherit the position from me, whether you like it or not!'

'I don't want it. I don't want to be involved with the Merchant Corporation, nor do I – '

'I, I, I! Me, me, me!' Elanora interrupted. 'Listen to yourself! You nasty, selfish, spoilt, little girl! This is not about you!'

'I'm sorry if it sounded – '

'Be quiet!' Elanora commanded. 'Your fate was sealed the day your twin brother died. You are the sole remaining member of the Merchant family and as such, you will be responsible not only for the daily fortunes of an international corporation, but also for the lives of thousands of its employees. *Understand or not understand, ah?*'

'*Understand, Grandmother.*' Georgina did. Her grandmother's fury had finally hit home, and Georgie felt truly penitent. How could she have been so foolish to think she could escape her responsibility? She was the granddaughter of the Merchant Mistress and hundreds of people, from local household staff to company workers in foreign cities, would be relying on her guidance and good judgement. How could she have ever contemplated the selfish life she'd been planning?

'Good.' Elanora nodded. 'For years those employees and their families have depended upon the Merchant Company to put rice in their bowls, some for decades. Why do you think I arranged for you to work at Raffles Hotel? Why did I have you study business administration? And why did I allow you the run of *my* house in Singapore?'

'I'm sorry, *Ju Mo*.'

'Did you think I paid those ridiculous sums of money for your education in Europe so you could run away from your responsibilities when the time came to face them?'

'I said, I'm sorry, Grandmother.'

'Then say it as if you mean it!'

'I'm sorry!' Georgie wailed as the tears began to flow. Her shame was complete. 'I'm truly sorry, *Ju Mo*.' She had never before in her life felt the true wrath of the Merchant Mistress and her resistance crumbled utterly.

'It's all right, my darling.' Elanora's voice was suddenly soft, motherly. She had won. 'It's all right. But let's have no more talk of running away. Whether you like it or not, you will become the Merchant Mistress. It is the way things must be. It is *joss*.'

Her grandmother was right, Georgie thought. She had been selfish. She had hidden herself away in Singapore and wallowed in self pity, dreaming of the life she had so wanted to share with Jeremy, but life didn't work that way, did it? Jeremy had been killed at Sha Tau Kok, one year ago tomorrow, she thought. And for the last year she had wanted to die, too. She'd imagined their life together, the children they would have had, the house they might have lived in. She had allowed the thoughts to consume her.

She sat still, the tears flowing down her cheeks and absent-mindedly toyed with the necklace around her neck.

'Where did you get that?' The question cut through the air like a whip.

'What?' Elanora's voice brought Georgie back to the present. 'Oh, this?' She held the necklace away from her neck for her grandmother to see. 'It was Jeremy's. It was in his personal effects given to me by the Police Commissioner, at his funeral.'

'Where did he get it? Do you know?'

'Yes, I do.' Georgie remembered the story, she remembered it vividly.

龍

Durien Phumkumpol had been gathering the plates from the table when she'd noticed the necklace Jeremy was wearing.

'It is very beautiful,' she remarked pointing at it. Durien liked pretty things.

'What is?' Jeremy asked. He and Georgie, more than a little distracted with each other, had failed to notice what had caught the woman's attention.

'Your necklace.' She pointed again. 'Very beautiful.'

'Yes, it is, Durien, and it means a lot to me.'

'It means a lot to me, too,' Georgie murmured as Durien took the plates to her food hut.

'How come?' He was bewildered.

'It hovers before my eyes during moments of ecstasy.'

'Oh, I see.' He grinned wolfishly. 'Good God, does it really?'

'Yes.' She squeezed his hand. 'Really.'

He moved to put his arms around her.

'Not just yet, sport,' she laughed, pushing him away. 'Tell me where you got it.'

'What?' he asked, his eyes focused on her bare breasts.

'The pendant, you idiot. The symbol of my ecstasy.'

'Oh right. The pendant.'

The memory of the night came flooding back to Jeremy. 'I was six years old,' he said. 'My grandmother's place in Battersea had been bombed by the Luftwaffe – '

'Your grandmother? Was she hurt?'

'She was killed. So was my mother.'

'Oh.' Georgie was taken aback. 'I'm sorry.'

'My mum's name was Mavis,' he said inconsequentially. 'Mavis Higgins.'

'I know,' she replied. 'It's on our wedding certificate. Oh, my darling, how awful for you.'

'Yes. It wasn't a particularly good night for the Higgins clan. My grand-uncle Charles was murdered the same night.'

'Murdered?'

He nodded.

'Did they catch the killer?'

'No, they never did solve the crime; it became yet another unsolved murder on the books of Scotland Yard. There were many at that time, you know. Murders I mean. What better time to murder someone than during a world war?'

Georgie wasn't sure whether his tone was still light-hearted or whether there was a touch of cynicism in it, but either way she felt inadequate, at a loss for words. She moved her seat around the table beside his and sat with her arm around him. 'Where was your father during all this?' she asked.

'I've always told people he was away at the war, but he wasn't. Alfie Bent was a small time crook and ladies' man who got my mother pregnant and did a runner. They located him after the war, and, I've got to hand it to him, he took me in and looked after me, in his own inimitable fashion. He's dead and gone now. He was anything but an ideal parent, but he fed me and clothed me.'

He was serious now, Georgie could tell. 'And so, you adopted his surname?'

'No. I used my mother's surname right up until I applied to join the Hong Kong Police.'

'Why?'

'This is something I've never told anybody,' Jeremy turned and kissed her cheek, 'but now I've got a wife, I suppose I'll have to tell you everything.'

'I should hope so.' Georgie kissed him back.

'My grand-uncle, the one who was murdered, was once the Commissioner of Police in Hong Kong. Charles Higgins. That's where I get my middle name from, Jeremy Charles Higgins, now Jeremy Charles Bent.'

'But why change it? Why did you feel it necessary?'

'I wanted to make it on my own in Hong Kong. I didn't want anyone to know I was related to Grand-uncle Charles, so I changed my name. And I'm glad I did,' he smiled thinly. 'Apparently old Charlie was a bit of a lad, which is probably why he was murdered.'

'I've heard of Charles Higgins,' Georgie said. 'My grandfather Richard spoke of him.' She hugged him. 'So, tell me about the pendant,' she insisted.

'It was a strange night, that night.' Jeremy shook his head as he remembered. 'My mum and gran, gone in an instant. I was lucky. I'd gone to stay the night with my friend who lived nearby. Bertie Ogden was his name; isn't it funny the things you remember? Anyway, I heard the bombs crashing all around and I got frightened and ran home. The whole street was ablaze. There were fire hoses all over the road, hissing like snakes and the flames must have been thirty feet high. I thought they looked like dragons.' He looked out over the sea, lost in the past. 'It's funny how you remember things, isn't it?'

'Yes, it is,' she said softly, 'go on.'

'Well, I was standing in the street and people were yelling and screaming, and then, I saw the figure of a man standing not twenty yards away, a black silhouette against the flames. He came and picked me up and I remember asking him if he was God, and he said "No." Then I saw the wings on his hat and I asked him if he was an angel. He just shook his head and said "No" again. Then he said, "But I'll look after you, I know where you'll be safe."

'He took me to the Sisters of Mercy in Earls Court and left me with the nuns. But before he left, he gave me this.' Jeremy toyed with the necklace. 'And that's about it,' he shrugged. 'I never saw or heard from him again. All I know is that he was a pilot in the Royal Air Force, and thank God for him. That pilot saved my life. Wherever he is today, God bless him.'

'Yes, God bless him,' Georgie repeated solemnly. 'If it wasn't for him I might not be married to the most wonderful man in the world.'

'The most wonderful man in the world?' Jeremy laughed, hauled back from the past.

He took her in his arms and carried her to the hut, and once again, the last thing Georgina saw before ecstasy overwhelmed her was the gold and silver medallion dangling before her eyes, the tiny dragon breathing flames around the pearl in its mouth.

龍

'So there you have it, *Ju Mo*.' Georgina blinked away the threat of tears. 'It was a gift to a lost little boy in the London Blitz.' Her memory of Jeremy was as strong as ever, but she would not cry. Not any more. She had cried for long enough. Elanora was right, she had responsibilities to face. She looked at her grandmother and was surprised to see a tear rolling down her cheek.

'It's a wonderful story, isn't it, *Ju Mo*?'

'Yes.' Elanora nodded. She drew a handkerchief from her sleeve and wiped her eyes. 'It truly is a wonderful story.'

A shiver of joy ran through Elanora. She'd forced James from her mind over the past year, but as a mother, the thought that he had committed that one, solitary, act of kindness made her feel extraordinarily happy. Perhaps she could mourn for him after all.

She smiled at his daughter. She would tell Georgina the story of the medallion when the time was right. But not now, she thought. Georgie had enough on her plate for now.

Georgina reached out and took her grandmother's hands in her own. '*Ju Mo*, if it wasn't for that young pilot, I might never have loved and married the most wonderful man in the world.'

'That is true, my darling.'

Georgina looked down at the beautiful harbour glistening in the sunlight.

'I wonder who he was?' she whispered.

ACKNOWLEDGEMENTS

Dear Reader,

An enormous thank you to you for buying an Australian book by an Australian author. Good on you!

I would like to thank Judy Nunn, for her love, her honesty, her friendship and the use of her brilliant literary mind.

My thanks also go to my publisher, Meredith Curnow, whose smile could light up a cathedral, and for believing my claim that I can talk to animals; to my editors, Roberta Ivers and Annabel Blay, who struggled so diligently over my saliva-stained manuscript; to my publicist, Peta Levett, who is simply the best at what she does, and who tolerates me because I make her laugh; and to all the staff at Random House Australia who continually support my literary efforts.

I would like to thank Peter Comptom for his wonderful aeronautic advice. If you ever need to sabotage an aircraft in flight, Peter's the man to talk to. Thanks too, to Colin Julin, as always, for continually thrusting me into the vanguard of computer technology, even though I don't understand it; to Katya Quin, for use of her wonderful maiden name; and a special thanks to Tanya Creer for her brilliant cover art work, *The Ming Tigers*. The computer generated image was constructed painstakingly and lovingly, one hair at a time, by a master of computer graphics.

Once again my gratitude goes to my mates from the Royal Hong Kong Police: Bill Bailey, Les Bird, Mark Ogden, Paul Keylock and Steve Tarrant, firstly for their friendship of

thirty years and secondly for their continued encouragement
. . . *Doh jei, Daai Loh*.

Thanks too, to my Tasmanian mates: John Everard for the
last forty years; Lee Renshaw for his wise advice; and David
Johnston whose text messages prove unequivocally that there
is a higher order of lunacy than mine.

I would also like to thank my friend Tang, an orang-utan
who lives in Taronga Park Zoo, for his encouragement. He
told me, as he sat happily eating his signed copy of this book,
that my literary efforts were food for thought. An elephant,
who also read this book, stated that she would never forget
it. However, two tigers, on seeing the front cover design,
claimed it was defamatory and refused to read it at all.

Finally, having reached the bottom of the acknowledgement food chain, my thanks must go to that group of dys-
functional misfits, the Australasian Primates, those denizens
of Sydney's deep and the would be Illuminati of this country,
for explaining to me why it is that I have opposable thumbs
. . . Wassail!

Bruce Venables